The cattle drive from Texas to Kansas was long and exhausting. But it was going well, even though Charles Goodnight had not originally planned on having a couple of women along.

Along the trail death waited for one of the women, and a charge of murder which provoked a situation so explosive that Goodnight's dream was nearly wrecked. Fortunately, he had with him a quiet, insignificant little fellow – named Dusty Fog!

Revised list of J.T. EDISON *titles in chronological and categorical sequence:*

Ole Devil Hardin series

YOUNG OLE DEVIL
OLE DEVIL AND THE CAPLOCKS
OLE DEVIL AND THE MULE TRAIN
OLE DEVIL AT SAN JACINTO
GET URREA

The Civil War series

COMANCHE
THE START OF THE LEGEND } *
How Belle Boyd Became The Rebel Spy }
YOU'RE IN COMMAND NOW, MR. FOG
THE BIG GUN
UNDER THE STARS AND BARS
THE FASTEST GUN IN TEXAS
A MATTER OF HONOUR
KILL DUSTY FOG!
THE DEVIL GUN
THE COLT AND THE SABRE
THE REBEL SPY
THE BLOODY BORDER
BACK TO THE BLOODY BORDER

The Floating Outfit series

THE YSABEL KID
.44 CALIBRE MAN
A HORSE CALLED MOGOLLON
GOODNIGHT'S DREAM
FROM HIDE AND HORN
SET TEXAS BACK ON HER FEET
THE HIDE AND TALLOW MEN
THE HOODED RIDERS
QUIET TOWN
TRAIL BOSS
WAGONS TO BACKSIGHT
TROUBLED RANGE
SIDEWINDER
RANGELAND HERCULES
McGRAW'S INHERITANCE
THE HALF BREED
WHITE INDIANS
THE WILDCATS
THE BAD BUNCH
THE FAST GUN
CUCHILO
A TOWN CALLED YELLOWDOG
TRIGGER FAST
THE MAKING OF A LAWMAN
THE TROUBLE BUSTERS
DECISION FOR DUSTY FOG
DIAMONDS, EMERALDS, CARDS AND COLTS
THE CODE OF DUSTY FOG
THE GENTLE GIANT
SET A-FOOT
THE LAW OF THE GUN
THE PEACEMAKERS
TO ARMS! TO ARMS! IN DIXIE
HELL IN THE PALO DURO
GO BACK TO HELL
THE SOUTH WILL RISE AGAIN
THE QUEST FOR BOWIE'S BLADE
BEGUINAGE
BEGUINAGE IS DEAD
MASTER OF TRIGGERNOMETRY
THE RUSHERS
BUFFALO ARE COMING
THE FORTUNE HUNTERS
RIO GUNS
GUN WIZARD
THE TEXAN
OLD MOCCASINS ON THE TRAIL
MARK COUNTER'S KIN
THE RIO HONDO KID
OLE DEVIL'S HANDS AND FEET
WACO'S DEBT

The Floating Outfit series cont'd

THE HARD RIDERS
THE FLOATING OUTFIT
APACHE RAMPAGE
THE RIO HONDO WAR
THE MAN FROM TEXAS
GUNSMOKE THUNDER
THE SMALL TEXAN
THE TOWN TAMERS
RETURN TO BACKSIGHT
TERROR VALLEY
GUNS IN THE NIGHT

Waco series

WACO'S BADGE
SAGEBRUSH SLEUTH
ARIZONA RANGER
WACO RIDES IN
THE DRIFTER
DOC LEROY, M.D.
HOUND DOG MAN

Calamity Janes series

CALAMITY, MARK AND BELLE
COLD DECK, HOT LEAD
THE BULL WHIP BREED
TROUBLE TRAIL
THE COW THIEVES
THE HIDE AND HORN SALOON
CUT ONE, THEY ALL BLEED
CALAMITY SPELLS TROUBLE
WHITE STALLION, RED MARE
THE REMITTANCE KID
THE WHIP AND THE WAR LANCE
THE BIG HUNT

Waxahachie Smith series

NO FINGER ON THE TRIGGER
SLIP GUN
CURE THE TEXAS FEVER*

Alvin Dustine 'Cap' Fog series

YOU'RE A TEXAS RANGER, ALVIN FOG
RAPIDO CLINT
THE JUSTICE OF COMPANY 'Z'
'CAP' FOG, TEXAS RANGER, MEET MR. J.G. REEDER
THE RETURN OF RAPIDO CLINT AND MR. J.G. REEDER

The Rockabye County series

THE SIXTEEN DOLLAR SHOOTER
THE LAWMEN OF ROCKABYE COUNTY
THE SHERIFF OF ROCKABYE COUNTY
THE PROFESSIONAL KILLERS
THE ¼ SECOND DRAW
THE DEPUTIES
POINT OF CONTACT
THE OWLHOOT
RUN FOR THE BORDER
BAD HOMBRE

Bunduki series

BUNDUKI
BUNDUKI AND DAWN
SACRIFICE FOR THE QUAGGA GOD
FEARLESS MASTER OF THE JUNGLE

Miscellaneous titles

J.T.'S HUNDREDTH
J.T.'S LADIES
J.T.'S LADIES RIDE AGAIN
MORE J.T.'S LADIES
IS-A-MAN
WANTED! BELLE STARR
SLAUGHTER'S WAY
TWO MILES TO THE BORDER
BLONDE GENIUS (*Written in collaboration with Peter Clawson*)

**Title awaiting publication*

J.T. EDSON
Omnibus Volume 6

comprising:

FROM HIDE AND HORN

TRAIL BOSS

GUN WIZARD

J.T. EDSON OMNIBUS VOLUME 6
A CORGI BOOK 0 552 13607 7

TRAIL BOSS and GUN WIZARD originally published in Great Britain by Brown Watson Ltd.

PRINTING HISTORY – FROM HIDE AND HORN
Corgi edition published 1969
Corgi edition reprinted 1972
Corgi edition reprinted 1978

PRINTING HISTORY – TRAIL BOSS
Brown Watson edition published 1961
Corgi edition published 1968
Corgi edition reprinted 1969
Corgi edition reprinted 1982

PRINTING HISTORY – GUN WIZARD
Corgi edition published 1969
Corgi edition reprinted 1970
Corgi edition reprinted 1974
Corgi edition reprinted 1981

Corgi Omnibus edition published 1991

Corgi Books are published by Transworld Publishers Ltd., 61–63 Uxbridge Road, Ealing, London W5 5SA, in Australia by Transworld Publishers (Australia) Pty. Ltd., 15–23 Helles Avenue, Moorebank, NSW 2170, and in New Zealand by Transworld Publishers (N.Z.) Ltd., Cnr. Moselle and Waipareira Avenues, Henderson, Auckland.

Printed and bound in Great Britain by
Cox & Wyman Ltd., Reading, Berks.

From Hide and Horn

For Mike Muse and his box of doom,
disaster, subtle violence and sudden death.

Author's note:

The events recorded in this book follow on from GOODNIGHT'S DREAM and tell how he made it come true.

FROM HIDE AND HORN
COLONEL GOODNIGHT'S TRAIL CREW

Charles Goodnight	trail boss.
OD Connected	OD
Dusty Fog	segundo.
Mark Counter	point rider.
The Ysabel Kid	scout.
Red Blaze	trail hand.
Billy Jack	trail hand.
Swinging G	G
'Rowdy' Lincoln	cook.
'Turkey' Trott	cook's assistant.
'Boiler' Benson	trail hand.
Eddie Quinn	trail hand.
'Spat' Bodley	trail hand.
'Austin' Hoffman	trail hand.
Eph Horn	horse wrangler.
Ross Phares	horse wrangler.
Will Trinka	night hawk.
D4S	D4S
Dawn Sutherland	trail hand.
Vern Sutherland	trail hand.
Josh Narth	trail hand.
Bench P	P
Tod Ames	trail hand.
'Jacko' Lefors	trail hand.
Lazy F	F
Solly Sodak	trail hand.
'Pick' Visscher	trail hand.

Double Two	**22**
Swede Ahlén	trail hand.
Burle Willock	trail hand.
Flying H	⌣H⌣
Shermy Sherman	trail hand.
Alex Raymar	trail hand.

CHAPTER ONE

YOU HIRE CHEAP, YOU GET CHEAP RESULTS

Bearers of bad news are rarely welcome and the tall, lean man clad in travel-stained range clothes shuffled his feet uncomfortably as he finished his tale of misfortune and failure. Seated at his desk, Joseph Hayden glared coldly at the man.

Rooms in the small hotel at Throckmorton, Texas, did not usually offer such facilities. Nor, especially since the end of the War Between The States, did they normally house guests of wealth and social prominence. So the manager had willingly complied with Hayden's requests. Small, dapperly attired to the height of current Eastern fashion, Hayden had a hardness of face and cold eyes. He invariably spoke in a clipped voice which showed an expectancy of receiving instant obedience.

'So Goodnight's managed to regather his herd, has he?' Hayden said at last.

'That's what the feller I met on the way here told me,' the westerner, a typical cattle-country hard-case, replied. 'He allowed that Mr. Wednesbury had just got to the cabin when about thirty Swinging G cowhands jumped them. Your partner and all but one of the others went down in the fighting 'n' the feller allowed he was lucky to get away alive.'

'I'll just bet he was,' Hayden sniffed, having no illusions about the quality of the men his penny-pinching late partner had insisted on hiring. 'Goodnight hasn't got thirty men, counting his ranch crew and the extra help he hired for the trail drive.'

'He's got Cap'n Dusty Fog backing him,' the man pointed out, his tone indicating that he was giving a perfect explanation for Wednesbury's defeat and death.

Maybe Hayden had never worn a uniform, and spent the War years building up a sizeable fortune, but he had heard the name mentioned by his hired man.

During the last years of the War, Dusty Fog had risen to a prominence as a military raider and fighting cavalry commander equalled only by Dixie's other two experts, Turner Ashby and John Singleton Mosby. At the head of Company

'C', Texas Light Cavalry, Dusty Fog had caused havoc, loss and despair among the Yankee Army in Arkansas. In addition to his excellent military record, he was rumoured to have twice helped Belle Boyd, the Rebel Spy, to accomplish dangerous assignments.* With the War ended, he had returned to Texas and taken over as segundo of the great OD Connected ranch. Circumstances soon sent him into strife-torn Mexico on a mission of international importance, which he brought to a most satisfactory conclusion.†

In addition to his past military glories, people spoke of Dusty Fog as a tophand with cattle. They told many tales of his ambidextrous prowess, lightning-fast way of drawing a pair of 1860 Army Colts and wonderfully accurate shooting. Also frequently mentioned was his uncanny bare-handed fighting skills, which rendered bigger, heavier, stronger men helpless in his grasp.

Hayden did not know how many of the legends about Dusty Fog might be true. Nor did he particularly care. Except that Dusty Fog was Goodnight's nephew and so a factor to be reckoned with when plotting the downfall of the stocky, bearded, trail-blazing rancher from Young County.

'Is the man with you?' Hayden inquired.

'Nope,' the hard-case answered. 'He allowed that he wasn't staying anywheres close to Goodnight in case somebody was took alive and talked. Last I saw of him, he was headed East like the devil after a yearling.' Then, feeling he ought to express his condolences, he went on, 'I'm real sorry about Mr. Wednesbury, Boss.'

'So am I,' Hayden replied. 'I'll put a mourning band on for him. What did you learn around Mineral Wells?'

'Not much at first. The Sutherland gal come in with Mark Counter and the Ysabel Kid, trying to talk some of the ranchers' wives to get up a herd and send it to Goodnight. They weren't getting any place, then Wardle, Hultze and the others got back from chasing the cattle Chisum stole. Seems like Goodnight'd offered to let them send cattle and men on his drive to Fort Sumner. So's they'd have hands who knowed how to trail cattle and money enough to pay for another big drive.'

'Where to?' Hayden demanded.

* Told in *The Colt and the Sabre* and *The Rebel Spy*.
† Told in *The Ysabel Kid*.

'I heard up to the railroad in Kansas,' answered the hard-case and made a deprecatory gesture. 'Only I figure somebody'd been joshing the gal who told me. Hell! They'd never take cattle right up there.'

Although Hayden did not show it, he disagreed with the speaker. Conditions were sufficiently bad in Texas for men to take desperate chances in the hope of improving them. Having supported the Confederate States during the War, most people in Texas found themselves left with a worthless currency following the South's defeat. Texas had no major industries capable of competing on the national market, nor mineral assets which might help its people to return to solvency.*

All they had was cattle. The longhorns grazed in enormous herds on land capable of supporting them and many more; a potential source of wealth if they could only be sold. At first there were only the hide-and-tallow factories willing to take the cattle—at three or four dollars a head, calves thrown in free. They bought by the herd, killing, stripping off the hide and tallow, then dumping the meat and remains of the carcasses into the Brazos River.

Charles Goodnight and Oliver Loving found another market. With something like 11,000 Indians on reservations needing to be fed, the U.S. Army in New Mexico wanted all the beef they could buy. So the Texan partners had decided to make a stab at supplying that need. They had made two successful drives, pioneering a trail and learning many valuable lessons, before word of their efforts leaked out.

No cattleman, Hayden had recognised the potential source of profit offered by delivering beef to the Army. Longhorns could be bought for less than five dollars a head in Texas and sold at Fort Sumner for eight cents a pound on the hoof. With an average-sized steer—the Army wanted neither cows nor yearlings—weighing about eight hundred pounds, there would be a very fair return on his outlay.

Along with his partner, Wednesbury, Hayden had gone to Fort Sumner in the hope of obtaining contracts to supply the cattle. Although Loving had died from a wound gathered in a Comanche Indian attack, Goodnight had put in a bid to deliver three thousand steers by early July; relying on rancher John Chisum to fill the number for him. There would still have been

* It would be many years before oil became a factor in the Texas economy.

a good opening for Hayden, but he wanted much more than that. Before him lay a vision of enormous wealth. By buying cheap from the impoverished ranchers of Texas, he hoped to make a vast fortune.

Figuring Goodnight to be a threat to that vision, Hayden had tried to remove him. With the aid of the unscrupulous Chisum, Hayden had hoped to plant eleven hundred head cf stolen steers into Goodnight's shipping herd and have their owners find them. By bad luck, Goodnight had learned of the thefts in time and turned the stolen cattle away. Although Hayden's men had managed to stampede the Swinging G herd, the attempt was only partially successful and the losses had been made up. Determined to attend to Goodnight's ruin himself, Wednesbury had taken some men to Young County and died with nothing achieved. Not even the loss of the eleven hundred head stolen by Chisum had slowed Goodnight down, it seemed. In some way the rancher had not only made his peace with the irate owners, but persuaded them to make good the missing cattle.

From what Hayden remembered of Goodnight, he did not lightly discard the idea of the alternative destination for cattle mentioned to his hired man. Goodnight had foresight and was aware of the crying need for beef on the Eastern sea-board. While it would not be possible to trail cattle that far, they could be shipped east on the transcontinental railroad.

If the long drive could be made, Hayden saw a second, even greater, market opened. The forts of New Mexico were less accessible to the owners of the eastern and southern ranches than from his present location. Kansas would be open to all. Nor, using it, would the Army become flooded with stock so that they could lower their prices. If Goodnight's actions in taking along men from his neighbours' ranches was anything to go on, he intended that everybody would benefit from the markets he opened.

That was the last thing in Hayden's mind. The longer he could keep the markets to himself, the greater would be his profits. From the money the herds brought in, he could buy property, take over ranches from bankrupt owners, and build himself a cattle empire.

Let Goodnight pave the way and others would follow. So he must be stopped or, coming from a breed which did not know the meaning of the word 'beaten', killed. Let Charles Goodnight, honoured scout of Captain Jack Cureton's famed company of Texas Rangers and master cattleman fail, and others would hesitate to try. The problem facing Hayden was how he might best achieve his intentions.

'Can we get men down there in time to stop the Mineral Wells cattle reaching Goodnight?' Hayden asked, breaking in on his train of thought and seeking for the means to deal with the rancher.

'Not afore they get to him,' the man admitted.

'Then why didn't you do something before you came here?'

'How d'you mean, boss?'

'You could have followed them and stampeded the herd.'

'With Mark Counter trail bossing it and the Ysabel Kid riding scout?'

Looking blankly at his employee, Hayden saw a flicker of consternation cross the other's face. Yet Scabee had shown courage, if not initiative, on more than one occasion since they first met. Hayden wondered who Mark Counter and the Ysabel Kid might be. If he had lived for any time close to the lower reaches of the Rio Grande he would have known the answer to the latter part of the question.

Born in the village of the *Pehnane* Comanche, only son of a tough Irish-Kentuckian mustanger-cum-smuggler and his Creole-Comanche wife, the Ysabel Kid had been raised and educated among the Wasps, Quick-Stingers or Raiders—the white man's translation of *Pehnane*—band. From his maternal grandfather, Chief Long Walker of the fabled Dog Soldier war lodge, the boy had learned all those things a Comanche braveheart must know.* He could ride any horse ever foaled and knew ways to bring a strange, hostile mount to his will. Given expert instruction in the handling of a variety of weapons, he also knew how to walk in silence through the thickest brush, follow tracks barely visible to less keen eyes, locate hidden enemies and conceal himself in minute cover. One thing he had never been taught was to nurse too great a respect for the sanctity of human life.

Fortunately for the peace of Texas, he had never made use of his knowledge in the manner of a *Pehnane* brave. However, he put much of his training to use helping his father as a smuggler or, during the War, delivering cargoes, run through the U.S. Navy's blockading squadron into Matamoros, to Con-

* Told in *Comanche*.

federate officials north of the Rio Grande. During that time he had gained a reputation for being one tough, very capable and deadly *hombre*. Maybe he did not rate high in the use of a revolver, but none could fault his handling of a bowie knife, or be-little his ability with a rifle. Young he might be, yet the hard-cases along the bloody border grew silent and well-behaved in his presence.

With the War over, the Kid had intended to resume the family trade. Bushwhack lead cut down his father and, while hunting for Sam Ysabel's killers, he had met Dusty Fog. Lone-handed smuggling held no attraction for the Kid, so, having helped Dusty complete the important mission, he accepted the other's offer of employment. Many folk slept easier in their beds knowing that the Ysabel Kid now rode on the side of justice. His talents were given to the OD Connected and utilised by Ole Devil Hardin to help friends in trouble. It would have gone very hard for any man the Kid had found acting in a suspicious manner in the vicinity of the herd he helped to guard.

While he would quickly achieve a fame equalling that of Dusty Fog or the Ysabel Kid, at that time Mark Counter was less known than his companions. Son of a wealthy Big Bend rancher, Beau Brummel of the Confederate Cavalry, Mark was known as a tophand with cattle, something of a dandy-dresser, yet immensely strong and exceptionally able in a rough-house brawl. Less was known of his skill as a gunfighter. Nor, riding as he did in the shadow of Dusty Fog, would he ever gain his just acclaim. Yet men who were in a position and possessed knowledge of such things would say that Mark was second only to the Rio Hondo gun wizard in the matter of fast draw and accurate shooting.

Like the Kid, Mark helped Dusty on that important assign-ment. Instead of returning to his father's R Over C spread, he took on at the OD Connected. Not just as a hand, but to ride as part of the floating outfit, the elite of the crew. On the enormous ranches like the OD Connected, four to six men—tophands all—were employed to travel the distant ranges in-stead of being based on the main house. Being aware what was at stake, Ole Devil Hardin had sent his floating outfit to help Goodnight. Although Hayden did not know it, the floating outfit had been mainly responsible for the failure of his plans.

'So Goodnight will be moving out soon,' Hayden commented coldly. 'And with a full three thousand head.'

'Sure, Boss,' Scabee admitted. 'Anyways, you've got our cattle on the trail by now, ain't you?'

'Yes, and with Chisum handling the drive. He knows the trail to Fort Sumner as well as Goodnight does. And he's got a good four days' start. But I don't mean to take chances. I'm going to make sure that Goodnight doesn't arrive.'

'You figuring on taking men after the Swinging G herd, Boss?'

'Not me personally. I'm going after Chisum and joining him on the trail. A man who'd betray his friend won't play square with an employer. So I'm going to be with him when he reaches Fort Sumner.'

'Then who——'

On his arrival at Throckmorton, Hayden had found that a suite was an unknown quantity at the hotel. Explaining his needs, he had had three ordinary rooms converted into quarters for himself and his recently-departed partner. Each of their bedrooms had been connected by a door to the room in which he now sat interviewing Scabee. Suddenly the hard-case cocked his head in the direction of what had been Wednesbury's quarters and chopped off his words. Down dropped his right hand, drawing the Remington Army revolver from its holster on his gunbelt and thumbing back the hammer. Lining the gun at the door, he glanced at his employer.

'I just heard somebody in there, Boss.'

'Go and see——' Hayden commanded, but the rest of the order proved to be unnecessary.

Slowly the door opened. While the sitting-room had a lamp glowing over the desk, Wednesbury's bedroom lay in darkness. Standing inside, so that only his empty hands could be seen clearly, was a shadowy figure.

'Good evening,' it said.

'Oh!' grunted Hayden, recognising the voice. 'It's you!'

'It's me,' admitted the newcomer. 'I hope you don't mind, but I can never resist the chance to eavesdrop.'

'How much have you heard?' Hayden demanded, but waved back Scabee who snarled a curse and began to move towards the bedroom.

'Almost everything your uncouth friend's said. Ask him to put the gun away. If he kills me, you'll have lost your only chance of stopping Goodnight.'

'Do it, Scabee,' Hayden ordered. 'I know this man.'

'You near on got killed, feller,' Scabee growled, returning the Remington to its holster. 'I like to shot you when I heard you behind the door.'

'If you're no better than the others Mr. Hayden hired,' the man answered, still not showing himself, 'I wasn't in any great danger.'

'What do you think, having eavesdropped on us?' Hayden said, ignoring Scabee's indignant muttering. 'Come in.'

'I'll stay where I am if you don't mind,' the man told him. 'The less who know me the better I like it. As to what I think; the work was amateurishly handled and badly bungled.'

'Maybe you could've done better?' Scabee challenged.

For a moment the newcomer did not speak, then he said, 'I'm trying to think how I could have done *worse*. Well, Mr. Hayden, have you considered my offer?'

'You're asking a high price,' Hayden commented.

'As you've just found out, you hire cheap, you get cheap results,' the man told him. 'My price is high because I guarantee success. If I don't produce, you don't pay me.'

'Just how do you figure on taking Charlie Goodnight, fancy pants?' demanded Scabee.

'My way,' the newcomer replied calmly.

'For what you're asking, I'll want to know more about your way than that,' Hayden warned.

'First, you tried to stop Goodnight gathering his herd and made a complicated plan to do it. That was a mistake. You were going against him on his home ground for one thing. Instead of stopping him, you just warned him of danger. You ought to have let him get the herd well along the trail, then busted him. But the way things turned out, it's happened for the best.'

'How's that?'

'Well, Mr. Hayden, due to your efforts, Goodnight is taking along cattle for five of his neighbours as well as his own——'

'And that's for the best?' Scabee sneered.

'It is,' agreed the shadowy figure. 'Those ranchers have their hopes raised high and are looking to a rosy future. When Goodnight fails to get through, they'll be badly disappointed. So badly that none of them will have the heart to try again, and their experiences will scare off others from trying. And you'll be able to go on buying their cattle dirt cheap, sending them to the Army in New Mexico or up to Kansas with a near monopoly on doing it.'

'How did you know——?' Hayden gasped.

'I guessed, but I see that I have found your motives.'

'Go on,' requested the impressed Hayden.

This was a vastly different kind of man from the dull-witted, unthinking hard-cases who came so cheaply and carried all their brains in their triggerfingers. The speaker in the bedroom had intelligence, drew correct conclusions and came with excellent references.

'I'll stop Goodnight reaching Fort Sumner,' the man promised without a hint of boasting. 'How I do it is my own concern. For what you pay me, I supply everything I need——'

'Does that include the men?'

'*All* I need, Mr. Hayden,' the man repeated. 'You will deposit my money with Bossaert at the saloon along the street. Not until you are satisfied that I have fulfilled my end of the bargain do you authorise him to give it to me.'

'Do you trust him?' Hayden inquired.

'Another saloonkeeper was asked to hold money for me, but when I went to collect, claimed he had been robbed.'

'What'd you do to him?' Scabee wanted to know.

'Told him how sorry I was for his bad luck. Losing my money was only the start of it.'

'How come?'

'He did quite a good night's business next day. The trouble was that three of his customers died and the rest were so sick because of his liquor that he lost all his trade and got lynched by indignant citizens,' the man explained. 'Yes, Mr. Hayden, I can trust Bossaert. He knows that *nobody* has ever double-crossed me without very rapidly wishing he had not.'

CHAPTER TWO

I'VE NEVER SHOT A MAN ON THE TRAIL

'That's one right forceful and determined gal, I told you, Dusty,' Mark Counter declared admiringly, nodding to where Dawn Sutherland was carrying her low-horned, double-cinched saddle towards the Swinging G corral.

'She sure is,' grinned Dusty Fog, also turning his eyes in the direction of the girl.

Tall, slender, but blossoming into full womanhood, Dawn Sutherland wore a man's tartan shirt and levis pants, the turned-up cuffs of which hung outside her high-heeled riding boots in the approved cowhand fashion. On her blonde hair, cut boyishly short before her return from Mineral Wells, a white Confederate Army campaign hat's brim threw a shadow over her tanned, pretty face. About her middle was a military gunbelt with a Cooper Navy revolver in its open-topped holster. Dusty had cause to know that the gun was no mere decoration. If her free-striding walk and the way she carried the heavy saddle, with a forty-foot hard-plaited Manila rope coiled at its horn and a twin-barrelled ten-gauge shotgun in the boot, was anything to go on, she was a healthy, fit and strong young woman.

'If you think that blow-up with Colonel Charlie just now was something to watch, you ought to have seen the one with her pappy when she told him she was coming,' Mark chuckled. 'I thought that lil gal was fixing to whup us all, tooth 'n' claw, to get her way. She'll make a hand, Dusty.'

'How about the rest of them?' Dusty inquired, indicating a group of ten assorted, but fairly representative cowhands hovering in the background.

'They handled the herd from Mineral Wells easy enough,' Mark answered. 'Which, afore you tell me, I know it's nothing to what's ahead. Swede Ahlén there,' he nodded to a big, powerfully-built blond man, 'he's the Double 2's segundo. Hultze and the other ranchers figured they should have one foreman along. Swede's not pushy and's willing to take orders as long as he figures the man giving 'em's giving the right ones.'

'Do the rest of them listen to him?'

'Most do. Bench P, Lazy F and Double 2 are all pards, but the Flying H and D4S get along all right with them. Young Vern Sutherland's a mite wild, but he'll likely grow out of it when she stops being his *big* sister. That flashy-dressed, good-looking cuss's Burle Willock from the Double 2. He's a good hand. They all are but *he* knows it.'

'I'll mind it,' Dusty promised.

Faced with the post of segundo, second in command to Goodnight, on the trail drive, Dusty did not regard Mark's comments as snooping or a breach of confidence. With seven ranches involved, even though four of them had sent only two men each, he would have to stay constantly alert against inter-spread rivalry. One of the cowhand's prime virtues, which Dusty greatly admired, was his loyalty to the brand for which he rode. Yet he must persuade the trail crew to put aside thoughts of their respective outfits and weld them into a smoothly functioning working team as quickly as possible. Only by doing so could they hope to complete the six hundred mile journey to Fort Sumner.

So every detail Dusty could learn about the men and their relationship to each other would be of the greatest help in keeping the peace and achieving unity.

Sure the drive to Fort Sumner had been completed before, but never with such a large herd or small crew. On his previous drives, Goodnight had used at least twenty trail hands to handle a thousand to fifteen hundred head. Experience had led him to believe the number was grossly excessive. Penny-pinching did not account for the view. So many men tended to get in each other's way and caused confusion in an emergency. With that in mind, Goodnight planned to deliver three thousand five hundred head with a crew of only eighteen trail hands, his segundo, cook, cook's louse and three horse wranglers. If his gamble paid off, a herd and crew of the same general size could complete the longer journey to Kansas with a sufficient margin of profit to make the attempt worthwhile.

Much depended on Dusty as segundo for the drive's success. Never a man to flinch from responsibility, he meant to do everything in his power to see his uncle's scheme put through.

If Dusty and Mark studied and discussed the Mineral Wells cowhands in a surreptitious manner, the return scrutiny was much more frank and open. In fact, Dusty could guess at the thoughts uppermost in the newcomers' minds. How did one reconcile the Dusty Fog of legends with the actual man. Such a reputation should go with a giant figure, capable of physically dominating any company and of commanding appearance.

Dusty Fog stood five foot six in his high-heeled boots. While his clothes had cost good money and were those of a tophand, he contrived to give them the appearance of somebody's cast-offs. A new black Stetson, low of crown and wide brimmed in the Texas fashion, rode on his dusty blond head. His face was handsome, if not exceptionally so. If one chose to look closer, the cool grey eyes and strength of his features told the tale of the real man within. Around his waist was a finely-built gunbelt with a silver Confederate States Army buckle. Its carefully designed cross-draw holsters supported two bone-handled 1860 Army Colts. Efficient outfit though it might be, the gunbelt did nothing to lessen the small Texan's insignificant appearance—in times of peace.

If Dusty Fog failed to look the part, Mark Counter might have posed for a painting of the popular conception of a hero. Six foot three in height, his golden blond, curly hair and almost classically handsome features topped a truly splendid physical development. A great spread of shoulders tapered down to a slender waist and long, powerfully muscled legs. Decorated with a silver concha-studded band, his costly white Stetson hinted at his affluence. Around his throat was knotted a tight-rolled green silk bandana. His broadcloth shirt—its sleeves hinting at the enormous biceps under them—and levis pants had obviously been tailored to his fit, while his boots were the best money could buy. Like Dusty, he wore a gunbelt made by a master craftsman and supporting matched ivory-handled Army Colts of Best Citizens Finish in the contoured holsters.

Over the years Dusty had grown used to the surprise people showed when meeting him for the first time. He reckoned he could win over the newly arrived cowhands and effectively deal with objections to one of his stature giving orders to larger, more imposing men.

There was, however, one disturbing element. It had been Dawn Sutherland who brought Goodnight the first warning of the stolen cattle and received an account of his dream to rebuild Texas' war-shattered economy. The idea had been that she should return to her home near Mineral Wells and persuade the local ranchers to send men and cattle to accompany the Swinging G herd. However, Dawn planned to do more than act as messenger, then sit passively in a corner while the men-folk went off. Oldest child, she was aware of her responsibilities. A riding accident had lamed her father and he might never recover sufficiently to make extended journeys. Regarding her younger brother as a mere child—he lacked two years of her nineteen—she decided that it fell upon her to go on the drive and learn how to handle a trail herd. Despite arguments, pleadings by her mother, objections from her father and brother and warnings of the difficulties her presence might cause to the male trail hands, she had remained adamant. In the end, to Vern's protests, her parents had given permission for Dawn to go. Nor had Goodnight been any more successful in dissuading her.

Dawn's presence might raise problems. A good-looking girl could easily stir up the unruly, lusty younger element of the crew. However, from what he had seen, she knew how to take care of herself and steer clear of romantic troubles. It was still, however, something more added to Dusty's burden at a time when he could have done with things taken off not added.

There had been only one incident of note on Mark's visit to Mineral Wells. Two days before the return journey was begun, he and the Kid had recognised a man whom they had last seen as part of Chisum's trail crew, with the stolen cattle. On learning that the man had been asking questions about their presence in town, they had discussed what should be done. Discarding his companion's simple, if drastic, solution, Mark had decided on keeping the man under surveillance. So the Kid had followed him when he left town and did not return in time to assist on the short drive to Young County.

While Dusty approved of Mark's decision, being interested to know if the death of Wednesbury had ended the threat to the drive, the Kid's absence deprived them of his services as a scout. He would catch up to them on the trail, having collected a relay of horses from the D4S before setting out after the snooper, and, fortunately, the need for his presence would be less during the earlier days of the journey.

A stirring and change of the Mineral Wells men's point of interest diverted Dusty from his thoughts. The cowhands were looking to where their trail boss had left the main house and stood on the edge of its porch with a sheaf of papers in his hand.

Charles Goodnight had the build of a Comanche warrior, middle-sized, stocky, powerfully-framed but far from clumsy. Apart from his neatly-trimmed beard, his face held some of that savage nation's qualities in its keen, hard eyes and impassive strength. He dressed little differently from the cowhands, except that his vest was made from the rosette-spotted hide of a jaguar which had foolishly strayed north and tried to live off his cattle. Matched rosewood handled Army Colts rode in the holsters of his gunbelt and he knew how to use them.

'The Kid's not back yet?' Goodnight inquired as his nephew and Mark walked across to join him.

'No, sir,' Dusty replied. 'He'll follow that feller and see who he meets if it can be done. Then he'll come back and catch up with us on the trail.'

'We shouldn't need him for a week at least,' the rancher said. 'And I'm like you, I'd like to know if Wednesbury's partner is still in the game. Get the hands to come here, Dustine.'

'Yo!' Dusty gave the old cavalry response to an order.

Sensing what was in the air, big Swede Ahlén led the other men up before Dusty had time to speak. Forming into a rough half circle before the porch, they waited eagerly to hear what Goodnight had to say.

'I'd best make a few things clear to you,' the rancher announced. 'You've handled herds and know what it's all about. Well, this drive'll be much the same—except that it's longer and with more cattle than you've ever tried. There's only one way we'll get through. By working together and obeying orders. I've made out these Articles of Agreement which I want you to read and sign. They'll be binding from the moment you put on your signature until the drive's over. Binding to you and just as completely to me.'

'Would you read 'em out to us, Colonel Charlie?' Ahlén requested, his voice as Texan as any of the cowhands'. 'Some of us're a mite shy on schooling.'

Nodding soberly, the rancher complied. Maybe Goodnight had never served in the Army, or risen to higher rank than sergeant with the Texas Rangers—his title being honorary, granted in respect for his courage, integrity and qualities of leadership*—but he had a strong sense of responsibility to the men he hired. On his previous drives, he had established a code of conduct for boss and crew, setting it down in writing that all might know exactly where they stood.

In a clear voice Goodnight began to read the various paragraphs of the Articles. First he stated, in plain terms all could follow, what he as trail boss undertook to do. Then he went on to stress the importance of instant obedience to the orders of himself or his aides, Dusty Fog as segundo, or Mark Counter in the small Texan's absence. While reading the duties of the trail hands, Goodnight watched the Mineral Wells men. Nods of agreement with the various points came from the older, steadier listeners, showing that they at least accepted the Articles as satisfactory. All saw the need for the ruling that hard liquor would only be carried in the chuckwagon and used for medicinal purposes; a drunken cowhand being a danger to himself and menace to the safety of the whole drive.

At last Goodnight stopped reading. Yet something in his attitude warned the listeners that he was not finished. Whatever came next must be real important. So they waited in silence and he continued, but with a grimmer emphasis.

'If any member of the crew kills another, he will be tried by his companions and, if found guilty of murder, hung on the spot——'

'*Hung!*' repeated Burle Willock, the word bursting out in a startled pop.

'I've never shot a man on the trail,' the rancher replied.

Being aware of the stresses and strains to which a trail crew found themselves subjected, Goodnight had found the last article a stout deterrent to trouble. The threat of hanging carried a grim finality which went far beyond that of being shot. Only criminals, murderers, horse or cow thieves and the like were hung. It was a death of disgrace. So the men would be inclined to think twice and decide wisely, Goodnight hoped, when they knew the fate awaiting them if they broke the article.

'Any man who doesn't agree with the articles needn't sign them,' Goodnight said after the rumble of comment at the last article had died away. 'But if he doesn't, he'll not be coming on the drive.'

* Dusty Fog's youth prevented him from qualifying for the title 'Colonel'.

'They're fair enough for me, Colonel,' Ahlén declared and walked forward.

'By cracky, I'm on,' announced Dawn's tall, gangling, tow-headed younger brother crowding up on the big blond's heels.

Man after man followed, each writing his signature or making his mark on the master copy and his own sheet of the Articles. Even Dawn signed, calmly ignoring the rancher's cold-eyed disapproval and oblivious of his attempts to will her into a change of heart.

Helping his uncle take the signatures, Dusty became aware of a commotion at the bunkhouse. Shouts, curses, crashes and other sounds of a struggle preceded the appearance through the door of a fighting pair of cowhands. Locked together, they crashed to the ground and rolled over flailing punches at each other. Recognising the men as Spat Bodley and Austin Hoffman, two of the Swinging G's detachment on the drive, Dusty could guess at the cause of the trouble.

Before Dusty could make a move to intervene, while Mark raced towards the fighters, a peace-maker came on the scene. Long experience had taught Rowdy Lincoln how to deal with such disturbances. So the well-padded, big, jovial-faced cook emerged carrying a large bucket which he up-ended over the struggling pair. The arrival of the cold, dirty water shocked the breath from the cowhands and caused them to release their grasps as they knelt facing each other. Giving them no time to recover, Mark swooped down on them. Taking hold of each cowhand by the scruff of his neck, the blond giant hoisted them erect and hurled them apart.

'Quit it!' Mark growled, looming ominously between them.

Even a hot-head like young Austin Hoffman had sense enough to know when to surrender. Anybody who could pick up two grown men and toss them aside with such ease deserved to have his wishes respected. No less astute, Spat stood breathing heavily and glaring at his opponent.

Coming up on the run, Dusty went by the Mineral Wells men and halted at Mark's side to ask, 'What started it?'

'Hell!' Austin sniffed indignantly. 'Spat there can't take a joke.'

'Some damned joke——' Spat growled. 'And if you——'

'Tell it, Rowdy!' Dusty snapped, glaring the cowhand to silence.

'Boys were talking about the drive, and Austin said something about how lucky they was to have Spat along, him being such a tophand at fetching help. That was when Spat jumped him.'

Annoyance bit at Dusty and he prepared to stamp out a potential cause of further trouble on the drive. Spat Bodley was an amiable man, most times, and a skilled trail hand. The comment which had goaded him to violence referred to his having twice been sent to collect help for companions in trouble. On the first occasion he had returned just too late to prevent Oliver Loving receiving a fatal wound. The second time, he had brought help just in time to save Dusty's life.

Since Loving's death, Spat had grown increasingly touchy about mentions of his part in the affair and reacted with growing hostility to talk of his fetching help. For the first time, his objections had reached the point of physical violence. Dusty wanted to avoid any repetition. There were not enough trained trail hands on the drive for him to leave either man behind; and that, while the easy way out, would not solve Spat's problem. So Dusty thought fast and put his decision into words.

'Go and clean out the barn, Spat!'

Normally such a menial task would have been performed by the horse-wranglers. Knowing why he had been given it, Spat went without another word. Dusty turned cold eyes to a slightly defiant Austin, but addressed his next words to the cook.

'You were saying that new back-house hole wants to go down deeper, Rowdy?'

'It could do with a couple of foot deeper, cap'n,' Lincoln admitted.

'Take Austin here and he'll do it for you.'

Shock twisted at the cowhand's face and he gasped, 'Me! On the blister end of a shovel. I'll be damned——'

'I'm telling you to do it!' Dusty cut in coldly. 'It's that, or go ask for your time.'

Knowing that Goodnight would support his nephew's statement, Austin made a fast decision. Work was not easy to find in Texas, especially highly-paid work like trail-driving, and riding for the Swinging G carried a certain significance. It meant such a man was a cowhand of high quality. Folks would think twice before hiring a feller whom Colonel Goodnight had fired.

Nor did Austin discount Dusty's own part in the matter. Unlike the Mineral Wells men, he had come to know the small Texan very well. Not only had Dusty demonstrated his strange, uncanny almost, bare-hand fighting skill, but two days earlier had been captured by a pair of Wednesbury's men and escaped. Even having his hands bound behind his back had not prevented Dusty from gaining his freedom, killing one of his captors and taking the second prisoner. So Austin figured that Dusty Fog did not need the backing of any man to enforce his intentions.

'I hates digging,' Austin said, trying to carry off the affair in a light manner. 'But I hates work-hunting worse. Lead me to it, Rowdy, and watch me make like a gopher.'

'Have you any work needs doing, Rowdy?' Dusty asked before the cook left.

'Just a few things to load on the bed-wagon is all, cap'n.'

'Take three of these fellers to help you,' Dusty ordered, indicating the onlookers. 'Swede, have half of them that's left to help the wranglers. Mark, take the rest to spell Uncle Charlie's men on the herd until night-fall.'

'Yo!' answered Ahlén and Mark echoed the word, then they turned to give their orders. Mark included Dawn in his party, for she was to be classed as an ordinary hand and take her share of the work.

That evening the whole trail crew were gathered for supper when Austin came into the cookshack. No cowhand took kindly to digging and the youngster scowled unpleasantly around. Watching the expression on Austin's face, Dusty prepared to ram home the point he wanted to make.

'Do you know why I made you do it?' Dusty asked, making sure his words carried to all the men.

'For starting that fuss,' Austin guessed.

'That was only a lil part of it. I figured you should learn how it feels to be made do something you hate doing. That's what happened to Spat, with Oliver Loving and again with me. He didn't leave either time because he was scared, but because he was ordered to do it. Spat hated like hell having to obey—and it was a damned sight harder thing to do than dig a back-house hole. But he's a good hand and he knows that orders have to be obeyed. So he did what he was told. And each time, he turned right round then came back after he'd done what he was sent to do.'

'I never thought——' Austin began.

'You should try it some time,' Dusty told him. 'It's easier on the hands than riding the blister end of a shovel. And the rest of you can get this. Spat's full capable of standing up for his-self, but I don't aim to have him doing it on this drive. The next man to mention it, even as a joke, I'll fire and run off without pay; even if it happens while we're driving through the gates of Fort Sumner.'

'Reckon he'd be mean enough to try it, Boiler?' Burle Willock asked the grizzled Swinging G cowhand seated at his side.

'You'd best believe he'd *do* it,' the old timer grunted and rose to walk away.

'He talks big, don't he, Jacko?' Willock grinned to one of his cronies. 'Only I noticed that he let Mark Counter stop that fight.'

'Leave us not forget he's Colonel Charlie's nephew,' Jacko Lefors warned.

'Likely *he'll* not let us forget *that*,' Willock replied. 'Thing being, how'll he stack up on his own. Could be we'll find out afore this here drive's through, Jacko boy.'

CHAPTER THREE

IT'S JUST PART OF GROWING UP

Although the sun had barely peeped above the eastern horizon, Dawn left the Swinging G ranch house accompanied by Mark and Dusty's cousin, Red Blaze. A tall, well-built young man, Red had a fiery thatch of hair, a pugnaciously handsome face and sported a bandana of such a violent clash of colours that he might have been colour-blind. He wore range clothes of good cut and twin walnut-handled Army Colts hung butt forward in low cavalry-twist-draw holsters. One of the floating outfit, and Dusty's second-in-command during the War, he had a name for hot-headed, reckless courage and a penchant for becoming involved in more than his fair share of fights. So much so that few people recognised his virtues. Dusty knew him to be steady enough when giving a job of work and willingly trusted him to carry out any task he received.

Maybe the hour was early, but Vern Sutherland was already sitting his *tobiano* gelding, a black horse with three clearly defined patches of white on its body.

'Come on!' the youngster greeted enthusiastically. 'Time's a-wasting. Let's get moving.'

A hot flush crept to Dawn's cheeks and she snapped, 'Climb down and stop acting *loco*.'

'Yah!' Vern answered hotly. 'I don't know why you had to come along!'

'Because I figured we should have somebody in the family who knows about trailing cattle, that's why!' Dawn told him.

'What about me, huh?' Vern blazed. 'I'm——'

'You pair want to wake up Colonel Charlie 'n' Dusty?' Mark put in.

'Well look at him!' Dawn snorted, knowing the two men were awake and already preparing to leave for the herd. 'Acting like a kid going on a Sunday-school picnic for the first time.'

Ignoring the comment, Vern grinned at the two cowhands. 'What say we——'

'Have you fed yet?' Mark interrupted.

'Ain't hungry!' Vern replied.

'You will be comes nightfall,' the big blond stated. 'Go and eat, we're just headed there.'

'Sure, Mark,' Vern said, reining his horse around and sending it running towards the cookshack. Just before he reached the wall he turned the *tobiano* in a rump-scraping swing and rode back to halt before the trio. 'How about that?'

'Not bad,' Red Blaze commented dryly. 'Trouble being, you'll tucker the hoss out afore we get to the herd.'

'Nah!' Vern scoffed. 'Ole Toby here eats work. He'll be running when the rest're worn down to their hocks.'

'Fool kid!' Dawn snorted as her brother turned and galloped back to the cookshack. 'Don't pay him no never mind. He's just trying to make out he's a man.'

'We all start out that way,' Mark assured her and looked pointedly at Red. 'Only some of us stay like it.'

'Don't you pair get at it again,' Dawn groaned, for their bickering had kept her entertained the previous evening. Then she became serious. 'Mark, Red, will you do something for me?'

'If we can,' Red promised.

'Help me set Vern right.'

'How do you mean?' Mark inquired.

'You've just seen how he acts——' Dawn began.

'It's harmless enough,' Mark said tolerantly. 'We're all excited. This's a big thing we're starting out to do.'

'Yes, but——' the girl started.

'Now listen, Dawn gal,' Mark interrupted her. 'Your pappy asked me what I thought about having Vern along, and I said I reckoned he'd make a hand. I didn't say it just to please Vern —or rile you. I meant what I said. If your pappy's leg doesn't get better, young Vern'll have to grow up fast; and I reckon going on this drive'll make him.'

'He's a fool kid——' Red continued.

'He's only young——' Dawn corrected hotly, bristling indignation.

'Now me,' grinned Red. 'I thought *you* was the one worrying about *that*.'

'And anyways,' Mark went on, 'give him time. He'll likely grow out of it. Like I said, most of us do in the end.'

'You men always stick together,' Dawn sniffed, her good humour restored.

'We have to,' Red explained. 'It's the only way we can keep

half-ways ahead of getting trampled underfoot by you women.'

'Vern's not wild,' Dawn stated as they drew near the cook-shack. 'And all that talk he gives about whooping it up in saloons's just talk. He's not been around them anywhere nears as much as he'd have you think. Fact being, he's only snuck in a couple of times when he's been sure pappy wasn't around.'

'It's just part of growing up,' Mark replied. 'And when you get to Vern's age, you don't want a bossy sister only a year older 'n' you trying to run your life.'

'I'm near on *two* years older!'

'Sure. But try to forget it. The more you ride him, the harder he'll set on showing the rest of us fellers that you're wrong.'

'Mark's right on that,' Red informed the girl. 'I've got two older *brothers* and I didn't cotton to them trying to run things.'

'I'll mind what you say,' Dawn promised and they walked into the building.

All the men present were eating heartily and appeared to be in the best of spirits. Seated near the door, tall, lanky, mournful Billy Jack of the OD Connected predicted all kinds of doom and disaster. Nobody took any notice of him, knowing it to be a sign that he felt all was well in the world. Under that dolorous exterior lay a bone-tough fighting man and skilled cowhand. One of the floating outfit, Billy Jack had been Dusty's sergeant major in the War and appearances in his case were very deceptive.

With the meal over, the trail crew headed for the corral. Ropes swished and hooley-ann loops* sailed through the air to drop about the necks of the horses selected for use while moving the herd out. In very quick time, every hand had caught and saddled his horse; the hooley-ann being a roping throw designed to allow several of the crew to operate at the same time around the corral. One of the first ready was Dawn, snaking her *bayo-tigre* gelding from the milling crush and throwing on its rig with practised speed.

Already Dusty and Goodnight were riding towards the herd. Studying the steers with experienced eyes, the rancher sought for signs of restlessness. Despite the addition of the Mineral Wells stock, the assembled Swinging G animals seemed quiet enough. Goodnight's foreman, John Poe, who would be staying in Young County to gather cattle for another drive, rode up. He told his boss that the night had been quiet and unevent-

* Described in *Trail Boss*.

ful, apart from the inevitable attempts by some of the wilder cattle to regain their freedom.

'You can expect that from the sort of *ladinos* we've been hauling out of the thorn-brush,' the rancher said.

'Sure,' Poe grinned. 'Way some of 'em act, you'd figure they didn't want to go and feed up all them hungry Apaches in New Mexico. Anyways, none of them got away.'

'I didn't think they would,' Goodnight replied, flashing a rare smile at his segundo and foreman. 'Here's my crew. We'll move out straight away, Dustine.'

'Yo!' answered Dusty, and rode to meet the approaching party.

For a long moment Goodnight sat silent, then he sucked in a deep breath. This was the start of what might easily be the salvation of Texas, or a fiasco. Whichever way it turned out, he felt it was well worth the try. Turning to Poe, the rancher offered his hand.

'I'll see you when I get back, John.'

'Everything'll be ready for you, Charlie,' Poe replied as they shook hands. 'Good luck.'

'Likely we'll need it,' Goodnight said.

'All right!' Dusty said to the trail crew. 'Head 'em up. Let's move 'em!'

'Yeeah!' Vern whooped, wriggling on his saddle in excitement and eagerness.

'I said move 'em, not spook 'em!' Dusty barked. 'Hold it down and save that whooping for when we hit Fort Sumner.'

'Sure, Cap'n Dusty,' the youngster answered, face flushing with shame at the public rebuke. 'I——'

'You heard,' Mark growled in Vern's ear. 'Get to it.'

Much as Dusty would have liked to make up for the sting of his words, the chance did not arise. Along with the other hands, Vern rode to his position and made ready to start. When setting out the order in which the hands would work that day, Dusty had allocated Dawn to the swing, the forward third of the herd. Approaching her place, the girl became aware for the first time of just how many three thousand head of longhorns amounted to. She had seen gathers almost as large, during communal round-ups, but nobody had ever thought of moving so many from place to place.

The range ahead seemed blanketed with steers of almost every imaginable animal colouration. While every bit as much creatures of a herd as buffalo or pronghorn antelope, the Texas longhorn showed none of their uniformity of appearance. No two steers in that vast gathering looked completely alike. Apart from the occasional muley, however, they all had one thing in common, a set of spreading, powerful and needle-sharp horns.

Not that Dawn found time to sit in awed contemplation. Already the men were riding towards the cattle, gently urging them to move. Slowly, yet surely, the tremendous collection of steers started to walk in a westerly direction. At the point, Mark Counter and Swede Ahlén closed in on either side of the first steer ready to turn it anyway the trail boss signalled.

Commencing the first day's drive was always a trying time for the trail crew. So far the steers had not settled into a cohesive travelling unit. The Swinging G stock were still unsettled by the arrival of the Mineral Wells herd not thirty-six hours back. Due to the way they had been collected,* a number of Goodnight's contingent were *ladinos*, outlaws long used to free-ranging in the thorn-brush country. Given time, they might have become accustomed to herd life. Unfortunately, time was a commodity in very short supply if they were to reach Fort Sumner by the end of June. The drive had to be got on its way.

To an unknowing on-looker, everything might have seemed to be in wild confusion. There were steers which objected to being moved from such easy grazing, or *ladinos* striving to return to their wild existence, demanding attention and keeping the trail hands fully occupied.

Horses spurted, twisted, pivoted and galloped into a muck-sweat, cutting off would-be bunch-quitters and turning the departing steers back into the marching column. After the resting mass had been converted into a mobile line, there was a continuous changing of positions. The better travellers shoved their way by the slower, less fit, or plain lazy remainder. Already some of the steers, particularly those from the Mineral Wells area, had teamed up with 'travelling partners'. Finding themselves separated, the partners would shatter the air with their bawling and try to balk against moving forward until reunited. They added to the confusion, as did the 'lone wolves'. These steers appeared to have only one aim in life, to amble up as far as the point, cut across before the leading

* Told in *Godnight's Dream.*

animals, make their way down the other flank to the drag and repeat the circle. More than one cowhand started to chase a 'lone wolf', thinking it was trying to escape, and retired cursing on discovering its harmless purpose.

Yet the drive continued. Following the cattle came the remuda, available for when a hand wanted a fresh horse from his work-mount.* Bringing up the rear were the chuck- and bed-wagons, driven by Rowdy Lincoln and his tall, lanky, freckle-faced and excitable louse, Turkey Trott. Towards evening they would speed up their teams, pass along the side of the drive, find a suitable camping-ground and prepare a hot meal—the first since breakfast—for the crew.

Throughout the day Dusty and Goodnight seemed to be everywhere. Sometimes at the point, then among the swing or flank men, or back with the drag, either the rancher or the segundo would materialise wherever he was needed most.

Two hours after moving the herd off its bed-ground, Dusty heard a sound that called for investigation. Two steers faced each other in menacing attitudes among the bushes to the flank of the herd. Pawing up dirt, throwing back their heads and cutting loose with as masculine bawls as their castrated condition allowed, they prepared for hostilities. It was a situation which demanded an instant attention on the part of the nearest trail hand. Like some human beings, longhorns could not resist the temptation to watch a good fight. So other steers would attempt to quit the herd as spectators.

Yet stopping the contestants would not be without risks, as Burle Willock well knew. When one of the fighting steers decided to quit, it would not linger. Twirling around, it would leave like a bat out of hell, giving all its attention to its rival and oblivious of anything ahead. Only by such tactics could the loser hope to protect its vulnerable, unprotected rear from a severe goring by the victor. Not even a cutting-horse—most agile of the equine breed—could equal the turn-and-go prowess of a longhorn under those conditions. Nor did the flight necessarily follow a fight. Should one of the steers be bluffed out by the other's aggressive mien, it would take just as drastic evasion measures.

So Willock hesitated before going in too close to the animals. Not so Dusty Fog. Charging up, he made straight for the steers. Dusty sat a buckskin gelding, noted through the Rio

* Texans did not use the word 'string' for their work-horses.

Hondo country for its cattle-savvy, and it knew just what to do. Ignoring the chance of a fear-inspired charge, the horse rushed forward, slammed a shoulder into the nearest steer and knocked it staggering. Seeing its rival at a disadvantage, the second steer attacked. Letting out a squeal, the buckskin's victim fled for the safety of the herd.

'Stop it!' Dusty roared, guiding his horse after the triumphant assailant.

While Willock chased and turned the fleeing steer, preventing it from rushing among the other cattle, Dusty caught up with the victor. Knowing only rough treatment would calm the beast, Dusty rode alongside its rump. By catching and jerking at the steer's tail, he caused it to lose its balance and crash to the ground. On rising, as was mostly the case after a good 'tailing down', the steer forgot all its anti-social notions and went quietly into the moving line.

Shortly before noon, Vern Sutherland pushed his *tobiano* down a draw after three steers which had escaped. In a foolhardy attempt to show how good a horse he rode, he had not changed mounts since starting out. While the *tobiano* overtook the steers and swung them back in the direction of the herd, it was tired.

Hearing a low snort to his left, Vern turned his head and saw a big black *ladino* coming towards him. Everything about the animal showed its mean nature and it clearly aimed to fight its way to freedom. The *tobiano* faced the steer, but Vern knew it was too leg-weary to deal with such a dangerous proposition. For all that, the youngster sat his ground. While he carried a holstered Colt and knew how to use it, he made no attempt to do so. The sound of a shot might easily cause the herd to stampede.

On his way to the drag, Goodnight saw the youngster's predicament and raced his *bayo-cebrunos** gelding to the rescue. Unshipping the rope, with one end ready-tied to the saddlehorn, he shook out its loop and gauged the distance with his eye. The rancher approached from the side of the steer as it began its charge. Rising to stand in his stirrups, as a means of making a more accurate throw, Goodnight sent the rope curling through the air. As the loop fell and tightened about the steer's neck, the rancher cued the *bayo-cebrunos* with his knees and brought it to a turning halt. Manila twanged taut between

* *Bayo-cebrunos:* a dun colour, shading into smokey-grey.

longhorn and saddlehorn. Fixing to keep anything he roped, the Texan always tied his lariat securely to the horn and relied upon his saddle's double girths to hold all firm. Braced ready for the impact, the *bayo-cebrunos* kept its feet. Not so the steer. Stopped unexpectedly with its feet off the ground, its legs shot sideways and it slammed down hard on its flank.

'Get them others back to the herd!' Goodnight called to Vern. 'Then go pick a fresh hoss from the remuda.'

'Yo!' the youngster answered and turned to obey.

There were other incidents calling for Dusty's or Goodnight's attention. In the late afternoon, they combined to help Dawn deal with a group of extra-determined *ladinos* which broke away. Only the girl's deft riding-ability held the bunch together long enough for the men to reach her. She felt no shame at needing the assistance. Not even the most experienced tophand cowboy could have handled the steers alone.

'Good work, Dawn,' the rancher said.

'Real good,' Dusty echoed, and grinned at the girl's dirt-smudged features. 'And as a reward, you can take first spell on the night herd.'

'How can you stand being so good to me?' Dawn yelled at the small Texan's departing back. Then she gave a resigned sigh. 'It could be worse, I might have been on the middle watch.'

CHAPTER FOUR

WE'LL NEVER BEAT HIM TO SUMNER

Knowing the importance of getting longhorns off their home ranges as a means of quietening them down, Goodnight had insisted that the herd be pushed hard all day. When he called a halt towards sun-down, they were some fifteen miles from their starting point. After leaving the Swinging G's holding area, none of the trail hands had dismounted for longer than it took to transfer a saddle to a fresh horse, or relieve the needs of nature. At mid-day, Rowdy had taken the chuck-wagon forward and handed out cold food to the crew as they rode by, so that they could eat but still stay on the move.

Even with the herd watered and brought to a stop in the open area selected by Goodnight for the night's bed-ground, only Mark, Dawn and two of the hands rode back to where the cook had set up camp. Until the four—first part of the night guard—had eaten a meal, set out their bed rolls and returned, the remainder of the hands continued to circle the herd and quieten any restless urges the hard-driven steers still felt. Later, when the cattle were broken to the trail, there would normally only be two riders at a time on night guard. Until then, and in periods of necessity later, the number would be doubled.

When the quartet arrived to take over, the rest of the crew trooped gratefully to the camp. Dusty went with them, but Goodnight stayed by the herd to make sure the guard knew their duties. First caring for their mounts, the trail hands took and picketed their night horses ready for instant use if the need arose. With that done, they made their way to the big main fire. There Rowdy or Turkey supplied each man with a plate generously loaded with thick, savoury stew and cups of coffee in which a spoon would almost stand erect.

Little was said until the plates had been cleaned and hunger satisfied. Then the hum of conversation arose.

'How do you like being on the trail, Vern boy?' demanded Willock in a condescending manner, winking at his crony, Jacko.

'It's great!' the youngster answered enthusiastically,

although he did not particularly care for the swaggering Double Two cowhand. Then, realising that he sounded too eager for a man of the world, he tried to adopt a more non-chalant tone. 'It's about what I figured it'd be.'

'Is, huh?' Willock sneered, flashing a superior grin around the circle of watching and listening men. 'It gets sorta rough though. Unless you've got the boss on hand to save you from them mean old steers.'

'Yeah?' Vern flashed back, cheeks reddening at the sniggers which rose from Willock's friends. 'Well I didn't see you doing so all-fired much about them two steers that was fighting—until Cap'n Dusty come and split 'em out for you.'

A low chuckle of laughter rose at the response, coming from the men less close to Willock. Annoyance twisted at the flashy cowhand's face and he lurched to his feet.

'If you'd done more working and less sitting watching, us *men*'d've had a heap less work to do!' Willock snarled, looking mean and hooking his right thumb into his gunbelt close to the butt of the low-hanging Army Colt. 'I don't take much to carrying——'

Watching the incident, Dusty scented potential trouble. Across the fire, the D4S's third member, a dour, middle-aged man called Josh Narth stirred slightly as he squat on his heels. No swaggering trouble-causer, Narth had been a long time with the Sutherland family and could be counted on to side with his boss' son. So Dusty set about nipping the discord in the bud.

'All right, you pair,' Dusty said in a carrying voice as Vern also rose. 'Let it drop.'

'What's up?' Willock asked, looking to where Dusty heel-squat cradling a coffee-cup. 'Don't you reckon the hen-wrangler there can take a bit of funning?'

'He can take it, and hand it back,' Dusty replied. 'Only it's starting to look and sound like *you* can't take what he gives.'

'Hell!' Willock spat. 'We've been car——'

'The young 'n' did all right today,' Red Blaze remarked. 'He didn't need any carrying, what I saw of him.'

'Shy out of it, Red,' Dusty ordered, but noticed that most of the hands muttered agreement with his cousin's statement.

'Yeah, Red!' Willock went on viciously. 'Shy out. Unless you figure this D4S bunch can't——'

'That's another thing!' Dusty interrupted and gave Red a

glare which prevented him from rising and carrying the matter further. 'From now on I don't want to hear any more talk about the D4S, Double Two, Bench P or any other damned kind of bunch. This drive's going to be hard enough with us all pulling together. So you can forget about riding for some spread or other back to home. From here to Fort Sumner we all belong to *this* outfit.'

'Them your orders,' Burle asked, 'or Colonel Charlie's?'

A low rumble of sound came from Swede Ahlén's throat, but he said nothing. Maybe he was segundo at the Double Two, but on the trail drive he rated as an ordinary hand. So he sat back and waited to see how Dusty meant to deal with the cowhand's insolence.

'Feller, you're——' Red began, again making as if to stand up.

'Stay put, Cousin Red,' Dusty ordered.

'Sure, *Cousin* Red,' Willock sneered. 'Leave us not forget that frying-size there's got a right pretty sister along——'

Whatever else the cowhand intended to say was never uttered. Tossing the dregs of his coffee into the fire, Dusty put down the cup and came to his feet.

'All right,' he said, in the soft tone which every OD Connected cowhand came to know so well. 'I figured that sooner or later I'd have to prove to somebody how I got this segundo chore for more'n just being Colonel Charlie's nephew. So tonight looks as good a time as any to do it.'

As Red or Billy Jack could have warned Willock, if they had been so inclined, there were stormy times ahead for him. When Dusty's voice took on that gentle, almost caressing note, it was long gone time to hunt for the cyclone-shelter. Willock did not have their knowledge of the small Texan's ways, but did have his own reputation for toughness to consider. So he stamped in gaily where angels—or as near angels as any member of the OD Connected could be—feared to tread.

'So what's that supposed to mean?' Willock demanded truculently.

'Way I see it,' Dusty replied. 'You figure to be wild, woolly, full of fleas and never curried below the knees. So I'm fixing to give you a chance to prove it. Guns, or bare hands. Whichever way you want.'

That placed the issue as straight as anyone could ask for. Looking around, Willock read eager expectancy on the faces of the other Mineral Wells men. No hint of concern for their segundo's safety showed from the two OD Connected riders, only complete confidence in Dusty's ability to handle Willock's play no matter how he made it. That, and mocking pity at the cowhand for his stupidity. Even as Willock watched, Billy Jack turned and addressed Ahlén.

'How do you stand on this, Swede?'

'He roped the hoss,' Ahlén replied immediately. 'Let him ride it.'

Along with the other newcomers, Ahlén recognised some of Dusty's potential, but wondered if all the stories heard about his fighting prowess were true. While none of them felt inclined to make the experiment personally, the Mineral Wells crowd were not averse to watching Willock give it a try.

Slowly Dusty began to walk around the fire. Watching the other coming his way, Willock became aware of a strange change taking place. Suddenly he found that he faced a real *big* man, not an insignificant nobody who held post as segundo by virtue of being Goodnight's nephew. In some way, Dusty gave the impression of having taken on size and heft until he towered over the biggest of the crew.

'If the button can't——' Willock commenced, hoping to turn the fight to the less dangerous Vern Sutherland.

'Vern's not in it any more,' Dusty warned him, continuing to advance. 'It's between you and me.'

Fear bit at Willock as the small Texan delivered the ultimatum. The cowhand became increasingly aware that his salty reputation was strictly local and did not extend beyond his home ranges. Dusty Fog's name was State-wide and, as Willock now realised, had been well-deserved. So Willock wondered how he could back down, avoid the clash, without being laughed off the drive. There was no half-way about it. Either he ate crow or took a licking for his pains. The idea of facing Dusty with a gun in his hand did not for an instant enter Willock's head.

Silence that could almost be felt had dropped on the camp, broken only by the thumping of Dusty's boots as he walked. Then old Boiler Benson spoke.

'Hosses coming, Cap'n Fog,' he said, silently cursing the sound as it would most likely prevent Willock receiving a badly-needed lesson in manners. 'Not from the herd, along our back trail.'

Immediately he heard the words, Dusty laid aside all his thoughts on Willock's redemption. With Goodnight still at the herd, it fell on the segundo to prepare for meeting and dealing with unexpected, possibly unwelcome visitors. So Dusty turned from the cowhand, ready to rattle out orders.

For his part, Willock let out a sigh of relief. He decided that he owed the approaching riders a vote of thanks, no matter what brought them to the herd. In another five seconds, he would have been forced to make a hateful decision and either way he had gone would have been unpleasant. So he listened to the approaching hooves and mentally raised his hat.

'Come all you fellers, you cowhands from Texas,
Bring on your young ladies and gather around,
I'll tell you a story so sad and so gory,
Of how Juan Ortega got put under ground.
Ole Juan was a rowdy who never looked dowdy,
He dressed caballero and died in his boots,
Though his past was real shady, he loved but one lady,
Her love caused the death of this king of owlhoots.'

Getting ready to leap to their *big* segundo's orders, the trail hands settled down when a pleasant tenor voice lifted over the sound of the hoof-beats. Clearly whoever came did not intend to surprise the camp. Dusty relaxed before the end of the first line, as did Red and Billy Jack, for they had identified the singer's voice.

'It's Lon,' Dusty told the old-timer.

'That's the Ysabel Kid,' Solly Sodak of the Lazy F said, wanting to air his superior knowledge to the man at his side. 'He sure sings purty.'

Satisfied that he had given notice of his coming, the Kid did not continue with the 'so sad and so gory' story of Juan Ortega. Looking through the darkness, the men by the fire soon made out enough to solve the matter of the multiple hoof-beats. Though he was alone, the Kid had four horses trailing after him with their hackamore reins tied to his mount's saddlehorn.

Sitting afork his magnificent, huge white stallion—which, despite its saddle and bridle, looked as wild as any free-ranging mustang—the Kid rode into the light of the flames before stopping. Swinging his right leg up and across the saddlehorn, he dropped lightly to the ground. In his right hand he gripped the new type of Henry rifle—soon to achieve fame as the Winchester Model of 1866, or the 'old yellowboy' by virtue of its brass frame—given to him while helping Dusty in Mexico. An improvement on the original Henry, the rifle was much admired and several of the Swinging G's men swore they would save sufficient money from their end-of-trail pay to purchase similar weapons.

Travel-dirty, showing signs of having ridden far and hard, the Kid stood for a moment looking around the camp. From hat to boots, all his wearing apparel was black, including the gunbelt, which carried a walnut-handled Colt Dragoon revolver butt forward in the holster at the right side and an ivory handled James Black bowie knife sheathed at the left. Hair as black as the wing of a deep-South crow gave more hint of his Indian blood than did his red-hazel eyes and handsome, almost babyishly innocent cast of features. The eyes were alert, constantly watchful, almost alien in such a face. Dressed cowhand style, he gave the impression of latent, controlled, deadly danger; as a cougar did when sleeping on a limb.

'See you've got a fresh relay, Lon,' Dusty greeted, knowing the four horses led by the Kid were not those he had taken to Mineral Wells.

'Left the others at the Swinging G and got some that warn't so tuckered out,' the dark youngster explained. 'Where-at's Colonel Charlie?'

'Out with the herd. He'll likely be back soon. Do you want to see him about something real important?'

'Sure. But it can wait until he gets back. I'll tend to my mount and eat. Then if he's not back, we'll ride out and meet him.'

'I'll come and help you with 'em, Kid,' Vern offered.

'Gracias,' grinned the Kid. 'We'll split it up fair. You tend to the relay and I'll see to ole Nigger here.'

'I wouldn't have it any other way,' Vern replied, walking across but waiting until the Kid released the horses and handed over the reins. Anybody who took liberties like approaching the white stallion too closely would right soon come to regret the indiscretion.

Talk welled up around the fire as the Kid and Vern departed towards the remuda with the horses. Looking around, Dusty noted gratefully that the tension had gone from the atmosphere. The Kid's arrival had given Willock a chance to let the show-down against Dusty pass without losing face. So the cowhand resumed his seat during the conversation and stayed quiet, studiously avoiding making any movement or sound that might catch the small Texan's attention.

Not that Willock needed to worry about that. Satisfied that he had made his point, Dusty was quite prepared to let the matter drop. Later he might be compelled to prove himself by physical means, but felt content to wait until the moment was forced upon him. Dusty knew, as did the whole crew, that Willock had backed water. He would gain nothing and only increase any resentment Willock felt by emphasising the point. So, as far as Dusty was concerned, the incident had run its course and was at an end.

Helped by Vern, the Kid made good time in attending to the needs of his five horses. Leaving his stallion to roam free for the night, secure in the knowledge that it would come when needed, he turned the other four in with the remuda. Then, carrying his saddle, he returned to the fire. In passing, Vern exchanged scowls with Willock. However they both knew better than to resume their quarrelling. They had come out of the first time without punishment, but Dusty would not deal so gently with them in future.

The Kid had finished his meal and spread his blankets alongside Dusty's, then was about to suggest he and Dusty went out to meet Goodnight, when the rancher returned. Hearing his scout's request for an interview, Goodnight collected a meal and went to the bed-wagon. With his plate on the tail-gate, he stood with the Kid and Dusty in the light of the lantern which hung from the canopy's rear support. Interested eyes studied them from the fire, but none of the crew offered to come across and satisfy their curiosity.

'Looks like you've been moving, *Cuchilo*,' Goodnight remarked, using the Kid's Comanche man-name 'The Knife', granted with regard to his skill in using one.

'Some, *Chaqueta-Tigre*,' the Kid answered, returning the compliment by addressing the rancher as 'Jaguar Coat', given to him by his *Nemenuh** enemies in the days when he rode with Cureton's Rangers. 'I trailed that feller clear up to Throckmorton, only he was travelling so fast I couldn't catch

* *Nemenuh:* 'The People', Comanche Nation's name for themselves.

up to him, and I hadn't seen hide nor hair of Chisum neither. Got to thinking maybe the feller'd quit the Long Rail on account of them stolen cattle. Anyways, I was out of makings and with Throckmorton so close, I reckoned I'd ride in and buy some. I'm right pleased I did now.'

'Apart from not believing the part about you *buying* tobacco,' Dusty put in, 'you're starting to get me interested.'

'What I learned was——' the Kid began, speaking the deep-throated *Pehnane* dialect which Goodnight understood but Dusty did not.

'Talk U.S., you damned slit-eye,' Dusty grinned. 'I apologise, you did buy some tobacco—once.'

'Cut the fooling, blast you!' Goodnight grunted, eyes sparkling good-humouredly. 'You're worse'n two old women.'

'I accepts that apology, sir,' the Kid replied, bowing to the rancher. 'Like I said, I'd got to thinking that feller'd quit Chisum and was getting all set to bawl Mark out for wasting my valuable time when I got back. Only it come out that ole Mark's smarter'n I figured—which he'd have to be comes to a point——'

'Is he always like this?' Goodnight groaned.

'You're seeing him at one of his better times,' Dusty assured his uncle.

'Anyways,' the Kid continued, after giving a lofty sniff. 'Seems like Chisum'd been to Throckmorton, with them Mineral Wells steers and left again—trail bossing a drive for some dudes who'd been around town for a spell.'

'Did you see the dudes?'

'Nope, Colonel, they'd pulled out afore I got there.'

'Where was Chisum driving to?' asked Dusty, although he could guess at the answer.

'Out to Fort Sumner. He'd left two days afore I got there, the dudes followed him later.'

'Damn it to hell, Dustine!' Goodnight barked. 'You know what this means?'

'Yes, sir. Chisum's got near on a week's head start on us.'

'It means a heap more than that. Chisum knows that trail as well as I do. He can stick to a route we'll have to follow and make sure that everything's spoiled after he's passed and afore we reach it. We'll never beat him to Sumner.'

Dusty and the Kid exchanged glances which showed their complete agreement with Goodnight's coldly logical summation of the situation. With Chisum so far in the lead, they could not hope to push their herd fast enough to pass and beat him to their destination. Nor would Chisum hesitate to use foul means to slow them down. Unscrupulous he might be, but he was also a master cattleman and would know ways to effectively hinder a following trail drive. However, Dusty, the Kid and Goodnight sprang from stock which did not mildly admit defeat. So they gave thought to how they might still beat Chisum to Fort Sumner despite his advantages.

'I near on went after Chisum and gave him a mite of trouble collecting his herd after the stompede,' the Kid remarked.

'Which stompede?' Dusty ejaculated.

'The one I was going to start,' the Kid said calmly. 'Only I figured you white folks'd likely not think I was playing fair. And that I'd best make speed to tell Colonel Charlie what I'd learned.'

'Damned *Pehnane*,' Dusty grunted. 'You'd be better hunting buffalo with——'

'Hey though!' interrupted the Kid, coming as close as the other two had ever seen to showing emotion. 'If Chisum's using your trail, Colonel, he'll be going up the Clear Fork of the Brazos and across to the headwaters of the Pecos, won't he?'

'That's the trail Oliver Loving and I blazed,' Goodnight admitted bitterly. 'And, knowing Chisum, that's the way he'll go.'

'Only you allus went up it earlier in the year,' the Kid went on.

'We did!' Goodnight breathed, beginning to guess what the dark youngster was leading up to.

'And you never had any Injun trouble between the Clear Fork and the Pecos?'

'Not on that stretch.'

'Only this's the time of the year when the *Kweharehnuh*'ll* be making their big buffalo and antelope hunting,' the Kid went on. 'If I know them, which I figure I do, they'll not take kind to having a damned great herd of cattle drove through their hunting grounds.'

'That's for sure,' Dusty agreed. 'Which only makes things worse for us. Even if he manages to sneak his cattle through, Chisum'll make good and sure that the *Kweharehnuh*'re all

* *Kweharehnuh:* Antelope band of the Comanche Nation.

riled up by the time we get there.'

'So why go?' said the Kid.

'Because there's only one other way,' Goodnight explained. 'And it'd take us a damned sight longer to head south and circle around the Staked Plains. We'd still not get to Sumner on time.'

The Kid's face was as gently innocent as a church-pew full of well-behaved choir-boys and his voice mild as he said, 'I wasn't figuring on going '*round* the Staked Plains.'

CHAPTER FIVE

BAD AS IT IS, IT'S OUR ONLY CHANCE

For a long moment neither Dusty nor Goodnight spoke. Taken any way a man looked at it, the Kid had made a mighty startling—some would even say, considering his knowledge of the terrain involved—even crazy suggestion. The Staked Plains were a rolling, arid, semi-desert area between the South Concho and Pecos Rivers. Baked by the heat, parched for the want of water, the stunted vegetation offered poor grazing and little shade for the cattle and many hazards existed along the route they would be forced to follow. Under no circumstances could it be termed the kind of coutry into which a trail boss would willingly direct his herd.

At last Goodnight let out a long breath and said, 'It's near on ninety-six miles from the South Concho to the Pecos, Kid. With nothing but spike grass, horned toads and gila monsters from one side to the other.'

'I knowed that all along,' the Kid answered. 'Back when I was a button with the *Pehnane*, I hunted desert sheep around it.'

'We'll not be hunting around it, we'll be trailing cattle *across*,' Goodnight pointed out. 'There's not much drinking water, but plenty of alkali and salt lakes scattered about. Let a thirsty herd get just a teensy smell of one of 'em, and there'd be a stompede that nothing could stop. And any steer that drinks from one of them lakes'll be buzzard bait in twenty minutes.'

'I know that, too,' the Kid admitted.

For all his words, Goodnight was clearly giving the suggestion his close consideration. Watching his uncle, Dusty could almost follow the other's train of thought. Novel, wild, impractical though the Kid's idea might have sounded at first hearing, it was possibly their only chance of beating Chisum to Fort Sumner. The very nature of the animals in the herd made that so.

Unlike the pampered beef breeds which would follow them, the Texas longhorns lived an almost completely natural existence. Left to forage for themselves upon the unfenced ranges, they had over the generations developed the survival instincts of wild animals. In nature only the fittest survive. So any longhorn that reached maturity was perfectly capable of standing up to hardships and the rigours of climatic conditions.

Maybe, just maybe, the Kid had offered a solution to Goodnight's problem. Crossing the Staked Plains would be desperately risky, but better than no chance at all. No Texan ever cared to go down without fighting.

'Damn it!' Goodnight growled. 'I'd hate like hell for Chisum and that slimy cuss Hayden to lick me this easy.'

'And me,' Dusty agreed. 'Especially after they cost me the price of two new Stetsons.'

'Two?' grinned the Kid. 'Don't tell me that you lost that one you bought after them fellers shot up your old woolsey?'

'Somebody put a hole in the new one,' Dusty explained, ignoring the suggestion that he would wear a cheap, poor quality 'woolsey' hat. 'You haven't got kin around here, have you?'

'Damned if *I* don't start talking Comanche soon!' Goodnight groaned. 'Kid, if you could find each of those lakes afore we come to it, we could point the cattle up-wind until we get by and they won't smell the water.'

'It'll not be easy doing, Uncle Charlie,' Dusty cautioned.

'Don't I know it?' demanded the rancher grimly. 'But, bad as it is, it's our only chance of licking Chisum to Fort Sumner.'

'Which we all want to do, for more reasons than one. I tell you, Uncle Charlie, if we fail there'll be few who chance trying. And Chisum'll cheat 'em blind on taking their stock to sell for them.'

'There's one thing in our favour,' Goodnight said. 'It's good grazing and easy going from here to the South Concho. So we'll let the steers take on fat and tallow up to there. After that, we'll push them day and night without stopping until we hit the Pecos. It'll be all of three-four days to get across.'

'By then the crew'll've learned plenty about their work,' Dusty replied and remembered something. 'Hell's fire. We've got Dawn along. Maybe we should send her back.'

'Whee doggie!' chuckled the Kid. 'So that lil gal made it, did she? Way she talked 'n' acted going home, I got to figuring she had it in mind to come along. And I sure admire you, which ever of you's the one who's fixing to make her go back. That's no *Nemenuh naivi** as's been trained right 'n' proper from the cradle-board to do as the men-folks tells her regardless.'

'What does delegation of authority mean, Dustine?' Goodnight inquired.

'You do it, I'm scared to, I've always been told. Poor ole Mark, I hope she don't chaw his ears off when *he* passes the word.'

'Does she have to go back?' asked the Kid. 'She's got sand to burn and spunk enough to see it through.'

'Having her along might even help,' Dusty went on. 'No matter how tough the going, the fellers won't quit while she's sticking it out—and stick she will.'

'We'd best ask her how she feels about it, anyways,' Goodnight decided. 'And do it tonight, so's she's close enough to the Swinging G house to make it back without an escort; happen she wants to go.'

'I'll bet my next month's pay that she's still with us at Fort Sumner,' the Kid offered, looking at Dusty. 'Are you on?'

'No bet. And, anyways, you've already drawn most of your next month's pay to buy shells for that fool rifle.'

'Injun-giver!'

'Are you figuring on telling the rest of the hands, Uncle Charlie?' Dusty asked, ignoring his friend's comment.

'What do you think?' asked Goodnight.

'I'd say no, was it me,' Dusty decided. 'At least until after they've been on the trail a mite longer.'

Goodnight nodded soberly. Told of his intention of taking the herd across the Staked Plains, while still new to the notion of handling it, the Mineral Wells men might figure that they faced an impossible task. After a few weeks on the trail, they would have widened their experience and, more important, gained at first hand complete confidence in the abilities of their trail boss and his segundo. Knowing they were led by competent, trail-wise bosses, the men would be more willing to risk the dangerous crossing.

'I think you're right,' the rancher said approvingly. It seemed that his nephew had learned the lessons of leadership well; small wonder Dustine had done so well during the War and since. 'When Dawn comes from the night herd, I'll tell her what we've decided and ask what she wants to do. Then I'll ask her not to tell any of the others.'

* *Naivi*: unmarried Comanche girl.

'It'd be best,' Dusty agreed.

On her return from riding the night herd, Dawn found herself taken to one side and told of Goodnight's intention to cross the Staked Plains. Without attempting to influence her one way or the other, he warned of the difficulties and dangers they would face. At the end, the girl stated her determination to see the drive through. Then she promised not to mention his plans, even to her brother. After a meal, she went to where her blankets were spread in the bed-wagon. Allowing her to sleep there was the only concession the men made to her sex, but agreed it was less embarrassing for all if she did not sleep among the male members of the crew.

Taking his horse—the big paint stallion which had crippled Ole Devil Hardin before Dusty tamed it for use as his personal mount*—from the picket line, the small Texan rode out to the herd. He had waited to see the girl's response to Goodnight's question, and left grinning a little at the calm manner in which she heard the startling news then gave her answer. As he drew near to the bed-ground, he could hear the droning, near-tuneless singing which experience had taught cowboys soothed the cattle and prevented them from becoming frightened by the unheralded appearance of a rider from the darkness.

'Now say, you fool critters, why don't you lay down?
And quit this for-ever moving around,
My hoss is leg-weary, my butt-end aches like hell,
So I could feel the bumps if I sat on a smell.
Lay down, you —— bastards, lay down,
Lay down; you —— —— ——† sons-of-bitches, lay down.'

Looming from the blackness, riding at a leisurely walking pace, Swede Ahlén brought his song to a stop and grinned a greeting as he saw Dusty coming his way.

'That sure was a beautiful tune, Swede,' complimented Dusty. 'And the chorus would make a deacon proud.'

'You should've heard the words Dawn was singing when we come out to relieve her,' Ahlén answered, still grinning. 'It like to start ole Billy Jack and me to blushing.'

'I'll have to come out and listen next time she's on,' Dusty

* Told in *The Fastest Gun in Texas.*
† The reader can supply the missing words.

decided. 'Everything all right?'

'We've been quiet enough so far. Knowed we would be, Billy Jack was saying how he figured we'd have a stompede come half an hour.'

Turning in their saddles, the two men looked across the night-darkened range. Before them, the cattle were assembled in a loosely-formed square with a rider patrolling each side. Experience and good luck had allowed the trail boss to pick a nearly perfect location, clear of ravines or draws into which a restless steer might blunder, or where wild animals could hide. Nor was there any wooded land, always a source of trouble and danger, close by. Some of the steers lay quietly chewing their cud, others slept on their feet. Here and there, a restless animal stirred a flurry of complaint as it moved from place to place in search of choicer grass on which to chew. However, having been pushed hard all day, allowed to feed on the way and carefully watered, the majority of the herd showed no inclination to travel.

Yet Dusty and Ahlén were aware of how easily the peaceful state could be changed. A sudden, loud, unexpected noise, the wind-carried scent of a passing predatory animal—be it cougar, wolf, black or grizzly bear—the appearance of a rattle-snake from a hole down which it had slipped during the day, any of them might send the cattle racing off in wild stampede. That was more likely to happen, however, when the steers were hungry, thirsty, riled up or disturbed for some reason; but the men knew better than to take unnecessary risks.

'Let's hope it stays that way,' Dusty said after a moment's study of the herd. 'Unless you feel like taking a gallop after them, that is.'

'Happen I get to feel that way, I'll find me a tall tree and bang my head again' it to knock my brains back in,' Ahlén grinned. Then he became sober and continued, 'Say, Dusty. Burle Willock's got a big mouth, but he's a good hand.'

'If he wasn't, I don't figure you'd've brought him along,' Dusty replied.

'Yeah. Waal, I had me a lil talk with him afore I come out here and I don't reckon, what he said back, he'll give you any more lip or fuss.'

'That's all I ask. I don't like billing in on things like that tonight, but it had to be stopped. Young Vern Sutherland's aiming to prove how he's a man-grown on the drive and I'd hate like hell to see him get pushed so that he acted *loco* trying to do it.'

'Burle was more'n a mite rough on him, and hadn't any call to talk about having to carry him. Vern did all right today. Damn it though, I've just now remembered——'

'What's up?' Dusty asked.

'Burle figures to be a real ladies' man,' Ahlén answered. 'He got into some fuss with Darby Sutherland over making up to Dawn the wrong way. Darby licked him good and he's a bad forgetter.'

'He'd better forget until this drive's over,' Dusty warned. 'How d'you stand if I have to pick up his toes, Swede?'

Ahlén knew what Dusty meant. Generally the term was used to describe the punishment handed out to a remuda horse which continually broke out of the wranglers' rope corral, or a fractious steer making trouble in a herd. Rather than have the difficult one stir up its companions, or teach them its bad habits, the boss would order one of his cowhands to pick up its toes. To do this, the man roped the animal by its fore-feet, bringing it crashing down with sufficient force to knock some sense into it or break its neck. In the latter case, the boss considered the loss of the awkward one justified in that it preserved the majority's good behaviour.

While Dusty's intentions in Willock's case were somewhat less drastic, his words conveyed the desired meaning to Ahlén. If Willock did not mend his ways, the small Texan intended to teach him a sharp and painful lesson.

'Maybe we ride for the same brand back to home, Dusty,' Ahlén answered soberly. 'But if it's to do with the working of the herd and just between you 'n' him, he's on his own. I know you won't play favourites when it comes to picking up toes.'

'You can count on it,' Dusty assured him. 'Well, I'll be moving on to see if Billy Jack's fell off his hoss and broke both his legs yet.'

'Way he was talking coming up here, he's figuring on that, or worse, happening any ole time,' Ahlén replied. 'Tell him to keep happy and cheerful.'

'What do you want me to do?' Dusty asked. 'Spoil his night.'

For a moment Dusty wondered if he should tell Ahlén about the decision to cross the Staked Plains. Then he decided against doing so. Not that he distrusted the big man. Dusty knew Ahlén to be shrewd, capable, regarding him as one of the best hands in the crew and well worthy of the post of ranch foreman.

The latter was the deciding factor in not speaking. First quality of a ranch's foreman was the ability to put his own spread's interest foremost on all things. Being aware of the risks involved in making the crossing, Ahlén might feel it his duty to prevent his boss' stock being submitted to them. From what Dusty had seen, the other Mineral Wells men, with the possible exception of the D4S contingent, would follow Ahlén's lead. The big blond could either be a calming influence, or stir them up.

In the final analysis, the decision on whether to inform Ahlén or not lay with Goodnight. So Dusty concluded it would be best for him to go along with his uncle's original plan. With that in mind, Dusty left Ahlén to continue patrolling and drifted on in search of Billy Jack.

'Howdy, Cap'n Dusty,' the lanky cowhand greeted, halting his doleful and even more profane chorus of the night herders' chant as the small Texan came up. 'Nice night, if it don't blow up a blue-norther or twister afore morning.'

'Sure,' Dusty agreed. 'Everything going all right?'

'Up to now,' Billy Jack answered, in a tone which expressed amazement that such should be the case. 'Likely they'll all've died off by morning.'

'Happen they have, Uncle Charlie'll likely peel your hide.'

'Shucks! I knowed that I'd get blamed regardless. Did the Kid learn anything wherever he'd been?'

'A mite.'

'Is that Wednesbury's partner still around, you reckon?'

'Not that I know of,' Dusty replied. 'He wouldn't get word about Wednesbury's try failing until it was too late to hit at us on the holding ground.'

'He'll know by now,' Billy Jack announced in gloomy satisfaction. 'Likely got him a whole mess of hard-cases coming after us by now.'

'Could be,' Dusty admitted. 'Only Lon didn't see any of them on his way here and he watched real good.'

Knowing Billy Jack, Dusty did not expect him to be comforted by the news. Letting out a long, tormented sigh, the lanky cowhand waved a languid hand at the resting cattle.

'This here herd'd spook real easy happen they come boiling

up at us with guns a-roaring. Even if they ain't got any of that new-fangled diney-mite with 'em.'

'Don't *you* let 'em do it,' Dusty commanded.

'How'd I stop 'em?' Billy Jack wailed.

'Why, look to the heavens with the light of righteous truth, brother,' Dusty suggested, sounding like a hell-fire-and-damnation circuit-riding preacher delivering a sermon, 'and shout, "They can't scare me, my soul is pure!" Then charge 'em head down and horns a-hooking.'

'What if they figure I'm a stinking liar?' Billy Jack wanted to know, then he brightened up. 'Anyways, they'd probably drop me in the first volley.'

'We'll give you a swell burying,' Dusty promised.

For all the light manner in which they discussed it, neither underestimated the danger. There had been at least two dudes involved in the bid to capture the Army's beef contracts, one of whom now lay in a grave at Graham's boot-hill. Dusty did not expect Wednesbury's partner—or partners—to give up after the earlier set-backs, there was too much at stake for that. Those men were not interested in the welfare of Texas, but meant to carve a fortune out of the State's misfortune and poverty. There would be other tries at stopping Goodnight reaching Fort Sumner. So the trail crew needed to maintain a constant vigilance and be ready to counter force with force should the need arise.

At the moment Dusty gave his promise of a fine funeral, a disturbance started close to where they sat. Coming on to a resting muley, one of the steers decided to drive it away out of sheer ornery cussedness. Instantly Billy Jack dropped his mournful pose and started his horse moving. Dusty waited until sure his help would not be needed, then rode on in search of the next member of the night guard.

Seeing the slim figure of Vern Sutherland approaching, Dusty brought his horse to a halt. There had been a slight stiffness in the youngster's attitude to him after the incident with Willock and he could guess at its cause. A faint grin twisted at the corner of Dusty's lips as he thought of the diverse nature of a segundo's work. It entailed far more than merely attending to the cattle, or ordering the trail hands to perform their tasks.

'Hi Vern,' Dusty said.

'Cap'n!' Vern grunted and made as if to ride on.

'Hold it. Is something up?'

'Naw—Hell, yes there is. You didn't have to bawl down Burle Willock on my account. I could've took him.'

'I didn't bawl him down on your account,' Dusty corrected. 'I made *both* of you quit doing something that somebody'd've been sorry for had it been done.'

'I can handle a gun——!' Vern began hotly.

'So can most folks in Texas,' Dusty interrupted. 'Trouble being too many of 'em only learn *how* to shoot, not *when*.'

'Burle Willock don't scare me!'

'And you don't scare him, so you're even,' Dusty replied. 'But, happen you pair make any more fuss on this drive, I'll make a stab at seeing if I can scare you both.'

'Sure, Cap'n,' Vern muttered, figuring that Dusty could make good his threat. 'Only I don't cotton to having folks ride me.'

'Ride you!' Dusty barked. 'Did you hear the way they all rode Rowdy about his cooking?'

'Sure.'

'Did he get riled?'

'No. He's only a cook——'

'You try doing without him. Or wait until you've got a bust leg, or some other hurt,' Dusty interrupted. 'Then see how "only" he is. Rowdy's as good a man as anybody on this drive. And because he is, and knows it, he takes a joke or more about his food. You're young, Vern, the youngest hand on the drive. So you'll get hoorawed some. But the fellers know that you're doing a man's work and figure you're grown enough to take a lil funning. Remember that next time somebody does it.'

'Willock didn't mean it funny,' Vern protested.

'Nor did you when you answered,' Dusty pointed out. 'Which I don't blame you for doing it. Sure, you've got to stand up and not be pushed around. All I ask is that you don't go to pushing back—afore somebody else starts.'

'I'll mind it,' Vern said.

'It'd be as well,' Dusty replied. 'See you around, Vern. Don't let Billy Jack give you the miseries.'

Continuing his tour of the night guard, Dusty knew that he had caused Vern to think. He hoped that the youngster would take his advice and steer clear of further clashes with Willock. The drive would be difficult enough without adding a feud to its problems.

CHAPTER SIX

THE YAP-EATERS'RE TOUGH HOMBRES

With only the barest touch of dawn's light showing, Rowdy Lincoln and his louse set to work rousing the trail hands. Already the coffee-pots were steaming on the fire and the aroma of breakfast wafted to the groaning, cursing men the cook's racket tore from the arms of sleep.

Laying in his blankets, Vern listened to the comments hurled at Rowdy's head and began to see more than ever the point Dusty had made to him the previous night. So the youngster decided that he would avoid being touchy or easily riled in the future. If a mere cook could take joshing of a rough kind, a cowboy who was also a trail drive hand should be able to do just as well.

'Come on!' Dusty shouted, striding towards the bed-wagon and banging his fist against the side. 'It's near on noon and the crew're dying of sun-stroke waiting to put their gear away.'

'Looking for somebody?' Dawn inquired, walking from the far side of the wagon. 'Us women-folk're used to getting up early.'

Collecting their food and coffee, the trail hands stood or squatted around the fire and began to eat. They ate without the formality of washing or shaving, stowing away the hot refreshments in the knowledge that they would receive no more until the herd had been bedded down that evening.

Having eaten, the hands dumped their plates and cups into the tub of hot water placed for that purpose. Then they rolled their blankets, secured the bundles holding their individual belongings and headed for the bed-wagon. Each hand was responsible for seeing his, or her, bed roll went into the wagon. On the first failure to do so, the cook would attend to the matter and give the owner a tongue-lashing on their next meeting for his idleness. If the offender continued to leave his bedding unrolled, the cook was within his rights to drive off and leave it.

Already fed, the two day wranglers had collected the 'cable' from the bed-wagon. Taking the long, stout rope to where the night hawk held the remuda, the two men set up a temporary corral. Supporting the cable on forked sticks spiked into the ground, they formed it into an open U shape. Into that flimsy enclosure, the night hawk guided the horses.

Having been taught early the futility of fighting against a rope, the horses made no attempt to break through the slender barrier. So they milled around but remained inside the U while their users came to make the first selection of the day. With the trail hands, less the four on night guard, mounted and gone, the wranglers let the night-horses join their companions. They did not start the remuda moving straight away, but waited for the night herders to return and change mounts.

Having relieved the night watch, the fourteen remaining trail hands took up their positions and watched for Goodnight's signal to start moving. Removing his hat, Goodnight swung it once counter-clockwise over his head, then pointed it forward above the ears of his horse. Instantly Mark and Ahlén cut loose with a deep-throated, sing-song chant which, they hoped, would eventually come to be regarded as marching orders by the steers.

'Ho, cattle!' boomed the two men. 'Ho! Ho! Ho! Ho!'

Closing in, the trail hands began the business of getting the herd on the move. There was much the same kind of confusion as on the previous day, with an additional source of concern for the crew.

Even among the de-prided and impotent steers there was an in-born desire to lead. So, up towards the point, the largest or more aggressive of them started jockeying for position. It was a time of danger, calling for constant supervision by the swing and point riders, with powerfully muscled bodies thrusting and shoving in contests of domination.

Led by Dusty, Billy Jack, Red, Dawn and two more hands worked their horses in among the cattle ready to halt any serious conflicts. While most of the disputes, due to the press of advancing animals from behind, ended quickly, the work was not without risks. Separating two steers about to meet head-on, Dawn had her leg pinned between the saddle and the flank of a third longhorn. Saying a few things a well-bred young lady did not usually utter, the girl slashed at the steer with her rope and it drew away. Then she turned aside the rivals by the same means. Narrowly avoiding the stab of an angry steer's horns, Billy Jack's horse was butted by a muley and let fly with both hooves against the offender's jaw hard enough to make it allergic to butting for some time to come. In doing so, the horse nearly threw its rider. Recovering his balance with masterly skill, Billy Jack found fresh trouble. In passing, the steer stuck its horn up the left leg of his pants. The material tore before worse damage was done and the doleful cowhand spent the rest of the day moaning about his misfortune in having a new—well, not more than six months old—pair of levis torn to doll-rags.

Finally one steer, a ten-year-old heavyweight with a dark brown body and head and shoulders of black seemed to be asserting its dominance over all the others. Twirling like a flash, it met the challenges of potential rivals with such force and determination that all were scared off without fighting. At last it stalked off ahead of the rest and none questioned its right to do so. Falling in on either side of the self-appointed leader, Mark and Ahlén guided it in the required direction.

With the leadership determined, the cattle continued to move with increased ease and Dusty's party withdrew to the sides of the lines. Riding ahead, Dusty joined his uncle as Goodnight sat on a small rise to one side of the route.

'What do you reckon, Uncle Charlie?' Dusty inquired, nodding towards the point of the herd.

'I've seen that big cuss around. He always lived close to the house, so he's used to folk being around him. He's not mean, or snaky. Happen he can hold on to the lead, we'll be all right.'

Like all herd-dwelling animals, the longhorns tended to follow the dominant male's directions. So a steady, well-behaved, sensible lead steer was invaluable on the trail drive. It would set the most suitable pace, obey the point riders' instructions without fuss and hold the rest of the cattle together by the strength of its presence.

Another day's hard pushing saw the trail herd thirty miles from the holding ground on the Swinging G. There was some horse-play around the camp-fire that night, but of a harmless nature. Dusty watched Willock to see how the cowhand was accepting the bawling out. From all appearances, Willock had decided to forget it, for he made no trouble and acted pleasantly enough in Dusty's presence. Yet he displayed a veiled hostility towards the entire D4S contingent, ignoring them completely. Nobody else seemed affected by Willock's attitude, so Dusty said nothing.

The events of the morning had prevented Dusty from suggesting to Goodnight that they should tell Ahlén of the change in their route. At night-fall, Dusty had put the matter from his mind and it was not raised.

The start of the third day's drive went off somewhat more smoothly and ended with the big brown and black steer even more firmly established as the leader. Due to its colour, the trail crew started to call it 'Buffalo' and it rapidly justified Goodnight's faith in it. It had all the qualities needed to lead the herd, being of a tractable nature where human beings were concerned and having the size, speed and bulk to handle dissidents or challengers, without being aggressive or bullying.

On the fourth day Goodnight allowed the pace to slacken. They were now well beyond the steers' regular stamping grounds, which caused a sharp reduction in the desire to return. Even the *ladinos* began to lose their eagerness to bolt, faced with unfamiliar surroundings, and took comfort from the companionship of the mass around them. While there was still the occasional attempt to break away, they grew infrequent and were easier to deal with. 'Lone wolves' still prowled and circled the flanks of the herd, but the rest of the steers were gradually becoming accustomed to the trail.

By the end of the first week, the three thousand four hundred steers left—the early stages of a drive, with an inexperienced crew, always saw losses by desertion or from other causes—had settled into as near perfect a travelling unit as any trail boss could desire. Retaining its position as lead steer, Buffalo strode at the head of a long, multi-hued line of walking beef which stretched snake-like across the range. Following Buffalo came the chief contenders for his post of honour, the biggest, strongest, most energetic of the steers.

With each passing day, the order of seniority among the steers became more firmly established. Once on the move, they ambled along in the most convenient manner to their needs. Unless bunched together for some reason by the cowhands, they picked their own line of march as long as it was in the required direction and grazed as they walked. However, while a steer could drop back then revert to its original position, any attempt to advance beyond its station was resented and discouraged by the beasts ahead. So at any given time of the day a steer could generally be found in the same position relative to its companions. Even when thrown off the trail, stopped to allow more extensive feeding than possible on the march, or after being bedded down for the night, they would resume their positions on the drive's continuing.

The muleys soon formed themselves into a group for mutual protection, bedding down clear of their horned kin, and foraged separately. Bringing up the rear, the weak, foot-sore or plain lazy animals formed a lachrymose bunch which needed to be constantly urged on by the drag riders.

Everybody on the drive worked hard from sun-up until late in the afternoon. Even after that most of the hands faced a spell of riding the night herd. The cook and his louse might have things easy during most of the day, but made up for it by being the first of the crew awake every morning. Good at their work, they saw to it that the others were well-fed and kept the coffee on the boil all night for the benefit of the riders coming to or from the herd.

Not only the steers improved with the travelling. All the trail hands gained confidence and experience as the days went by. Dusty watched them all and drew his conclusions from what he saw. Although there was, naturally, some inter-ranch rivalry, it stayed on a friendly basis.

Despite his start, Willock proved to be a good man at his work. He did tend to show off a mite and try to impress the others with his skill, but avoided incidents of the kind which had almost brought him into conflict with Dusty. Only once did his path close with Vern's; even then only slightly.

Apparently Vern had taken Dusty's comments of the first night to heart. He still reacted eagerly and showed boyish enthusiasm for his work, but not so much as on the first day of the drive. It seemed that Dawn too had profited from advice, for she might glance in annoyance when Vern acted in what she regarded as an unbecoming manner but never condemned him publicly. Left to himself, the youngster matured fast. He took part in the horse-play around the camp, giving as good as he got. When joshed about his youth, he no longer grew angry and commented instead on the age or senility of his tormentor. Only once did he almost fall from grace.

On the tenth day Goodnight allowed the herd to rest and graze. With Dusty's permission, Vern left camp on a hunting expedition in the hope of varying their diet. Shortly after noon he returned at a gallop on a lathered horse.

'I saw some dust shifting down that way, Cap'n,' the youngster breathlessly announced, pointing along their back trail. 'And there was something flashing in it.'

'Best go take a look,' Dusty decided and ordered some of the men to saddle up fast.

'Reckon it's that Hayden feller?' Vern asked excitedly, having been included in the party.

'I hope it's not,' Dusty replied. 'Let's ride.'

Guided by Vern, the party rode east. On their way, they met the Ysabel Kid returning from a circle around the area. The Kid confirmed about the dust and explained the 'metallic' flashes seen by Vern. About three miles away a large band of pronghorn antelope were grazing. What Vern had taken for the flickering of the sun on weapons was the flashing of the animal's white rumps as they signalled to each other in the manner of their kind.

Going back to the camp, the men told what had happened. Willock sneered about the mistake, but had sense enough to keep his comments to himself. All the older hands agreed that the youngster had done the right thing by returning. So their comments about his behaviour held no sting. He redeemed himself by resuming his hunting in the late afternoon and returning with a bull elk, the meat of which made a welcome change from longhorn beef.

Having what appeared to be the easiest job on the drive, the Ysabel Kid came in for his fair share of ribbing whenever he appeared at the camp-fire. Ranging far ahead, or circling the herd at a distance, it was his duty to locate natural hazards, human enemies or any other kind of danger. He also had to report to the trail boss on the condition of the land ahead, so that the route offering the best, easiest travel could be selected.

With the possibility of further trouble from Hayden, the Kid kept an extra careful watch on the rear. Nor did Vern's abortive alarm cause the dark youngster to relax. However, day after day rolled by with no sign of their enemies. The weather stayed fine and the whole crew were in good spirits.

For all that he covered more miles than any of his companions in a given day, a convention had grown up in the camp to accuse the Kid of spending his time asleep in the shade of a bush and only catching up when sure all the work had been done. When the Kid tried to produce his leg-weary horses as vindication of his true hard-working qualities, Billy Jack countered by fabricating a story about a pretty girl the dark youngster visited each day.

Usually the Kid did not return until well after dark. So Dusty and Goodnight, out ahead of the herd, regarded his appearance with apprehension when he came towards them in the late afternoon of the fourteenth day. Nothing showed on the Indian-dark young face and its owner might have been no more than returning in the normal course of events. Yet Dusty and the rancher guessed that the Kid bore grave and disturbing news.

'All right,' Dusty said resignedly as his *amigo* halted the leggy *bayo-lobo** horse he was using that day. 'What's up ahead.'

'Plenty of good grass, a stream of clear water and a mighty pretty place to bed down just by it.'

'Now the bad news,' Goodnight ordered.

'Saw some smoke ahead a ways,' the Kid complied.

'Indians making it?'

'Could be, Colonel. It was a fair ways off and I didn't take time to go closer. Figured you'd want to know.'

'You figured right. What do you reckon?'

'There wasn't enough smoke for white folks to be making it. Or for a whole village. I'd say it's a small bunch. Out raiding seeing's how they're down this ways.'

Which meant, as Dusty and Goodnight knew, the braves were on a horse-stealing mission. Not a comforting thought when the herd had along almost seventy good horses in its remuda. During his time with Cureton, Goodnight had gained a considerable knowledge of the Comanche as enemies. However, he was willing to yield to the Kid's superior wisdom.

'What're our chances, Lon?'

'I dunno,' the Kid answered frankly. 'Down here's the borders of the *Kwehärehnuh* and *Yamparikuh* stamping grounds. Could be a bunch from either. I'd bet my money on it being Yap-Eaters, not Antelopes, at this time of the year.'

'The Yap-Eaters're tough *hombres*,' Goodnight pointed out.

'Sure, but us *Pehnane* were allus closer to 'em than to the Antelopes. Happen it's either band and not just a bunch of *tuivitsi* on their lonesome, I might be able to get us by them. It'll likely cost us some cattle, and maybe a few of them extra hosses I asked you to fetch along.'

'It'll be worth them to get by without fuss,' Goodnight stated. 'Only a bunch of hot-headed young bucks aren't likely to listen to reason.'

'Nope,' agreed the Kid. 'But, happen them *tuivitsi*'ve got a *tehnap* along, he might be.'

* *Bayo-lobo:* dun approaching wolf-grey colour.

'Can you get up close enough to talk, even if there is one along?' Goodnight asked, knowing that even *tehnap*, experienced warriors, were inclined to shoot first and ask questions a long ways second when dealing with white men.

'I've got my medicine boot along,' the Kid answered. 'When they see that, they'll sit back and listen.'

'You want to handle it alone?' asked Dusty.

'Nope. I'd like to have you along to talk for Colonel Charlie. There's another thing, you mind how them renegade Tejases took on when they saw what our new Henrys could do?'

'I sure do,' Dusty grinned, recalling how the repeated fire from their Winchesters had scared off a band of Indians while on a mustang-catching trip.* 'It's likely those Yap-Eaters won't have seen rifles like them yet either.'

'Go with him, Dustine,' Goodnight said, even though he might be sending his favourite nephew to an unpleasant death. 'Make any kind of deal you have to and I'll back you on it.'

'Yo! When do you want to start, Lon?'

'As soon as we've fed, I'd say. Further we are from the herd when we meet 'em, the easier we can dicker.'

Accompanied by Dusty and the Kid, Rowdy speeded up his team and made for the site selected as their night's camp ground. There he and his louse broke all records in producing a meal. So well did they work that Dusty and the Kid rode out of camp just as the first of the night watch came from the herd.

'Back to four of us on night herd,' Willock muttered sullenly, watching the Kid and Dusty pass by. 'There's something in the air!'

'What's up, Rowdy?' inquired Raymar of the Flying H, having seen the decorative buckskin case across the Kid's bent left arm. 'What's Lon got that medicine boot on his rifle for?'

'Had he?' countered the cook and raised his eyes piously to the sky. 'So help me, I never noticed.'

'There's something bad wrong!' Willock insisted.

'That stew don't smell no worse'n any other night,' Spat Bodley objected. 'And if it's anything else, we'll likely get told soon enough.'

However the four men had to return to their duties with curiosity unsatisfied. Goodnight gave them no more than the usual orders before following the rest of the crew to the camp.

* Told in *.44 Calibre Man.*

There he addressed the party at the fire and warned them what the Kid suspected.

'Comanches!' Dawn breathed.

'Shucks, they don't fight at night, sis,' Vern protested. 'Everybody knows that.'

'They may not fight, but they move and raid in it,' Goodnight warned him. 'Only, afore you start looking for war-whoops behind every rock, I don't reckon they're close enough to make fuss for us tonight. Sure, I know I doubled the guard. I'd sooner have you all out riding the night herd and see nothing than get two men jumped and the cattle scattered.'

'Uncle Charlie's got a real kind heart,' Red whispered to Dawn. 'You've just to look real hard to find it. Most of my uncles're like that.'

Despite his comment, Red fully agreed with Goodnight's precautions. So did the rest of the listeners. Throwing a glare at his nephew, the keen-eared rancher continued with his orders in case of an attack.

'What repeating rifles have we along?' Goodnight asked, wanting to make sure he knew the correct figure. 'All my boys're carrying Spencers, down to Rowdy and Turkey——'

'*Up* to Rowdy 'n' Turkey,' corrected the cook, a privileged member of rangeland society. 'That's the right way to say it.'

'I've a new Henry,' Mark announced.

'Pappy let me bring along our Henry,' Vern went on, not without a touch of pride. 'But Dawn's only got her old scatter-gun.'

'It's a right handy tool though,' Dawn continued tolerantly.

Altogether the party could muster twelve repeating rifles and carbines, the rest of the crew being armed with muzzle-loaders, single-shot breech-loaders or just their hand-guns. Quickly Goodnight arranged the positions of the trail crew so that the repeaters would be evenly shared between the swing, flank and drag. Should the Indians come looking for trouble, the flank and swing riders on each side were to join their respective point man at the head of the herd. The drag hands and wranglers had orders to gather at the wagons. That way there would be controlled groups of defenders delivering volley firing instead of scattered individuals shooting.

'Hey, Colonel Charlie!' Rowdy Lincoln suddenly hissed. 'There's somebody moving out there to the east.'

CHAPTER SEVEN

THIS IS WHY YOU WON'T TAKE OUR CATTLE

Having wanted mounts which they could trust and rely upon under any conditions, Dusty had collected his big paint stallion from the remuda while the Kid whistled up his magnificent white. From his war-bag in the bed-wagon, the Kid had produced a long, heavily fringed buckskin pouch decorated with medicine symbols. With that on his rifle, it told all who knew the *Pehnane* that he belonged to the Dog Soldier lodge. So any insult or injury inflicted upon him would bring reprisals from the rest of that savagely-efficient fighting brotherhood.

With a good meal inside them and a reserve of pemmican in case of emergency, the two *amigos* wasted no time in heading across the range. Two miles beyond the herd, the Kid brought his horse to a halt as he wished to take certain added precautions before visiting the Comanche camp.

In addition to gathering the medicine boot from his gear, the Kid had donned a pair of *Pehnane* moccasins. Clearly he did not intend relying on such a flimsy disguise. Dismounting, he handed Dusty the buckskin-encased Winchester, removed his gunbelt and hung it across the white's saddle. Then he stripped off his hat, shirt, bandana and levis. That left him clad only in the moccasins and a breechclout of traditional *Nemenuh* blue. Formed of a length of cloth drawn up between the legs and passed under a belt at front and rear, with loose-hanging flaps trailing almost to knee level, the garment served him instead of conventional white man's underclothing and allowed a rapid transition to an Indian warrior when necessary.

Stripped of his cowhand regalia, the Kid looked almost completely Indian. Nor did the gunbelt lessen the likeness after he buckled it on. Many a brave-heart warrior wore such a rig, looted in battle. Satisfied with his appearance, he made a bundle of his clothes and fastened them to the saddle's cantle. Catching the rifle Dusty tossed to him, he vaulted astride the white's seventeen-hand high back.

'Let's go,' the Kid suggested. 'This way, happen any of 'em see us, they'll be more likely to talk first.'

Holding their horses to a fast, mile-devouring trot, they rode to the west. Night came, but the Kid had seen enough of the suspicious smoke to have fixed its position firmly. Despite the darkness, he led the way in as near a direct line as possible. After about three hours' riding, he signalled Dusty to stop.

'It's not far ahead now, so you'd best stay put until I've been in and let 'em know how things stand.'

'Go to it,' Dusty replied. 'Only if they're all *tuivitsi*, you come back here *pronto*.'

'You can count on it,' the Kid assured him.

'What do you want me to do?'

'Wait here. I'll move in on foot. Watch ole Nigger and come up with him when he starts moving. He'll soon enough let you know if there's anybody sneaking around. Should there be, try to settle 'em without too much noise.'

'Is it all right if I whomp 'em on the head with my carbine?' Dusty inquired, sliding the Winchester from its saddleboot.

''s long's you do it polite and thank 'em for letting you,' replied the Kid.

With that the dark youngster dropped from his horse's back. He landed and disappeared into the blackness with the minimum of sound. Cradling the carbine on his left arm, Dusty remained astride the big paint. At his side the white stallion stood like a statue, only its raised head, pricked ears and constantly moving nostrils testifying to its alertness as it sought for any warning scent or sound.

Advancing on noiseless feet, the Kid looked no less wild and vigilant than his horse. He came across no guards, nor expected to find any despite the increasing evidence which reached his ears of the Indians' presence in the vicinity. Almost half a mile from where he had left Dusty, he received his first sight of their quarry. Reaching the lip of a draw, he looked down its gentle slope at the fire which had sent up the smoke that brought him from the herd.

A touch of relief crept over the Kid at what he saw, along with a feeling of satisfaction at having his judgement verified. There were only men around the fire on the bottom of the draw. Not more than thirty of them, stocky, medium-sized and wearing clothes made from buckskin, elk hide, but not antelope. Naturally the bulk of the party consisted of *tuivitsi*, young, comparatively inexperienced warriors. Yet the Kid could see sufficient *tehnap* and a war-bonnet chief present to ensure that his medicine pouch would be respected and himself allowed to speak unmolested. They were a well-armed band, if a touch low on firearms and with no repeating rifles. By their dress, they came from the *Yamparikuh* band, not the *Kwe-harehnuh.*

Continuing just as quietly down the slope, the Kid halted while still in the darkness. So far none of the party gave any sign of being aware of his presence, but he wanted to announce himself before appearing.

'Greetings, men of the *Yamparikuh,*' the Kid called, speaking the *Pehnane* dialect perfectly. 'I come in peace to your fire.'

At the first words, several of the *tuivitsi* sprang to their feet and reached for weapons. None of the *tehnap* moved and the chief showed no sign of agitation, accepting that only a member of the *Nemenuh* could come so close undetected.

'You may come,' the chief replied.

Given permission, the Kid walked into the fire's light. He heard several startled comments as the men saw his tall, slim, un-Comanche figure coming out of the night. However the *Nemenuh* had adopted enough captive children into the tribe, turning the boys into warriors every bit of 'The People' as if they had been Comanche-born, for the Yap-Eaters to accept his *bona-fides.* And that *was* a Dog Soldier's medicine pouch covering the visitor's rifle. Halting before the chief, the Kid raised his right hand in the peace greeting.

'I am one called *Pinedapoi,*' the chief introduced. 'Are you *Nemenuh*?'

'My grandfather is Long Walker of the *Pehnane,*' the Kid answered. 'I am one called *Cuchilo.*'

'You speak a honoured name. Long Walker is a respected chief of our people. And I have heard of *Cuchilo.*'

'The fame of *Pinedapoi* has reached my ears,' the Kid countered politely.

'It is said you are a white man now,' a leathery *tehnap* put in.

'I have friends among the white men and live in their lodges,' the Kid admitted. 'But I am still *Nemenuh.*' He paused to see if there would be a challenge to his statement. None came and he went on, 'My blood-brother waits in the darkness, wishing to speak with the chief and braves of the *Yamparikuh.* He is a name-warrior among his people. His name is Magic

Hands.'

'The man who broke the medicine of the Devil Gun?' askea *Pinedapoi*.

'He is the one,' confirmed the Kid.

During the War, a pair of fanatical supporters of the Union had obtained an Agar Coffee Mill gun and hoped to use its rapid-fire qualities to lead the Indians in Texas on the war-path. Dusty had learned of the plot, attended the council at which the gun was to be displayed, killed the fanatics and prevented the full-scale uprising they had planned.*

'He may come,' *Pinedapoi* declared, for such a fighter as 'Magic Hands' would be welcome even though a white man and nominally an enemy, and without the added advantage of being blood-brother to a member of the *Phenane* Dog Soldiers.

The Kid pursed his lips and gave a shrill whistle. In the darkness, Dusty saw the white stallion toss its head and start to walk forward for no reason apparent to him. Following the horse, he booted his carbine. Riding towards the Yap-Eaters' camp, Dusty felt a touch uneasy. Cold black eyes in impassive, slightly Mongoloid faces studied him from head to toe. At a signal from the Kid, the stallion halted on the fringe of the firelight. Taking his cue from Nigger, Dusty stopped his paint, dropped from the saddle and let the reins dangle free. With his horse ground-hitched, he walked to where the Kid and the chief waited.

'Why are you here, Magic Hands?' *Pinedapoi* asked in Spanish after the formalities had ended.

'I am with *Chaqueta-Tigre*,' Dusty explained in the same language. 'We are taking a herd of cattle to the Army's forts beyond the Staked Plains.'

'So that the soldiers may eat well and be strong to fight against the Comanche?' suggested the chief. 'Or to make your home on the Indian lands?'

'Neither. To feed the Indians who live at peace on the reservations.'

Before Dusty could elaborate further, a *tuivitsi* rose and pointed to the south. All the other young braves came to their feet, talking and showing excitement. The older warriors scowled their disapproval at such behaviour before strangers and retained their impassive postures.

'We've got callers, Dusty,' the Kid said quietly. 'A wagon

* Told in *The Devil Gun.*

and two-three riders. Could be we've picked a mighty poor time to come calling.'

'Could be,' Dusty agreed. 'Only it's too late to pull out now.'

In a short time the newcomers appeared and Dusty found that the Kid had guessed correctly about the composition of the party. Three riders flanked a small wagon and two men sat on its box. They were Mexicans, evil-faced and looking out-of-place in the tarnished finery of their *charro* clothing. All carried revolvers and knives at their belts, while one of the riders nursed a Spencer carbine on his knees.

'Damn the luck!' grunted the Kid. 'It's Hugo Salverinas and his bunch. They're *Comancheros.* That's Salverinas on the wagon. The driver's Andrés. The short cuss riding on the right's Carlos, the one with the Spencer's called León and the other's Cristóbal. If the Devil put worse on this earth, I've sure never met 'em.'

Which, considering some of the people met by the Kid during his short but hectic life, sounded very damning for the new arrivals. *Comancheros* were Mexican *bandidos* who combined trading with the *Nemenuh* and raiding on their own account. Merciless killers, they had been all but quelled by the Texas Rangers before the War and returned due to the inefficient policing offered by the corrupt Davis Administration currently controlling the State.

Dusty could not see a bunch of *Comancheros* taking kindly to finding two Texans in the Comanche camp. Nor could the Kid, so he moved slowly from his companion's side and squatted on his heels by the fire. The wagon came to a halt and Salverinas directed a cold glare in Dusty's direction. Short, heavy-built, cruel-featured, the man carried himself with the air of one who knew he was on safe ground.

'Who is this?' Salverinas demanded, pointing at the small Texan but apparently taking the Kid for one of the *Yamparikuh.*

'He is a friend,' *Pinedapoi* answered, sounding just a touch annoyed at the tone of the *Comancheros'* leader.

'Why is he here?' Salverinas went on without leaving the wagon's box.

'Why are *you* here?' countered the chief.

'We met Apache Scalp and four braves,' Salverinas explained in a milder voice and his men swung from their horses. 'They told us where you are camped and we came to bring you news. Not far from here is a large herd of cattle. If you take them for us, we have guns, powder and lead for trading.'

'What do you say to this, Magic Hands?' *Pinedapoi* asked, the conversation having taken place in Spanish.

'He is sending many of your braves to the Land Of Good Hunting, chief,' Dusty replied. 'We want no trouble with your people. And you have too few braves to attack *Chaqueta-Tigre's* herd with any hope of winning.'

'They are not more than twenty-five men,' Salverinas put in. 'You have thirty here and more around if you need them.'

'We are all well-armed,' Dusty warned. 'Not only with hand-guns. We have many rifles.'

'The *Yamparikuh* have faced rifles before——' Salverinas began, as Dusty hoped he would.

'But not such rifles as our men carry,' the small Texan stated, dipping his left hand into a pocket and producing something which he handed to the chief. 'This is why you won't take our cattle.'

'What is it?' *Pinedapoi* inquired, turning the metal-case Henry catridge between his thumb and forefinger.

'A bullet such as our new rifles fire. Each of them can be loaded and fired many times without reloading——'

'We have such a rifle here!' Salverinas barked. 'It holds seven bullets and they cannot be loaded quickly.'

'Our rifles are of a new, better kind,' Dusty told him. 'And it will not be *you* who face them.'

Squatting on his heels to one side of his companion, the Kid grinned and slid the medicine boot from his rifle. Trust old Dusty to say just the right things. *Pinedapoi* and the *tehnap* particularly could see how the metal-case bullets might speed up the reloading process, even beyond that of paper cartridges which required that the weapon be capped separately. While a Comanche had few peers for courage, once he passed the *tuivitsi* stage he also knew the value of caution. Using single-shot rifles and the new bullets, a respectable rate of fire could be achieved. High enough to make attacking men armed with such weapons a costly business.

Equally aware of the Comanches' qualities, Salverinas read the signs as well as had the Kid. The *Yamparikuh* would hesitate to throw their lives away, but he saw another way by which he might achieve his ends.

'This small *Tejano* must be very important if he comes and

speaks for the men with the cattle,' Salverinas said, jumping from the wagon. 'Take him prisoner and his friends will pay well to have him returned.'

'I can't do that,' *Pinedapoi* objected. 'Magic Hands is my guest.'

'But not mine!' Salverinas spat out. 'If I take him——'

'That is between you and him,' the chief answered calmly.

'Get him!' the *Comanchero* ordered and the three men left their horses to move in Dusty's direction.

Instantly the Kid rose, landing lightly on spread-apart legs. He held the Winchester in his right hand, thumb over the wrist of the butt, forefinger inside the triggerguard and the remaining three fingers curled through the loading lever's ring, its barrel directed at the ground. Mutters rose from the watching *Yamparikuh* as they realised that he held some new kind of rifle.

For their part, the three Mexicans studied the new element which had entered the game. At that moment the Kid did not look white. The fire's light played on his all-but naked, hard-muscled and wiry body, its torso marked with the scars of old wounds. Standing before them, he looked like some great cat ready to pounce, or a Comanche Dog Soldier on the prod.

'*Pinedapoi* said for your boss to take him, *pelados*!' growled the Kid.

Although the words came in English, with the exception of the final insulting name—used in that manner it meant a corpse or grave robber—the trio understood. More than that, they knew no Comanche was addressing them. Sure he looked and acted like the saltiest brave who ever put on the paint and rode the war trail, but he spoke Texan like one of the Alamo's defenders. To men from the Rio Grande's bloody border country, the combination brought a name to mind.

'*Cabrito!*' ejaculated León, conscious of his Spencer's comforting weight and the fact that he held it in a better position of readiness than did the dark young Texan.

'That's me,' agreed the Kid. 'Now, happen you want to take a hand, get to it.'

Quickly Salverinas assessed the situation and knew that, *Cabrito* or not, he must act. The Comanches had no respect for a coward or a boaster. Should he fail to back up his suggestion, he would be lucky to leave the camp alive. Taken any way he looked, things seemed to be in his favour. Not only was he fast with a gun, but his driver had already slid the short-barrelled shotgun from its boot on the side of the wagon box. That small *Tejano* wore two guns, yet hardly seemed dangerous. Which left the Ysabel Kid. *Cabrito* was good, Salverinas did not deny that. So were the three men facing him. It was worth a chance. With the two Texans dead, the *Yamparikuh* would attack and scatter the herd. That ought to provide pickings for the *Comancheros*; not the least being the opportunity to obtain some of the repeating rifles.

'Get them!' Salverinas ordered, stabbing his right hand fast towards the ornate butt of his holstered Colt.

That left the others with no alternative but to fight. *Cabrito* would not waste time in asking what their intentions in the matter might be. So León started to swing his Spencer into line, confident that he was in a better position than the Kid to aim and fire. To the right of the trio Carlos reached for the fighting knife sheathed at his belt. On the left, Cristóbal put his trust in the power of his Army Colt.

Working with lightning fast precision, the Kid selected the men in order of their threat to his life. Fom his findings, he made his plan of campaign and put it into effect. First to go, without any argument, must be León for he already held a weapon in his hands.

Up swung the Winchester's barrel, its foregrip slapping into the Kid's left palm as if drawn there by a magnet, to line unerringly on the man with the Spencer. Flame lashed from the muzzle and a flat-nosed B. Tyler Henry-designed bullet tore its way into León's chest before he could complete turning his Spencer towards its mark. Wanting to impress the *Yamparikuh* with the magazine capacity and rapid-fire potential of the Winchester, the Kid fanned the lever through its loading cycle. In trained hands, the rifle could throw out two bullets per second; and the Kid possessed the necessary skill to achieve that performance. Working the barrel across to deal with the next danger, he got off four shots which all found their way into the reeling Mexican's body. Thrown backwards, León died without managing to line his Spencer or get off a load in return.

Blurring down the lever, the Kid watched an empty cartridge case flick out of the ejection slot in the top of the frame. Automatically counting his shots, he swung the barrel at the second most dangerous of the trio. Cristóbal might be trying to draw his revolver, but the Kid knew Carlos would beat him into action. Out came the knife, with Carlos drawing it rearwards for a deadly underhand throw. Only a bullet, propelled by twenty-eight grains of prime du Pont powder, flew faster than even the best-designed knife. Again the Winchester spat and Carlos jolted under the impact of lead. Already the knife was flying in the Kid's direction. On firing, he flung himself aside. While moving, he continued to shoot. Steel nicked his arm, so close did it come, but he had carried himself clear of the worst effect. Another bullet struck Carlos, turning him around and tumbling him on to his face.

Cristóbal had his revolver drawn, but he hesitated before trying to use it against a fast-moving target. Bringing it up, he aimed from shoulder high on where he figured the Kid would land. As he fell, the Kid stopped shooting. Aware that he could not use the rifle from waist level while on the ground, he thrust it forward. Seeing the Kid land, Cristóbal made a hurried last moment of adjustment of his aim and fired. To miss. As soon as his body touched the ground, the Kid rolled over and the bullet ploughed into the dirt where he had been an instant before. Settling on his belly again, he cradled the butt of the Winchester against his shoulder. A cold red-hazel eye peered from the rear sight to the blade at the muzzle end of the barrel. When both were set to his satisfaction, which took a bare half second, his forefinger gently squeezed the trigger. Striking Cristóbal in the head, the bullet from the rifle instantly ended further attempts on the Kid.

Ignoring the blast of shooting sparked off by the Kid, Dusty sent his hands flashing across. Fingers closed on the white handles of the waiting Colts and a thumb coiled around the spur of each's hammer. Almost faster than the eye could follow, the long-barrelled Army Colts left Dusty's holsters. Only one of them roared. From waist high, in what would soon become known as the gun-fighter's crouch, Dusty fired his left hand revolver.

Shock twisted at Salverinas' face as he realised that the insignificant cowhand so lightly dismissed was a *big*, lightning fast, dangerous man. Then a .44 ball spiked a hole between the Mexican's eyes. He turned involuntarily, the gun still not clear of his holster, and tumbled to the ground.

Slower than the others to assess the danger, the driver completed the freeing of the shotgun and started to throw it to his shoulder. Salverinas had advanced from the wagon, which permitted Dusty to deal with him from the gun-fighter's crouch. Not wanting to chance shooting by instinctive alignment over the distance separating him from the other Mexican, Dusty took the time to swing his right hand Colt to shoulder level. The wisdom showed as the gun spat. Caught in the chest by its load, the man tilted backwards. With a roar the shotgun sent the charges from its barrels harmlessly into the air. Then he fell into the wagon, his feet sticking into the air, twitching for a few seconds and going still.

Two *tuivitsi* sprang to the heads of the wagon's team, preventing them from bolting. After a glance to make sure that Salverinas was out of the game, Dusty turned to look at the Kid.

'Did they get you, Lon?'

'Just a nick,' the dark youngster replied, coming to his feet. 'Throw me some more bullets and we'll start to dicker with *Pinedapoi*.'

CHAPTER EIGHT

YOU ARE RESPONSIBLE FOR OUR DEATHS

Listening in the silence which followed the cook's warning, the girl and men about the trail camp's fire detected faint sounds to the east. Then they awaited Goodnight's orders, being all too aware that none of the crew, or other friends that they knew of, should be moving about in that direction. There might be a simple, or harmless explanation for the sound, but the bearded rancher did not aim to risk it being so.

'Grab your rifles!' Goodnight barked. 'Drag and right side men stay by the wagons. Wranglers head for the remuda. Rest of you, out to the herd if anything busts. Move it!'

Swiftly the party scattered. So that all might gain experience in every aspect of trail driving, the crew had been alternating their positions from point to swing, flank or drag. Yet there was no confusion, each member snatching up a firearm and heading to the appropriate group. Holding her shotgun, Dawn slid under the bed-wagon and rested its twin-tubes on a spoke of the rear wheel. A moment later Billy Jack, carrying a Henry 'liberated' on the battle-field during the days when he had ridden as Dusty's sergeant major, dropped to her left side. Showing excitement and a touch of eager anticipation, Vern joined them. Red Blaze, armed with a Spencer obtained from the same source which had supplied Billy Jack's Henry, stood by the tail gate. The remainder of the wagons' defenders had also selected places from which they could fight in reasonable safety.

'Likely we'll all be killed 'n' scalped comes morning,' Billy Jack muttered to the girl.

'How'd I get you for a partner?' Dawn whispered back.

'Just fortunate, I reckon,' the lanky one answered. 'Being with me, you're sure to get killed early.'

By which time the suspicious noises in the night had come closer and were identifiable. Listening to the rumble of wheels mingled with the beating of hooves, Vern let forth a snort of disappointment.

'A wagon and hosses!' the youngster announced. 'I never heard tell of Injuns riding the war trail in a wagon.'

'There's always a first time for everything,' Red told him.

'Hello the fire!' called a voice from the darkness. 'Can we come in?'

'It's white folks!' Vern sniffed and began to wriggle forward.

'Stay put until Colonel Charlie tells you different!' ordered Billy Jack in a low, grim tone far removed from his normal plaintive whine. In that moment he let Dawn and Vern see him as he really was, a bone-tough, competent fighting man. Such a change did it make that Vern froze as if turned to stone.

'Come ahead,' offered Goodnight. 'But do it slow, easy and with your hands showing.'

Time dragged by, with the trail crew remaining at their posts. While the second group had joined their night horses, Mark had not led them out to the herd. He was waiting to make sure that doing so would be necessary. From what he had just heard, the need ought not to arise; but he kept the men by their mounts until certain of it.

Drawn by a pair of powerful horses, a small covered wagon came into the light of the fire and stopped. It was driven by a medium-sized, dapper, handsome man, with an exceptionally beautiful, black-haired young woman seated at his side. From all appearances, neither of them belonged to the range country. The man wore a well-cut town suit which set off his slender frame to its best advantage, derby hat, spats and walking boots —as opposed to the high-heeled cowhand variety. A wide brimmed, flower-decorated hat graced the woman's head. Draped across her shoulders, a black cloak hung open at the front. Under it she wore a stylish black dress with a décolleté which seemed more suited to a fancy dude ball than for riding in a wagon on the West Texas plains. Jewellery sparkled at her ears, neck, wrists and fingers, while the dress displayed a truly magnificent figure.

A second man rode alongside the wagon. No dude this, but a product of the West. Tall, well-made, clad in range clothes and with a low-hanging Army Colt at his right thigh, his surly features and general attitude told a story to eyes which could read the signs. A cattle-town loafer, a hired hard-case, but no cowhand. Not the kind of man one would expect to find with such elegant travelling companions.

For all his surprise at the sight, Goodnight retained his poise and remembered the social conventions.

'Get down and rest your horses, ma'am, gents,' he said. 'Food's on the fire and you're welcome to spend the night here.'

'My thanks, sir,' the driver replied, swinging deftly to the ground and walking forward. 'My name is Edmond de Martin and the lady is my sister, Barbe.'

'My pleasure, ma'am,' Goodnight said, formally removing his hat and bowing to the girl. He was conscious that the men had come from their places of concealment, or returned from the picket line, and stood staring with undisguised interest at the wagon; or rather at its occupant.

'Good evening,' Barbe greeted. Like her brother, she spoke with a slight foreign accent. 'Would somebody please help me down?'

Watching with a mixture of amusement and disapproval, Dawn could not remember when Vern had moved with such alacrity. Nor were the majority of the men any slower in offering their services. Soon most of the crew milled around the wagon like cattle attracted by the blood call, pushing, shoving and trampling on each other's feet in their eagerness. Letting out a sniff, Dawn stalked over to the crush.

'Back off afore you turn the son-of-a-bitching wagon over!' she snapped. 'Come on. You can't all lay hold and lift her down.'

Barbe flashed a surprised glance at the speaker and lost her smile for a moment. Hostility mingled with the surprise on the newcomer's face before it regained its original expression.

'The young—er—lady is right, gentlemen,' Barbe said, causing a hurried withdrawal of the closest men. 'If one of you will help me——?'

'Thin out there, some of you!' Goodnight ordered. 'See to Miss de Martin, Dawn, Swede. Mark, take out pickets for the night.'

'Yo!' Mark replied. 'Come on, move it some of you.'

'Are you expecting trouble, Colonel Goodnight?' asked de Martin, watching the men scatter. His sister descended from the wagon with the minimum of aid from Dawn. 'I assume that you are Colonel Charles Goodnight?'

'I am, sir. My apologies for not introducing myself sooner.'

'I judge by how you acted as we approached that you are expecting trouble.'

'There may be Comanches about,' Goodnight admitted.

'Don't alarm your sister. I doubt if we're in any immediate danger, but I'd sooner not take chances.'

'That's wise,' de Martin agreed. 'And if there are Indians about, I am doubly fortunate in finding you tonight. With Mr. Heenan for our guide, my sister and I have been following you for the past ten days or so.'

'May I ask why?'

'To accompany you to Fort Sumner.'

'To accomp——!' the rancher spat out.

'Yes,' agreed de Martin. 'If you will join us, I can explain over supper.'

'I invited you first,' Goodnight pointed out. 'It won't be anything fancy——'

'We'll be delighted to accept,' de Martin said. 'My sister is not the world's best cook—if you know what I mean.'

'I'll be gallant and say "no",' Goodnight smiled. 'Rowdy's food is plain, but well-cooked.'

'Then perhaps we can add a little comfort of our own?' the newcomer answered, also smiling. 'We have a table, chairs, a few tolerable wines. Why be uncomfortable when a few luxuries weigh so little extra?'

Knowing that to deviate might cause resentment, Goodnight always lived and ate at the same standard as his men when on the trail. However he could see no harm in accepting de Martin's offer as it would only happen once. During the meal, he intended to show the newcomers the impossibility of their accompanying the drive.

'My thanks for your offer,' the rancher said. 'And I gratefully accept.'

'We have a table and a few other things in the wagon, gentlemen,' Barbe called, looking around the camp. 'If I could have——'

'I'll see to it,' Dawn put in, before another rush could commence.

'Lend her a hand, Turkey, Boiler,' Mark confirmed, selecting fast. The cook's louse was an unprepossessing young man and the grizzled old timer's interest in women had been tempered by years of experience. 'The rest of you stay put.'

Although Mark had an eye for a beautiful woman and was anything but averse to female company under the right conditions,* he saw the danger of allowing the men to compete for

* This is proved in *The Wildcats* and *Troubled Range*.

the favours—small though they might be—of the newly arrived girl. So he held down his own impulse to go and help, giving the chore to the men he felt most suitable to handle it. Before the drive it had been decided that Mark would take over as segundo in Dusty's absence, so nobody questioned his right to give the orders.

Clearly the de Martin family believed in travelling comfortably. Looking at the interior of the wagon, Dusty smiled a little. There was a wide, well-padded bed fastened to the front end and the rest of the space held a variety of boxes and trunks. Barbe pointed out a small collapsible table and three folding chairs, fussing over her male helpers until they had removed and set them up. Then she opened boxes to produce a fancy candelabra, plates, cutlery and wine glasses.

While setting out the table, Barbe more or less ignored Dawn. Nor did the western girl show a greater inclination to offering friendship. Turning, Barbe started to walk by the end of the wagon towards the darkness beyond it. As if struck by a thought, she stopped and looked back.

'Er—Miss—I—I want t——' Barbe spluttered, dropping her eyes with becoming modesty to avoid the men's gaze.

'Come on then,' Dawn replied. 'I want to go myself.'

'I suppose you have lost all your clothes and have had to borrow those—garments?' Barbe remarked as they walked away from the camp.

'Nope,' Dawn answered. 'I'm working on the drive, and they're better'n fancy do-dads for handling cattle. Say. Did the dress-maker run out of cloth, or have you grown some since you bought that frock?'

Barbe swung her head sharply in Dawn's direction, fluttering a hand to the exposed upper section of her bust, but read only bland innocence on the other's face. Giving a low sniff, she flounced ahead and Dawn followed, grinning slightly. In Dawn's opinion, their first clash could be called a draw.

When the girls returned, they found Goodnight and de Martin waiting by the table. Refusing an invitation to join them, Dawn continued to walk towards the fire. She arrived in time to hear Heenan describing what 'that fancy French gal' wore beneath her gown. One of the listeners remarked, as Dawn came up, that Heenan appeared to be remarkably well-informed. A sly grin came to the hard-case's face and he explained that there was a small slit in the wagon's canopy which offered a view of the interior.

'When she's getting undressed——' Heenan began, rolling his eyes ecstatically and chopped off his words as he became aware of the girl's presence.

'I'll put rock-salt into *anybody* I see sneaking around that wagon after she's got into it,' Dawn announced grimly.

'And I'll load the gun for her,' Mark went on. 'Only it won't be needed. As soon as I tell her brother, he'll have that slit covered over.'

Taking in the great spread of the blond giant's shoulders and the way the ivory-handled Colts flared so perfectly in their holsters, Heenan held back the comment which had started to rise. Not until Mark walked away accompanied by the hands he selected for the first spell of picket duty did the man make his views known.

'I never figured Cap'n Fog'd be a spoil-sport.'

'That's Mark Counter, not Cap'n Fog,' Vern told Heenan.

'Only, was I you,' Billy Jack went on. 'I'd mind what he said.'

Goodnight enjoyed the meal, finding Barbe's presence pleasant and decorative while her brother was a sparkling conversationalist. For all that, the rancher was not sorry when the girl said that she would retire for the night and rose. He wanted to talk with de Martin about returning to wherever they came from.

Seeing the other girl going to the wagon, Dawn made a decision. Mark had not spoken with the rancher about Heenan's comments, so Dawn went over to the table.

'Well I'll be——!' Goodnight growled as the girl delivered her news.

'So will I,' de Martin went on, a flicker of annoyance crossing his handsome face. 'Leave it to me, I will attend to the matter straight away.'

'I hope I done the right thing, Colonel,' Dawn said worriedly. 'I don't go much on running to the boss and telling tales.'

'You did right,' Goodnight confirmed. 'If those fools'd've tried to sneak a look at Miss de Winter, there could have been trouble.'

'Figured there might be,' Dawn admitted. 'They'd likely've started fighting for who got the best place to look from. *Men!*'

'I've attended to it, Charles,' de Martin announced, dropping from the wagon after Dawn had returned to the fire. 'That damned Heenan—still, he got me to you. And you're probably wondering what a dude like me can possibly want that I should follow you all the way from Young County, and ask to accompany you to Fort Sumner.'

'The notion *had* crossed my mind,' Goodnight admitted, accepting the cigar de Martin offered.

'It's simple. I'm a photographic artist, a good one if I say so myself, and have been commissioned by General Vindfallet to go to Fort Sumner to produce illustrations for a book he is writing about life on the western frontier.'

'That figures, knowing Vindfallet; him writing a book, I mean.'

'The General isn't entirely unaware of its value socially,' de Martin smiled. 'And, as I have a certain reputation in my line, he contacted me. I must admit that I was dubious at first. But he suggested that I should join and accompany you. He also promised to write and inform you of our coming.'

'I never had any letter from him!' Goodnight stated.

'Probably it was lost in the mails,' de Martin suggested. 'He seemed so confident it would be all right that I made no other arrangements. Then, when I reached your ranch, after an unavoidable delay, I found that you had already left. Heenan had escorted us that far and said that we could easily catch up with you, so we came along.'

'I'm sorry——' Goodnight began.

'I realise that it is something of an imposition, Charles. More so in view of Vindfallet's letter not arriving. But my professional reputation depends on my completing this commission. So I am determined to do so at all costs. Even if it means completing the journey alone and with Heenan as my guide.'

'You don't know what you're saying. If you've any sense, you'll turn around and take your sister back East.'

'That isn't possible. Barbe won't agree. You see, I must go to Fort Sumner and we have no kin-folk. There is a certain man forcing his attentions on her and if she was left alone, unprotected— You understand?'

'Yes. But——'

'I don't see why she can't come along. You have that young lady with you.'

'Dawn Sutherland was born out here and knows what she's

facing.'

'My mind is made up, Charles!' de Martin declared. 'My sister and I go on, with or without you. I say now that I understand your objections and hold you no ill-will if you refuse to take us, for you must have the best of reasons not to. But if we try it alone and are killed, there will be those who say you are responsible for our deaths.'

Annoyance flickered across the rancher's face as he thought of the position General Vindfallet had placed him in. If the rancher refused to take the de Martins, his men would certainly protest. Some of them might even consider the only right response would be to escort the brother and sister. Even if Goodnight persuaded the cowhands to change their minds, he would have a worried, discontented crew.

Yet he could hardly take a delicate, well-bred and beautiful city woman over the hell of the Staked Plains. Nor, equally certain, could he turn Barbe and her brother loose to fend for themselves. In addition to all the other hazards on the way to Fort Sumner, Heenan would be a mighty bad choice for a guide. Already he had spied on Barbe and apparently could not wait to start boasting of it. At the first hint of danger, he would probably desert the couple. Or, when certain it could be done safely, kill the brother and do far worse to the sister.

'All right,' Goodnight said grimly. 'I'll take you along—but on my terms.'

'They are?' de Martin asked.

'First that you sign the same Articles of Agreement as the rest of the crew. Second, that you and your sister obey without question all orders given by me or my segundo.'

'Accepted, and I'm sure Heenan will agree also.'

'Heenan?'

'He's going to Fort Sumner to enlist in the Army for reasons I have not questioned, but seem pressing. As he came with me instead of going north and joining an Army supply convoy, I feel a certain responsibility for him.'

'He can stay,' Goodnight grunted.

'I will keep him in my employment, he helps attend to the wagon and does other such work for me.'

'Like I said,' Goodnight answered. 'He can go along, as long as he signs and sticks to my conditions.'

'I'm sure he will.'

'One more thing, Edmond. Would you ask your sister to

wear something less—revealing. Those men of mine have enough on their minds without—— You understand?'

'I do. And I'll mention it to her in the morning.'

'If you want, I'll ask Dawn to sleep in the wagon with your sister,' Goodnight offered.

'Doesn't she have duties with the herd?'

'She rides her spell on night herd, but I can leave her off it.'

'That won't be necessary. We'll be in your camp area and I'm sure I can rely on the behaviour of your men.'

'You can!' the rancher said stiffly. 'Now, much as I hate breaking up this pleasant evening, I've things to do.'

On Mark's return from setting out the pickets, Goodnight told him that the de Martins would be accompanying the drive.

'Across——!' the blond giant began, then closed his mouth before making any reference to the Staked Plains.

'All the way,' agreed Goodnight. 'De Martin's set on getting there and stubborn enough to try it with Heenan for a guide——'

The sound of approaching hooves chopped off further conversation. From the direction they came, the riders might be the first part of the night guard returning. Yet they were pushing their horses at speed, and that could mean trouble. Mark and Goodnight tensed slightly, hands straying gun-wards. Then they relaxed. Instead of coming straight into camp, as would be the case if they brought bad news, the riders halted at the remuda. Soon after, the first of them appeared. Carrying his saddle and striding out fast, Burle Willock darted expectant glances around as he made for his bed-roll.

'Where's she at?' the cowhand demanded. 'We heard tell that there's a right pretty lil city gal around here.'

'There for sure is,' Jacko Lefors informed him. 'Ain't she something to see, boys? Got apples on her the size of melons and ain't scared of showing them around.'

Mark scowled, realising what had happened. Hearing about the de Martins from their reliefs, the younger members of the first watch had made a fast ride in to see Barbe. They had, at least, shown sufficient good sense to leave their horses at the remuda instead of galloping straight up to the fire. Then Mark saw the red flush on Dawn's cheeks and moved towards her.

'Some of you should wash your mouths out with soapy water!' the girl snorted.

'What's up, Dawn gal?' Willock sneered, grinning wolfishly. 'Getting jealous 'cause we don't say things like that about you?'

'Anybody who did'd right soon answer to me for it!' Vern snapped.

'And I'll be stood at his side on it,' Narth went on.

'Josh, go help Heenan there with de Martin's horses!' Goodnight growled before more could be said. 'Vern, help Rowdy check up on the ammunition. And all of you hear me good. Those folks're coming with us to Fort Sumner. They're *my* guests. I'm saying no more than that.'

It was enough apparently, for the subject of Barbe's attractions was dropped. Although Dawn almost mirrored Mark's reactions to the news, she said nothing.

'Mark,' Goodnight said, leading the way from the fire and beyond the crew's hearing. 'We'll have to do something about that girl. Those fool young hands'll be swarming around her like bees to honey—— Unless they figure that she's spoke for by you.'

'Spoke for?'

'Damn it! I shouldn't have to explain *that* to one of Big Ranse Counter's sons. I want for you to make it look like Miss Barbe and you're real close friends. And I don't reckon any of them, even Austin, Vern or Willock'd be *loco* enough to lock horns with you over her.'

A slow grin crept on to Mark's face as he considered Goodnight's words and their implications. Since the drive had commenced, the hands had seen sufficient examples of the blond giant's exceptional strength to be fully aware of his potential. So he was ideally suited to carry out the rancher's orders.

'I'll give it a whirl, sir,' Mark promised. 'Now don't that go to prove what a loyal hand I am, making a sacrifice like that?'

'Remind yourself *not* to ask for a bonus for doing it,' Goodnight answered dryly.

CHAPTER NINE

HE MUST BE BURLE WILLOCK'S KIN

'Indians coming, Colonel Charlie,' announced Billy Jack with almost gloomy satisfaction as he rode to where the rancher was sitting on a knoll ahead of the trail herd.

Not wanting to give the hands time to think about the newcomers, Goodnight had insisted on getting the herd moving in the usual manner on the morning after the de Martins' arrival. Before Barbe had made her appearance, much to their disappointment, the cowhands had been taken out to the herd. There Goodnight had given them orders which temporarily drove all thoughts of the girl from their heads. Faced with the possibility of an Indian attack, even the three men Goodnight had named the previous night had enough good sense to concentrate on the business in hand.

It was almost noon, with the cattle continuing to move westward. Sent ahead to act as scout in the Kid's absence, Billy Jack had just returned to report on his findings. Galloping from the point, Mark reined in his horse and looked to the rancher for orders.

'Throw the herd off the trail!' Goodnight said. 'Signal to the drag men to drop back to the wagons, then you and Swede get your men up on the point.'

'Yo!' Mark replied, turning his horse and riding away.

After the cattle's forward progress had ceased, Goodnight watched the trail hands taking up their allotted positions. Then the rancher and Billy Jack turned their attention to the distant riders.

'Cap'n Dusty 'n' the Kid's with 'em,' Billy Jack commented, relief plain in his voice.

Even as the lanky cowhand spoke, the Kid rode ahead of the others and stopped his white stallion. Raising his rifle into the air with his right hand, he put his left up as if to shield his eyes from the glare of the sun, then indicated the men behind him.

'He wants us to show the Indians our rifles when they come,' Goodnight translated. 'Best do it, I reckon. Fog back and tell the men I said it's all right for them to let the Comanches look, but that none of them have to do anything that might spark off trouble.'

'I'll warn 'em good,' Billy Jack promised.

Left alone almost a quarter of a mile in front of the herd, Goodnight watched and waited for the Indians to arrive. A more prudent, or less knowledgeable man would have taken off the jaguar-skin vest that had become so well known to the *Nemenuh.* Wise in Indian ways, Goodnight did no such thing. The Comanche admired a brave man, even if he might be an enemy, and would feel the more respect if they saw he did not fear to let them know he was *Chaqueta-Tigre* who had caused their people grief on occasion.

'How!' Goodnight greeted as the Comanches halted and their chief accompanied Dusty and the Kid forward to where the rancher waited.

'How!' the chief answered.

'This's *Pinedapoi*, chief of the *Yamparikuh* and his *hunters*, Colonel,' introduced the Kid, laying emphasis on the next-to-last word. '*Pinedapoi,* this's *Chaqueta-Tigre*. The chief has come to see the guns-which-shoot-many-times.'

'Take him to look at them,' Goodnight offered, also speaking the Comanche tongue but using the dialect of the *Tanima*, Liver-Eater, band with which he was most familiar. He could guess at the reason for the request and willingly gave his permission. Then he turned to Dusty, 'How did it go?'

'Easy enough in the end. Lon showed them how a Henry can pour out lead, and be reloaded as you shoot. After that it was just dickering.'

One of the improvements to the 'New Model Henry' was that it could be loaded through a slot in the frame instead of following the old, slower way of retracting the spring and opening the entire tube on hinges. With the new rifle, one could load and fire in the manner of a single-shot, but still retain a full magazine of sixteen rounds against an emergency. As Dusty claimed, the Comanches had seen the advantage of the improvement and been much impressed.

'We can go through then?' asked the rancher.

'Yes. I've offered them six good horses and a dozen head from the herd. It's to show our hearts're good, not a tribute.'

A subtle difference which Goodnight understood. Passing through another hunting party's area, Indian braves would share their meat as a sign of good faith. But, if strong enough to enforce their will, they did it voluntarily. Tribute implied that the people giving it had no other choice. The *Yamparikuh* would be less inclined to make trouble with 'good heart' givers than for people who paid tribute.

Hearing a noise behind them, Dusty and Goodnight looked around. One of the braves rode from among the *Yamparikuh* and stared at the cattle. Taller and heavier than the majority of his companions, he had an air of truculence about him. Dressed in the style of a dandified, successful young warrior, he carried a war-axe and long-bladed knife balancing themselves on his belt and was one of the few firearms' owners. Judging by the scalp of long, lank black hair which decorated his knife's sheath, he had met with victory on a previous mission. Holding a tack-decorated Mississippi rifle in his right hand, he pointed towards the herd with his left and made an explosive comment to his companions.

'Damn it!' Goodnight growled, *sotto voce* to Dusty. 'He's seen Buffalo and allows that'll be the wohaw he takes from us.'

For his part, Dusty had already identified the brave as Apache's Scalp, a *tuivitsi* approaching the status of *tehnap*. He had been the man who directed the *Comancheros* to the camp, and had returned with his companions shortly before the party set out to meet the herd that morning. The small Texan had liked little he had seen of Apache's Scalp so far; and the suggestion did nothing to change his feelings.

'The hell he does!' Dusty breathed. 'I can't see the crew parting with ole Buffalo, can you?'

'No,' admitted Goodnight. 'We'd best see what the Kid has to say about it.'

Since assuming its post as lead steer, Buffalo had become very popular with the crew. Calm, intelligent, with none of the vicious traits which so many of its kind possessed, Buffalo had led the herd and proved invaluable. Losing it, even if the trail hands allowed that to happen, would mean that the rest of the cattle would be disturbed until a new leader asserted itself. So Dusty knew that they faced a tricky situation and started to think how it might be averted.

Going to where the right flank's party waited, *Pinedapoi* saw the repeating rifles held by some of its members. The Kid had one of them work the lever of his Spencer carbine to eject bullets, then display the remainder of its load by opening the magazine in its butt. However, having examined León's weapon, the chief already knew that it would be capable of a rate of fire almost as fast as that of the Henry. With the first inspection over, they rode on in the direction of the wagons and remuda in its rope corral.

Following the orders delivered by Billy Jack, Red Blaze had all his party formed up before the wagons. In the rear of the men stood Barbe, wearing a more demure dress than on her arrival, and Dawn, gripping her shotgun. De Martin was at Red's right side, holding a Sharps breech-loading rifle. To Red's left, Heenan had his right hand thumb-hooked close to the butt of his revolver.

'What's that stinking red varmint want?' Heenan demanded.

'Don't ask me,' Red replied, Spencer carbine hanging at arm's length in both hands. 'All of you mind what I say. No shooting unless I give the word.'

'Some of us might be a mite choosier 'n you about having stinking Injuns rub hoss-droppings in our faces,' Heenan growled. 'If it'd've been me, I'd've started throwing lead as soon as they come into range.'

'You're not handling things, *hombre*,' Red reminded him. 'So you just stand fast and do like I told you.'

'I'll think on it,' Heenan promised, his hand crawling around towards and fingers gripping the Colt's butt.

Alert for any trouble, Red had been watching Heenan from the corner of his eye. Suddenly he swung his arms forward and propelled the carbine around so that its metal-shod butt crashed with some force into Heenan's groin. With a croaking yelp, the man removed his hand hurriedly from the Colt and clutched at the stricken area. Buckling at the knees, he collapsed to the ground where he lay moaning in agony.

'You just stay down there,' Red ordered. 'If you didn't mean to draw, I'll apologise most humble later on.'

'What's the idea?' de Martin hissed, staring at the writhing hard-case.

'If that damned fool'd pulled and started shooting, we'd be up to our knees from the neck down with riled-up Comanches,' Red answered. 'Which, with your sister along, I don't reckon you'd want to happen.'

If the chief had noticed the incident—and he could hardly have missed it—he regarded Red's actions as a sign of good faith. After studying the various weapons, *Pinedapoi* passed on in the direction of the third and final party. Pushing away from the wagon against which she had been standing, Barbe stormed up to Red.

'Why did you hit him?' she hissed.

'To stop him getting us all killed, ma'am,' Red replied. 'It seemed like a good thing to do at the time—and still does.'

'Mr. Blaze acted correctly, my dear,' de Martin went on. 'Heenan acted in a foolish manner and might have endangered all our lives.'

'Get him to the wagon, two of you,' Red ordered. 'And tell him if he's any complaints to come and see me.'

Although the message was delivered, Heenan declined the offer. He scowled whenever he saw Red, but made no attempt at taking reprisals.

After seeing the number of men armed with repeating rifles or carbines, *Pinedapoi* realised the wisdom of accepting the 'good heart' gifts. The main body of the *Yamparikuh* band had split into a number of family or clan groups and scattered in search of horses and hunting. Any force less than the band's full fighting strength would meet crippling losses or be completely wiped out facing so many guns-which-fire-many-times in the hands of the calm, clearly competent Texas ride-plenties. Accepting the gifts would save *Pinedapoi* from losing face or authority when the story was told. The Comanches admired bravery, but knew the difference between it and life-wasting stupidity.

'Take our gifts and we leave the white brother in peace!' the chief ordered on rejoining his men.

'I want the wohaw that looks like a buffalo,' announced Apache's Scalp.

'No!' Dusty snapped, guessing what the young buck was saying when he heard the word 'wohaw'.

That was the name Indians gave to cattle, being derived from the commands 'Whoa' and 'Haw' used by bull-whackers to guide their draught-oxen.

'You won't let us have our gifts?' asked *Pinedapoi*, brows knitting ominously.

'Not the one that looks like a buffalo,' Dusty replied.

At Dusty's side, the Kid tensed slightly. Dressed once more in his cowhand's clothing, he looked young and innocent—but as ready for action as a cougar crouching to attack.

'Apache's Scalp says that he wants that wohaw,' the chief pointed out, sounding just a touch uneasy. 'He has a strong head for it.'

'No!' Dusty repeated and saw the *Yamparikuh* fingering their weapons. 'It's my medicine animal.'

Instantly the hostile gestures came to a halt. Dusty's words had put his refusal in a light the Indians understood. No man, especially a warrior of Magic Hands' standing, would allow his medicine animal—a bringer of good luck—to be taken from him. Just as the small Texan had expected, Apache's Scalp intended to force the issue. The *tuivitsi* was at an age when he wanted to prove himself the toughest and boldest brave-heart ever born. Although he had heard the story of the Devil Gun council, and about the fight with the *Comancheros*, the young buck chose to regard both as fabrications. Such a small man, white at that, could not be capable of a warrior's deeds. Combined with his natural truculence and dislike of all palefaces, Apache's Scalp was marching straight into the trap laid for him by Dusty.

'I am going to take the wohaw anyway!' the *tuivitsi* announced and the Kid translated the words. He slapped a hand on the hair dangling from his knife's sheath and continued, 'Think well before you try to stop me, small white one. This is the scalp of an Apache I wear.'

To the Comanche, taking an Apache's scalp ranked high among a warrior's deeds. In the case of the savage warriors from the desert country, the old saying, 'Anybody can scalp a dead man' did not apply. A brave who killed an Apache considered he had done very well and wanted people to be aware of the fact.

'He was a deaf Apache,' Dusty scoffed, with the Kid for his interpreter. 'With age in his bones and no sight in his eyes.'

Snarling in rage, Apache's Scalp made as if to raise his rifle. Three-quarters of a second later, he looked down the muzzle of Dusty's left hand Colt and wondered how it came to be lined on him. With his usual speed, Dusty had drawn and cocked the gun at the other's first hostile movement. The small Texan sat holding the *tuivitsi*'s life in his hands.

'Throw away the rifle!' Dusty ordered.

'It's for you to chose,' the Kid warned after delivering the command.

Slowly, with every evidence of sullen reluctance, Apache's Scalp flung his rifle aside. Dusty felt a touch of relief, for he had not wished to kill the brave. However, he knew that a stronger lesson might be needed to settle Apache's Scalp and prepared to give it. Backing off his paint stallion, Dusty holstered the Colt. Before the *tuivitsi* could decide what to do, Dusty tossed his right leg across the saddlehorn and jumped clear of the horse. Never taking his eyes from Apache's Scalp, he unbuckled and removed his gunbelt to hang it on the paint's saddle.

'Tell him the buffalo-wohaw gives me real big medicine, Lon,' Dusty ordered. 'So much that I don't need weapons to handle a *tuivitsi*. Then tell him that if he still figures to take my medicine to come right ahead and try it.'

Apache's Scalp listened to the words with growing disbelief and fury. Then he flung back his head and let out a roaring curse.

'He must be Burle Willock's kin,' the Kid remarked disgustedly to Goodnight as the brave sprang from his horse. 'That much stupidness runs in families.'

'Soon I have a white man's scalp to wrap around my war-axe!' screeched Apache's Scalp and snatched that weapon from his belt.

'This is between the two of them, *Chaqueta-Tigre*?' asked *Pinedapoi*.

'It is,' Goodnight confirmed and raised his voice in a bellow as he saw some of the cowhands moving restlessly. 'Nobody interferes. Mark. Swede. Shoot down any man who tries to use his gun.'

'Reckon them Injuns'll stay out of it?' Willock muttered as he sat at Mark's side.

'As long as we do,' the blond giant answered. 'Which we're going to, even if I have to do what Colonel Charlie told me.'

Advancing with his war-axe ready, Apache's Scalp became aware of the change in his opponent. No longer did the ride-plenty look small, but was big, powerful and dangerous. Maybe there was truth in his words and he did gain medicine power from the buffalo-wohaw.

Balancing lightly on the balls of his feet, Dusty watched the Comanche closing in on him. From all appearances, Apache's Scalp had been well-taught and handled the war-axe efficiently. Yet Dusty also figured that the *tuivitsi* would be reckless, proud of his skill and likely to act in a rash manner should things go wrong.

Which was what Dusty intended would happen.

Across and up lashed the war-axe's blade, but Dusty took a step to the rear and carried himself beyond the arc of its two-foot handle. Swiftly, with little loss of momentum, the brave reversed direction, chopping savagely across. Again he missed as Dusty avoided the blow. Going forward with the force of it, he was carried past the small Texan who slammed a quickly snapped side-kick to his ribs in passing. Apache's Scalp stumbled, caught his balance and whirled fast as Dusty moved towards him.

Snarling in fury, the *tuivitsi* attacked. Time after time the deadly axe, its edge as sharp as many a barber's razor, licked in Dusty's direction and met only empty air. The blows became wilder, less well-timed as their maker's rage and frustration increased. Watching every move, Dusty figured that he could lure his attacker into some ill-advised move and where he could bring the fight to an end. The spectators on both sides were getting more excited by the second. Yells of encouragement rang out in English and Comanche, but so far neither side showed any sign of objecting to the other's presence. Which was one of the reasons Dusty wanted to terminate the affair quickly.

By what seemed to be an accident, Dusty slipped in the course of evading a slash. Out shot the Comanche's left hand to catch hold of Dusty's shirt at its open neck. With a screech of triumph, Apache's Scalp swung up his other hand and prepared to drive the axe into the Texan's skull. It seemed that nothing could save Dusty. Certainly the *tuivitsi* knew of no way in which his intended victim might escape.

Which, unfortunately for him, was not the sum lack of Apache's Scalp's knowledge. He did not know about the small Oriental who worked in the Rio Hondo country as Ole Devil Hardin's personal attendant. Nobody could say what caused Tommy Okasi to flee his native Japanese islands, for he never mentioned the subject. No matter why he left, he brought along a thorough education in his country's unarmed fighting skills. More than that, he had passed on to the smallest male member of the Hardin-Fog-Blaze clan the secrets of *ju-jitsu* and *karate*. With such knowledge, virtually unknown outside the Orient at that time, backing his powerful muscular development, Dusty could deal with men of greater weight and superior strength. The ignorance was to cost Apache's Scalp dearly.

Startled yells rose from the watching trail hands, mingled with Mark's and Ahlén's demands that orders were obeyed. Throwing up his hands inside the *tuivitsi*'s left arm, Dusty crossed his wrists and interposed them between the down-driving war-axe and his head. Caught in the upper V formed by the wrists, Apache's Scalp's forearm halted without achieving its purpose.

Before the *tuivitsi* realised the danger, Dusty slipped free his right hand to grasp the immobile wrist. Pulling it forward and downward, the small Texan twisted himself to the right. Taking a rearward step with his right foot, Dusty hauled even harder on the trapped limb and pivoted on his left leg to drag Apache's Scalp off balance. Giving the other no chance to recover, Dusty propelled his right knee around to drive it into the exposed and offered belly.

An agony-filled belch broke from the *tuivitsi*'s lips as the knee arrived. Having withdrawn his left hand from the X-block position when the right gripped Apache's Scalp's wrist, Dusty knotted it into a fist which he drove with all his power just below the other's rib-cage. Dropping the axe, the *tuivitsi* blundered by Dusty on being released and fell to his knees.

Dusty followed his victim grimly. Although they watched with considerable interest and commented excitedly among themselves, none of the *Yamparikuh* braves offered to intervene. Going against another man's declared medicine power, Apache's Scalp must stand or fall alone. Despite their lack of interference, Dusty knew he must end the fight quickly.

Raising his right arm, Dusty kept the hand open, its fingers extended and thumb bent across the palm. Down it whipped and he slashed the heel of the hand into the side of the *tuivitsi*'s neck above the vagus nerve. Apache's Scalp stiffened as the blow landed, then collapsed limply forward. Rolling him on to his back, Dusty bent and took the knife from its scalp-decorated sheath. Amazement showed on the *Yamparikuh* faces as the small Texan walked towards them. Springing from their horses, two of the *tuivitsi* ran by him in the direction of their motionless companion.

'Is that one dead?' asked *Pinedapoi* as Dusty offered him the knife hilt-first.

'No. He will wake soon,' the small Texan answered. 'Does any other want to take the buffalo-wohaw?'

Although he could not understand the majority of grunted

answers, Dusty concluded that they expressed a complete disinterest in gaining possession of his medicine animal. Discovering that Dusty had spoken the truth about Apache's Scalp's condition, *Pinedapoi* stated his complete satisfaction. Nor did Apache's Scalp show any inclination to resume his demands, having received what he regarded as convincing proof of the medicine's capabilities. So, with a further exchange of compliments, the *Yamparikuh* departed taking their 'good heart' gifts.

'They'll not trouble us any more,' the Kid stated. 'Especially with you giving *Pinedapoi* that extra hoss and three head.'

The bonus had been handed over by Goodnight as a compliment to a wise and brave *Nemenuh* chief. It was the kind of gesture Indians liked and would increase *Pinedapoi*'s determination to keep his promise of peaceful passage for the herd.

Not until the herd had been started moving did the Kid realise that he had failed to satisfy his curiosity on a certain point.

'Say, Colonel. Who's the dude and that fancy gal back with the wagons?'

CHAPTER TEN

YOU COULD LOSE THE WHOLE DAMNED HERD

'And if she takes to Mark, which I reckon she might, we shouldn't have any trouble over her,' Goodnight concluded after explaining to his segundo and scout about the de Martins' presence.

'Could be,' Dusty agreed. 'The only fellers big enough to make fuss for him are Swede, Sherm Sherman or Tod Ames and they're old enough 'n' steady enough not to try it.'

'It all depends on the gal, though,' warned the Kid. 'Women're mighty peculiar critters.'

During the next three days, Barbe de Martin seemed determined to prove false the Kid's views on female peculiarity. While the younger hands swarmed about her on the first morning, trying to attract her attention with displays of roping or riding skill, they kept their distance once Mark made his intentions plain. No mean hand at the flirting game, and possessed of the attributes most likely to attract women—handsome face, magnificent physique and wealth—he found little difficulty in drawing Barbe to him.

The situation lasted only three days. On the evening of the third, Mark and Barbe were walking in a small valley clear of ths camp. He had already found her to be a lot freer with her favours than expected and had wondered if maybe the man back East was the one doing the forcing. However, instead of flying into his arms at the first opportunity, she acted hesitant. A low gasp broke from her as he slipped an arm around her waist.

'What's wrong?' he asked as she drew away from him and clapped a hand to her side, face showing pain.

'I—I fell and banged myself in the wagon this afternoon,' Barbe replied.

'Is it hurting bad?'

'No. But you pressed it and it stung. Mark——'

'Yes?'

'Nothing can come of our friendship, can it?'

'How do you mean, nothing?' Mark asked warily.

'I mean when we get to Fort Sumner, you'll go your way and I'll go mine,' Barbe explained.

'It's likely,' Mark admitted.

'It's certain,' she smiled. 'I've seen you with your friends. You wouldn't leave them to come East and live. And I couldn't stay in this wild land. So nothing can come of our friendship, can it?'

'Likely not. But it's real pleasant.'

'It's *too* pleasant,' Barbe said, darting a glance around her. 'Mark, you wouldn't marry me. Would you?'

'I reckon you're going just a touch too fast,' Mark answered. 'We've not known each other——'

'You wouldn't,' Barbe sniffed. 'So I think that it is better we end this now. You would be too easy to fall in love with, Mark. Neither of us want that, do we?'

'Maybe not.'

'I could too easily find myself deeply involved, Mark. So we must stop doing this. We must.'

A slight sound reached Mark's ears, coming from some bushes about thirty yards away. Gently thrusting the girl from him, the blond giant faced them and his right hand Colt flowed from its holster in the effortless-seeming, yet lightning fast way which separated the expert from the average in the *pistolero* arts.

'Don't shoot, Mark!' called de Martin's voice and he walked into view with a shotgun tucked under his arm. 'I was walking and heard voices, so I came over to see who it was.'

'Edmond!' Barbe said, sounding startled. 'I—I was just talking with Mark about the matter we discussed this evening.'

'And does he agree?'

'We understand each other. Don't we, Mark?'

'I reckon so,' Mark replied, holstering his Colt.

'If I thought it would work and Barbe be happy, I would be the first to say "Go ahead", Mark,' de Martin stated. 'But, as her elder brother, I was naturally concerned. I've nothing against you personally, and feel that you would have been a suitable choice. But Barbe is a city-girl. She could not settle in this land and I doubt if you would like living in the East. Come, Barbe. We'll go back to the camp.'

Watching the brother and sister fade off into the darkness, Mark felt as if a cold hand had touched him. The way things sounded, he had been under consideration as a matrimonial prospect and had only narrowly avoided acceptance in that light.

'Whooee!' the blond giant breathed, mopping his brow with a bandana. 'Mark boy, you've got to stop being a loyal hand making sacrifices happen you get asked to handle another chore like that.'

'They do say the first sign's when they start talking to themselves?' drawled the Kid's voice.

Spinning around with hands driving to his guns, Mark halted the draw uncompleted and glared indignantly at the dark youngster who materialised from the darkness. Familiarity did not lessen the surprise the Kid could hand out when he made one of his silent appearances.

'Blast you, you danged *Pehnane*!' Mark spat out, letting the revolvers return to leather. 'I near on killed you, jumpy as I am over that narrow escape I've just had.'

'It was narrower than you think,' the Kid replied. 'Her brother was hid up behind that bush, listening to every word you said.'

'The hell you say!' Mark growled.

'Left camp just after you did, toting his shotgun. I thought he might be fixing to do some hunting and tagged along. When I saw his game, I waited unknown to him. Figured maybe you'd like to have a witness on hand.'

'Thanks, Lon. I reckon they'd fixed together to have Barbe break off with me and Edmond come along in case I'd got notions to the contrary. Let's get back to camp and tell Dusty what's happened.'

On hearing of the incident, Dusty agreed with Mark's ideas about de Martin's motives and that there would be no point in the blond giant continuing his efforts. If he attempted to carry the matter further, the other hands might consider that he was trying to force unwanted attentions on the girl. Figuring that and wanting to raise his standing in Barbe's eyes, one of the impressionable young men might intervene. Which would spark off just what Goodnight was seeking to avoid.

So, although Barbe threw yearning or even inviting glances his way, Mark made no further attempt to resume their close acquaintance. Seeing his attitude, the younger hands swarmed in like hounds around a coon on a tree-stump. In the main, the competition was shared between Vern Sutherland, Austin Hoffman and Burle Willock, with Jacko Lefors trailing along out of deference for the latter. By careful manipulation of their duties, Dusty made sure that the trio only rarely found themselves in camp at the same time. Barbe also showed interest in Red Blaze, but achieved nothing. Being aware of Mark's narrow escape, Red figured the girl might consider him a matrimonial prospect. There were two things scared Red: being left afoot and the risk of being tricked into marriage. So he steered clear of Barbe.

If his sister mingled with the younger hands, although ignoring Dawn, de Martin gained the confidence and friendship of the older, staider members of the travelling community. He had knowledge, was willing to listen and learn, so got on well with the senior trail hands. As the drive continued, he used his photographic equipment to gather material for Vindfallet's book and his own use. Various members of the crew posed self-consciously before the camera, including a blushing Dawn, and he took long-range pictures of the herd. Goodnight vetoed a suggestion that de Martin should go closer to the cattle as he did not want them disturbed by the blazing flare of magnesium which supplied the necessary light to process the photographic plate.

On went the drive, gathering unbranded—therefore ownerless—cattle which came their way to replace those given to the *Yamparikuh*, used for food, or lost in travelling. Goodnight wanted to keep the size of the herd at around three thousand five hundred head. That would leave him a margin of safety against the crossing of the Staked Plains.

With each passing day, the rancher grew increasingly aware that he must soon tell the crew of his plans. He had noticed that Ahlén, Sherman and Ames in particular had begun to spend time studying the stars at night, or paying extra attention to the route they followed in the day-time. Soon they would start suspecting the continued western course. So he wished to explain his motives before they discovered for themselves which way they were to go.

Black clouds filled the sky as Goodnight left Dusty to handle the bedding-down of the herd. He wanted to make a large circle and check if there was any danger from the approaching storm. On his return to camp, he intended to break the news to the crew.

Satisfied that even a heavy rainfall would cause him no inconvenience, the rancher left his horse with the remuda and walked towards the camp. Immediately he knew something was wrong. Normally the crew, less the herd's guard and night hawk, would be gathered about the fire, eating, making insulting comments about the food or discussing the events of the day. Instead they appeared to be split into three groups. The Swinging G hands and men from the OD Connected's contingent were around Dusty. To the rear of the others, the de Martins and Heenan stood together. With the exception of the D4S trio who had the night herd with Billy Jack, all the Minerals Wells men formed the third party.

'I doubled the night watch, Uncle Charlie,' Dusty remarked as the rancher approached him.

Before any more could be said, Ahlén strode over. 'What's all this about us taking the herd across the Staked Plains, Colonel?' the big man demanded.

'I'm sorry, Colonel,' de Martin called. 'I thought that you had told your men the way you intended to go, or I wouldn't have drawn their attention to it on my map.'

'Now lookee here, Colonel Charlie,' Sherman went on, joining Ahlén. 'We've got our bosses' stock to think about and we don't figure to see them killed off.'

'Your bosses don't have any stock in this herd,' Goodnight said quietly.

A low rumble followed, from the Mineral Wells men, in echo to the rancher's surprising comments. Ahlén and Sherman exchanged glances, then gave their full attention to Goodnight. Behind them, the rest of their party awaited the next developments. To Dusty's rear, the OD Connected and Swinging G hands stood alert, watchful but in no way openly threatening. It was an explosive situation, calling for the most delicate handling.

'Would you mind making that a mite clearer, Colonel?' Sherman asked, politely enough yet clearly determined to receive an explanation.

'It's simple,' Goodnight answered. 'Before we left, your bosses signed all their cattle over to me so that I could claim the legal right to sell them at Fort Sumner.'

'And you figure we can reach it, Colonel,' Ahlén said, 'going across the Staked Plains?'

'It's our *only* hope of reaching it in time,' Goodnight told him. 'Chisum is headed there, going by the trail Oliver Loving and I blazed. He's got almost a week's start on us and we'll never lick him going on his heels. Our only hope is to cross the Staked Plains.'

'You could lose the whole damned herd!' Sherman warned.

'It's a chance I'm willing to take,' Goodnight assured him.

'You've known about this from the start?' asked Ahlén.

'Since the night the Kid rode in.'

'And you didn't mention it to us?'

'I wanted you boys to learn about trail herding first. To let you see what could be done. Well, you've seen and you've learned. If I hadn't faith in you, I'd've turned north after the first week and said to hell with the contract. But I've got faith in you and I say that you boys can take the herd across the Staked Plains if it can be done.'

'Does Miss Sutherland know of the route you intended to take?' de Martin asked without leaving his sister's side.

'I told her the first night,' Goodnight replied. 'Just her. Not her brother, or my hands. She said she wouldn't turn back and I don't reckon she will.'

'*We're* going on, anyways!' Dusty put in and the men at his back mumbled their agreement. 'The OD Connected and Swinging G don't want it sticking in our craw that Chisum got the better of us.'

Dusty spoke deliberately and in a definite challenge, implying that the drive would continue no matter who deserted. No cowhand with loyalty to his brand could mildly allow another outfit to make good on such a boast. Guessing what his cousin had in mind, Red took up the stirring process and continued it.

'I sure wouldn't want it!'

'Maybe it don't mean anything to some folks that Chisum getting there'll be selling their bosses' cattle,' Mark carried on from Red's statement.

'Damn it, yes!' Ames growled, slouching forward. 'Chisum'll maybe have our cattle along.'

'Ain't no "maybe" about it,' drawled the Kid. 'He's got 'em.'

'In that case, I'm for licking the bald-headed son-of-a-bitch there and taking 'em back when he arrives!' Ahlén growled.

'And me!' Sherman went on, slapping a hand on his thigh. 'Whooee! Won't it be a pistol to see his face when he comes and finds us-all waiting.'

Once started, agreement to Goodnight's plans came fast and the dangerous tension ebbed away. No cowhand cared to let a rival spread out-do him. Added to that, the idea of beating Chisum to Fort Sumner and retrieving their employers' cattle appealed to their sense of humour or justice.

'There's one thing you gentlemen are forgetting,' de Martin announced, walking forward. He brought Barbe with him, an arm draped protectively across her shoulders. 'My sister and I are with you. I don't mind the hardships and dangers for myself. But is it fair to risk the life of a beautiful woman?'

Slowly Barbe turned her eyes around the circle of men. On her face was an expression of pleading which begged all the big, strong men to protect her. Although Dusty and Goodnight retained attitudes of stony indifference, they knew that de Martin would gain support.

'Damn it! That wouldn't be right!' Willock declared and was favoured by a weak smile of gratitude from Barbe.

'It for sure wouldn't!' Austin went on, not wishing to let a rival gain so much of an advantage over him.

'I warned you that the trip would be dangerous,' Goodnight told de Martin.

'But not that you meant to cross the Staked Plains,' the photographer replied. 'I'm afraid that I can't risk Barbe's life on such a crossing. We will turn north until we find the Army's trail to Fort Sumner.'

'Not alone you won't!' Willock declared and the rumble of agreement included members of both the original parties. 'Some of us'll come with you.'

'What about the herd?' demanded the practical Ahlén.

'Hell! We can easy enough catch up with you after we've seen these folks safe,' Willock answered, still basking in Barbe's admiring gaze. 'Me 'n' Jacko——'

'I'm going along!' stated Austin grimly.

'What for, to help take pictures of the Comanches killing you off?' interrupted the Kid, for de Martin had been instructing Austin on the use of the camera in order to be photographed with his sister and various members of the crew. 'Because, feller, that's what'll happen if you go north from here, or even back east.'

'Them Yap-Eaters let us through this far, Kid!' Austin protested, seeing his chances of a pleasant trip slipping away.

'Only 'cause they didn't have enough men along to do different,' the Kid pointed out. 'That won't be the way if you pull out. You don't have a chance in a thousand of getting through.'

'You reckon so, Kid?' gulped Jacko, impressed by the dark youngster's vehemence and respecting his knowledge of matters Comanche.

'You'd best believe it, happen you want to keep Miss Barbe's scalp from hanging on some *tehnap*'s lodge pole.'

'But if you came as our guide, Lon——' de Martin hinted.

'Which I don't aim to, even if it'd help. I took on to ride scout for Colonel Charlie, like these fellers took on to drive the cattle. So I'm keeping my word and doing just that.'

Almost instinctively the Kid had said the right thing and struck a nerve among Barbe's protectors. To leave the herd would be betraying their trust and given word. That was something not even irresponsible cusses like Willock, Jacko or Austin wanted to do. Sensing their wavering, Dusty decided to offer them a way out that avoided a loss of face.

'Take it this way, Edmond,' he said to de Martin, but making sure his words carried to the trio. 'Your only safe bet is to stick with us. But if *you* want to expose Barbe to the danger of being killed—*or worse*—by the Comanches, we'll let these three fellers go along.'

That dropped the entire decision into the photographer's lap. If he insisted on going away, it would be his stubbornness which endangerd his sister's life. Like Dusty, de Martin could see the uncertainty shown by her champions.

'If you're sure there's danger——' de Martin began.

'I'd take my lodge oath on it,' the Kid said with quiet sincerity.

'Then we will accompany you, Charles,' the photographer decided.

'It'll not be easy, I won't pretend otherwise,' Goodnight said. 'We'll all be on a strict allowance of water and if it runs short, the horses get first crack at it. That way alone we'll get across alive.'

Watching the de Martins, Dusty read nothing on the man's face. However Barbe showed anxiety and seemed to be on the verge of speaking. Her brother swung his head around and she closed her mouth. Swinging on her heel, she stalked towards their wagon and disappeared inside it. Muttering an apology, de Martin followed her.

'Come and get it!' boomed Rowdy with masterly timing, rattling a spoon against his cooking-pot. 'Come and get it afore I feed it to the other hawgs.'

'Come on, boys!' Mark yelled. 'I'm going to put some fat on afore I start to cross the Staked Plains.'

CHAPTER ELEVEN

YOU HIT NEAR ON AS HARD AS MY PAPPY

'That was close!' Dusty breathed as he and Goodnight watched the rush for the chuck-wagon.

'Real close,' the rancher agreed. 'I meant to tell the men about crossing as soon as I got back tonight. Only it looks I got beat to doing it.'

'I'm sorry about that, Uncle Charlie.'

'How did it happen?'

'Harmlessly enough. De Martin got talking about how far we've covered and his sister fetched out an Army map. She asked me if I could show her where we're at. I couldn't lie about it with Swede and Sherm there. And as soon's I'd showed her, they knew we weren't on the trail you blazed with Oliver Loving.'

'I should have told them earlier,' Goodnight declared.

'It all came out right in the end,' Dusty answered. 'Lucky for us Edmond saw sense. We couldn't've spared those three or four young cusses who aimed to go along with him.'

'No,' Goodnight agreed. 'And they'd've likely been fighting among themselves over Barbe afore they'd gone two miles. It'd've happened before now but for the way you've been keeping them apart. You're doing a good job, Dustine.'

'Looks like we'll miss the main storm,' Dusty said.

'It's coming heavy up north, for sure,' Goodnight replied. 'And don't try to change the subject.'

'No, sir. Further we go, the more I think we've lost Hayden's men by coming this way.'

'I like a segundo as takes orders,' smiled Goodnight. 'You could be right. Or maybe he figures that seven-day head start has us licked. Tell the Kid to keep watching our back trail regardless.'

'I'll see to it,' Dusty promised. Then he felt the first patter of rain and went on, 'Here it comes. I'll get my fish and ride out to the herd.'

Dressed in his yellow oilskin slicker, with the fish picture trade-mark that produced its name, the small Texan visited the night guard. He found that they had taken warning from the cloud-laden skies and carried protective clothing along. For the first time Billy Jack, Vern and Narth learned of the change in the route, although the former had suspected something of it for a few days. It did, however, furnish him with material for a mournful discourse on their probable fate While Vern expressed amazement at his 'female' sister keeping a secret, Narth took the news more seriously. Yet, such was the faith they had attained in Goodnight and Dusty, that none of them considered the decision unwise, or that it would be other than successfully completed.

Although the trail drive missed passing through the centre of the storm, it ran into continuing rain. For a week, with rain falling in varying degrees of severity, the cattle were kept moving westward. In one respect the inclement weather proved a blessing. All the trail hands were kept too busy to brood over Goodnight's failure to inform them of his plans. Nor did the younger hands find time to resume their rivalry. If it came to a point, Barbe did not show to good advantage in the wet weather. Possibly her bedraggled appearance would have evoked sympathy, except that everybody was in the same condition. So Barbe's whining and complaining produced little response other than irritation.

Through all the bad weather, Rowdy and Turkey performed miracles. Every day they managed to produce two hot meals and a plentiful supply of hot coffee for the crew.

At last the rains ended and, as if wishing to make up for the inconvenience, the sun blazed down on the sodden land. Finding an area of reasonably dry ground, Goodnight halted the herd for a day. With the cattle held under the minimum of a guard, the remainder of the party spread out and dried their clothing. Next day the journey was resumed.

Excitement, anticipation and a little concern filled the trail crew when they learned that the South Concho lay only a day's drive ahead. For several days the pace had been slackened and the cattle encouraged to graze on the lush, rich, fattening buffalo grass. In the manner of their kind, the steers took advantage of the good feeding and blossomed into top condition. Which was just what the rancher wanted in view of what lay ahead.

'We could push straight on across, sir,' Dusty suggested as they watched the herd go by and start spreading on the bed-ground appointed for the night. 'At dawn, I mean.'

'No,' Goodnight replied. 'They need a rest up to let them take on all the food and water they can. We'll stop here for four days.'

'The longer we're here, the more time the crew'll have to think about how tough the crossing's going to be,' Dusty warned. 'There'll not be much work to keep them occupied while we're in camp.'

'A good rest won't do them any harm any more than it will the steers,' Goodnight replied and grinned at his nephew. 'I reckon *you* can find something to keep them occupied.'

'I'll have to,' Dusty answered. 'If only to keep them from thinking about the Staked Plains—or about Miss Barbe.'

'Here's what I'll do, Dustine,' the rancher decided. 'I'll take Swede Ahlén, Sherman and one from each of the other Mineral Wells spreads along with me and the Kid on a scout. That'll leave you short-handed enough to keep the rest of 'em busy.'

'Sure,' Dusty agreed. 'Best take Austin along. That'll be one of the rivals out of my hair.'

'I could take them all——'

'That'd make it too obvious, sir. Anyways, it'd be best to take men who'll learn something from what they see. I can manage Vern, Jacko and Willock. Austin as well, comes to that.'

'I'll take Austin,' Goodnight smiled. 'You do what you have to for the rest.'

With the herd bedded down close to the South Concho, the trail hands gathered for the evening meal. On being told that they would accompany the rancher on his scouting mission, all but Austin agreed that it was a wise precaution. The Swinging G hand saw that his rivals would be left a clear—or reduced—field for Barbe's favours, but reluctantly concluded that he must obey orders.

'Sooner them than me!' grinned Vern, heel-squatting by the fire. 'All we've got to do here's ride round nice 'n' easy and watch them ole steers getting fatter.'

'I sure wish I'd your faith,' Dawn told him, darting a glance at Dusty. 'Is that all we've got to do?'

'That,' Dusty replied and saw relief creep on to various faces. 'And a few other lil things.'

Listening to Dusty listing all the work he wanted doing, the cowhands lost their relieved expressions. Yet they knew that he was not inventing tasks out of ornery cussedness. Every chore he mentioned needed doing and would increase their chances of safely crossing the Staked Plains. Naturally none of Dusty's audience intended to let their feelings show.

'Would that be all, Cap'n Fog, sir?' Billy Jack asked mildly. 'You ain't forgot something now, have you?'

'If he says "yes",' Dawn hissed in the lanky cowhand's ear, 'I'm going to make all them bad things you're expecting come true.'

'They will anyways,' Billy Jack replied, after Dusty had admitted that for the moment he could not think of further tasks. 'You see if they don't.'

'Anyways,' Dawn said. 'We can sleep in real late comes morning. Why, Cap'n Dusty says we don't need to roll out until full dawn.'

'I'm riding the last watch on night herd,' Billy Jack informed her, steadfastly refusing to accept that life held any bright side for him.

Next morning the majority of the trail crew enjoyed their extended spell in bed. Goodnight's party left while the rest ate a leisurely breakfast. Before the men could depart on the tasks assigned to them by Dusty the previous night, Barbe left her wagon. She wore a dainty black Stetson, frilly-fronted white blouse and an Eastern-style riding-skirt. Followed by her brother and Heenan, she crossed to the fire and flashed a dazzling smile at Dusty.

'As we are to be here for a time, I would like to go riding. Could you give me an escort, please, Captain Fog?'

'I'll——!' said at least three eager male voices.

'Dawn'll do it,' Dusty interrupted.

'Shouldn't a man go along, Dusty?' de Martin inquired. 'Not that I don't trust Dawn, but——'

'It'll be safe enough,' Dusty replied. 'Don't take Miss de Martin more than a mile from the camp, Dawn. And take along a rifle in case you get a chance to shoot some camp-meat.'

'Yo!' Dawn answered. 'Come on, gal. I'll pick you a hoss from the remuda.'

'Thank you, but Mr. Heenan says I may use his,' Barbe replied, a touch coldly. 'It is saddled and waiting.'

'Come on, it's time some of you started working!' Dusty growled. 'Half the day's gone and nothing done. Cousin Red, you're segundo on the herd. Take your crew and let the night herders come in afore Billy Jack starves to death.'

'Vern, Jacko, Burle, Spat. Let's go.'

Watching Red's section leave, Dusty wondered if he had made the right decision sending the first three out together. Yet they would be safer away from the camp than continually thrown into close contact with Barbe in each other's company. Red and Spat would act as restraining influences while they handled the comparatively easy work of holding the herd on the eastern banks of the river.

Although understanding why Dusty had given her the task, Dawn did not care for it. A friendly-natured girl, she had tried to be sociable with Barbe on several occasions and been, if not completely snubbed, shown that the other girl had no desire for her company. Coming from two entirely different environments, they had nothing in common that might have drawn them closer. So, while willing to carry out her orders, Dawn made little attempt at conversation as they rode away from the camp. Concentrating on keeping her seat, Barbe spoke little and Dawn concentrated upon watching for signs of deer, elk or pronghorn antelope.

Evidently the presence of the herd had temporarily driven away the wild animals, for Dawn and Barbe circled the area and approached where the herd was held without the western girl seeing anything suitable to shoot for camp-meat. Dawn made as if to turn away, but Barbe asked if they could go closer and see the cattle. Not wishing to appear obstructive, Dawn agreed. As they rode nearer, Burle Willock saw them and headed in their direction. Removing his hat with a flourish, the cowhand bowed over his saddlehorn.

'Howdy, Miss Barbe,' he greeted. 'It's sure pleasing to see you out here.'

'My! What a tremendous lot of cattle!' Barbe replied, looking around. 'There seem to be so many more when you see them like this. What do you do if one of them tries to run away?'

'Turn him back. I can right easy show you.'

Before Willock could make good his promise, Vern came galloping up from the opposite direction and Jacko rode their way.

'Hey, Miss Barbe!' Vern said, bringing his horse to a sliding stop.

'Ain't you supposed to be up that ways, watching them draws?' Willock demanded coldly.

'So?' Vern challenged. 'You're reckoned to be out on that rim comes to that.'

Moving his horse forward, Willock halted it alongside Vern's mount and thrust his face forward grimly. 'You get back to what you should be doing, *boy*!'

'Don't you go giving me no orders!' Vern spat back.

'Quit it, the pair of you!' Dawn snapped. 'Red's coming——'

'Now you back off, *sonny*!' Willock snarled, drowning the girl's warning. 'This time you don't have Dusty Fog on hand to take you p——'

Even as Dawn opened her mouth to repeat the warning, Vern flung himself at Willock. Locked together, they slid sideways from the horse and lit down fighting. Leaping from her saddle, Dawn darted towards the struggling pair.

'Quit it, you fools!' she yelled, trying to separate them as they came to their feet. 'Cut i——'

With a surging heave Willock threw the girl from his arm. She sprawled on to her rump in time to see Vern drive a punch into the other cowhand's face. Sent back a few paces, Willock caught his balance and went into a half-crouch. When Vern charged in recklessly, the more experienced Willock caught him by his vest. Partially trapping the youngster's arms, Willock jerked him closer and butted him between the eyes. Shoving the dazed Vern, Willock sent him reeling to tumble over his sister. Continuing to roll, Vern got clear of Dawn and started to rise. With a grin at Barbe, who sat watching with detached interest, Willock moved forward meaning to hand Vern the beating of his life.

The chance did not come. Having seen the girls' arrival and movement by the cowhands in their direction, Red Blaze wasted no time in making for them. His first intention had been to chase the men back to their work, but the fight gave him a more serious purpose. Maybe Red was a hot-head who revelled in fighting, but he never did so at the expense of his duties. So he raced his horse towards the others, ready to end the fight.

Without a glance at Jacko, who had already ridden up and dismounted clear of the combatants, Red quit his running horse and relied on its trailing reins to halt it. On landing, he hurled forward and shoulder-charged Willock. The force of the impact lifted the unsuspecting cowhand from his feet and flung him aside. From doing so, Red pivoted fast to meet the approaching Vern. Lashing around his right arm, Red delivered a backhand blow which sent the youngster spinning. From dealing with Vern, Red started to turn on Willock. What he saw made him put the cowhand out of his thoughts for the moment.

While Jacko was a good cowhand, he was not bright. Loyal to his friends, he regarded Red's treatment of Willock as unreasonable or part of a plot by the D4S to gang up on the Double Two hand. So he rushed to Willock's defence and reached for his Colt. In addition to recognising his own danger, Red knew that a shot might spook the herd and would certainly provoke a gun-fight. So he did not hesitate. Leaping forward as the other tried to clear the revolver from its poorly-designed holster, Red kicked him in the groin. Trained from his earliest days to respect firearms and that he must never pull a gun without the intention of using it, Red figured everybody should follow the same rule. Acting on it, he stopped Jacko in a painful, but most effective, manner. Letting out a croak of agony, the cowhand folded over, forgot drawing his Colt and collapsed face down on the grass.

'All right!' Red barked, swinging to face Willock once more. 'If you want to fight, get up and try me.'

Winded by the charge, Willock shook his head. He knew enough about Red to figure taking him would be far harder and much less certain than licking Vern. So, having no desire to let Barbe see him beaten, Willock declined the offer.

'I—I ain't got no fuss with you, Red. It's betw——'

'Get your hoss and head back to camp!' Red interrupted. 'Tell Dusty to send me three men out here.'

'Sure,' Willock answered sullenly and obeyed without offering to help the moaning Jacko.

'Whooee!' Vern groaned, standing up and rubbing his cheek. 'Red, you hit near on as hard as my pappy——'

'Go watch those draws until somebody comes out to relieve you!' Red snapped. 'And if any of the cattle've strayed down 'em, I'll kick you 'round the camp when I come in.' With that he turned from the abashed youngster and went to help Jacko rise. 'Sorry, feller, but I had to stop you firing off that gun.'

'G-Get your hands off!' Jacko muttered, holding the injured area and shrugging himself away. 'I'll——'

'Take your hoss and head back to camp,' Red said. 'See Rowdy and ask him to give you something for your hurts.'

'I—I won't be forgetting——!' Jacko began, then moaned and staggered to one side and vomited. When he had finished, he stumbled to his horse, dragged himself into the saddle and rode awkwardly after the departing Willock.

Red frowned then gave his attention to the girls. Standing up, Dawn went to the waiting *bayo-tigre* and mounted.

'If you pair don't have anything better to do,' Red said coldly. 'Stay clear of the herd. Get going.'

'How dare y——!' Barbe began in a loud voice.

'He's right,' Dawn put in. 'Turn your hoss and let's get going.'

For a moment Barbe glared furiously at the other girl and met cold challenge. Then the dark-haired girl swung her mount and rode after the cowhands. Dawn turned to Red and sighed.

'Damned fool kid!' she said.

'Who me?' asked Red.

'You too. Only I meant that damned fool kid brother of mine. He'd've got licked for sure happen you hadn't cut in.'

'And still might, him and Burle both, when Dusty hears what's come off. You'd best get going back to camp, Dawn. One I'm sorry for's Jacko.'

'I reckon he's sorry for his-self,' Dawn said without humour. 'Only you had to stop him and he's lucky you didn't do it with a gun. We'll not come out here again.'

Catching up to Jacko, Dawn tried to show him what might have happened. He only snarled back at her and, wisely, she let the matter drop. Leaving the cowhand, Dawn went after Barbe to catch her just after she joined Willock.

'He had no right to talk to you like that,' Barbe was saying when Dawn arrived. 'It was shameful and——'

'Yeah!' Willock answered. 'I'm not going to forget it.'

'You mustn't antagonise him, Burle,' Barbe warned. 'After all, his uncle is leader of the trail drive.'

'Yeah!' Willock muttered. 'Goodnight and his kin run the drive.'

'Which they don't do bad at it,' Dawn commented, deftly inserting her horse between Barbe's and Willock's mounts.

'Depends,' Willock grunted.

'What on?' Dawn asked coldly.

'How good friends you are with 'em,' the cowhand answered. 'There's some of us get on better with 'em than the others do.'

'What might that mean?' Dawn demanded.

'Look who's been sent back to the herd,' Willock told her.

At that moment they saw Dusty riding towards them. Halting his horse, the small Texan asked Willock what brought him and Jacko away from the herd.

'Maybe you'd best tell him,' Willock said to Dawn, a hint of challenge in his voice.

Sucking in an angry breath, Dawn did so. 'Sure, if you don't have the guts to,' she answered. 'Him and Vern got to tangling back there. It was Vern who started the fight——'

'I think that it was no more than a harmless piece of horseplay and neither were to blame,' Barbe put in, smiling in her most winning manner at Dusty. Then she put on a frown. 'But your cousin had no right to treat them so roughly. He kicked that poor cowboy in the—— Well, he kicked him savagely.'

'Jacko tried to pull a gun on Red,' Dawn put in and Willock, annoyed at his crony for drawing Barbe's sympathy, nodded agreement.

'Then he got what he asked for and's lucky it's not worse,' Dusty said, showing no signs of being won over. 'What happened?'

'Red sent me 'n' Jacko back to tell you he wants two more——'

'*Three* more!' Dawn interrupted and corrected Willock. 'He said three more. Only reason he didn't send Vern along was he figured you pair'd be *loco* enough to start fussing again on the way in.'

'And he'd likely've been right,' Dusty said, his voice almost mild. 'It sounds like there's not enough work for you knobheads* out at the herd. I'll have to see if I can't find you something to fill the time.'

By that time Willock had come to know Dusty real well and he stifled a groan. One way or another, he figured that he, Jacko and Vern were going to pay a stiff price for their stupid attempts to gain Barbe's favours.

* Knobhead: generally an exceptionally awkward mule.

CHAPTER TWELVE

HE'S NOT WEARING A GUN

Burle Willock found his guess to be correct. Making sure to divide the work evenly, Dusty kept the trio fully occupied. He did so well at it that all of them barely found time to do more than glimpse the source of their rivalry in passing from one chore to the next. At night they found themselves riding guard on the herd or sent to man the lonely picket points Dusty had set out to prevent any chance of a surprise attack. In that manner he kept them away from the camp fire at those times when Barbe was near it. More than that, Dusty had taken each of the trio aside on their return to the camp and given his opinion of their conduct, intelligence and general worth. None had enjoyed the interview. However, Jacko appeared to realise that he had got no more than he deserved and might have been far worse off. The other two promised to mend their ways and seemed to be making a try at doing it. If Barbe felt like going riding again, she never mentioned it.

The work went ahead fast. After a thorough check on each horse in the remuda, a party under Billy Jack started work on replacing missing or badly-worn shoes. Under old Boiler Benson's knowing eyes, saddlery was inspected and repairs carried out. Then the cook organised the unloading of the chuck- and bed-wagons, bracing each of them in its turn so that its wheels could be removed and the axles greased. On the morning of the fourth day only the de Martins' wagon remained to be put in a condition where it could survive the hazardous crossing.

Wanting to see if they had learned their lesson, Dusty let Vern, Willock and Jacko help the photographer empty the wagon. Having Mark in charge, he felt that any trouble would be dealt with promptly. Although Vern and Willock scowled at and studiously pretended to ignore each other, they gave every appearance of having profited by the lessons of the past days.

Boxes and trunks came from the wagon, while Barbe hovered around. One of the boxes gave off a familiar clinking sound which drew interested looks from Willock and Jacko.

'Thirsty work this, Jacko,' Willock commented, flickering a gaze at Barbe as they spoke.

'Sure is,' Jacko agreed, running his tongue tip over his lips. 'And nothing but water to take for it.'

'You have nothing but water?' Barbe asked.

'Nary a thing but that 'n' coffee,' Willock agreed. 'Colonel Charlie don't allow no hard liquor on his drive.'

At that moment Mark came into sight around the end of the wagon and the conversation ended. The work went on without incident and towards evening they started to reload the wagon. While passing a box up to where Turkey stood at the tail gate, Vern heard the sound of approaching hooves. Both of them turned to look, each expecting the other to retain his hold. Instead neither did, so the box fell and burst open. It held items of feminine underclothing and a large, leather-bound book. The latter bounced and landed open at the feet of de Martin and Dusty as they walked towards Goodnight's returning party.

'You clumsy b——!' Barbe began furiously, then chopped off her words as de Martin glared at her.

Bending down to help gather the scattered contents, Dusty found himself looking at several photographs in the book. All appeared to be of a wedding and in one de Martin stood at Barbe's side. He wore a top hat and fashionable suit while she was dressed in white, with a veil over her hair and bouquet of flowers in her hands. Before Dusty could do more than glimpse the picture, Barbe snatched the book from him and slammed it shut.

'I'll take that!' she said, going to place it in the box.

'I'm sorry, Dusty,' de Martin said. 'But there are a few photographs which Barbe regards as embarrassing. That was a picture of our cousin's wedding. Barbe was maid-of-honour and I was best man. It *was* disappointing. The rumour that the best man has the first night just isn't true.'

'I found that out for myself,' Dusty admitted, watching a spluttering Vern and Turkey blushingly help Barbe pick up the remainder of the contents. They hurriedly handed over the various garments and she packed the box then let them place it in the wagon. 'I'd best go and see what Uncle Charlie found out.'

'May I come with you?' de Martin asked.

'Feel free,' Dusty replied and called some of the men to give orders that they should take care of the new arrivals' horses. 'How'd it go, Uncle Charlie?'

'No worse than we expected,' Goodnight replied. 'There's been some rain up this way, but we'll still have three days of solid dry driving to reach the Pecos. We'll start the crossing at sun-up tomorrow.'

'May I offer a suggestion, Charles?' de Martin put in.

'Go to it.'

'If Dusty doesn't have any further plans for us, how about letting all hands have a night's relaxation?'

'How do you mean?'

'I understand that Rowdy plays the fiddle and has one along. Perhaps we could have a social evening. Of course Barbe and Dawn won't be able to partner the whole crew for dancing——'

'That's easy enough settled,' Dusty smiled. 'We'll put a heifer-brand on some of the boys.'

'I don't follow you,' de Martin said.

'It's the way we have out here, usually being short on women for dances and such,' Goodnight explained. 'So some of the fellers have a white rag tied around their left arms and dance "lady" fashion.'

'Not many of them object to being heifer-branded, seeing's how they get to sit with the ladies,' Dusty went on. 'Although they most times wind up looking at the bar most unladylike.'

'That won't happen tonight,' Goodnight stated. 'They can fun all they like, but there'll be no drinking.'

'With Rowdy keeping his medicine bottle locked up tight in the wagon, they won't have anything to drink,' Dusty replied. 'I'll fix things up, if it's all right with you, Uncle Charlie.'

'Go to it,' the rancher authorised. 'Ask Miss Barbe and Dawn to lend you a hand while you're at it.'

News of the proposed evening's entertainment was greeted with considerable enthusiasm by the trail crew. Dusty warned them that night herding would continue, but agreed to leave off the pickets. Knowing that the cattle came first, the cowhands raised no objections. Especially when they discovered that he had organised a rota which allowed everybody to spend as much time as possible at the festivities.

Due to the shortage of 'for real' lady partners—heifer brands formed a poor substitute—Dawn was excused taking her turn on the night herd. Following the range-land custom, she and Barbe were permitted to select the men who wore the heifer brands. Although Dusty did not care for the girls picking Vern and Willock, they produced a mighty good argument in favour of their choice. That way neither cowhand could partner Barbe, removing a cause of friction between them. So Dusty gave in, it being the ladies' prerogative to select their own company.

Certainly the dance began with reasonable decorum. Barbe wore the dress in which she had presented herself on the night she arrived and Dawn produced a gingham frock brought along to use on reaching Fort Sumner. The music was supplied by Rowdy on his battered violin, Turkey playing a jew's harp and Swede Ahlén giving backing with a blow-fiddle.* Perhaps the sounds they emitted would not have been acceptable in a fancy Eastern hotel, but the uncritical audience buckled down to dancing with vim if not grace.

After a few dances, somebody called on the Kid for a song. Once he had obliged with such of Juan Ortega's story as was fit for mixed company, other members of the crew responded with their party-pieces. Everything was going smoothly and in such good spirits that Dusty relaxed. It seemed that Vern and Willock had forgotten the fight. Certainly they made the most of their 'heifer-brand' positions, by allowing their 'partners' to bring them cups of coffee or the minor luxuries Rowdy had been able to produce at such short notice for the 'guests'. Even Heenan appeared to be joining in the fun for Dusty saw him handing a cup of coffee to Willock in an interval between the dance sets.

'And I tell you there ain't nobody can lick Swede Ahlén at Injun-wrestling!' Solly Sodak of the Lazy F announced in a loud voice during a lull in the noise and brought every eye his way.

'Mark there can,' objected Red Blaze, having been involved with the cowhand in a discussion for some minutes. 'Which I've got five whole dollars to prove it.'

'How about that, Swede,' called Sodak. 'Are you going to help me get rich at ole Red's expense?'

Once brought up, the subject aroused much interest and demanded settlement. Never averse to putting his skill and strength on display, Ahlén suggested that he and Mark should satisfy the bettors promptly.

Producing his sturdy chopping-block and muttering dire

* Blow-fiddle: An empty whiskey jug used as a kind of wind instrument.

warnings of what would happen if it be damaged in any way, Rowdy set it in position by the fire. Taking up their places on either side of the block, each of the contestants rested his right elbow on the chopping surface and gripped the other's raised right hand. Appointed judge, Rowdy waited until the audience had formed around the block and gave the order to start.

'I've got ten dollars's says it lasts for more than twenty minutes,' a man said and another took the bet.

Certainly all knew that they faced a lengthy session of Indian-wrestling, for the contestants were evenly matched. Mark's slight advantage in strength was counter-balanced by Ahlén's extra experience. Excitement filled the audience as the seconds ticked away and they were oblivious of anything but the two men at the chopping-block. Straining in their efforts to force down the opposing hand, Mark and Ahlén put all their considerable strength into beating the other.

Shortly after the contest began, Willock became aware that Barbe was not in the crowd. Looking around, he saw her going towards the de Martins' wagon and edged back to follow her.

Laughter, advice—mostly impractical or impossible—and offers of further bets flashed noisily among the spectators. So great was the racket that it drowned out the sounds of cursing, shouting and scuffling from behind the de Martin wagon. Dusty as first to become aware of the trouble, although up to that point he had not noticed certain absentees from the crowd.

Suddenly Willock reeled into sight from behind the wagon. Catching his balance, he drove out a blow at the head of Vern as the youngster followed him. Running into Willock's fist, Vern went backwards and sat down hard.

'Don't shoot him!' Barbe screamed, appearing beyond the two cowhands.

Spitting out a curse and mouthful of blood, Vern stabbed his hand towards his side. Already moving in to attack, Willock skidded to a halt, drew and fired. Vern rocked backwards as lead ripped into his chest and sprawled on to the ground.

Dusty went through the crowd as if it did not exist. At the sound of the shot, Mark and Ahlén released each other. The rest of the crowd forgot the contest, bets, everything except what met their eyes as they faced the de Martins' wagon. A concerted rush followed on the small Texan's heels. Faster than the rest, Dawn reached her brother almost as soon as

Dusty. She went to her knees at Vern's side, staring at the wound and reading its serious nature.

Tense and watchful, yet without making a hostile movement, Dusty faced Willock. Every sense the small Texan possessed warned him of danger. After shooting the youngster, Willock had recocked his revolver. Now he stood on spread-apart legs, with an over-casually balanced stance that, taken with the loose-lipped, slobbering grin on his face, screamed a deadly warning to one experienced in such signs. For all that, Dusty could not believe Willock was drunk no matter how he looked or acted. Silence fell on the crowd behind Dusty as they waited for him to make a move.

'What happened?' Dusty asked quietly.

'The fodder-forker pushed his luck too far is what,' Willock replied, his voice slightly slurred but tuned to sound tough and mean.

'Vern's dead!' Dawn gasped, looking at the two men.

'So he was going for his gun and I stopped him!' Willock growled. 'That's——'

'He's not wearing a gun!' Red Blaze put in, having moved forward to kneel at Dawn's side. 'His holster's empty.'

Angry comments rumbled up at the words. Looking over his shoulder, Dusty saw Narth moving forward with the Swinging G cowhands flanking him. At the same time, Jacko and two other Mineral Wells men came together. Dusty was suddenly aware that all but Ahlén of the older Mineral Wells men were riding the night herd. That deprived him of what might have been a restraining influence. Dusty's sense of danger increased. There was trouble in the air, a peril to the success of the herd as serious as any Hayden's hired guns might have caused. One wrong word or move might easily explode the whole camp into blazing gun-play.

'If that's right——!' Narth began grimly.

'I'll handle it,' Goodnight interrupted, joining Dusty. 'Put the gun up, Burle, and let's talk this out.'

'What's to talk about?' the cowhand demanded truculently. 'I pulled on him when Miss Barbe yelled. How was I to know he didn't have a gun?'

'Easily enough,' de Martin commented, walking to his sister's side from the rear of the wagon. 'You'd seen Vern loan me his gun so that I didn't go unarmed into the bushes.'

'Why you——' Narth spat out, right hand dropping to his

Colt's butt.

Fingers like steel grasped Narth's fist, crushing it in a powerful grip and preventing him from drawing the gun. Twisting his head, the cowhand looked into Mark Counter's face and heard the other's soft-spoken warning.

'Leave it be, *amigo*. Colonel Charlie'll see the right's done.'

Slowly Dawn raised her head. No tears came, but her face held lines of grief and anger. Lifting her eyes to Goodnight's, she said in a bitter voice, 'What're you going to do about it, Colonel? He murdered my brother.'

Again the low rumble of comment rose. Every man in the camp knew of the last grim article in the contract they had signed before leaving the Swinging G. Looking back, Dusty saw two separate groups starting to form. About half of the men, Goodnight's hands included, moved to where Narth stood by Mark. The second party consisted of Willock's cronies and looked to Ahlén for guidance. As the accused cowhand's segundo, Jacko and the others wanted to know where the big blond stood in the affair.

So did Dusty, come to that, and he asked, 'How about it, Swede?'

'We can take him——' Austin began.

'Open your mouth again!' Dusty blazed, swinging towards the speaker. 'And I'll close it with my boot—— Mark, take Austin, Spat and Eddie to the night herd. Eph, Ross, go help Will Trinka on the remuda.'

'Get to it!' Goodnight went on, knowing what Dusty wanted to do.

Slowly, showing their reluctance, the Swinging G men turned to obey. Usually Eph Horn and Ross Phares would not be sent to assist the night hawk with the horses but Dusty wanted to give Ahlén proof that he would deal fairly with Willock and not rely on the hands loyal to Goodnight to enforce his demands.

Swiftly Dusty looked around. Kneeling at her brother's side, Dawn was silent. It seemed that she had realised what her words might cause, for she never took her eyes from Goodnight's face although she said no more. From her, Dusty turned his attention to the de Martins. They and Heenan once more stood clear of the two factions. Considering what had happened, Barbe seemed remarkably calm. She watched the scene before her with an almost detached interest.

Diverting his thoughts from the girls, Dusty studied the trail hands. His dismissal of the Swinging G men had lessened the tension slightly. Yet everything depended on how Swede Ahlén answered Dusty's question. If he stood by the Articles of Agreement, Willock's supporters would go along. If not, the small Texan did not care to think of the result. Swede Ahlén held several lives and the safety of the whole trail drive in his big hands. Should he go back on his word about the contract, Josh Narth would want to dispense his own justice. While Willock's cronies might stand for Goodnight or Dusty dealing with the situation, they certainly would not permit another trail hand to do so.

After what seemed an age, although it followed on the heels of Dusty giving his orders to Mark, Ahlén spoke.

'Put up the gun, Burle. We're going to hold a hearing on the killing.'

'The hell you are!' Willock spat back, making no attempt to comply. What chance do I have? You've seen how all that bunch stand together.'

Ahlén stiffened slightly, looking at the cowhand's face and moving to stand between Dusty and Goodnight. 'He's liquored up. Watch him. He's dangerous when he's wet.'

Hearing the words, Dusty and Goodnight let out low breaths of annoyance. Under the Articles of Agreement, no liquor could be carried by the trail hands. Yet Willock showed every sign of being drunk and, according to his foreman, was a bad *hombre* when in that condition. Which altered nothing in the basic issue. It only made the situation more dangerously explosive.

'All ri——' Goodnight began, making as if to step forward.

'Keep back, all of you!' Willock snarled, his Colt making an arc that took in the three men before him. 'I'm full to my guts with this drive and I'm quitting. Who's coming with me?'

'Nobody,' Goodnight said quietly. 'And you're not going either.'

'Who'll stop me?' snarled Willock.

'I will,' Goodnight answered.

'No, Uncle Charlie,' Dusty put in gently. 'The segundo handles the men. I let this start, so it's for me to see it through.'

There was another, unmentioned point. Without its trail boss, the herd could not get through. So Dusty figured if anybody was going to be shot, he could be better spared than his uncle.

'I'll kill the first to move!' Willock snarled.

'Then you'll have to do it,' Dusty replied and took a step forward.

'You'll have to drop us both,' Ahlén warned, advancing in line with Dusty. 'Don't be *loco*, Burle. Leather it. You know Colonel Charlie'll give you a fair hearing.'

Backing off before the steady advance of the two men, Willock looked from one to the other. Drunk he might be, but not sufficiently for his condition to have driven all sense and thought from his head. Swede Ahlén had never professed to be a gun-fighter, but possessed the gritty determination to push through anything he started. Yet, more menacing to Willock at that moment was the *big* blond man ranged at his segundo's side. A quick glance warned Willock that he could not expect help from his cronies. Even Jacko stood silent and clearly willing to accept Ahlén's assurance that justice would be done.

Sweat ran down Willock's face and indecision played on it. Watching him, Dusty knew that he might go either way. If he should be drunk, impossible as it seemed, he could either surrender or make a rat-like fight against what he regarded as a trap.

For each pace the two men advanced, Willock retreated a stride. To Dusty it seemed that the barrel of the cowhand's Colt started to dip. At that moment a shot rang out. Lead ripped into Willock's head, spinning him around and tumbling him lifeless almost at the small Texan's feet.

Smoke curled up from the revolver in Heenan's hand and he said, 'I thought he was fixing to start throwing lead.'

CHAPTER THIRTEEN

WHERE DID YOU HIRE HEENAN?

Throwing a look at the Mineral Wells men, Dusty prepared to draw if they showed signs of hostility. None of them made a move, but stood staring at the still body at the small Texan's feet.

'You stupid son-of-a-bitch!' Ahlén growled at Heenan. 'He was giving it up.'

'It didn't look that way to me!' the hard-case answered, holstering his gun. 'Hell! If he'd thrown lead, this whole camp'd've gone up smoking. And if he'd run, we were standing in his way.'

On the face of it, Heenan had acted in a sensible manner. The moment Willock had squeezed his trigger, the rest of the men would have become involved. That would place the innocent by-standers in considerable danger. Nor would their position have been any safer if Willock had elected to escape, for they stood in his path to freedom.

'You can hardly blame Mr. Heenan, Swede,' de Martin put in. 'I thought that Burle meant to shoot you.'

'Best get two graves dug,' Dusty said quietly. 'Lon, take after Mark, then go on to Billy Jack and tell them everything's all right here.'

'Yo!' replied the Kid, whistling for his stallion and darting into the darkness to meet it.

Slowly Dawn rose and turned her grief-lined face towards Dusty. It was not her first brush with violent death, or even the first time she had lost somebody close to her, so she held control of her emotions and showed no sign of breaking down. That might come later. Right then she had other things on her mind. From Dusty she turned to Barbe, eyeing the girl with cold mistrust.

'How did it start?' Dawn demanded.

'They—they followed me,' Barbe replied hesitantly. 'I had come to the wagon to help Edmond collect his camera so that we might photograph the fun. I thought that they wanted to help——'

'So did I,' de Martin went on. 'When I said I wanted to go into the bushes, Vern loaned me his Colt——'

'Who started the fight?' Jacko interrupted.

'Finding out now won't do anybody any good,' Dusty put in. 'Burle Willock'd been drinking. Where'd he get the liquor?'

'Could he have had it with him all the time?' asked de Martin. 'Waiting for a chance to celebrate, I mean.'

'Not him,' Ahlén grunted. 'He wasn't a booze-hound, but he liked it enough to have drunk any he'd brought long afore tonight.'

'None of the others in the crew had any either,' Dusty said. 'Except Rowdy. Go see if your stock's still there, Rowdy.'

'Sure, Cap'n,' answered the cook and went to obey. On his return, he held out a partially-filled bottle of whiskey. 'That's what there was left in it after I yanked a tooth out for Sherm Sherman.'

'Which leaves you, Edmond,' Dusty drawled.

'How dare you imply that my brot——!' Barbe started hotly.

'Dusty is right, dear,' de Martin cut in. 'I do have liquor in my wagon and this is a serious matter which needs clearing up. You can inspect my stock, Dusty. I have kept it under lock and key since Charles explained his no-drinking article.'

With that the photographer led the way to his wagon and insisted that an inspection be made of his liquor supply. As he had claimed, it was securely locked in a trunk to which he carried the only key. Leaving the wagon, Dusty remembered something he had seen earlier and turned to Heenan.

'You took Burle a cup of coffee——'

'Sure,' agreed the hard-case. 'Two of 'em. Hell, it was all part of the running, us treating the heifer-brands like they was for-real women-folk.'

'Mr. Heenan has no liquor with him, Dusty,' de Martin stated. 'He was broke when he came to work for me and I refused to advance his wages to buy a bottle.'

'It—it's all my fault!' Barbe put in, sniffing and looking pathetically at the men. 'You all blame me——'

'No, ma'am!' Jacko hastened to assure her. 'We ain't none of us blaming you.'

'Those boys've been fussing over you——' Dawn began.

'And I did my best to stay away from them after that fight!' Barbe whimpered. 'You all know that. I never went near either of them. And tonight it was I who suggested that they played at being women so that I wouldn't have to dance with either of them. You all know that.'

'We all saw it,' Sodak agreed. 'Ain't nobody blaming you, Miss Barbe.'

'There for sure ain't!' Jackie confirmed, directing a grim, challenging look around him.

Barbe threw the young cowhand a look of abject relief and complete gratitude. Then she clasped her handkerchief to her face, turned and ran to her wagon. Sobs shook at her as she climbed inside.

'You'd best see to her, Edmond,' Goodnight said. 'Rowdy, take some of the crew and have two graves dug. We'll have to bury—Vern—tonight, Dawn.'

'I—I know!' Dawn replied. 'Oh Colonel Charlie, he was only a boy——'

Showing a gentleness known by only his closest friends, Goodnight took the girl in his arms and led her away from the bodies. Quietly Rowdy assembled a working party and, for once, none of the cowhands objected to riding the blister-end of a shovel. Watching them go, Dusty let out an angry growl which brought Ahlén's eyes to him.

'Damn it, Swede!' Dusty said. 'Where did he get that liquor?'

'I wish I knew,' the big cowhand answered. 'Whoever gave it to him near on blew this whole drive into the air.'

Red-eyed from crying, stiff-faced and tight-lipped, Dawn took her regular place among a silent trail crew on the morning after the double killing. She had seen her brother buried the night before and sobbed almost to sun-up in the bed-wagon, but insisted at breakfast that she was able to take her share of the work-load. If anything, her brother's death had increased her determination to see the drive brought off successfully.

'Ho, cattle!' Mark and Ahlén chanted at the point. 'Ho! Ho! Ho! Ho!'

Showing satisfaction almost, Buffalo lurched into motion. There was a short period of inevitable confusion until the steers reassumed their positions in the line. Wending their way to the banks of the South Concho, the cattle drank and crossed without any trouble to resume their westward march on the other side.

'We've not lost more than half-a-dozen head,' Dusty told his uncle as they gathered to compare their totals after making a trail count on the western side of the river.

'You've done well, boy,' Goodnight congratulated.

'Not all that well,' Dusty said bitterly, thinking of the two graves close to their deserted camp-site.

'Very well!' Goodnight insisted. 'Including last night. A wrong word or move there would have seen more graves on the Horsehead Crossing.'

Early in their stay, one of the hands had found a horse's skull near the river and stuck it up in a tree to give the area a name it would bear in future.

'Swede did most of it,' Dusty said. 'If he'd not backed us, there'd've been powder burned last night.'

'Swede's got a good head on his shoulders, like you. That's why I stayed out of it and let you two call the play. I'm damned if I know what I'll say to Darby Sutherland when we get back home.'

'I know how you feel, sir. That was one chore I hated in the War; and I only had to write letters, not tell them face to face. It'd be best if we watched the crew real careful for a few days, Uncle Charlie, and try to make sure that nothing else happens to stir them up.'

'It would,' Goodnight agreed. 'Once we get on to the Staked Plains, they'll have more than plenty to keep them occupied.'

'Sure. I wonder where Willock got the liquor from?'

'He could've caried it all along. After being off it for so long, he'd not need much to make him drunk.'

'I asked Miss de Martin why she shouted about not shooting,' Dusty said. 'She reckons she can't remember doing it. I didn't push it, she likely feels bad enough about what's happened.'

During the day, Dusty kept a close watch on the crew. They were subdued in their manner, but worked together with no sign of remembering the split of the previous night. So far they had not got on to the real Staked Plains, but the grazing grew poorer while the heat increased. By good fortune they found a water hole and let the cattle drink before bedding down for the night.

Despite Dusty's comments, Barbe seemed to have recovered from her shock by night-fall. Returning from a visit to the remuda, Dusty heard talking beyond a clump of bushes. Recognising Barbe's voice, he would have walked on but her companion's words brought him to a halt.

'Colonel Charlie won't let me do it,' said Austin Hoffman. 'He wouldn't let Edmond take pictures close to the cattle.'

'But you could do it, Austin,' Barbe answered. 'And it would make both my brother and I so grateful if you did.'

'They'd not let me do it either,' Austin protested.

'Couldn't you do it without them knowing?'

'How?'

'Take the camera and hide close by. Then photograph the herd as it comes towards you.'

'That'd mean being on foot,' Austin gasped.

'Are you afraid?' Barbe asked and Dusty could sense her bristling at the arguments.

'No. But I'm not *loco* neither,' Austin replied. 'Any one of them critters'd charge me on sight——'

'It would be worth the risk, Austin,' Barbe purred. 'Just think what such a photograph would mean. The first of its kind, taken at considerable risk. Why it would make you famous. Then, with the flair you show for photography, you could open a studio in Austin, or even in some Eastern city where I could live. Don't you see, Austin?'

At which point Dusty decided to let his presence be known. So he gave a rasping cough and heard a hurried scuffling among the bushes.

'Who's there?' Dusty called.

'It's only us,' Austin answered, coming through the undergrowth with the girl trailing behind him. 'We're just going back to camp.'

'I'll come with you,' Dusty said. 'Hey, I just now remembered, Austin. There was a Hoffman in the Texas Light, maybe you're kin to him?'

'My uncle,' Hoffman confirmed, looking just a touch relieved and showing no sign of yielding to Barbe's glances at the bushes. 'What do you know, Miss Barbe, Cap'n Dusty knowed my uncle in the War.'

'How interesting!' Barbe said in a tone which carried a knife's edge.

'Say, Miss Barbe,' Dusty drawled. 'You don't know if Edmond's figuring to take any pictures of the herd in the next few days?'

'He may be,' Barbe answered, darting a suspicious glance at the small Texan and reading nothing on his face.

'I'd best ask him not to,' Dusty said. 'Especially close up. That powder going off near them might start a stompede and none of us'd want that to happen—now would we, Austin?'

'We sure's hell wouldn't,' Hoffman agreed vehemently.

'I'm sure pleased that I met up with you, Miss Barbe,' Dusty went on in a matter-of-fact tone. 'It'll save me looking up your brother special to warn him. You can do it for me.'

'I will,' Barbe promised, but her voice dripped ice and she left the men as soon as they drew near to the camp.

'How much did you hear, Cap'n Dusty?' Austin asked as soon as they were alone. 'Afore you coughed, I mean.'

'Enough to figure it was my business to cough,' Dusty replied. 'Don't try it, Austin. Even if you don't get killed by a steer, you'll stompede the herd. Either way, you'll never get that fancy photographic studio in some Eastern town.'

After the cowhand had left him, Dusty stood for a moment and looked at the de Martin wagon. However, he put off his intention to see the photographer with a warning not to use Barbe as a lure to get risky pictures taken. There would be time to do that later. So Dusty walked across to the main fire and heard Goodnight talking to the crew. One of the hands had just been complaining about his bed being so rock-studded that he doubted if he could sleep.

'Getting to sleep's not going to worry you for a spell after tonight, anyways,' the rancher announced.

'How come, Colonel Charlie?' the cowhand inquired.

'Because when we move out tomorrow,' Goodnight explained and something in his voice brought all other conversation to a halt, 'we won't be stopping until we reach the Pecos.'

An almost numbed silence followed the words, as the trail crew gave thought to the implication behind them. Even the de Martin party had heard, for they approached the fire. Dawn could see concern on the girl's face and wondered what caused it.

'You mean that we just keep the herd going,' Ahlén said. 'Without bedding down, or for water, until we get to the other side, Colonel?'

'That's just what I mean,' the rancher agreed. 'You saw the lie of the land, Swede. There'll barely be enough water for the horses and crew. So we keep the cattle going for as long as it takes us to hit the Pecos.'

'How about food for the hands?' Sherman wanted to know.

'Rowdy'll pull ahead with the wagon, throw up a meal and you'll eat it in the saddle. Those cattle have to be kept moving all the time.'

'How about my sister, Charles?' asked de Martin. 'Do you expect her to be subjected to such conditions?'

'There's no other choice,' Goodnight answered.

'What you could do,' Dusty suggested, 'is stop back at night, then catch up during the day. Your wagon'll be able to make better time than we can with the herd.'

'Would that be safe?' de Martin inquired.

'Safe enough,' Dusty replied. 'There're no Indians up this way and we'll be leaving a trail a blind man could follow. If there should be a sand-storm, I'll get Lon back to guide you.'

'We'll see how it goes first,' the photographer decided, taking Barbe's arm as she opened her mouth. 'Come, dear. I think we had better get a good night's sleep, don't you?'

'If you say so,' Barbe answered, her voice brittle.

'Edmond's got a right smart idea,' Dusty remarked as the couple walked away. 'We're all going to need our sleep with what's ahead. I don't know about the rest of you, but I'm riding herd on my blankets right now.'

The feeling appeared to be generally accepted and soon the camp had settled itself down for what would be their last night's sleep until they reached the Pecos.

Always a light sleeper, and never more so than when acting as a scout, the Kid woke as some slight, alien noise reached his ears. The normal camp sounds had left him undisturbed. Neither the changing of the night guard nor one of the crew leaving the camp to relieve himself had woken the dark youngster. Yet faint foot-steps brought him from his sleep. Apart from a casual-appearing roll over in his blankets, he gave no sign of the change in his condition. Looking around, he saw nothing apparently changed. The crew still slept around the fire, except for the empty beds of the night herders. Yet somebody had sneaked away from the camp, of that he felt certain.

In a swift, silent movement, the Kid quit his blankets and rose. He wore moccasins, was bareheaded, fully-dressed and held his bowie knife. Glancing at the rifle and Dragoon Colt on his bed, he decided they would not be needed. So he flitted into the darkness without disturbing the other sleepers.

Whoever had woken the Kid was going towards the bedded-down herd a quarter of a mile from the camp. On fast-striding, noiseless feet, the Kid followed. At last he saw a crouching figure moving through the darkness. Not fifty yards from the nearest of the steers, the figure halted. Something metallic glinted in its hand and the rapidly-approaching Kid knew what it was.

'Drop it!' hissed the Kid.

'What the——?' snarled a familiar voice and the figure spun around, right arm bending to point at the dark youngster.

Knowing what the other had planned to do, the Kid did not hesitate. Up then down swung his right hand. Leaving it, the bowie knife flashed through the air. Such was the weight, balance and cutting edge of the great knife, powered by the Kid's trained right arm, that it severed a way through the snooper's ribs and sank its clip point into the vital organs they protected. Reeling, the night-sneaker let his revolver drop unfired. Vainly his hands tried to draw out the knife during the brief time he had left to live. Buckling at the knees, his legs deposited him face down on the ground.

'Who-all's that?' called a voice and Mark Counter rode from the darkness.

'You had a caller,' the Kid replied, rolling over his victim and retrieving the knife. 'Likely Dusty'll be interested to know who it is.'

Which statement proved correct. On his return, the Kid found the cook and louse already preparing breakfast. Going to Dusty, the Kid shook him gently until he woke. Hearing what his dark *amigo* had to tell, Dusty rose immediately.

'Let's go and see what de Martin's got to say,' Dusty growled.

'His bed's not under the wagon,' the Kid said as they walked that way. 'I missed seeing that.'

'Where the hell is he then?' Dusty asked.

De Martin supplied the answer by looking from the rear of the wagon's canopy. With ruffled hair and his torso bare, he gave signs of having been recently woken. Yet he had always bedded down under the wagon, except during the rainy period.

'What's wrong?' the photographer asked.

'Can you come out here, Edmond?' Dusty said.

'Of course. Just a moment,' de Martin agreed and ducked back out of sight. The Texans heard him talking with his sister, then he appeared wearing a bath-robe which had been much admired by the cowhands on previous occasions. 'What is it?'

'Heenan,' drawled the Kid.

'What about him?' asked the photographer.

'I just now killed him for trying to stompede the herd.'

There was no doubt that the words came as a shock to de Martin. Nor had the Kid done anything to lessen their impact, wanting to see how the other reacted.

'I—I don't understand!' de Martin gasped.

'Nor do we,' Dusty assured him. 'Where did you hire Heenan?'

'In Graham. It was soon after we learned that Charles had already left with his herd. Heenan came to me and offered to act as my guide. From what he said, I formed the opinion he wished to leave Texas to avoid a feud. As he asked a reasonable wage, I agreed.'

'You took a big chance, hiring a stranger like that,' the Kid remarked.

'It seemed safe enough,' the photographer answered. 'I knew that we would soon catch up with the herd. Please, Dusty. Can we continue this later? My sister was so disturbed at the thought of crossing the Staked Plains that I spent the night in the wagon to calm her. I wouldn't want her made more nervous.'

'I reckon we can,' Dusty decided. 'Let's go, Lon.'

'What do you reckon, Dusty?' the Kid inquired as they walked away.

'If Heenan was working for Hayden, coming with Edmond and his sister'd be a good way to get accepted by us,' Dusty replied. 'Then he waited his chance, or for help to catch up. When it didn't come, he figured to scatter the herd. After the trouble at Horsehead Crossing, the crew'd not be too eager to gather the steers and go on.'

'Even if they did, it'd slow us down so we'd not get to Fort Sumner on time,' the Kid went on. 'I'll bet on one thing, though. De Martin didn't know what Heenan planned.'

'That's for sure,' Dusty agreed. 'Nobody could act as surprised as he looked. Come on, we'd best go tell Uncle Charlie what's happened.'

CHAPTER FOURTEEN

IF THIS KEEPS UP, I'LL GO MAD

When told of Heenan's attempt at stampeding the herd and death, Goodnight agreed with Dusty's views about the former. However, the urgent nature of the drive's next phase soon pushed all thoughts of the incident from his and Dusty's heads. To avoid complications, they passed the word that Heenan had deserted during the night. Filled with the knowledge of what lay ahead, the trail hands accepted the excuse and were not greatly interested in why the hard-case had gone.

When the cattle started moving that morning, there began an epic journey in the history of the West. For years to come, the first crossing of the Staked Plains by a trail herd would be spoken of with awe. Certainly the people involved would never forget it. Just as Goodnight had warned, they kept going without a pause by day or night.

At the point, Boiler Benson and Billy Jack took over the usual leaders. The giant strength of Mark and Ahlén was of more use with the drag. There they and other men tailed up steers which had fallen or just lay down to quit, or pushed aside the stronger steers to ease the path for the weaker. Masked by bandanas to try to keep the churned-up dust from clogging their nostrils and mouths, the remainder of the crew found work in plenty. Heat-crazed steers fought among themselves or showed the savage aggression of stick-teased rattlesnakes. More than one of the trail hands owed his life to the speed and sure-footedness of his horse, when attacked by a raging longhorn. Snatching meals in the saddle, dismounting only when nature could no longer be resisted, they rode on and on, ever west.

Ranging far ahead of the others, dependent upon his *Pehnane* upbringing and the ability of his horses, the Kid sought out the deadly alkali or salt lakes. Once located, he checked on the wind's direction and passed the word to Goodnight who changed the line of march to pass so that the smell of water was not carried to the cattle. In that way they avoided the greatest danger of all. Fights could be stopped, charges evaded, the weary kept moving or the 'downners' hauled up and made to walk. Let the thirsty cattle get but one sniff of the water and they would have pushed to it with a force that no man nor horse could hope to halt.

Through the three days of the drive, Dawn took her share of the work, risks and hardships. In fact, the way she plunged herself into the thickest, hardest of the gruelling toil, it seemed that she sought to fill both her own and her dead brother's places. Not only did she work hard, but her presence acted as the spur Dusty had hoped it would. What cowhand would quit, no matter how tired or dispirited he might be, when he saw the girl carrying on? At times Dawn being on hand prevented an exhausted cowboy from just giving up. Although every muscle, fibre and bone ached with weariness, the girl continued to ride the herd.

On the morning of the fourth—and they hoped last—day, Dusty sent Dawn back to see if the de Martins were all right. His main reason for the order was to take the girl from the dangers of the herd, if only for a short time. Reluctantly she agreed and rode away through the dust of the drag.

Even the girl did not realise just how tired she was. Once clear of the constant exertion and the ever-present need to remain alert, she found trouble in keeping her eyes open. In fact she actually went to sleep, only her years of riding training keeping her balanced in the saddle. The sound of a female voice raised in anger jolted Dawn awake. Staring ahead, she found that her *bayo-tigre* gelding was approaching her destination. The de Martins' wagon stood with its team unhitched and flaps opened so that the approaching girl could see inside. Dressed in a robe, a dishevelled Barbe faced de Martin furiously.

'If this keeps up, I'll go mad!' the black-haired girl was screaming. 'You said it would all be over before we had to——'

At that moment the photographer slapped his sister hard across the cheek. The force of the blow knocked her sprawling on to the unmade bed, sobbing in pain. Then he heard the sound of Dawn's horse. Whirling around, he snatched a Remington Double Derringer from the top of a trunk to line it in the newcomer's direction.

'Oh it's you, Dawn!' de Martin greeted, lowering the little hide-out pistol.

'Cap'n Dusty sent me back to see if everything's all right,' Dawn replied, wondering where a dude like the photographer had learned such fast, efficient gun-handling.

A muffled croak broke from the weeping Barbe, but de Martin went to her side and laid a hand on her shoulder. 'It is,' he assured Dawn. 'My sister was just a little hysterical and I had to quieten her, but we're all right.'

'Will she be all right?'

'Yes. I can take care of her.'

'Can I help you hitch up your team, or anything?'

'No!' de Martin stated emphatically. 'You've probably got enough on your hands with the herd.'

'That's for sure,' Dawn admitted. 'Well, if there's nothing I can do——'

'Not a thing,' de Martin insisted. 'In fact, I can probably cope with Barbe better alone——'

'Sure,' Dawn said. 'You'll find the chuck-wagon maybe a mile and a half along the trail. I'll get back to the herd.'

With that, she rode in the direction of the herd. Curiosity made her turn in the saddle when about a hundred yards from the wagon. De Martin was bending over his sister talking in what Dawn felt to be an angry manner. Figuring it was none of her business, the girl continued to ride after the herd. Before she had reached the drag, something happened to make her put the de Martins out of her mind.

Up at the point, Billy Jack and Boiler Benson saw Buffalo start to sniff the air in a restless manner. At a signal from the old-timer, Goodnight and Dusty rode up. They too noticed the change in the lead steer's behaviour and turned worried faces to each other.

'There's a lake among the broken country ahead!' Dusty said worriedly. 'If the wind's changed——'

'Yes!' Goodnight answered and the one word was encyclopaedic in its inference.

More of the leading steers raised their heads, joining Buffalo in excited bawling. The sounds rose to a crescendo as the leg-weary longhorns increased their pace. From a weary, dragging gait, they changed to a hesitant trot, then to a faster run. Soon the front section of the herd was racing forward with a dogged, blind determination that knew no stopping.

'God damn all fool —— —— —— steers!' Goodnight cursed impotently and profanely as the tired cowhands tried to halt the rush.

A mile fell behind, then two, with no sign of the cause for the steers' behaviour. At last Billy Jack saw the sun glinting on something ahead. For all his previous gloomy predictions, the cowhand felt a sickening sense of frustration and rage. After so long they were in danger of losing most of the herd. Unless——

'It's not a lake!' Billy Jack screamed the words above the sounds of hooves, bellowing steers and shouting men. 'By the Good Lord, it's the Pecos!'

'It's the Pecos!' Catching the words, another of the hands sent them ringing through the air. 'It's the lovely, son-of-a bitching Pecos!'

So it was. Instead of a lake with misery and death in every mouthful, the water ahead was the Pecos River. Scented almost three miles back by the steers, it had drawn them on and given the inducement they needed to reach it.

By that time the herd had spread itself into a long, segmented line as the fitter steers drew ahead. Even the drags had caught the fever of excitement and were pushing along at their best possible speed, although Mark and his eight-strong party still found the need to help the weakest.

Down to the river's bank rushed the leading cattle. Buffalo and the first of the steers plunged in without hesitation, only to be pushed through by the crush from behind. Yet even that was not as dangerous as it might have been, for they went on, turning back and moving up or downstream until they found a place to enter and drink.

Among the cowhands accompanying the front of the herd, Dawn followed the cattle towards the Pecos. Knowing her strength limited her usefulness in the drag, she had pushed on along the line to help try to stop the rush. Keeping with the men, she rode into the river. Profane hilarity filled the air as rider after rider flung himself from his saddle to disappear beneath the surface. Coming up, gasping and spluttering, Dawn looked around her. While the Pecos River lacked the sparkling, crystal-clear quality of a snow-fed mountain brook, none of the crew thought the less of it. At that moment they would rather be drinking its water than the finest whiskey money could buy.

'We've done it!' Dawn screamed, throwing her arms around the nearest man and kissing his bristle-stubbled cheek. 'We've done it!'

'We for sure have!' whooped the recipient, Billy Jack, then realised that such enthusiasm would ruin his image. 'I'll bet either them or us drown or get bogged in a quick-sand, mind.'

'Get 'em out of it and to work, Dustine!' Goodnight ordered through his water-sodden whiskers, pounding his grinning nephew on the back. 'The rest of the drive're coming and'll need handling.'

The Staked Plains had been crossed, the Pecos River lapped around their hips, but there was still work to do. Gathering the cowhands, including a bright-eyed, wildly-happy Dawn, Dusty set half to control the arriving cattle, move those that had watered away from the river and hold them. The other half went back with him to meet the drag. It said much for the self-control of the riders in Mark's party that they had stuck to their posts and continued with the gruelling work of keeping the drag moving.

Not until noon did the last of the herd quench its thirst and cross the river. The chuck- and bed-wagons had arrived and come to the western bank to join the cattle and remuda. Last on the scene were the de Martins, helped over in their wagon by laughing, delighted men. There had been losses during the final rush, but not heavy and still more than sufficient steers remained to fulfil the Army's contract.

'All right!' Dusty told the assembled trail crew. 'You've done real well and deserve a rest. So I'm giving you a holiday. Right through to tomorrow at sun-up.'

'I dearly love a generous, kind-hearted boss,' Red Blaze whooped. 'Danged if I don't celebrate by having me a bath.'

The idea caught on and a steady stream of cowhands left the camp carrying a change of clothing and, if they owned such refinements, towels. Going to the bed-wagon, Dawn climbed in. It had been cleared of bed rolls by men wanting clothing or the means to reload their soaked revolvers. So she opened up her war bag with the intention of following Red's suggestion. First, however, she figured to let the men get through. Lying on her blankets, she drifted off to sleep.

Voices woke the girl and she stayed still for a moment until her sleep-dazed senses cleared. Looking out of the wagon, she concluded the time to be late afternoon. Then she rose, listening to what was being said.

'Barbe has gone along the river to bathe, Jacko,' came de

Martin's cultured tones. 'Can you go and ask her to come back?'

'Sure can,' agreed the cowhand, sounding just a touch too eager. 'Which way did she go?'

'Upstream, among those bushes,' de Martin explained. 'I'd go myself, but I want to take some photographs.'

'Shuckens, I don't mind doing you 'n' Miss Barbe a favour,' Jacko protested.

'I can just bet you don't!' Dawn thought as she waited silently. 'Not when there's maybe a chance of seeing her taking a bath.'

Before lying down to rest, the girl had removed her boots. She slipped on a pair of Indian moccasins, picked up the clothing set out earlier, draped her gunbelt across her right shoulder and left the wagon. Already de Martin was strolling towards the fire and Jacko was going at a fair speed in the direction of the bushes. Dawn darted after the cowhand and he turned as he heard her coming.

'Hey, Jacko,' Dawn greeted. 'Say, Cap'n Dusty wants to see you.'

'What for?'

'I dunno. He said for me to tell you if I saw you.'

'Reckon I'd best go and see what he wants,' Jacko muttered in a disappointed voice. 'If you see Miss Barbe, ask her to come back to help her brother take some pictures.'

'I'll do just that,' Dawn promised.

Watching the cowhand stalk indignantly back to the camp, Dawn shook her head and let out a long breath. If her actions should be questioned later, she would claim that she had delivered the false message as part of a joke. One thing was certain to her way of thinking. For a smart big-city feller, de Martin sure showed a bad judgement of human nature in picking Jacko to fetch his sister. If Barbe was still either bathing or dressing, Dawn could not see the cowhand acting polite and warning the unsuspecting girl of his presence.

'I'm damned if I know why I'm bothering,' Dawn mused. 'Only it don't seem right for him to be watching her.'

Finding a path, Dawn followed it. She made no attempt to walk quietly, not wanting to startle the other girl by an unannounced appearance. Hearing a frightened feminine cry, she sprang between two bushes and skidded to a halt at the sight that confronted her.

Barbe stood on the other side of a sandy clearing, clad in a flimsy silk shift over the briefest, most daring underclothing Dawn had ever seen. Not that the shift offered anything but the scantiest concealment. Its hem had become spiked on the branches of a bush and was drawn high enough to expose her bare, very shapely legs to the tops of the thighs.

'I—I'm caught. Can you help m——?' Barbe began, making ineffectual attempts to free herself. Then she looked up at Dawn and puzzled annoyance creased her beautiful face. 'It's you!'

Maybe Dawn was a country-raised girl, with no more formal schooling than her mother had been able to supply, but she possessed her fair share of natural intelligence. Taking in the scene, she drew some rapid conclusions and did not care for them. Everything about Barbe's attitude hinted that she had been expecting some other person to come on to the scene.

'Just who the hell did you think it'd be?' Dawn demanded, dropping her clean clothes and crossing the clearing to drape her gunbelt over the top of the bush which trapped the other girl. 'Let me help you get loose.'

Gripping the hem of the shift, Dawn tugged it free from the bush and ripped the material. With an angry hiss, Barbe started to pull away from the other girl and added further damage to her garment. Staggering back a few paces, Barbe's face twisted into an expression of rage which shocked Dawn.

'You did this on purpose!' Barbe spat out, moving forward and holding out the torn edge of the shift. 'You cheap little——'

'Don't start mean-mouthing me, you man-chasing bitch!' Dawn flared back. 'Pulling a play like this, you could have—— Hey though! How the hell did you know your brother wouldn't be coming out to fetch you? That fancy skirt didn't hang itself on the branch by accident.'

'You mind your own business!' Barbe yelled. 'I've had enough of you, the whole stinking bunch of you!'

'Which I can't say I reckon a whole heap on you,' Dawn replied and started to turn away. 'Get dressed. None of the men'll be coming.'

Barbe spat out something in a language which Dawn did not understand, but figured it to be anything except complimentary. Then the dark-haired girl caught the blonde by the arm and jerked her around. Up drove Barbe's right knee, aimed at

Dawn's groin. Giving the angry oath had been a mistake on Barbe's part. Always a tomboy and with experience gained in childhood scuffles, Dawn turned half-expecting such an attack. So she continued to swing her body and the knee struck her hip instead of its intended target. The force of its arrival sent the slim girl staggering away and with an effort she retained her balance.

'All right!' Dawn hissed. 'If that's how you want it——'

Clearly that was just how Barbe wanted it. Letting out another string of what Dawn assumed to be French profanity, the dark-haired girl flung herself forward. Caught by a stinging slap across the face, Dawn cut loose with both hands to retaliate in kind. Then their fingers sank into hair, tugging and jerking while their feet or knees flailed at the other girl's legs and body.

For a few seconds the girls staggered backwards and forwards clinging to hair. Gasps, squeals and curses broke from them as each tried to throw the other to the ground but retain her own footing. In the matter of hair-pulling Dawn had the advantage. Her short-cropped locks offered a less secure gripping area than the long black tresses of her rival.

Feeling her fingers slipping from Dawn's hair, Barbe raked her nails down the other's cheeks and closed her hands on the other's throat. Pure instinct made Dawn release her hold and transfer her fingers to Barbe's neck. Reddish blotches formed where their fingers gouged into flesh, yet neither showed signs of releasing her hold. Guttural, croaking sounds broke from their mouths as the choking grips grew tighter.

Dawn had been surprised at Barbe's unexpected strength, but was still the stronger of the two. Slowly she forced Barbe back, digging her thumbs into the other's throat and bending her rearwards. Desperately Barbe released Dawn's neck and clawed wildly at Dawn's wrists. Pain brought a screech from Dawn's lips and she hurled the other girl from her.

For a moment Dawn thought Barbe had had enough. Then the beautiful-faced girl attacked again. Launching themselves at each other, they collided with a sickening force. Without any form of planned attack, they grappled wildly for a grip to bring the other girl down. Locking her wiry arms around Barbe's waist, Dawn tried to crush her. Struggling wildly, the black-haired girl encircled the blonde's neck with her right arm and twisted until she held Dawn in a headlock. With her own arms around Barbe's middle, Dawn could do nothing to prevent herself being trapped. Once again Dawn found herself being choked, but with less chance of reprisal. Nor could she use Barbe's method of effecting an escape. Riding with the trail herd did not allow her to grow long fingernails.

Croaking and gasping, Dawn broke off her bear-hug. Her hands roved wildly in an attempt to break the hold. Reaching Barbe's head, Dawn's left hand buried into the hair. Taking a firm hold, she jerked Barbe's head backwards and at the same moment kicked the other hard behind her right knee. Braced on stiff legs, Barbe was thrown off balance when her leg suddenly bent forward. Before she could recover, Dawn had jerked free and they both sprawled in a heap on the sand.

With barely a pause the girls began to roll over and over. It was a wild, mindless tangle in which fists, flat palms, knees, feet, heads and teeth were used indiscriminately. Dawn's shirt ripped down the back and flapped free of her levis, while Barbe's scanty clothing—even less suitable for such treatment—suffered even greater damage. The shift hung in tatters, while the bodice of her underclothes had ripped to bare her torso.

Exhaustion rather than modesty or shame at her behaviour made Barbe try to end the fight. How it happened was impossible to decide, but in some way they had each obtained a head scissors on the other. With legs locked about the other's head, they rolled four times and then came apart. Sobbing for breath, Barbe tried to crawl away. Dawn lurched to her feet and flung herself forward. Taking a double handful of the black hair, she dragged Barbe upright. Then she released the girl and swung a punch. Hard knuckles crashed into Barbe's nose and she stumbled backwards with hands going to the source of the pain.

'My face!' Barbe screamed, going to her knees. Through the tears of pain which misted her vision, she saw Dawn approaching. 'No! No! Don't hit me again!'

Slowly a feeling of revulsion filled the blonde, bringing her to a halt. Yet she wanted to give Barbe a warning to prevent a further recurrence of the flirting which had caused Vern and Willock's deaths.

'All right!' Dawn said, breathing hard and standing over the crouching girl. 'What the hell kind of game are you playing at?'

'Do-don't hit me again!' Barbe whined. 'Don't hit me and I'll tell you everyth——'

The flat crack of a light-calibre revolver chopped off her words. Struck in the head by a bullet, Barbe pitched sideways. Exhausted by the fight, Dawn reacted sluggishly. For a moment she stood and stared with unbelieving eyes at the other girl's spasmodically jerking body. A soft thud nearby brought Dawn's head around and she saw her Cooper revolver lying on the sand, smoke curling from its muzzle. Faintly she heard shouts and the sound of running feet coming her way. Without thinking, she bent over and picked up the revolver.

Still too dazed to realise fully what she was doing, Dawn turned with the smoking Cooper in her hand. She stood holding the gun, looking in exhausted incomprehension at Barbe's body when the first of the men from the camp burst into the clearing. Everything seemed to be whirling around before Dawn's eyes. Then as her legs buckled under her, she heard a voice from what seemed a long way off.

'My God! She's murdered my sister!'

CHAPTER FIFTEEN

SHE HAS TO STAND TRIAL

Attracted by the sound of the shot, Dusty Fog led the rush of men to investigate its cause. Bursting through the bushes, he came to a halt and stared at the scene that met his eyes. Behind him, the trail hands also stopped and were shocked to silence by what they saw. Dusty knew the shock would not last. Even before de Martin came shoving through the rear of the party, the small Texan knew he faced a delicate and dangerous situation. Angry, startled comments rose from the other men as the photographer made his accusation. Even as Dawn collapsed alongside Barbe, Dusty swung around.

'Back off, all of you!' Dusty ordered and his eyes went to the big shape of the cook. 'Rowdy, see if there's anything you can do.'

Coming prepared to deal with any kind of trouble—although not of the type they found on arrival—all the trail hands held guns. So did Dusty. Yet it was not the threat of the long-barrelled Army Colt in his left hand which caused the men to obey. At such a time they needed a leader to guide them and Dusty was that man.

Although the majority of the group obeyed, de Martin ran towards his sister and Josh Narth went to Dawn. Dusty raised no objections, knowing they showed a natural and understandable concern for the girls' welfare. Holstering his Colt, Dusty watched the men do the same. Shock, horror, disbelief and lack of comprehension showed on the tanned faces which Dusty had come to know so well. Staring fixedly at where Rowdy bent over Barbe, Jacko muttered under his breath.

The cook's examination of the black-haired girl did not take long. Looking at de Martin, Rowdy said gently, 'There's nothing I can do for her.'

'Lord!' the photographer moaned. 'Why did it happen? Why? Why?' Then he flung himself to his sister's side and started to sob with his head buried against her naked bosom.

'Dawn's just swooned,' Rowdy said after looking at the slim girl. 'We'd best have her took back to camp, Cap'n Dusty.'

'When I've looked around,' Dusty replied. 'Do what you can for her here.'

'What the hell started them fighting, Dusty?' Mark asked, moving to his *amigo*'s side.

'That's what we're going to have to find out,' Dusty replied. 'It looks straight-forward enough, but——'

'Yeah?' Mark prompted.

Before Dusty could reply, de Martin looked up. Grief twisted at his face and his eyes were red with tears. Slowly he raised a hand to point at where Narth had propped Dawn in a sitting position against his knee.

'What are you going to do about her, Dusty?'

'How do you mean?' Dusty asked, turning from the men as they holstered their revolvers.

'She murdered my sister——'

'Mister!' Narth growled. 'I'm taking it that grieving's what made you say that——'

'It's true!' de Martin answered. 'Look at the signs. She must have attacked poor Barbe, beat her and then shot her!'

'Why you——!' Narth began and started to rise but was prevented from doing so by Rowdy catching his right shoulder in a paralysing grip and holding him down.

An angry growl rose from the trail hands and Jacko moved forward, right hand grabbing at his revolver. Instantly Mark brought out his off side Colt, throwing down on the cowhand long before Jacko's gun cleared leather.

'Back off, friend,' the blond giant advised. 'All you can do is make things a damned sight worse.'

'You would have tried Burle Willock for shooting her brother!' de Martin went on in a loud voice. 'Is she to be treated differently?'

'No!' Dusty stated firmly. 'She's not!'

'Damn it, Cap'n Fog!' Narth yelled, struggling futilely against the numbing pressure of the cook's powerful fingers. 'You're not——'

'I am!' Dusty insisted and looked over his shoulder. 'All of you'd best go back to camp. There's nothing you can do here.'

'Come on, boys!' Mark said, dropping his Colt back into leather. 'Do what Dusty wants. It'll be for the best.'

'Yeah!' agreed old Boiler Benson. 'There's nothing we can do here.'

Turning, talking quietly among themselves, the men walked away. Last to go was Jacko. For a moment he stood staring at Barbe's body. Then, with a strangled gasp, he swung on his heel and stumbled dazedly after his departing companions.

'Josh. Help Rowdy take Dawn back to camp,' Dusty went on, watching the cowhand go. 'She's to be kept in the bed-wagon until I get back.'

'Damn it, Cap'n!' Narth blazed. 'If you reckon I'm going to stand by and see her hung——'

'Let's hope it doesn't come to that,' Dusty interrupted quietly. 'But she has to stand trial, Josh. Uncle Charlie may be away with the Kid, but I'll do everything that he would.'

'And Colonel Charlie'd do just what Cap'n Dusty's doing,' the cook pointed out, sharing the small Texan's unspoken wish that Goodnight had not ridden out with the Kid to scout the land ahead ready for continuing the drive in the morning. He lifted the girl in his arms. 'Come on. You can stay with her.'

'Don't try anything *loco* like trying to run out with her, Josh,' Dusty warned. 'All that'll do is make things even worse.'

'I'll mind it,' Narth answered quietly and followed Rowdy across the clearing.

'Stay with your sister, Edmond,' Dusty told the photographer gently. 'There's not much a man can say at a time like this. I'm real sorry——'

'Thank you, Dusty,' de Martin replied without raising his head. 'Dawn must have hated poor little Barbe to do this.'

'Maybe,' Dusty replied. 'I'll know more about it after I've talked to her.'

'Then you don't mean to try her?'

'Yes I do,' Dusty corrected, picking up the girl's revolver and looking at how the gunbelt hung over the bush. 'Maybe you'd best come with me——'

'And leave her?' de Martin moaned, indicating the body.

'It'd be for the best. I'll have her brought in.'

Taking the photographer by the arm, Dusty helped him rise. For a moment de Martin seemed ready to resist. Then he let out a croaking sob and walked away. Dusty was about to follow. Looking down, he decided to cover the body's naked bust and bent to do so. Something caught his eye and he looked closer at the body, studying one of the injuries with extra care. Removing his calf-skin vest, Dusty draped it across the naked torso. With that done, he followed and caught up to de

Martin. Together they made their way back to the camp.

The change in the atmosphere struck Dusty immediately on his arrival. Up to the sound of the shot disturbing them, the crew had been a happy, contented whole. Now tension twanged the air like a snapped bow-string as the trail hands formed groups who sat or stood conversing in low tones. Surrounded by Willock's cronies and others of the Mineral Wells men, Jacko scowled at the bed-wagon with savage concentration. Leaving Dusty, de Martin went slowly in the direction of his wagon. Coming to his feet, Jacko walked over to the photographer's side.

'Mark!' Dusty said as the big blond approached him. 'I want you to go out to the clearing and stay there.'

'Sure.'

'Take Pick Visscher with you. Both of you stay there until I send somebody to relieve you. You're to let nobody—and I mean *nobody*—touch *anything* out there.'

'Yo! I'll take out a tarp and cover the body.'

'Sure. But don't move or touch anything.'

'It's done,' Mark promised and went to the Mineral Wells men. They showed some surprise at his words, but the stocky Lazy F cowhand rose without argument and accompanied him.

Walking across to the bed-wagon, Dusty felt the uneasy stirrings which warned him of danger. Once again the trail crew faced a split in its membership, for some of the men would be sure to back up Josh Narth in Dawn's defence. Others, especially Jacko's bunch would remember Willock and be equally insistent that Dawn should face trial. Dusty cursed. In addition to Goodnight and the Kid being away, Ahlén was riding the herd with Sherman, Red and Billy Jack. That deprived him, as had sending Mark to guard the clearing, of possible steadying influences and of men on whom he could rely.

On entering the wagon, Dusty found Dawn recovered sufficiently to be able to talk. Sitting on her bed, she dropped a cloth into a bowl of water and turned her half-washed, frightened face in the small Texan's direction.

'D-Dusty!' Dawn gasped. 'I didn't kill her.'

'Best tell me what happened then,' Dusty replied. 'All of it from why you went at each other on.'

After listening to the girl's story, from her decision to deliver de Martin's message instead of allowing Jacko to do so up to Barbe's death, Dusty stood up

Narth looked at the small Texan in a challenging manner and asked, 'You believe her, don't you, Cap'n?'

'Can you be ready to face a hearing in half an hour, Dawn?' Dusty said, ignoring the question.

'Damn it——' Narth started to growl.

'We're only a week at most to Fort Sumner, Cap'n Dusty,' Rowdy put in. 'Can't it wait until we get there and let the legal law handle it?'

'Some of the crew wouldn't hold for waiting,' Dusty warned.

'We could hold them!' Narth stated grimly.

'Not without gun-play,' Dusty pointed out. 'This drive's too important to ruin when there's a way out.'

'Nothing's important enough for you to hang Dawn!' Narth spat back.

'Josh!' Dawn put in quietly. 'I told the truth about what happened and I'm ready to face up to whatever comes. I know Dusty'll do the right thing.'

'You can count on it,' Dusty assured her. 'Now stay in the wagon. Get cleaned up and changed. I'll send for you when I'm ready.'

Swinging himself to the ground, Dusty looked around the camp. He saw Jacko and the Mineral Wells men gathered around de Martin and walked their way. Glares varying from quizzical or challenging to frankly hostile on Jacko's part, met the small Texan.

'Dawn told her story——' Dusty began.

'Which you have accepted as true!' de Martin interrupted.

'Which I listened to,' Dusty corrected. 'She reckoned that she heard you asking Jacko here to go fetch your sister back to camp——'

'I did. I wanted Barbe to help me take some photographs.'

'Only Dawn allowed that you shouldn't ought to be sending a feller to fetch her when she might still be undressed.'

'The idea never entered my head,' de Martin protested. 'I knew I could trust my sister and Jacko both to behave in a proper manner.'

'Dawn acted as she thought was for the best,' Dusty replied, seeing the rest of the crew gathering around. 'When she arrived, she found your sister dressed kind of skimpy and had got that shift, or whatever it is, tangled up on a branch. Dawn allows that she tore it getting it loose, which riled Barbe and made her jump her.'

'My sister wouldn't do such a thing!' de Martin insisted and Jacko rumbled agreement.

'What do you reckon happened then?' Dusty inquired, knowing the trail crew were hanging on to every word he and the photographer said.

'I don't want to say anything prejudicial to Dawn before her trial—if she is given one——'

'She's going to be,' Jacko put in grimly. 'You can count on that.'

'Go on, Edmond,' Dusty requested as if the cowhand had not spoken.

'All right, Dusty. You asked me to. From the start Dawn was jealous of my sister. You've all seen how she snubbed and ignored Barbe. Until Barbe came, Dawn was queen of the camp. Only Barbe ended all that. With such a beautiful woman around, the men stopped taking notice of Dawn and she hated Barbe for it. Then she may have blamed my sister for her brother's death. So when she heard Jacko and I talking, she saw a chance to take her revenge. She lied to Jacko to send him away, went to where my sister was alone, unprotected, vulnerable, and attacked her.'

'Your sister put up a hell of a fight for a lady,' Dusty commented.

'Fear and desperation must have lent her strength,' de Martin answered. 'She fought back with such fury that Dawn was afraid of being beaten, so pulled the gun and shot her.'

'And that's how you reckon it happened?' Dusty asked.

'There's no other way——'

'Unless Dawn told the truth. She hung her gunbelt over the bush——'

'Doubtless thinking that she could easily thrash Barbe without needing it,' de Martin countered.

'The holster was on the side of the bush away from the clearing,' Dusty pointed out. 'Dawn'd've had trouble getting to it in a hurry. And she allows that somebody else shot Barbe, then threw the gun over the bushes and she picked it up.'

'Is that likely?' de Martin demanded, directing his words to the assembled men. 'Who else but Dawn had reason to want my sister dead?'

'Nobody!' Jackos stated and there was a general rumble of agreement.

'Can you prove any of what you have told us, Dusty?' de Martin went on.

'There was no sign on the ground, but the sand'd been churned up in the fussing,' Dusty replied. 'There was some sand on the gun.'

'Gathered when she dropped it and collapsed,' de Martin suggested.

'Seems like you're tolerable set on making out Dawn didn't do it, Cap'n Fog,' Jacko growled. 'I don't mind there being all this talk when Burle Willock shot Vern Sutherland.'

'Perhaps Dusty doesn't think my sister's death should be treated in the same manner as the killing of Dawn's brother,' de Martin went on.

Angry murmurs rose from the assembled men, deep and menacing as the first rolling thunder-claps heralding the coming of a storm. Then Dusty spoke and his words brought silence in their wake.

'When you talk about your "sister", Edmond, don't you really mean your wife?'

Although the small Texan's comment cleary shocked de Martin, he recovered fast. After a brief flicker of shock and surprise, the photographer's face took on a puzzled expression.

'I don't——' he began.

'It's no good, de Martin!' Dusty interrupted. 'I saw the photograph in that book. Remember?'

'Yes. But I explained——'

'That's how I know,' Dusty stated. 'If you and Barbe had been brother and sister, you'd not have bothered. But if you were man and wife, you'd not want me thinking so. I didn't cotton on to it at the time, or until today in fact.'

'Why today?' de Martin asked in a brittle voice.

'You put your love-bites where they shouldn't've been seen,' Dusty explained. 'Only you didn't count on her getting herself stripped to the waist.'

'Dawn could have bitten her in the fight!' de Martin spat out.

'And did. Only the other bites'd been done a heap earlier,' Dusty replied. 'Anyways, there's an easy enough way to prove what I've said. Go find that book with the photographs in it, Solly.'

One of the older, more mature Mineral Wells hands, Solly Sodak was all too aware of the danger in the situation.

Wanting to help avert trouble, he nodded and moved to obey.

'Here, Solly,' de Martin said, reaching into the off side pocket of his jacket. 'I'll give you the key.'

While speaking, the photographer grasped something in the pocket and twisted up the side of the jacket to point it in Dusty's direction. Thrusting himself aside, the small Texan missed death by inches. Flame spurted from the front of de Martin's pocket and a bullet fanned hot breath by Dusty's cheek in passing. Across flashed Dusty's left hand, moving as soon as he began to step away from the danger. The right side Army Colt left its contoured holster and bellowed on the heels of the crack which sounded from de Martin's pocket. Shock and disbelief twisted at the photographer's face as lead ploughed into his chest. He reeled under the impact, bringing his hand into sight holding a smoking Remington Double Derringer. Fortunately for him, he dropped the weapon as he tumbled backwards.

'H-how—how did you——' de Martin gasped as Dusty came towards him.

'I've known that you were carrying that stingy gun ever since you started doing it the morning after Heenan died,' the small Texan replied.

'What the hell's going on?' croaked Jacko, staring from Dusty to de Martin and back.

'You mind how we've been expecting that Hayden feller to make fuss for us since the drive started?' Dusty asked and nodded in the photographer's direction. 'This's who he sent to do it. Him and his wife.' Then Dusty turned his eyes to where Rowdy, Dawn and Narth were running from the bed-wagon. 'See what you can do for him, Rowdy.'

Night had come and de Martin lay on the comfortable bed in his wagon. Looking at the men and girl gathered by him, he read their thoughts which gave added confirmation to his belief that death was close to him. Rowdy had done everything possible, but knew it to be only a matter of time before the end came. So the cook had raised no objections when de Martin asked to see Dawn, Dusty and Jacko.

'You're a smart bastard, Dusty Fog,' de Martin said admiringly. 'Nobody else suspected me.'

'I'd been starting to after you sent Heenan to stompede the herd that night,' Dawn objected.

Irritation showed on the dying man's face and he spoke indignantly. 'I don't mind you thinking I'm a no-good murdering son-of-a-bitch, Dawn. But I'd hate for you to think I'd be stupid enough to make a fool play like that.'

'You're saying that Heenan acted on his own, huh?' the girl asked.

'With a little prompting from my dear, stupid wife.' de Martin agreed. 'I'm sorry, Jacko. But I knew her far better than you ever could.'

'Damn you!' Jacko spat out. 'You killed her!'

'Yes. She was so scared of Dawn that she was about to tell what she'd been sent to do. I had to shut her mouth, so did it in a way that might let me earn my fee for wrecking the trail drive.'

'By getting us fighting among ourselves, same's you've been trying all along,' Dusty guessed.

'It was a technique I developed in the last year of the War to create dissent among various Southern outfits, and have used to some success in the East since then. So I thought that it would work with no trouble, especially when I learned that several different ranches were involved. I felt that the inter-outfit rivalry could easily be fanned into open conflict. What I didn't take into consideration was the high quality of leadership Colonel Goodnight and you showed, Dusty. That was a smart move at the start, having Mark take charge of Barbe. Yours, I presume?'

'Uncle Charlie's, but I'd likely've done the same.'

'I don't doubt it. The scheme nearly worked better than you expected. My dear wife had the morals of an alley cat. She was falling in love with Mark, or as near love as her cash-box mind could conceive. Her simple little brain got the notion that marriage to a rich rancher's son might be preferable to that with a professional trouble-maker. Fortunately I knew how to handle her. She yearned to have her love handed out roughly—— I'm sorry, Dawn. This is hardly for your ears.'

'I'll live through it,' the girl answered, blushing a little.

'Let us say that I persuaded her to remain as she was,' de Martin said. 'So she met Mark with the reason I had taught her and I hovered in the background. If she had failed me, or offered to betray me, I'd have killed them both and been the tragic brother who found his sister being raped, then shot her by mistake along with her attacker. Mark had a narrow escape that night.'

'So did you,' Dusty told him. 'The Kid was watching you watching them. I'll give you one thing though. At that time we figured the way you wanted us to and hadn't got round to suspecting you.'

'I'm good at my work,' de Martin stated. 'And who'd suspect a man involved in a business like photography? Anyway, I set Barbe to work on the younger hands. She worked on Vern and Burle and in the end caused the fatal fight. Only you stopped the trouble, Dusty——'

'And Heenan killed Burle so we'd not learn he gave Burle the whiskey.'

'As soon as he saw Burle show signs of surrendering,' de Martin agreed. 'I'd arranged for that when I supplied Heenan with the whiskey. You smoothed off the trouble I hoped to start over the crossing of the Staked Plains. Lord, how I had to work to keep Barbe from breaking down during the rains and across the desert. I had promised her we'd have our business done before we needed to cross. You spoiled that. I was willing to settle for tricking Austin into something that would stampede the herd, but you stopped him.'

'He'd refused before I cut in,' Dusty corrected.

'Be that as it may, the idea failed. So Heenan decided to act on his own. If I'd have been stupid enough to plan that try, I'd certainly not have let you find me in the wagon. Barbe wanted convincing about the crossing and I was doing it when you came back. I hoped to do something on the desert, but Barbe wouldn't let me out of her sight. I think Dawn saw one hysterical outburst——'

'Sure,' the girl confirmed.

'Anyway,' de Martin continued. 'We crossed and on reaching the Pecos I put another scheme into action. I sent Barbe off into the bushes with instructions on what to do. Then I asked Jacko to collect her. The idea was that I should see Austin and express worries about having seen Jacko sneaking off in the direction Barbe had gone to bathe. Naturally Austin would have investigated, to find Barbe struggling to "protect her honour" from Jacko, having enticed him into a position where she could do so.'

'Only I went, not Jacko,' Dawn said.

'Seeing Jacko coming after me handed me a hell of a shock,' de Martin replied. 'When he told me why, I wondered if you'd become suspicious. So I followed and watched the fight. I must say that I was pleased at the thrashing you gave Barbe. I also saw a way of getting rid of her. She was getting a little too unstable for our kind of work. When she looked like blabbing, I picked up your gun from its holster and shot her. Then I tossed the gun near you, waited until you had picked it up, slipped away and joined on to the rear of the men coming from camp.'

'She was your wife!' Dawn gasped.

'Not a very satisfactory one,' de Martin answered. 'I saw a way to get rid of her without the risk of a legal come-back and to finish my work. With Barbe dead, I knew I could stir up bad feelings. Jacko and some of Willock's friends, pointed the right way, would demand that "justice" was done. There would be others just as determined that they must protect Dawn.'

'You came close to doing it,' Dusty said.

'Not close enough,' de Martin objected weakly. 'Otherwise I wouldn't be laying here.'

'Why've you told us all this?' Dusty asked.

'Why am I betraying my employer, you mean?' de Martin sighed. 'It's simple enough. I've the greatest admiration for you, Dusty. You've licked me all the way along the line—— And I'd hate like hell to die without figuring you'll take care of the man who caused me to be killed.'

CHAPTER SIXTEEN

IT LICKS BEING HUNG AS A COW THIEF

'John Chisum's coming, Colonel Charlie!' the Ysabel Kid announced, entering the Yellow Stripe saloon where Goodnight sat with his trail hands waiting to start the evening's festivities.

It was the second day after the drive's arrival at Fort Sumner. The Army's cattle buyer had expressed his complete satisfaction with the three thousand, three hundred and twenty-eight steers which had survived the journey from Young County. In addition to purchasing the whole herd at the promised eight cents a pound on the hoof, Colonel Hunter had agreed that Goodnight had fulfilled the contract made on the rancher's last visit. Buffalo had not been sold, the crew refused to part with him.

Dusty and Dawn had stayed with de Martin until he died. During the hour or so he had lingered, the man cleared up everything which puzzled them; including how he simulated such grief at Barbe's death. While burying his face against his dead wife's body, he had rubbed sand into his eyes and achieved the desired effect. He had also signed a statement which implicated Hayden as his employer.

After de Martin's death, the remainder of the trip had gone by without incident. Receiving payment for the herd, Goodnight had paid out to his crew more money than most of them had ever seen. It would be a long time before the town of Fort Sumner forgot the celebrations which followed.

Coming to his feet, the rancher looked at Dusty and Mark. All around the room, the trail hands moved towards their leaders with hands loosening revolvers in holsters.

'Let's go see him!' Austin Hoffman suggested.

'Hold it!' Goodnight barked, halting the concerted movement towards the bat-wing doors. 'John Chisum saved my life, way back. So if he hands over the Mineral Wells cattle, we take them and call it quits.'

'That's good enough for us, Colonel Charlie!' Ahlén stated and the others of the various ranches concerned rumbled their agreement. 'We'll play it any way you say.'

Needing beef urgently to feed the reservation Apaches, Colonel Hunter had split up and dispatched the herd to various agencies as soon as he had completed the purchase. So there was nothing in the Army's big holding corrals to warn John Chisum that he had been beaten to Fort Sumner. Tall, thickset, bald, with coldly calculating eyes which belied the jovial aspect of his face, he dressed like a saddle-tramp and wore no gun. Swinging open the gate of the nearest corral, he rode aside and allowed his men to drive the herd in.

'That's got 'em here!' declared Chisum's tough-looking segundo, watching two of the hands close the gate on the drag of the herd. 'I wonder if that second bunch got through the *Kweharehnuh*?'

'I sure hope so,' Chisum answered with such sincerity that he might have been telling the truth. 'Fact being, I hope ole Charlie Goodnight makes it——'

'He has!' the man ejaculated, pointing with a thumb.

Turning, Chisum stared to where Goodnight, Dusty, the floating outfit and Ahlén were walking from between two of the houses which stood about fifty yards from the corral. Not all the floating outfit, Chisum noticed, for the Ysabel Kid was absent. If Chisum felt any concern, either by the Kid's absence or Goodnight's presence, he gave no sign of it as he rode to meet the approaching party. Behind him, the hard-faced, well-armed trail hands followed like buffalo-wolves on the heels of their pack leader.

'That's not Targue, the segundo he had in Graham,' Dusty remarked to Goodnight. 'Nor any of that bunch he had along.'

'They're the same kind though,' the bearded rancher replied.

'Howdy, Charlie,' Chisum greeted. 'Well I swan if I ever expected to see you here. How'd you lick us?'

'Could be we passed you on the trail one dark night,' Goodnight answered.

'You're joshing me!' Chisum chuckled. 'It's good to see you and right pleasing that you'd come to say "Howdy" to ole Uncle John after a long drive.'

'That's not all we're here for,' Goodnight warned. 'We've come to take the Mineral Wells cattle off your hands.'

'To——' Chisum began, conscious of a stirring among the twenty hard-cases—selected for gun-skill rather than cattle-savvy—at his back. 'Now I know you're joshing, Charlie. Even if I'd got them steers along, you've got no right to 'em.'

'This's Swede Ahlén, segundo of the Double Two,' Goodnight introduced. 'He and I've got power-of-attorney notes to take possession of all Bench P, D4S, Lazy F, Flying H and Double Two cattle wherever we find them.'

'That's not funny, Charlie——' Chisum began mildly.

'It's strange how different folks see things,' Dusty put in, noticing the increased signs of hostility among Chisum's hands and indicating the building from between which his party had appeared. 'The Ysabel Kid and those fellers there thought it was.'

Muffled, startled exclamations and curses broke from the Chisum hands as they looked in the required direction. The Ysabel Kid and other men carrying repeating rifles had appeared on the roofs of the buildings. More cowhands, also toting shoulder-arms, came from between the houses and formed into an efficient fighting line which covered the Long Rail's riders more than adequately. With sickening certainty the hard-cases knew they were licked. At their first hostile move, the rifles by and on the buildings would pour a devastating hail of fire upon them. Although his men showed their alarm, Chisum retained his jovial poise. Yet he remained alert for a chance to escape from the trap in which he found himself.

'You did say that you drove our stock here for us, Mr. Chisum,' Ahlén drawled, after giving time for the realisation of their position to sink into the Long Rail riders' heads. 'Now didn't you?'

'We're allowed to pay you five dollars a head for doing it,' Goodnight went on.

'Five dollars?' Chisum yelped, aware that each steer would bring upwards of sixty dollars at eight cents a pound on the hoof. 'I'll b——'

'Look at it this way, Mr. Chisum,' Dusty interrupted. 'The Army's buyer knows none of the Mineral Wells ranchers have sold you any of their cattle. So Colonel Hunter's going to be mighty suspicious when he finds more than a hundred head from each of those spreads in your herd.'

'Five dollars ain't much, Charlie,' Chisum groaned, knowing that at least three-quarters of his herd belonged to the ranches Goodnight had named.

'It licks getting hung as a cow thief,' Ahlén stated bluntly.

'And it'll give you enough money to pay off your loyal

hands,' Dusty drawled.

At that moment Chisum almost reached bursting point and lost all control of his carefully-held temper. Dusty's words had smashed the bald rancher's last hope of goading the Long Rail crew into fighting. Faced with the threat of losing their pay, they might have taken a chance of going against the rifles. Without that inducement, they would be only willing to let things ride. Rage seethed and boiled inside Chisum, but he struggled to fight it down.

'I sure admired to've brought your cattle for you, Swede,' Chisum gritted in a feeble attempt to sound his usual jovial self.

'Figured you would be, when you saw it our way,' Goodnight said. 'Colonel Hunter's on his way here. So I'll pay off your boys and let them go get a hard-earned drink or three. My crew've quenched their thirsts and they'll tend to things from now on.'

'One thing, you Long Rail gents,' Dusty put in. 'The town marshal's appointed Mark, the Kid and me as deputies. We don't mind what fun you have as long as you keep it as fun. Understand?'

'Just in case you don't know us,' Mark went on. 'I'm Mark Counter and this's Dusty Fog.'

'We'll mind what you say, Cap'n Fog,' Chisum's segundo promised.

So departed Chisum's last faint hope of turning the tables on Goodnight. With money in their pockets, his hold on the hard-cases disintegrated. Burning with frustrated fury, he watched the men paid off and depart, then stood by while Hunter and Goodnight carried out the formalities for the sale of the herd.

'Where's Hayden, Mr. Chisum?' Dusty asked as they gathered in the Golden Stripe saloon waiting for Goodnight to bring the other rancher's money. 'You know, the feller who paid you to pull that game on Uncle Charlie, and who you took on to drive for at Throckmorton?'

'I don't know,' Chisum replied. 'As soon as I figured he was working——'

'Maybe I believe in fairies and Father Christmas, Mr. Chisum,' Dusty cut in coldly. 'But I've stopped believing in a whole lot of other things.'

'We figured that nobody could handle three thousand head in one herd,' Chisum said, only his eyes showing the hatred he felt for the small, soft-spoken young Texan. 'Split the herd into his stuff and them I'd brought. I went ahead, with Hayden following a mite to the north. Up between the Clear Fork of the Brazos and the Pecos we only just managed to sneak by a big band of *Kweharehnuh*.'

'And Hayden didn't——' Mark Counter suggested as he and the Kid listened to the conversation.

'I couldn't say.'

'Didn't you try to find out, Mr. Chisum?' inquired the Kid.

'Hell no! Them danged Injuns—sorry, Kid—them *Kweharehnuh* was thicker'n fleas on a hound-dawg. I'd got my own men to think about and couldn't risk lives sending to see what might be happening to Hayden's herd. I sure hope they come through all right.'

'I just bet you do,' drawled the Kid.

The conversation lapsed and Chisum stood moodily staring around the room. No pleasure filled him at the scenes of celebration and merriment. Nor did his feeling of frustration lessen when Goodnight came over with the balance of the money for the herd. It made a pitifully small pile when compared with the amount the bearded rancher had received and which Chisum had fondly hoped would come his way.

Taking the money, Chisum stalked with what dignity he could muster across the room. With his head full of thoughts on how he might avoid a repetition of his misfortunes—the simple way of not taking other people's stock never occurred to him—he failed to see the bat-wing doors open and three men enter to block his path.

'So you made it, Chisum!' said a cold, angry voice.

Jolted from his considerations of how he might use power-of-attorney notes to his own advantage,* Chisum stared at the three figures before him. Dirty, dishevelled and hard-travelled they might be, but Chisum recognised them. Hayden no longer looked dapper, with his torn, filthy clothes and haggard face unshaven. Flanking him, big, burly Targue and Scabee looked mean as all hell. A bloody bandage encased the latter's head and did little to make him appear any pleasanter. While the two hard-cases wore belt guns, their hands were empty. Hayden held a Henry rifle before him and his forefinger entered its triggerguard as he addressed the bald rancher.

'Joe!' Chisum yelled. 'Joe Hayden! Thank the merciful

* Chisum's solution is told fully in *Slaughter's Way*.

Lord that you got through.'

'It's no thanks to you that we did!' Hayden snarled. 'Why in hell didn't you send back word to us about those Indians?'

Silence fell on the room and every eye turned towards the door. Slowly the customers and staff inched into positions which would allow them to take cover hurriedly in case of gun play. Chisum was sickeningly aware that he did not have a man in the room who he might call 'friend'. Not even Charles Goodnight, for the rancher had made it clear when handing over the money that he considered his debt paid in full. Maybe Chisum did not wear a gun, but cowardice had never been one of his many vices. So he showed no fear and prepared to play the game out to the tricky end.

'I did send!' Chisum declared in tones of sincerity, well-simulated shock crossing his face. 'You mean that he didn't get to you?'

'You know damned well "he" didn't!' Targue spat out. 'You let the *Kweharehnuh* jump us so's you could push on clear while we fought 'em.'

'Now would I do a meanness like that?' Chisum wailed. 'Lord, those words grieve me. Here I've been a-pining and sorrowing at the thought——'

'Of how you'd spend the money you'd get for my herd!' Hayden snarled. 'Chisum, when I found out what you'd done on us, I swore I'd find you and kill you.'

Having helped fight off the *Kweharehnuh* raiders until rescued by an Army patrol, Hayden and his two men had set out after Chisum. They had lost their herd and wanted to get a share in the money for the bunch the bald rancher drove. Picking up his trail, they had read the story of his desertion and their purpose had changed to one of vengeance. Although Hayden had planned a more subtle way of dealing with Chisum, being confronted by the rancher holding money which must have come from selling the herd drove all thoughts of his plan from his head.

'I—I'm not wearing a gun!' Chisum announced.

'Nobody'll hold that against me when they learn why I killed you!' Hayden spat back.

And the damnable part, to Chisum's way of thinking, was that the other spoke the truth. Once told of his desertion, no Western jury would convict Hayden for taking such extreme revenge. Something of an expert in killers, Chisum knew from the expression on Hayden's face that the man intended to carry out his threat. For once—and what might be the last time—the bald rancher's charm and smooth tongue had failed him. Given time, he might have been able to talk Hayden out of the murderous mood—— Only he doubted if the required time would be granted to him.

'Mr. Hayden!' Chisum heard somebody say and Dusty Fog's voice had never sounded so pleasant to the rancher's ears.

Turning his head slightly, Hayden glared angrily at the three young men who came towards him. While he failed to recognise Dusty, Mark or the Kid, his companions rapidly and correctly identified all three of the Texans.

'Well?' Hayden demanded.

'I've business with you,' Dusty stated while the Kid at his left and Mark on his right allowed him to do the talking.

'Make it later,' Hayden ordered. 'I don't know you.'

Taking advantage of the interruption, Chisum began to edge away from the men at the door and clear of the three Texans. He had learned enough since his arrival to figure why Dusty had intervened and meant to make the most of the chance presented to him.

'No,' Dusty agreed, coming to a halt and conscious of Chisum's actions. 'You don't know me, but we had a mutual acquaintance. De Martin he called himself, but you'd know him better as Soskice.'

Shock jolted Hayden's attention from the bald rancher to the small Texan. While he did not know what his visitor at the Throckmorton hotel had planned to call himself while working against Goodnight, the man's name had been Soskice. Mastering his surprise, Hayden gave a disinterested shrug.

'I've never heard of either of 'em.'

'He'd heard of you,' Dusty said. 'Fact being, he took an oath on his death-bed that you'd paid him to make trouble and bust up Colonel Goodnight's trail drive. I don't reckon he lied.'

'He sure as hell didn't!' Chisum screeched, estimating that he was in a position from which he could safely start things popping. As he spoke, he flung himself towards the nearest customers and caused a hurried scattering among them.

'Damn you, Chisum!' Hayden screamed and started to swing the Henry's barrel in the rancher's direction.

On either side of Hayden, Targue and Scabee sent hands

fanging down to their revolvers. No less promptly, the floating outfit went into action. Ahead of all the others, before the Henry completed its turn and spoke, Dusty's matched Colts roared. He shot at Hayden. Not to save Chisum, but to prevent the financier from committing wholesale murder. In his crazed condition, Hayden would have sprayed the Henry's magazine around the room without regard for who or what he hit. So Dusty sent his bullets the only way possible under the circumstances. Both of them drove into Hayden's head, spinning him through the bat-wing door with the rifle unfired and dropping from his hands.

A split-second later, Mark's revolvers echoed the double crash. Caught in the chest by the lead from the blond giant's guns, Targue pitched backwards to collide with wall then tumble lifeless to the floor.

Neither the Kid nor Scabee could count themselves in the class of gun-skill shown by Dusty and Mark. While their hands closed on the waiting guns' butts simultaneously, the Kid's old Dragoon cleared leather and spoke first by a slight margin. Slight, maybe, but it proved just fast enough to save Dusty's life. Out of a sense of self-preservation, Scabee had selected the small Texan for his target. The sledgehammer impact of the Dragoon came while the hard-case was still squeezing off his trigger. Knocked sprawling by the force of the blow, Scabee fired with his gun out of line. Passing between Mark and Dusty, the bullet ended its flight among the bottles behind the bar. Torn open by the round, soft lead ball, Scabee collapsed on to Targue's body.

'You saved my life, Cap'n Fog!' Chisum gasped and his gratitude was not entirely assumed.

'Saved you hell!' Dusty spat back and, thick-skinned though he was, the rancher writhed under the icy contempt in the small Texan's voice. 'They could have killed you by inches for all I cared. I was thinking of two young cowhands who didn't finish the drive. But for Vern Sutherland and Burle Willock, I wouldn't've lifted a finger against Hayden until he was through with you.'

CHAPTER SEVENTEEN

GOODNIGHT'S DREAM

And so one of the earliest large trail drives ended, paving the way for Goodnight's dream to come true. On their return to Texas, the trail crew used their knowledge to organise and carry out other shipments. Word of Goodnight's success passed across the Texas ranges, along with his belief in the possibility of a market at the Kansas railroad towns. In the years which followed, almost a quarter of a million longhorns walked the trail carved by the Swinging G to Fort Sumner. More than double that number went north to Kansas and further herds spread across the western plains. The money brought in by the longhorn herds helped the Lone Star State to throw off the poverty and desolation left by the War. Truly it could be said that, guided by men of vision like Colonel Charles Goodnight, Texas grew from hide and horn.

Trail Boss

For Dorothy, who has put up with me for years.

CHAPTER ONE

BRING BACK A TRAIL BOSS

'BRING back a trail boss.'

The words beat a tattoo in Thora Holland's brain, beat it in rhythm to the hooves of the chuckwagon's team as she sat on the hard, uncomfortable seat.

A trail boss was the thing the Rocking H wanted, just one man.

But not any man would do.

A trail boss was a man amongst men; only a trail boss could cope with the many problems of trailing three thousand head of half-wild Texas longhorns north to the shipping pens at Dodge City. To do that he had to be tough, aggressive, intelligent and quick to deal with any emergency.

On any drive he needed all those qualifications; he needed them even more so on this drive. This Rocking H herd would have to be taken all the long miles north, up through the Texas Panhandle, over the North Brazos, the Red, the Cimmaron, the Canadian and other smaller rivers. It would have trouble with these as the season was early and the winter snows would still be raising the river level. These problems were enough, but there were others, not the least of which was Jethro Kliddoe and his bunch of reb-hating Kansas border ruffians.

Thora shivered at the thought of Kliddoe; the name struck a chill into her. Kliddoe and his men would be something more than the ordinary hazard for the trail boss to handle.

The trail boss was needed to handle the drive; but where could an Eastern woman find such a man?

Thora thought of all she had heard about the duties of a trail boss and the creed by which he was judged. Ben Holland, her husband, had told her of it often. How a trail boss left Texas with a herd, fed beef to the hands all the way north, lost a few head on the trail and still reached the shipping pens with more than he started out.

Ben Holland knew this creed well enough. Before his accident his name as a trail boss was assured. Then bushwhack lead left him a cripple in a wheelchair. With Ben on his feet there would have been none of this worry about getting a crew to go north with the trail herd.

It had been in Dodge that Ben was shot. The ambush had been well laid, but the bushwhacker showed caution. The charge from his ten-gauge shotgun crippled instead of killed.

That was some trip, Ben's last drive north the previous spring. In Dodge he ran foul of a pious assistant deputy called Wyatt Earp. Earp was about to pistol-whip a drunken young Texas cowhand, but Ben intervened. There was no trouble. Earp declined to fight a sober man of his own size; but he made muttered threats.

After Ben was shot Bat Masterson investigated, but found nothing to help him in his search. He was a friend of both Earp and Ben Holland and checked on Earp's whereabouts to prove one thing or the other. Earp had left Dodge the morning after the clash. There was nothing to connect him with the attempted murder.

Masterson tried to find who did the shooting. Ben was well liked by folks in Dodge and had no enemies. Only one significant point came out of the business. After his return to Dodge, while Ben was being taken back to Texas in the wagon, Earp passed word that Rocking H must not use the Dodge City pens again.

That was just one more problem the trail boss must handle if he took the herd to Dodge. Just one more trial in the arduous task ahead of the Rocking H trail boss.

It was a true saying, Thora thought, that it never rained but it poured. With all this against them, they get trouble nearer at hand. Ben's crew had made an early round-up, and had collected their trail herd; they had only completed road branding it the day before. Then their neighbour, Thad Toon of the Double T, an old enemy of the Rocking H, made his move. Toon had begun his roundup after Ben's crew started theirs and was trying to catch up on their lead. He knew that by fair means he could not get his herd on the trail first, so he made his move. Hiring a fast-gun killer, he had set up camp in the town of Granite and passed word that any man hiring to Rocking H would be buying grief.

With Ben off his feet, and without a leader, it had worked. No man had offered to hire.

That was the sort of problem Ben could have handled easily, had he been on his feet. Now it lay to Thora to do the best she could. It had taken much argument and pleading before Ben would allow her to go into Granite and try to hire men. At last Ben had given in; and so she was sat here this cold morning by the side of Salt Ballew, the cook, headed for Granite.

She made a pretty picture sitting on the hard seat of the Rocking H chuckwagon. A tall, mature woman with golden blonde hair hanging from under the brim of her Stetson hat. Not even the heavy coat she wore could hide the rich, fullness of her body, the gentle swell of her breasts, the slimness of her waist and the strong, firm curves of her hips and legs.

Turning she looked at the man by her side. He was as typical a product of the Texas range as she obviously wasn't. Salt Ballew was six-foot-odd of oak brown sinew and whang leather. His range clothes were clean, well worn and around his waist was a gunbelt supporting his old Dance Bros. percussion revolver.

Salt was handling the team with the same relaxed competence that showed in everything he did. He was as much at ease, and as capable whether he was cooking up a meal out in the open in a half gale, driving a two-mule team, or sitting round the fire in the cookshack and spinning tall tales about the Mexican War. He looked what he was, an old-time range cook, master of his trade, hard, tough, ornery and respected by the crew for it.

'Will we get the men, Salt?' she asked.

'Men's there, Miz Thora,' he replied, his lazy drawl a contrast from her Eastern accents. 'Want work, and r'aring to go. But they wants a leader, which same we can't give them. Sort of men we wants won't just foller any man.'

'I'm going.'

'Sort of men we wants won't foller no woman. We needs the best happen we have to face Earp and his friends.'

Thora thought this over for a moment. 'A lawman can't stop us from taking the herd into Dodge, just for a grudge, can he?'

'Law don't come into it. There ain't much law for Texas men north of the Indian Nations. Anyways, Earp ain't the law.

He's just one of the extra hands they takes on while the trail driving season's on. But he surely wants to make hisself a name as a lawman. There's plenty of ripe pickings for a man who can. So he's making this play against the Rocking H. If we don't take the herd, he's made his play. The Rocking H has a name and the man who can scare off Ben Holland's somebody. If we go up we've called his bluff and he'll have to show down.'

Thora had long since learned to listen when Salt Ballew gave out his wisdom, for it was mostly right. He had experience in the West and she had need of that experience now.

'How about Thad Toon?' she inquired, she had only met him once.

'Thad ain't bad. Jest a mite ornery 'n' none too bright. He ain't been overfond of Ben since we built up our herd with all that unbranded stock, after the war. Ben even offered to throw in with Thad to cut out all the range, but Thad got mean and wouldn't. Ole Thad's been waiting all this time to get evens.'

'With Ben in the wheelchair he should stop us,' Thora agreed, bitterly. 'I'm going to see the sheriff——'

'Thad don't want to stop us going. Jest wants to get off afore we do.'

'Is that important?'

'Surely is. First off gets the pick of the grazing all the way north. Gets the best prices in Dodge. There's a lot to being first herd into Dodge.'

Thora knew something of the loyalty of the cowhands to the brand, and knew that every ranch crew wanted their own spread to have the best possible record and reputation in matters concerning the cattle business. However, the Rocking H couldn't spare the men and the trail-drive crew would be strangers who did not have that same loyalty.

'Can't the law help,' she asked, 'with that gunman in town threatening any man who takes on for us?'

Salt sent a spurt of tobacco at a small rock before replying 'Ain't much the town marshal can do. Anyways, the men'd hire, happen we had a trail boss. It'd take more than a hired gun to stop hands going up trail.'

Thora sat back. She hardly noticed they were almost into the town of Granite. There was so much she didn't know about the cattle business and so much she was going to have to know if she was to get that herd to market. That was work for a man and a highly skilled man at that—not for a young woman who'd only been in the West for three years.

Thora was aware of her limitations. She had never been west until meeting Ben in Chicago. They married after a short courtship and he had brought her to his ranch in Texas. At the ranch she was accepted as the boss's wife. The hands treated her with respect, yet they didn't accept her as one of them. She was a Yankee knowing nothing of cattle business.

That hadn't mattered with Ben on his feet, where all she needed to do was run the house. Now she was to take her husband's place and learn the cattle business under the most difficult of conditions.

'Excuse me, ma'am,' a voice, a soft, pleasing Texas drawl came from her side of the wagon.

Thora and Salt both looked at the speaker, but they saw him with different eyes.

Thora saw a small, insignificant man riding a big paint horse. She noted a black, low-crowned, wide-brimmed hat on dusty blonde hair. The face was handsome, young looking and friendly. Around his neck was a long, tight-rolled blue bandana, the ends falling over his faded blue shirt almost to the waistband of his levis. The cuffs of his levis were turned back and hung outside his high-heeled riding-boots with their big spurs. She hardly noted the gunbelt and doubted if he could use the guns in the holsters.

Salt was looking at the same man, but he was looking with rangewise eyes that knew cowhands. He saw a face which was young, yet old in wisdom, cool grey eyes which looked right through a man, a mouth which had grin quirks at the corners, yet was firm. The jaw below showed strength of character.

The cook's eyes went to the hat—was an expensive JB Stetson; that hat had cost plenty. Next he looked at the boots and the double-girthed Texas saddle; they were expensive and the maker of them——

Salt's eyes went to the gunbelt and a whistle of surprise came from his lips. That gunbelt had been made by the same man who made the saddle and boots, a man famous for his leatherwork. But that buscadero gunbelt told a man things. Ole Joe Gaylin of El Paso had made the belt. He would sell his boots and saddles to anyone who had his prices, but they were high. His gunbelts were something again. Joe Gaylin wouldn't sell them to just anyone, he chose the men who wore his gunbelts. To wear a Joe Gaylin gunbelt a man had to be somebody. That belt, with the matched bone-handled Colt 1860 Army revolvers, butt-forward for a cross-draw, had been made by Joe Gaylin.

The horse told Salt more about the small man. It was seventeen hands of paint stallion, not the horse for a beginner to try out on. A man had to be better than average happen he wanted to stay on top of that horse, and not end picking its shoes out of his teeth.

So where Thora saw a quiet, insignificant young man riding a big paint horse Salt saw a tophand whose twin, bone-handled guns, rope and Winchester 66 carbine had all seen expert use.

'I hear you're hiring a trail crew, ma'am,' the small man went on.

'We are!' Thora managed to hide her disappointment that this small man should be the first to offer his services. He didn't look the sort who could face hired killers.

'There are three of us,' the small man indicated the others.

Salt and Thora turned and looked. They had been so interested in this small man that they hadn't heard the other two riding on the other side. Thora nodded in approval; these were the sort of men she wanted.

Both were tall, one six foot, the other three inches more than that. The latter took Thora's eyes right away, he would catch the eye in any company. Thora thought he was the most handsome man she had ever seen. His hat was a costly, low-crowned, wide-brimmed, white JB Stetson, set back on his curly golden blonde hair. His clothes were expensive and he was a cowhand fashion-plate from the silver concha decorated hatband, through his multi-hued silk bandana, expensive doeskin shirt, new levis and fancy-stitched boots. Around his slim waist was a hand-carved gunbelt with a matched brace of Colt 1860 revolvers, the butts flaring to his hands.

Salt studied the dandy rig of the cowhand, noted the width of the shoulders, the slim waist. The fancy dress of the big man might have turned Salt off, but that too was a Gaylin gunbelt. The man rode a blood bay stallion as big as the paint, rode it easily, being a light rider in spite of his size.

To Salt it all read clear; here was another tophand.

The third man was lean and lithe, but he looked as tough as whipcord. He appeared to be about sixteen years old, his face young, almost babyishly young. Yet the red hazel eyes were not young, they were old, cold and dangerous. Salt saw more than just a young, black-dressed boy on a magnificent white stallion.

The young man wore all black, from his hat to his boots. Even his gunbelt was black, only the butt forward, walnut grips of the old Dragoon Colt at his right side and the ivory hilt of the bowie knife at his left relieved the blackness.

Salt felt uneasy as he looked this young man over. He wore a cowhand's rig all right, but Salt felt that he had learned the cattle business along the Rio Grande on dark nights.

The old Dragoon Colt told a man things, happen he knew what to look for. In the year of 1870, Colt's 1860 Army revolver had been on the market for long enough and enough of them had been produced to have seen most of the old four-pound Dragoon guns put aside as out of date. For a man to be wearing one these days usually meant that he was behind the times and was looked down on for it. Somehow, Salt got the idea that this didn't apply to the black-dressed boy. In a tight fix it would be to the hilt of the bowie knife his hand would fly to first, the revolver second.

They were a pair to draw to, those riders—tophands both, and fighting men from soda to hock, Salt thought. Yet strangely the third man, the small, insignificant Texas man at the other side, wasn't out of place in such company.

'I think we could use you,' Thora replied, having decided that, if these three took on, others might be willing to join. 'Have you ever been to Dodge City?'

'No, ma'am,' the tallest of the trio replied. 'Hays once, Newton once.'

'Happen we're lucky,' the black-dressed boy went on. 'We'll find where she lies.'

Salt craned his neck, trying to discover what brands the horses wore, particularly the big paint, but couldn't see it. He had a vague, uneasy feeling that he could name these three young men. If his guess was right the Rocking H were having more luck than they could rightly expect.

The cook glanced ahead to where three men had left one of the saloons and were looking towards the wagon. In a few minutes, he thought, a man would know just how good his guessing was.

Thora caught Salt's eye and looked ahead; she felt a sudden panic as she watched the three men stepping from the side-walk and moving out until they blocked the trail. Two of them, she knew; the man at the right, big, well-dressed, wide-shouldered, hand resting on the butt of his Colt, was Thad Toon, owner of the TT.

The man at the left of the trail was shorter, stocky and hard-looking. That was Joel Hendley, Toon's foreman, a tough man and handy with his old Navy Colt.

It was the rider in the centre of the trail who caught and held Thora's attention. He was a tall man, dressed in the style Wild Bill Hickok affected in town. His hat was a low-crowned JB Stetson, his black coat, frilly-bosomed shirt and tight-legged white trousers were all well-tailored, his store shoes shining. Around his waist was a silk sash and a pearl-handled Remington revolver was thrust into it. It was the face which held her eyes. A face which was cold, expressionless with eyes as hard and unfeeling as a snake.

Thora had seen gunfighters before, she knew without being told that this was the killer who had been hired to prevent men taking on to drive for Rocking H. She looked at the three young men; they were lounging in their saddles, looking over the Double T riders without any knowledge of their danger. She could not let them be shot down by this hired killer.

Toon stood silent for a few moments, then looked Thora and Salt over. Finally, he spoke to the three young Texas cow-hands.

'That's the Rocking H wagon you're riding with,' he said softly.

'Now me, I thought it was the President's carriage. Was all set to take off my hat and cheer,' the dark boy on the white horse replied.

Toon looked up sharply, taking in every detail of the mocking-voiced youngster. 'I put the Injun sign on that spread, sonny. Likewise passed the word that nobody hires to them.'

'Waal, now,' the tallest of the trio's voice was a deep, southern drawl. 'That's for the lady to say, her being from the Rocking H and all.'

'Funny bunch, huh?' Hendley growled before his boss could speak. 'We got us a real bunch of funny men here, ain't we, Ed?'

'Yeah.' The hired killer's voice was harsh and menacing. 'We sure have Joel. Likely they'll laugh themselves to death.'

The small man had been watching all this. He spoke, his voice mild. 'You mean you're asking us not to hire to Rocking H?'

'The boss here don't ask cowhands nothing,' the hired killer answered. 'He's *telling* you—and I'm here to see you does as he tells you.'

'Mean he's ordering us?' There was a deceptive mildness in the big cowhand's tones.

'Just that.'

'Well now, I never was much of a hand at taking orders. Fact being that ole General Bushrod Sheldon always said I was the worse order-taking soldier in his command.'

'That means you aims to take on agin the boss's orders?' asked the killer tensing slightly, his hand lifting.

Toon flashed a glance at the hired gun. He didn't want these three young men shooting if he could help it. Like Salt, he could tell good hands when he saw them and he had need of good hands for his own trail drive.

'This here's Ed Wren,' he said warningly.

If he expected any sign of fear, or any other emotion, at the mention of the name, he was sadly disappointed. Not one of the three gave any sign of ever having heard of the man called Ed Wren.

The three young Texans still remained lounging in their saddles; they studied the hired killer. Then the dark young man replied, his tones mocking and sardonic.

'Waal now, seeing's how we're all so cosy and being real formal like, allow me to present us. I'm Loncey Dalton Ysabel. This here gent on the blood bay's Mark Counter.' He paused for a couple of seconds, to let the names sink in, noting the worry lines which were forming on two of the faces. 'This here,' he waved a hand towards the small rider. 'Ain't nobody much at all. Happen you never even heard of him.' He paused, then:

'His name is Dusty Fog!'

CHAPTER TWO

THE IMMORTAL WORDS OF COLONEL SAM

'DUSTY FOG!' In all her life Thora had never heard four voices put so much different expression in just two small words. There was wild elation in old Salt's whoop as his suspicions were confirmed. Toon's startled croak showed his worry, and there was fear and uneasiness in Hendley's tones. Only the hired killer's voice held a sneering disbelief.

To Thora alone the name meant very little, at the moment. She tried to remember what she had heard about a man called Dusty Fog.

'*Him!*' The hired killer jerked a contemptuous thumb at the small Texan. 'A short runt like that, Dusty Fog! Who the hell are you——?'

'Mister!' There was a flat and sudden menace in the small man's soft-drawled words. 'Leave us remember the immortal words of Colonel Sam Colt:

> *'Be not afraid of any man,*
> *No matter what your size.*
> *When danger threatens, call on me,*
> *And I will equalise.'*

Ed Wren scowled; he wasn't used to prospective victims spouting poetry at him. 'Meaning?' he hissed.

'When ole Colonel Sam brought out his first six-gun, back to Paterson in the old days, he made you and me both the same height.'

Thad Toon licked his lips nervously. 'Now easy, Dusty.' He, for one, didn't doubt who this small, soft-spoken young man was. 'We ain't after no fussings with you three; our fight's with the Rocking H.'

Thora's mouth opened to claim the three men were hired to her; she closed it again when she realised that she had not told the three cowhands whether they were hired or not. She wanted to say something and try to avert the trouble which plainly was coming. Before she could do so, Dusty Fog took the matter out of her hands.

Without taking his eyes from the hired killer, Dusty reached back and unstrapped the bedroll from behind his saddle. Holding it one-handed, he said, 'Excuse me, ma'am. Cookie, throw her in the wagon.'

Salt rose and reached over in front of Thora to take the bedroll, a broad grin of pure delight on his seamed face. He took the bedroll and swung it back into the wagon with a delighted, 'Sure thing, Cap'n Fog, suh, sure thing.'

Thora got the feeling that she had somehow missed something, a sign of some kind. There was a stiffness in the three men standing before her, a tension in the air that hadn't been there before. She alone didn't know the full significance of Dusty's action. The others knew it well, too well. They knew that when a cowhand threw his bedroll into the wagon he became part of the outfit, and any trouble the spread got into was his trouble. It meant that he was fully committed to the brand; their fun his fun; their fight now his fight.

Toon and his two men knew it and they knew that they would have to fuss with Dusty Fog, Mark Counter and the Ysabel Kid if they fussed with the Rocking H.

Mark and the Kid had handed their bedrolls up to the cook, just to show where their feelings in the matter lay. The action had not gone unnoticed by Thad Toon; he was even more disturbed by the action, for he knew much of those three young men.

Dusty watched the hired killer all the time and spoke to Salt. 'Start the wagon, Cookie.'

Salt reached for the ribbons, his eyes watching the Double T men ahead. 'They's in the way, Cap'n.'

'Happen they'll move.'

Thora had a sudden feeling that she should say, or do something to stop this small man getting hurt. Before she could make up her mind to say something Salt had twitched the reins gently against the sides of his mules. The wagon started to move, flanked by the three cowhands.

Toon and Hendley stood still for a moment. Then they moved aside, having decided that war was off for this day. Ed Wren stood firm, his hand lifting, for he was paid to fight. He was a paid killer and had his reputation to consider. To back out of a fight would mean that his future employers would remember and not pay so well. He thought of this and made his move.

It was a good move in any company; any but the present.

Thora saw the dandy-dressed killer's hand lash across his body to the butt of his gun. The move was fast. Faster, to her terrified eyes, than any other she had seen.

The crash of a shot made her start up, the concussion of the explosion jarring at her nerves and the acrid smell of burnt powder coming to her nostrils. Ed Wren pitched to one side, blood running from the side of his head. His gun fell from his hand, unfired, and landed in the dust of the trail. He crashed down by the side of it an instant later.

Twisting round, Thora looked down at the small Texan. Somehow, Dusty looked taller than any other man here. He sat lounging in the saddle, his left hand holding a smoking revolver. Dusty lifted the gun to his lips and blew smoke from the barrel, then spun it round and holstered it.

The big paint moved forward, passed in front of the wagon and halted in front of Thad Toon. Cold grey eyes looked down at the rancher and a soft voice drawled, 'I only creased your hired man, mister. The next time I have to shoot, I'll kill—and it won't only be the hired man I go after.'

The Rocking H wagon carried on and Thora leaned over to see what was happening back along the street. Mark and the Kid stopped their horses and were watching whilst Dusty spoke to Toon. She turned back to Salt. 'Who did they say he was?' she asked.

'Why, Miz Thora, ma'am. That's Cap'n Dusty Fog of the Texas Light Cavalry.'

The name didn't mean much to her, she was still confused by all that had happened. 'Is he really fast with a gun?'

'Waal now, Miz Thora,' Salt scratched his jaw thoughtfully, 'I wouldn't go and say he was fast, ma'am. See, take men like Wes Hardin, King Fisher, Bill Longley or Ben Thompson, they're real fast with a gun.'

'Well?'

'Ma'am, sides of Cap'n Fog they're only l'arning.'

Thora gulped, and sank back in her seat. The men named were the best exponents of gunwork Texas had produced. She wondered what kind of men she had hired.

Salt could have told her something about them, things he had heard in the years since the war.

Dusty Fog might look like a quiet, unassuming young man. He might be passed over unnoticed in a crowd, but not if the crowd were painted for war. At fifteen, he had joined the Texas Light Cavalry in the War Between the States: a year later he had been a Captain, and for two years had made a name for himself. It was a name that ranked with Turner Ashby and John Singleton Mosby as the supreme raiders of the Confederacy. Where Ashby and Mosby had fought in the more publicised East, Dusty had led his men to harass the Yankee troops in Texas and New Mexico. In doing so he had caused many a Yankee commander to wish that he was dealing with an older and more conventional fighting man.

After the War Dusty had been selected to go into Mexico and bring back Bushrod Sheldon and his men, who were serving Maximillian. That was where he had teamed up with Mark and the Kid. Since then, they had ridden for Dusty's uncle, Ole Devil Hardin.

Mark Counter could have carved a name for himself in the annals of border gunfighting, had he not chosen to ride with Dusty. He had been a Lieutenant under Sheldon and was said to be the finest all-round fighting man in the West. He was faster than most with his guns, a better than fair shot with a rifle and as a fist-fighter had few equals. He was a tophand and knew cattle if anything better than Dusty did. His father owned the biggest ranch down in the Texas Big Bend country, but Mark preferred to ride with Dusty and the Kid as part of Ole Devil's floating outfit.

The Ysabel Kid was last, but by no means least, of this trio; they tell many tales of the Ysabel Kid down in Mexico. He might look young and innocent, but men who had seen him in a fight knew how far the innocence went. He was good with his old Dragoon gun, the finest exponent of the art of cut-and-slash since James Bowie went to his death at the Alamo. It was with his rifle that he excelled; there was a saying down on the Rio Grande about the Kid and his Winchester 66: 'When the Ysabel Kid hits his mark it is ordinary; when he misses it is a miracle.'

There was more than just a bone-touch fighting man to the Ysabel Kid; he was acknowledged as a first-rate tracker and reader of sign and as a student of Indian ways. His knowledge of Spanish was only exceeded by his mastery of six Indian tongues.

All in all, although Thora didn't know this, Dusty Fog, Mark Counter and the Ysabel Kid were good friends to have in a fight; they were also real bad enemies.

The three young men rode up alongside the wagon again and not one of them gave so much as a look behind them at Toon and Hendley. Dusty smiled up at her, and he looked young and insignificant again. 'Didn't have a chance to tell you before, ma'am, but Uncle Devil sent me along to be trail boss when he heard about Cousin Ben's trouble.'

Thora frowned; she was willing to accept Dusty as a hand, but he looked too young to be able to handle the dangerous task of being a trail boss. Then she remembered how fast Ed Wren had grabbed for his gun, and how this small man had beaten him to the shot—also the worried look on Toon's face when he heard who the small man was.

Whatever misgivings Thora might have had, Salt Ballew didn't show any. He greeted Dusty's words with a yell of delight. 'Yowee!' he howled. 'We don't have us no more worries now, Miz Thora. Men'll come in faster than a Texas blue norther when they hears Cap'n Fog's riding trail boss. We'll certain be plumb belly-deep in pick of the town.'

Thora thought this over for a moment, she could not remember her husband ever mentioning anybody called 'Devil' and wondered who he was that he should send men to help her out. 'Do you know Ben?' she asked more to cover her lack of decision than for any desire of information.

'He's nodding kin,' Dusty replied. 'Met him one time when he came to the Rio Hondo for the Christmas turkey-shoot.'

Thora nodded; she could see how she had not heard much about this relative of her husband. Since coming west she had learned something of the kin system of the South. Nodding kin were distant relations and she wondered why one would take the trouble of helping out the Rocking H.

The town marshal stepped from his office; he had been a witness to all that had happened along the street and seen the shooting. Now the wagon had arrived, he stepped out to have a word with them.

Salt halted the wagon and the three cowhands also stopped, each lounging in the saddle and looking down at the marshal. Looking back, he asked, 'He dead?'

'Nope,' Mark replied. 'All cooks look like that.'

'Not Salt. I know he ain't but half dead—and that only from the Stetson down. I meant Ed Wren.'

'Just creased,' Dusty answered. 'You should keep such evil-doers out of your town, Frank.'

The marshal didn't take any offence at this and turned his attention to Dusty. 'I try, I try. So the sooner you three hellers light out the happier I'll be. I can do with you here the same way I can use a hole in the top of my head.'

'That'd be what I'd call an improvement.' the Kid replied.

Thora started to get to her feet; she knew the marshal was a fair and brave man and expected to see her three hands thrown into jail for the shooting. They didn't seem to be trying to avoid it, with their attitude towards the marshal. 'Capain Fog is my trail boss,' she put in hotly, then realised she had committed herself now. 'We only came to hire hands, after that we'll be going. You know that Thad Toon had that man in town to stop us hiring——'

'Yes, ma'am,' the marshal interrupted with a wink at the three cowhands. 'I know what Thad's been saying and wondered just when somebody'd take up that fancy-dressed gunslick.' He looked along the street to where Toon and Hendley were carrying the gunman towards the doctor's house. 'I'll have a few words with Thad. Don't you worry none, Miz Thora, with Dusty here as trail boss you'll get your crew, the town's full of men all looking for work.'

'Thank you.' Thora saw that her crew were in no danger of being arrested. 'I'm sorry it came to shooting.'

The marshal grinned. 'So's ole Thad I reckon.' The grin faded. 'You heard that Kliddoe's got a new bunch and working the Dodge City area?'

'We heard.' Dusty didn't sound any too worried by the prospect. 'I reckon we'll just have to hope and pray we slip by him.'

The marshal could see that trio of hell-twisters doing any praying over a thing like that. He lifted his hand in a cheery salute. Then he turned to head down the street, to tell Thad Toon something to his advantage.

Granite City wasn't much different from a hundred other such towns in the West. The business section, comprising stores, saloons and the jail, shared the main drag with the

Granite Hotel—the finest, in fact the only, hotel in town. Outside this imposing building Salt halted his team.

Mark helped Thora down from the wagon and then the three young men attended to their horses. They returned to join her on the porch and Dusty pulled a chair up for her, then sat on the rail with his back to the street. For a moment Thora thought that he was showing a lamentable lack of precaution, presenting his back to anyone coming towards them. Then she saw that Mark and the Kid were lounging on either side of her and all were in a position to cover the others' blind spots. She saw that Salt was down at the store getting last-minute purchases for the drive.

Dusty asked for permission to smoke and then rolled three smokes one after the other. She watched his hands at work and realised that he was using his right hand now, not his left. She didn't know it but Dusty was completely ambidextrous. He had trained himself to be that way since his early school days. It had been part of his defence against his lack of inches, a defence which had driven him to become the chain-lightning gun-handler that he was.

'Do you know what they say about the herd?' she asked.

'Sure, they're offering five-to-one it doesn't get through, back in Fort Worth.' Dusty replied. 'I've ten dollars on it.'

'There's a lot against our getting through.'

'Man'd say you called that right. I heard about Cousin Ben getting gunned in Dodge. Word has it that a friend of Earp, skin-hunter called Shag Moxel, boasted he'd done it.'

'Yeah,' the Kid put in. 'Happen we'll know the truth when we get up there.'

'You mean that, knowing about Earp's threat, you're willing to go to Dodge?'

'Sure.' It was Mark who answered her startled query. 'Earp doesn't mean a thing. And don't tell me about him arresting Ben Thompson in Ellsworth: I was there and know what happened. Earp's just a loud-mouth who likes a badge to hide behind. He's not even a regular lawman in Dodge, just one of the extra hands they take on in the trail season.'

'Mark's right!' Dusty agreed. 'Earp talks big but he's not big inside, unless he has the backing. Kliddoe scares me more than Earp, and he doesn't scare me all that much.'

Thora licked her lips. Kliddoe was one man she didn't want

to talk about. 'What will you do now?'

'Hire us some men, unless you have enough.' Dusty looked along the street as he spoke. 'Who was that *hombre* we had words with back there?'

'Thad Toon, owner of the Double T. He's our neighbour and wants to get his herd moved out first.'

'Does, huh?' Dusty's smile made him look even younger. 'He won't get his wanting.'

Thora felt a momentary misgiving at taking on this young man: he would never be able to handle the crew. However, Salt approved of having Dusty Fog as trail boss and Ben had told her to take the cook's advice on such things. She knew that Salt would never lead her wrong on a matter as important as this.

'How many men will we need? The herd is about three thousand head.'

'How many of your own men are you sending?'

'Salt, his assistant.' Thora answered, 'and myself.'

Three faces looked at hers; it was the first and last time she ever saw them show any surprise. 'You, ma'am?' The Ysabel Kid sounded as if he didn't believe his ears.

'A trail drive's no place for a woman, ma'am.' Mark took it up. 'It's not even a fit place for a man, happen he's got any sense at all.'

Dusty didn't speak but watched the young woman's face as she answered them. 'I'm the only one who can be spared. We can't do without Salt and his assistant, but we have to. Ben doesn't want me to go, but I can be pretty persuasive when I have to. He's come round to my way of thinking by now. Besides'—her face was flushed—'I have a reason for wanting to go along, a reason that I haven't told Ben. I know a surgeon in the East who may be able to help Ben. I've made arrangements to meet him in Dodge and bring him home to the Rocking H.'

'We could bring him for you, ma'am,' Mark suggested.

She shook her head. 'Doctor Burglin wouldn't come with you. He's rather eccentric and thinks that cowboys aren't to be trusted. He won't come unless I go and fetch him myself.'

'All right, ma'am—if that's your reason, you come with us,' Dusty drawled.

Thora had two other reasons, but she didn't tell them to

these three young men; either one would have turned them off, she thought. She wanted to know more about what they were going to do now. 'How many men will you need?'

'About another eighteen or so,' Dusty replied. He studied the woman's face for a moment, seeming to be uncomfortable about something. 'There's one thing I want understood, ma'am. And I want it understood right from the start. Uncle Devil always taught me one thing, in everything from a Cavalry regiment to a trail drive there can't be but one boss. There can't be two.'

'Well?'

'You can come along with us, but I want it understood that either you or I handle the chore of trail boss. If I am it's my duty to hire, work and fire every man we take on. If you come, you're classed as a hand, the same as the rest. You take my orders.'

The two looked at each other for a time. Then she drew herself up proudly. 'Captain Fog, my father was a regular officer in the Army and I spent most of my early life in army posts. I learned the same rule as you. If you are the trail boss I will take your orders.'

Grins flickered on three tanned faces. Mark held out a hand the size of a ham. 'You'll do, ma'am.'

'Reckon you will,' Dusty agreed. 'Now we'll get the trail crew rounded up. We've got a whole heap of miles to cover, ma'am, and "Captain" sounds real formal, I'm Dusty, this is Mark and Lon.'

'And I'm Thora to my friends,' She felt warmer towards the three men now.

'Mark, you'n Lon head down to the shanties and roust out a nigger for night-hawk. Pass the word as you go along.'

The two men stepped forward obediently and Dusty moved so that he had his back to the wall. He took a chair and sat in it, leaning against the wall.

'How will you get the eighteen men we need?' asked Thora.

'Hire them.'

'But do you know that many men in town?'

'Likely know some. We'll get all we want.'

Thora sat back, she wondered how Dusty would set about hiring strangers for a difficult business like trail-driving. She didn't want him to think she doubted him, so she changed the subject. 'How long have you three been together?'

'Since just after the war. We teamed up in Mexico and, when we came north, decided to stick together. Uncle Devil took us on as a floating outfit and we've been riding for him since then.'

'Floating outfit?' She looked puzzled. 'We don't have one. What do you do?'

'Work round the spread until winter, then head out for the back country. There's five of us and a cook, riding greasy sack most of the time.'

'Greasy sack?'

'Sure, we take our food along in sacks on a mule, instead of with a wagon. Call it trailing a long-eared chuckwagon down our way.'

Thora relapsed into silence and watched Mark and the Kid entering a saloon. They soon came out and Thora went on talking, 'Lon, the Kid, is he as dangerous as he looks?'

'Worse!' There was a smile flickering on Dusty's lips. 'He's the only man who scares me.'

'Is he—er—is——' She floundered to a stop, not knowing how to carry on or frame her next question.

'Is he white?' The smile had gone and the voice was cold. 'He's white clear through, ma'am. His paw was Irish–Kentucky, his mother Creole–Commanche—but he's the whitest man I know, ma'am.'

'I didn't mean to insult your friend!' That one word, 'ma'am' had been a warning to her. She was coming to dangerous ground. 'I haven't been west long enough to have any prejudice against mixed blood. My mother was French and my father Scottish. That is a mixture, too.'

'Sure, Thora.' The drawl was back, soft and easy again. 'We'll soon be getting our crew.'

Thora saw that Mark and the Kid were headed towards the shanties where the coloured workers of the town lived. She also saw that several cowhands were walking along the street towards the hotel. The men came along; they didn't stop or say anything to Dusty, just walked past and then turned and went back towards the saloon once more.

Then she saw a tall, dark man coming along the street towards the hotel. He wore a low-crowned, black Stetson and his clothes were old, untidy, yet his boots were new-looking.

His face was lean, dark and dangerous-looking. He ambled along in a slouching stride, his eyes all the time flickering round and his hands brushing the Remington revolver at his left side and the bowie knife at his right.

She felt a sudden fear; the man looked cold and dangerous, like the pictures she had seen of Quantrel raiders. He must be an outlaw the way he acted, probably a killer. To her horror, Dusty lifted his hand in greeting.

'Howdy, Kiowa?' he said, 'You riding?'

CHAPTER THREE

ON CHOOSING HANDS

THE dark man halted at Dusty's words and glanced at the girl before he replied, 'Nope!'

'Need a point man or scout—along of Mark, or ahead with the Kid. You take that?'

'Yep!'

'You heard the word about this herd?'

'Yep!'

Thora had been watching the dark face, which showed no expression at all that she could read. She wondered why Dusty had picked this dark, dangerous-looking man from the crowd. Of course Dusty knew him, but that meant little to her. If she had been hiring, she would have taken someone more presentable.

'Wagon's down there by the store. Throw your bedroll in and come back here.' Dusty jerked his thumb in the direction of the Rocking H wagon as he spoke. 'I want to light out as soon as we've got the rest of the crew. Who all's in town?'

'Billy Jack, Red Tolliver, Basin Jones and a few more you'll likely know. Want for me to herd them in, happen I see 'em?'

'Be right obliged.' Dusty was getting amusemenc in watching the obvious disapproval on Thora's face.

Kiowa slouched off to collect his horse, moving like a buck Apache on the warpath. Two clean, neatly dressed young cowhands came by, both looked hard at Dusty. For a moment Thora thought they were going to ask Dusty for work, but they passed on. She felt disappointed; they were the sort of men she would have hired, not that dark man.

A tall, gangling man was coming along the street now; she noticed him only because of the tired, miserable and careworn look on his face. She wondered if he had just had very bad news, for every line of him gave that impression.

Once more Dusty raised a hand in greeting. 'Howdy, Billy Jack,' he said. 'You riding?'

The gangling man halted and hitched up his gunbelt as if the low-tied brace of Colt 1860 Army revolvers were a burden to him. He looked even more miserable at the thought of work being forced on him. 'You say so, Cap'n.'

'Point man along of Mark most of the time. You know this is the Rocking H herd, and what they're saying about it?'

'Nigh on skeers me to death,' Billy Jack answered dolefully, his prominent Adam's Apple jumping up and down. 'Where at's the wagon?'

'Down there by the store. Kiowa's trailing with us.'

'That makes my day.' Billy Jack turned and slouched about, still looking the picture of dejection.

'Do you know him?' Thora asked. Dusty nodded. 'Then is he always like that?' she went on.

'This is one of his good days,' Dusty replied. 'You should have seen him the day General Robert E. Lee commended him for bravery in the field.'

'Him?' Thora gasped, her surprise making her lose her grammar for a moment.

'Yes'm. Billy Jack was the best top-sergeant I ever had.'

Thora stirred uneasily in her chair, Dusty watched her out of the corner of his eye and guessed what she was thinking. Had he planned it this way, it couldn't have happened better, for she disapproved of his first two choices. Yet she didn't speak; if she took this she would take any orders he gave. This was why he didn't explain his reasons for picking them.

Thora watched a handsome, tall young man coming towards them. He wore the dress of a cowland dandy and belted a low-tied, pearl-handled Army Colt. After passing the first two over, she doubted if Dusty would take this man. However, he raised his hand. 'Howdy, friend! You riding?'

The man halted. He raised his hat to Thora, then shook his head. 'Take on, if you'll have me.'

'Point's all filled, but we'll take you.'

'*Gracias*. The name's Dude.'

'Wagon's by the store, Dude. Throw your roll in.'

Thora watched Dude walk away and her frown deepened; it was plain to her that Dusty didn't know the man, yet had hired him. She shook her head, it was all beyond her. The next two men Dusty hired were both well-dressed youngsters, and they also were strangers to him. Why he took them and passed over a couple who looked, to her eyes, like them, she couldn't tell. Dusty's next choice was an untidy-looking man who was also a stranger to Dusty. He came after two who might have been his brothers had passed by and been ignored.

There were seventeen men hired when a thin, freckled youngster riding a sorry-looking paint came up. He halted the paint and asked. 'You looking for a wrangler, Cap'n?'

Dusty looked the youngster over; he was wearing cast-off clothing that had seen better days, tucked in his belt was a worn old model Navy Colt; worn though it was, the weapon was clean and cared for. 'Sure. You reckon you can handle it.'

'Sure I can,' the boy sounded eager; 'I been wrangler on a couple of spreads. Was going to say on a couple of drives, but I wouldn't lie to you, Cap'n.'

Dusty bent forward to hide his smile, then jerked a thumb to the wagon. 'Your folks say you can go, you head down for the wagon and throw your gear in.'

The boy shook his head. 'Ain't got no folks, Cap'n. Comanches got them when I was a button.'

'But how have you lived since then?' Thora gasped, not having run across an Indian-orphaned waif before.

'Folks took care of me 'til I was old enough to fend for myself. Then I took out and worked for a cattle spread. Got me a hoss and lit out to see some of the range.'

'You eat today, boy?' Dusty inquired, and the boy shook his head. 'Best get a meal then, afore we head for the spread; you'll likely be needing one——' He stopped, the boy looked embarrassed and hung his head. Dusty pulled a couple of dollars from his pocket and said, 'Here, it's a spread rule that we always pay the wrangler some in advance, happen we get a good one.'

The boy took the money eagerly. He was very hungry, but didn't want to let his hero know how near the blanket he was. He turned his horse, muttering his thanks, and rode off towards the livery barn. There, before he went to get himself a much-needed meal, he bought the horse the first grain feed it had had in many days.

Thora shook her head: there were many facets to this small man's character that she didn't know of. 'Did you hire that boy out of pity?'

'Nope, I reckon he'll make a hand. He'll handle the remuda all right and comes Dodge he'll have filled out plenty on regular food. Next time he goes north he'll be riding as a hand and, maybe in time, he'll be riding trail boss.' Dusty saw a familiar face and greeted another old friend. 'Howdy Red, I'd about given you up. You riding?'

Thora watched the final man walking towards the wagon. The men were all standing round it, some helping Salt to load the supplies. Even from the hotel, Thora could see the delight on her cook's face and knew Salt was satisfied with the men.

'That's eighteen,' she remarked. 'All we need.'

'Sure, now what's worrying you about the men?'

She turned a startled face to him and then laughed. 'You knew all along I didn't understand how you picked the men. I still don't. Every time I thought I had your system worked out, you spoiled it.'

'There's only one system when you're hiring a man. Look at his boots, then at his hat, then at his hands,' Dusty replied. 'A good hand always buys the best boots and hat he can, no matter what the rest of his rig is like. The two who followed Kiowa along. I reckon you'd have hired them. I didn't, they were nothing but milk-cow riders. Sure they'd got good, clean clothes, but their boots were ready-mades. A hand worth hiring buys his boots made to measure; he knows the extra money spent is worth it. Same with his hat; he buys the best JB Stetson he can afford. A cheap woolsey might look good, but come a good rain and the brim starts to flop down. That happens when you're riding to head a stampede in a storm, well it doesn't happen more than once. But with a good Stetson you're safe; it'll hold its shape as long as you have it. You can't wear it out; it'll happen take on some weight with age and get so's you can smell it across a wide room, but it'll never lose its shape.'

Thora saw Dusty's point. 'But what about their hands?'

'A cowhand handles a rope. It burns callouses into his hands. That shows he's handled a rope regular.'

Looking down at Dusty's hands, she saw the marks; but there were other callouses on his forefingers. 'And the other callouses, on the fingers?'

'They're from a handling a gun.'

'I see.' She decided to study the boots and hats of the men when they rejoined Dusty. 'But about the dark man—Kiowa, I think you called him.'

'Kiowa?' Dusty grinned. 'I've know him since I was knee-high to a grasshopper. He rode for Uncle Devil's OD Connected until the country started to get too crowded for him.'

'How do you mean?'

'Folks started to build another town thirty miles away. He allowed that the Rio Hondo was getting worse crowded than Chicago and pulled out. But there isn't a better hand at the point and I can't think of three better at riding scout. If it comes to Indian savvy there's only one man in this town who licks him.'

'Then shouldn't you have hired that one?'

'Didn't have to—it's Lon,' Dusty answered.

'Oh!' Thora could see that her trail boss had thought of about everything. 'Will we have Indian trouble?'

'Could have. One time you go through the Nations and you're plumb belly-deep in them all the way. Next time, there isn't a feather in sight, 'cepting that can whistle and fly. But one thing I do know. If we get hit by Indians it won't be because they sneaked by Lon and Kiowa.'

Mark and the Kid came round the corner of the saloon, followed by eight or so Negroes. Before they came to the porch, Thora had asked another of the questions which had been puzzling her. 'But why didn't the men just come up and ask for work, instead of just walking past?'

'Men as good as Kiowa and Billy Jack don't need to ask for work. There were a couple I know went by, tophands both of them, but I didn't want them. So they just walk by. If I want to hire them I ask; if I don't, well nobody's feelings get hurt.'

Mark stepped up on to the porch and pointed to the Negroes.

'All want to take on as night-hawk,' he remarked.

Dusty rose and went to the edge of the porch to look over the eight men, then asked each one what he could do. Seven out of the eight proudly announced their good behaviour and sterling Christian ways. The eighth was a tall, lean, grinning man, wearing an old, collarless shirt and a tattered pair of Confederate army trousers.

'Cap'n, sah,' he said, pushing back his beat-up old rebel kepi. 'I drinks, I smokes, cusses and chouses them lil ole darkie gals bow-legged but I can sho' herd hosses.'

'You handle a big remuda at night?'

'You has it, I'll handle it.'

'Got a hoss?'

'Got me 'n ole mule that can see in the night like a hoot-owl.'

'What do we call you?'

The black face split almost across in a grin. 'You calls me what you likes, sah, as long as you calls me for meals good 'n' regular!'

One of the other Negroes snorted; he didn't take kindly to losing a plum chore like this and sought to discredit the fortunate man. 'Cap'n, sah. That there Tarbrush he ain't fittin' company for gawd-fearing folks.'

'Well then.' Dusty dipped his hand into his pocket again, 'I'll tell you what I'll do. Happen we find any of those god-fearing folks where we're going, I'll surely keep him well away from them.' Taking out a coin, Dusty tossed it to the man. 'Here, either put it in the church box, or buy the rest of the boys a drink.'

The seven unfortunate job-seekers turned and ambled off happily, headed for the shanty-town sloon, to drink the gift away. Tarbrush stood and watched them go. He sighed. 'Most wish I hadn't been hired now,' he remarked as he turned to go for his mule and few belongings.

Salt returned with the rest of the crew and Thora studied each man; she found that Dusty's three pointers in choosing hands were correct. 'What now?' she inquired.

'I'll take the boys in for a drink. Then we'll light out for the Rocking H,' Dusty replied. He turned his attention to Salt. 'How near to ready for rolling are you?'

'Herd's road-branded and ready to go, Cap'n.'

'I mean the chuckwagon.'

'Waal, I've been sleeping with my sourdough keg for the past two weeks and she's riz to please the eye. I'm full loaded and me louse's back at the spread putting antelope grease on the hubs of the bedwagon. You say the word and we can light out come sunup tomorrow.'

Dusty looked at the men who formed a half-circle at the foot of the porch steps. All stood waiting for him to speak.

'All right, boys, I'll read you the scriptures here instead of at the spread. Then, if any of you don't like them, you can pull out and save a ride. First, I'm trail boss. And the name, as you likely know, is Dusty Fog. Miz Holland here's going with us as spread's rep.' There was a startled mumble from the men, Dusty waited until it died then carried on:

'She'll be treated as one of the hands. Mark's my segundo, and the Ysabel Kid rides scout, helped by your good friend, Kiowa. Billy Jack or Kiowa will be at point with Mark. The rest of you will ride swing, flank and drag turnabout. The remuda's held at the Rocking H for any of you who need a mount. We'll hold us a choosing match as soon as we get there, taking it in the order you took on. Some of you have rode for Colonel Charlie Goodnight, and you'll know his way. I learned under him and it's my way too. I want to pull out tomorrow so we haven't time to draw up articles. If any of you don't know Colonel Charlie's rules and want to, ask Billy Jack, he'll likely tell you.'

The men muttered their agreement to this. Every man had heard of the stringent rules of conduct laid down by the old master of trail drive work, Colonel Charles Goodnight. They covered the man's life from the time he signed on to when he paid off, and protected both his and the owner's interests. They all agreed with the rules, for they knew that their lives would be made easier by following them.

'How about likker, Cap'n?' It was Dude who asked.

'Any toted goes in the wagon and Salt'll hand it out.'

This was agreed upon by all the hands. A trail drive was dangerous enough without having a drunk on it. 'If that's all, I'll buy a drink. Then we head back for the spread.' Dusty stepped aside and the men all started forward across the porch towards the hotel doors.

'Hey, you!'

A man rode towards the porch, a big, heavily-built man wearing dirty range clothes and belting a low-tied Navy Colt. He halted the bay he was riding and the other two horses stopped at the same time; they were all nervous-looking animals, the whites of their eyes showing.

'Who's bossing the drive?'

Thora bit her lip as she looked the man over; she had seen him before somewhere, but couldn't remember where. Dusty was also studying the man and replied. 'I am.' His attention was now on the muzzles of the horses, not the man.

'You need a wrangler?' The question was directed to Thora more than Dusty. 'Man across the street telled me the lady was boss.'

'I'm trail boss—and we're full-hired.'

'Yeah?' The newcomer's face twisted in a sneer. 'Waal, happen the lady'll make you change your mind. See, a friend of her'n telled me to look her up and mention his name.'

'Mister'—Dusty's voice was still the same soft drawl but there was a subtle difference to it now—'Miz Holland hired me as trail boss on the understanding that I handled the hiring and firing of the crew. We've got a wrangler and, even if we hand't, I wouldn't take on a man who uses a ghost-cord on his mount.'

Thora stared at the horses; she had heard the ranch crew talk about ghost-cords. She could see the marks the thin cord had made as it was tied around each horse's tongue and gums, under the lower jaw and the ends carried back to be used as reins. The ghost cord was an instrument of torture and no cowhand worth his salt would use one. The ranch owners also hated the use of the cord, for it either broke the horse's spirit or turned it into a killer.

The man spat into the dust, his hand falling casually towards his side. 'Is that right?'

'Try it!' Dusty's flat, barked warning was accompanied by a click as his right-hand gun came out and lined.

The man stared at the long barrel of the Army Colt; it had come out faster than he had ever seen a gun drawn before. Having expected to take the other by surprise, it came as a sudden and nasty shock to him that he had failed, and failed badly.

'All right,' he growled, holding his hand well clear of the

gun and turning his face to Thora's. 'Happen you can talk some sense to your trail boss. Like I said before, this friend of your'n——'

The colour drained from Thora's face, she knew who the man was, and who the mysterious friend was. If the Texans heard the name they would never drive for her.

'I'm getting quick sick of you.'

Thora hadn't noticed the Ysabel Kid moving forward to her side. He stood there now, his soft-drawled words biting through the other's speech and halting it.

Looking the dark-dressed, innocent-featured youngster over the man made a mistake. He thought he was dealing with some dressed-up button who was still wet behind the ears. 'Shy out!' he hissed. 'I'm talking to the white——'

The Ysabel Kid went over the hitching rail in a smooth dive which carried the man from his saddle and brought them both crashing to the ground. Whilst the man landed hard on his back, the Ysabel Kid lit down on his feet with an almost catlike agility. Crouching lightly on the balls of his feet, Loncey Dalton Ysabel waited for the man to come up and carry on.

Cursing, he came up, his hand fanning towards the butt of his gun. Even as he did so, Dusty roared out, 'Lon! No!'

The sun glinted on eleven-and-a-half inches of razor-sharp steel as the Kid lunged in. His knife made a ripping arc faster than the other man's hand dropped. At the last instant, it swerved and cut through the holster flap. The weight of the Colt swung the severed holster over and the man's hand clawed at an empty space. The gun slid from leather and fell into the dust. Turning, the man leapt towards the rifle stuck in his saddleboot.

Mark Counter vaulted the rail, his hand shooting out to grip the man by the collar and hurl him backwards. 'Don't be loco, *hombre*!' he snapped. 'Lon could just as easy of killed you the first time. Don't tempt him any more—he fails real easy.'

The man looked up and saw just what Mark meant. The Ysabel Kid was still standing in that knife-fighter's crouch, his dark face as hard and savage as a Comanche Dog soldier looking for a paleface scalp. He had seen a couple of knife-fighters, this big man, and knew that here was a master hand, one that it would be best to steer clear of.

Slowly he relaxed, his face twisted in a mask of hatred. 'All right,' he snarled, 'I'm going and I won't forget this.'

'Happen you won't,' the Kid growled back. 'Not when things are even you won't.'

The man mounted his horse and turning it headed off.

The trail-drive crew had been interested spectators of all this. Billy Jack looked sheepish and holstered his right-hand gun. Salt leered at the miserable-looking rider, he for one being satisfied. His judgment had been vindicated. In a fight, it had been the Bowie knife the Ysabel Kid first reached for.

The cowhands trooped into the bar, and Dusty stood by Thora, watching them go. In Texas in the 1870s, a lady didn't enter the barroom and she would have to wait until they returned. She was pleased to note that the diversion had taken the men's minds off the statements the newcomer had made.

Dusty stopped at the door and turned back. 'You look worried, Thora. Don't be. That kind of bum always tries a game like that. He'd knew you were from the north and allowed he could get taken on if you thought he knew some friend.'

'What do the men make of what he said?'

'About the same as I did. It's your business and none of our'n.'

Thora watched Dusty enter the bar and sat down, her legs feeling suddenly weak. The man had known a friend of hers all right—a friend? A man she hated, a man who could lose her every man Dusty had hired. She felt sick and scared, realising that in the future she might meet this mysterious friend.

Dusty found himself leaning on the bar alongside Billy Jack. The tall hand still looked as miserable as ever.

'Thought we'd see us some blood out there,' Billy Jack remarked, his tones showing that he was disappointed that they hadn't. 'The Kid's knife's enough to turn a man's blood cold. Happen you should have let him use it; I just recollected where I last saw that hombre. Couldn't place him at first, then I got him.'

'Where?'

'With Kliddoe!'

'Kliddoe?' Dusty spat the word out. 'You sure on that?'

'Nigh on. Leastwise, he looked powerful like one of the

bunch that got clear when ole Shangai Pierce and his crew hit them.'

Dusty shook his head, 'I can't see that, *amigo*. No Kliddoe man dare show his face in Texas.'

'Thought that myself,' Billy Jack agreed. 'He looked powerful like one of them. He warn't from the south either.'

Before Dusty could go further into the matter he was called on by one of the other men to clear up some point of a drive they had been on together. Then, when this was cleared up, he told the men to get their horses and they would head for the Rocking H.

In a saloon along the street, Toon and his foreman sat by the window and watched the cavalcade of men riding by, headed for Rocking H. Toon wasn't in any too good a temper; and it didn't improve when he saw that not only had he failed to stop the Rocking H hiring, but that they had taken the cream of the hands in town.

'What now?' Hendley inquired.

Toon thought it over for a moment and an idea formed in his mind. 'Go down to the Doc's and pay off Wren first thing. Then we're going to slow Rocking H down some.'

Hendley stiffened. 'You ain't going against that bunch with guns, are you?' There was a lamentable lack of enthusiasm in the foreman's tones.

'Nope, brains. You get me that damned half-breed Dan Twofeathers. Get him here real fast. If he don't want to come, tell him I'll have him jailed for slow-elking.'

'What have you in mind, Thad?' Hendley had uneasy visions of stampeding the Rocking H herd, and of the consequences. He was brave enough, but the thought of matching lead with that crew was more than he could stand.

'Suppose they was to lose something real important to them?' Toon answered. 'Something that'd take them a week or more to replace, and that they can't do without.'

'Like what?'

'Like their sourdough keg.'

CHAPTER FOUR

CHOOSING MATCH

BEN HOLLAND sat in his wheelchair and looked over his range. He was on the porch of his house accompanied by his foreman, a tall, hard-looking man called Sam Starken. Their attention was on the dust cloud which was coming rapidly towards the ranch and along the town trail.

Ben was still healthy looking, and his wide shoulders set back squarely. His time in the wheelchair had left hard, bitter lines round his mouth and there were worry creases around the corners of his eyes. Even Thora didn't know how worried Ben had been since his return from Dodge. The worries of the ranch were not great, Sam Starken and the crew being able to handle anything that came up on the home range. Getting the herd to market was another thing though. That herd meant badly-needed money to the Rocking H, money that couldn't be got in any other way.

'That's Miz Thora,' Sam Starken growled. 'Got what looks like a full crew along with her.'

Starken pushed his boss to the edge of the porch and Ben felt worried as he watched the men coming towards the ranch. Thora wasn't experienced in matters of this sort, and there was no telling what sort of men she would take on. At best, he hoped that they might get enough hands to allow him to send half the crew along and keep the new men on Rocking H to handle the cattle.

The first thing that became obvious was that the riders Thora was bringing were at least all good horsemen. As they came nearer, both men began to recognise some of them.

'Damned if the gal ain't a living wonder,' Ben growled huskily. 'She's done took on Kiowa and Billy Jack both. There's a pair to draw to.'

Starken gulped hard: he knew the two men by reputation, but there were certain others he knew as friends. He could hardly believe the evidence of his eyes. 'Got Red Tolliver there, 'n' Duke Lane. If that ain't Basin Jones, I'll swan! Took with Kiowa and Billy Jack them three'd make a dandy full house.'

Ben could not think how Thora had managed to hire such men; even the small man on the big paint had the air of a tophand. This last rider looked vaguely familiar to Ben, but he couldn't place the face.

The party came to a halt before the ranch house and fanned out into a rough half-circle. Ben looked around and felt even more amazement as the correct calibre of the riders became apparent to his range-wise eyes. They must represent the pick of the town; in fact, they would be hard to match in Texas.

The handsome, blonde giant on the blood bay swung down and turned to help Thora from the wagon. She came forward and the small man on the paint rode up. 'Howdy, Cousin Ben,' he greeted. 'Uncle Devil heard you needed some help and sent me along to ride trail boss for you.'

Then Ben knew who the small man was and knew how these riders came to be here. 'Howdy, Cousin Dusty.' He held out his hand as the small man dismounted. 'Real obliged to you for coming. This here's my foreman, Sam Starken.'

'Howdy, Sam.' Dusty appraised the man with one quick, all-seeing glance, then got down to business. 'Miss Thora allows the herd is ready to move. Happen you'll let me take a horse from your remuda. I'll head out and look it over.'

'Sure, Dusty.' Starken liked a man who got right straight down to business. 'We'll head out soon as you're ready.'

'Mark, Billy Jack.' Dusty barked out, 'I want you along with me. Lon, you take four of the hands and roust out the cable from the bedwagon, Lil Jackie, Tarbrush, I want the remuda handled as soon as I get back.'

The Kid turned to Thora and sighed. 'That's how you tell a trail boss, ma'am. He can't rest hisself and it surely hurts him to see the help rest.'

Dusty looked his pard over in some disgust. 'You've rested most of all your wicked and sinful young life. Time comes when a man has to start you in to working.'

Dusty, Mark and Billy Jack each cut a horse from the Rocking H remuda, saddled it and headed, with the foreman, to look over the herd. Thora went to stand by her husband and watched them go. 'Did I do all right?'

'Honey, nobody could have done better.'

She flushed at the praise, then shook her head. 'I'm not too happy about either Billy Jack or Kiowa. I wouldn't have taken them on. But Dusty did and I promised not to interfere. Do you know either of them?'

'Heard of them both,' Ben answered, a grin flickering round the corner of his lips in a way which Thora hadn't seen since his return from Dodge. 'Billy Jack rode segundo for Shangai Pierce that last drive, when they cut Kliddoe's gang to doll rags. Kiowa used to ride for Ole Devil Hardin and for Clay Allison. They're tophands, both of them, and they could get took on as segundo most any place they chose to go. There aren't many better trail drivers in the west.'

Thora turned her attention to what the other men were doing, some of the men were by the corral, examining the horses of the remuda, whilst others were helping unload their bedrolls from the wagon. The Kid and four men were at the second wagon and taking out a thick rope.

Turning back, she told her husband what had happened in town. Ben listened without a word, only speaking when she asked, 'How did Toon know I'd hired Dusty? In fact, I hadn't even told Dusty he was hired.'

'You didn't have to tell him. When a hand throws his bedroll into the wagon he's hired and part of the crew.' Ben replied. 'I'm not sorry that Dusty didn't down Thad—he ain't all that bad a *hombre*.'

'The other man who came,' Thora licked her lips before she went on, 'I recognised him. His name is Blount and he rode for Kliddoe. I was afraid he was going to tell the men about me. The Kid stopped him just in time.'

Ben gripped her hand, seeing the fear in her eyes. 'Honey, you don't need to go north with the herd. You know that Kliddoe's out again and that Dusty won't let him collect any head tax.'

'I know.' The little she had seen of Dusty Fog told her that. 'But, if it comes to the worst, I may be able to do something to help.'

Starken escorted Dusty, Mark and Billy Jack out to the bottomlands where half the crew were holding the herd. Dusty looked the herd over from a distance; then they rode nearer and circled around. The cattle were all steers, long-horned, half-wild and well meated up. They would stand the long drive north with no trouble and, given luck, would reach Dodge City in first-class shape.

'Be around three thousand head?' Dusty guessed.

'We road-branded three thousand two hundred, but happen a few more will have got in.'

Mark had made an even more careful study of the cattle than Dusty had.

More than the trail boss, the segundo had to be concerned with the cattle. Dusty, as trail boss, would have many problems on his mind; he had to handle the men, the remuda, any emergency that might come up. Mark was the man who would be mostly concerned with the cattle themselves.

'Look real well, Sam,' he finally remarked. 'You don't get so much tick trouble this far north?'

'Not much and none this time of the year,' Sam replied. 'They'll likely not die off afore you get to Dodge.'

'Reckon your boys can handle the night herd for us, tonight, Sam?' Dusty inquired as they headed back towards the ranch. 'I'd like to give the trail crew a decent night's sleep.'

'Sure, I aimed to keep half the crew out. Don't figure Thad Toon be loco enough to try scattering the herd, but he might.'

'If he does,' Dusty growled, 'he'll surely wish he'd never been born.'

The Ysabel Kid saw Dusty coming back and called, 'Set up that cable over here.'

The four hands took up the heavy rope and carried it to the place Lon had pointed out. One man was at each end, and the two others pulled the centre back to form a loose U shape. This was the only corral they would use all the way north. To someone who didn't know Western horses this might look like a flimsy enclosure, but every horse in the remuda had learned early and painfully what a rope was.

Little Jackie and Tarbrush sat their mounts on either side of the corral gate as the Rocking H wrangler opened it and allowed the horses to come out. The two riders came on either side and, without fuss or bother, hazed the horses into the cable corral. The horses halted and milled around, and the four rope-holders shook the cable a few times just to remind the remuda what it was.

'Boy handles the remuda all right,' Mark drawled as they watched the corralling of the horses.

'Sure, time he gets to Dodge he'll have made a hand, and next time he goes, he'll be ready to ride the herd,' Dusty answered. Then, he frowned and growled, 'Look!'

A big black gelding cut back from the milling horses, out of the corral and broke for the open range. Mark started his horse forward but Jackie had alredy turned it back towards the corral.

'Red, take the cable over there a piece. Jackie, Tarbrush, bring them in again.'

Red Tolliver, at the cable, acknowledged the order with a wave. Then he lowered his end of the cable. The other holders let the rope go down and backed off to reform the loose U a couple of hundred yards away. Again the horses were brought in and, once more, the black broke back out.

'All right, move the cable again.' Dusty sounded grim.

On the porch, Thora and Ben were watching. The rancher explained to his wife all that was happening. They saw the new cable set up again; the remuda was driven in and then the black broke out once more. Ben's hands gripped the arms of his chair and, in a roar which was echoed by every watching man, he yelled, 'Takes his toes up!'

Dusty had reached forward and unstrapped his rope as the third coralling commenced. When the black broke back out, he was ready—and so was the wiry dun roping horse he had borrowed for the ride to the herd. A touch sent the little horse leaping forward. It knew just what it was supposed to do as it moved to the rear and left of the big black.

The sixty-foot rope came alive in Dusty's hands, a medium-sized loop building, forming and sailing out. The noose passed across the horse and slightly ahead of its right shoulder, then dropped into position to trap the feet. Dusty gave his rope an inward twist as the noose dropped. This turned the loop to hit against the horses knees, and then trap the feet.

Up to that moment, the black ran blithely on, confident that it was the master of its destiny and the two-legged things were impotent against it. Then its forelegs suddenly locked tight together and it landed with a bone-jarring thud, trapped by Dusty's well-executed forefoot throw.

Thora leapt to her feet as the horse smashed down, her face shocked and angry, 'Did you see that?'

'Sure did, honey. That Dusty can handle a rope.'

'But he could have broken that horse's neck!' She gasped, 'It was a dangerous thing to do.'

'Reckon Dusty'd rather have bust the horse's neck than have him break out like that. Breaking out's the worst thing a remuda horse can do. It's catching and can ruin the remuda.' Ben watched Dusty release the black and point out another place for the cable corral to be set up. 'I'll bet he doesn't break back out again.'

Thora watched the shifting of the cable again and, once more, the horses were driven in. This time, she noticed, the big black didn't try and break back.

Tarbrush and Little Jackie rode around the cable corral and the Negro turned to the youngster. 'You watch real careful now, Jackie boy,' he warned. 'They's going to have their choosing match and we've got to know who all has what.'

Dusty rode forward and looked round the milling horses. A wiry, smallish bay caught his eye and he spun his rope up to catch the horse, then lead it out. Releasing the bay, he headed back and picked out the rest of his mounts. The other hands watched the choosing, and noted with approval that their trail boss was taking the rough string. Every horse he picked bore the look of a fighter, a horse it would take a good man to handle.

In a choosing match the men took turn in order of seniority with the ranch; in this case, in the order they had been hired in town. Mark had second choice; he picked out the biggest horses, five of them, including the big black. These joined Dusty's mounts in the care of the wranglers and the Ysabel Kid rode out.

Ignoring the remuda, the Kid went straight to the ranch house and halted before the porch. 'Ben, you got anything with a mite of speed? I don't want to take cowhorses for riding scout.'

'Got just what you do want, *amigo*,' Ben replied. 'Comanche war relay that I bought off a brave. They're in the small corral, at the back of the spread. You go and look them over.'

There was joy in the Kid's heart as he headed round the house and looked over three horses in the small corral. Riding scout was a dangerous enough task any time; and the horses a man had could mean the difference between living to be old and ornery and making a hair decoration on some scalp-hunting buck's belt.

The three horses were small, rough-coated and wiry, yet

they were alike in one thing. Each was powerfully muscled and looked as if it could run for ever. More, they had been trained as a warrior's relay by a tribe who were horsemen without equal. The three horses had been trained to run together, their rider on one and the other two following him. All in all, they were just what the Ysabel Kid wanted when he rode scout for the herd. Opening the corral gate the Kid drove the three horses out and headed them towards the group of horses being held by Little Jackie and Tarbrush.

Little Jackie watched the increasing remuda and felt nervous. He could see there was much more to handling a trail-drive remuda than there had been to working as ranch wrangler. However he would have one advantage in that the remuda would not increase in size much; on the drive, they would not have many visitors, whilst, at a ranch, there was always a chance that someone would ride up and add his string to the wrangler's cares. The youngster watched the horses and realised that he would have to remember every man's mount and know all their habits. He would have to learn, and learn fast, which were the bunch-quitters, the fighters, the nervous and the mean horses, if he was to do his work properly.

Each man took the horses he would need and added them to the trail remuda. Then Dusty picked out ten spare horses. The ranch wrangler cut out Thora's mount for her and added them to the bunch belonging to the trail crew.

The sun was going down but the men still had time to ride out some of their mounts and get the bedsprings out of their backs. Each man cut out one of the horses, saddled it and then hopped aboard, hoping for the best.

What followed was a display of riding that would have drawn big crowds in the East. Here, it drew only sarcastic jeers and cheerful advice from the watchers.

The horses bucked, leapt, sunfished and tried to get rid of their riders; occasionally one was successful but the man got back to his feet and mounted again. To let a horse end a winner gave it bad habits and encouraged it to try again.

'Ketch my saddle!' Billy Jack went off his horse and howled the time-honoured cry as he lit on the ground.

It was Dusty who obliged by returning the doleful one's saddle along with the ranch horse. 'You resting already?' he asked.

'Why sure, likewise wondering when we're going to see the trail boss ride any of his string.'

Dusty laughed, tossed Billy Jack the reins and then rode to the remuda to cut out one of his string. He took the conceit out of the horse in chunks and then went on to do the same with the others.

The trail hands were correct in their guess; Dusty had taken the rough string, every horse here was a fighter as well as a trained cowhorse. The hands also had their views confirmed; Captain Fog was the best horseman of them all and he would have little or no trouble with his mounts.

The night was coming in fast when Dusty rode the last of his string to the side of the two chuckwagons and looked down at the cook and his fat, cheerful young louse.

Salt was unaware that he was being watched and proudly displayed a five-gallon wooden keg to his lousse. 'This here's the best danged sourdough keg you'll ever see,' he said proudly. 'You kin sleep with it tonight and make sure you take care of it.'

Hobie accepted the keg reverently, for he knew the value the trail crew would set in it. The sourdough keg was the most important item the chuckwagon carried and was Salt's most treasured possession. In the keg was fermenting dough, ready for bread—or biscuit-making; it took time to prepare and without it the crew would be on short rations.

Wrapping the keg in blankets, Hobie asked, 'When you going to let me make up a keg of my own?'

'Happen you're careful and l'arn well, in about ten, fifteen years.' Salt answered, then looked up. 'Howdy, Cap'n.'

'You pair all ready to roll first thing tomorrow?'

'Allus ready,' Salt replied. 'And, comes Dodge, we'll slap ole Sam Snenton's brand on this here ole keg.'

'Happen you haven't poisoned us all before that,' Dusty scoffed. 'You keep them fool knobheads back where they belong and don't crowd the remuda. Iffen you don't, I'll likely slap my brand somewhere and it won't be on a keg.'

Before Salt could think up any reply to either suggestion that he would let his mules get too close to the remuda, or that he might poison the crew, Dusty had turned the horse and headed for the remuda.

The two wranglers watched the trail boss come up and

Dusty pointed towards the stream behind the ranch house. 'Hold them down here tonight,' he ordered as he stripped off the saddle, then turned the horses in with the others. 'Keep my paint and Mark's blood bay away from the others.'

'Yes, sah, Cap'n.' Tarbrush rolled his eyes and waved his hand towards the Kid's big white as it grazed away from the others. 'I surely hopes Massa Kid ain't going to put his hoss in with the rest of the remuda.'

'He isn't.' Dusty could see that his night-hawk had a keen eye for the character of a horse. 'He'll stay clear—and Jackie, don't you ever try and touch that white, happen you want to keep both arms.'

'Boy,' Tarbrush waited until Dusty strolled away with his saddle slung over his shoulder, 'them is the truest word you'll ever hear. That hoss there looks meaner than two starving devil-cats.'

Ben and Thora entertained the three young Texans at the house that night. After the meal was over, they sat in the dining-room and talked. Thora brought in coffee for the men and stopped as she heard them discussing the happenings of the day. She came in as they were mentioning the man who had tried to get taken on as wrangler.

'Wisht Billy Jack'd spoken sooner about him being a Kliddoe man,' the Kid said mildly. 'I'd have spoken loving words with him.'

Thora frowned; she didn't want to let them get thinking about the man again, so she asked, 'How does Kliddoe work?'

'Ole Yellerdawg?' The Kid sniffed. 'He takes head tax on the herd.'

'Head tax?'

'Sure, it's an old game,' Mark explained. 'Came out when the first drives went north after the war. He used to come on the herd backed by fifty or so men and claim he'd been sent out by the Governor to take head tax on the herds. He had a real legal-looking bit of paper and his men backed it up. It worked for a spell—either the drives paid off or they fought and they were outnumbered. Then Stone Hart and his Wedge crew called his bluff, that was over Abilene way. They drove over the Kliddoe bunch and got through. Kliddoe went into hiding after that, the Governor came out flat-footed and said he wasn't aware that Kliddoe worked for him. Wall, we got word that Kliddoe started after your drive last year, but he ran into bad luck. Shangai Pierce's scout found where they were at and, when Kliddoe tried to take the herd, they had him whipsawed. Kliddoe and some of his men got clear. Shangai and his boys gave the rest a coat of molasses and feathers and turned them adrift. They missed Kliddoe though—he got clear.'

'Trust ole Yellerdawg!' The Kid sneered. 'Regular ole Yankee hero, him. Real loyal blue-belly.'

All eyes went to the dark youngster, Ben and Thora wondering at the vicious hardness in his voice. Thora wondered where the Ysabel Kid had known the Yankee leader, Jethro Kliddoe. 'Do you know him?' she asked.

'Never met him. Came across a real good friend of his in the war though.'

'What happened?' Thora had asked before she realised that she had gone beyond the bounds of frontier friendliness.

'He died happy, I guess.' The Kid rolled a smoke as he replied. 'One day I'm going to meet ole Yellerdawg—and, when I do I'll make him wish his maw never met his pappy the one time she did!'

Dusty and Mark remembered other times when the name of Kliddoe had been mentioned. Every time that same alum-bitter snarl had come into their pard's tones, although he had never told them why he hated Kliddoe.

'Reckon we'd best turn in,' Dusty remarked. 'You'd best get some sleep, Cousin Thora, likely you'll be needing.'

'What time will we be leaving tomorrow?' she inquired as the three Texans rose.

'Soon after sunup as we can,' Dusty replied. 'See you in the morning.'

The rest of the trail crew were in their bedrolls already; they were getting a good night's sleep for what might be the last time until the drive was over.

Dusty, Mark and the Kid spread their rolls away from the others—not through any sense of superiority, but because they didn't want to disturb the rest. Dusty looked around the area, then snapped the clips of his tarp and went to sleep.

The Ysabel Kid woke. There was no half-waking-half-sleeping period for him, just a swift transition from sleep to full alertness. He didn't move, just lay still waiting to locate the sound that had wakened him. It wasn't the distant sound of the night-hawk riding his rounds; that sound had never stopped and hadn't wakened him. It wasn't the stamping and movement of the trail crews' night horses. Slowly he emerged from his bedroll, his old Dragoon in his right hand. The sound which had wakened him came from the dark bulk of the two waggons and it was towards these he made his way. The rest of the crew were still all asleep around the dying embers of their fire.

The few seconds delay caused the Kid to curse himself several times in the next few hours.

From the chuckwagon sounded a muffled yell, then a thud. Dark shapes moved from the rear of the wagon. The Kid wasted no time; he darted forward and barked, 'Hold it!'

There were three shapes. Leaping from the wagon, they ran into the blackness towards a smaller, darker shape—either a buggy or a buckboard, the Kid guessed. One of the men threw something into the back of the wagon and then leapt aboard. The other two grabbed horses and all set off away fast.

The old Dragoon boomed in the darkness, flame lancing from the muzzle. He knew he had missed and raced to the side of the wagon; but he was too late to get in another shot.

Men yelled and shouted and the camp was awake. Dusty was the first man to join the Kid. 'What the hell, Lon?'

A groan from the back of the wagon stopped any reply. Dusty and the Kid went to the tailboard and Dusty lit a match. Hobie lay on the bed of the wagon, blood running from a gash in his scalp. The blankets were all thrown about and, in the last instant before Dusty had to throw the spent match to one side, he saw what was missing.

The small Texan cursed savagely. The sourdough keg was gone.

CHAPTER FIVE

MR. TOON LEARNS A LESSON

DUSTY took in the sight and made his decision right away. Even as the other men gathered round, asking questions and yelling for lights, he snapped, 'Lon, Kiowa, get it back.'

Neither man wasted time in obeying this casually given order to do the almost impossible. Kiowa didn't even know what was missing, but he didn't wait to ask about it. Indian smart, he had his night horse staked near to hand, saddled, and only needing the girths drawing tight. He ran for the horse even as the Kid's shrill whistle shattered the night and brought the big white horse running to him.

Mark came up. He tossed the Kid his gunbelt and then stood back, holding the rifle. He knew that in a delicate matter of this nature Mr. O. F. Winchester's ·44 brainchild was of as much use as old Colonel Sam's heavyweight thumbuster, or Mr. James Black's razor-edged bowie knife.

Salt was by the chuckwagon. He howled in fury when he saw that his precious keg was gone. Running to where the night horses were tethered he grabbed one without asking who might own it. Tightening the girths, he swung into the saddle and headed for the wagon to get his old Sharp's carbine . . .

The Kid was afork his white without bothering with such refinements as saddle or bridle. He thrust the Dragoon into his waistband and strapped on the belt, then holstered the revolver and caught the rifle Mark tossed to him. Then he and Kiowa lit out into the night.

Salt tore by the crew, waving his rifle and yelling, 'I'll get 'em.'

'They're on our side,' Mark called after him.

The rest of the trail crew whooped their approval, even Basin Jones who owned the horse Salt had taken. Dusty turned to the men and gave his orders: 'Fix young Hobie's head, Dude,' he snapped. 'Rest of you get back to sleep.'

Thora came up wearing a long house coat and Indian moccasins on her feet. 'What happened?' she asked.

'Somebody stole the sourdough keg.'

Thora felt like sobbing; this was the final blow. To get so

near to starting the herd and then to find that they would be delayed until Salt could make up another keg seemed like the height of injustice to her. She was near to tears as she said, 'Then we can't start tomorrow.'

Dusty looked off into the darkness to where, growing fainter all the time, he could hear the sound of horses running. 'We'll pull out at dawn just like we said we would. Somebody thought they could slow us down by taking the keg. They were wrong.'

'But we can't manage without it?' Thora objected, having heard how important the keg was.

'We'll have to,' Dusty replied. 'Besides I sent Lon and Kiowa after the men who took it. Likely they'll get it back, happen old Salt don't get too much in their way.'

'Salt?'

'Sure. He lit out of here afork old Basin's night hoss like the devil after a yearling.' Dusty turned to where, by the light of a lantern, Dude was attending to the cook's louse. 'How is he?'

'Reckon he'll live,' Dude answered. 'Who'd you reckon did it?'

'I'm reckoning, not saying.' Dusty grinned at Thora as he replied. 'Know one thing though. Happen Lon and Kiowa find them, they'll surely wish they'd never done it at all.'

'But they can't find the men in the dark,' Thora put in.

The same sentiments were being expressed about a mile from the ranch, where Salt finally caught up with the other two, who had stopped their horses and were seated silently. 'Can we find them?' Salt growled.

'Yeah, Kid,' Kiowa sounded dubious, 'my Grandpappy's kin were fair hands at reading sign, but they never tried it at night.'

'Kiowas never was wuth a cuss at reading sign day or night,' the Kid jeered back. 'But us Comanches are some different. Anyways I'm not trying to read sign, I'm letting this ole Nigger hoss of mine do it.'

'Dangnab it, if I ain't see-rounded by Injun varmints,' Salt cursed. 'Get to it, damn ye, or do you want to take time out to get your warpaint on. That there keg's too dang good to be taken by any robbing skunk.'

The Ysabel Kid allowed his big white to follow the sounds which were too faint for even him or Kiowa to locate. He rode at the head of the party, sitting the horse alert and ready for instant action. The other two followed, confident that the big white stallion would not only locate the men they were after, but would also steer them clear of any ambush.

The time passed slowly, and the men rode on, only Salt being aware of the direction in which they were travelling. He began to mumble out curses as he became more sure of the direction they were taking.

The Kid and Kiowa ignored him for a time. Then, drawing their horses to a halt, they studied the cook. 'What're you on at now?' the Kid finally asked.

'Toon's spread's down thisways. It must have been him that took the keg.'

'Me, I figgered it was Santanta,' Kiowa scoffed.

'Naw, I reckoned it was ole Dingus James'd come up from Clay County just especial, that fool keg being so valuable,' the Kid put in.

Salt spluttered in silent fury, the entire conversation having been carried out in whispers. He swore by several sacred objects that two certain Injuns would suffer for those insults to his beloved keg when they got back to the spread.

The ranch house loomed black against the surrounding darkness, a single small light showing that folk were out and about. Off from the ranch house, some half a mile away, was another larger, darker mass.

'That's real lucky,' the Kid remarked, 'he's holding his herd right close up.'

They rode their horses nearer to the ranch, keeping to a steady walk and making as little noise as possible. The Kid halted and allowed the other two to come alongside him. The door of the house opened and a man came out, going to the buggy and the two horses which could be seen outside.

'Get's on Injun style,' Kiowa remarked as the man mounted one of the horses and headed off into the darkness.

Salt too had noted the right-hand mounting of the horse and decided that a half-bred gentleman called Dan Twofeathers had best start looking for a new home real soon.

The door closed again and only the light in the window showed that Thad Toon was still not abed as befitting a man with work to do the following morning.

'Le's go down'n get 'em,' Salt growled.

'That's real smart,' the Kid scoffed. 'And, afore we gets in there, they could likely bust up that fool keg and throw it on the stove.'

'Holding their herd over thatways, we could happen——' Kiowa began.

'Yeah.' The Kid had an idea; it was audacious, but, given some luck, it might work. He went on speaking rapidly, but Salt couldn't understand a word.

The two horses started forward again and Salt spat out an angry curse as he realised he didn't know what was happening, 'Hey, you danged Injuns. What you fixing to do?'

The Ysabel Kid stopped his horse and twisted round, then lifted his hand in a mocking peace sign. 'Stay right here, white brother. Keepum bad paleface inside stone wickiup.' He paused and a wicked grin played around his lips. 'Happen you can hit the house from up here with that rusted-up ole Beecher's Bible.'

Looking down at his highly prized Sharp's carbine, Salt prepared to defend its virtues. Before he could open his mouth the other two had faded into the blackness.

Sim Hogan of the Double T liked to ride night-herd; it gave him a chance to whistle without anyone asking him to stop. He was a keen and ardent whistler, though there were certain members of the Double T crew who, with no appreciation for the arts, insisted that he was out of tune most of the time. Out here, riding along one half of the sleeping herd, he could whistle to his heart's content—for the cattle never complained and he didn't go near enough to his pard, Kenny, to hear his views.

Halfway along the line of Sim's patrol stood an old cottonwood tree, a very useful growth and one he much approved of. A man could ride behind the thick old trunk and, hidden from the herd, light up a smoke without risking scaring the cattle and starting a stampede.

Thinking about the use of the tree reminded Sim that it was some time since last he had a smoke. Turning his horse's head towards the tree, he steered it under the thick branches and stopped the movement. Sim bent forward and took out his makings. He had just started to roll a smoke when, from the branch above, something lashed down and thudded on to his head. Sim slipped sideways from his saddle and fell to the ground without a sound. Before the cowhand hit the earth a dark shape dropped into the saddle of the startled horse. Strong hands gripped the reins and a soft, soothing voice stopped it from spooking.

Riding the other flank of the herd, Kenny saw a horse coming towards him. Thinking Sim wanted to talk, the cowhand rode to meet him, noting idly that the whistling was in tune at last. He grinned, then the grin froze on his face as he got an uneasy feeling all was not well here. The proof of his feeling became more clear to him as the other man rode towards him.

Sim might have learned, in a sudden and miraculous way, to whistle in tune; but he would hardly have changed his riding style to do it. Even if he had changed the way he sat a horse, he couldn't have changed his clothing in the short time he was behind the tree.

Kenny's hand dropped to his hip. He spoke softly, 'Sim?'

'Guess again!' The soft drawled reply was backed by a sound, the sound a Colt made when it came back to full cock.

The rider was close enough in now for Kenny to see that he was a tall, young man dressed all in black. In the stranger's hand, as Kenny had rightly guessed, was a Colt. The Double T cowhand had little but contempt for old Colonel Sam's second Hartford Dragoon model revolver, considering it both overheavy and out of date. This contempt did not extend to open criticism when one was lined on his belly at hardly any range at all.

'What the——?' he began.

'Silence is golden, friend,' the stranger replied. 'We wouldn't want to go and wake up all them poor li'l ole cows, now would we?'

Before Kenny could make any reply the stranger gave a low whistle and a riderless white horse came out of the darkness, followed by a tall man riding a big buckskin. A man Kenny thought he recognised. A man who apparently could see better than the Double T man in the dark.

'Howdy, Kenny boy.' It was the voice of Kiowa all right. 'What now, Kid?'

It took Kenny a moment to realise that it was the dark boy on Sim's horse Kiowa was addressing.

'Take his gun,' the Kid replied.

Kenny suffered this indignity without argument; he did not know who the dark man called Kid was, but he did know Kiowa. They had once ridden for the same brand and Kenny knew better than to fool with the dark, dangerous man called Kiowa. He noticed that although Kiowa had a rifle in his saddleboot, he also carried a second—and wondered why all the armament? He saw when the other man changed from Sim's mount to the big white, Kiowa tossed the rifle to him.

'Never knowed you was a rustler, Kiowa,' he remarked as the other man striped the caps from the nipples of his gun, then dropped it back into his holster.

'Just l'arning from the Kid here. We'll head back and pick up your bunkie.'

Kenny stiffened as the import of the words hit him. His voice was brittle and angry, 'Is Sim dead?' he asked.

'Have a lump on his head come morning,' the Ysabel Kid replied. 'I don't reckon he'll take much hurt, but it evens us for our louse.'

By the time they reached the tree, Kenny had learned about the raid and the stealing of Rocking H's sourdough keg. As a loyal member of the Double T, he was both amused and delighted at the ingenious way his boss had attempted to slow down the Rocking H trail-herd. Then the amusement and pleasure died off as he thought of what would have happened if any of the other spread's crew had been killed in the attempt. Kenny knew from experience of what Kiowa would have done; he didn't think the other man would have been any less easy in extracting his revenge.

'What you fixing in to do with us?' he asked.

'Waal now,' the Kid answered, 'we just happens to want you to take a message in to your boss.'

Inside Toon's room at the ranch the light was still on. The keg and a full bottle of whisky stood side by side on the table. Toon was at peace with the world and he grinned at his foreman as he poured out two large drinks. 'That went off real neat, Joel.'

'Yeah, but comes daylight the Ysabel Kid and some of the others'll be reading sign and coming out here.'

'We can handle them.' There was confidence in Toon's tones. 'The boys'll fight if they have to. Rocking H can't prove we took their keg and I sent into Granite for the law. Telled Dan Twofeathers to tell the town marshal to get out here and lend a hand. Rocking H'll be on my land and he'll have to turn them off. If they gets here before the law, we'll bust their keg and burn it.'

Hendley relaxed. He looked the keg over and slapped it with a hard hand. 'Say, let's us hide this keg out until they've gone. Then we can take it north with us and leave it at Sam Snenton's place. The Rocking H won't never dare show their faces in Dodge again.'

Toon whooped in delight as he saw what would happen. The Rocking H would be the laughing stock of the range country, the crew who had lost their sourdough keg. Ben Holland would never hear the end of it.

'Yeah,' he agreed. 'We'll do just that. It'll even us some with Ben Holland and his crew.'

'Kid might not be able to trail us.' Hendley's optimism rose as he drained down the drink. 'The wind gets up come dawn. it'll blow the sign right off.'

'Yeah.' The optimism was contagious and Toon sat back with a happy beam on his face. 'Rocking H, the crew that lost their sourdough keg!'

The rosy dreams were shattered as the door was thrown open and Kenny came in, half dragging, half carrying his pard from the night-herd.

Toon watched Kenny lay his pard on the floor and straighten up, then yelled, 'Kenny, what the hell are you doing here, away from the herd?'

The reply came from a different source, not from Kenny. It came from the darkness outside in the sound of a wild yell.

'Hi, Toon! Hey, Toon! You've got our keg in there, we've got your herd out here. Do we trade?'

Toon and Hendley stared at each other as if they couldn't believe the evidence of their ears. Then Toon growled, 'Kenny, get into the bunkhouse'n——'

'Happen there's any evil designs in there,' the voice went on, 'we got Brother Kiowa out here lined on the hawgpen door, right ready 'n' willing to ventilate any gent who shows his fool head. Out front, ole Pastor Ballew's got him a right true bead on the door with his rusted up ole Sharps.'

'Leave us also remember them poor, dear, lil ole cows,'

Kiowa's voice came to them from the rear of the building, 'which same're like to be up and headed to hell and gone comes shooting and you getting out of your house.'

Toon and his men knew this, even without Kiowa's friendly reminder. Like Kiowa said, come shooting the herd would be up and running. Even if it wasn't, Kiowa or one of the others could slip away whilst the remainder pinned down the ranch crew, it would only need one man to scatter the herd. Rocking He might be delayed by the loss of their keg, but not as much as the Double T would be. That herd would be scattered and would take some finding. It would call for another, complete round-up to gather them in again and cut the road-branded stock from the other cattle.

Crossing to the window, Toon looked out. It was still some time to dawn and, in the blackness, he could see nothing of the men who were laying up out there. 'How do we know you won't scatter the herd when I've sent the keg out?'

'You don't,' the comforting reply came back promptly enough. 'But you don't have any choice. Time you fight your way out, there won't be any herd left.'

'He's right, damn him!' Hendley spat the words out bitterly, 'Even if the marshal gets here by dawn, they'll have scattered the herd.'

'Send it out, Toon.' Even at this range, they could tell there was a harder note in the Kid's voice. 'We're getting quick sick of waiting.'

'Send your ramrod out with it,' Kiowa's voice went on. 'I ain't stampeded a herd since the last time, and that's some too long.'

Toon stamped across the room, his face black with anger. He picked up the whisky bottle, and with a savage curse, smashed it on to the floor. Then he gripped the keg and for a wild moment, was tempted to smash it, or to empty it out. Sanity came back to him; he knew that the Rocking H men held the whiphand and that he had to give in. If he damaged, or emptied the keg, they would find out soon enough and the revenge would be small compared with the loss of his herd.

Hendley took the keg from the table, warning Kenny to keep the rest of the ranch crew quiet and not let them do anything foolish like shooting at the watchers. An idea was forming in his mind as he carried the keg to the door. Kenny opened the door and allowed the foreman to go out. He was told to shut it again and keep it shut.

It was dark now, darker than it had been all the night, as Hendley stepped off the porch and stood allowing his eyes to become accustomed to the darkness.

A man came towards him, a dark shape emerging from the black of the night; Hendley was pleased to see it was old Salt Ballew, not either the Ysabel Kid or Kiowa. The half-formed plan was far safer now. All Hendley had to do was wait until the cook came close, then drop the keg and grab him. With the Kid, or Kiowa, that would have been deadly dangerous; but even though Salt was a tough handful, he would be easier meat.

Grinning, Hendley moved forward to meet Salt. He would show the Rocking H how the game should be played. They might be smart and have the best cards; but, shortly, they were going to lose their ace in the hole and be left sat with a dead hand.

Something touched Hendley's back, something with a sharp point. A soft voice said, 'Far enough, friend. Set her down.'

Hendley almost dropped the keg, his startled gasp bursting out unchecked. He let the keg fall to the ground and then stood very still. That thing sticking in his back might only be a sharpened bit of whittling wood, *might* be. It might also be, and was, eleven and a half inches of razor-sharp steel from Mr. James Black's Arkansas forge. It was the Ysabel Kid's bowie knife and held in a position just handy to remove his kidneys if he even blinked too hard.

Salt came up and bent over the keg. He rasped a match on his pants and, in the glare, looked it over with loving care. Hendley gulped and offered a silent prayer that his orders regarding no shooting were obeyed without question. He knew that, if anyone shot at Salt, his own life was due to come to a painful and messy end. Joel Hendley was brave enough in the face of gunmen, but that wasn't a gun in his back. The thought of the knife going home unnerved him.

'She all right, Salt?' the Kid inquired.

'She be,' Salt sounded grim. 'But if she hadn't been I'd've surely killed you in inches, Joel Hendley.'

'Back off, Salt,' the Ysabel Kid warned. 'And take that danged fool keg along with you. We'll be long gone afore they can get after us.'

Salt grabbed the keg and departed fast. Hendley watched the cook go, then heard a fresh sound. It was the noise of a horse retreating into the night. Soon after, there was another commotion down by the corral. Once more, hoof-beats sounded. This time, of many horses. Hendley cursed under his breath as he realised what was happening. The remuda was being driven off into the open range.

'Left you two tied, for the night-herd,' the Kid explained. 'Rest won't scatter that far, I reckon.'

'Reckon so. Thanks for the two.'

'That's all right,' the Kid answered as he lifted Hendley's gun from its holster and tossed it to one side, 'Dusty'd want it that way. Who war it hit our cook's louse?'

'The breed.' Hendley was wondering if there was any chance of taking the Kid by surprise. The knife moved from his back and he stiffened just a little, ready to try and make a move.

'Yield not to evil temptations, brother,' that soft voice warned. 'It'd only get you hurt real bad. She's still out ready.'

Hendley relaxed again. His only hope was to stall for time and wait for a chance when the Kid came to take his departure. 'Your man hurt bad?' he inquired.

'Nope.'

'Good, the breed didn't have to hit him. I was for taking a quirt to Twofeathers, but we was in a hurry. Take it kind that you didn't hurt young Sim real bad.'

The Kid whistled shrilly, then replied, 'Had Hobie been hurt, we'd have been some less friendly.'

Hooves thundered and a big white horse raced round the side of the house, travelling at a dead run. Hendley knew this was the chance he had been waiting for. He spun round ducking and flailing a looping blow which he hoped would catch the young man. His fist hit only empty air and the force of his blow staggered him off balance.

The Kid stood, not just behind, but some distance back. He had been as keenly aware of the danger at the time of his departure as had Hendley, and to avert it moved back silently. He looked down with a mocking smile and drawled 'You been learning from beginners, friend.'

Saying this he whirled and ran forward, caught the mane of the big white and vaulted aboard, sheathed his knife and sent his mount racing away into the night.

Hendley dived for his gun and caught it up. He came up to one knee and lined it, easing back the hammer. Then he shook his head, lowered the hammer again and rose, shoving the gun back into leather. ''Twouldn't be right, not after they left us two horses for the night-herd.'

Toon, Kenny and some more of the crew came out of the house as they heard the sound of the horse. They listened as Hendley, with many a lurid curse, told of how the Ysabel Kid had handled the entire business. They cursed the black-dressed, baby-faced rider from the Rio Grande, but there was admiration for a master in their curses.

'Get the crew out,' Toon howled at the end. 'We'll take out after them and get the——'

'Get nothing, we *won't*,' Hendley contradicted. 'For one thing, there ain't but two horses left—and them for the night-herd. For another, and more important, them's the Ysabel Kid and Kiowa out there. The man who goes after that pair in the dark's asking for more trouble than plenty, and then some.'

Kenny nodded his sage agreement. 'Was I a praying man, I'd say Amen to that.'

CHAPTER SIX

POINT THEM OUT

'AREN'T they back yet?' Disappointment tinged Thora's voice as she stood on the ranch-house porch in the cold pre-dawn light.

Out front all was activity, Hobie and the Rocking H's temporary cook had been up some time and the rest of the trail-drive crew had been turned out to get a hot meal. Dusty, with a plate loaded with ham and eggs, answered Thora's query; 'Nope, but the crew have to be fed so we can make a start.'

'A start?' Thora stared at her trail boss. 'We can't start without Salt. Hobie can't handle the wagons *and* the cooking.'

'Then he'd surely best learn, and fast.' Dusty replied, 'Tarbrush can handle the bedwgon today and, afore we need food, Salt'll likely be back.'

'But what if they can't get the sourdough keg back?'

'Salt'll have to throw up another as fast as he can.'

Mark came up carrying two plates; he handed one to Thora and they entered the house to sit down at the table. Ben Holland was all ready in the room and he greeted them. It never occurred to him that the Ysabel Kid and Kiowa might fail to get the keg back. He watched the worried lines on his wife's face and smiled, 'You get fed, honey. There won't be another chance before night.'

Thora sat down and started to eat. Through the window she watched the wranglers bringing the remuda in and realised something. 'Tarbrush has been out all night. He can't drive the wagon all day.'

'Reckon he'll just have to get used to it,' Dusty replied as he started to eat his breakfast.

The meal was over and the two Texans pushed back their chairs. Dusty held out his hand to Ben. 'See you down the trail, Cousin Ben.'

After Dusty and Mark had left the room Ben pulled Thora's head down and kissed her. 'Now don't you get to worrying. You'll be all right, Dusty will get you through.'

Dusty and Mark stood watching the other men as they collected their horses from the cable corral which had been set up, using four sticks as supports. The wranglers were having no trouble with the remuda due to the time taken the previous night.

Each cowhand came up carrying his rope and looking for one of his mounts to pass by. Then the hand brought his rope up with one quick twirl in front, then up towards the right and overhead, and sent the loop out to turn flat and drop over the head of the chosen horse. This throw, the 'hooley-ann' was always used for catching horses in a corral. It was the best throw for the purpose, for the loop went right out, small and accurate, and dropped over the horse's head with the minimum of fuss. Using the 'holley-ann' throw several men could all be roping at the same time without unduly exciting the rest of the remuda.

Dusty took his big paint for first horse. The stallion and Mark's blood bay had come in separate from, but following, the remuda and ran to their masters without needing roping. Dusty saddled his horse and then, as Tarbrush rode by on his mule, yelled for him to take the bedwagon.

'How's the remuda?' Mark inquired.

'Handled wuss,' the Negro replied cheerfully. 'You all done got a big ole claybank that don't like us none at all.'

Mark and Dusty could feel some sympathy for the Negro; both knew they wouldn't take to riding night-hawk. Tarbrush would spend the night riding herd on the remuda and try to get what sleep he could in the back of the bedwagon as it bounced along behind the herd.

Today he wouldn't even get that chance, unless Salt came back in time to let him.

Dusty swung into his low-horned, double-girthed Texas rig and sat watching Mark leading the hands out to the herd. Turning in his saddle, he saw Thora had one of her horses and was mounting it. The horse bounced a few bedsprings out of its system without giving her any trouble, and she rode to join him.

'Ready to go?' Dusty asked.

'Yes, as soon as you are. How do we do it?'

'Just get round them and point them in the right direction. I can show you better than tell it.'

They rode after the crew, side by side. Thora gave Dusty a warning, 'You'll have to expect a lot of questions from me. By the time I get back to Texas, I want to know all about trail-drive work.'

'You'll likely know,' Dusty drawled. 'But the first thing you have to learn is that we don't drive the cattle—or won't after we get them off their home range. After today all we'll have to do is keep them pointed the way we want them to go and let them amble along, grazing as they go. The hands'll only need to keep the herd moving, stop them from straying, keep strays from joining the herd. Keep the stock from getting too bunched, or too scattered. That's all there's to it.'

Thora laughed; Dusty made it sound all too easy. She waited for him to tell her more, but they were in sight of the herd and there was no more time to waste on idle chatter.

The cattle were just beginning to stir from their night's rest and the trail hands sat their horses ready.

Thora watched Dusty. The small man halted his big paint

and then took off his hat to wave it.

'Head 'em up!' he yelled. 'Point 'em north.'

At the order, all the hands started their horses towards the herd. Shrill yells came from the men as they urged their mounts towards the cattle. Steer after steer came up and started to move, milling and circling. Then a big red beast slammed through the others, horns swinging, and bowling lesser creatures from the way. He was watched with keen and knowing eyes. Mark and Billy Jack moved in on either side of the big red steer and headed him towards the north. This would be the lead steer, the others would follow him and, if he was able, he'd keep his place all the way to Dodge.

The rest of the cattle were up as riders came at them. They started to move and any attempt at going in another direction was met by a fast-riding man with a swinging, stinging rope. The swing men moved into position as the cattle lined out, then the flank men dropped into place. At the rear the drag riders for the day, cursing in the rising dust, brought the rear up.

'Have to hold them bunched for a spell,' Dusty told Thora as he watched the herd start to move. 'Cattle aren't like humans—they don't cotton to leaving their home section and seeing what's over the next hill.'

To Thora, the scene below was one of confusion, but it was orderly confusion. The cowhands rode fast, twisting and whirling their horses like the masters they were.

Dusty turned his horse and headed off, leaving Thora watching. She rode towards the herd, wondering what she should do to help and afraid to try anything that made a nuisance of herself.

A steer broke from the line and cut off for the open range. There was no hand near and Thora felt her horse quiver. She shook the reins and allowed the trained cowhorse to get after the steer. Thora saw the horse knew what to do and sat back to allow it to work. Heading after the steer, her horse caught up alongside it, and then cut round to turn it back towards the herd. Thora urged the horse to a bit more speed. This was a mistake. She came alongside the steer and a pair of long, sharp horns lashed round at her.

Jerking her leg away from the lashing horn, Thora lashed out with her quirt at the steer's nose, landing hard on it.

Bellowing, the big animal turned and headed back for the safety of the herd.

Thora's first essay into cattle work had not gone unnoticed. The handsome young cowhand called Dude had been on the point of cutting out to fetch the steer in and had been an interested witness instead. He whirled his cowhorse by with a yell of, 'You'll make a hand, ma'am.'

Thora's face flushed red, she hadn't realised that she was being watched. She turned the horse to head along the line, and another broke out. Dude allowed it to go and she brought it back again. 'The next one's yours,' she called.

Dude waved a cheerful hand, he had been told by the trail boss to keep an eye on Thora, but could see that he didn't need. Thora was making a hand.

Dusty sat his paint and watched the herd moving. From a distance, he had watched Thora start work and was pleased with what he saw. Turning the paint, he headed back towards the ranch where the remuda waited.

Lil Jackie watched the trail boss approach and licked his lips nervously, waiting for his first orders. The horses of the remuda were restless, milling in the cable corral and waiting to be allowed to move out after the herd.

'Bring on the remuda, boy,' Dusty ordered. 'Let them go easy and don't let them get out of hand. If they do, and you can't hold them, light out for the herd as fast as you can and get one of the hands to help you turn them. Don't let them run into the drag; that could start a stampede!'

Dusty stayed watching the remuda for long enough to make sure his wrangler could handle the horses. Then he rode to the two wagons. Hobie was seated on the box of the chuckwagon, a bandage round his head but a cheerful look on his face.

'You ready to roll?'

'Sure thing, Cap'n. Want for me to move out?'

'Nope, sit here until fall.' Dusty watched some of the Rocking H hands coiling the cable.

The two wagons started forward as soon as the cable was inside the bedwagon. Tarbrush sat on the box of the second and relaxed, he was a fair judge of horse-flesh, and also of mules. From all the signs, he could have gone to sleep and this team would follow the chuckwagon. That was the way they had been trained, the way Salt had them trained.

Dusty whirled the big paint and rode back towards the herd. He passed the remuda and gave Little Jackie a friendly wave. Then he was up with the drag men.

The hands were still holding the herd tightly bunched and hazing them along. This was only necessary on the first few miles; after that, they could allow the cattle to scatter more and let them feed as they moved. The odd steer still tried to break back out of the line, but the hands rode too fast for this to happen. Thora, her face smudged with dust, came alongside Dusty as he headed for the point. 'How's it going?' she asked.

'Fair. We'll likely have a couple of head left when we reach Dodge.'

They rode side by side until they reached the point where Mark and Billy Jack rode on either side of the big red steer. Mark turned as he heard the hooves.

'You fixing to run a trail count, Dusty?' Mark asked.

'Sure, soon as we get off the home range,' Dusty agreed.

'Trail count?' Thora inquired.

'Sure, we want to know how many we've got along.'

'Is that important—I mean, to know exactly how many we've got along with us.'

'Why sure, you know what they say about a trail boss?' Thora nodded in reply to Dusty's question and he went on; 'I don't want you to think I haven't done the right things.'

Thora smiled; it looked as if the Texans driving for her were starting to accept her as one of them. Looking back at the long line of moving cattle she remarked, 'We're making good time, aren't we?'

'Sure,' Mark agreed. 'But we won't drive them thisways again, not unless it's a real emergency. Likely make us fifteen miles today, then slow down to between ten and twelve. It won't hurt the cattle any to haze them like this today, they've been held down in the bottomlands and are fat and sassy. They'll be leg weary tonight, ready to bed down.'

'The ole red there looks like he'll make a lead steer, Mark,' Dusty put in.

'Sure, happen he stays on top there won't be much trouble from the others.'

Dusty pulled his horse off to one side, then sat back to watch the herd moving past. Thora joined him for there were a lot of questions she wanted to ask and this seemed like a good time to ask them. 'Won't we lose time if we stop to count the cattle?'

'Would *if* we stopped. But, as we don't, we won't.'

'Then how do you do it?'

'We'll show you, let you try your hand at it later.' Dusty suddenly stiffened slightly and looked around the range.

'What is it?' Thora had seen the languor fall off Dusty before and knew it meant trouble in the air.

'Nothing. I just got the feeling we were being watched.'

Thora looked around the rolling country; there was enough cover for any amount of watchers, but she could see nothing to disturb her. Neither could Dusty, but he had that instinct which came to men who rode dangerous trails.

They had covered three miles from the ranch by then and Dusty headed back along the line, making for the remuda. Others of the hands were taking a chance to go back and collect a fresh horse. Dusty watched the hands change mounts. Mark rode up afork the black which had caused the trouble at the rope corral. Halting Mark asked, 'Any sign of Lon?'

'Not yet. What do you reckon to the herd?'

'Ben picked out good stock. Happen we get the sourdough keg back we'll have most all we need.'

'Why, sure.' Dusty turned to scan the range again. 'You get the feeling we're being watched?'

'Had it myself,' Mark admitted. 'But I haven't seen anybody. When Lon gets here, you'd best have him light out and check.'

'I'll do just that,' Dusty agreed. 'Bet you a dollar they get it back for us.'

'Not me.' Mark had the same faith in their dark comrade. 'Happen he found him a pretty girl and stopped on to sing to her.'

Dusty saw three riders top a distant rim and, even at that distance, recognised them. 'Looks like her pappy done run him off with a shotgun.'

'Sure.' Mark would have liked to wait and hear the result of the Ysabel Kid's adventure, but he had work to do. 'I'd best get back to the point.'

Dusty headed back to meet the three riders. Passing the two wagons, he told them to halt. Salt was carrying the keg; Dusty could see that now, although he knew the three wouldn't have returned without it. He waited and speculated idly on how the recovery had been made.

'You took your time,' he growled as the men rode up.

'For them few kind words of praise and encouragement, sir, we surely thank you,' the Kid replied. 'It makes us feel real good to know we was missed and wanted.'

Kiowa grunted in sympathy and inquired as to their next duties. Salt held his keg and looked pleased with himself, but he didn't get a chance to speak.

'Take out for the rims ahead, Kiowa,' Dusty ordered. 'You fed?'

'Called in at the spread and took us a bait.' The Kid answered. 'Then come as fast as the oldster could make it.'

'Oldster?' Salt bellowed. 'Oldster! Why, you danged Injun, here's me done all the work and this is how I gets treated!'

'This's nothing on how Basin's going to treat you,' Dusty warned. 'He had to take a spare saddle after you lit out on his night horse, and he allows he's getting galled by it.'

Salt headed for the chuckwagon and Hobie climbed down. He looked relieved when he saw the keg and, after taking care of the cowhorse, went to take over the bedwagon. Tarbrush stretched and ambled round to climb in the back of the wagon and try to get some sleep.

The Kid and Kiowa changed horses at the remuda, then rode back to where Dusty was waiting for them. Thora came back at a dead gallop and brought her horse to a halt beside Dusty's. She looked at the Kid as he came riding up and asked. 'Did you get it?'

'No ma'am. Mr. Toon done killed all three of us.'

'You smell like it!' Thora couldn't have said a better thing if she had tried. The Kid was treating her as an equal and a member of the crew. Thora felt pleased that she had been able to think of and get out an answer at him.

The Kid told roughly what had happened at Toon's spread. Thora got a far more accurate version later from Salt Ballew. The way the Kid told it, he had spent most of the night holding the horses, while Kiowa and Salt did all the work.

She nodded her approval when she heard that the trio had left Double T horses for the night-herd and had not stampeded the herd. Toon might not be friendly, but he was a neighbour and had enough troubles without adding to them.

Dusty was also pleased with the way the affair had been handled, he knew there was far more to the story than his pard told. He also was pleased that the Double T herd had been left alone. Knowing the Ysabel Kid and Kiowa, he quite expected that when Mr. Toon went out to look for his herd he would be finding it scattered all over the range.

'Light back there and see if you find sign of anyone following us, Lon,' Dusty ordered, 'Kiowa, head out for the rims.'

Thora watched the two men head off to obey their orders, then asked: 'Couldn't you have let them get some rest before you put them out to work?'

Dusty grinned; the young woman had a whole lot to learn about the trail herd work and about trail hands. They wouldn't miss the night's sleep and would be very lucky if they reached Dodge without missing more than the one night in their bedrolls. Tarbrush was different; he would be out every night riding the remuda, and so he had to try and get his sleep in the daytime.

The Kid rode the horse of his Comanche relay back, paralleling the line of the herd. He rode slowly and watched the ground, checking every bit of sign as he came to it. Once his sign-wise eyes saw where a coyote had chased a jack rabbit, in another place a couple of antelope had grazed their way along. He saw other signs, but none of them had been made by human or horse.

On reaching the rim where they first caught sight of the herd, the Kid halted and stood up in the stirrups to look around. The range was still and, apart from the dust of the herd, there was no sign of life. He rode across the churned-up, hoof-scarred trail of the herd and, at a distance of fifty or so yards, started to ride parallel to it, headed back towards the herd.

After covering about half-a-mile the Kid came on proof that Dusty had been right. He found tracks of three horses where such tracks should not have been.

The Kid swung down and remembered just in time that he wasn't riding his big white. He held the reins of the Comanche war pony and bent to check the tracks. His first guess had been right; there were three horses here, but only one of them had been ridden.

The watcher had been up to no good, that was clear to the

Kid in a few minutes of tracking. A man didn't keep to cover all the time if his intentions were honourable. This man stuck to every bit of cover he could find.

The watcher had stopped his horse, then turned and ridden off at a tangent. The Ysabel Kid could read the reason for that. From here the man would get his first view of Kiowa, Salt and himself, and had pulled out rather than risk being caught.

Taking the trail and following it, the Kid rode slowly and cautiously along. He was as alert as the man who trained the war pony and no less savage. If he found the watcher somebody was going to get badly hurt.

The tracks ended in a rocky-bottomed stream. The watcher was smart enough to figure that he might be followed, so had taken this simple but effective ruse to slow his trailer. It was no great trouble, though a long matter, to refind the tracks. The Ysabel Kid would be able to pick out the hoof-marks of the three horses among a hundred others. All he needed to do was ride in ever-increasing circles until he found the sign again.

That would take time, more time than the Kid could give at the moment—he had to report his findings to the trail boss.

Dusty heard the Kid's report and sat silent for a time, frowning as he tried to judge the implications. Like the Kid, he had all but forgotten the man with the three ghostcord-broke horses. There was no real reason to connect the two. Many men owned a three-horse string, or mount—as the Texans called it.

'Happen you or Kiowa's best watch the back trail real careful for a spell, Lon. It might be the scout for a bunch of rustlers.'

'Looks that ways. I don't figger on it being anyone from the Double T, they've had their belly full of us,' the Kid replied. 'Want for me to follow him all the way if he comes again?'

'Not if it'll keep you away from the herd for too long.' Dusty turned his paint and they rose towards the point. 'Take over from Mark for a spell while we make a trail-count.'

Thora joined them just in time to hear this. 'You weren't joshing me about counting the herd?'

'Nope.'

'But can they manage to count all these while the herd keeps moving?'

Dusty watched the Kid heading for the point at a better speed and turned back to the woman with a grin. 'They're surely going to try.'

CHAPTER SEVEN

TRAIL COUNT

THORA watched the Texans riding towards the point of the herd. She followed and saw Mark and Billy Jack leave their places to ride ahead some two hundred yards, then halt facing each other about fifty yards apart. Turning, she looked back along the long, winding line of cattle and shook her head. It didn't seem possible that any man could count all the animals as they walked by.

Spurring her horse forward, Thora passed the herd and headed to where Mark now sat his horse, leg hooked round the saddle-horn and relaxed. In his hands was a long length of cord. Billy Jack sat hunched in his kak, looking, if possible, more miserable than usual. He too held a length of cord, the end trailing down.

Dusty turned and yelled, 'Thin the line!'

The hands stopped crowding in on the herd. Slowly, the pace dropped and the cattle scattered until they were ambling along, grazing as they went. The trail crew still rode watchfully and were ready to handle any steer which showed a desire to head back to the Rocking H.

Watching the herd approach, Thora wondered if Dusty was having a joke at her expense. What she had seen so far of the trail boss made her doubt this. She waited to see if the count could be made with any degree of accuracy. One of the reasons she had wanted to come on this drive, one she hadn't mentioned to Dusty, Mark and the Kid—was that she meant to write a book about the trail-drive work. She had written one book, about her first year on the ranch, and it was bringing in useful money for her. This second book should do even better, for she knew how little the Eastern folks really knew about the skill needed to trail a herd of cattle.

She watched Dusty and the Kid bring the lead steer through the gap between the counters. Mark pointed to the red steer and said, 'One!'

Sitting his horse Mark continued to count and point as the cattle went by. At one hundred, he tied a quick knot in the cord, without taking his eyes from the herd, or losing count. Thora sat behind him, trying to make her own count; but she lost it and saw that trail-counting was far more skilled than she had imagined.

Mark counted on. At one thousand, he threw a loop instead of a knot in the cord and went on with his counting. He did not know that he was being watched and was oblivious of the fact that Thora had headed up the line again. All his attention was on the moving line of cattle. As segundo, Mark was eager for his count. It not only let him check how many head he was running, but also gave him a chance to see if any of the herd were lame, or showed signs of distress at the travelling.

The steers passed, each counted by Mark and Billy Jack as they went by. The segundo missed nothing; he picked out trouble-causers, nervous, sluggish cattle. In the early two thousands, he spotted a black steer with trouble in every inch of its body. There was a mean look about that steer, which would mean that he needed watching, or he'd stir up some bad trouble.

There were muleys in the herd, Mark noted. That was to be expected if not desired. A muley cow, one which had lost its horns, was not in any great favour on a trail drive. In fact a muley was always trouble. The hornless steer, amongst its horned brothers, was forced to the edge of the herd on the march and chased from its bedding place at night by any steer which felt ornery. If there were many muleys, they tended to bunch together for protection and baulk at the slightest excuse. Also the muleys tended to lose weight faster and feel the heat more than horned stock. Taken all in all, they were not what Mark wanted to see in his herd. One good thing about them was that they wouldn't last all that long.

Mark counted on, the swing men passed him, then the flank riders. The line of knots grew in the cord and the third loop was formed. Then the drag men, masked with their bandanas, to keep the rising dust out of their nostrils, passed by. Mark could always feel sympathy for the drag riders. He had ridden on the drag himself, and expected to do so again. Of all the duties of trail herding, the drag was the most onerous. The drag man rode in churned up dust, while the other hands were out in the fresh air. On some drives the drag men were poor-quality cowhands, who couldn't be trusted with any more exacting work. On this drive, there was no such disgrace. Every man, with the exception of Dusty, Mark, the Kid and Billy Jack, would take a turn at the drag.

The herd passed by. Mark totalled up his line of knots before turning his horse and heading along the line. On the other side of the herd, Billy Jack was also riding to make his report. Neither man took any notice of their friends' jeering comments on folks who had an easy life. The trail boss was waiting to hear the result of the count and a man didn't keep him waiting. Not twice anyway.

Dusty turned and saw the trail-counters coming, and waved a man up from the swing. He rode out and waited with Thora by his side. She was waiting to hear how close the count came to the number Ben had told her was in the herd.

Mark was the first to arrive. He lifted his hat to Thora with exaggerated politeness, then said: 'At an off-hand guess, I'd say three thousand, two hundred and thirteen.'

Billy Jack cut round in front of the herd and came back to the trail boss. He could not have heard what Mark said, of that Thora was certain. Her smile died as he drawled, 'Three thousand, two hundred and twelve.'

Thora looked startled, her eyes taking in each unsmiling face. Dusty nodded in agreement with the count. Ben had told him there had been a tally of three thousand, two hundred and thirteen. The Rocking H crew had not been idle to keep the herd at the correct figure. Dusty had been expecting that there would have been a few strays, or even a few odd cattle which had sneaked in to join the herd.

'Bet you missed than dun muley in the eight hundreds,' Mark told Billy Jack. 'He went by with two big steers on each side of him.'

'Saw him,' Billy Jack answered mournfully. 'Tell you where you went wrong. There was a zorilla in the two thousands; he busted back and got pushed in behind us. I bets you counted him twice.'

Before Thora could ask the questions which welled into her

head, the two men had returned to their places at the point. She turned her attention to Dusty. 'Did they really count the herd?' she asked. 'Or did you tell them the number just to have fun with me?'

'They did, and I didn't,' Dusty answered. He knew that many of the things cowhands did and regarded as ordinary, appeared wonderful to the eyes of a greener.

'Could they count any number of cattle that way?'

'Why, sure.'

'What was the biggest herd you ever saw counted?'

'Well now,' Dusty frowned as he thought back, 'reckon it was six thousand, seven hundred and sixy-one head. The first round-up we made at home after the War. That was the first herd we brought in.'

'Who counted it?'

'My cousin, Red Blaze.'

'Alone?'

Dusty looked uncomfortable, he seemed to be blushing under his tan, 'No, ma'am, I helped.'

Kiowa came riding back at a fast gallop and halted his horse by Dusty's.

'Water ahead there, Cap'n,' he growled. 'Aint but a lil bitty river, ain't but hardly swimming water.'

'Good.' Dusty was once more the self-assured trail-boss. 'We'll water the herd there, then push across. How about a bed ground?'

'Couple of good places over the other side. The Kid's headed out to make a pick.'

Thora turned. She had not noticed that the Kid had headed out as soon as he left the point. Even now she could see him crossing the river. 'Ben and the hands always talked about the trouble they could run into when they had to cross water.'

'Depends on the river. That one won't give us much trouble,' Dusty replied, then turned his attention to Kiowa: 'Take over the point, and tell Mark to come back here.'

Mark rode back and joined Dusty. 'River ahead, *amigo*,' he remarked. 'We'll be watering the herd there, I reckon.'

'Can't think of a better place. We'll thin the line down a mite, then try and bring them in in bunches. Many muleys along?'

'Fifteen at most, fair average for a herd this size.'

'What's wrong with muleys?' Thora asked. 'I heard Ben and Sam talking about them. Sam said you might find them some use.'

'They're trouble all the way,' Mark replied. 'See, cattle are some like humans. In every bunch there's a bully; and, being a bully, he likes to pick his man. That means the bully goes for a muley that can't fight back. When it happens at night, you get trouble. They stir the herd up and the night-herd has work on. Get it happening on a stormy night and you can end up with a stampede. So, as soon as we can, we eat the muleys.'

'Eat them?' Thora stared at the two young men.

'Sure.' Mark pointed back to the chuckwagon. 'Ole Salt isn't going to be able to head for town when he wants fresh meat, so he has to get it from the herd. He can either take good stock that'd likely get to Dodge and sell, or he can take him a muley that happen wouldn't make it anyway. 'Course that might not make sense to a real smart Yankee like you, but it surely does to a half-smart Texas boy like me.'

Thora sniffed disdainfully. She realised that Mark was joshing her and felt pleased; it proved the men liked her.

'At least, we won the war,' she pointed out.

'Sure,' Dusty agreed. 'By forging our money.'

'Well, if you were only half-smart and let us, that was your fault.'

Thora whirled her horse and headed along the line before either of the men could think of an answer to this jibe. Dusty whooped and slapped his big pard on the shoulder.

'That told us, *amigo,* Cousin Thora's making a hand.'

'She's making a *Texan,*' Mark corrected, paying her the greatest compliment he could think of.

Dusty and Mark headed back to the point of the drive. They were watching the water and calculating its distance from them. There were other factors to be watched at the same time. The wind was blowing across the herd and there was little or no chance of their winding the water. With the cattle in the present condition, that wouldn't be too dangerous; but, with a thirsty herd, it was.

The hands were tense and alert now, more than at any other time. Every man watched his opposite number, and also glanced ahead to see any signs Dusty might be giving. It was tricky business watering three thousand head of cattle. The herd first had to be moved just right, not too bunched or too scattered. When the leaders went down to water there must be no rush, or they would be pushed across before they drank their fill.

Dusty pulled out to one side of the herd and waved Thora to join him. They sat watching the hands working the herd. Thora could see from Dusty's relaxed gaze that that all was as he wanted it.

'Uncle Charlie Goodnight always told me that the two most important things in trailing cattle are grazing and watering, and watering the most important of all.'

Thora had not realised that Dusty was related to the old Texas trail-drive master, Colonel Charles Goodnight, although she had heard of the old-timer. Almost everything that was known about trail driving was part of his findings.

Dusty had served his apprenticeship with Goodnight in the early drives after the war. Three times, he had ridden with Goodnight, the first two as a hand, the last as segundo. It had been a hard school, but the finished product showed it had been well worth it.

Dusty watched the men headed back for the remuda to get fresh horses, and called to Dude: 'Stay back with the remuda for a piece. See that the button can handle it.'

Dude waved a cheerful agreement and headed on back to the remuda. Handling the horse herd was not the work for a skilled man, but Dude knew better than argue with his trail boss. He knew why Dusty wanted him back there. Little Jackie was fresh to this kind of work and might make a mistake. With a herd new to the trail, this could be dangerous. Little Jackie would get help, today; from then on, he would be on his own.

Every man got himself a fresh horse from the remuda; they all knew that a fresh animal could mean all the difference in the highly exacting and very difficult task of watering three thousand, or more, head of half-wild Texas cattle.

The cattle were still moving along at an easy walk, but the hands came in to cut the first three hundred or so from the rest and move them towards the gentle banks of the stream. The herd couldn't just be allowed to come down with a rush, as the first cattle would be forced over before they could get their fill. Each separate bunch had to be brought in upstream of the last batch, so they all got clean water.

The lead steer and the rest of the first bunch were brought down and slowly allowed to get to the water. The riders waited until their cattle had drunk their fill, then moved them across. Even as the leaders started to swim, the water from above came down muddy as the second group were brought in.

Thora rode with the men, allowing her horse to work the cattle and doing her share. She came up behind one of the hands just as he cut loose with a string Texas oaths hot enough to singe the hair of a bull buffalo. The hand stopped in mid-stride as he saw Thora was behind him; his face turned red and he headed his horse into the water again.

Thora realised that her presence might be an embarrassment to the men at such times. She knew that they cursed to relieve their feelings under the strain of working the cattle. To stop them cursing would not help their work any. She wondered how she could get around this problem and decided to ask Dusty to pass the word round that she——

A steer bellowed near at hand. She whirled round and saw the animal was down in the muddy water and floundering wildly. Jerking her rope from the horn, Thora headed into the water. She slipped out the noose and flipped it, from close range, over the head of the steer, then threw a quick dally round the saddlehorn. From then on the matter was taken out of her hands. The trained cowhorse she was riding turned and headed for dry land, hauling the steer behind him.

Thora watched the steer get to its feet on dry land and felt satisfied that she had helped it. The horse knew what to expect, which was more than she did. Bellowing, the steer was up; its head went down and it charged straight at its rescuer. Thora saw the long horns lashing up. Grabbing the saddlehorn, she hung on as her horse danced aside and slammed iron-shod hooves into the steer's ribs as it shot by.

Luckily for Thora her dally slipped and she saw her rope trailing off behind the steer, headed for the open range.

Dusty and Dude had witnessed everything and the trail boss shook his head to the hand's suggestion that he should go after the steer. 'No need for that,' Dusty remarked.

Thora went after the steer, caught it and turned it back towards the herd. Riding in close, she tried to get her rope free, but the steer avoided her. Her face flushed red with anger and she started in to call the errant animal everything she could lay tongue too. In her youth, as she had told Dusty, Thora had been raised in Army camps. Now the half-forgotten learnings of those early days poured from her lips.

Dude rode up and rescued her rope for her and, for the first time, she realised that several hands had been interested and amused listeners to her. They now were all regarding her with broad grins. Tossing her head back she made for the herd. One of the hands gave a wild yell and, whooping, the rest of the riders headed for the battle again. Without realising it, Thora had passed yet another test.

From that day on, the men cursed the cattle freely, whether she was there or not. They treated her as an equal while riding the herd. In camp, none of them would have thought of using anything stronger than a damn, and would have tromped any stranger who spoke out of turn; but with the cattle, Thora was one of them. They cursed freely and without embarrassment. So did Thora.

The herd was watered and moved across the stream and Little Jackie brought his remuda down. Tarbrush was awake and helping; he had come out before the first of the herd were brought down and Dude returned to work the cattle.

Last across came the two wagons. Salt knew the herd would be bedded down very soon and decided that he would make his camp on the banks of the stream. He wanted to have a meal ready for the first pair of night herders when they returned. Salt had plenty work to do, he had to prepare his camp and get the meal ready for the first men back. The hands had been in the saddle all day without food. If he was late in handing out the meal, Salt knew he would hear a few things about himself from the trail boss. He also guessed Captain Fog would do it real good.

Halting the wagon, Salt gave his orders to Hobie. They were to put the wagons in position to make a windbreak for the camp. Salt's two teams knew this as well as he did, and moved into place without fuss. Salt climbed down from his wagon and nodded in approval. The water would be clear soon and he would find plenty of dry wood to make a fire in the small *bosque* downstream. Near to hand were two trees which were far enough away from each other to be used as supports for a picket rope for the night horses.

'What now?' Hobie inquired as he climbed down to join his boss.

'Unhitch the teams, fix up the picket line, roust out the cable, start and collect me some firewood. Then, when I've got a fire going, you turn all the bedrolls out of the wagon. Then get some water. When you done that, I'll find you some work.'

The herd had been formed again after crossing the river and were moving on; but now Mark and Billy Jack crowded in on the lead steer and slowed him down.

Dusty rode out ahead of the herd and the Ysabel Kid joined him to point out the bedground he had chosen. The Kid's judgment in such matters was sound and Dusty saw no objection to the open stretch a half-mile or so ahead. The ground was clear and there were no trees around; the cattle would settle down here with no trouble.

'Make a circle, Lon,' Dusty ordered. 'Kiowa's headed out the other way. Don't let him shoot you in the leg.'

'Not me. I'm smart.'

The Kid whirled his horse and was gone before Dusty could answer this modest claim.

Dusty watched the Kid fade into the distance and knew that his pard would find any signs of undesirable company. The Ysabel Kid was also well capable of handling the said company with either his old Dragoon or his Winchester, if such handling proved to be necessary.

Turning, Dusty headed back for the herd and found that Mark was out on one flank, while Red Tolliver rode the point with Billy Jack. Mark sat his horse and watched the handling of the herd carefully. He had to ensure that the cattle were neither too bunched, nor too scattered, as they were brought towards the bedground.

Slowly, imperceptibly to a casual onlooker, the herd's pace dropped. The big red steer halted and behind him, the rest of the herd came to a stop. The hands started to ride in a circle around the cattle now, each man crooning out as he waited for the herd to settle down. Here and there a steer settled down on the ground and the others started to chew their cud.

Thora rode to join Dusty and Mark as they sat watching the hands circling the herd. Two hands rode from the herd, then made for the wagons by the stream.

'First night-herd,' Dusty remarked as he saw Thora watching them. 'They're headed back to get their food.'

'When do the rest of the hands get their food?'

'When the night-herd comes back.'

'Fair day's drive,' Mark put in. 'Allow we've made sixteen miles. But we won't make that distance again, not in one day.'

'Nope,' Dusty agreed, then pointed to the herd. 'See that black steer; he's the trouble-causer Mark was talking about.'

Thora watched the big black charge a muley and drive it from its bedding place. A passing hand eyed the black malevolently and snarled a curse at it. He halted his horse to wait for the cattle to settle down again, then resumed his riding.

'All right, black boy,' Mark drawled softly as he watched the steer snorting and moving restlessly. 'You keep on the way you're going, and ole Salt'll turn you into a stew come nightfall tomorrow.'

The hands carried on their riding around the herd as the sun went down and the night-herd came riding back. Then and only then did the men leave the herd and head back for the wagons and the food which awaited them.

Dusty warned the two night herders about the black steer and made a round of the herd with Thora, then headed for the flickering camp-fire by the river.

Tarbrush was holding the remuda down by the river and Mark had cut Thora a night horse ready. By the time she had changed her saddle, Thora felt hungry enough to eat the horse—Texas double-girthed rig and all. She left her night horse on the picket-line with the others and noticed that Dusty and Mark left their own horses standing away from the others, not even tied. The Ysabel Kid materialised as she was about to leave her horse; he had his big white and let the horse join the other two.

Mark pulled the chuckwagon tongue round until it lined on the North Star as Dusty and Thora came into camp. She watched and asked, 'What's the idea of that?'

'What we call following the tongue,' Mark replied. 'Line the wagon tongue on the North Star at night, and that gives us our direction for the next day's travel.'

The hands were all eating and Dude looked up as the Kid went to the table. 'Where you been all day, Kid?' he asked.

'Ain't seen hide nor hair of you.'

'Now that ain't right, Dude,' Basin Jones objected. 'You knows we saw him and Kiowa asleep under that bush.'

'That's right,' the Kid agreed. 'That's where we're some smarter than cowhands. They ride herd, we sleep.'

Thora went up; she had been warned not to try and eat her food off the bench at the back of the chuckwagon. This was the sole property of the cook and the privilege of eating off it was the highest compliment he could pay to any man. Not even the trail boss could eat from the bench; if he, or any man tried, he got told to move in impolite terms.

The plate of stew Salt handed her looked very good and was almost thick enough to be cut with a knife. She barely noticed this as she mopped up the food with unladylike speed. There were grins from the hands as she handed up her plate for a second helping.

'Ben won't know you, eating thatways, when you gets back to home, ma'am,' Red Tolliver remarked as the second plate disappeared. 'Ain't but Lil Jackie cleared away his plate as fast as you.'

'Yeah, and the language when that poor lil ole cow took off with her rope,' another man put in. 'It war fit to set a man to blushing.'

'Evil associations,' Thora replied, 'I was never like this before I met you bunch.'

The men finished their food and each dropped his plate into the bowl of water. Then each went to where the bedrolls were laying in a pile and sorted his own out. They went back and chose their places round the fire, each man noticing who was on either side of him. This was the order they would sleep in all the way to Dodge. The men would need to know who were their neighbours. This was so that when they came in to relieve the night-herd they could get the right men without waking up the rest of the camp.

'I spread your roll for you in the bedwagon, ma'am.'

Thora turned to find Hobie standing by her side. She dropped her plate and cup into the water bowl and went to the bedwagon. Inside, a lamp hung from the roof and she looked at her home until she got back to the Rocking H. There was some gear in the wagon, a couple of spare saddles, a keg of good enoughs—this was the name given to the assorted sizes of ready-made horse shoes which would be used in cases of emergency on the drive. The other gear consisted of oddments needed for the drive.

Near the gate of the wagon her bed was laid out ready for her. On the floor was a tarpaulin sheet which would serve instead of a mattress. On this were laid four blankets and three thick, quilt-like suggans. For a pillow she had her warbag, which contained her spare clothing for the drive.

Thora sighed, there wouldn't be much comfort for her on this trip, that was certain. She sat down on the hard bed of the wagon, then moved on to her bed. On an impulse she lay back, to test how comfortable it was, deciding to have a few moments' rest before she joined the men round the fire.

Half an hour later, Salt came round the back of the wagon, climbed in and covered her with the suggans. Then he put out the light and left her to sleep until roll-out the following morning.

The trail crew unrolled their bedrolls now. Each man had much the same—two or three blankets and a couple of the thick, quilt-like suggans, with a warbag for their pillow.

Billy Jack had his bed made up and he watched Mark unroll his tarp. The big segundo spread the seven by eighteen tarpaulin sheet out on the ground. The tarp had snaphooks down on side and eyes on the other. In wet weather it would be wrapped around the blankets, and if the sleeper was on reasonably well-drained ground, he would sleep dry even in the rain.

Tonight was fine and Mark spread a blanket on the tarp then lay the others ready to get into them. Billy Jack eyed the top suggan and remarked, 'That's a right smart suggan you got there, Mark. Don't recollect you having it when we rode for Colonel Charlie.'

Mark looked at the suggan with some pride. 'No, I didn't.'

Dude studied the material which had made up the suggan; it appeared to have been constructed from the remains of three gingham dresses, several highly coloured satin frocks and some less nameable items of female apparel.

'Man'd say you've got a tolerable heap of lady-friends—and some of them dressed a mite loud for ladies!'

'Got it up to Quiet Town while we were there,' Mark explained to Dude as the other men moved in closer. 'Miz

Schulze and Roxie Delue done made it for me while they were getting over the fight in Bearcat Annie's.'*

The trail drive hands had all heard of the great fight in Bearcat Annie's saloon in Quiet Town, Montana. Three townswomen had fought it out with the owner of the saloon and her girls to enable Dusty, Mark and the Kid to get into the saloon and take a gang of gunmen. From the look of the suggan it had been some fight.

The men yarned for a time about this and that, then rolled into the blankets. Dusty left the camp to check on the remuda and allow Tarbrush to come for a cup of coffee.

CHAPTER EIGHT

MR. ALLISON MEETS CAPTAIN FOG

THE herd moved on steadily to the north, following the tongue. For the first few days, Thora was so stiff and sore that she could hardly bear to move. She gritted her teeth and clung in the saddle all the long days, collapsing into her bedroll at night. The hands watched her dogged courage with admiration, and every one of them felt relieved when she at last got over the stiffness.

Across the rolling Texas plain the herd moved, covering ten or so miles a day. They crossed the forks of the Brazos, the Prairiedog Fork of the Red and carried on up the sparsely-settled lands of the Texas Panhandle. The herd became broken in to the trail, and there was no trouble. The trail crew were a closely knit and compact team. There had been little or no trouble with the cattle, and Thora was getting to be a good hand.

Sometimes the herd would be visited by riders, either cowhands or ranch-owners. All seemed to be surprised to see a herd so early in the season and most of them either knew, or had heard of Ben. They stopped for a meal if they came in at night, also staying the night if they wished. All offered their

* Told in *Quiet Town* by J. T. Edson.

best wishes and most were of the impression that the Rocking H crew would handle kliddoe and Wyatt Earp both.

Thora was a source of interest to the visitors; she didn't know how her crew regarded her as a good luck charm and proudly pointed her out to the visitors as the best dang cow-nurse the West had ever seen.

One thing Thora noticed was that, although they were eating the muleys, the herd seemed to grow. Any unbranded stock they came across was added to it. Dusty insisted that all branded stock should be chased off as soon as it was located, but unbranded animals were held at the drag until they could have the Rocking H road brand run on them.

For fourteen days the weather held good and clear. Then they ran into rain. Not just rain, but torrential streams pouring down and flooding over the land. Thunder rolled and lightning flashed as the trail drive hands unstrapped and got into their yellow fish slickers, and rode with their head bent, hunched miserably in the saddle.

Dusty saw one man riding without his fish and headed back. It was Dude. The handsome young hand looked up as the trail boss appeared by his side and asked where his fish was.

'Like this, Cap'n,' he replied. 'I bought the damned thing new in Granite just afore we left. Toted it every day and near to got it torn yesterday when a steer hooked at me. So I left it behind today.'

'That's asking for rain. Head back and get it.'

Dude turned and headed for the bedwaggon; he would never have gone without Dusty's permission and knew there were trail bosses who wouldn't have given it—not when it meant taking his place in line while he went.

Salt watched Dude ride up and told him in no uncertain manner just what he thought of a hand who left his fish in the wagon. Dude thanked him politely and rode to the bedwagon, where he collected his gear quietly to avoid disturbing the sleeping night-hawk. Dressed in dry clothing and wearing his fish, Dude headed back for his place by the herd.

Thora rode alongside the herd; she was uncomfortable and cold, but she kept to her place like the men. She wondered how much longer Dusty would keep moving in this rain. She found out fast enough.

For five more days it rained just about all the time. The

herd was kept moving through the wet, soaking grass and fording rivers which were, to use the trail-drivers' term, over the willows. The crew used every ounce of their skill at each crossing and the losses to the herd were, by masterly handling, slight. The hands got what sleep they could, for there was no chance of finding some place dry to make a camp. Never were there less than four men with the herd and two men always rode with the remuda. In the five days, Tarbrush and Little Jackie never seemed to be out of their saddles, and even snatched a brief nap whilst riding.

There was only one consolation about this rain; it beat from the south and helped to keep the cattle headed north.

Throughout all the time Salt worked wonders; every morning before the herd was moved on, he had a hot meal for the hands; and again, at night there would be hot food when the men came in. Yet, for all of that, tempers frayed amongst the crew. The hands were touchy as teased rattlers and mean as starving grizzlies. Red-eyed from lack of sleep, dirty and unshaven, they rode, hard-eyed and silent.

It was at this time Thora saw more than ever what made a trail boss. Dusty was always there; he got less sleep than the other men and always seemed to be in his saddle. Now he was soft-spoken and diplomatic; then, when need be, he became hard, savage and dangerous.

The crew were round the fire on the fifth night of the rains, each man standing morosely, eating his food. Dusty watched them sensing their mood and knowing that a spark could cause bad trouble.

Each man was gulping down his food, wolf savage and angry, wet and miserable. Little Jackie came from the side of the wagon, headed for the warmth of the fire Salt had made. The boy was cold, wet and more than half-blinded by the brim of his cheap woolsey hat falling down. He crashed full into Dude, spilling his food down the rider's new fish.

Dude roared in rage as his own plate of stew went down his fish front. The back of his hand lashed round, staggering Little Jackie backwards into Red Tolliver.

'What the hell!' Red roared, pushing the wrangler aside and facing Dude, who was moving in, fists clenched.

Dude's face darkened with sudden anger, his hand dropped

towards his hip. Red's hand fanned down and like the other man's, clutched his fish over the butt of his gun. With a roar of rage, he hurled himself at Dude. They met like two enraged bulls.

Dusty and Mark hurled forward to stop the fight; for in these conditions, such a thing could start a full-scale battle. Mark caught Red by the scruff of the neck and hurled him backwards, then spun round to face Dude. But Dusty was there first.

'Cut it, Dude!' Dusty roared, catching the other's arm and spinning him round.

Dude snarled and swung a punch which had enough power to rip the top of Dusty's head off, had it landed. The punch ripped through empty air as Dusty ducked under it. The force of the blow put Dude off balance and Dusty's right slammed into his stomach. Dude doubled over and the other fist smashed up on to his chin. Dude looked like he was trying to go two ways at once. His feet shot from under him and he landed flat on his back in the mud.

Red Tolliver stood scowling at Mark, fists clenched and lifted. Then slowly he relaxed and a grin came to his face.

'All right, Mark. I ain't fighting you, 'cause I never fights nobody bigger'n me. That's 'cause I'm a noble, true-blue Texan. And 'cause I'm scared of getting licked.'

The tension was broken then and the men were all grinning again. Billy Jack ambled over and looked at Dude, who lay with the rain dripping on his face.

'Ain't nothing like rain for cooling a feller's temper,' he said mournfully, 'and ole Dude, he sure looks cooled.'

Dude sat up, shaking his head and holding his jaw, then managed to get up. 'Where at's the mule?' he growled. 'Salt, I telled you to keep them knobheads out of the camp.'

'What mule?' Salt growled as he washed off the plates and refilled them with stew.

'The one that kicked me.' Dude backed off hurriedly as Little Jackie carried the plate to him. 'You keep clear of me, boy. I don't want no more spilled down me.'

'If you feels that bad about it, pour one on me,' Jackie answered. 'It ain't wuth much more than that, anyways.'

The tension was eased around the fire now. Dusty went to

Dude and listened to Salt talking to the hand.

'I sure wish it was steak.'

'Way my jaw feels, I don't,' Dude replied, then went on hopefully: 'You ain't got a steak have you?'

'Cook you an ole boot was you to ask real nice.'

'Mean you ain't been doing that all along?' Dude turned his back and faced Dusty, before the irate cook could think up an answer. 'Sorry if I hurt your hand, Cap'n. I don't know what you did to me, but you sure did it right.'

'That's all right. Don't you forget your fish again—that was what started all this,' Dusty answered.

The rest of the hands gathered around the fire and began to swap tall tales about the wettest time they had ever run across. They were still at it when the Kid returned with news that the weather appearing to be clearing.

The following morning the Kid's prophecy was proved correct. The sun came out and the crew were given a day to dry out their wet clothing before moving on once more.

The day they crossed the line into the Indian Nations, Kiowa came back with word that they were still being dogged by a man who was riding a horse and leading two more. The Kid had found sign that the man was still on their trail, but that he was keeping his distance. Dusty refused to allow his scouts to take time out to hunt the man down; he didn't want them too far away as they were now coming into Indian country. However, he told the Kid to take his string and make a circle to warn any other drives that might be within three days trail of them to be on the lookout for the watcher.

Mark and Dusty discussed the watcher as they rode at the point

'Further we get from Texas, the better I like the idea of him being a Kliddoe man,' Mark drawled as he scanned the range ahead.

'Sure. Had he been a rustler spy, we'd have known before now. They wouldn't want us this far. It'd be like Kliddoe to have a few men in Texas to dog the first herds and point him to them.'

'Happen you should let Lon and Kiowa go after him.'

Dusty thought this over for a time, then heard a disturbance from back along the line. He didn't take time to answer Mark, but turned his horse and headed back fast.

Thora was waiting, the black steer roped and snapped. 'He started to gore a muley,' she snapped, 'reckon he'll make us a dandy stew, or a couple of steaks.'

Dusty laughed as he watched her lead the steer back to the chuckwagon. Thora was acting like a seasoned trail drive hand now. She left the steer in Salt's care and headed along the line to take her place in the swing.

The herd was bedded down soon after, even though there was more than half a day left for them to travel in. Dusty was satisfied that the herd was ahead of any other. He wanted to give the hands time to mend any damaged gear and rest the remuda and herd.

The hands settled down around the cook-fire, making the most of their brief rest from the trail driving. Men lounged around, talking. None of them took much notice of the approaching buggy, nor of the man who rode by the side of it.

'Hello, the wagon!' the man yelled.

'Come ahead, friend.' Dusty gave the customary permission to ride up, without which no stranger would come into camp.

The buggy was driven by a thin, tired-looking and work-worn woman of indeterminate age. She had the look of a very poor squatter—the sort who ran maybe a hundred head of stock and tried to eke out a living with the calf-crop.

The man was big, well-dressed and powerful-looking. He sat a big roan horse and looked arrogantly around. His right hand thrust back the lapel of his coat to show the marshal's star on his vest.

'The name's Garde, Town Marshal of Timbal. Who's herd is this?'

'Rocking H,' Dusty as trail boss, replied, 'Miz Holland here's spread, I'm the trail boss.'

Garde had known that without telling; known it as soon as he rode into the camp. He wondered why so small and insignificant a man could be holding down so important a position as trail boss. He looked round the camp, but he was no cattleman and cowhands were just cowhands to him. To a man who knew Texans in general, and cowhands in particular, the men at the fire would have told much. To Garde, they looked like any other such group, and he had never found much trouble in handling cowhands in his town.

'This here's Mrs. Crump,' he growled, waving a hand to the woman. 'She had all her stock run off, sixty head. Went a couple of nights back and, you being the only trail herd in the country, I reckon they might have got mixed in with your'n.'

'So?' Dusty's tones were soft and silky.

'I want to cut your herd,' Garde spoke to Thora not Dusty.

'Certainly.'

'No, ma'am!' Dusty spoke softly.

'What do you mean, Dusty?' Thora turned to her trail boss, but she felt nervous. That word, 'ma'am' was there. She knew she had blundered badly somewhere.

'The herd doesn't get cut.'

Thora knew that tone, too. It was hard, flat and it meant Dusty would brook no interference with his orders. She didn't know that every Texan regarded having his herd cut as an insult, and that any attempt was liable to end with gunplay. She also didn't know that Garde of Timbal wasn't highly thought of by Texans. The man was one of the kind of lawmen who never gave the cowhand a break. In his town, just to be a cowhand was likely to end a man in jail with a broken head.

The trail hands looked on, waiting for the outcome of this matter. Not one of them expected Dusty to allow any man to cut his herd. Much less when it was a loud-talking Yankee who boasted that he jailed Texans one-handed.

'The lady said I could,' Garde pointed out, but he now knew who this small man was. He also knew that cutting the herd would be far harder than sneaking up behind a booze-blind cowhand to buffalo him with a pistol barrel.

'And I say you can't,' Dusty replied, his voice, to Garde's ears, still soft and drawling. Dusty turned his attention to the woman. 'We haven't seen your stock, ma'am. There's only our brand here.'

There Garde had it laid out before him as plain as he could ask. He could now call the play in one of two ways; either he took Dusty's word, or he didn't. It was as easy as that.

Except that, if he didn't take Dusty's word, it meant he was calling the Texan a liar.

'There ain't another trail drive around.' Garde spat the words out, wishing he had brought a posse with him.

'Not ahead there ain't.'

None of the crew had noticed the silent arrival of the Ysabel Kid. He had returned shortly after Garde and been standing in the shade of the wagon, listening to all that was said.

'That means the herd'll still be round,' Garde answered. 'There war three men took them, and three ain't going to risk crossing the Injun Nations with sixty head.'

'Said there warn't a drive ahead, mister,' the Kid corrected. 'I never mentioned behind. There's one back there, three days' drive behind us. I done talked to their scout, real nice feller called Smiler—mostly 'cause he never does.' The Kid's words were mocking and got more so as he went on, savouring the shock he was going to give this loud-mouthed Yankee John law. 'Hoss he war riding carried a real cute brand. I read it to be CA.'

'CA!' Garde's tones were husky as he breathed the letters out, 'CA, but that's——'

'Yeah,' the Kid interrupted, being highly pleased with the effect of his words. 'The old Washita curly wolf, Mr. Clayton Allison—complete with Brother Jack 'n' Brother Ben.'

The marshal of Timbal looked round the circle of tanned, unfriendly faces, reading pleasure at his dilemma in every one. It was one thing to ride into an unknown trail camp and try to look big. It was another matter entirely heading up and asking Mr. Clayton Allison, even without Brother Jack and Brother Ben, if he could cut the CA herd.

The old woman had been looking at the men around the fire. For the first time she spoke: 'Them three ain't here. I reckon we'd best go and see the other herd.'

Garde lost what little bluster he had left, all in one go. The name Clay Allison meant something to him and to every other Yankee lawman. Allison was a rich cattleman whose business in life was the running of his ranch in the Washita country. His hobby was the hunting out—and either treeing, or killing —of Yankee lawmen. If there was one place in the West where no Yankee had best go and flash his fancy law-badge, Clay Allison's trail camp was that place.

'Sorry, Mrs. Crump, but they're thirty mile off, right out of my bailiwick.'

Dusty looked the man over in some disgust, and stepped from where he had lounged against the side of the wagon.

'You'd likely not have come here, had we been Allisons,' he snapped, turning away. 'Mark, get the herd moving again. Keep them going until night.'

'Sure.' Mark and every other man there had been expecting the order. With a herd behind, the Rocking H must be kept moving.

Garde scowled as he watched the men going into action. He wanted to make something of the stealing of the cattle and saw his chance going. His only reason for coming out here was to make a name for himself. The local election for the post of sheriff was approaching, and he needed the publicity to help him get the post.

Dusty watched the hands preparing to move out, then turned his attention back to the woman.

'Tell you what I'll do, ma'am. I'll head back to Clay's camp and we'll talk to him. If the men have brought the cattle to him, he'll give you them back again. Clay Allison never stole a thing in his life.'

Mrs. Crump stared at the young Texan; she was a nester and never thought any cowhand would offer to help her. However, she could see no chance of getting help from Garde, and agreed to let Dusty handle the matter for her.

It was dark when Dusty rode alongside the woman's buggy towards the flickering light of the CS fire. He called the usual greeting and the tall, well-dressed, handsome man with the black moustache and trim beard called for him to come and take something.

Dusty rode in, he helped the woman down and they came into the light of the fire. The small Texan looked round at the tanned, grim-faced group; he noted the two lean, handsome young men who were Clay Allison's brothers flanking Clay. His eyes went on taking in the lean, dark Indian scout and Allison's segundo, Smiler. The other men were all hard, tough-looking hands with the look of first-rate cattle-hands about them. That figured, for Clay Allison only took on the best.

There had been much written and told of Clay Allison's wild drinking and his whisky-primed fun and games. Yet no man ever saw him drink when working his cattle; him or any of that tough, rough and handy crew who rode with him and would have died for him.

Allison looked Dusty over, noting the gunbelt which had been made by his own maker. He ignored the soft whisper that run round the men about the fire. Even as Dusty accepted the proffered coffee cup from the cook, and introduced himself, the men were telling each other who he was.

'Trail boss for the Rocking H?' Allison remarked. 'Thought I heard a buggy with you. How far behind are you?'

'Three days. But we aren't behind, we're ahead.'

'The hell you say!' Jack Allison growled, 'I thought we were the first up trail.'

'Could still be,' a medium-sized stocky man put in. 'Hold him here and see how far they'd get without their trail boss.'

'That's real smart, Smith,' Clay scoffed. 'You just up and try it. This here's Cap'n Fog all right, happen you reckon it isn't.' He ignored the man again and turned back to Dusty. 'Mind you, Cap'n, saw you one time in the war.'

'The day we took the Yankee General, you brought the word where we could find him,' Dusty agreed. 'You didn't have the beard then, but I'd know you any place. Reason I came back to your herd was that some damned cow-thieves ran off sixty head of stock and Garde from Timbal came to us. Reckons they'll be taken north with a herd. He got to crying and took on like to wet us out. So I said I'd come back here and ask you if anybody'd come and asked to trail with you.'

'That so?' Clay flashed a look at the tough who had spoken before. 'Now who'd you reckon'd be robbing them poor ole Injuns like that?'

'Injuns?' Dusty spat the word out. 'You don't reckon I'd leave my herd and come back here for Injuns. It was an old nester woman and they took every head she owned.'

Allison came to his feet, his mouth a hard, tight line in the light of the fire. 'Is that right?'

He wasn't speaking to Dusty, but to the tough who had suggested holding up the Rocking H herd. The man and two more were on their feet, hands driving down towards the butts of their guns.

Dusty dropped his coffee cup and started his draw the instant after Clay Allison's move was made. The firelight glinted on the barrels of guns and the exploding powder rocked the silence of the night. Ahead of those of Allison and the other men, and before the falling cup hit the ground, Dusty's matched guns roared throwing lead into Smith and the man on his right. Clay Allison's gun roared out in echo to Dusty's. The third man hunched forward, then dropped.

For an instant there was silence as the men all watched the small Texan who had shaded their boss. There was no move until the cook stepped forward to pick up the fallen cup, wash it and refill it.

Allison holstered his gun and told some of his men to get the three bodies moved out of the camp. Then he turned to Dusty. 'I never could stand a liar.'

Dusty explained why he had come here and called the woman in from where he had left her. Clay Allison sat down again and told how Smith had brought the sixty head to his herd the previous day. Saying that they took the herd from the Indians, Smith offered to help work the CA herd to Dodge in exchange for safe conduct through the Indian Nations. There was nothing unusual in this arrangement; small ranchers often took on with larger drives on the same terms. Clay Allison was not even worried by the fact that the cattle had been stolen from Indians. He and most other western men regarded Indians as something to be killed off, and a man who robbed the Indians as something of a hero.

'Trouble now being that the sixty head's all mixed up with my own stock,' he mused as the woman was seated by the fire. 'I don't want to lose a day by cutting herd. So, if it's fair with you, I'll take the cattle north with me and sell them. Pay you for them now.'

The woman agreed to this eagerly; it solved her problem of getting the stock to Dodge.

Dusty finished his coffee and waited until Clay Allison had finished dealing with the woman and came back to sit by the fire.

'Kliddoe's ahead,' Dusty remarked.

'Heard about it. You aiming to do something?'

'Happen.'

Allison grinned wolfishly. 'If you need any help, send word back and we'll come running.'

'We'll do that.'

'You've been having luck, or Ben did. We heard about his trouble and allowed to stop over to Granite and talk some sense to Thad Toon. Then we heard he'd got a crew and come on. Thought we'd be ahead of you. What you reckon Earp'll do when you hit Dodge?'

'You know Earp.'

'Sure, full of wind and bull-water. Say, did you hear the word Bat Masterson passed about me?'

'I heard,' Dusty agreed. 'But I don't reckon Bat sent it—not unless it came to you direct.'

'You've got a whole heap more faith in him than I have. You know him real good?'

'Met him a couple of times. Nice feller—fair with the cowhands. Waal, I allow it's long gone time for me to head back to the herd.'

Ben Allison grinned and winked at his brothers. 'Know something, Clay? Ole Smith had a real good idea, keeping Dusty here.'

'What'd you have to say about that, Dusty?' Allison asked.

Dusty smiled, then he threw the cup into the air, shouting, 'Lon!'

The flat bark of a rifle echoed the shout, and from the darkness came a spark of light. At the peak of its flight, the cup spun off course and landed, neatly-holed, at Allison's feet.

Clay Allison roared with laughter at the startled faces. 'That's the Ysabel Kid out there, I reckon,' he remarked. 'Smiler said he'd talked with the Kid, but there warn't no mention of working for a drive.'

'Lon's like that, modest. Reckon if your boys aren't going to hold me, I'll light out, Clay.'

Allison rose and held out his hand. Dusty shook it then said his good-byes and left the camp.

The Allison brothers watched the small figure disappear. Then Ben turned to Clay, 'I never reckoned I'd see you licked to the draw, but I seed it tonight.'

Clay Allison nodded, his face thoughtful. 'I never allowed to see a man draw and use two guns as well as that either.'

They listened to the sound of hooves fading into the night. Jack Allison laughed. 'That Dusty Fog sure showed us how the game should be played. I nigh on jumped clear out of my skin when that rifle went off.'

'Yeah.' Clay Allison had not been annoyed, but amused, at

Dusty's caution in leaving the Kid out there in the darkness. 'Know something; he don't need any help to handle Kliddoe and Earp both.'

CHAPTER NINE

STAMPEDE

'WHAT'S wrong with the herd, Dusty?' Thora asked as she watched the cattle walking past her.

'Dry driving—and those.' Dusty jerked his thumb towards two lean, grey shapes which flashed through the bush.

'What were they, coyote?'

'Wolf!' Dusty sounded grim. 'They're hanging on to our flanks and waiting for a chance to pick up the stragglers.'

A week had passed since the meeting with Clay Allison; and the Rocking H herd was now getting deep into the Indian Nations. The rains of the south did not appear to have hit this far north, for water was very scarce and the cattle had been on short rations for three days. The last day had been dry driving, so the cattle were disturbed both by lack of water and the lean, big wolves which clung to the flank of the herd.

The wolf-pack, with the inborn cunning of their kind, realised the cowhands couldn't risk using guns; so they loped along the flanks of the herd, watching and waiting for a steer to drop out.

Thora watched the staggering cattle and the tired, hard-eyed men who rode by them. There was so little she could do to help them. She returned to her place on the flank, where she rode to relieve a man who was badly needed at the drag. It was the first time she had seen Dusty to speak to for two days. The trail boss was constantly on the move. At the point rode Kiowa and Billy Jack, for Mark was riding the drag. The Ysabel Kid rode a constant circle round the herd, hurling his horse at any wolf he saw and breaking the pack off, trying to scatter them without shooting.

The drag was now the key-point of the drive. Mark rode there and had not left his place for two days. He was tireless in his work here, a veritable tower of strength. The other men had each taken a turn at the drag and been relieved; but Mark stayed here, tailing up the weakened steers.

It was hard and gruelling work, riding in the dust-choked rear of the herd. Now and then a steer would go down stubbornly, waiting for death. When this happened, one of the drag riders would come in, lean out of the saddle, grip the animal by the tail and haul it back to its feet.

The weaker stock were all at the rear now and the drag men kept them going, trying to stop them dropping and pushing stronger stock out of the way of the weak ones.

Through all the dust and the lung-ache it caused, Mark worked on. He did the work of three men; every other hand who rode the drag tried to keep up with him but none could.

The Ysabel Kid rode to where Dusty sat his horse, watching the herd and trying to decide how he could ease the burden on the hands at the drag. The Kid brought news that was both good, and dangerous. In one of his wolf-chasing circles he had seen, in the distance, the waters of the North Canadian river. The waters were not high just now, but they were still high enough to make trouble for the herd in its weakened state.

The biggest danger was that the herd might get scent of the water. If they once did——

Sending for Mark from the drag, Dusty held a quick conference.

'Canadian's ahead. Reckon you'd best take the point with Billy Jack. And send Kiowa to the drag.'

'Sure,' Mark agreed, 'we'll have to hold that ole lead steer down until he can't but hobble. If the herd gets a smell of that water——'

'Yeah, we'll have us some real fun then. Happen we're lucky, they won't.'

Mark looked back to where Little Jackie was bringing the remuda along, and beyond to where the two wagons moved at the rear. Tarbrush came from the bedwagon and joined the youngster. Mark turned back to Dusty and said, 'We'd best get the remuda down there and watered before we bring the herd in.'

'Why sure, the hands are going to need fresh horses when we try to hold the cattle in. Take the point, *amigo*; if we can't hold them, push them right across, then turn them at the other side. Don't let them start a merry-go-round in the water.'

Mark knew this without being told; he knew that, although it was always desirable to get the herd milling round on land, if it ran in stampede, the same did not apply to when the cattle were in water. If the stock started to mill in the water they would close in and tighten. The loss through drowning would be terrible for there was little the hands could do to stop it.

'Only good thing is the sun'll be in their eyes,' Mark pointed out. 'That'll hold them from going in, but it'll give us hell when we want to get them across.'

Dusty turned and left Mark to handle the point. The trail boss rode back along the line and to the remuda. Tarbrush and Little Jackie waited for their orders. Neither had managed to get much sleep in the past few days, but both managed a grin as Dusty rode up.

'Get the remuda up to the head of the drive,' Dusty ordered. 'The Canadian's ahead and I want the horses watered ready for the hands to make a change. Keep them well to the flank of the herd.'

'Sure will, Cap'n.' Like most of the crew, Lil Jackie used Dusty's Civil War rank when he gave them orders.

Tarbrush didn't take time to speak; he flashed Dusty a salute and kicked his heels to the sides of his mule, then started the remuda swinging around the flank of the cattle and headed for the water ahead.

Dusty turned and looked back at the two wagons, which were ambling along behind the herd. Salt and Hobie each had a horse saddled ready and fastened to the side of the wagon. If they were needed to handle the cattle they would leave the two mule teams to follow and ride the horses into action. Salt had insisted the mules were watered, even at the expense of the hands. He had trained the mules well and, with them not being thirsty, could rely on them to follow the herd and not spook at all.

Just what started the trouble was never discovered. It may have been one of the wolf-pack that cut in close without being seen. Perhaps the horses got either scent, or sight, of the water ahead. Whatever the cause, the result was the same. One minute the remuda was under full control, and moving at an easy half-gallop, the next they were running in full stampede and out of all control.

Dusty saw what happened. He whirled his horse and sent it racing after the remuda. Three of the cowhands came from the herd fast, all making for the remuda.

Then the cattle spooked and were off running.

'All hands and the cook!' Mark's bellow rang out over the noise of the cattle. *'Stampede!'*

Salt and Hobie piled from their wagons and afork their horses, to go after the herd. The two-mule teams never even showed any sign that they were alone; they just walked along, following the herd.

The ground shook as the rumble of three thousand sets of racing hooves churned up the dust. Every rider joined in the mad, wild race to get to the point and help get the herd milling round. Thora was caught in the rush and rode like a master through the whirling dust.

'Shout, Miss Thora, *shout*!' a voice roared out.

She let out a wild screaming shout and, faintly over the thunder of the hooves, heard men yelling. She yelled and shouted out until her throat ached and her voice cracked. On the other side of the herd, her opposite number yelled back and listened; whilst she yelled he knew she was all right.

Every hand hurled along the line, trying to get to the point. This was no easy task, for a spooked Texas longhorn could run almost as fast as a good horse.

Dusty allowed his horse to run. Then, from the corner of his eye, he saw something that made him bring the cowhorse whirling round and headed at a tangent. He slammed the paint into Lil Jackie's horse knocking it staggering. The wrangler had drawn his gun. He lost it, then heard a roar of: 'Don't ever try and shoot—you'll spook the herd worse.'

At the opposite side of the herd, Dude was riding fast and well on his way, when his horse put a foot into a prairie-dog hole and went down. At the first sign of the fall, Dude kicked his feet free from the stirrups and lit down rolling. Coming up, he knew he was still not out of the woods and was in trouble—bad trouble. A Texas longhorn feared a man only so long as he was afork a horse. One on foot was easy game and ripe for stomping.

The steer lunged out of line, long, sharp horns swinging

down to hook Dude from belly to brisket. The cowhand grabbed for his gun but it had jolted loose and lay in the dust by his horse.

From out of the whirling dust a big blood bay stallion loomed, ridden by Mark Counter. Cutting in behind the steer, Mark leaned over, caught hold of its tail and heaved. The steer was thrown off balance and lit down hard. Dude felt a hand grip his collar and pull, then he was dumped across the back of Mark's horse. The steer got up winded, and stood for a moment, shaking its head. Then it headed back into the rushing line.

Mark brought Dude clear of the herd and the cowhand yelled: 'Let me down, Mark. Get after the herd.'

Mark dropped Dude to the ground and hurled his blood bay back after the herd. Dude was clear of the cattle but still in trouble. From behind, came the rapid patter of feet and he whirled to see a wolf coming at him.

Dude saw his revolver and knew he had no chance of getting to it in time. The wolf left the ground in a leap and then gave an anguished howl and crashed to one side. Faintly Dude heard a rifle cracking and saw a scene he would remember to the day he died.

Riding his white stallion as if he was part of it came the Ysabel Kid, his rifle cracking at the wolves. At each shot, a wolf went rolling over on the ground. It was an exhibition of marksmanship which would have been hard to equal.

The wolf-pack were cutting in, trying to get at the stragglers of the herd and at the mule-teams pulling the wagons. The Kid came at them with his deadly rifle cracking. Now the herd were running, there was no reason for the Kid not to shoot. He cut down on every wolf he saw.

Dusty had dropped back behind the herd and seen Dude's trouble. He headed for the remuda and caught one of Dude's horses from that racing mass, then brought it back.

'All right, Dude?' he asked as he tossed its rope to the cowhand.

'Likely live, Cap'n.'

'That being the case you'd best get afork that hoss and get back to work.' Dusty looked at the lamed horse. 'Can you get your saddle out?'

Dude walked to his horse and looked down; he removed the

saddle. Picking up his gun he sighed, shook his head, then shot the horse. Saddling the mount Dusty had brought, Dude called: 'Tell Mark and the Kid I'll happen buy them a drink in Dodge.'

At the point Mark and the other hands had turned the leaders of the stampede. The idea was to make the cattle mill round, the leaders getting into the centre of the herd and, like a coiled spring, get tighter and tighter until at last all movement ended. The dust died away and the hands sat their horses, looking round to see if anyone was missing.

Thora rode to where Dusty and Mark sat watching the herd. Her face was pale and she was gasping for breath. 'How bad is it?' she managed to get out.

'Twarn't nothing but a lil bitty stampede,' Mark replied.

For once Mark wasn't belittling the matter. The stampede as such things go, hadn't been too bad. Mark had heard of stampedes where more than half the herd was lost. What he didn't say was that only the superb handling of the crew prevented it from being far worse. The cattle had run for almost a mile; but they had not scattered too badly and only the weaker members of the drag had been left behind.

Dude came up, hazing several of the weaker stock ahead of him. Despite his two narrow escapes, he was as cool and collected as ever. 'Say, Mark. Next time you hauls me across your saddle, just watch how you does it. I've got ideas about how time should be spent in Dodge, and you ain't helped it none, if you follows me.'

'I wouldn't, not less the wind was right,' Mark growled. He could see the smile on Thora's face. ''Course, you had to be riding a company horse when you lost it.'

'That's me, smart.' Dude raised his hat to Thora and headed back to help collect the rest of the drag.

Dusty made a circle of the herd and surveyed the damage. Three steers had been killed and one more had to be shot. That was a small price to pay for what might have happened if the trail hands had been less quick off their marks.

The remuda had run to the river and were now watered. The hands took turns to collect fresh mounts and, when all were afork fresh horses, started to move the weaker stock down to the river and water them.

When the time came to move the cattle across, there was

trouble. The steers baulked and fought against being pushed into water when they could not see the other bank. Dusty sent the remuda across ahead, then drove the cattle in.

The hands closed in and helped the weaklings over, one man on each side of any steer that looked as if it might be in trouble. One steer went under in the swift water, but was hauled ashore on the end of a rope.

The rest of the herd was cut in groups of a hundred or so and brought down to the river, watered, then pushed over.

Salt managed to get his wagons over between two groups and started preparing the camp for the night.

The darkness was closing in when the last of the cattle were moved across the river and bedded down. Dusty was the last man, as always, to leave the herd.

The Ysabel Kid came over the river just as Dusty arrived. The scout was bloody and, across the rear of his saddle, were the skins of several wolves. He presented the pelts to Thora, who was sitting by the fire.

'They'll sell in Dodge, happen you get ole Salt to fix 'em.'

'Thank you most to death,' Salt answered dryly. 'Whyn't you go out and shoot a couple or so buffler and maybe a silver-tip or two, me not having nothing better to do than cure hides for you?'

Thora stretched back; she was tired but didn't feel like going to bed just yet. 'Well, if you've got nothing better to do, get on with them. The crew are fed and all you'll do until morning is stand in front of the fire and spin windies.'

'I hired as cook, not as skinner for some danged Injun that goes round killing everything he sees,' Salt objected. 'Anyways,' he was examining the skins as he spoke, 'they ain't wuth a cuss, none of them.'

'How'd a cook know that?' The Ysabel Kid walked off before Salt could answer this.

'Head-shot, every one of them,' Salt grinned at Thora, 'they'll sell for as much as the steers we lost.'

Mark sat on his haunches and rolled a smoke. A black-sleeved arm reached over his shoulder and took it on completion. With a sigh of resignation, he rolled another, which Dusty accepted.

'Been a fair sort of day,' the trail boss remarked.

'If there's any more cigarette-rustlers round here it'll be a worse night,' Mark warned. 'Don't you pair ever buy any?'

The Kid lit his smoke, then drawled. 'I got thinking today.'

'That's good, Dusty. We work and the Kid here thinks.'

'I treats that remark with the contempt it deserves, Mr. Counter.'

'Yeah, Mark,' Dusty agreed. 'First time Lon ever got round to thinking, so we'd best set back and listen to him.'

The Ysabel Kid took this as permission to go ahead and expound. 'More I think about it, the more I reckon that *hombre* with the three-hoss string is a Kliddoe scout.'

'I'll give you that,' Dusty agreed. 'Seen any more of his sign?'

'Not for a spell now. I allow he cut round us and looked over the CA herd. Smiler allowed he'd seen sign of a man with a three-hoss relay. I make it this way: He followed us until he was real sure which crossing of the Canadian we'd make, then went back to look over any other herds that were coming. Soon as he saw the CA he headed back round us to tell his boss.'

'Sure,' Mark agreed. 'Happen he knows cattlemen, he'd want to stop well clear of CA. I'd as soon have Kiowa or you catch me than Smiler, was I a Kliddoe man.'

'Shucks, Smiler's of a sweet and loving nature, most times. But he sure acts Kaddo mean when he's riled. Which same he would be should he catch him a Kliddoe man.'

'Know something?' Dusty looked at the other two, 'I'd just about forgotten ole Kliddoe. What with the rains down south, then the dry driving up here. I reckon it's time to remember him now. We're but three days at most from the Kansas line. It's come time we found where Kliddoe was at.'

'Sure,' Mark agreed. 'And when we find his camp, we'll cut in on him and make him think the hawgs have jumped him.'

'Happen we will,' the Kid's voice was soft, yet the other two had never heard it so latently dangerous sounding since the day he faced the second of the men who killed his father. 'I've got something to show his Yankee friends, that's so proud of their great and noble 'n' loyal Federal hero. They'll likely be real pleased to hear it.'

Dusty and Mark looked at their friend for a time. Both remembered other occasions when he had let slip the name of the Yankee hero, Kliddoe. Always the mentions had been made with the same soft voice, the bitter twist to the lips and that mean, savage, cold-eyed Comanche look on his face.

'You'd best take out and find them come dawn,' Dusty put in.

Before the Kid replied he came up, his hand twisting back round the butt of his old Dragoon gun.

'Easy, Kid. It's us!' a voice yelled from the darkness.

Dude, Red Tolliver and the rest of the hands came out of the darkness. In the firelight they all looked clean and were now wearing clothes that weren't inch deep in trail dust.

'Water's colder'n a blue norther,' Dude remarked. 'But it surely beats trail dirt.'

Dusty and Mark had been thinking the same thing and they collected a change of clothes from their warbags. The Kid joined them and they all bathed in the cold water of the North Canadian.

It was a far cleaner and shaved crowd who gathered round the fire to drink and yarn. Thora went down after the men had finished and, by the time she returned, only Dusty, Mark and the Kid were awake, the rest all being wrapped in their bedrolls. The three men came to their feet with exaggerated politeness as she came up to the fire.

'Howdy, ma'am,' Dusty began. 'Where did—— Oh, it's you, Thora. I thought it was a lady, not seeing you a couple of inch deep in trail dust.'

Thora sniffed disdainfully and went by with a jeer of: 'If you worked, you'd get dusty too.'

Dusty watched her climb into the bedwagon, then turned his attention to the others. Mark was spreading his bedroll down ready to get into it as soon as he had turned out the next night-herd. Dusty shook his head and said: 'I shouldn't have taken that bath until morning. Don't feel tired now. Reckon I'll head out and look over the herd. You pair turn in.'

'Ain't tired now, myself,' the Kid growled. 'I reckon I'll take my mount and light out tonight. Got me a hunch that something's going to happen real soon.'

Dusty had a whole lot of faith in his pard's hunches. They had a nasty habit of developing into full-blown, real come-up happenings. He told the Kid to light out, if that was how he felt, and not to get lost. Then he winded up with: 'Happen you get to Dodge before we do. Tell that nice Mr. Earp we're powerful sorry, but we've just got to use his fair metropolis.'

'I'll do just that,' the Kid promised. 'You roll my bed up for me, come morning. Ole Salt'll cuss me like to peel my hide if he has to do it for me.'

Dusty watched his dark friend fade into the night, then heard Mark waking the relief night-herd. The four hands rose cursing the drive, the cattle, the trail boss and the segundo.

Going out with the four men, Dusty talked with the old night-herders. 'They're settling down real quiet now, Cap'n,' one remarked.

'Sure, happen they're all quieted down come dawn, we'll go back to a two-man herd come night again.'

Crossing to the remuda Dusty allowed Tarbrush to slip into camp for a cup of coffee, then returned himself. The camp was all silent and Dusty built the fire up, then rolled himself into his bed and went to sleep.

Far to the north, the Ysabel Kid slid from the back of his big white stallion, removed the saddle and turned the horse loose. Picketing the Comanche relay near to hand, he settled down. Using the sky for a blanket and the ground for a mattress he was soon fast asleep.

CHAPTER TEN

LONCEY DALTON YSABEL RIDES SCOUT

THE Ysabel Kid rode his big white stallion and led the three-horse Comanche relay tied in line one behind the other. The dark youngster was never more Indian than when he rode as he was now, on the scout for whatever he could find. He was very alert as he rode through the Indian Nation brush country, for here was a land ideal for ambush. It was from the shelter of the coulees and brush that the Kliddoe men would lay up, ready to swarm upon the unsuspecting Texas men who drove their herds along.

The land ahead held a curious fascination for the Kid. Not for him to ride blithely and unseeingly over a rim, or into a coulee. He approached each with Indian caution and examined the ground ahead carefully. This alert caution was inborn to him and came naturally when in the country of an enemy. It was what kept a man alive on the blood-drenched banks of the Rio Grande country the Ysabel Kid had been born and raised in.

The big stallion stopped, snuffling softly and tossing back its head as it sniffed the breeze. In the same instant, the Ysabel Kid slid from the saddle, his Winchester joining him as he went into the shelter and cover offered by an old scrub oak. Except for one click, as he threw open the lever and slapped a shell into the breech of the rifle, there was no other sound or movement from him.

The white stallion knew what it had to do without telling. Turning, it trotted off back the way it came, leading the Comanche war relay after it.

Lying flat under the scrub oak, the Kid placed his ear to the ground and listened. At first, he could only hear the sound of his own four horses moving away; then, when the white found cover and that sound ended, faintly from the other direction could be heard two more horses approaching.

The Kid knew what was happening now. Nigger would have led the other three horses off into cover and was waiting for him to give his next orders. The white would not move until he whistled; then it would come back fast. The other two men, if it was two men, would be headed this way for the same reason he was following it. The way was the easiest; an old Indian war-trail, which allowed ease of travel with a fair amount of concealment.

Time dragged by and the Kid looked back to where, in the far distance, the dust of the trail herd rolled into the air. Then gave his full attention to whoever was coming this way.

Two men came into view. The Ysabel Kid's lips drew back in a savage grin as he recognised one as the man with whom he'd had words in Granite City, Texas. The other was a tall, lean, sullen-looking though handsome man, dressed like he was advertising a leather shop. He wore the rig of a cowhand dandy, this one, from his high-crowned, snow-white Stetson to the soft, expensive levis tucked into shining boots. Yet he didn't sit his big palomino gelding like a cowhand.

The two men were riding along, talking and showing such a complete lack of caution that the Kid thought they were slighting his abilities. He listened to their talk and was enlightened as to who they were. He also got proof that his guess about the watcher all the way north had been correct.

'Where at's this herd, Blount?' the dandy asked.

'There, under that dust. 'Bout a day's drive off and coming fast. They'll be all set-up for the Colonel in two days. Then there's another herd behind them 'bout three days. Allison's CA, that one.'

'That don't make us no never mind. Uncle Jethro'n me, we knows how to deal with them sort. We'll take us head-tax toll, or herd, from both of 'em.'

Blount nodded in sycophantic agreement. 'Sure, Cawther. We'll do us just that. The one I wants is that black-dressed 'breed——'

'Friend, you got your want!'

The Ysabel Kid left cover in a lithe bound that would have done credit to a buck Apache. He landed before the two men so fast and so quiet that they got the idea the ground had opened to sprout him, full-growed Winchester rifle and all.

Both men brought their horses to a sliding, riding halt, hands stabbing at the butts of their guns. The dandy was the faster of the two, and he got first attention from the Kid's old rifle. The Winchester spat once, held hip-high, throwing two hundred grains of best quality B. Tyler Henry flat-nosed lead bullet through the dandy's shoulder.

Blount's gun was out. He jerked the horse's head round as the Kid fired a second shot. His own bullet missed the black-dressed youngster by inches as the Kid hurled himself to one side. The Kid's bullet was intended for Blount, but killed the horse instead.

Kicking his legs free as the horse went down, Blount swung his revolver in an attempt to line on the Kid. Loncey Dalton Ysabel didn't wait for such a move. The lever of the rifle flipped open, flung out the empty case and replaced it with a loaded bullet. The Kid dropped while he was doing it and fired as he landed. Blount's bullet passed over the Kid's head, then Blount rocked over backwards.

Cawther Kliddoe had slid off his horse, and was trying to get his gun with his uninjured left hand. The Kid glided in like a Comanche headed for a white-eyed scalp-taking.

'Fool idea!' he warned and brought the metal-shod butt of

the old Winchester round to smash against Kliddoe's jaw.

The Dandy went over backwards and lay still. Bending over, the Kid pulled the fancy, silver-mounted Navy Colt from the leather and was about to throw it away. Then he remembered that Little Jackie had lost his old gun on the stampede and was in need of a new weapon.

Looking down at the unconscious man, he said: 'And you kin to ole Yellerdawg Kliddoe, you deserves to lose this gun.'

With the gun tucked into his waistband, the Kid took stock of the situation his enterprise had brought about. When he came out from under the bush, he had possessed no set plan. A challenge had, unwittingly, been thrown at his head and he had replied to it. The net result of his impulsive appearance was one very tough, very dead spy, plus one wounded and unconscious nephew of Jethro Kliddoe, leader of the Kansas Border tax collectors.

The sound of hoof-beats brought the Kid whirling round in time to see Kliddoe's Palomino headed back in the direction it had come and travelling at a fair speed. This did not enter into the Ysabel Kid's sense of the fitness of things at all. He knew that, throughout the West, a riderless horse coming home was a serious cause for alarm. The last thing he wanted was for Jethro Kliddoe to be given anxiety about the well-being of his favourite nephew.

One glance was enough to show that Kliddoe would not be going any place, and so the Kid was free to act. He gave a shrill whistle and the big white stallion came crashing towards him. Running forward, the Kid drew his bowie knife with his left hand and carried the rifle in his right. The Kid went up into the saddle like he was jumping a foot-high fence. The knife slashed, cutting loose the Comanche relay and, before the severed lead rope had fallen, the white was running.

The Kid sat his racing white and sheathed the knife, then booted the rifle. Next, he unstrapped and shook the kinks out of his rope while the white closed the distance with the running palomino. The chase was not prolonged; that palomino wasn't trying to get away and, even had it been, the gelding never breathed that could outrun that big white stallion, even when the latter was carrying its rider.

The Kid built up his noose and sent it flying out to drop over the head of the palomino. Bringing the two horses to a halt, he squinted ahead over the range. A rising column of smoke caught his eye; smoke where no smoke should be. The Kid made a careful note of its direction, then headed back to the scene of his encounter with the Kliddoe men.

The Comanche relay were grazing, and Kliddoe still lay where he had fallen. The Ysabel Kid hardly noticed them as he rode back, for he was very thoughtful. That smoke would most likely mark the camp-site of the Kliddoe men. That was far more likely than it having been caused by a nester's cooking fire. The locating of the Kliddoe camp was now a certainty. Even without the smoke, there were tracks to be followed.

Swinging down from his horse, the Kid checked on how far away the herd was. He attended to his horse, then gave his attention to the wound in Kliddoe's shoulder. The young dandy was groaning his way towards consciousness, and the Kid talked as he worked.

'You never up and went and left me,' he said to the groaning and uncomprehending man. 'Now did you, friend. I'm real pleased that you didn't, 'cause you're our lil ole ace-in-the-hole. You're going to help take the pot for the ole Rocking H, less I miss my guess.' He stopped and made a quick check around, then went on: 'Ole Dusty's going to be real pleased to see you. Just think about that now, a Texas boy pleased to see you. I bet you never thought to hear that. Almost worth getting shot for, warn't it?'

Cawther Kliddoe had recovered enough to lay still and look up at the dark face whilst he listened to the soft, drawling Texas voice. He raised himself on his good elbow and spat out: 'You'll get your'n! Wait and see!'

'Waiting long and lonesome and so are you.'

'Uncle Jethro'll fix you and your bunch.'

'Not him. Ole Yellerdawg don't want, nor like, no war, happen the other side's ready and got guns. And, if he wants war, I reckon we can hand him some along of one real dead kinsman.'

The full import of those words didn't hit Kliddoe for a few seconds for he was looking at a face as cold, emotionless and menacing as any Comanche Dog soldier. The face of a killer born and efficiently raised.

Spitting out curses, Kliddoe tried to boost his courage. The words died an uneasy death as a hair was plucked from his head and a bowie knife came into a dark hand. The Kid placed the edge of the knife to the hair and cut. Kliddoe had seen a barber do this same thing with a fresh honed razor, the result was the same, the hair split in two pieces.

'Hombre!' The Kid's voice cut in, mean and menacing as a silvertip coming out of its winter sleep. 'You ain't got the brains of a Texan, the looks of a desert canary, but happen you got the sense of a seam squirrel. You get shut and stay shut. Rile me any more with your wicked words and vile accusations and I'll cut your tongue out. After what your uncle and his crowd did to my pard in the war, I'd as soon do it as not.'

Cawther Kliddoe shut his mouth tight. He was remembering tales told of a handsome, innocent-looking youngster who rode a white stallion and handled a rifle like a master. They were not tales to hearten a prisoner of this man, rather they were tales liable to make such a prisoner wish he had been captured by raiding Comanche or Kiowa braves.

Time dragged by. The Kid lounged in the shade of the bush, watching and waiting for the herd to come up. Kliddoe managed to drag himself, first to the dead horse to get a drink, then to shade and lay back moaning and holding his shoulder.

Dusty rode ahead of the herd. He saw the horses and read from what he saw that his young friend the Ysabel Kid had found some trouble. He halted his paint and looked down at the wounded man. 'Borrowing neighbour, Lon?' he inquired.

'Kin of ole Yellerdawg hisself,' the Kid replied proudly. 'And I called it right about that hombre with the three-hoss relay. You might as well have let me kill him down in Granite. I got round to doing it anyways.'

'Sure.' Dusty was long used to the callous way the Ysabel Kid showed when dealing with enemies. 'You were right, for once. I'll write the folks to home and tell them you've finally been right.' He turned his attention again to the wounded man. 'Looks like some deck's gone shy its joker. Happen it's ole Kliddoe's stacked pile, he'd like to get you back alive.'

'Yeah, he might at that.' The Kid sounded doubtful. 'He might like this *pelado,* but I can't see why.'

'What Cousin Betty calls fascination of the horrible.' Dusty passed over the suggestion that Kliddoe was in border slang, a corpse robber. *Pelado,* in correct usage, meant a skinner of dead animals; but, used in the way the Kid spoke, it meant robber of the dead.

The Kid told what he had seen and what had happened since he met up with Kliddoe and Blount, 'Allow I can find their camp now, was I to try real hard.'

'Sure. But wait until after you've fed. You look all gut-shrunk and needing food.'

They mounted the wounded man on to his horse and escorted him back to meet the herd. The trail-hands were all too busy to take any notice of the three riders. The country through which they were now moving was thick enough to keep all hands busy. Thora saw the men and left her place on the drag. Her face paled under the tan and trail-dirt as she saw the wounded man.

'What is it, Dusty?' she gasped.

'Not much. Happen you could call it old Yellerdawg Kliddoe's favourite nephew, come to call.'

Cawther Kliddoe was staring at the trail-dirty young woman and hardly recognised her as the erstwhile belle of York, Pennsylvania. He grinned triumphantly, and sneered, 'Howdy, Cousin Thora!'

Thora's stomach felt suddenly cold; she looked at the two Texas men, but could read nothing in either of their faces. She wondered what they made of this greeting from a man who they hated.

Kliddoe grinned evilly at the cowhands. 'Yeah. She's my kin. What do you reckon about that?'

'I've got kin I wouldn't spit on, too.' Dusty spoke to Thora, not Kliddoe. He turned and waved to Salt Ballew, who was coming up with his wagons. 'Hold her in a spell, Salt.'

'You reckon being kin to Miz Thora'll buy you anything, *hombre*?' The Ysabel Kid's voice was soft and deceptive.

'Sure, them hands won't take it kind to know they've been working for my kin.' Kliddoe leered triumphantly at the two Texans. 'So, afore I tells them, you'd best——'

The Kid jumped his big white forward, slamming into the Palomino. His hands shot out and dragged Kliddoe from the saddle. They hit the ground with Kliddoe held flat and the Kid kneeling astride him, knife in hand. Gripping the other man's nose, the Kid held on until Kliddoe opened his mouth.

'You're going to have trouble telling without a tongue.'

'Lon! No!' Thora screamed as the knife went towards Kliddoe's mouth.

Dusty flung himself from his horse yelling: 'Quit it, you damned crazy Comanche.'

The Kid slammed Kliddoe's head back against the ground in disgust, then rose and sheathed his knife. He turned and grinned sheepishly at Thora, his young face innocent and almost babyish. She could hardly believe, looking at that face, that its owner could be so deadly and dangerous. She didn't doubt that, without Dusty's intervention, Kliddoe wouldn't have had a tongue in his mouth that moment.

'Sorry, Miz Thora.' The Kid managed to sound contrite. 'I forgot ole Dusty don't like the sight of blood.'

Salt climbed down from the wagon; he didn't know what was happening, who the wounded man was or why the Kid had taken such drastic action. If he was surprised at all it was only that the Kid had allowed himself to be swayed from his purpose and that the stranger still kept his tongue.

'What about him?' he asked.

'Throw him in the bedwagon, and see he don't get loose,' Dusty replied. 'Then I want some food for Lon.'

Salt grabbed Kliddoe and hauled him erect, then pushed him towards the bedwagon. He did not know any more about the prisoner than before, but all he needed to know was that Dusty didn't want the man to get away.

Tarbrush woke up as the prisoner was pushed in. He yawned and sat up, scratching himself, looking at the white man who was dumped in. Kliddoe scowled and waited until Salt had gone back to his wagon, then growled: 'Let me loose, nigger.'

Tarbrush scowled. 'I ain't heard that word since I took on with the herd,' he said softly. 'Why'd I let you all loose for?'

'Because I'm a Kliddoe, and we fought in the War to set you niggers free.'

Tarbrush rolled his eyes. 'You did now, did you? I'se been wanting to meet one of you. I never asked to be set free and, from what my ole pappy telled me, I'd have been better if I wasn't free. He telled me how them folks what had him treated him. He didn't have to ride no night-hawk for his food.'

Kliddoe had an idea that the freeing of slaves hadn't met

with this Negro's approval. 'You get me loose, you black——!'

The words ended as Tarbrush folded a useful-looking fist and warned, 'You stop all this here fussing, white boy. Cap'n Fog wouldn't want you to let loose. You jest get shet and let me sleep in peace or I'll beat you most ugly.'

Kliddoe closed his mouth and sat in sullen, glowering silence as the Negro went back to sleep. The wagon lurched forward, Kliddoe twisted round to look out. He wasn't so tightly fastened that he couldn't get loose; then he could get out over the back of the wagon and escape. The chuckwagon pulled in behind the other, instead of travelling front. On the box, sat Salt Ballew, his carbine across his knees and a desire to commit mayhem in his heart.

Thora and Dusty watched the Kid eating. For a time both were silent. Then she turned a pale face to his. 'Dusty.' Her voice was tremulous. 'It's true about my being related to Jethro Kliddoe. I should have told you earlier but I hoped that we might get by without seeing him. I recognised Blount back in Granite and knew why he had come. He meant to blackmail me into taking him along. Then he could let Kliddoe know just where we are.'

'I figgered you knew him.'

'What will the men say about my being related to Kliddoe?'

'What should they say?' Dusty answered. 'They hired to drive for the Rocking H, not your kin. Besides——' Dusty stopped, his face flushed red and his shoulders shook as he started to laugh. It was some seconds before he could stop enough to speak, 'I'm kin of your'n too. That makes me——'

Then the Kid saw what Dusty was getting at and whooped in delight. 'That means you're kin to ole Yellerdawg, Dusty. Just wait 'til I tell Mark about that.'

Thora's mouth dropped open and she turned a startled face to meet Dusty's laughing gaze. Under the kin system of the deep south, Kliddoe, through his relationship with her, was kin to Dusty Fog.

'We'd best tell the hands who we've got for kin tonight,' Dusty suggested. 'Likely, they'll all quit on us in disgust.'

The Ysabel Kid finished his meal and rose. He went to the big white and vaulted into the saddle. The woman watched him go; she had come to know him pretty well by that time. There was no change of expression on his face, but she knew he was going to do something which pleased him.

Riding his Comanche relay and the big white, the Ysabel Kid covered miles faster than any one horse could have.

There was no trouble in following the two Kliddoe men's tracks, not to a trailer of the standard of the Ysabel Kid. The men had not tried to hide their trail, and it would have taken better than them to fool him.

The tracks curved away from the direction that smoke rose in, but the Kid took a chance and headed straight for the smoke. His guess paid off, for he came on the tracks of the two horses again on a gentle slope. The opposite side of the slope was where the smoke originated.

The Kid left his horses standing out of chance view and, rifle in hand, moved forward. He travelled across the ground like a scalp-hunting Indian, flitting from cover to cover, alert for anything that came his way. Although he watched for Kliddoe sentries, there were none out; and he wondered if he had guessed wrong.

Topping the rim cautiously, he knew that he guessed right. From his place on the boulder and tree-covered rim, he looked down on Jethro Kliddoe's camp. For a time, the Kid examined the land to see if he had missed any sentries. Then he decided that Kliddoe wouldn't bother with such things, not until his scouts brought news that the herd was near.

The camp was at the bottom of the valley, a line of small tents along a small stream. There was a large Sibley standing away from the rest, which would be Kliddoe's residence whilst here. The horses were picketed away from the camp, and a skilled man would have no trouble in getting by the Kliddoe sentries to let them loose. If the worst came to the worst, a stampede of the horses would set Kliddoe and his men afoot long enough to allow Rocking H and CA to get by safely.

From all the Kid could see, there appeared to be about thirty or so men in the valley. Mostly, they had the look of poor farmers, not the usual type Kliddoe trailed with. Only five of the men around the main fire were of the hulking, dirty and untidy kind of scum Kliddoe used for his work. They would be all who were left after Shangai Pierce and his men hit the Kliddoe gang the previous year.

The other men would be new recruits and there were few

repeating rifles evident amongst them. The Texans all, with the exception of Salt, had either a Winchester, Henry or Spencer, that would give them a big edge if it came to war.

The Kid studied everything about the camp with disapproval. It would appear on the face of things that Kliddoe was slighting his ability as a scout. The 'Colonel' should have been keeping his men out on guard, alert and watchful for the arrival of the Ysabel Kid. The failure to take these precautions was open invitation for Loncey Dalton Ysabel to do something about it.

Of course, Kliddoe's logic was easy to follow and to his Yankee mind quite right. He figured he had the Texans outnumbered and they didn't know the location of his camp, or where he would strike from.

It was good, sound reasoning, but it was only half right.

The Texans were outnumbered, but they knew where he could be found. Or would, happen a dark young man called Loncey Dalton Ysabel could ride his Comanche relay back and tell the news to his trail boss.

The flap of the Sibley lifted and the great man himself, Colonel Jethro Kliddoe, stepped out. He stood at the door, a fine figure in his Union Army uniform, complete with shiny close-top holster and the sabre at the other side. He stepped forward to walk amongst the men and he was never to know how near to death he walked.

Up on the rim, a rifle came up and cold, red-hazel eyes fondly aligned the sights on the trim blue uniform. A finger closed lovingly on the hair-trigger as the sights made a perfect picture over Kliddoe's heart.

Prudence held the finger. The Ysabel Kid knew he could shoot, kill Kliddoe and be long gone before pursuit could be organised. He also knew more would be lost than gained by dropping Kliddoe now. The men down in the valley would regard a murdered Kliddoe as a martyr, slain by the brutal unreconstructed rebels, and would paint for war. Besides there was an old, creased letter in the Kid's warbag to be fetched out and read to Jethro Kliddoe and his men before the great, noble and loyal Yankee hero died.

The letter was in the Kid's mind as he backed from the rim. It had been all of ten years since it came into his hands. For all that time he carried and treasured it, but had never got near enough to Kliddoe to return it to the correct owner. That letter was going to come a big surprise to a lot of folks; and Jethro Kliddoe wouldn't be the most surprised by it.

CHAPTER ELEVEN

COLONEL KLIDDOE MEETS KIN

'Boys.' Thora looked round the circle of tanned faces she now knew better than the men at the Rocking H. There was a hint of nervousness in her voice as she prepared to tell them her secret. 'I haven't played square with you. When you took on, I told you we would have trouble with Kliddoe. I didn't say that I was related to Jethro Kliddoe.'

If she expected the words to cause any great sensation amongst the men she was disappointed. Not one face changed expression or showed any great amazement at her words.

Red Tolliver was whittling a stick with the quiet concentration of a man doing a useless but enjoyable task. He tossed the stick into the fire and looked up. 'Ma'am, I've got me a cousin who votes Republican, but I don't boast about it.'

'Should think not,' Billy Jack agreed. 'You'd likely turn a man offen his food, talking about things like that.'

'I got me an uncle who drinks sasparilly,' Dude confessed, hanging his head in shame.

'Some place back to home I've got me a kinsman who goes to church,' a tall, lean hand from the Big Ben country admitted sadly.

'What the boys are trying to say, Thora,' Dusty finished for the men, 'is they don't give a damn who your kin might be. I'm your kin, too, but they don't hold that against you.'

''Cepting when he turns us out for night-herd,' Dude remarked.

The Ysabel Kid looked up from eating. 'Question now being what we does about said Colonel Kliddoe.'

'Not knowing what you found out today, if anything,' Dusty

replied, 'there but three things we can do. Turn back to Texas, try to get round without him finding us, or pay.'

'Pay?' Lil Jackie howled, disappointed that his hero should even consider such a thing.

'Sure, boy,' the Kid replied. 'Pay—with Colt coinage and Winchester bank drafts.' He turned his attention to Thora and went on: 'There's one thing I reckon you'd best know now, Miz Thora. Happen we meet up with Kliddoe, and I get half a chance, he's going to get hurt real bad. I had a pard in Mosby's regiment. Kliddoe caught him. He warn't but sixteen. Apaches couldn't have done wuss to a man than Kliddoe's bunch did to that boy.'

Thora watched the dark, emotionless face, then she replied, 'I probably hate Kliddoe even more than you, or any other man here. It was through Kliddoe that my father was disgraced and killed himself.'

'How d'you mean, Miz Thora?' the Kid asked.

'My father was Colonel Langley Bosanquet. You may have heard of him?' she looked around the fire at the men.

There was silence for a time, then Dusty nodded. 'The Quaker Wagons Massacre. We heard about it. Kliddoe wiped out five wagons of Quakers, allowed he thought they were some of our people.'

'Sure,' Mark agreed. 'We heard, too. Ole Bushrod Sheldon was still yelling about it when I last saw him. Swore it showed what sort of folk the Yankees were. Never laid blame on your father, always swore it was Kliddoe who did it.'

'The Court Martial didn't.' Thora's tones were bitter. 'My father was the senior officer and it was made out that Kliddoe was under his command. He swore on oath that father gave him orders to attack the wagons. My father's orders were for him to attack the Confederate troops wherever he found them. Kliddoe was a good friend of the Custer crowd and the Boy General stands by his friends. They had to lay the blame on someone, and my father didn't have many influential friends. So they broke him and dismissed him from the service. It broke his heart; he shot himself three days later.'

'Don't reckon Yankees would have listened to much again Kliddoe in the war,' Billy Jack remarked.

'No more than a reb would have listened to the truth about Quantrell.'

'Like to say that not all the south thought of Quantrell as a hero,' Dusty interrupted. 'Uncle Devil, my pappy and Colonel Mosby, always knew him for what he was. They led the group that outlawed him after Lawrence.'

Thora accepted this, then went on: 'I want to see Kliddoe face to face and ask him if he lied about the orders. I want to prove what kind of a man Kliddoe really is.'

'Ma'am.' The Kid spoke gently, yet his voice had the ring of truth. 'Happen we're real lucky and Dusty comes up with something you're going to get your proof.'

Before Thora could question this statement, Dusty had moved into the centre of the group. 'All right, Lon. Tell it.'

The Kid told it, with the aid of a bowie knife-drawn map in the soil. He told of all he had seen in his trip and finally sat back waiting to hear what Dusty made of things.

'Thirty of them, we were expecting fifty,' Dusty mused.

'That's a tolerable handful, even for us Texans,' Thora remarked.

'Sure.' Dusty turned to Mark. 'How many hands you allow you'll need to keep the herd moving? Counting Hobie and Lil. Jackie?'

'Ten, twelve. In this brush we can't do it with less. With that few they'll have to move fast or we'll lose stock in this scrub country.'

'Sure, but we can't stop, not with CA three days behind us.'

'We'll handle it. You can't get round Kliddoe; he'll miss them two scouts and get more out. He can ride faster than we can move the herd,' Mark drawled. 'Go right ahead, we'll handle the herd for you.'

Dusty had known Mark would say that. Now all that remained was to select his men and explain what he wanted. It was a good plan, if it could be worked.

If it *didn't* work, there would be stirring times round Kliddoe's camp real soon.

'I'm taking Kiowa, Billy Jack, Dude, Basin, Red and Frank. With Lon and me that should be enough. The rest of you, keep the herd moving. Ole Tarbrush's going to miss sleep again; he'll handle the remuda. Lil Jackie and Hobie'll ride the drag. This is how we play it.'

Billy Jack lounged against the side of the bedwagon and

watched the small rider who held the attention of every man here. He remembered other similar scenes in the war: A bald-faced youngster in Captain's uniform standing in the centre of a group of attentive men, planning some fresh attack against the Union forces. Captain Dusty hadn't changed much since the days when he led the Texas Light Cavalry in raids that rivalled the best of John Singleton Mosby and Turner Ashby.

Thora sat back and watched the scene; it was one she never forgot. Often, on the long drive north, she wondered why these men, all bigger and many far stronger than Dusty, followed him and accepted his orders. Now she knew, knew from her own knowledge of great leaders. She had met Grant Sheridan and even Lincoln; all had that same air Dusty possessed—the air of a born leader. It was that which had made Dusty a Cavalry Captain at seventeen. It was that which made him a trail boss.

'I would like to go along with you, Dusty,' her voice sounded unnaturally loud to her.

'It'll be no place for a woman,' Red Tolliver pointed out.

'Somebody told me the same thing about this drive. But I've managed so far and haven't been too much of a nuisance.'

'You surely ain't!' Basin Jones agreed.

'You've made a hand, Thora,' Dude whooped.

'Then I claim the right as a hand.' Thora stood in the light of the fire, head thrown back and meeting the eyes of the men. 'I claim it as much as the Ysabel Kid can claim it.'

'I backs the claim,' Billy Jack was on his feet, standing erect, hands hanging by the butts of the matched Colts. In the firelight, he was transformed. The miserable, hang-dog look had left him for once, showing what he really was—a bone-tough Texas fighting man. 'Likewise I passes my word Miz Thora'll be safe.'

'All we asks is that you stops back until we've got them hawg-tied.' Duke spoke softly. 'Then you can do most anything you likes with them.'

Thora saw the pride in every face as they met her eyes. Never had she seen the hands of Rocking H look at her with so much respect. She smiled round the faces. The attacking party's worries at having her along were not that she would spoil things, but that she might get hurt.

'Right, talk's over,' Dusty snapped. 'Get the gear I want set up, Billy Jack. Use some of the boys to help you. Red, get out to the remuda and collect a couple of horses. I want to pull out in less than an hour. Lon, I'll let you take care of Cousin Cawther. Look after him real good.'

Fifty minutes later the raiding party were mounted and ready for war. Dusty paused as the others rode out, held his hand out to Mark. 'I'd like you along, *amigo*. Reckon the next drive we handle you'd best be the trail boss, you're missing all the fun.'

'Sure.' Mark crushed his pard's hand. 'You just take care of the boss lady. And Lon.'

The sun was just rising, flooding Kliddoe's camp with light when the great man himself stepped from his Sibley to look around the camp. The first of the trail drives might be within striking range that day, so he was already dressed in his uniform. He turned his attention to the picket line and saw his nephew's palomino wasn't there.

'Cawther not back yet?' he asked one of the men.

'Nope. Thought he'd be in last night, but him and Blount never showed.'

The news didn't worry Kliddoe unduly; his two scouts might be making sure the herd didn't swing off at the last minute.

Looking round the camp, Kliddoe wondered how these new men would react to their task. The old crew had either gone under, or scattered, last year after the disastrous attempt to head-tax the herd of Shangai Pierce. The new men were of different stock from the savage crowd who had ridden with him in the war. Only five of these old hands remained; they were separate from the rest, for they couldn't get on with the new men.

Most of the new men had fought in the war, but they had fought in more conventional groups than his Raiders. They were poor squatters and only took on with him to make a stake for moving west. They might not like the idea of taking tax from the Rocking H herd, if they knew of his relationship with the owner. That was one of his worries; a couple of the men had served in Langley Bosanquet's regiment in the War and they might or might not recognise Thora. However, they all firmly believed he was appointed by the Governor of Kansas Territory to take head-tax on the north-bound Texas herds, and so would believe they were acting in the right.

Suddenly a man jumped to his feet and pointed up the rim. The others all leapt up, grabbing for weapons.

Kliddoe spun round, following the gaze of the man. On top of the rim, sat three men on horses. The centre one was Cawther Kliddoe, his arm in a sling. The other two were young Texas cowhands.

'Kliddoe!' the smaller of the Texans yelled. 'Tell your men to lay down their weapons. Look up here and see what I mean.'

Kliddoe and his men looked to where the Texan pointed, and all attempts to draw weapons ended. The top of the rim had several men, dark shapes hidden behind rocks or under scrub oaks. Each man was only in evidence by the shape of his hat and his rifle barrel which lined down on the camp.

A man at the rear of the group pulled his gun out. Then, from behind the camp, top the other rim, a rifle cracked. Kliddoe and his men turned to see other men lining weapons down on them from behind. The man whose attempt to draw a weapon had brought the shot stood fast. The bullet had hit between his feet.

'Any more shooting, and poor lil ole Cawther gets his,' the dark youngster on the big white called. He sat close to Cawther Kliddoe, yet the watchers could see something metallic glinting close to their wounded friend. 'I've got him on the point of ole Annie Breen here. And she'll likely cut him in half, happen there's trouble.'

'Do what they ses, Uncle Jethro!' Cawther howled, 'this here Ysabel Kid'll do for me, if you don't.'

A man clawed at his belt, trying to get his revolver out. Dusty's right hand flipped and his long-barrelled Army Colt cracked. For a fast took, off-hand shot at long range, the aim was good and lucky. The bullet sent dirt flying under the feet of the man.

'Hold it, all of you!' The Kid's yell cut across the distance as Kliddoe's men prepared to get into action. 'Next to draw gets ole Cawther here cut in half. Then the boys on the rim'll down Jethro.'

'Drop your guns, all of you!' Dusty barked out. 'I'll give you the count of five. Then we start into shooting.'

On the third of the count, Cawther Kliddoe screamed for

the men to let fall their guns. He knew how large the raiding-party was; but he also knew that he was number one mark for them. Jethro Kliddoe's men might fight off the Texans, but he wasn't going to be alive to see it.

Jethro Kliddoe was in an awkward spot. His men were waiting for his guidance, ready to follow whatever lead he gave them. With his old bunch, if he had been in no danger, he would have started shooting and let Cawther take his chance. With the old hands, that would have been their only thought. These new men were not of that sort. They wouldn't expect their leader to endanger the life of his favourite nephew.

There was another thought in Kliddoe's mind. He was under no delusion as to how the men of the South regarded him. Every Texas man on that rim would be lining his rifle, ready, willing and more than able to send lead into the hated Kliddoe.

With this in mind, Kliddoe took the only course left open to him. He stepped forward and removed the revolver from his holster to toss it into the dust.

'Move aside, Kliddoe. Let each of your men drop his guns, then get clear of them.'

Kliddoe took the orders, and man after man dropped his weapons, then moved to one side. Every rider was disarmed and stood clear of the weapons before the next move was made. Four more riders came over the rim and the group rode down the slope. The sullen Kliddoe men watched the riders coming nearer, but none made a move.

Dude and Billy Jack rode forward to perform their part in the plan Dusty had made. They swung down from their horses and, taking a rope each, threaded the end through the trigger guards of the weapons, until all were fastened together in two piles.

A big, burly man stepped forward from the Tax Collector ranks. He hadn't the look of a Kliddoe tough, rather of a hard professional non-com. 'You can get away with this. We've been appointed by the Governor to take tax on the trail herds. Colonel Kliddoe has a warrant to do it.'

'You're wrong, Sergeant Marples.'

The big man stared at Thora, as if he was seeing a ghost. Then he stepped forward and looked harder. 'Miz Thora, by all that's holy! What're you doing here?'

'Taking my trail herd to Dodge.'

'*Your* trail herd?' Marples twisted round to face Kliddoe. 'Did you know whose herd it was?'

'He surely didn't,' the Ysabel Kid sneered. 'His scout never told him about trying to force Miz Thora to hire him down in Texas, and how he dogged us all the way north.'

'Scout?' Marples turned his attention to the dark youngster who sat with a bowie knife resting against Cawther Kliddoe's belt. 'What do you know about Blount? And where is he?'

'Gone, friend—to a far happier place than this. I surely hope it don't get too hot for him.'

'You killed him?' Jethro Kliddoe asked.

'He ended that way.'

'Hold it!' Dusty's bark cut across the angry mutter of the Kliddoe men. 'You all reckon that Kliddoe is working for the Governor in this here head-tax collecting?' The men growled their agreement. He went on: 'That warrant is a fake. Stone Hart, of the Wedge, proved that once, and Shangai Pierce the second time. Kliddoe's got no more right to tax the trail herds than I have.'

'You rebs would say that,' Marples growled.

'Friend,' the Kid's voice was that deceptive mild tone again, you stand behind Kliddoe because he's a real, noble Yankee hero?' Marples nodded, and tried to speak but the Kid went on. 'Waal, I've got something to show you. Happen it'll make you real proud to know Colonel Jethro Kliddoe. If friend Billy Jack here'll tend to Cawther.'

Kliddoe watched the thin, miserable-looking man take the knife and assume position as guard on his nephew. Then he stared at the thing the Ysabel Kid took from his saddle-horn. He recognised the object and felt a sudden panic. If this dark boy possessed that thing, he must have something more—something that spelled finish for Jethro Kliddoe.

The Ysabel Kid dropped lightly from his saddle; in his hands he held a third model Colt Dragoon with an attachable canteen stock fitted to the butt. The gun was a finely-engraved piece and, in the walnut of the stock, was a silver plate. All too well, Kliddoe knew what was engraved on it.

'This here Dragoon came into my hands in the War. Me'n my pappy were riding scout for Colonel Mosby and we got us a Yankee Captain. Pappy gave me this gun. The butt-plate reads: "To Mason Haines, from his good friend, Jethro Kliddoe."'

The Kliddoe men all looked at each other. Three or four of them, including Marples, knew who Haines had been.

'So that's what happened to Cap'n Haines?' the big man growled.

'Sure.' The Kid didn't take his eyes from Kliddoe's. The dark young face was emotionless as he savoured the moment he had waited for since the day he first came by the gun. 'It wasn't the gun that got us all interested. It was a letter we found in the canteen that got us.' Reaching into his vest pocket, the Kid removed an old, yellowed envelope. 'Yeah, Kliddoe. I've still got the letter. Ole Devil kept me too busy to bring it to you afore this.'

Kliddoe didn't move or speak. His face had lost all its colour. The end was very near, if the men believed that letter.

'What does the letter say, Lon?' Thora asked, her face as pale as Kliddoe's.

'It's addressed to William Clarke Quantrell,' the Kid replied. He ignored the sudden gasp from the listeners as he opened the envelope and took out the letter. 'It reads: "*Will meet you outside Lawrence on the night of August twentieth. Am only bringing ten men as I am not sure how many more I can trust. Warn Anderson and Todd we are coming, as we will have to travel in uniform. Your information about the wagons was a dud. They were all Quakers, and not worth robbing. The only way I can avoid trouble is to lay the blame on Bosanquet.*" The letter is signed "Jethro Kliddoe", and marked with his seal.'

'That's a lie,' Kliddoe began. 'I never——'

Marples and another man moved forward. 'Let's have a look at that letter.'

The Kid passed over the letter without a word. Both men studied the broken, but still legible, seal on the back. Then they glanced at the writing. The second man took a paper from his pocket and compared the writing on it with that of the letter.

'That's Kliddoe's all right—and that's his seal!'

Marples spat in the dirt at Kliddoe's feet. 'Yeah. And now I think about it, you was away from us when we heard about the attack on Lawrence.'

Thora swayed in her saddle. The world seemed to be spinning round her. She could hardly believe her ears, but knew that her father's name was cleared by the letter that proved Kliddoe a traitor. More, it implicated him in the sacking of the town of Lawrence, Kansas, along with the gangs of Quantrell, Anderson and Todd.

Marples leapt forward to catch the girl and help her from her horse. 'I never believed your father ordered that attack.'

The other men turned on Kliddoe, their faces showing hatred. They stopped as Kliddoe's sabre came out and made a flashing arc. 'Get back, all of you!' he snarled. 'I'd rather be killed by these rebel scum than by you. Go ahead, shoot me down. There's not one of you would dare face me with a sabre.'

'Well now, I wouldn't say that.'

The soft-spoken words cut across the shouting of the crowd and stilled it as they turned to see who had spoken.

Kliddoe studied the small man on the big paint stallion. 'Who might you be?'

'The name is Dusty Fog, Captain, Texas Light Cavalry. Is there another sabre in the camp?'

'There is, in my Sibley.' For a moment, there was a gleam in Kliddoe's eyes.

'Get it, Lon,' Dusty ordered. 'Dude, take this gent here and collect Kliddoe's horse. Let the gent saddle it and fetch it back.'

Marples and the Texan walked away towards the horse-lines to pick Kliddoe's mount. Dude was relaxed and showed no suspicion that any foul play might be contemplated by Marples, and the northern man ignored the gun in the Texan's holster.

The Kid crossed to the Sibley to collect the sabre. He had wanted to settle with Kliddoe himself, but Dusty had taken the play from him by accepting the challenge. He promised himself that he would sit out as long as Kliddoe played fair; but at the first sign of treachery, he would be free to take whatever hand he felt was required in the matter.

Thora came to Dusty, who smiled down at her worried face. 'Dusty, you mustn't go through with this. Kliddoe is good with a sabre.'

'He called us rebel scum.' Dusty's eyes were cold. 'No man can call me that and live.'

The Kliddoe men were talking amongst themselves. The original five moved away from the rest watching the two piles of guns on the ground. One of the other men stepped forward to address Dusty: 'Cap'n Fog, we all know you by reputation. You fought as a soldier in the War and behaved with honour. We don't see any need for you to go through with this and, if you'll let us, we'll take Kliddoe in for trial.'

'Thank you, sir. But this is between Kliddoe and me. He called the play, so we'll let them fall and see how they lie.'

The Ysabel Kid returned to hand over the sabre to Dusty. He looked around, then glanced at Cawther Kliddoe, 'Didn't you tell these gents how many men were up on the rim?'

CHAPTER TWELVE

CAPTAIN FOG SHOWS MORE TALENT

At the Kid's words every man looked up towards the rim. The figures with the rifles were still there, alert and motionless. Motionless. Every Kliddoe man looked harder, slowly it came to them. There was only one man on each side of the rim. The rest of the attacking force were nothing but dummies, hats stuck on bedrolls. In the half light of the dawn, with the rifles sticking out, they had been enough to fool Kliddoe and his men.

For a moment there was silence. Then Marples threw back his head and roared with laughter. Man after man of the new Kliddoe men joined in the laughter, slapping each other on the back in their delight at the neat way they had been tricked.

'You danged rebs!' Marples gasped at last. 'You're trickier than a city three-card monte man.'

Kliddoe removed his belt, then stripped off his coat and rolled up his sleeves. He felt admiration for this small, soft-talking Texas man who had fooled him. Taking the sabre, he walked to his horse. He was in bad trouble and likely would die one way or the other. His one wish was to kill the man who had outwitted and ended him.

Dusty unbuckled his gunbelt and handed it to Marples in silent tribute to the man's honesty. Then he checked the girths of the saddle, patted the neck of the big paint and swung up. Kliddoe watched Dusty, a secretive sneer playing round his lips. He rode out into the open away from the camp. The Texan followed. They halted, facing each other, some thirty yards apart. Kliddoe lifted his sabre in a mocking salute and noted that the Texan at least knew how to hold and salute with a sabre.

Lounging easily in the saddle, Dusty hefted the long sabre. It was sharp enough and balanced well, but he would have preferred to be using his own, Confederate Haiman-made sabre for a serious fight.

Billy Jack stepped forward and asked formally: 'Are you ready, Colonel Kliddoe?' Kliddoe nodded. 'Captain Fog?' Dusty agreed. 'Then fight!'

The two horses leapt forward as Billy Jack's words cracked out. Kliddoe sat erect in his saddle, sabre held at the guard, ready for use. In contrast, Dusty appeared to be lounging in his kak, his sabre loosely pointing along the neck of his horse. It was plain that he was the better horseman of the two and, in an affair of this kind, the better rider had an edge.

Kliddoe hurled his big black horse full at Dusty's mount, trying to knock the paint off its feet. Too late, he realised just how big the stallion was. At the last moment, he tried to swing the black clear, but Dusty slammed his paint into it and staggered it. Kliddoe brought round his sabre in a backhand slash at the Texan's head. Dusty parried the cut, deflected it, then flickered out the point in a trust. It was Kliddoe's turn to parry now; he caught the blade and turned it just in time, then spurred his horse past. Dusty cut at Kliddoe and almost scored a hit as the other man rode clear.

The paint was as fast on its feet as many cutting horses and came round before Kliddoe got his black round. They came together, the Yankee rising in his stirrups to get more strength behind each blow and to take advantage of his extra reach. He was revising his opinion of the fighting qualities of his opponent. At first, he had thought Dusty had the basic rudiments of the sabre. Now he knew different; the Texan was very good.

Dusty for his part, was alert, watching every move and thanking the providence which had caused him to keep up his sabre-practice down in the Rio Hondo country. Steering the paint by knee pressure alone, Dusty used the point of his weapon in flickering thrusts. He knew he had to tire the other man. Kliddoe fought savagely, his sabre cutting and slashing; but all the time, that flickering point kept him back and gave him trouble.

They separated and rode in a circle, the paint turning the faster. Kliddoe hauled back on the mouth of his horse, making it rear high, hooves lashing down at Dusty. The Texan slid over the flank of his paint, out of the saddle even as the hooves hit his saddle. Then the paint was past the black. Dusty was still holding the saddle-horn with his left hand. He bounded lightly and went afork with a leap. Bringing the paint round, he headed back at Kliddoe.

The blades licked and glinted in the early morning sun. Kliddoe was still trying to get an advantage from his extra reach, but Dusty's fast-moving point was something he couldn't get by. The watchers studied the fight; some of them knew sabre work, and could see that both men were even in skill. Only the Texan's superior riding was tilting the balance. However, Dusty knew that his paint was tiring. The big horse had been worked hard against the grain-fed freshness of Kliddoe's black.

With this in mind, Dusty started to attack himself, forcing the paint in, point licking at Kliddoe with a speed and precision that drove the bigger man back.

Desperately, Kliddoe beat at the sabre. Then, with his left hand, he forced Dusty's blade down on to his saddle. Raising the hilt of his weapon, he smashed it down on the blade. A moan went up from the crowd as Dusty's sabre smashed, the broken blade falling to the ground.

Kliddoe screamed in triumph and he slashed at the Texan. His blade was parried by the broken stub of blade, then Dusty was by him and clear.

Hauling on the reins, Kliddoe brought his horse round, tearing at its mouth. Dusty rode clear, but even now was bringing the paint round again. He threw the broken sabre to one side, then sent the paint at Kliddoe. The other man rode forward, guessing what Dusty would try. The Texan was going to swing by on the left, to avoid a sabre cut, and hang over the side of his saddle. Rising in his stirrups, Kliddoe twisted himself slightly, ready to cut at the leg as the Texan went by him.

Nearer the two horses came, hooves thundering and dirt flying as they closed on each other. Kliddoe saw the Texan was looking to his left and prepared to cut down, severing Dusty's leg, if he rode Indian style over the flank.

At the last moment Dusty's paint swung. Kliddoe gave a startled curse; the horse was going to his right. He tried to turn back, felt a pair of hands grip his leg and haul his foot from the stirrup. Then he was falling from his horse, landing hard, but he still held his sabre as he came up.

Dusty came from his saddle before the paint halted. He landed lightly, turning to face Kliddoe. The other men started to run forward to stop this unfair fight. Kliddoe saw this and rushed in. He swung wildly and Dusty avoided the blow. Throwing the sabre aside, Kliddoe made his supreme bid. The little derringer he had hidden in his waistband came out, lined.

Coming into the attack Dusty saw that he was too late; the murderous single-shot weapon came up to line on him. A shot roared and Kliddoe staggered forward as lead hit him. An instant later the Ysabel Kid's bowie knife sank in between his shoulder-blades.

Marples hefted Dusty's Colt, then said apologetically: 'I'm sorry, Cap'n Fog. Didn't figger you can lick a hideout gun with your bare hands, so I cut in.'

The men swarmed forward eagerly. One stopped and collected the two parts of the broken sabre. Examining the blade, he spat out a curse: 'Some hero—the blade of the sabre'd been weakened.'

The broken sabre was passed from hand to hand. Man after man saw the tell-tale marks where the blade had been weakened in forging. It was an old trick of professional dualists. Both blades were the same. They would hold up under normal fighting, but a sharp blow at the right spot snapped the steel.

'And we reckoned he was some feller!' a man growled.

The five old Kliddoe men and Cawther were ignored during

the fight. They saw their chance now and dashed for the piles of weapons. One cut the rope and threw guns out to the others. From up the slope a rifle cracked; Cawther Kliddoe went down as he clawed up a revolver.

The crowd saw that had happened and scattered. The five Kliddoe toughs had their guns. These were firing at their erstwhile comrades, even as the Texans got into action. Billy Jack was the first man started, his right-hand gun throwing lead an instant ahead of Dude's. Then the other men joined in. Three of the Kliddoe men went down in the first roaring Texas volley. The fourth crumpled up to a fast-thrown shot by Marples and the fifth sent Billy Jack's hat flying from his head. Just who got this last man was never discovered. There were five holes in him, when the men checked. Any one of these would have been fatal.

Stepping forward, Marples handed Dusty his gunbelt. 'Cap'n Fog, sir, there's been a lot of foolishness done by men like Kliddoe since the war. He kept us thinking that we were still fighting you rebs. I reckon it was for his own profit, same as he fought in the war. I'll give you my word that there'll be no more head-taxing done on the border.'

Dusty buckled on his gunbelt again, then held out his hand to Marples. 'That'll be all right with us. Kliddoe and his old bunch have all gone under, I reckon you can tend to them. We'd best get back to the herd.'

'Joe, walk the Cap'n's paint until it cools,' Marples snapped. 'Bill, you saddle a hoss for him to ride back to his herd.' Turning to the Kid, he took the old letter from his pocket. 'I'd like to keep this. I aim to see that Colonel Bosanquet's name is cleared.'

'You'll have trouble, friend,' the Kid answered. 'Custer and his bunch won't want it showing one of their friends played both sides.'

'I'll do it,' Marples promised, his voice grim. 'I know a few folks who'd be willing to help. One of the Colonel's friends is our Senator—he'll see the truth is known.'

There were tears in Thora's eyes as she shook hands with the big ex-sergeant. She knew that he would try and clear her father's name. 'I don't care if they don't clear him publicly,' she said, 'as long as our friends know father didn't order that attack.'

The Kid looked at the letter, a half-smile on his lips. 'You take good care of it, friend. I have all these years.'

'You coming, Miz Thora?' Billy Jack asked.

'Reckon so.' She turned her horse and followed.

Billy Jack turned to Dusty. 'You nigh on skeered me to death, Cap'n. Back there, when that sabre got bust. 'Course I knowed you could handle him.'

'That why you near to poked my eye out with that ole Colt?' Dude asked. 'Trying to line on Kliddoe.'

'Warn't doing no such thing. I was just trying to see that my sights was on straight. Anyways, you'n Basin near to beat my head in waving your guns round.'

'Sure. We was thinking our sights warn't too straight neither,' Basin drawled. 'Taken all in all, I reckon we done a good day's work.'

The horses were headed at a good pace, making for where the dust cloud marked their herd.

'I never thought I'd see the day when I'd be pleased to know you three fellers,' Thora remarked. 'It was a lucky day when you came along. I'd almost made my mind up to tell you we didn't need any men, back in Granite. I thought you looked too young to ride a herd. I'm pleased that you took on. I can't believe that my father's name is cleared. It's hard to believe the Kid would keep that letter all this time.'

'Lon's a strange man,' Dusty replied. 'When you call him Comanche, it isn't far out. He's got the patience of any Injun. In all the years we rode together, he never talked much about Kliddoe; but, every time we took a trail herd north, I reckon he hoped to meet up with him. If we hadn't one day, he'd have asked Ole Devil if he could go out and return the letter. And that would have been the end of it.'

They rode on in silence for a time, but Thora was too full of happiness to try and hold anything back. 'You knew all along that I was hiding something, didn't you?'

'Sure, even half-guessed what it was. That was your third reason for wanting to come on this drive.'

'Yes. I didn't know we would meet up with Kliddoe. And I thought, if we did, that I might be able to prevent bloodshed.' Her face flushed red, but she had to talk, and so went on. 'My other reason is, I wrote a book about ranch life. It's selling well. I wanted to do another about trail-drive work.'

'A book about *this* drive?' Dusty looked startled.

She nodded, her eyes gleamed with delight. 'Don't worry—I won't put anything in it to embarrass you and the boys. I didn't when I wrote my last book about the Rocking H.'

'A book—all this bunch in a book. Folks won't believe it.'

The Ysabel Kid halted his horse and waited for the other two to catch up with him. 'Waal, that's Mr. Toon and Colonel Kliddoe done handled. Don't but leave us Marshal Earp to tend to.'

'That's right,' it was a shock to Thora to suddenly remember Earp's warning to the herd. 'What do you aim to do about him, Dusty?'

'Nothing.'

'Nothing?' Thora stared at the trail boss. 'But he——'

'He's in Dodge, and we're not there yet, so how can we do anything about him?'

'But how about when we get there?'

'Ah!' Dusty looked wisely at the Kid. 'That's some different, isn't it, Lon?'

'Sure. Earp's made a lot of talk about the Rocking H not coming to Dodge, but he can't back it none. Earp never was a fighting man, except when he's got the backing. Which same he won't have in Dodge. He won't try and touch us, now he's lost the edge.'

It was Dusty who explained: 'Dodge gets its money from three sets of folk! Texas trail drives, buffalo hunters and railroad men. So they want us in there—not chased off by some two-bit loudmouth.'

'And it means that, if he chouses us off, the big, brave Mr. Earp won't never get no shiny badge to pin on his chest—which same he wants so bad. See, Mr. Earp dearly loves to hide behind a star,' the Kid finished.

'You mean there won't be trouble?'

'Didn't say that,' Dusty warned. 'Earp could likely get some help, happen he tried. I don't figure Luke Short, Billy Tilghman, or Bat Masterson will side him in this, but he might get some others to join in. But apart from those three there isn't one he could get who's worry a weaned calf. Up to and including Doc Holliday.'

'Doc Holliday?' Thora frowned. 'He's a dangerous killer, isn't he?'

The Ysabel Kid laughed, his wild Comanche laughter ringing out. 'Ole Doc? Ain't never killed anybody that I knows of. He knows how to look mean and happen he got loaded enough with brave-maker, he'd kill a drunk, but that's all.'

'Bat Masterson doesn't like Doc; he'd be real pleased to get a chance to move him on again. Could do it, too,' said Dusty.

They came up towards the herd; the hands had for once forgotten all about cattle as they gathered round the raiding-party, to hear the news. Mark rode out to meet his friends. He grinned as he saw the looks Dusty was giving the crew.

'Meet Kliddoe?' he asked.

'Sure. See you've still got some of the herd.'

'Nope, we lost all our'n. These belong to CA.'

'Way this lot are sat round, I'd say that was to be expected,' Dusty growled and rode by. Thora called that she was headed for the wagon, and rode back along the line.

'What happened?' Mark inquired of the Kid.

'You should have seen it, Ole Kliddoe allowed to get himself a real edge. Offered to take on all hands with a sabre.'

'Poor man.' Mark suffered no illusions about Dusty's skill with a sabre. 'I surely hope he knews better now.'

'He l'arned. He l'arned.'

The trail crew were all excitedly talking and none noticed the grim-faced trail boss as they listened to Billy Jack's stirring story of what happened to Kliddoe.

'*Gentlemen!*' The voice was cold and grimly incisive. The hands all turned to meet a pair of unpleasant grey eyes. 'May I ask just what the hell you were hired for? I might be wrong when I allow it's to ride herd, not to sit on your tired butt ends and whittlewhang like old women at a dance.' The crew looked sheepishly at each other and Dusty's voice rose to an angry roar: 'Let's get the herd to Dodge, then you can talk your fool tongues out.'

The remuda was scattered for Lil Jackie was with the other hands. The youngster sat his horse and listened, tight-lipped but unspeaking as Dusty told him in pungent and hide-searing terms just what he thought of a wrangler who allowed the remuda to scatter damn near back to Texas.

Dusty caught one of his string and saddled it, then looked round to make sure everything was meeting with his approval. The hands were shifting the cattle once more, and the remuda was collected. Then he headed back to the wagons. Thora's excited story of the raid was interrupted in mid-flight by a voice. 'Howdy, Mr. Ballew,' Dusty greeted sarcastically, almost mildly. 'Would it be asking too much for you and your fool louse to get moving so that comes bedding-time you've got a meal for the hands?'

Salt twisted round to observe the trail boss eyeing him. 'Yes, sir, Cap'n. I means no, sir, Cap'n. I'll do just that.'

'Today'd be real nice,' Dusty growled. 'I know Thora here's a woman and can't help jawing, but you're a man and can.'

Thora poked her tongue out, turned her horse and headed for the herd. Halfway there, she remembered that she had not changed mounts and turned for the remuda. She found Lil Jackie subdued, but not over worried by the bawling out.

Dusty sat easily in his kak and watched Hobie sprinting to his wagon. Then, hearing a horse approach he turned to find Ysabel Kid riding up. He looked the dark youngster over in disgust and said, 'Huh! The scout, and what may Mr. Loncey Dalton Ysabel be scouting back here?'

'Now don't you go abusing me, Cap'n, suh,' the Kid warned. 'You'll likely make me wet my pants. I heerd all the ruckus down here and thought the Injuns had jumped us. It warn't but you abusing the poor, fool ole cook. I'll light out after we've had a bite to eat.'

'Thank you most to death,' Dusty replied. He turned in his saddle to look round and make sure everyone was working. Seeing nothing to offend his sense of things, he relaxed. 'There's no need for you to go out. Besides, Thora told me she aims to write a book about the drive, and wants to know all about trail-driving.'

'Not from me she don't!' The Kid was emphatic. 'I don't want my name in no book.'

'Why not? I'll ask her to write you up real good. She can tell a few lies about you. Make you out a real nice young feller instead of a dead mean ole Comanche Dog soldier.'

'It ain't the lies that'd worry me,' the Kid objected. 'She might tell the truth about me.'

'Well, who'd that hurt?'

'*Me!* If word gets out I've been herding legal cattle, and by daylight, all my kin down on the border'll cut me dead when they see me.'

Dusty slapped the Kid on the shoulder. 'Say, now we've got these loafers to work, happen we'd best head up to the point and tell Mark what happened today.'

Salt watched Dusty and the Kid ride off towards the point and pulled aside to allow his assistant to catch alongside. Hobie gave a scared glance ahead to make sure the trail boss couldn't see them idling, then waited to hear what his lord and master had to say.

For a time Salt Ballew was silent. Then he spat out his chaw of tobacco and spoke: 'If you lives to be as old as me, which same ain't likely, you'll never work for a better man than him. He ain't tall, and he ain't the loudest talking man you'll ever see. But son, he's a trail boss.'

The chuckwagon lurched forward again and Hobie started his own team to follow. The cook's louse wasn't given to deep thinking, but he agreed with what Salt had just said.

Captain Fog was a trail boss.

CHAPTER THIRTEEN

MR. ODHAM HAS A PLAN

Dodge City got the news over the prairie grapevine. A trail drive was within two days of the town. The word ran through the saloons, gambling houses, dance-halls and other places of business around the cowboy capital. They heard the word from the former Kliddoe tax-collectors. That Kliddoe was dead interested them but little: he had been a menace who had slowed down the flow of money into the town. Of the word in the letter they took little interest; the War was long over and Texas money was badly needed in town.

Throughout Dodge the news was greeted with hurried checks on the items for sale.

It was a time of feverish activity in Dodge, the local citizens making the preparations. Doc Holliday spent time practising with his new, shiny faro box, checking that it would, in the words of the crooked gambling house catalogue: *'Bear any inspection while ensuring the top card was always under control and would prevent any flash from the bottom card whilst it was being dealt.'*

At the Texas House, first call of every herd-crew, Sam Snenton cleaned the head of his famous SS brand, in readiness for burning his mark on the sourdough keg of each spread. His pretty, dark wife, Selina, ran a final check that the kitchen held all the choice delicacies the Texans and the cattle-buyers would require, and ran an approving eye over the eight pretty girls who waited at the tables.

The cattle-buyers were there, well-dressed men from the Eastern syndicates. They came in for the season, wallets bulging with notes and bank drafts, ready to buy the long-horn cattle the Texans brought into the shipping-pens.

Maurice Odham wasn't one of the big buyers. He was a hanger-on, like a wolf following the flanks of a buffalo-herd. He would hang on in Dodge, ready to flash in and cut any small profit he could for himself. He reached Dodge a week or so before the big buyers, in the hope that a small herd might turn up for him to buy. In the time he spent wandering round the saloon, he heard much that interested him. Now, as he made his way to the Texas House on Trail Street, he had an inspiration.

The Texas House was faced, across the street, by Ed Sciffen's Buffalo House. The Texas House was Odham's original destination, but he remembered all he had heard. The man he wanted to see was not to be found in Sam Snenton's place.

Crossing the street, the small cattle-buyer pushed open the batwing doors of the Buffalo House and looked round. The man he wanted was standing at the bar. Wyatt Earp glanced at Odham, then ignored him. The big cattle-buyers were important people in Dodge, and Earp was always polite to them. Odham wasn't one of the important ones, and could have no use to anyone with plans, so Earp ignored him.

'Howdy, Marshal Earp.' Odham knew the other liked to be addressed as if he was a regular marshal. 'Barkeep, two drinks.'

'What do you want, Odham?' Earp growled.

'I heard the Rocking H was down trail. They didn't take your warning. They'll be here in a day or so.'

Earp grunted and moodily took his drink. He knew Rocking H were coming, knew it all too well. 'So?'

'Well, after all you've said about them, folks are wondering what you aim to do.'

'When I'm ready, I'll tell them,' Earp replied. Yet, for all of that, he knew what he was going to do. When definite word had reached Dodge that Rocking H were headed for the shipping-pens, and would be first herd in, Earp made a round of the town. He found a startling lack of enthusiasm amongst his friends when he mentioned stopping the herd.

He'd tried every man he could think of, knowing that tophands would be needed to handle the crew of the Rocking H. Luke Short, Doc Holliday, Dave Mathers, they all had the same answer: They didn't aim to stop the first herd coming in, as they were feeling the financial pinch along with the rest of the citizens of Dodge. The final blow had been delivered by Bat Masterson, sheriff of Ford County. Bat and Earp were friends, but the sheriff had his position to think about. He was a different kind of man to Earp, with none of the other's sanctimonious piety. More, he was popular with all classes in Dodge, liked and respected by the Texans as a fair and honest man. Bat's words struck a chill into Earp's heart. The City Fathers didn't consider it advisable to hire Earp as assistant deputy marshal any more. They would also look with some disfavour at a man who caused any delay in the arrival of the first herd.

So Earp found himself in an unenviable position. He had sent word out against the Rocking H, in the assumption that Ben Holland would not last the long trip back to Texas—or, if he did, couldn't send a herd again for some time. Now Earp was left, without the protection of a law badge, to face the consequences.

Odham watched Earp's face, then turned to the bartender. 'Any skin-hunters left around town?'

'Shag Moxel and his boys,' the bar-dog answered. 'They lost their stake, bucking the tiger. Camped over towards the creek.'

'Thanks!' Odham murmured and left the room.

For a time Earp stood silent. Then he tossed some money on the bar. 'Len, I've got to go down track to Kansas City for a few days. If Shag and his boys come in, let them drink that up.'

Len watched Earp leave the room and dropped the glasses into the tub under the counter.

Odham drove the livery barn buggy across the range at a fast clip. He whistled a tune and watched the cloud of dust which marked the progress of the first herd to Dodge. In his mind was an idea that he had used many times before in other trail-end towns. They had been good days—just at the start of the trail herds when every man could throw a herd together in Texas did so and headed north.

The livery barn horse kept up a steady trot. Odham handled the reins with half his attention on what he would say to the woman who owned the herd. The crew might not listen to him, but she would.

A tall, black-dressed young man, riding a big white stallion, was approaching. Odham watched him, and decided he would be the scout for the herd.

The Ysabel Kid studied the buggy with some interest, his red-hazel eyes taking in every detail. He rode forward and halted his horse across the path of the buggy.

'Howdy?' he greeted.

'Where at's your herd?'

'Under the dust there, less'n they lost 'em all,' the Kid replied. 'You're a cattle-buyer ain't you?'

'I am.' Odham puffed out his chest pompously. This cowhand was regarding him with less favour than a cattle-buyer deserved. 'How's the drive been?'

'Fair. I saw you one time in Hays.'

This wasn't what Odham had expected; he had hoped that none of the hands would know him. Certainly, he now hoped none would know of his business methods whilst in Hays City.

'I want to see your boss,' he remarked, as casually as he could.

'Take you back to see him.'

Dusty, Mark and Thora were riding out ahead of the herd. They were relaxed and taking things easy over the last few miles. Mark left the point to Kiowa and Billy Jack, claiming that, as he missed out on all the fun, he was going to take things easy for the last few miles of the drive.

'Won't make Dodge today,' Dusty remarked. 'We'll bed down out there a piece, and take the herd in tomorrow. Be there around noon.'

'Why'd you have a double night-herd and both scouts out

last night?' Thora asked. 'I thought we were out of trouble.'

'Just being careful. There used to be a bunch working the trail-end towns. They laid up a few miles out and hit the herds, stampeded them on either the last night or the second last. They'd usually get away with a few dozen head, or more. See, the trail-crews weren't expecting trouble that near to the town.'

'What'd they do with the cattle?'

'Hold them to the end of the season, then run them in. They'd try to alter, or counter-brand, the cattle. There were some buyers who would take a herd without asking too many questions.'

'Yeah!' Mark put in. He was looking ahead, at the Kid and the man who drove the buggy alongside him. 'And one of them's coming up right now.'

Dusty looked at the man in the buggy, his memory for faces being as good as those of his two friends. He recognised the newcomer. A half-smile played around his lips as he guessed why Odham was coming. 'Sure, Mark, we know him, I wonder if he's going to try his old game on us?'

'He'd never chance it,' Mark scoffed.

'What game is that?' Thora asked.

Before the Texans could reply, the buggy was up to them. Odham might have wondered why such a small, insignificant man rode at the place of honour, but he knew this man. 'Howdy, Cap'n Fog. I'm Sidney Odham. We met in Hays, I think.'

'I remember.' There was little friendship in Dusty's voice.

'I'd like to talk with the owner.'

'This is Mrs. Holland.'

Odham raised his hat politely, a warm, ingratiating smile on his face. He glanced at the cattle going past, fat, well-meated stock. They would command a high price in Dodge City. If he could play his cards right, the price would roll into his pockets.

'Mrs. Holland, I came out here to talk business with you. After seeing your herd, I'm really sorry to tell you that it isn't safe for you to take them into Dodge City.'

'Not take them into Dodge?' Thora glanced at Dusty and Mark—they looked impassive, but Dusty winked at her. 'Why shouldn't we take my herd into Dodge? I'm worry we can't offer you a meal, unless you can stay until we bed down.'

'That won't be necessary. What I came here for was to save you the embarrassment that awaits you. I will buy your herd from you right now.'

'Buy the herd?' Thora felt foolish, repeating the words, but couldn't think of anything else to say. Dusty and Mark weren't helping her with their silence. 'But that isn't usual, is it?'

'Not under normal circumstances. I would have waited in Dodge. But when I heard that Marshal Earp was taking on men to stop your herd using the pens, I thought I would come out and meet you, buy the herd and save you any further trouble. After all it is common knowledge that Marshal Earp ordered you never to use this town again. When a man of his calibre gives you such an order it is hardly prudent to go against it.'

'I didn't think Earp could prevent our using Dodge,' Thora objected but she was beginning to see the light now. Dusty and Mark still kept their faces impassive and unreadable and the Kid lounged in his saddle looking more Indian than ever.

'He can't under law of course, but in Dodge he and Sheriff Masterson are the law. You know of how they stick together. I saw Marshal Earp leaving the sheriff's office only yesterday, I daresay he'd been making arrangements to stop your herd coming to Dodge. I realise that your men could fight their way in—but think of the trouble and the bloodshed.'

'How much a head you figger on paying?' Dusty put in.

'Well, I have to hire the men to——'

'How much?'

'Fifteen dollars, I will have to——'

'*All* of fifteen dollars?' Dusty looked amazed at such generosity. 'Why thank you 'most to death.'

'That's real neighbourly of you, friend,' Mark agreed; but his voice held irony, not gratitude. 'You rode all these miles out here to take the herd off our hands, and save Thora some trouble. I allow we owe you a vote of thanks. What do you reckon, Lon?'

The Ysabel Kid looked Odham over with the same kind of pleasure he might give a bed-sharing gila monster. Pushing the big white to the buggy, he leaned forward to look Odham over. 'Yep, let's us give him one right now. Just like ole Stone Hart's Wedge did that time at Hays. Mister, you've got a heart like a winter's night—cold, dark and hawg-dirty!'

'What's wrong, Dusty?' Thora asked, though she had a fair idea.

'Not much. This kind-hearted gent here come all the way from Dodge, with us less than a day's drive out, and offers to buy the herd from us.'

'Sure.' Mark finished; 'for less than half we can make for it in Dodge.'

'Mrs. Holland, I'd prefer to deal with you, not hired hands. I came out here to save you from some trouble——'

'You came to make some easy money,' the Kid growled. 'Now just take off, or I'll ram a boot down your neck.'

Odham scowled and only his knowledge of the ways of Loncey Dalton Ysabel prevented further objections. He scowled round at the herd, then back at Thora, 'I'm sorry you take this attitude, Mrs. Holland. I've tried to help you, but——'

'I'm sorry, too. But, when I took Dusty on as trail boss, I agreed that he would handle the herd. I'm merely Rocking H's rep, and so I've no more to say about selling the herd than any other hand. If you want to buy the cattle, you must talk with Captain Fog.'

Odham scowled, for he knew that what Thora said was the truth. If she was riding as the representative of the spread, she could not sell the herd; only the trail boss could do that. He also knew that any attempt to fool, or buy, cattle from Dusty Fog was doomed for disaster straight off. Turning the buggy he set the horse moving and drove back across the range towards Dodge.

Away from the herd, he laid his whip to the horse and let it run. In his heart, there was black rage against the Texas men who rode for Rocking H. His plan had been to persuade Thora to sell and they foiled it neatly.

The horses were lathered by the time he reached Dodge; circling the town, he found what he was looking for.

The camp of the buffalo-hunters was on the bank of a creek —just a wagon, a fire and some untidy bedrolls. The seven men who lounged around the fire were all dressed in buckskins, dirty and unshaven. One was tall, heavily-built and ugly-looking. He looked up as Odham drove up to the fire. 'What do you want?' he growled.

'You Shag Moxel?' Odham knew the answer without needing the surly nod the other gave him. 'How's things, Shag?'

'Not bad.' Moxel took the whisky flask Odham offered, drank and then spat appreciatively. 'You from Dodge?'

'Sure. I saw the trail boss of the Rocking H. He's looking for you.'

The skin-hunters looked up from their places round the fire. Shag Moxel's brows drew into lines as he asked, 'Is he now?'

'Reckon we can handle him, don't you, Shag?' one of the other men asked.

'Could, if we'd got enough food to stay on,' Moxel agreed. 'There ain't no hunting round Dodge, and we've got to head out after the herds.'

Odham took out his wallet, peeled off some notes and passed them to Moxel. 'Here. Call it a loan. Go into town and get yourself some food. You watch for their trail boss. You can't miss him—he rides a paint.'

Moxel took the money and looked up suspiciously. 'Why're you doing this for us?'

'I don't like cowhands. Besides, we don't want folks saying you ran out of Dodge and from the Texans.'

Moxel reached over and picked up the old ten-gauge shotgun from his bedroll. He broke open the weapon. 'Nope—we don't.'

Thora watched the cattle-buyer heading away, then turned her attention to the three lounging Texas men. 'Just what was all that about?' she asked. 'I didn't get half of it.'

'I never thought he'd pull that old game with us,' Mark replied. 'It went out with the Colt Dragoon.'

'What game?'

'One he played a couple of times, maybe more, in the early drive days. He'd leave Hays, or whatever town Kliddoe was working near, and look for a small herd, one without many men. Then he'd warn them Kliddoe was waiting, and offer to buy the herd,' Mark explained.

'At about half the market price,' Dusty put in.

'Sure. Worked real well, for a piece. The small owners hadn't the men to fight off Kliddoe, and couldn't afford to pay, so they sold to Odham and reckoned they were lucky. Odham worked it well. Then he made a mistake. The small ranchers back to Texas pooled together. Stone Hart gathered their herds, made a big drive and came north. He faced Kliddoe down, him and his Wedge crew. Then, the following day, Odham met him with the news Kliddoe was ahead, reckoned he'd buy the herd. Wedge sent him back to Hays without his pants!'

'He just faded out after that, turned up in a couple of other trail-towns, but word had gone out about him. The small owners didn't try to drive alone; they pooled and hired Stone Hart's Wedge, or somebody like that, to bring their cattle to market,' Dusty finished.

Dude and Lil Jackie rode up. The cowhand raised his hat to Thora and asked, 'Can the button head into Dodge, Cap'n? There's some of us left without smoke or chaw.'

Dusty studied the eager face of the youngster, then glanced down at the fancy Navy Colt stuck in his belt. Lil Jackie had changed almost beyond recognition since joining the herd. Salt's cooking and plenty of it, gave him a filled-out look. The trail hands, with typical cowboy generosity, had supplied him with a change of clothing. Dude had given the wrangler a good hat and burned the old woolsey which caused him to be drenched with stew and knocked down by the trail boss.

The boy had changed; he looked older, fitter, and was well able to handle himself in either the rough horse-play of the camp or the hard work of the remuda. He sat his paint horse and waited eagerly to hear his fate.

'All right, boy,' Dusty said. 'Bring me a sack of Bull Durham and don't you get yourself into any trouble. If I find you in jail when we get to Dodge, I'll take the hide off you.'

Lil Jackie whooped his delight, kicked his spurs into the ribs of his horse and headed off for Dodge. Dusty watched him go and then turned to the Kid. 'Ain't no more scouting to be done, is there?'

'Nope. You reckon I'd best go to Dodge after the button and see he says out of trouble?'

'Reckon you'd best watch the remuda. See they keep out of trouble.'

CHAPTER FOURTEEN

SHAG MOXEL'S INDISCRETION

'THE button not back yet?' Dusty asked as he stood eating his breakfast on the last day of the drive.

'Not yet, likely stayed in Dodge the night and's headed back now,' Mark replied, then looked round the camp. 'Reckon we'll make Dodge this week, happen these bunch don't fall asleep on the trail.'

The cowhands jeered derisively and headed for their horses. There was a light-hearted mood in the air as they headed the cattle up ready to pull out on the last stage of the journey. Every man was thinking of the various uses they had for the money they'd get when the herd paid off.

Kiowa and Tarbrush handled the remuda this final day, leaving the Kid to ride ahead with Dusty and Mark. It was the last day and already, in the far distance, they could see the sun shining on the roofs of Dodge City.

The Kid stopped his horse, squinting his eyes as he stared ahead across the range.

'Two riders,' he said, pointing across the range. 'Sits like Bat Masterson and Billy Tilghman.'

Dusty and Mark could see the two riders, but not well enough to make any guess as to who they might be. They both felt admiration for their keen-eyed friend, and knew his guess was most likely correct.

'Best go and meet them, then,' Dusty suggested. 'They'll likely want to warn us not to rope Trail Street and haul it down to the Cimmaron.'

Masterson and Tilghman rode towards the Texans, and neither man looked over-eager for this meeting. They knew that there were stormy times ahead, and hoped they could stop the worst of it.

'Howdy, Bat, Billy!' Dusty greeted. There were few Yankee lawmen he would have greeted so warmly. These two were good, honest lawmen; both played fairly with the Texas men, and so gained Dusty's respect for he knew handling trail hands at the end of a drive was exacting and dangerous work.

'Howdy, Dusty!' Masterson replied. He felt definitely uneasy, and glanced at Billy Tilghman. 'We've got some bad news for you.'

'Mr. Earp ain't gone and died of his meanness, has he?' the Kid inquired, watching the two lawmen with the wary attention of a part-reformed border smuggler.

Masterson didn't smile; his face was grave, his eyes not meeting those of the Texan. 'You sent your wrangler into Dodge last night?'

'Sure,' Dusty felt uneasy. Masterson was a good enough friend not to be nervous like this. 'Don't tell me you had to throw him into the hoosegow for treeing the town.'

'No. He's been killed!'

'Little Jackie—dead!' The easy slouch had left Dusty now.

'When did it happen, and how?' The slit-eyed, mean Comanche look was on the Kid's face again and the savage growl in his voice.

'Last night, he was riding out of town and got shot in the back.'

'With a ten-gauge?' Dusty's voice dropped to a soft drawl; but Masterson had heard it go soft like that before. When it did, the time had come for trouble. It meant bad trouble, and hunt for the cyclone cellars.

'With a ten-gauge,' Tilghman agreed. He was one of the bravest men ever to wear a law badge but he knew he wouldn't face any of this trio in their present mood.

'Where at's Earp?' the Kid's savage, Comanche growl cut in.

'He left town on the noon train yesterday. I saw him go,' Masterson replied.

'How about Shag Moxel?' Dusty put in, accepting Masterson's word.

'Still in Dodge. Saw him at the Buffalo House. His bunch allow he was with them all night. Sciffen reckons they were playing poker in his back-room. We can't prove anything——'

'Prove?' The Kid spat the word out. 'Had it been Earp or one of his stinking *amigos* who got downed, there wouldn't be no looking for proof. It'd just be find the first Texas neck and stretch it.'

'Not while I'm wearing a badge,' Masterson snapped, his temper rising. 'I tried to find out who killed your boy. Give me time and I may yet do it.'

'No offence, Bat,' the Kid replied. 'I just feel mean as a razor-back hawg. We took that kid on in Texas, and brought him north. He worked hard and was making a hand. Then some lousy back-shooting skunk puts him under.'

Thora rode across to the party; she could read the signs real well for a Yankee gal, and she knew that, when Dusty stopped lounging in his saddle, trouble was coming.

'Jackie dead?' she gasped when Dusty told her. 'Who did it?'

'I don't know, but it's surely time we found out.'

'Hold hard now, Dusty. Moxel's got six men with him. I don't want no war starting in Dodge.' Masterson snapped.

Dusty faced the sheriff, his eyes cold and expressionless. 'You should have told that to the man who killed Jackie. *Before* he did it.'

'Wasn't the button riding his paint?' Mark's deep drawl cut in.

'Sure,' Tilghman knew trouble was coming and wanted to stop it if he could. 'We've got it in the city——'

The words died an uneasy death as Tilghman and every man here looked at the huge paint stallion Dusty sat.

'Hell!' Masterson spat out. 'That buckshot was meant for you.'

'And there'll likely be more of it,' Dusty replied. Turning to Thora he went on. 'I want——'

'Take every man, if you need them,' she answered, before he could finish. 'I want the men who killed Jackie.'

'Won't need but Mark and Lon. You aiming to stop us, Bat?'

Masterson sat silent for a time. He knew that any attempt to halt Dusty, Mark and the Kid would end in gun-play. Then he shook his head; it wasn't fear that made him take this attitude, but his sense of fairness. The murder last night had been aimed at Dusty, not at the wrangler. Dusty would be in danger, unless he found the murderer and found him real fast.

'No, Dusty, I'm not going to stop you. I let Moxel stay on when I should have run him out of town. I was near certain he gunned Ben down, and hoped I'd get some proof. He kept quiet, and then this happened.'

'It was Moxel then?'

'I don't know enough to take him to court, but he's a friend of Sciffen. And his bunch would say whatever he told them. The town's yours for three weeks. Billy and me aims to go round the county on Tax Assessment. You'll be gone when we get back, I reckon.'

'We'll be gone,' Dusty agreed. 'Us and Clay Allison both.'

Masterson nodded. 'Heard he's coming north. I also heard some damned fool says I've passed word that he shouldn't use Dodge. I never passed any word.'

Dusty knew this without being told. He could guess that the story had been spread by someone who wanted to see a gun-fight, or wanted some excitement. 'I'll tell ole Clay.'

Masterson knew that, if he stayed in Dodge, there would be shooting and while not being afraid of Allison, was a realist. If he killed Allison, a lot of other men were going to look for him, and the reputation he gained. If he died, the City Fathers of Dodge would give him a first-rate funeral, but would only mourn him long enough to put in a replacement sheriff.

This way he could be out of Dodge while Clay Allison was there and not lose face by it.

The Kid jerked his rifle free and kicked his white forward, then stopped in disgust. The others all turned to see a fast-departing man headed for Dodge.

'Who was it?' Thora asked.

'A skin-hunter. He must have followed you, to see what was happening, Bat,' the Kid replied. 'That proves Moxel shot Jackie.'

'Likely,' Dusty agreed. 'Thora, you're trail boss. Billy Jack'll be segundo. Keep the herd moving. We'll meet you outside Dodge.' Turning to the other two members of Ole Devil's floating outfit he snapped, 'Let's go!'

Thora watched the three young men riding towards Dodge, then turned back to the lawmen. 'I think we could offer you breakfast and coffee back at the wagon, if we hurry.'

'Thanks, Mrs. Holland. Like to say that Dodge City wasn't behind the word Wyatt put out about Rocking H. There's times I think Wyatt talks too much.'

The skin-hunter who had followed Masterson and Tilghman from Dodge made good time back to Dodge. He pulled up outside the Buffalo House, leapt up the steps and crashed through the doors.

'You were right, Shag. Masterson went to the Texans and told them.'

Moxel turned. 'That means they'll be coming after us.'

Apart from Moxel's men, only the owner, Ed Sciffen, and his barman, Len, were in the saloon. Word had gone round Dodge that trouble was coming and, with that strange premonition which was peculiar to the frontier crowds, people stayed clear of both the Buffalo House and Sam Snenton's Texas House across the street.

Sciffen, a contrast to the untidy, dirty skin-hunters, with his elegant gambler dress, looked worried.

'What you aiming to do, Shag?' he asked. 'You got the wrong man last night.'

'I was telled the gunslick rode a paint. When I saw a Texas man riding a paint, and toting a fancy gun, I reckoned he was the one.'

'It wasn't Dusty Fog,' Sciffen warned. 'But he'll be here, looking for you.'

'We stopping to fight?' a tall, gangling skin-hunter asked.

'Sure, but we takes them *our* way,' Moxel replied, leering round at the others. 'Where'll be the first place them Texans head for, if they come looking for us?'

'Texas House, like they allus does,' Len suggested.

'That's right. We've seen all them Dodge City john laws pull out after Masterson went. Them Texans won't go to the jail, having seed Masterson. They'll come straight to the Texas House and ask Snenton where we are. I wants Blinky and Herb up on the roof. Bert and Case'll be along the street a piece, one on each side. Then we'll have 'em.'

'Snenton'll warn them,' a man growled.

'No, he won't. 'Cause you'n moe'll be in thar with a gun lined on that pretty wife that Snenton's so fond of. All right, Rut?'

Rut nodded, then went on: 'Where'll you be?'

'Right here at the bar. Me'n ole Len's going to have our ten-gauges lined on that door. That'll be the only way the Texans can run. Where you going, Sciffen?'

The saloon-keeper had left the bar and was walking across the room. He stopped. 'Got me some office work to do in the back.'

'All right. But, happen you don't come out when the shooting starts, I'll burn your place down.'

Sciffen tried to smile, but he was cursing the luck which made Wyatt Earp his customer. Earp had left money for Moxel's bunch to stay on with, and now Sciffen was deeper in trouble than he ever had been before. He went into the back room, opened his desk-drawer and lifted out his short barrelled Webley Bulldog revolver. He knew that he had to help Moxel, whether he liked it or not.

The Texas House was empty at this early hour and Sam Snenton was helping his wife to make the final arrangements for the arrival of the cattle-buyers at lunch time. Snenton was tall, wide-shouldered and heavily-built. He was a happy man, dressed in a spotless white shirt and comfortable jeans. Around his waist was an apron; but, tucked in his waistband out of sight, was a Remington double derringer.

The place was quiet, except for the occasional noise made by Hop Lee, the Chinese cook and general handyman, working in the kitchen. The dining room was large, and tables were large enough to accommodate six men each. Behind the bar, burned in the woodwork, were many brands—for this was the first place every Texas trail-drive crew made for when they hit Dodge at the end of the drive. Nearly every ranch-owner in Texas had left his brand burned on the wall back-board. Amongst them was P. and C. brand of Mark Counter's father's Big Bend outfit. In a place of honour was the OD Connected brand of Ole Devil Hardin. Snenton was proud of that back-board, it had come with him from Hays, Abilene and Wichita. On hooks made from the horns of a Texas steer hung the famous brand he used to mark the sourdough kegs of the different spreads which came to Dodge.

Selina Snenton was small, dark-haired and pretty. It was her capable business sense that turned this place into a financial success, for Sam was a genial host and liable to forget to collect pay for the meals eaten by a crew. She brought a solvency to the business, whilst he handled any trouble with a fast-pulled gun, or a punch like a Missouri mule-kick.

Two men entered the dining room. She turned and frowned. They were skin-hunters, part of Moxel's bunch. 'We're not serving yet, gentlemen,' she said.

Snenton turned and frowned; he disliked the Moxel bunch

and tried to keep them out of his place. 'Best come back in a couple of hours, if you want food. We won't have any until then.'

The men moved to either side of the door, both drawing their guns. Rut growled: 'Just stand still, Sammywell, and nobody'll get hurt.'

Snenton did what any man with gun-savvy would have under the circumstances. He stood still, but his hand dropped casually towards his waistband. 'What's the——?' he asked softly.

'Stand real still, Sammywell, if you don't want the missus hurt,' Moe snarled, cocking his gun and lining it on Selina. At that range he could hardly have missed.

'All right. But, if this is a stick-up, you've picked a real poor time. We banked last night.'

'Ain't sticking you up, Sam,' Moe answered. 'We wants to wait here for some friends what's likely to arrive sudden and unwelcomed if we don't do it for 'em.'

'Friends?' Sam Snenton felt suddenly cold. He had heard of the killing of the Texas boy, and guessed why the skin-hunters were here. 'Your friends wouldn't come here.'

'These friends would. See, they're them Texans what's coming after ole Shag for killing their pard last night.' Moe had been drinking and was slack-jawed through it.

'Moe!' Rut growled. 'Shut your face and get across the room. Set at that table with your gun on Miz Snenton. Set down, ma'am. I'll keep watch out the winder.'

Selina sat at the table and the man took a chair near her, his gun resting on the top of the table. She looked down at the cloth and asked, 'Did Moxel kill that boy last night?'

'Sure. Allowed it was Dusty Fog, after him for gunning Ben Holland last year,' Moe replied. 'Ole Shag'd downed Holland, but the charge was weak.'

'Why did Moxel shoot Ben Holland?' Snenton asked casually.

'Shag don't like Texas men. He heard Holland was tough, and wanted to try him out.' Moe grinned as he talked, a drunken leer. 'Last night he saw that kid on the paint. He figgered it was like the little fat feller said. Dusty Fog was in town looking for him, so he got out his ole ten-gauge and dropped the boy.'

'And you reckon to take Dusty out here?' Snenton watched the men, waiting his chance. 'Knowing Dusty, he'll head straight to the jail, to ask Bat Masterson instead of coming here.'

'Naw, they won't,' Rut sneered. 'Ole Shag's real smart. He had Bert follow Masterson and Tilghman out of town. They went to the herd to tell them Texans. They'll come here first. Ole Shag's smart—he'll take him some reb scalps.'

'Like hell!' Snenton scoffed. 'Moxel's no good without it's dark and he's behind a man.'

'Yeah?' Rut was bursting with misplaced pride in his boss. 'He knows they'll come here fust. He's got the sweetest lil ole gun-trap a man ever saw laid on here. Two boys up the street, two on the roof of the Buffler House. Me'n Moe here, and him in the saloon—at the bar with the bar-dog and two scatters. We've got them rebs whipsawed.'

Snenton knew to be sure; from the window he could see the two men moving on the Buffalo House roof. He also knew, as did Moxel, that the Texas men would come here looking for information. That was as natural for a Texas man in Dodge as it would be for a homing pigeon to make its way back to the loft it left. The three or more Texas men would come riding towards the Texas house—right into an ambush that gave them no chance of escape.

Snenton tried to sound mocking, but he knew the skin-hunters were right in their thinking. 'You don't reckon Dusty Fog'll fall for a play like that?' he asked. 'The skin-hunter doesn't live who can do anything better than Dusty Fog. He'll bust your trap, like it wasn't there.'

'Be that so?' Moe growled. 'Well, when they buries them Texans you'll know you wuss wrong.'

'They're coming, Moe.' Rut's voice was urgent. 'Folks's clearing Trail Street.'

Selina watched the man at the table. He was sweating now. She waited for a chance to do something; for she knew, and liked, Dusty Fog.

Rut pulled a handkerchief out and rubbed the sweat from his face. He shoved the bandana back into his pocket and rubbed his palm against his trouser leg.

'Scared, Rut?' Snenton asked. 'Don't reckon it'll work now, do you?'

Rut snarled a curse and looked back out of the window. He knew the reputation of those three Texas men who would be leading the attacking party. If there was the slightest flaw in their plans, things would be going real bad for Shag Moxel's men.

From the kitchen came a wailing, high sound, which bit into Rut's nerves like a red-hot knife. He had never heard Hop Lee, Snenton's help, singing, or he would have known that this was an Oriental version of some popular ballad.

'What the hell is that?' Moe croaked.

'Our kitchen help,' Selina answered, her hand dropping below the level of the table and holding the edge of the cloth.

Rut roared out for the man to be quiet, but Hop Lee was used to the Occidental barbarians showing a lack of appreciation for music. He had long since learned the only thing to do was ignore them and carry right on with his song.

'Lee doesn't know any English,' Selina remarked.

The skin-hunters listened to the wailing notes for a time. It was bad enough waiting for the Texans, without having that banshee call jarring at the nerves. Rut gave in. 'You know how to make him understand?' Selina nodded. 'Then stop him—and quick.'

That was what Selina had wanted Rut to say; she and her husband both knew Hop Lee spoke good enough English. Speaking in the fluent Mandarin dialect Hop Lee had taught her Selina gave rapid orders. The singing stopped abruptly. The room was silent, except for the ticking of the wall clock. The two skin-hunters were sweating freely now, both wondering why Shag Moxel had chosen to remain in the comparative safety of the Buffalo House, instead of fighting out on the street. The bottle-poured Bravemaker was laying cold on them.

'They're coming down Trail Street now!' Rut hissed. 'Keep that gun lined on the woman.'

Snenton half-turned; he saw the kitchen door slowly opening, a slim yellow hand pushing it. Catching his wife's eye, Snenton nodded. The time was coming to take action. Selina gripped the table-cloth. She was pale, her face showing the strain. Looking out of the window, she saw three men riding into view.

Moe's hand jerked as Selina heaved on the table-cloth. The

gun was out of line and the woman dropped to the floor. Moe roared out and tried to bring the gun into line. At the same moment, Snenton drew and fired at Rut, missing him. Hop Lee threw open the kitchen door, his hand swinging forward, a meat-cleaver flying from it. Moe's gun swung down, then he pitched to one side, the cleaver having split his head open. He was dead before he hit the ground.

Rut twisted round as the bullet slammed into the wall. He saw the double-barrelled derringer in Snenton's hand. Panic hit him. He twisted back towards the door, tore it open. At the same moment Snenton roared out. '*Ambush*. Dusty!'

CHAPTER FIFTEEN

MARK COUNTER THROWS A BARREL

THE word ran round Dodge City faster than a wind-swept prairie fire. Trouble was coming soon. The Dodge City police force, those tough, rough handlers of drunks, got the word. They had seen Masterson and Tilghman go from town, and took their departure right after. Not one of the police force wanted to be here when Rocking H came to town, looking for the men who had downed their pard. It wouldn't be a safe location for a lawman who was supposed to stop shootings in Dodge City.

By the time the three members of Ole Devil's floating outfit rode into town, Trail Street was as clear of human life as Death Valley on a real hot summer's afternoon. The street was deserted, not even a horse standing at the rail of a saloon. Yet, in every building, from every window, faces looked out, watching the three men riding slowly towards the Texas House.

As always in these matters, Dusty rode in the centre of the trio, Mark at his right and the Kid at his left. They rode slowly, relaxed in their saddles. For all normal signs, they might have been three drifting cowhands, coming into town for a spree. The Kid alone gave the lie to that; he rested his old rifle across his knees. In affairs of this nature, he preferred his rifle to an opener and, after that, he might use his old Dragoon to take the pot. Dusty and Mark left their rifles booted; they were trained Cavalry men, and preferred their Colts for combat in the saddle.

Moxel's guess had been correct in one thing; and so had Snenton's. The three Texans were headed for the Texas House, but they weren't riding blindly into a trap. All three of them sat their horses in the relaxed, easy way of the cowhand. They appeared to be looking ahead, but never had they been more alert than they were then. All could read the signs; they *knew* Moxel was waiting for them, ready and prepared to fight.

A movement and a splash of colour where no such movement, or colour, should be—caught the Ysabel Kid's attention. He saw the two men on the roof of the Buffalo House an instant before Dusty and Mark picked them up.

'Two up there on the roof of the Buffler House, behind the false front.' The Kid just breathed the words out.

'See them,' Mark answered, just as softly. 'Two more ahead there—one on either side of the street.'

Dusty was silent, he too had marked the four men. The pair up on the roof were dismissed from his calculations as a factor in the game. Those two men were as good as dead; or, if they weren't, the Ysabel Kid was losing his skill with a rifle. Yet, there should be more men. Moxel had six men in his bunch, and only four were in sight. The rest might be in the Buffalo House. If that hadn't been Sam Snenton's Texas House across the street from Sciffen's place, Dusty would have expected men there, too. But Snenton would never allow a Texas man to be attacked from his place.

'Waiting for us, just like you said,' Mark went on, just as quietly as before. He had long since stopped marvelling at Dusty's ability for putting himself in the place of the other man, then thinking as he thought. It was an ability which had long stood Dusty in good stead, and it stood by them today.

'Yep, only four of them. The rest must be in the Buffalo House,' Dusty replied. 'Is Moxel out on the street?'

'Nope, he's a big, heavy *hombre*—less'n Red Tolliver called him wrong,' the Kid answered. 'Red allows to have known Moxel in Wichita.'

They were in front of the Texas House now. All halted

their horses, knowing it wouldn't be long before the shooting started. The Kid watched the men on the roof, but his Indian intuition warned him all was not well.

From inside the Texas House a shot sounded and a voice yelled, 'Ambush, Dusty!'

The Ysabel Kid left the saddle of his white in a dive, his rifle crashing even as he fell. Up on the roof one of the two men reeled back from out of cover, a hole between his eyes. Even as that man went down, all hell tore loose on Trail Street.

At the shout, Dusty and Mark sent their horses leaping forward, both drawing their guns as they charged at the two men along the street. The door of the Texas House was pulled open and a man leapt out, gun in hand.

Rut landed on the street, his revolver lining on the fast-rolling Ysabel Kid. He fired one shot, the bullet joining the dust-spurts following the rolling black shape. Then a shadow fell on Rut and he heard the wild, terrifying scream of a fighting stallion. Rut twisted round. A scream broke from his lips as he saw a huge white stallion rearing over him, iron-shod hooves smashing down at him. The scream stopped as the hooves thudded home. Rut went down with the white horse, fighting screams shattered the air, smashing at him with battering hooves.

The Kid rolled over, lead licking dust spurts behind him. He rolled right up to his feet, his rifle lining up and beating a rapid tatoo. On the false front boards of the Buffalo House a line of holes formed, creeping nearer to the buffalo-hunter. The eighth hole sent splinters flying into the man's face. The Kid's rifle sights lined as the skin-hunter stepped back in an involuntary movement. The rifle kicked back against the black shirt and a skin-hunter went down dead.

The skin-hunters on either side of the street leapt out, guns coming up. Mark cut down on the one nearest to him, the long-barrelled Army Colts throwing lead into him. The man slumped forward, dropping his short carbine. The other spun round, his gun fell from his fingers and he clutched up at his shoulder. Dusty rode nearer, his smoking Colts lined and ready. The skin-hunter turned and ran, staggering from the pain of his wound. For an instant, he was close to death. Dusty's Colt lifted and lined, the V notch in the hammer lip and the low, white brass foresight covering the man's back. At that range, Dusty could hardly have missed. Then the Texan holstered his guns and turned the paint to head back along the street.

The Ysabel Kid lowered his smoking rifle and, for the first time, noticed the fighting screams of his white stallion. He whirled round and yelled: 'Back off, Nigger! Back off there, hoss!'

The white backed away, nostrils flaring and angry snorts blowing out loudly as it pawed and stamped the bloody ground. The skin-hunter wasn't a pretty sight, the white stallion's flaying hooves had shattered his head almost to a pulp.

'Kid, Snenton coming out!'

Sam Snenton wanted to come out of the Texas House and took this elementary, but necessary precaution. The Kid had seen one enemy come out of the Texas House; he wouldn't wait to argue if the door opened again to let out some other unheralded figure. Even after his yell, Snenton found the Kid's rifle lined on the door when he came out.

'Howdy, Sam. Nice company you keep in thar.'

Snenton stepped out, looked down at the bloody remains of Rut and twisted his face wryly. 'Moxel's in the Buffalo House,' he said as Dusty and Mark rode back. 'Sorry about this. They had two in my place. Didn't get a chance to warn you until just afore you stopped.'

'Them two in your place, weren't but the one came out,' Mark pointed out. 'The other one still inside?'

'Sure.'

'He going any place?' the Kid inquired.

'Nope—tangled with Hop Lee's cleaver.'

The Kid grinned. He vaulted on to the hitching rail and tried to see into the Buffalo House. Climbing down, he shook his head. 'Can't see a thing in there.'

'Both got a scattergun, and they'll cut down any man who goes through that door,' Snenton put in. 'Rut and his pard talked some.'

Dusty swung down from the paint. He looked at the Buffalo House and called: 'Moxel, your hired men are all dead. Come out and see how you stack against a man who's facing you.'

In the saloon, Moxel licked his lips. He still stood at the bar for he had been sure that his gun-trap couldn't fail. Crossing the room, he looked out of the window, the three Texans were still on their feet; Snenton was also there. Moxel knew that his men were all done. He hefted the shotgun and moved to stand with his back to the far wall. Cocking the hammers of the heavy weapon he yelled: 'Come in here, and git me!'

'I'll do just that,' Dusty shouted back and started forward.

Mark lunged forward, enveloping his small pard in a grip which gave Dusty no chance to struggle. 'Hold hard, boy!' Mark growled. 'Try any of Tommy Okasi's tricks on me, and I'll toss you through the Texas House wall. This is for us all—you can't lick two scatterguns.'

'Mark's right, *amigo*,' the Kid agreed. 'You always keep telling me not to rush in, head down and pawing dirt.'

Dusty stood still; he knew better than try and break Mark's grip on him. The big Texan was fully aware of the tricks Ole Devil's Japanese servant, Tommy Okasi, taught Dusty; but holding him like that was fairly safe.

'All right, you pair of wet hens. What do we do?'

Mark let loose. He looked round and his gaze stopped on the large water-barrel which stood before the Buffalo House. The barrel was supposed to be kept full of water, in case of fire. 'Is that full?' he asked.

Snenton shook his head; he was a member of the Dodge City Fire Department and knew Sciffen. 'I told him to get it filled a week back, but I'd bet he hasn't.'

'Good that's all we want. Let's go. Real Army tactics.'

The Kid looked puzzled; he had never been an officer as had the other two, and his sole tactic in the Army had consisted of shooting faster than any Union soldier he came across. 'What the hell're you getting at?'

'It's called diversion, then attack, *amigo*,' Dusty explained.

They crossed the street and halted just in front of the Buffalo House sidewalk. Mark stepped forward and looked into the barrel; it was empty. He bent and lifted the heavy object, his muscles writhing and bulging as the weight came up. 'Ready?' he gritted through his teeth.

'Willing and able,' Dusty replied, stepping forward on to the sidewalk.

The Kid ducked under the hitching-rail and stepped up on

to the sidewalk. He flattened himself against the wall by the far window. Lifting his old Dragoon, he prepared to take action.

Mark tensed, lifted the barrel up over his head and threw it right through the window. The entire pane of glass shattered and, from the dark interior of the saloon, three shotgun blasts boomed out. The barrel hit by three heavy charges of buckshot burst, staves flying in all directions.

From the directions of the shots, Dusty knew where the men stood in the saloon. Two shots came from the rear wall—that man's gun was empty—but only one had been fired from the bar. Dusty knew the bar-dog might still have one more shot in his weapon, but that didn't halt him.

The batwings burst open. Dusty came through in a flying dive, his old bone-handled Colt guns out ready. In his flashing dive across the room, he saw the bar-dog behind the bar; and, backed against the wall, stood a big burly man in buckskins. The bad-dog saw, too late, what the thing which smashed the window was, and he swung his shotgun round. Dusty landed on the floor and threw over a table, blocking him briefly from the man at the bar.

Moxel dropped his shotgun and clawed at the Colt in his belt. Dusty rolled over on the floor; he fired his first shot while his right shoulder was still on the floor. The second roared as he rolled on to his stomach; and a third as he went over to his left side. Moxel slammed back into the wall as the first bullet hit him. He tried to lift his gun but two more shots hammered lead into him. Slowly, he slid down the wall, his guns dropping from his hand.

Len, the bar-dog, jerked his shotgun round, then the other front window smashed. The Ysabel Kid's old Dragoon boomed from the broken pane, throwing its charge at the man behind the bar. Len felt as if a red-hot anvil had struck his arm. He spun round, the shotgun falling and crashing as it struck the ground, sending the nine buckshot charge tearing harmlessly into the roof. The bar-dog stared numbly down at the smashed, mangled remains of his arm.

Mark followed the barrel through the window. He fired fast at the man who came from the back-room, short Webley Bulldog gun throwing lead at Dusty.

The lead slammed into the floor near Dusty's face. He rolled over, thumb easing back the hammer of the Army Colt. He held his fire; Mark's bullet beat him. Sciffen, the owner, hit the wall, blood oozing from a hole in his shoulder. He dropped his gun and screamed at the Texans not to shoot him.

'You all right, Dusty?' Mark asked.

'Likely live!' Dusty got to his feet, holstered his guns and rubbed the trickle of blood from his cheek. 'Splinter nicked me.'

Sciffen looked up at the tall, powerful Texan who had crossed the room and now towered over him, 'Don't hurt me again, Texas,' he moaned. 'Get me a doctor.'

'Get one for yourself,' Mark replied. 'You aren't hurt bad. Allow you bar-dog needs a doctor more than you.'

The Kid entered the saloon and walked to the bar. He looked over it with detached interest. Mark joined him, looked over at the smashed, torn arm and growled, 'You danged Injun. Damned if I don't buy you a civilised gun!'

The Kid grinned; he was used to this reaction when he used his old Dragoon and a soft, round lead ball. 'You do that.'

The three Texans walked from the saloon together. From houses, stores and the other places where they had been hiding, men and women poured out to view the remains of Moxel's gang.

Sam Snenton and his wife came from the sidewalk before the Texas House. 'Moxel's dead?' it was a statement not a question. 'He was the man who gunned your wrangler, and Ben Holland. Moe, one of his gang, told us in there. He'd been drinking, and talked more than he aimed to.'

'Earp in on it?' Dusty asked.

'Not that I know of,' Snenton replied. 'They never said. I wouldn't spit in Earp's eye, if his face was on fire, but I don't figger him on a play like that. Way I see it was, Earp knew Ben was bad hurt and reckoned he'd never get back to Texas alive. That was why he put out the word. He reckoned to make a big play of it when Rocking H didn't come up this season. I don't reckon he'd got so far as hire Moxel to do the shooting.'

'You've got more faith in him than we have,' Dusty growled. 'You might be right though.'

'With Moxel and his bunch all down, there's no way to find out,' Sam Snenton replied, feeling relieved that the trouble was over. 'Earp pulled out of town yesterday at noon, and Moxel hasn't been in for a couple of days. Leave it lie, Dusty.'

'Not quite!' Dusty looked round at the citizens of Dodge. 'Where at's the Mayor? I've got things to say to him.'

'Be up to the Long Branch, I reckon.' Snenton answered and decided his judgment might have been out when he reckoned the trouble was over. 'Do you want to see him?'

'We do!' Dusty sounded grim.

'I'll come with you.' Snenton was one of the City Fathers and, whilst having an idea what Dusty wanted, didn't want to miss hearing it. He turned to his wife, 'You looking peaked, honey. Feeling all right?'

'Yes.' She watched one of the undertakers who was coming along the street. Her face was pale and she kept her eyes from the victim of the Kid's white stallion. 'I don't want to go back inside until——'

'That's right, honey.' Snenton's voice was gentle. 'You stay out. Go shopping until after Hop Lee's cleaned the place up.'

Mark pulled an old boot from his saddle pouch; it was small and dainty. 'Could you take this to the Leathershop, Miz Selina. Tell Jenkins I want a pair of Texas style hand-carved boots making, stars and all, I want them ready for tonight.'

Selina accepted the boot and looked at it, then at Mark's large expensive footwear. 'They look a mite small for you.'

'Not him, they useta call him ole fairy feet,' the Kid scoffed.

'I'll see to it,' Selina was pleased to have something other than killing and bloodshed to occupy her mind. 'I don't know if Jenkins can do it in the time.'

'You ask him to try, just for us,' Mark drawled, a grin flickering on his lips. 'Tell him, if they aren't ready, we'll have Kiowa and Billy Jack come sing to him.'

The Mayor and other civic dignitaries were gathered at their table in the Long Branch saloon. They looked up with well-simulated pleasure as Sam Snenton and the rest of the Texans entered. The City Fathers were not over-eager for this meeting; all could guess there would be some trouble.

Dusty, Mark and the Kid halted in front of the table. For a time all was silent. Then Dusty spoke: 'I'm trail boss for the Rocking H herd out there. The name is Dusty Fog. Last night my wrangler came here and was murdered. A year ago my kinsman, Ben Holland, was gunned down in this town. The man who shot both of them is still here. I've just killed him.'

There was silence again. Dusty had thrown down the gauntlet, but not one of the Dodge City men wanted to take it up. 'We're real sorry about what happened,' the Mayor said ingratiatingly. 'And we should give you a vote of thanks. Moxel had just about frayed his cinch here. We——'

'I didn't finish.' Dusty's drawl cut off the words unsaid. 'I hold this town responsible for what happened. The man who was suspected of gunning Ben was left to stay on here. Then, after he killed again, you tell us he'd frayed his cinch. Mister, you're going to see how Texas men feel about it.'

The men at the table looked at each other, not one spoke for a long time. They had seen their police force take it on the run from town and knew Dodge City was in danger of being painted with the Stars and Bars, then pulled apart board-by-board and scattered over the range.

'Couldn't you hold your men in, Cap'n Fog?' one man asked nervously.

'Why the hell should I?' Dusty's soft voice bit at the men like a bullwhacker's whip. 'You never played square with Texas men here. You've taken their money and, when they were broke, either had them jailed, or run out of town. Now you're going to see riled-up Texans.'

'But—but——!' the mayor spluttered.

'I'll tell you what I'll do. That boy who died today. I want him buried in the real graveyard, not in boothill. I want him to have a real headstone. On it you'll put *'Lil Jackie, the wrangler. He never lost a horse*. Will you do that?'

The Mayor and council nodded their agreement. Headstones were expensive items in Dodge, but not so expensive as refusal would be. The City Fathers knew that Dusty's word, once given, would never be broken.

'We'll do it, Dusty,' Snenton promised.

'I'll talk to the boys,' Dusty said. 'Let's go.'

The three young Texans walked out of the saloon, their boot-heels thudding across the sidewalk. Then, with a creak of saddle-leather, they rode out of Dodge.

Thora and Billy Jack rode at the point of the herd. They were on either side of the big red lead steer. Billy Jack pointed ahead to the sprawling town by the shining metals of the railroad. 'There she be, Miz Thora,' he said proudly. 'There's been trail-end towns before, and there likely'll be trail-end towns again, but there ain't but one Dodge City.'

Thora nodded soberly: she was still feeling the death of the young wrangler; it spoiled the drive for her, made her almost wish she had never brought the herd. 'We should have sent more men,' she said.

'Dusty wouldn't have wanted that,' Billy Jack replied, 'he's the trail boss and it was him that let Lil Jackie go in. We don't hold that against him, but that's how he thinks.'

'Did he tell you that?'

'Didn't have to; I know how he thinks. Don't you worry, the skin-hunter warn't never born who could lick Cap'n Fog.'

Thora managed a smile; Billy Jack's face wasn't quite so miserable as usual. 'I don't reckon there is. Say, I wonder where those old boots went.'

'Did you lose a pair of boots?' Billy Jack asked innocently. 'You should take better care of your gear.'

Thora glanced at him, but she couldn't read the face. Billy Jack had taken the boots and given them to Mark with orders to get a pair of real Texas made-to-measures for the boss lady. 'Look!' She pointed. 'It's Dusty, Mark and Lon—they're all right!'

'Sure. Didn't you reckon they would be?'

CHAPTER SIXTEEN

A TRAIL BOSS

THE shipping pens at Dodge. A crowd was waiting to welcome the Rocking H, first drive of the season. The Mayor and his council were assembled, and many other local citizens were there. All eyes were on the long line of cattle, the tall, tanned riders, handling the herd with such easy familiarity. And on a tall, tanned, beautiful woman who rode as well as any of the men. For a moment there was silence. Then as Thora chased, caught, turned and returned a reluctant steer back to the herd the cheers rang out.

Thora's face flushed in a blush as she saw the familiar stubby shape of Doctor Burglin standing talking to an affluent-looking cattle-buyer. She stopped blushing and smiled broadly when the fat, purple-dressed and much bejewelled madame of Jack, while showing off some of her pretty assistants in a rig.
a downtown cat house yelled a delighted greeting to Billy

Dusty yelled: 'Mark, Billy Jack, get ahead. Make a count.'

Thora joined Dusty by the pens and watched the herd coming between the two counting men. The cattle-buyers surged forward and the local people cheered. A speech of welcome from the Mayor took her attention from the herd and she managed to say a few words of thanks for the greeting. Then she was having her hand shaken and requests made to buy her herd on all sides.

Mark and Billy Jack came up, thrusting through the crowd. They halted before Thora. 'Boss,' Mark said, 'at a rough guess I'd say three thousand, two hundred and fifty.'

'Don't make it no more'n three, two, forty-nine,' Billy Jack objected. 'I bet's you've been using the Big Bend count again.'

'That's why I'm right. That Brazos count always ends up wrong.'

'Brazos count?' Thora looked at each man, wondering if there was something here she hadn't learned.

'Why sure,' Mark's solemn face should have warned her. 'See, these Brazos hands, they count the horns and divide by two. Now us Big Bend men know that, when you do that you miss the muleys.'

Thora frowned, 'I'm being took, but I'll bite. How do you do it?'

'We count the legs and divide by four.'

'Which same works real well, unless you've got four steers with a leg short each,' she put in thoughtfully.

'What difference would that make?' Mark had been so sure he had put one over on Thora, that he asked before he thought what she'd said.

'It would make you one short in the herd.' Thora turned before Mark could recover. Dusty was standing behind her, smiling as he listened.

'Waal, Thora, that's your herd to Dodge.'

'Why sure. We left Texas with three thousand, two hundred

and thirteen. I'd tell a man you'd fed us beef all the way north. I reckon I'm sprouting horns. You lost a few and you've made Dodge with more than you left Texas, Captain Fog, sir, you are a trail boss.'

Gun Wizard

CHAPTER ONE

Johnny Behan's Dilemma

TOMBSTONE CITY, Arizona Territory. A hot, sprawling, wild and wide open town. The great mines, the Toughnut, the Contention and the others poured forth their wealth and sent their workers into town to spend wages. The cattle spreads of Cochise County, Texas John Slaughter, the Clantons, the McLauries paid off their hard-riding crews and most of that pay went over the many saloon bars in Tombstone City. From out Galeyville way, up in the hills, came the rustlers, happy-go-lucky followers of Curly Bill Brocious and Johnny Ringo. They came to Tombstone all these men, all with money in their pockets, money they wished to spend on fun, on gambling and occasionally on tweaking the nose of the local law.

Johnny Behan held post of sheriff for Cochise County; a stout, affable man who would have preferred politics to handling a law badge. He was a good lawman for all of that and willing to put up with a reasonable amount of hell-raising in the interests of greater peace and quiet.

Behan was a Democrat in a town which was mostly Republican and had been put in office by the Territorial Governor when Cochise County first was formed. This did not meet with the approval of the Republican clan, so they formed the so-called Law and Order Party. Prominent amongst these public-spirited citizens were certain men who had gained something of a name for themselves in the cattle towns of Kansas. They were the Earp Brothers, Wyatt, Morgan, James and Virgil, the latter being town marshal. They were a hard bunch and harder with the backing of men like Bat Masterson, Sherman McMasters, Doc Holliday and their like.

The fast-growing town sat back and rubbed eager hands in anticipation of what Johnny Behan would make of this development. In this they were to be disappointed, for Behan was far too loyal to his oath of office to involve in bickering and trouble making with another officer of the law.

So things stood when the owners of the big mines produced

their inspiration, their idea to bring some fame—and not an inconsiderable sum of Eastern money—to help further develop their holdings.

They were rich men by any standards, these mine owners, powerful men with an influence that reached to and beyond the Territorial capital. In the way of rich and powerful men they craved for the atmosphere of culture and refinement much wealth demanded.

The Bon Ton Theatre at one time or another brought the most talented and famous performers of the day to tread its boards. The drama and noble words of Shakespeare, the thundering notes of great operatic stars, the wail of some maestro's violin at one time or another held entranced the mine owners and their workers alike in this centre of culture set in the heat and dust of the Arizona hills.

The homes of the mine owners were as good as could be found in any Eastern city. The meals they served were cooked by chefs who had worked in the kitchens of great European houses and their table service as good as could be found in the land.

These then were the men who decided they would organise and run the Cochise County Fair.

No ordinary county fair would do for them. For their glory it must be the greatest, the most magnificent county fair ever held anywhere in the whole United States. There would be tests for cooking and preserve making for the womenfolk, a chance for them to display their talents with needle and dress-cutting shears. For the men would be trials of speed in sinking a drill bit into the hard soil, contests with shovel and pick. There would be a prize-fight by two pugilists who were spoken of throughout the country. There would be contests for the cowhands, too, riding bad-bucking horses, roping, throwing and hog-tying cattle. There would be a chuckwagon race which would attract great attention, for every ranch prided itself in the ability of its cook to handle the traces of a racing chuckwagon team.

Not that the mine owners cared for such things, but they knew that to the Eastern visitor the cowhand had a glamour that the mine worker never had. There was another reason for the inclusion of the cowhand sports. John Slaughter, Texas John, ranched near Tombstone and would be quick to take offence at any slight to his loyal hands. Texas John was just as rich and autocratic as any mine owner and something of a power in the county. On no account must he be slighted in any way.

With their plans arranged, the mine owners were struck with

a sudden thought. Nothing they were offering was different than could be shown at the fair of any county. Cochise County must offer something more, something which would be guaranteed to bring the rich Easterners out West, where they might be persuaded to invest in the mines.

One of the owners came up with the suggestion of a rifle shoot. It would be a match that would attract the best shots in the West. Tests for skilled handling of repeating rifles more than for the long-ranged work of such weapons as the Sharps Old Reliable or the Remington Creedmore rifles. There was one prize which would bring in the best men and that would be the prize the Conchise County Fair would offer. So accordingly an order was rushed to the Winchester Repeating Firearms Company for one of the specially constructed "One Thousand" Model of 1873 rifles.

An uneasy feeling came to the organizers of the Fair that this match might be equalled and one of their number brought out the pièce-de-résistance, the idea which they were sure would make their fair a success.

In the East nothing was so talked about to do with the West than the speed and accuracy of the gunfighter with his Colt. The mine owners decided they would try and draw in the masters of the tied-down holster for a match. Put up such a prize as would draw the fast men to Tombstone to compete in a shooting match to prove who was the fastest and best shot of them all. The prize would be a pair of matched and gold inlaid Colt Peacemakers and a good sum of money also. There would be other prizes, for the Eastern firearms companies would donate freely so as to have their weapons on show before so large an audience. The shooting match would be as good a test of skill as could be arranged, long range shooting, handling guns with either or both hands, then if Colt's factory could fix it, a test to decide who was the fastest double draw of them all.

The news of the shooting match burst like a bomb over the West, spread by the telegraph wires and word of mouth and boosted in every newspaper throughout the wild range country. Within a month the names of fast men were coming in to be entered and if all held well the shooting match, the Fair along with it, would be a show long remembered in the West.

Johnny Behan saw in this apparently harmless Fair a threat to his office. There was soon to be an election for the post of County Sheriff and already Wyatt Earp was boasting he would claim the post. Earp stood high in the betting among the entrants for both rifle and pistol shooting and if he won would command a veritable landslide of votes. Earp, for all his faults, was a fine shot with rifle and fast with a revolver. Also he owned that long-barrelled Peacemaker presented to him by Ned Buntline and that would lend him a big advantage over the more conventional weapons used by his opponents.

Behan was no gunfighter, he could draw and shoot in about a second, but that was only rated as fast among people who'd never seen a real fast Western man in action. Such a man, and Earp was one, could almost halve that time and hit his man at the end of it. If Earp won the two, or even one, of the events he would be carried into office on the strength of it; then with his brother Virgil as town marshal, Tombstone would find itself under the heel of Kansas-trained lawmen.

There did not appear to be any way Behan could stop this happening. He knew he could never gain the lightning fast reactions and co-ordination of mind and muscle which went to make a real fast man with a gun. His deputies were brave and good men, but under no stretch of the imagination could they be termed fast. Burt Alvord was in town and highly fancied by some in both matches, but Behan could expect nothing from him. Alvord had been a Tombstone deputy until Behan fired him. The reason for the firing was that Alvord always brought his man in dead and was suspected of only bringing in such as could not pay their way by him. If the man could pay, there was more than a strong rumour that Alvord was not beyond escorting the man to the border and ensuring his safe crossing. If Behan enlisted the aid of such a man he would do himself more harm than good.

In desperation Behan put the problem to Texas John Slaughter, but received no sympathy or offer of aid. Slaughter believed in staying out of his neighbour's feuds and making sure he was respected for it. So the rancher had no intention of becoming involved in the political and office seeking feuds of the town—then he overheard Wyatt Earp boasting he would win both shooting matches, become sheriff and that those trouble-causing cowhands best watch out.

Slaughter made no reply, although he knew the challenge was directed at his head. He was not afraid; that small, tough rancher did not know where fear was kept, but he knew blood would be shed if he took Earp up on it. Instead of picking up the gauntlet, John Slaughter held his peace and headed for the telegraph office. What message he sent and to whom was never mentioned by the old timer who worked the key, even though the said old timer found the occasional ten dollar gold piece under his message pad on the unsaid understanding he let the Earp brothers know anything to their advantage or disadvantage. John Slaughter said nothing about the message either—but then he never did.

It was a fortnight to the day before the County Fair opened. Tombstone was already booming wide open at the seams and every stagecoach brought in more people. The rooming houses and hotels were either full or booked to capacity, every house filled with paying guests.

The Bucket of Blood Saloon was among the best in town, standing proudly on Contention Street. However, at this early hour of the morning it was empty of all but a lone bartender idly polishing glasses. He stood behind the long, shiny and polished bar which was his pride and joy, surveying the tables, the covered-over vingt-et-un, roulette and tiger-decorated faro layouts. His eyes went to the free lunch counter which was already set out for the customers. He turned and glanced at the display of bottles on the shelves which surrounded the mirror. A man could buy anything from root-beer to fine champagne in the Bucket of Blood. Turning, the bartender glanced at the stage to one side, with the pit for the three-piece orchestra before it. He nodded with approval, all in all Buckskin Frank Leslie's Bucket of Blood saloon stood up to a standard which would not have disgraced New York or Chicago.

The bartender was sure of that, he'd been imported from the East to take charge of the bar, instead of the leathery, stove-up old cowhand who usually fulfilled this honoured post. He was a man well skilled in his trade and had served drinks in good quality bars in New York and Chicago's Streeterville section. He could mix any of the better known drink combinations, serve them with style. He could chat amiably yet respectfully with the richest and touchiest customer, handle a rowdy drunk with either tact or muscle, depending on the drunk's financial standing; he could slip undetected a mickey finn into the drink of a dangerous customer—but he did not know cowhands.

The batwing doors opened and three men entered, three young Texas cowhands. The bartender's eyes went to them and saw nothing but the bare essentials. The low-crowned, wide-brimmed, J. B. Stetson hats, the clothes, the high-heeled, expensive, made-to-measure boots, the way they wore their guns, all told a story to a man who knew the West. To the bartender they were just three cowhands fresh in from the range.

Two of the men would have caught the eye in any company for all that. One of them, mused the bartender, would be about as fine a looking man as he'd ever seen. Full three inches more than six foot this man, even without the aid of his Kelly spurred boots or the costly white Stetson with the silver concha decorated band. He towered over his friends, his golden-blond hair combed neatly, his face almost classically handsome. His shoulders were broad in a great muscular spread which strained the tailored tan shirt, as did the powerful biceps of his arms. His cowhand style brown levis hung outside his boots with the cuffs turned back, his legs were long, straight, powerful and stood over the ground as if they owned it. Around his waist, hanging just right, was a brown leather gunbelt and in the holsters which were tied to his legs, ivory grips flaring so that his hands could reach them, were a brace of Colt Cavalry model Peacemakers. Fine looking guns, but plain, well cared-for fighting man's weapons.

The second of the eye-catching pair was not quite as tall, or as broad as the handsome blond giant. He was lean, lithe and gave the impression of having whipcord strength. All in black was this boy dressed, from hat to boots. Even the leather of his gunbelt was black and the only relief to the blackness came in the ivory hilt of the bowie knife at his left side and the worn walnut grips of the old Colt Second Model Dragoon revolver which was butt forward at his right. His hair was so black it almost shone blue in the light as he thrust back his Stetson. His face was young looking, innocent appearing and almost babyishly handsome. It was the face of a delicately reared youth in his teens—until a man looked at the eyes. They were cold eyes, old eyes, red hazel in colour. They were not the eyes to go with such a face.

The third man of the trio was smaller and the bartender hardly gave him a second glance. He was small, insignificant in appearance, not more than five foot six in height. His hair was a dusty blond colour, his hat thrust back from it. His face was tanned, handsome though not eye-catching. His grey eyes looked straight at a man without flinching. His mouth looked as if it would smile easily yet without any weakness and the face itself showed some strength. His figure was powerful, despite his lack of inches, his clothes were good quality, but he did not set them off as did his taller friends. His hat and boots had cost good money, as had that buscadero gunbelt with the matched white-handled Colt Civilian Peacemakers which were butt forward in the holsters.

Crossing the room, the three men halted at the bar before the bartender. "We'll take a beer each, friend," drawled the blond giant. "And call up a drink for yourself."

The bartender noticed the voice and accent. It was a deep, cultured Southern drawl, not the tone of a working cowhand.

"Would you gents be in for the County Fair?" asked the bartender as he served out the drinks with deft hands.

"We surely are, Colonel," answered the dark youngster.

The bartender was impressed by the pleasing tenor quality of the voice, but those eyes were disconcerting. There was something wild, alien, Indian almost, about them, which went with the free-striding way the young man crossed the room. It was almost as if he glided and gave the impression he could pass over heat-dried sticks without making a sound.

"Where'd a man enter for the events, happen he wanted to?" inquired the small man, glancing at the two big blackboards behind the bar. Each blackboard carried a list of names with the betting odds opposite each one.

"Right here's as good a place as any, although you can enter in any of the saloons. What'll it be for you, roping?"

"Not for us," replied the dark boy with a grin. "I never took to ropes since Uncle Obidiah died dancing."

"What'd ropes have to do with that?" demanded the bartender, playing his part by falling for the coming joke.

"He was dancing at the end of one."

The bartender joined in the laugh, then went on, "How about hoss busting?"

"That's all right for a man with a strong back, hard bones and a weak head," answered the big blond. "Which same I've only got the weak head."

"Well, I'll hazard a guess you're not interested in drill driving, hammer swinging or digging. I don't reckon pie making or dress sewing's much in your line either. Don't leave much else except the eating contest—or the shooting."

The three cowhands looked gravely at the bartender and he looked just as gravely back. Then they gave their attention to the two blackboards and studied the names of the contestants. The top men in both rifle and pistol shooting fields were already showing on the lists.

"Mr. Earp looks tolerable well favoured," said the dark boy sardonically. "Stands at even money for both. Look at that list. Tom Horn, Burt Alvord, old Steve Venard. Now there's three dandy cards to sit in with on the deal. It's like to scare a poor lil Texas boy out'n trying. Still, I've come this far so I might as well go in and make a fool of myself. Set me down on the board there, friend."

"What name'd it be, friend?" queried the bartender.

"Loncey Dalton Ysabel. What odds are you calling for lil ole me?"

That put the bartender in something of a quandary. His boss usually attended to the adjustment of odds, for Leslie knew by name or reputation every man who entered and could gauge his chances. At this moment Leslie was out meeting the troupe of show folks he'd brought in as a special drawing card for the County Fair.

"Let's say three to one, shall we?" he finally asked, making his choice with care. The odds were not high enough to arouse interest yet short enough to show the dark youngster no slight to his talents was meant. If they were wrong, Leslie could soon alter them on his return.

"Allow me to get some of that, friend," said the big blond and laid a ten dollar gold piece on the table. "Are you taking the bets?"

"That's my pleasure," grinned the bartender, accepting the money and making out the receipt for it. "What're you aiming to go in for?"

"Pistol shooting."

"What's the name, friend. I'll start you in at the same three to one."

"Mark Counter, and what odds on my standing second or third?"

"Leave it at the same three to one," answered the bartender, pleased to be making his boss some money. He marked the names on the board, then turned to the small man. "What'll you be trying for, mister?"

"Reckon I'll have a whirl for those fancy old gold mounted Colt guns too."

The smile died for a moment, then returned to the bartender's face. He understood. The small cowhand was wanting to make everyone notice him by entering for the Pistol Shoot.

"All right," boomed the bartender, wishing there was more of a crowd to share in the joke. "If that's what you want, that's what you get. Service with a smile, that's the motto of the Bucket of Blood. I reckon we'd best start you in at ten to one. We can always bring it down later."

In that the bartender hoped the small cowhand would take the hint that he was way out of his depth in entering the match. The three Texans exchanged glances, then two pairs of startled eyes turned to the bartender.

"Ten to one?" croaked Mark Counter.

"You mean ten to one he *don't* win?" went on Loncey Dalton Ysabel in a strangled croak of amazement.

"Sure, you didn't reckon I meant one to ten, did you?"

For a moment the two men stared at each other, then as if fearing the bartender would change his mind they dipped their hands into their pockets. Fifty dollars each of them placed on the counter and demanded the sum be scooped up and accepted. The bartender thought the two cowhands were going to costly lengths for a laugh. He started to write out the receipts on slips when a thought came to him.

Looking up at the small Texan, he grinned and said, "You know, I never got your name, friend."

The small man studied the bartender, a smile flickered on his face, while his two friends stood by with mocking eyes, waiting for the shock which was coming.

"I didn't tell you—but it's Dusty Fog."

CHAPTER TWO

On the Tombstone Trail

"HELLO THE CAMP. Can we ride through the water?"

Dusty Fog brought his big paint stallion to a halt as he called out the time-honoured range request for permission to approach a camp. Mark Counter, lounging in the double-girthed Texas rig of his seventeen hand bloodbay stallion, restrained the eagerness of the packhorse he led to get to the ford. The Ysabel Kid sat his huge stallion at Dusty's other side, graceful and relaxed afork a horse which was large and mean enough looking to scare a man.

It was the etiquette of the range that one called a greeting before riding into camp. The two covered wagons on the other side of the river, with the good team horses picketed to one side was a camp. There was a fire going, the scent of coffee and stew wafting on the breeze towards the three Texans. Around the fire stood three men and half a dozen women and it was one of them who turned to call out a reply:

"Come ahead and rest your saddles."

Dusty studied the people as he started his paint stallion across the stream. The party, in their camp up the slope, were not what he'd expect to see out on the open range country. A family of sod-busting nesters looking for a piece of new land might be out here. A bunch of miners travelling from Tombstone in search of work, a ranch trail crew returning from a drive, any of these might be out on the range. These folk were none of those categories.

The men wore stylishly cut Eastern clothes, it showed even though they were in shirt sleeves, or two of them were. The women, with one exception, were dressed in rather colourful and modish frocks which were not the wear of poor nester wives. These were show people unless Dusty missed his guess. Not a medicine show either, the wagons were too plain for that. These would be real showfolks, carrying their own scenery and props in the wagons with them. He was sure he could remember the big, henna haired, statuesque woman who called the reply to him, but he could not yet place her.

Swinging down from his horse, Mark Counter removed his white hat and bowed gracefully to honour the ladies, even though some of the party might not be such ladies at all.

"Howdy, folks," he greeted.

"Good afternoon, young men," answered the big woman coolly, studying them all with some care.

"Take it kind if we could night here with you, ma'am," Dusty said as he came from his saddle. "This's the best camp spot along the river. We've food in our pack saddle."

"Join us by all means," replied the woman. Her voice and actions were those of someone who was used to being seen and admired. "And don't worry about food. Cindy there always cooks theatre style, with plenty and to spare for all."

The girl by the fire looked around from the pot she was attending to. She was different from the other four girls who lounged about the camp. They were no different to the hostesses of any decent saloon or dance hall of any big Western town. She was tall, willowy, yet with a rich, entirely feminine figure which her modest gingham dress could not hide. Her hair was blonde, taken back shoulder long in a style which was attractive and yet not fussy. Her face was sweet, gentle and very pretty, with only the very lightest touch of make-up. Her smile of welcome was different from the interested glances the other girls directed towards Dusty, Mark and the Kid.

The three Texans attended to their mounts, stripping off the heavy double girthed Texas rigs and allowed the horses to go free and graze. Mark attended to the pack horse before they came back towards the fire.

The big woman was watching them with some interest still, a puzzled frown on her face. Then she smiled and came forward, extending a hand on which good rings glittered.

"I never forget a face," she said. "You're Captain Dusty Fog, aren't you?"

"That's right enough, Ma'am," Dusty agreed. "You'll likely remember Mark and the Kid here, they were in Mulrooney with me while you were there."

Now the four flashily dressed girls showed more interest. Those three names were well enough known throughout the West.

Dusty Fog, that small, insignificant and soft talking young man. Here stood a man who did not look the part his reputation called for. In the War Between the States, at seventeen, Dusty had carved himself a name which ranked with Turner Ashby and John Singleton Mosby as a fast riding light cavalry leader. Since the war Dusty's name came to rank with the tophands of the cattle business. He was the segundo of the OD Connected, Ole Devil Hardin's great Rio Hondo ranch and leader of Ole Devil's floating outfit, the handiest and toughest men of a handy and tough crew. Men spoke of Dusty Fog as trail boss, as town taming lawman and as being the peer of any of the wizards of the tied-down holster. They told how he brought law to Quiet Town, to Mulrooney, the wild trail end city. Whatever they told, it was all true. That was Dusty Fog, a giant among men despite his lack of inches.

Mark Counter had also carved himself something of a name throughout the cattle country. He was a tophand the equal of, if not better, than Dusty Fog. He was known as a fist fighter who could handle any man on any terms. They told of his giant strength, but they never mentioned his skill with his guns. A few, a very select few claimed he was almost as fast as Dusty Fog with his matched long-barrelled Colt guns. Beyond this select handful there were few enough whom could say how good Mark was with his guns, for he lived in the shadow of the Rio Hondo gun-wizard, Dusty Fog.

The Ysabel Kid, the last of the trio. Now there was a name to conjure with down on the Rio Grande. They once spoke of him as a one boy crime-wave, a border smuggler who knew every trail along the big river. He was the son of a wild Irish-Kentuckian father and a French-Creole-Comanche mother, and from that admixture of wild bloods came forth a dangerous young hell-twister. From his father's side he gained a love of fighting and the sighting eye of a woodsman of old. From his mother he inherited the ability to ride any horse that ever walked, to follow a track and ride scout among the best. From her French-Creole side also came a love for cold steel as a fighting weapon and the ability to handle his bowie knife in a manner of the man who designed it. All-in-all the Ysabel Kid was a fighting man with a skill beyond his years and far beyond his innocent appearance.

"I remember you," replied the big woman. "I'm Paula Raymond. Come and meet the rest of my people."

The introductions followed quickly. Paula Raymond was an actress and a good one, but she was never one to allow anybody take her place in the centre of things. The big, burly man with the heavy moustaches so necessary to a stage villain was her husband, Joe. The old man in the frock coat was a Shakespearean actor down on his luck and reduced to playing in low drama. He was distant as became one who had appeared on New York stages. The four gaily dressed girls were just called by their first names as being of insufficient importance to receive full introductions. That left the tall, wide-shouldered, tanned and handsome young man and the blonde girl to be presented.

"This is Miles Hamish, our hero," Paula said.

Hamish held out his hand, his grip was firm. Actor he might be, but there were hard muscles in his arms. He was clearly on his dignity, not willing to accept the cowhands as friends or anything but admirers.

"And of course the star, the female star," Paula went on, making the correction as there was just the smallest tightening of Hamish's lips at the words, "Cindy Alban."

The girl came from the fire with a warm smile on her face as she held out a hand to Dusty first, then each of the others. The three cowhands were polite, restrained in their greetings. To the other four girls they would have extended the same free and easy kind of friendship they'd given to the saloon girls of many a town. Cindy Alban was different. She was a girl a man dreamed about as he rode the circle around a trail herd in the Indian Nations when the stars shone down and the cattle lay bedded for the night.

"I'm pleased to meet you, gentlemen," she said in a voice which was gentle and pleasant.

"You're sure we're not putting you to any inconvenience, ma'am?" Dusty asked. "We've got food here in the pack and it won't take us but a minute to throw some in the pot."

"We wouldn't hear of it, Captain Fog," Paula answered. Clearly it was she who ran the troupe and made all the decisions. "We've enough for you."

"More than enough," Cindy agreed. "If you gentlemen would like to freshen up before the meal, I'm sure Miles will show you the place he used in the bushes there."

"Leave your saddles and wagons, boys," Joe Raymond put in. "You can either bunk down under the wagons with us men, or you can sleep by the fire."

"We'll use the fire, I reckon," Dusty answered. "It'd be a mite cramped under the wagon and ole Mark here snores like to wake the dead."

"Have it your way, then," Raymond replied and turned to discuss some point of stage procedure with the old man.

"You're a mite away from Kansas, ma'am," Mark drawled after they'd put the saddles by the wagons and dug out their washing and shaving gear.

"That we are. We've just played a most successful season in Texas and received a call from our old friend Buckskin Frank Leslie to be his stars for the Cochise County Fair. He also offers us a fortnight at the Bon Ton Theatre before the Fair, so we came along."

"Have you ever been to Tombstone?" asked one of the girls.

"Not for a year. We ran a herd of cattle out here for Texas John last year, just after the town started to boom wide-open at the seams," Mark replied.

"What's it like?"

"Wild, woolly, full of fleas and never curried below the knees, gal," drawled the Kid. "Just like Quiet Town, up in Montana after the War. Or Dodge, Mulrooney, Wichita or any of the trail end towns when the herds came in. Only with Tombstone the seasons lasts seven days a week, every week of the year."

"It'll be worse than ever with the County Fair coming off," Dusty went on. "I reckon every card-sharp, cheap hold-up man and would-be fast gun in the West will be headed there for the pickings."

Paula looked at the three young men. She'd seen the wild towns and from what Dusty Fog just said she knew she could expect some trouble in Tombstone. The other towns had been wild when the trail drive crews paid off, but the wilderness drew off between drives. In Tombstone it never died down and with the County Fair the pace would be increased.

"Are you entering for any of the County Fair events?" she inquired.

"I don't know, ma'am," Dusty replied. "I reckon we might be. Texas John asked Uncle Devil to send us along to win some of the prizes if we can."

"We were unsure of the advisability of calling off our Texas bookings," Paula remarked thoughtfully. "Even though Frank's terms are most liberal. However, he is an old friend, so we came along. The towns we have passed through on the way here don't give me any great hopes for Tombstone."

"Don't let them fool you, ma'am," warned the Kid. "Why, Tombstone's as fancy as Dodge City or Chicago."

Cindy looked up from the fire. "If you gentlemen wish to wash up before eating, you'd best go now. Are you going, Miles?"

"I just came back," Hamish answered.

"Reckon we can find the water, ma'am," drawled the Kid.

The three young men walked from the camp, down the slope and were soon in the bushes which lined the small stream. They had made a dry camp the previous night and so were in need of a wash and shave. The stream water was cold, but all three of them were used to washing and shaving in cold water. Mark stropped his razor, stripped to the waist, his mighty torso writhing with muscles. Watching them, the Kid grinned. The Kid scorned such affectations as shaving soap, lather brush and razor. To shave his needs were simple, water, the soap he used for washing and the edge of his bowie knife.

The horses had grazed down the slope towards the bushes and the big white was more like a wild animal than a domesticated beast. It never relaxed and repeatedly tested the wind with its nostrils as it grazed.

"Supaway, John?"

Paula Raymond looked up as the words were called from the slope above the camp. She heard startled gasps as the rest of the troupe saw who their callers were. Six ragged looking young Apaches sat their horses and looked down at the camp. The greeting they'd called was the usual one an Indian would give when approaching a camp in search of a meal.

"What tribe are you?" demanded Raymond.

This was a sensible precaution to take, or would have been with the semi-tamed Indians of the Oklahoma Territory. They were the kind of Indians Raymond was used to, the tribes which were under the firm heel of the reservation agents and the cavalry.

"We Lipan Apache," growled the squat, scar-faced buck who sat his horse ahead of the others. "Not bad Indians, we friends to all white-eyes."

Raymond knew that the Lipans were a branch of the Apache Nation, one which lived to the east of the main fighting tribes and one which had never taken up the war bow against the white man. They should be safe enough to allow into the camp. His eyes went to the men, noting that they were all young and the only weapons they appeared to have were the hunting knives in their belts.

"Come ahead," he finally said.

With the reservation Indians of the Oklahoma Territory it was always as well to invite them in for a meal. It saved trouble, for the braves could turn nasty if they were crossed, especially when away from the eye of authority. However, with the reservation Indians a few trinkets, some tobacco and food was enough to satisfy them and get rid of them. That was where Raymond made his mistake. He was no longer in Oklahoma Territory, he was in Arizona, almost the last frontier of the bad white-hating Indian.

The braves rode nearer, then dropped from their horses in the relaxed and easy way of their kind. They advanced on the fire, fanning out in a casual and innocent appearing manner, their faces blank of expression but their eyes on the white people.

"You want food?" Paula asked.

"We want plenty food," replied the squat brave. "No make

trouble for white-eyes if they give us plenty food, tobacco—and guns."

That gave a warning to Raymond. There was something bad wrong here. The braves were altogether too at ease and truculent. He did not like the way they came on towards the fire.

"We'll give you plenty food," he answered. "Tobacco. But we don't have any guns."

"No guns, huh?"

"No guns," Raymond agreed, spreading his arms and showing his gunless sides.

"That good," growled the scar-faced brave, then snapped an order in his own language.

At the words every Apache whipped out his knife and leapt towards the white people around the fire. There was sudden confusion, the three men jumping forward to try and protect the women, the four chorus girls running for the wagons, while Paula swung a wild hand which knocked the nearest brave to her staggering. Cindy Alban was nearest to the Apaches. She saw the scar-faced brave lunge forward and twisted to one side. His clawing hand touched the shoulder of her dress in passing, then she was free and running and he was after her. The girl saw him, looking back over her shoulder, saw she was cut off from the wagons and fled down the slope into the bushes.

Around the fire there was wild confusion. Raymond flung himself forward, his fist landing hard on the face of a brave. Hamish saw Cindy's peril but he was forced back by the attack of a knife-slashing brave. With remarkable agility the old actor avoided the rush of a wild young brave, tripped him and was tackled by another. It was a wild mêlée, but there would have been only one end to it had there not been help and very efficient help on hand.

By the stream Dusty, Mark and the Kid had finished their ablutions and were collecting their gear together. They were relaxed, discussing the chance meeting, when from the open the Kid's white stallion suddenly threw back its shapely head and gave an angry snort.

"Apaches!"

The one word came from the Kid in a Comanche-deep grunt. He took in the half-dozen braves with Indian-wise eyes, noting particularly the youth of the party, their lack of weapons and reading the signs right. This was a bunch of marauding young bucks on their first war trail, out after loot. They would not risk much in the way of a fight, at least until they were better armed. Raymond and his party would be safe enough as long as they kept up a bold front, gave some small tribute and did not let——

"Hell fire!" growled the Kid. "He's letting them into the camp. Get back there and *pronto*!"

That was the one thing Raymond should have resisted at all cost, allowing the bucks to get into the camp and see how poorly armed the troupe were. Feed them, give them tobacco, but never should Raymond have allowed them to get in close.

The attack started as the three Texans sprinted up the slope. Cowhand boots were never meant for running in, but for all of that the three were making good time. Then the Kid saw Cindy fleeing along the slope above him, saw her and the following brave disappear into the bushes and swung off at a tangent. Dusty and Mark could handle the other braves. The Kid was going to be needed far more by that pretty girl with the gentle smile.

Raymond leapt backwards, avoiding the slashes of the brave who was after him. He was no fool and had been in more than one brawl, but this time Raymond was up against a man who meant to kill him. He watched his chance, ready to slam home his hard fists, but did not get a chance. Hamish had the wrist of a second brave gripped and they were rolling over and over on the floor, each trying to get the other in a position where he could be finished. The old man went down under a third brave, the knife rose and drove down at the front of his old frock coat. Then the brave gave a startled yell, for his knife point sank in about half an inch and came to a stop. The old actor gave a sudden heave which threw the Apache from him and he rolled over, the bound copy of the Works of Shakespeare falling from his jacket. It had done its work by taking the force of the blow and preventing the knife from sinking home.

The women were backed against the wagons and two of the braves came at them, knives in hand ready for use. Paula clenched her hands but the four girls behind her, screaming in terror and clinging to her, prevented her from doing anything.

It was at that moment Dusty Fog and Mark Counter came on to the scene. They came through the bushes at just the right moment. Young Hamish's head hit the ground hard, he was dazed and the Apache tore free his knife hand, rearing up as he drew back the knife.

Dusty's left-hand Colt came out and roared in one flickering movement. Fast though the move was the Apache kneeling astride Hamish was caught by the bullet, jerked backwards and went down. Even before the Apache's body had hit the ground a second one, Raymond's attacker, crumpled and went down before the long-barrelled Cavalry Peacemaker in Mark Counter's right hand.

The two braves who were after the girls and the third, crouching to attack the old actor, saw the two men from the bushes, saw them and knew that no longer was this a safe game to play. They broke off the attack, sprinting for their horses and leaping astride the bare backs with an agility that was a joy to watch. One of them whipped back his hand, his knife raised to throw. Dusty and Mark both fired at the same moment and the young Indian was knocked flying from his horse, dead before his body struck the ground. Either bullet would have killed him.

Then the attack was over and the two living braves raced for safety. Raymond threw a glance to see if his wife was safe and turned a pale face towards Hamish and the old actor. Hamish was on his hands and knees, shaking his head to clear it and the old man was clucking his tongue as he studied the battered old book.

With the people of the troupe unhurt Raymond turned to look at his rescuers. He opened his mouth to say something as Paula pushed free of the hysterical girls and came towards the men. The words were never said. From the bushes came the sound of a shrill scream, then the most blood-curdling yell any of them had ever heard.

"What was that?" gasped Raymond, his face even paler.

Mark Counter pumped the empty cartridge case from the ejection gate of his Colt and slipped a fresh bullet in to replace it. "That was a dead mean ole Comanche getting riled up."

"Comanche!" yelped the showman. "They said they were Apaches."

"*They* were," agreed Mark.

It was at that moment all of them realized that Cindy was not in the camp.

"Cindy!" Paula screamed. "It's Cindy. He's got her. Get after her!"

Dusty and Mark did not move, they remained where they were loading their guns. "One way or another, ma'am," Dusty answered. "It's too late for that now."

Cindy had fled from the camp, running as she'd never run before. Behind her she could hear the patter of the Apache's moccasined feet as he chased her. The squat buck was not agile and the girl managed to keep away from his reaching, clawing hands, although she and he knew it was only a matter of time. They were in the bushes now, and the girl felt a branch strike her, then her foot caught in a root and she went down, rolling under a small bush. With terrified eyes she looked up at the leering, savage face of the Apache close on her. A scream broke from her throat, rose high and then ended abruptly.

There was a rush of feet and a black shape arrived in the open behind the Apache. Cindy's ears were jarred by a hideous yell which rang out from this black dressed apparition. It was a man Cindy dully thought she should recognize, a man whose black clothing was familiar but whose face was such as she'd never seen before. It was the hard fighting mask of a Comanche Dog Soldier and the yell was the coup cry of that same wild fighting warrior from the Texas plains.

The Apache also saw this sight of an Indian's face in white man's clothing. Saw it and the eleven and a half inch bowie knife blade which ripped at him. He started to make his parry, doing it with a speed which would have handled the attack of a white man—but it was not a white man who struck at him. It was the grandson of Chief Long Walker of the Comanches, war leader of the dread Dog Soldier Lodge who launched the knife blow, and the Apache never saw the day when he could teach a Comanche anything to do with the noble art of fighting with a knife.

Just a vital split-second too late the Apache began his parry and from then on it was all over. The great blade, sharper than many a barber's razor, went under the Apache's guard and sank home, biting into the knife-fighter's favourite target, the belly. The Kid felt his knife go home and ripped it across, feeling the hot rushing gush of blood against his hand, saw the Apache's face take on an expression of agony and drew back his hand. The knife blade was red in the Kid's hand and the Apache folded over, clutching at the middle as he went to the ground.

For a moment the Kid stood, allowing the wild Comanche blood to settle again. He tried to fight down the reckless streak of Indian in him but never, when he held a knife and faced an enemy, could he. Bending forward, he wiped the knife blade clean on the Apache's breechcloth, then straightened and looked at the girl who was crawling weakly from under the bush.

"You all right, Miss Cindy?" he asked. "I surely hope I didn't scare you too much."

The girl twisted towards him, recognizing him through the tears and the hysteria which welled up inside her. Desperately she tried to keep her eyes from the twitching, blood-oozing thing on the ground. She looked at the innocent, babyishly handsome face as if she could not believe her eyes. The clothes were the same but it appeared that an entirely different man had rescued her.

Then the reaction set in and with a cry Cindy flung herself into the Kid's arms and sobbed against his black shirt. He held her for a moment until she was over the worst of it and then turned her towards the camp.

"They told us they were Lipans," Raymond explained to the angry Kid who had brought Cindy back and turned her over to Paula, then demanded why the men had been fool stupid enough to let the Apaches get that close to them.

"Lipans?" barked the Kid. "Mister, they were Mogollons and real bad hats too."

"It's lucky we happened along," Dusty went on. "Let's get those bodies away from the camp and then we can eat."

It would not have mattered if Cindy had not cooked enough food to go around for only the three Texans felt like eating anything. The rest of them retired to the wagons and did not appear until night and even then they did not show any great desire to eat.

CHAPTER THREE

Mr. Earp Renews An Acquaintance

BUCKSKIN FRANK LESLIE stepped from the side walk and advanced to meet the two wagons and the three Texas men who approached him. The time was ten o'clock and the saloon keeper was going to meet his friends Paula and Joe Raymond. He'd had one of his swampers out on trail for the past two days looking for the wagons and on hearing of their approach came forth to greet his friends.

People going about their business stopped to look at the wagons and their escort with interest. Madame Paula knew the value of publicity and had the canopy off the lead wagon and all her troupe dressed in their show costumes in the back, with the exception of her husband, who drove the second wagon. Hamish, dressed in a fancy buckskin outfit drove the first one; he saw that the eyes of Tombstone's young ladies were on him and for once the feeling worried him. He had not said much since the fight with the Apaches and felt that he could have shown better in it. The four chorus girls and, to a lesser degree, Cindy, had shown much interest in the three Texas men who saved them and Hamish felt a little jealous. Always on the stage he played the handsome hero, saving Cindy from a foul plot of the villain. Then for the first time when he could have played the hero in real life he failed. Seeing Cindy laughing and joking with her rescuer he felt for the first time an awareness of her. No longer was she just a first-class competent actress who played her scenes without tantrums or trying to steal everything on the stage. Now she was a very real women and Hamish wished he had shown better when his chance came.

Buckskin Frank raised his hand in greeting. He was a tall, slender man dressed to the height of frontier gambler's fashion except that he wore a fringed buckskin jacket instead of the more normal cutaway coat. For all that the gunbelt around his waist was no ornament and the white handled Colt Artillery Peacemaker was a tool of speed and precision in his hands.

"Welcome to Tombstone, Madame Paula," he boomed out

in a voice which attracted the crowd and started them to gather. His eyes flickered to the three Texans, a glimmer of recognition in them. Then he got down to business. His old friends Dusty Fog, Mark Counter and the Ysabel Kid would not mind his ignoring them for the moment and there would be time to talk of the old days later. Turning to the fast gathering crowd he announced, "Ladies and gentlemen of Tombstone. As always I am bringing you the best entertainment possible. From tonight, until the start of the County Fair, Madame Paula's Talented Troupe will be presenting the latest drama plays at the Bon Ton Theatre and appearing in the Bucket of Blood Saloon. Now, presenting to you, Madame Paula Raymond——"

Dusty, Mark and the Kid backed off their horses to allow the show people the limelight. Leslie introduced the members of the troupe, doing it with a flair and shine that showed he was no mean showman himself. He saw the crowd growing and so saved Cindy until last. The girl would be a prime drawing card and would bring in the sentimental cowhand and mine worker's trade. She would be the sort of girl they dreamed about and would pay good money to see rescued from the clutches of the vile villain of the play.

Gallantly Leslie handed each of the girls down and shook hands with the men. Then he held out his hand, introduced Cindy and assisted her from the wagon box. The girl had barely set her feet in the dusty road of Tombstone when a voice spoke from the front of the crowd.

"Introduce me to the lady, Leslie."

Leslie turned on his heel to look the speaker over, although he did not need to do so. The man stepping forward was well enough known to Leslie. He was a tall, slim and handsome young man, his face tanned, although he did not have the look or the dress of an outdoor man. He wore an expensive black cutaway coat, frilly white shirt, string tie, fancy vest, white trousers and shoes. His hat was a good Stetson but he did not have the flair of a Western man in how he wore it. He also wore a fast man's gunbelt but to eyes which could call the signs he was not fast with it.

Behind this elegant dandy stood two men of a type Leslie and the three Texans knew well. They wore cowhand clothes, belted guns and these were what they worked with. They were hired guns, the sort a man would take on when he could not get good stock.

Slowly Leslie released the girl's hand and stepped away from her. The onlookers in the crowd started to fade back leaving the handsome man and his two hired guns clear to view. Every member of the crowd was suddenly prepared to hunt for cover—fast.

"I said introduce me," the handsome young man went on.

"I'd as soon introduce her to a Digger Indian."

There was a sudden reddening of the handsome man's face. His hand lifted, his fingers spread as they hovered above the butt of the gun. Leslie watched the man, saw the two gunmen moving slowly to be clear of their boss and sensed that Dusty, Mark and the Kid were moving their horses to a place where they could back him if backing was needed.

"Introduce me, Leslie," said the man.

"You go to hell, Rambeau."

The show people were seeing something they'd seen before and knew what they must do. Paula was first off the mark, gently gripping Cindy's arm and moving her back out of the possible line of fire. At the same moment the woman blocked Hamish who had started to move forward. The young actor saw his chance to make up for his failure on the trail. He meant to step in and demand the man called Rambeau to take himself off hurriedly. The young actor could fight but only with his fists in a rough-house brawl. He would have as little chance here if guns began to roar as a snowball had of keeping shape on a hot stove top.

Slowly King Rambeau's eyes went to the three Texans as they slouched comfortably in their saddles in a half circle behind Leslie. His lips drew back in a sneering grin which made the handsome face look evil as the devil himself.

"Took to hiring guns now, Leslie?" he asked.

"What're those two behind you, *hombre*?" asked the Ysabel Kid mildly. "A couple of Tombstone churchwardens?"

Rambeau's eyes lifted to the Kid, seeing there was no mildness in his face no matter how his voice sounded. "Tough boy, huh? Take that worn old relic of a gun from him, boys."

"Start right in any time you like, gents," offered the Kid. He was not a fast man with a gun but he knew he was able to deal with either of the hired men and their boss.

The gunmen made no move. They knew the signs and they read the warning in that gentle, mocking face. It was as menacing as the purr of a cougar with a belly full of horsemeat.

It was then the crowd parted and a tall, solemn-looking man came forward. In dress he looked like a prosperous trail end town undertaker and his moustached face was familiar. Round his waist was a gunbelt with a black handled Colt Civilian Peacemaker at his right side. At his left was the twelve-inch barrelled special Colt presented to him by Ned Buntline. The crowd stirred with expectation for King Rambeau was a crony of Wyatt Earp—and Frank Leslie was not.

Behind Earp, on the sidewalk, stood his brother Virgil, looking much the same and with the shield of town marshal on his jacket lapel for all to see. His face showed nothing of whether he approved or disapproved of what Brother Wyatt was doing.

Equally inscrutable was the face of the thin, sallow man who stood by Virgil Earp. This man wore the dress of a gambler and from under his coat, in a shoulder clip, was a ten gauge, twin barrel shot pistol. His pallid face was set in a cold and mocking grin as he looked on.

"What's the trouble, King?" asked Earp, stepping forward, by the two gunmen and halting at Rambeau's side. His eyes turned to Frank Leslie, glanced at the three cowhands then he snapped, "Making trouble again, Leslie?"

"This's private," Leslie replied. "Go peddle for votes some other place."

"Leave this to me, King," Earp said grimly, satisfied that his brother and Doc Holliday were on hand and that he had a good audience. "I can handle it."

Rambeau moved back a pace, his hand still hovering his gun. He hated Leslie both as a man and a business rival and this would be a good chance to force the play. Never would he have a better chance, two men of his own, Wyatt and Virgil Earp and Doc Holliday against Leslie and two cowhands, three if a man troubled to count that small runt on the big paint horse.

"Leslie," Earp began. "I'm getting——"

"Mr. Earp," Dusty cut in with an easy, gentle drawl. "You remember a skinhunter in Dodge, name of Shag Moxel?—— I'm the man who killed him."

Earp's face had flushed with annoyance at the interruption to his noble speech. Then the annoyance died and for an instant a flicker of something else took its place. Only for an instant was it there, then the face became an impassive mask again but Dusty had caught the expression. So had Mark, the Kid and Frank Leslie; caught it and read it for what it was.

"He's telling you true, Wyatt," said Doc Holliday from the sidewalk. "I was in town, didn't get called out on business like you and Bat. I saw him right after he did it."

There were times when Wyatt Earp wondered he ever took up with such an out and out ornery cuss as Doc Holliday. One thing Earp did not want was confirmation of the identity of the man who killed Shag Moxel. It still rankled Earp to remember how he'd left town when Dusty Fog came looking for the man who tried to kill his cousin Ben Holland. That was five years ago but Earp remembered every detail of it and so did Doc Holliday.

It was then a whisper ran through the crowd, loud enough for Earp to hear and give confirmation to his knowledge and memory.

"Yes, sir. That's him. The Rio Hondo gun wizard. That's Captain Dusty Fog."

"How're you calling it, Wyatt?" Holliday went on, always ready to fan up the flames and start the ball rolling.

There was death in the air of Tombstone that morning. It hung there poised and seething, just waiting for the first move to let it have its head. One move, one wrong word and guns would roar, men would die and the town of Tombstone would see its boothill grow.

Virgil Earp came forward but he came with hand away from his guns. He came as a peacemaker and not the kind which Colonel Colt's Hartford factory made so well.

"Break it off, Wyatt. Pull in your horns, King. If Buckskin Frank doesn't want to introduce you to the lady leave it lie. You're not fast enough to set in on a deal against a man like Captain Fog."

It was not clear to the crowd, or to Earp and Rambeau, which of them he meant by this last statement. The words did give Wyatt Earp a chance to get out of a real tight spot. Rambeau's two hired hands showed some relief now for they had a certain reluctance to match Colt courtesies with the four hard-eyed, deadly looking men who faced them.

The only one who showed any sign of making a play was Rambeau, then suddenly he knew that he would not get the backing of the Earps. He knew he would have to back out now or lose their not over-strong friendship. To the Earps Rambeau was a man who could be useful for passing out pro-Law and Order Party talk and for handing over generous sums to the campaign funds. He was nothing beyond that, having neither the gun-speed or ability to make himself a useful backer in any shooting which might be needed.

"All right, Virgil," he said. "Leslie's some touchy. I'll get to know the lady later."

With that Rambeau turned and walked away, followed by his men. Wyatt Earp was next to go, knowing he was leaving the field second best, but satisfied to be leaving it on his feet. Virgil stood for a moment, shrugged, turned and followed his brother.

The tension oozed from the watching crowd but talk rolled up among them. Leslie knew there was nothing more to be gained by standing here and so suggested to Madame Paula that she got her people into the wagon and headed for the rooming house where he'd booked them accommodation.

"Like to thank you for sitting in, Dusty," he said while the show folks climbed back into the wagon.

"Any time, Frank. Any old time," Dusty answered. "Where'd we be likely to find Texas John if he's in town?"

"He came in last night and he'll be in my place later. Go down and wait for him. I'll be along after I've seen my folks bedded down."

The two groups separated, Dusty, Mark and the Kid taking their horses to the livery barn and then making for the Bucket of Blood Saloon. They'd just finished making their bets when Texas John Slaughter came in. He was a smallish, tanned, hard looking man dressed in the style of a Texas cowhand, yet about him there was the unmistakable something which told other cowhands that here was a master of their trade.

Dusty came from the bar, holding out his hand which Slaughter gripped in a friendly shake. "Howdy John," Dusty said. "I came as soon as Uncle Devil got your telegraph message."

The rancher shook hands with Mark and the Kid after Dusty and then waved to a nearby table, suggesting they took the weight off their legs and talked things out.

"You know why I sent you?" he asked.

"Only what you said in the telegraph message," Dusty answered. "We've just signed in for the shooting. Though why you wanted us out from Texas just for that I don't know."

"See the boards, how Earp's favoured high for both shoots," drawled Slaughter. "He mustn't win either of them. If he does Tombstone and Cochise County'll toss their votes his way when they come to elect their sheriff. Then we'll be under Kansas lawmen and you know what that means."

"I wouldn't wish that on a carpet-bagging Republican," drawled Mark grimly.

"Was I a praying man I'd say amen to that," went on the Kid.

Kansas lawmen. They were an anathema to any Texas cowhand who'd trailed a herd north to the railheads. The men who ran the law in the trail end towns were for the most part northern sympathisers with a built-in hatred for those rebel Texas boys who came with the cattle. The hatreds of the Civil War were fanned afresh by the men who wore the badges of town marshal, kept alight by the way they treated the cowhands. To every Texan a Kansas lawman was a cold-blooded cowardly murderer at worst or a bribe taking pimp at best. Wyatt Earp's name ranked high on the list of Kansas lawmen and for him to run the law in Cochise County would mean bloodshed.

"Earp's after the sheriff's post then?" asked Dusty.

"Pushing all he can, him and the rest of the Law and Order Party. I wouldn't take sides, Dusty, but he's been boasting so loud and long I reckon it's time his bet was called."

"And you reckon we can stop him winning?" asked Dusty with a smile.

"Reckon?" scoffed Slaughter. "I'd be tolerable surprised if you couldn't."

While the men were talking, Buckskin Frank Leslie entered the saloon, having seen his people safely to their accommodation. He passed the table without more than a friendly greeting for a sudden thought had struck him while delivering Madame Paula. It was a thought which caused him to make a hurried and apologetic departure without even waiting for Joe Raymond to finish his unpacking and come for a drink.

The bartender laid aside the cloth with which he was polishing the glasses and came along to greet the boss, grinning broadly and jerking a thumb to the table.

"Those cowhands throw their money around," he said jovially, sure his boss was going to be pleased with his making money for the business. "Signed on for the shooting in the Fair. I set the two tall ones in at three to one, I didn't want to offend them by going any higher. The dark boy's took it to win on the rifle and the blond to come in second or third with the revolvers."

"Three to one?" gurgled Leslie, thankful the saloon had not been full of men who knew the West.

"Sure," grinned the bartender. "The best laugh was when that little feller took on for the Pistol Match."

Somehow, the bartender thought, the joke was falling flat. He could not think how or why. There was a look of horror almost on Leslie's usually expressionless face, for he was not looking at the bartender, but at the board on which the odds were written.

"Ten to one!" The words were torn from Leslie as if every one of them hurt him. "You laid odds of ten to one that *Dusty Fog* didn't win the Match?" He shot out a hand across the bar. "Give me that rag and chalk, quick!"

At the table John Slaughter was staring at Mark Counter in amazement.

"Ten to one, Mark?" he gasped. "You're jobbing me."

Mark grinned broadly for he was seated facing the bar and watching Leslie's agitated actions. "Was I never to leave this chair again, John, I'm telling you the bartender started Dusty at ten to one. I stand at three to one for a place and he put Lon in at three to one for a win with his old yellow boy."

Money jingled in Slaughter's pocket as he thrust back his chair. He could not see what was happening at the bar.

"I always thought you didn't gamble, John," drawled Dusty casually.

"So who's gambling? It's like finding money in the street."

For all that John Slaughter was cautious as he crossed the room, heading for the bar. He did not glance at the boards but leaned by Leslie, who was standing also with his back to the boards, looking just as relaxed and unconcerned.

"Fine day, Frank," Slaughter said.

"Real fine," agreed Leslie.

"They do tell me Dusty there's in for the Pistol Match at the Fair," Slaughter went on. "I reckon I might have a couple of dollars on him just for old time's sake."

With that Slaughter leaned back and offered Leslie a cigar. They were friends or the rancher would never have thought of playing things this way. It would make a good story to say he'd got the better of Frank Leslie and taken odds of ten to one that Dusty Fog did not win the shooting match. However, it had to be played careful or Leslie might see the board in time and alter the odds to something more in keeping, as would be his right.

"Yes, sir," Slaughter went on in the nonchalant, disinterested tone of a horse-trader trying to get a hundred dollar stallion for the price of a wind-broken plug. "Just lay this here two dollars on Dusty Fog for me, barkeep."

Slaughter offered the money, still without looking at the board and took the slip in return. Then he turned, a broad grin spreading on his face—and dying again.

"What the——!"

Leslie had made good with his time. Dusty Fog's name was still there but the odds showed a thick broad white mark where other writing had been erased. Now they stood not at ten to one, but at even money.

"Reckon the drinks are on you, John," Dusty remarked, coming to the bar.

"You saw what he was doing and never said a word," replied Slaughter. "Let me go against my principles and start betting——"

"You reckon you've worries," answered Leslie with a grin. "How about me if the place had been full? It's nothing but luck that nobody got any money down."

"I wouldn't go so far as to say that," drawled Mark as he

and the Kid joined the others. "Nope, I wouldn't say that at all."

With that Mark held the receipt so that Leslie could see it and read the amount on it. Leslie shrugged. One bet wouldn't break—then he saw the Kid also held out a slip.

"No." The word came in a strangled gasp. "Hank, you didn't take these bets, did you? You did? Oh well, we might break even on the bets we've got on already."

The Kid grinned and held out his receipt. "Is she worth fifty dollars as she stands, Frank?"

"Any time, right now if you like."

"Here, barkeep," laughed the Kid. "Throw this away and make it out at the right odds. Man, your face when you saw it, Frank."

Mark and the Kid exchanged their betting slips, giving away odds of ten to one without a thought. Buckskin Frank Leslie was their friend and they would not take advantage of the slip.

"Say, who was that handsome dude out there on the street?" Dusty asked.

"King Rambeau," Leslie replied. "He runs the King Saloon for the syndicate. Got him one of their top guns on hand, Iowa Parsons."

Dusty sipped at his beer thoughtfully. The syndicate were the unknown group who ran saloons, gambling houses and dance halls throughout Arizona. They controlled at least one place in every town and their take must have been high. Dusty was curious, the handsome saloon owner was not the usual type of man the syndicate put in charge of their places.

"Where's he from?" he asked.

"Ran a place in New York until he had to buy a trunk and head West. There's some talk that he's trying to work a private move, without the syndicate, although I don't know what it is. They shipped him Parsons in when Billy Clanton allowed he'd been cold-decked and it looked like trouble. Parsons has been here ever since."

Mark glanced in the mirror. He was rather more dishevelled than he cared to appear in public so he cut in before Dusty could ask any more about King Rambeau.

"I'm going for a haircut and bath," he said. "Then we can go and show the ladies of Tombstone what they don't have to go on missing."

"We'll come along, Mark," Dusty answered. "See you back here, John. What do you want us to do from now on until the Fair starts?"

"Come out to my place if you like," Slaughter replied.

"Leave it until you're freshed up. We'll have a night in town and then see what you reckon."

"That sits well with us," Dusty answered. "We'll see you later then."

Slaughter and Leslie watched the three young Texans leave the saloon and the rancher grinned. "Now there goes the three best men I know."

Leslie crumpled the two betting receipts in his palm and tossed them into a spittoon. "You're right about that, John," he replied.

CHAPTER FOUR

King Rambeau Makes Demands

DUSTY FOG walked with his two friends along Toughnut Street, making for the barber's shop Leslie recommended to him. He thought as he looked around that these wide-open towns were much the same. The faces changed but the general type of people remained the same. The same sort of crowds moved along the sidewalks, the same type of business premises flourished. There were mine workers, burly men with sleeves rolled up to expose their biceps and strong arms, with levis trousers that had the seam stitching reinforced with brass clips and with steel toed boots. There were cow-hands with wide-brimmed Stetson hats worn at just the right "jack-deuce" angle, over the offside eye, gay shirts and levis with cuffs turned back. There were townsmen of various types, the better class in good broadcloth suits, the others in lesser grades of suiting. Mingled among this crowd were drummers, salesmen in loud check suits and derby hats, and cavalrymen on furlough.

All in all the scene was one of constant change, of colour and what appeared to be unending numbers. It was Tombstone but it might just as well have been Dodge City, Quiet Town, Mulrooney or any of the other towns which boomed wild, woolly and wide open, then faded and were gone.

"Man, Tombstone's surely grown some since we were here last," drawled the Kid, watching the passing crowd as they strolled along.

"It's just like Dodge, Newton, Wichita or any of the big trail end towns when the herds were in and the crews paid off," Mark replied, giving a wink at a pretty young girl who smiled, then turned her sunbonneted head away as her mother gave an angry snort.

"More like Quiet Town," said Dusty with a smile, for he'd noticed the wink and its result. "There were never any mine workers in the trail end towns."

"Quiet Town," the Kid remarked. "Now there was a town. She was the wildest of them all."

Dusty could have agreed with that. Quiet Town, in Montana, and just after the War had been the wildest of them all. It had also been the first town in which he held the law badge and it was the first town he tamed, with the aid of his tough and handy deputies.

On a quiet side street they found the building they were looking for. It was a long, fairly new looking building and split into three parts. The first window had a display of male clothing, clothing to suit the cowhand, the mine worker, the town dweller or the professional gambler. Next door to this was the barber's shop and beyond it the bath house. This was an ideal arrangement and showed some considerable forethought on the part of its owner. It was situated handily to the edge of town and the men coming in from the mines or the ranches could enter one building, take a bath, then have shave and haircut and finally spend money on a change of clothing before going on to the pleasures of the town.

The barber's shop was crowded when Dusty and Mark emerged from the bathroom. They'd been before the Kid in the baths and so were ready for their haircuts while he was still soaking in the hot water. All three of the chairs were occupied and the barbers working fast while the lather boy attended to his stove kettle and worked up lather. In the seats around the walls sat the other customers, there were only two spaces left, one on either side of the street door of the building. Dusty took one and Mark the other, sitting back and listening to the conversation, the jokes and small talk which flashed between the barbers and the customers.

Time passed and a customer left the chair to allow the next man in. A tall, tanned, spare man in his early thirties rose to take a vacant chair. Dusty looked the man over, noting he wore cowhand dress of a style which showed he had money to spare, and was probably a rancher. There was something more about him, he walked with the stride of a horseman, but did not have that something which marked the born and bred cowhand. He did not wear a gunbelt either and that was strange; it was almost like seeing a man without his trousers, fact being there were men in Tombstone who might forget their trousers when rising in the morning—but they would never forget to strap on their guns.

The tall man was almost at the chair when the door of the shop opened and three men entered. One moved towards the vacant chair, the other two stopped with their shoulders against the door, their hands thumb-hooked into their gunbelts near the butts of the low-tied Colts.

Dusty had a good memory for faces and recognised the

newcomers. They were Mr. Earp's friend, King Rambeau, and his two gunmen. More, they were clearly looking for trouble with the tall man who was next in line for a haircut. Dusty glanced by the two gunmen and caught Mark's eye. By the slight inclination of Mark's head Dusty knew he was not alone in the recognition and was set for trouble.

"Just a minute, Brownlow," Rambeau said, dropping his hand to the back of the chair and turning it from the other man. "I've been looking for you. Haven't seen you for a couple of days."

The man called Brownlow's eyes met Rambeau's for a long moment. "That could be because I saw you first each time."

Dusty looked harder at Brownlow. He recognised the accent and it was not American. Those clipped, decisive and firm tones were British and upper-class British at that. Dusty had met some of these British gentlemen who had come West to find excitement and a new life. They were just what the word said, gentlemen in the strictest sense. He liked and admired their kind, it was their drive and spirit which made England the great country it was.

There was no hint of a smile on Rambeau's face and he kept his hand on the chair back, never taking his eyes from the other man's face. All talk in the shop had died down now, every eye on the two men. The barber, the burly owner of the building, drew back from his chair.

"Have you thought over my offer?" Rambeau asked.

"It didn't need thinking about. I'll take the chair and have my haircut."

"Not yet. I'm in a hurry and I want the chair."

" 'Fraid not," replied Brownlow. "I've waited my turn and so can you."

With that the man gripped the chair and turned it back towards him but before he could sit down Rambeau had kicked it so it spun back towards him once more.

"You don't get a haircut today or any other day, Brownlow. Not unless you cut me in on that herd."

There was no fear in Brownlow's face, only a slight tightening of his lips as he replied, "Do you run Tombstone now?"

"You haven't been able to hire a hand, have you?"

"I put that down more to your hired killer than to any effort on your part," Brownlow replied and his voice grew hard. "Move your foot and I'll have the chair."

Rambeau grinned, showing his coat clear of the gun butt. "I'm having it. Are you fixing to stop me?"

The watching men were silent. Not a Tombstone dweller here but who knew what was going on between Rambeau and the tall Englishman. There had been word passing around the town that no cowhand had better take on to drive cattle for Vance Brownlow on pain of offending Iowa Parsons, boss gun for King Rambeau. Why this was, not one man present, apart from the two main actors of the scene, could say. One thing was for sure, whatever their differences King Rambeau was now forcing the issue. The two gunhung men at the door would prevent anyone either going to fetch the law, or help Brownlow.

Rambeau's foot came down from the chair and he moved back a pace his hand lifting to hover his gun butt. Dusty watched the other man, saw how his feet moved slightly into what could have been a fighting stance. Dusty noticed the way the man stood but more so at the way the right fist was held. The hand was closed but the first knuckle extended beyond the others in what at first might have appeared an awkward manner. Dusty's brows drew together in a puzzled frown. Either that Englishman did not know anything much about defending himself with his hands, or he knew a very effective way.

"Make your choice," Rambeau sneered. "I'm either your partner and you can have the chair. Or I'm not and we settle it right now."

"On your terms, you armed and I'm not?"

Never taking his eyes from Brownlow the handsome saloonkeeper spoke to the owner of the shop:

"Barber, take one of your customer's guns and put it on the chair in front of Brownlow. I'll give him a chance."

The barber gulped. He knew something about guns and shooting and knew Vance Brownlow would have no chance in a fight, not like that. He would have to bend for the gun, straighten and line it. With a strange gun in his hand he would have no chance at all. The only difference would be that Brownlow would be armed, technically, and so Rambeau could plead self-defence.

"I'm waiting, barber," Rambeau went on. "You've got a real nice place here. You wouldn't want anything to happen to it, now would you?"

That showed the barber clearly where he stood. He must do as Rambeau demanded or his business would suffer for it. Rambeau worked for the syndicate, that was a common piece of knowledge around town, and the syndicate knew every method for making life uncomfortable for people who crossed them. He looked at the other customers of his shop, then at Brownlow, and licked his lips nervously.

Dusty Fog's right foot tapped on the floor in a casual and what might have been taken for a nervous gesture. Mark

Counter caught the sign and just slightly tensed, ready for the sudden action he knew was coming.

Faster than a striking rattlesnake and with much less warning Dusty made his move. His right hand lashed out and back suddenly. The way the hand was held looked strange to a man used to seeing fist fighters in action. Instead of clenching the fist Dusty kept his fingers extended, held together with the thumb over his palm. The hand, edge sideways, lashed around, aimed with skill and precision straight for the gunman's solar plexus. The gunman caught the first move from Dusty and dropped his hand towards his gun. He was a full half-second too late for the blow landed before the gun was clear. Awkward though the way Dusty struck appeared to the gunman the blow came like the bite of the edge of an axe. His hand missed the butt of his gun as he gave a croaking gasp and doubled forward, the breath forced from his lungs in a painful manner. Gasping in pain the man sank to his knees, his face an ashy grey colour and masked with agony.

The second gunman started to grab for his gun and almost made it. Fingers which gripped like the closing jaws of a bear trap clamped on to his arm. He gave what started as an angry curse and ended as a yell of agony as his wrist was crushed in powerful hands. Mark Counter came to his feet, swinging the gunman before him with no more trouble than if he was handling a baby. Then Mark brought the gunman's arm up behind his back. The man was bent forward, helpless in those hands. Mark turned again until they faced the wall. Then with a sudden surge of his muscles Mark sent the man hurling head first into the wall. The gunman's head hit hard and with a moan of pain he sank down.

Rambeau saw, reflected in the mirror, what was happening to his men. He started to swing around with his hand dropping and lifting his gun. He recognised Dusty and Mark as the two men who had backed Leslie on the street and once more they had crossed his path.

For all his gunfighter's belt Rambeau was not fast with his gun. The Colt was lifting as Dusty came to his feet, right hand flickering across his body. Yet from so far behind Dusty still had his gun out and lined before Rambeau cleared leather. The bone handled Colt was in Dusty's hand, the left holster empty, the hammer drawn back under his thumb and the four and three-quarter-inch barrel lined on Rambeau's middle froze the saloon-keeper's draw still not more than half done.

"Don't try it, Rambeau," warned Dusty.

It was at that moment Rambeau realised what Iowa Parsons had told him all the time since he bought the gunbelt.

Parsons' oft-repeated warning that Rambeau was not fast enough to tote a gun in such a rig was clear now. The saloon-keeper had come West after his saloon on New York's Bowery had grown too hot for comfort. He had come from a world where a gun was not yet considered as a useful tool for settling a difference and had started to learn, too late, the secrets of handling a smoking Colt in a Western corpse-and-cartridge affair. Slowly his hand came away from his gun and for the first time in his life he knew the raw ache of fear biting into him. He swore that never again would he be fool enough to strap on a gunbelt.

"I'll take the chair, Rambeau," Brownlow said coolly.

That put the play back in Rambeau's hands once more but he no longer fancied backing it. Without being told he knew murder was out, even murder done under the flimsy guise of self-defence. That small—small? Suddenly Dusty Fog was small no more in Rambeau's eyes, in fact he suddenly appeared to tower taller than any other man in the room to the saloon-keeper. That fast-moving Texan would never allow Rambeau to call the play with guns.

There was the prospect of standing up against Vance Brownlow in a rough-house brawl but no longer was that appealing to Rambeau. He was a skilled fist fighter who learned his game in the slums of New York but the Britisher was also skilled and his ways of fighting were something completely beyond Rambeau's understanding. He did not wish to get into a fight and risk having his handsome face marked up. Not when he thought of that beautiful young actress who arrived in town that morning. Rambeau was proud of his good looks and did not want them marked. Marked they would get if he stacked up against Vance Brownlow.

"I'll not forget this, Brownlow," he snarled, turning to cross the room to where Dusty's victim was getting to his feet, groaning and holding his stomach. He looked back at Vance Brownlow and went on, "You've done wrong, hiring a gun."

"I never saw either of these gentlemen before," Vance Brownlow replied. "I'm sorry, chappie, but I don't need a partner. Much less do I need one who puts nothing in and wants to take twenty-five per cent of all the profits out."

With that the tall Englishman sat in the chair in a gesture which clearly showed the interview was over as far as he was concerned. Rambeau's face showed anger but he kept clear his hand from the gun butt. Dusty Fogg stood to one side, his Colt back in the holster but that meant nothing as Rambeau knew. It had been in the holster before, but came out fast enough. Rambeau turned his anger on the gunman who was now on his feet.

"Get your pard up," he snarled, jerking a thumb towards the groaning man on the floor. "Let's get out of here."

The gunman gritted his teeth but bent and helped the other man to his feet. Rambeau jerked open the door and the two gunmen went by him; he stood for an instant, then turned and left, slamming the door behind him. The customers let out their breath in a long and concerted sigh which was echoed by the three barbers and the lather boy. This latter had stood from start to finish holding the lather-brush poised in the air.

"Excuse me, mister," said the prosperous-looking townsman who had been seated by Mark, rising to look at Dusty. "No offence meant, but I was wondering if you had entered for the pistol shoot?"

The man spoke with some care. It paid to do so when addressing such a remark to a man who wore two guns in a rig like that with the holster bottoms tied down. It was a saying in the West that a man who tied down his holster bottom was apt not to talk much with his mouth.

"Reckon I am, sir," Dusty answered.

"Wouldn't take it wrong was I to ask your name, mister?" the man went on in a polite and respectful tone. "I'd surely admire to lay a bet on you."

"No offence taken. The name's Dusty Fog."

"Dusty Fog!" the well-dressed man's repeating of Dusty's name was echoed by every other man in the shop. "I'll be back in a minute, Sid!"

The same idea apparently struck every other customer in the shop, including the two who were receiving treatment in the chair. There was a sudden rush for the door and Tombstone was presented with the spectacle of several citizens, including one with one side of his hair short, the other long and shaggy and the other with half his face still lathered, the barber's towels still around their necks, heading at a dead run for the Bucket of Blood Saloon.

Dusty watched the exit, then turned and grinned to the barber, who was by the cash drawer and taking money out.

"I'm sorry we cost you some trade, friend," he said.

"That kind of gunwork don't need no apologising for, Cap'n Fog," replied the owner of the shop. Then he turned to the lather boy. "Sammywell," he said, holding out the money, "head for the Bucket of Blood and ask the bartender to put this on Cap'n Fog in the Pistol Shoot."

The lather boy took the money and the other two barbers also handed over bets to be placed for them. The lather boy left the shop on the run and the barber waved a hand to the now empty chairs. A grin came to his face as he thought of the chance he had to win, for he was betting on Iowa Parsons and Wyatt Earp as well. Now it looked as if he'd covered all the bets.

"Take a seat, gents," the barber said. "Looks like you won't have to wait at all."

The Kid emerged from the bathroom and took a seat. He did not know what had happened, but was pleased to see he would not have to wait long for his haircut. His two friends and another man appeared to be the only customers and they were in the chairs now.

Vance Brownlow looked across to the two cowhands as they sat back, the towels in place and the barber's shears moving.

"I haven't thanked you two gentlemen yet," he said. "I hope you will allow me to show my appreciation by standing you a meal at the Eating House when we're done."

"No thanks are needed, friend," Dusty replied.

"I was watching how you hit that gunman, Captain Fog," Brownlow went on. "It's a remarkable coincidence but you used something like a karate trick I learned from a Japanese merchant in Hong Kong. I was a young subaltern in the Rifles out there."

"Now that's a real coincidence," Dusty answered and his two friends grinned as they listened. "I thought I was using the *tegatana* against his *suigetsu*."

"Gad!" Vance Brownlow ejaculated, twisting around in the chair and looking at Dusty with more interest. "I could have sworn that I was the only man in Arizona knew karate."

Dusty chuckled. "You'd best sit back afore you leave an ear on the floor. I learned karate and ju-jitsu down home to the Rio Hondo country. My Uncle Devil's man Tommy Akasi, taught me. I didn't know if the handsword would work against his solar plexus, but I reckon it did."

Vance Brownlow threw back his head and laughed, making the barber jerk back his clippers in a hurry to avoid cutting the rancher's head.

"I think it did at that. I hope you accept my offer of the meal down at Mother Handy's place."

"We never refused a meal yet," Dusty replied. "It's on your head though. Your friends'll likely cut you dead if they see you in the street, associating with folks like us."

Before the other customers returned Dusty, Mark and Brownlow were finished and the Ysabel Kid sat having his long black hair trimmed.

CHAPTER FIVE

Vance Brownlow Needs Hands

MOTHER HANDY'S EATING HOUSE stood on Toughnut Street, a large, white painted wooden building, clean looking and giving forth appetising smells which boded well for the meals served on the inside.

There was a good crowd in the Eating House when Vance Brownlow entered with the three Texans. He led them to a table by the central aisle and they sat around it, hanging their hats on the backs of the chairs. The waitresses, three pretty girls in black dresses and clean white aprons, moved among the other customers and did not give Brownlow's party a glance. At the door of the kitchen Mother Handy, a smallish, plump and white-haired old woman, neatly dressed, gentle in appearance, was giving the cook the benefit of a tongue lashing that did not fit in with her appearance at all. She turned, slammed the door and came down the aisle to halt by Brownlow's table, smiled at the men as they shoved back their chairs and started to rise.

"Sit down, all of ye," she said. "Vance, me darlin' boy, and when is it you'll be bringing us some of that good beef in?"

No question need ever be asked to Mother Handy's home country, not with a brogue thicker than a New York Irish policeman's on Saint Patrick's Day.

"As soon as I can gather in a trail crew," Vance replied, without looking at his guests. "Birdie's trying around town right now."

"Huh!" snorted Mother Handy. "I've been hearing why it is you can't get the men." Her eyes went to Dusty Fog, Mark Counter and the Ysabel Kid. For a moment she studied the Kid's Indian dark face, then she nodded. If three men like these, so obviously tophands, had taken on to ride for Vance Brownlow, he would get all the others he needed. She asked no questions, that was never done. "I can't offer you much by the way of meat, boys. The Folks in town are eating it faster than the local ranchers can supply it."

"Never heard tell that the Clantons or the McLowery boys had trouble raising beef, ma'am," drawled the Kid. "They do tell that every Clanton cow has at least five calves and even some of the bulls have young 'uns too."

"Well, I wouldn't buy nothing from the likes of them. I can prove all the beef I buy isn't stolen. I wouldn't buy no kind of dishonest goods."

"Smuggled wine isn't dishonest then, ma'am?" asked the Kid mildly.

The old woman snorted explosively, the sudden annoyance came and left her face as she laughed, holding out her hand to the Kid. "Lon Ysabel," she gasped. "The Saints preserve us. I heard you'd been killed down in Mexico just after the War. Sure and you're not still doing that awful and evil smuggling, now are you?"

For all the outburst there was a note which was more of hope than condemnation in the old woman's voice as she looked at the boy, who, with his father, had sold her more than one consignment of good wine on which no duty ever was paid to the U.S. Customs.

"Nope, I done retired," the Kid answered sadly.

The old woman opened her mouth to make a suggestion to Vance, then closed it again. She took their order for the meal, turned and headed for the kitchen to roust up the cook. Mother Handy liked Vance Brownlow and his pretty wife and hoped they would be able to get the men they needed. However, she could not interfere in their private business. If Vance had hired the three Texans all would be well. If he had not, Mother Handy could hardly poke her nose in and interfere.

"Would a man be out of line to ask what's between you and Rambeau?" Mark asked of Vance after the old woman walked away.

Before the question could be answered there was an interruption. The door of the room burst suddenly open and a small, plump yet pretty blonde woman entered and came across to the table. There was anger on her face. There was anger in the way she stamped down her dainty, high-heeled boots. Her white Stetson was thrust back from her head and hung on her back by the storm strap. Her blonde hair was cut short and curly, the hair style a woman living far from other women would choose as being easily cared for and need little attention. Her figure was plump, yet there was hard, firm flesh, not flabby fat. Her round, full breasts strained against the open necked tartan shirt and her hips strained the washed-out blue jeans which hung cowhand style outside her boots.

She halted at Brownlow's table, resting her hands on the top and looking straight at him. "I couldn't raise a single man, Vance boy," she said.

"I didn't think you would."

"I could have if that Iowa Parsons hadn't followed me every place I went," the woman went on angrily, her voice a Texas drawl under the anger.

"Did he say or do anything to you?" Vance snapped angrily and started to thrust back his chair.

"Nope, so pull in your horns. Parsons wouldn't let you get in close enough to get one of those ju-jitsu holds on him."

"This here Iowa Parsons, ma'am," put in Mark, still on his feet, as were the other two Texans, having risen when the woman approached, "they do tell he's a good friend of that nice Mr. Rambeau we're all so fond of and pleased to know."

To give the woman credit, she'd hardly noticed the three Texans in her annoyance. Now she studied them with eyes which knew cowhands in general and Texas cowhands in particular.

"He does," she snorted. "That fancy dressed, scent-smelling Arbuckle hires Parsons as his boss gun, and meaner, colder, back shooting Yankee sidewinder'd be hard to find, man or boss."

"Way you all get to talking, ma'am," put in the Kid politely and mildly, "a man'd think you didn't like neither of them."

"Don't like them!" the woman's voice rose a shade. "Don't like them. I tell you all. I'd as soon have the Earps, the Republican Party or two skunks settle on me than them pair. Why they make old Carpetbag Davis's dirty State Police look like good and honest Southern gentlemen."

Dusty smiled, a broad smile which was mirrored by the grins of his friends as they took their seats again. The woman was not English, that was for sure. She was as Texas as the Alamo, the Lone Star flag or any of the three young men from Ole Devil Hardin's Rio Hondo outfit. There was no doubting the State she hailed from, not with that accent or her reference to ex-Governor Davis's State Police, a force which had been brought to Texas to replace the Rangers after the War. The State Police had a career which varied from rank incompetence to extortion and robbery instead of one of crime prevention and the Police finally disbanded when Davis was forcibly tossed from office. They were a force for which the average Texan felt nothing but scorn.

"You wouldn't be from Texas, now would you, ma'am?"

Dusty asked as he drew out a chair for her to sit down.

"I surely didn't know it showed," she answered, taking the seat and looking at the men. "I've been trying to hide it since I married Vance. Anyways, that King Rambeau'd make a prissy Eastern schoolmarm cuss fit to throw her teeth."

The three men were then introduced to Mrs. Birdie Brownlow and Mark turned his attention back to Vance once more.

"You never got around to telling us about your problem, Vance."

"There's no trouble at all, much. I've got a herd of five hundred head, all prime beef. I want to bring them into Tombstone in time for the County Fair."

"Which same's not much of a problem," drawled the Kid. "Unless there's some more to it."

"There is just a trifle more," Vance agreed. "I was oversimplifying things a trifle. My place is ten days' drive from here, on the other side of the Carne River, which has only one decent crossing we can use to get here on time."

"And there's maybe half the Apache nation just sitting somewheres between our spread and Tombstone, licking their fat old lips and thinking how good that same herd's going to smell and taste in their stewpot."

"Which same'd make a tolerable large stewpot, taking five hundred head at one go," remarked the Kid.

Birdie gave him a cold look and then ignored him. "Trouble being we daren't weaken the ranch crew any to run the herd in," she told the other two, "which's why Vance and I came in a week back. Now Rambeau's sent Parsons out to make sure we don't get the men."

"Why'd he do that, 'cepting for meanness, ma'am?" asked the Kid.

"The price of beef is rising every day. Just before the Fair starts that herd will bring in five—six times as much as it would normally. I know it, so does Rambeau. He came to see me the first day into town and offered to get me all the men I'd need for twenty-five per cent of the gross price of the herd," Vance explained, sensing the others were becoming interested and feeling hope rise.

"Which same's a tolerable fair spread for a man who is running on nothing more than muscle, happen you didn't know," Birdie went on.

"Do tell, ma'am," drawled Mark. "I haven't been around much."

"That I could tell one eyed," she replied.

"Anyway," Vance spoke up, marvelling, as he always did, at the casual and relaxed way in which his wife became friendly with cowhands, "I told Rambeau he'd the wrong chappie and that I declined his offer. Then his man, Iowa Parsons, started passing the word he'd kill any man who hired to me."

The Ysabel Kid was seated so he could see the window of the room and through it he saw three men pass by. He saw the shape of one of them at the door and a grin came to his face.

"Do you reckon to be lucky, Vance?" he asked.

Vance Brownlow looked at his wife and smiled. "I think I am."

"You've never been luckier than now," drawled the Kid as the door opened.

The three men who entered were Texas cowhands, top-hands too, if the signs did not lie. In the centre was a tall, slim, somehow military looking young man. There was an air of command about him, the look of a man used to giving orders. His clothing was functional cowhand rig, yet expensive, and around his waist was a gunbelt built for speed, with a low tied ivory handled Colt Cavalry Peacemaker in the holster. His face was handsome, or would have been but for the sabre scar which twisted and marked his right cheek.

The other two were cowhands, Texas cowhands at that. Their hats were thrust back and both were red heads, the taller's hair a fiery thatch, the shorter's a rusty mop. The taller was handsome, wide shouldered, lean waisted and tall as the Ysabel Kid. He wore a gunbelt and in the holster at his left side was a staghorn butted Army Colt, one of the old 1860 percussion fired models, but still in a fast draw holster with the tip tied down. The last of the trio was not as tall, he was cheerily good looking, stocky and his low hanging, plain handled Colt was no decoration, even though he did not have the look of a real fast man about him. He was laughing at something one of the others had said, when he came to a halt, the laugh died and a hard expression took its place as he looked towards Brownlow's party.

"Say, Johnny," he said in a cold voice. "It's that Rio Hondo varmint. We owe him some from last time. Don't we?"

"We sure do, Rusty," replied the taller red head. "Let's hand it to him now."

The two men moved forward, their friend standing at the door with a half-smile playing on his lips as he watched them bearing down on Dusty Fog.

For his part, Dusty gave no sign other than to move back his chair so he was free from the table. The two cowhands were approaching, Johnny slightly ahead of Rusty. Then suddenly the taller man's hand lashed out, folded in a fist, at

Dusty's head. It was a blow hard enough to drop an ox and would have knocked Dusty clear across the room had it landed.

Dusty left his chair with the speed which had made his name a legend. His hands came up to trap the cowhand's wrist as it whistled towards his head. Jerking the arm upwards over his head, Dusty pivoted and turned, bringing the arm down once more. Johnny had no choice but to go over; he gave a yell as his feet left the ground, then he lit down again flat on his back. Rusty let out a yell and tried to get around his friend and into the attack.

Throwing back his chair, Vance started to come to his feet, wondering why Mark and the Kid were not offering to rise and help Dusty. He might also have wondered why two men wearing guns and so obviously able to use them, were fist fighting. Even before Vance could get round the table he was too late.

The cowhand called Johnny lit down on his back. To make sure he did not rise, Dusty moved fast. He released the wrist with one hand, but the other still held the arm stretched out and his foot lifted to stab down with the high heel gouging into Johnny's armpit in a painful manner. With Johnny out of action, Dusty was all set to deal with Rusty's attack.

Rusty's fist drove out right into Dusty's gripping hand. Dusty's thumb bit down on the spot just below the joining of the first and second fingers, on the nerve centres, Rusty gave a squawking yell, his arm was twisted until he was turned and Dusty held it bent up his back. Then Dusty hooked his foot between Rusty's leg and shoved him. Rusty gave a yell and went sprawling at the feet of the tall, scar-faced man. Looking down, the scar-faced man asked, "Don't you ever learn?"

Vance stood with his fists clenched, not knowing what was happening. He saw the Kid lean forward and look at the agonised face of Johnny and ask, "What you doing down there, Johnny?"

The red head managed a grin. "I'm good now, Dusty. Get your foot off'n me."

Mother Handy had emerged from the kitchen with a broom gripped in both hands when she heard the noise, but she could see there was nothing worse than cowhand high spirits, for Dusty was helping Johnny to his feet and the other two men were coming forward with grins on their faces.

"I sure figured we'd got you made there, Dusty," Johnny remarked, rubbing his hip. "Which same only goes to show, now don't it?"

Vance Brownlow stood still on his feet as the three newcomers began noisy and cheery greetings, shaking hands with Dusty, Mark and the Kid, demanding to know about friends and not waiting for any answer. At last Vance could not longer restrain his curiosity.

"Will somebody tell me what in the name of Sam Hill is going on?"

Dusty took a seat, sliding along to make room for Rusty and Johnny, who were bringing chairs from another table. The talk died down and Dusty gave a laughing answer:

"Vance, Birdie, meet Stone Hart, boss of the Wedge and two of his worthless hands, Johnny Raybold and Rusty Willis."

"The Wedge?" Vance repeated as he looked at the scar-faced young man whose name was spoken of as being one of the finest trail bosses alive. Then Vance remembered the Kid's remark about being lucky and guessed what the words meant.

"I'll take two of your specials, ma'am," said Johnny Raybold, the Wedge's scout, as Mother Handy came alongside them.

"How about your friends?" she answered.

"They'd be tougher than old leather to eat," Johnny drawled. "I'll just take two specials and apple pie to follow."

"Two is it?" yelped Mother Handy indignantly. "No man living can eat two of my specials hand-sitting."

"You wouldn't want to bet on that, would you, ma'am?" asked Rusty Willis eagerly.

"That I would not. But I'll make this agreement with you. If he eats the two specials I'll give him them free. If he doesn't I'll bend my broom over his head."

"She'll do it too, Johnny," warned Birdie.

"I'll just bet she will at that, ma'am," answered Johnny without sounding unduly worried. "Do I get the pie free to follow?"

The old woman gave Johnny a long stare of amazement, snorted and headed for the kitchen to make sure her always well-filled plates were piled up extra high to teach the red-headed upstart a lesson he'd never forget.

"You're a mite off your home range, Stone," the Kid drawled as they finished their meals and waited for Johnny to wade through his.

"Sure. We were offered a herd to drive for an outfit near hear. The Clantons. So I brought the boys along and came down here. We should have been back in town for the Fair, old Chow's entered his chuckwagon for the race. Anyway, I decided not to take the herd on."

"Wouldn't want to be out 'n' out nosey," drawled the Kid, "and ask why—why?"

"Their earmark's what'd be called a grub on the near and a sharp on the off. Then for brands they kind of go in for variety. Mexican maps and greaser madhouses and all from different herds.. With that kind of a herd a man's likely to wind up wearing a hemp bandanna at the cottonwood hoe-down."

Stone Hart did not need to explain the words to the others. Grub and sharp earmarks were rarely used on cattle. They were special ways of cutting an animal's ear, brutal and cruel, but little used in the normal line of cattle business. The grub was made by cutting both an under and over slope and left little of an ear to the animal. The sharp was done by cropping the ear to a short point, like that of a boxer dog. Both the earmarks had merit only to a man who wanted to remove the traces of previous and more legitimate earmarks from his cattle. Mexican maps and greaser madhouses were the terms given to the large and complicated brands the ranchers south of the border used on their herds. The Clantons' herd consisted of cattle branded with a variety of such brands, pointing that they came from different herds and were most likely stolen. For a man to be caught driving a stolen herd could bring him a hemp bandanna at a cottonwood hoe-down, or in plain and unvarnished English, to a hanging as guest of honour.

"Those Clantons will go too far one of these days," Vance remarked.

"You're not riding with anybody then, Stone?" Birdie put in eagerly. She was more concerned with getting their herd to Tombstone than with the possible end of the Clantons.

"No, ma'am, we're not."

For an instant Birdie was startled by the brusque way Stone replied and the way he did not, had not since he sat at the table, looked straight at her. She felt annoyed for a moment, then the annoyance died away. Stone Hart was seated so the unscarred side of his face was towards her. It was a handsome face and the scar was not as bad as he apparently thought. She realised that he must feel bitterly about it and would have liked to tell him that it was not so bad as he imagined, but common sense held her tongue. She knew he would resent bitterly any words about his disfigurement from a stranger.

"Would you care to handle a drive for me, old chap?" Vance asked, catching on to his wife's idea. "A small herd, five hundred head, A hundred miles or so to town and a few hundred Apaches waiting to stop us. I'll pay double the normal rate if you will."

"Pay us the normal rate," Stone answered with a grin. "I'm no Yankee to gouge a man when he's in a tight. Are you riding, Dusty?"

"I'm here for Uncle Devil, doing something for Texas John," Dusty replied. "I'd sure like to ride with you, *amigo,* but I'll have to see how he wants things playing first."

"How about you, Kid?" Stone went on, turning to the Kid. "Johnny's a fair scout, but he's always worked against Northern Indians and not against Apaches. I could use an extra scout."

"I'll ride if Dusty can spare me," replied the Kid. The thought of Apaches and danger never troubled him. He hoped to get a chance to ride with his good friends of the Wedge once more.

"Let's leave her lie on how Texas John wants us, Lon," Dusty suggested. "If you get a full crew, Stone, and we're free, we'll come along for the ride."

"Where's Doc and Waggles and the rest of the crew, Stone?" Mark asked.

"Made camp on a stream outside town. They allow it'll be cheaper than buying a hotel room."

"We'll go out there if you like," Vance suggested. "As soon as Johnny finishes eating. You're the trail boss, Stone. I'll take you out to my ranch, then lend a hand on the way in. Birdie won't stay in town now, or back at the ranch, so she can lend the cook a hand."

There were startled expressions on the faces of the Texas men as they looked at Vance. He wondered what he'd said to bring about such a change in them. He was soon to learn that Stone Hart's old cook, Chow Willicka, lived by two beliefs. The first was that no woman ever born, even his own mother, knew how to cook. The other belief was that women's cooking would plumb soon ruin a man's innards.

Birdie did not need to be told this, she'd heard cowhands talk of Chow Willicka, who was acknowledged a master of his trade. She knew his beliefs and decided to place a dainty and ladylike foot on them right now from the start.

"You can just set in and tell that fool old chow-spoiler he's going to have him a real-live female lady louse helping him on this trip," she warned Stone. "And if he objects or gives me sass I'll ram his biggest skillet so hard on to his head that his corns'll be pushed out of his boot soles."

The men all chuckled at the spirited words. They could see there would be stirring times around the camp fires on the drive when Chow Willicka and Birdie locked horns. The Kid was hoping they would be given a chance to ride with the Wedge if only to see the fun.

"How many will you need, Stone?" Vance asked.

"Normally I'd take a herd that size with just my regular crew, but with the Apaches out I'd like to take on a few, say four or five more riders. If that suits you."

"My dear chap, you're the boss. I'm just curious and interested," Vance replied and looked for Mother Handy, waving for the bill to be brought.

The old woman came to the table and found that Johnny's two plates were empty and that he was just finishing the last of the enormous slab of apple pie. He hardly showed any sign of consuming a meal which would have foundered many a man.

"I don't believe it," she gasped. "I just don't believe it. That boy must be all stomach, clean down to his feet."

The others all laughed, although the Texans were far from surprised at Johnny and his capacity for putting away food. Mother Handy joined the many other cooks who noted Johnny's trim figure and thought they could outfeed him. It was a thought which had saved Johnny more than a few dollars in eating houses from Texas to Kansas along the cattle trails.

"The boys'll be pleased, Stone," Rusty remarked. "Ole Peaceful allowed we'd all get into trouble and young Rin's been trying to borrow money to whup the tail off Buckskin Frank Leslie's tiger. They'll be right happy to get away from temptation, especially as they haven't much money left and the Fair's a fortnight off."

Deep down Stone agreed with Rusty. The failure to take the Clanton's herd had left his crew short of money and they would either have to head back to Texas or get work locally to raise money for the festivities. This way they would be away until just before the Fair and would pay off, have money in their pockets.

Vance paid the bill and came to his feet, the others taking their hats and also rising. Dusty meant to look around and find Slaughter, learn what the rancher wanted him to do. With that knowledge he could plan his future, whether to ride with Stone Hart and Vance or not.

The door of the room was suddenly kicked open and a man stepped in. Two more followed him, moving like wolves flanking an unstrung buffalo. The two men were hired killers, cheap, expendable, loyal only as long as the pay was good and the stakes did not rise too high.

The other man was also a hired killer, but as far above the

others as the ace is over the deuce in a high hand poker game. He wore a flat-topped black hat, a city shirt and vest, across which stretched a gold watch chain. His trousers and shoes equally pointed to the city, but that gunbelt was Western. It hung just right and told a grim story to a man who knew the signs as well as Dusty Fog did. That was a fast man's holster, but so was Dusty's, Mark's and, to a lesser degree, the holsters of the Ysabel Kid or the three Wedge hands. No, it was more than just the belt and holster. It was the gun and the way the holster hung. The leather of the holster was cut to a minimum, half the chamber, all the trigger-guard and the butt left clear and just right for an easy reach. The checking of the hammer tip had been filed off, leaving the spur so that it would slip free of the thumb easily. The gun and holster hung so the tip slanted forward and the butt of the gun looked too far back to a man who knew a little more about such things.

Dusty Fog knew more than a little about guns and holsters. That method was known as the walk and draw, it was favoured by professional town lawmen who rarely, if ever, rode a horse and did not need to bother about their guns jarring from the holster while riding. It all spelled one thing to Dusty. This lean, gaunt, dark faced man was a professional and fast—real fast.

"Dusty!" Vance Brownlow gasped as he felt Birdie grip his arm. His voice was no more than a whisper, as if he was mesmerised by that grim faced man before them. "That's Iowa Parsons."

"They say if any man can lick Wyatt Earp in the Fair's Pistol Shoot he's the one who'll do it," Birdie went on. "He's come to stop you hiring to us."

CHAPTER SIX

Shootout at Mother Handy's

THE GAUNT MAN called Iowa Parsons stood in the centre of the doorway, clearly blocking all exit, the two men flanking him making sure no one could slip by. Word had been brought to them that men were sitting in friendship and might be taking on to drive cattle for Vance Brownlow, and so they came along to lend their skill and backing to the man from the Syndicate, Iowa Parsons.

For a long moment Iowa Parsons studied each of the faces before him, reading in them their standing and ability. His eyes were cold and unfeeling as those of a cottonmouth snake's and his face was devoid of expression. He was a killing machine, cold, deadly and efficient. Vance Brownlow felt his wife's finger bite into his arm as the eyes looked at her, then he knew the chill of fear as Parsons looked at him. Vance was no coward, but he was no fool either. He knew that here was a man who would kill him without batting an eye or turning a hair to do it so fast that he would never know just what happened.

"Brownlow!" said Parsons, in a voice that had all the brutal finality of the croak of a buzzard dropping to pick the eyes from a corpse. "They tell me you've hired a fast gun to take care of you. Let's see him."

"I've hired no one," Vance began. "I——"

It was then Dusty moved forward, cutting off Vance's angry denial. "Nobody hired me," he said gently. "But I'm the one you want."

Parsons inclined his head in acknowledgment. His guess at Dusty's ability, capability and identity had been correct. With this thought in mind the killer began to give out a warning to the others, although he never took his eyes from Dusty's face. The slightest split second of inattention would be enough, against a man as fast as Dusty Fog, to be fatal. In that thought Parsons did Dusty far less than justice, for the small Texan would never take an advantage of any man. However, Parsons judged all men by his own standards.

"I passed a word about Brownlow here," he said. "There's only one way you can ride for him. By passing me."

Stone Hart was the leader of the Wedge and to him it would have fallen to take up the challenge, but Dusty had taken the play from his hands. Stone knew his own speed and limitations. He was a good man with a gun, but he was way out of his class against a man like the gaunt killer. He would send down his hand with all his speed, grip the butt of his Colt, perhaps even start to lift it—but he would be dead before he could raise it higher and long before he could get it lined for use. Now it all rested on Dusty, he'd called the play.

"Three to one, Parsons," Dusty asked gently, without relaxing his watchful attention on the killer, and with good cause. "Or do we make it three to three?"

"Call it any way you want, Captain Fog."

"Mark, Lon!"

At the words Dusty's two friends moved forward, Mark stepping to the right and the Kid to the left, halting on either side of Dusty and standing relaxed but ready.

The room fell silent, only the ticking of the clock on the wall sounded. The diners at the tables, the waitresses backed towards the walls and Mother Handy by the side of the cash desk, all were silent, hardly breathing, as they watched and waited for the next move in this deadly game.

"When you're ready, Mr. Parsons," said Mark gently.

The gunman facing Mark licked his lips. There was sweat pouring down his face, for suddenly the odds in the game became too even for his liking. It was an easy thing to scare off cowhands when backed by Iowa Parsons. It was no longer an easy thing when faced with even numbers, more so when the three were men like Dusty Fog, Mark Counter and the Ysabel Kid.

"I'm out," was all the gunman said and backed towards the door. He passed through it and went along the street to the livery barn, collected his horse, picked up his thirty year gatherings from the hotel and rode from town.

The Ysabel Kid's face split in a cold grin as he moved back. He was the slowest of the trio and could most be spared in this matter. There was no fear in this decision, for the Kid did not know fear. He would have gone up against Iowa Parsons even knowing he had no chance, if such a deed was needed. Right now it was not needed, for Dusty and Mark were quite capable of handling matters without his help. Now one of the other side had yelled "calf rope", and backed out and the play was one to one.

Parsons acknowledged the Kid's departure only in that it left him in a better position. Mark Counter stood on the other side of Dusty Fog, away from the man who stayed to fight. That gave Parsons an advantage, or so he thought, for Mark would have to be firing across his friend's front.

"We're leaving, Parsons," Dusty said quietly.

Iowa Parsons started his hand lashing down. It was a fast move, one which showed practice and skill. Dusty had watched the other man's eyes, saw the flicker which gave him warning and sent his hands crossing to the bone handles of his matched Colts. The twin Colts came into his hands, lining and flame licking from the four and three-quarter-inch barrels towards Parsons. Mark was moving and a split second behind the crash of Dusty's Colts, ahead of Parsons' move, the long-barrelled ivory handled Colt lifted from leather, hammer drawing back and filling to spew lead out.

The crash of shots shattered the silence of the room. Smoke laid down its whirling eddies around Dusty and Mark, but they knew that Parsons and his man had not made it at all. Parsons had brought his gun from leather, but it was not lined when the two 45 bullets smashed into him and hurled his body backwards through the door off the sidewalk and into the dirt of Tombstone's Toughnut Street. The other gunman spun around, crashed into the wall and went down, his gun not yet clear of leather.

The room was silent again after the shots flung back their lash echo from the walls. The raw, acrid smelling powder smoke wafted back in the breeze through the door, biting into Birdie Brownlow's throat as, with a cry, she turned to her husband and buried her face into his shirt, Vance's hands went around her, but his face had lost all its colour. Stone Hart and his two men stood stiff and silent. They'd all seen Mark and Dusty in action, but that speed gave a man pause to think no matter how often he saw it.

Dusty looked back at Vance, his face and voice hard. "Go and see about getting your crew, and take your lady with you."

It was left to Stone Hart to make the first move. Stepping forward, he laid his hand on Vance's shoulder, putting life into limbs which would no longer obey the dictates of the mind. Vance Brownlow had seen Wyatt Earp showing his speed and skill on a target in preparation for the forthcoming Pistol Shoot. Never had the rancher seen the real thing until this day. Now he'd seen it. That was no paper target which stood before Dusty Fog's bone handled Colts. It had been a living, breathing man, a man filled with hate and the urge to kill, a man who had killed for a price many times. Now all that was left of the man was a crumpled pile of clothes, an empty holster, a mass of quivering flesh, slowly spreading blood in the dust and dirt of Toughnut Street.

At the door, even as the crowd started to run along the street towards Mother Handy's Eating House, Stone Hart halted and looked back at Dusty Fog.

"I'll hold three places for you, Dusty," he said quietly.

"Do that, *amigo*," replied Dusty. "And if you send any of the boys in for supplies, send them in threes. It'll be safer."

Then Stone Hart was gone, taking Vance and the sobbing Birdie with him, followed by his two hands. Dusty glanced at Mark, who was standing over the second gunman, looking down to make sure he was beyond any help. Mark's eyes lifted and met Dusty's, he shook his head, walked back and joined his friends to await the coming of the Tombstone law.

It was Mother Handy with her broom who drove back the crowd of eager onlookers who were trying to enter the room and see the man who shot down Iowa Parsons. The old woman had spent all her life in the west and in her time had seen many of the fast men in action. She'd heard often of Dusty Fog's speed, but as far as she could remember had never heard of how good Mark Counter was with his guns. Good he was, she knew that now. Iowa Parsons was the man many had said would win the Pistol Shoot and yet he died of a case of slow. There was more, the old woman could swear that Mark's guns had cleared leather ahead of Iowa Parsons' draw and that the tall Texan could have faced him, drawn and walked away from it. The thought made Mother Handy frown, then she understood. Mark Counter rode in the shadow of the Rio Hondo gun wizard and his own skill went unnoticed.

The crowd parted and Mother Handy removed her broom to allow Texas John Slaughter and a stocky, rubbery looking man in a store suit, entrance. The man wore a gunbelt, but did not have the look of a real fast hand with a gun. On his lapel was the badge of County Sheriff; his name was John Behan. The old woman allowed the two men to pass her, then gave a warning that she would break the head of the first man who put his foot inside the door without good cause and followed them to the table where Dusty, Mark and the Kid waited.

"You, Dusty?" asked Slaughter, jerking his thumb over his shoulder in the direction of the grisly thing in Toughnut Street.

"He wouldn't have it any other way."

Behan nodded gravely at the words, turned and told some

of the crowd to remove the two bodies and get them to the undertaker's shop near the jail. Then he turned his attention back to Dusty.

"Parsons was a real fast man, Captain Fog," he said. "There's some it won't suit to think you took him fair."

"I saw it all, John Behan," snorted the old woman. "So just let any of that dirty Law and Order bunch try and make me out a liar."

At that moment Virgil Earp arrived. He came alone, with none of his brothers or their friends to back him. That was his way of showing good faith, for he'd been told who was involved in the killing and knew the situation needed careful handling if shooting was to be avoided. The Texans had little love for the Earps and what they stood for, Virgil knew that all too well. By coming alone he was leaving himself a way out in case some hot-headed fool wanted Dusty Fog and his friends arrested.

"What's all this, John?" he asked.

"You can read the signs, Virgil," answered Behan. "Iowa Parsons met up with a better man. That's all."

That was all, unless Earp wanted to carry it further. It was common talk around the town that Iowa Parsons had put the Indian sign on Vance Brownlow and said no man must hire to him. It was also common talk, so fast did news travel in a western town, that Vance had locked horns with Rambeau, the killer's boss and had been backed in it by the three Texans. That Iowa Parsons, so proud of his reputation as a fast gun killer and bender of wills, could not overlook. He must come out and face down the men who dared go against his word. He had done so, the end was on the street being borne off on to the cold slab in the undertaker's shop on the first leg of its last long journey. There was nothing to be made of the shooting. It was justifiable homicide. Dusty Fog had defended his life even to the extent of taking life from Parsons, and in the West that was no crime.

"You was first here, John," Earp said evenly, his face showing nothing of how he felt. "I've more than enough work of my own."

The crowd who watched from outside felt disappointed at the words. They all knew how the Earps and Behan stood. They also knew that any Texan was likely to be more friendly to the sheriff than to the Earps. So they'd hoped to see Virgil Earp take a firm stand on the dignity of the Town Marshal's office. In that case there would be more action, for no Texan would willingly surrender to a Kansas lawman. Now there was no chance of it, for Earp was walking towards the door, leaving John Behan in charge. The crowd broke up, some to go about their business, the others to head for the undertaker's shop and peer through the windows at the sheet covered forms on the slabs.

Behan waved a hand towards a table and suggested they sat down. The others all complied and he looked straight at Dusty, for a moment he looked, then turned his eyes to laughter:

"Texas John, can you get Captain Fog out to your place for a few days? At least, until this blows over."

"Sure. It'd be best, Dusty. Otherwise the *Tombstone Epitaph* will be asking why Johnny didn't arrest you or run you out of town if you stay on. The *Epitaph* is backing the Law and Order bunch and it'd be a good way to get at John here."

Dusty knew this to be true. The *Tombstone Epitaph* was a violenty pro-Earp paper and would make much of the fact that Sheriff Behan did not arrest the man who killed Iowa Parsons. Forgotten in the story would be the fact that City Marshal Virgil Earp, in whose jurisdiction the killing happened, did not make the arrest either. All the blame would be heaped on to Behan's head, the truth distorted and accusations of Behan being a friend of Dusty Fog thrown out, showing that the friendship was the only reason why Dusty was not arrested. The newspaper would use this incident, given a chance, to blacken still more the name of John Behan in the eyes of the voters.

"Stone Hart's taking out a herd for Vance Brownlow and running them into Tombstone," Dusty answered. "We'll ride with them and that way we'll be right clear of town until just before the County Fair."

Slaughter slapped his hand on the table in some delight and Mark grinned broadly, for he also saw what Dusty was getting at.

"The Earps and the *Epitaph* won't dare say a word if we come in with the herd," Mark drawled. "Reckon the trail drive crew'll be something special, having brought meat into town. Folks'll surely allow that Wyatt's trying to get men who might lick him in the shooting matches out of town so they can't enter. That'd sure lose him friends and voters."

"You're right on all sides, for once, Mark," agreed Slaughter. "We'll play it that way then. Comes the day you're going to be on hand to give Earp a real shock."

So it was decided and Dusty, Mark and the Kid left the Eating House to head for the livery barn to collect their horses and head out for Stone Hart's camp. The three young men walked along the street and there was some nudging and pointing as they passed. The word of the death of Iowa Parsons had made the rounds and in the Bucket of Blood saloon the bartender was amazed at the amount of people who came in to lay bets on the small and insignificant man he'd marked down at ten to one, but who now stood at even money, and whose odds Leslie was thinking seriously of putting even lower still.

Dusty, Mark and the Kid were passing a shop window, when they came to a halt and faced the glass, staring at the display inside. The shop was opposite the jail and a shotgun armed deputy sat on a chair on the jail porch, his undivided attention on the window.

The entire window space was taken up with a sloping surface on which, in niches, were set the prizes for the two shooting matches. There were cased pairs of Remington, Smith and Wesson, Merwin and Hulbert and other kinds of revolvers along the top of the slope, for the firearms companies of the East had given freely to have their weapons on show at the Cochise County Fair. Along the sides were various rifles, also donated as prizes; these framed the first prize of the Rifle Shoot and the first and second prizes of the Pistol Shooting match.

Resting on two pegs, framed by the red baize cloth, was the prize which brought the Ysabel Kid to a dead stop and put a look in his eyes that no woman ever had. It was a Winchester Model of 1873, .44.40 in calibre, yet such a weapon as the Kid had only seen the once. The woodwork was of the finest black walnut, polished and shone to reflect the scene, checked and engraved by a master craftsman. The metal work was of finest deep blue colour, engraved in a manner which pleased the eye. The sights were the finest, closest a man could ask for and there was a set trigger capable of the finest adjustment a man might want to make. Inlaid in the butt was a silver plate on which were the words, "Presented to", a space for the winner's name, "First Prize, Rifle Shoot, Cochise County Fair". On the top of the barrel would be engraved just four words, the greatest understatement in the history of the Winchester Repeating Firearms Company: "One of a Thousand".

Yet it was nearer to one in ten thousand that so perfect a barrel was found as to warrant the added care and attention which went to make such a rifle and give it the right to bear that title. That then was the prize in the rifle shoot. It was a prize the Ysabel Kid swore in the most solemn lodge oath of the Comanche Dog Soldier that he would win and own.

Beneath the box, in a case with a special leather holster, a brass skeleton carbine stock and a set of carbine type sights set on the frame over the chamber, was one of the long barrelled Colt Peacemakers such as carried by Wyatt Earp. It was the second prize in the Pistol Shoot.

Below this, in the centre of the window, in the place of honour, lay the first prize for the man with the fastest double draw of them all. The mahogany box lid was raised to show the brass plate on which was engraved:

"COCHISE COUNTY FAIR PISTOL SHOOT WINNER"

In the box, held and caressed by red felt, were a pair of matched, pearl handled, gold inlaid Colt Cavalry Peacemakers, their metal work of the finest blue citizen's finish and chased with gold in a manner that no other guns from the Colt factory ever had. They were fine guns and would make the winner proud to own them.

"Now there's what I call a fancy brace of guns, Dusty," drawled Mark. "I reckon they'll look swell on the wall in Ole Devil's study back home."

"There's only one thing to that, Mark," replied Dusty. "One of us has to win them first."

Mark laughed. "With luck I might get that long-barrelled Colt gun, but you'll be taking that fancy pair of guns with you when we leave."

The Kid could not tear his eyes from the rifle and had not heard a word his friends said. To the Kid a revolver was something just to be toted along for use when no great accuracy was called for and his knife would not answer the question. That rifle, that wonderful Winchester, was all he was interested in.

With a final glance at the window, Dusty turned and walked away. He knew that even if he won the guns they would never see use, but would be left with his Uncle. He had little use for the idea of the long-barrelled revolver, but Mark stood a good chance of winning it. Mark turned to follow his friend, then noticed the Kid was not following them. He turned back and saw the way the dark youngster stood. A grin came to Mark's face and he poked the Kid hard in the ribs with his forefinger.

"Hey, Lon," he said.

The Kid perked as if wakened from a deep sleep. He looked at his friend with unseeing eyes, then they were drawn back to the rifle again. Mark jabbed his thumb home again and the Kid swung around.

"Huh!" he growled. "What's wrong now?"

"Just a couple of Rambeau's men lining shotguns on you," Mark replied with a grin. "I never saw you look at any gal, not even Juanita Estradre, like you're looking at that Winchester there."

"You could be right at that, Mark. I'm going to have that rifle or die in the trying for it."

"Ambition's a wonderful and inspiring thing, *amigo*," drawled Mark, grinning broadly. "But give me the first choice of the remuda and I'll take me a pretty gal 'most any old time."

The Kid stepped from the window, crashing into something which gave a very feminine gasp and began to apologise. Then he saw the smiling eyes and pretty face of Cindy Alban through the mist which surrounded him. The girl staggered slightly and her escort, the young actor, Hamish, steadied her. Cindy's face held a smile but it flickered, for the Kid did not appear to recognise her. Without being vain about it, Cindy knew she was a pretty girl, not unattractive to the opposite sex. She felt rather piqued that this handsome yet so young looking boy should have forgotten her so soon. It was only that morning she'd been chatting gaily with him as he rode beside the show wagon; then he'd been polite, attentive, and now he hardly appeared to recognise her at all.

"I'm sorry, ma'am," said the Kid, then gave a start. "Why, it's you, Miss Cindy."

"It has been for the last minute or so," she replied tartly, then she realised the Kid was not even now giving her his full attention. His eyes flickering back to the shop window and that wonderful rifle inside. "Have I changed so much since this morning?"

"Yes, ma'am," answered the Kid absently.

"You'll have to excuse him, ma'am," Mark put in. "He's got a real bad attack of Comanche fever."

The girl looked anxiously at the Kid's face. It certainly did not show any sign of fever.

"Is he all right?" she gasped.

"Why sure, Miss Cindy. It's a disease that hits a Comanche when he sees a repeating rifle."

The girl glanced at the shop window and for the first time realised what was in it. She saw the way the Kid's eyes were drawn back to that magnificent rifle and her annoyance rose again. Then she started to smile as she remembered all he'd told her of his plans on the way into Tombstone.

"Well," she said with a smile, "I never ran second to a rifle before."

It was then the Kid came above water and he realised how he was acting. The grin which came to his face was boyish and infectious and the girl could not hold her annoyance any longer.

"Hi, Miss Cindy," he said. "Fancy meeting you here."

Cindy raised her eyes to the heavens. She could sense that Hamish had drawn back and took a delight in teasing him.

"Now he recognises me," she remarked. "I hope you can see me better on the stage tonight. I suppose you will be coming to the opening?"

"Waal no, ma'am. I don't reckon I will."

"Why not?" demanded Cindy. "Don't you want to see the play and hear me sing?"

"I'd sure enough admire to do both, ma'am," answered the Kid. "And likely will when I get back."

"Back?"

"Why, sure, Dusty, Mark and me have taken on to drive a herd of cattle in for a rancher. We'll be back before the Fair starts, so you can save me a seat up front."

The girl looked at the innocent face and tried to reconcile his appearance with what Madame Paula had told her of the Ysabel Kid. It was hard to believe so young an innocent a boy could be all Paula said he was. It was then Cindy remembered how the Kid came around the bush and faced the Apache to save her life.

"Say, Lon," drawled Mark. "Ole Dusty's moving on and looking back to us like he wants something."

"Reckon he does at that," replied the Kid, looking to where Dusty stood further along the sidewalk. "I'll likely see you when I get back, Miss Cindy—— If I make it."

The girl tried to read something in the face which was suddenly cold and as impassive as a Comanche Dog Soldier's. "Will it be dangerous?"

"Shucks, no. Maybe a lil bitty stampede or two. Maybe rustlers. Could be a few hundred head of Apaches after us. It won't be too dangerous."

"Said danger's going to start right now," growled Mark. "Happen you keep Dusty waiting much longer."

The girl tried to decide if the Kid had been teasing her and was not entirely sure. She managed a smile, saw the twinkle in the Kid's eyes and the smile grew broader and brighter.

"The best of luck then, Lon," she said. "I'll try and think about you once a night—for about five seconds. Take care of him, Mark."

The girl watched Mark and the Kid walk away, then she felt

Hamish's hand on her sleeve and looked at him with a gay smile.

"You look awfully serious, Miles," she said. "Don't you approve of my friends?"

"They're all right," was the grudging reply.

"For talking to, but for anything serious I prefer someone in my own walk of life. Say a tall, handsome hero who can save me from all the villains."

Hamish felt his cheeks burn and knew they must have reddened in a manner he'd not known since he first became an actor. He did not know what to make of the words, for twice when she'd been in peril he'd failed to do anything spectacular. Then he felt the girl squeeze his hand.

"Yes," she said gently. "A boy like the Ysabel Kid might be all right. But a man who'd rather look at a rifle than a girl—well, there's not much future for the poor girl, is there? Now come on or we'll be late for rehearsals. And when you kiss me ın the last scene," she looked up at him with sparkling eyes, "make it look as if you mean it."

Hamish started to walk along the street by the side of the girl. He was conscious of eyes turning towards him and the pretty girl by his side. That was how it should be, he was used to it. He squeezed her arm gently and felt the pressure back on his own. It did not look as if he need bother about the Ysabel Kid or any other man, now.

Dusty, Mark and the Kid rode up to the Wedge camp and received greetings from their old friends. Short, stocky Silent Churchman, who belied both names when roused; heavily moustached, miserable looking, medium sized Peaceful Gunn, who would always ride a good two inches out of his way to avoid trouble; tall, grizzled and capable Waggles Harrison, the segundo, all greeted the three riders delightedly. Doc Leroy, tall, slim, pallid and studious looking, his store coat with the right side stitched back to leave clear the ivory handle of his Colt Civilian Model Peacemaker, turned from where he was checking the supply of bandages and other gear he used for his doctoring chores, raised a hand in a cheery salute then went on with his work. The old cook, Chow Willicka, short, clean-shaven and quick, paused in his tirade against his regular louse, grunted as he saw who was here and went on with it once more. Young Rin, the wrangler, the night hawk and the four men Stone hired to supplement the crew for the drive, all looked on. They did not know who the three Texans were but they did know *what* they were.

Stone Hart sat with Vance Brownlow and his wife by the fire and looked up with a grin.

"See you made it, Dusty," the trail boss said. "I took on all the hands I need to ride the herd through. How about coming along as shotgun guard?"

"A good idea," agreed Vance. He'd been worrying about how Stone would get on if Dusty rode with them. Dusty had a reputation as being a trail boss and might not take to riding under another man. He did not know that Dusty would have been just as willing to ride as a hand and take orders as he would to take command. Dusty had been a soldier and knew that to lead men one had to be ready to take orders as well as give them.

"We'll ride with you like that," Dusty agreed. "When do we pull out?"

"Right now. I want to put a few miles between us and Tombstone," Stone replied. "There's a chance Rambeau might try and scatter the remuda, or shoot up the camp and I don't want to take a chance on any of the crew catching lead."

So it was arranged without fuss or bother. Dusty was to ride with Mark as a guard while the Kid went ahead as scout. The herd must be brought through and they aimed to see it was.

CHAPTER SEVEN

A Chance Offered

VANCE BROWNLOW rode between Dusty Fog and Stone Hart towards his old white-walled Spanish style house. The building was in the grand style of the old *hacienda* made by men who had plenty of good, cheap labour and wanted a home which would last for centuries. The house stood in the centre of large grounds and was surrounded by a high parapeted wall from the safety of which riflemen could pour lead down on any attackers. There was but one entrance to the grounds, through a large, steel-studded, heavy wooden gate which looked strong enough to stand up to an artillery pounding. All in all the place looked as if it was built to be used as a fort—and had been more than once.

It only took one look at the building down below to tell Dusty that Vance was no man's fool and that he could stay alive in this wild country as long as he had plenty of supplies, water from the well in the ground and ammunition. In the grounds of the house was a long line of stables in which the personal mounts of the cowhands were held, while the main remuda was out in the corrals, under the wall, where they could be covered with rifle fire if need be.

Looking around, Dusty tried to catch some sight of the herd, but could not do so, which surprised him. The country rolled up into the foothills about half a mile away, but all around there was little or no cover and certainly nowhere near enough for a herd of five hundred head to hide in. The herd must be held somewhere near the house or the Apaches would have jumped it before now.

"We made it safely," Vance remarked. "I thought they might try to hit us at the crossing of the Carne River."

"Lon said there was Apache sign up there, but it was old," Dusty replied. "I reckon that'll be where they aim to hit the herd. We'll all be too busy handling the cattle to keep a good watch."

"We've got to get the herd moving fast," Stone pointed

out, looking around him, clearly puzzled as Dusty had been, at the lack of sign of the herd.

"When do you mean to start out?" asked Vance as they rode through the gates, which had been opened by his foreman and a cowhand.

"At dawn comes the morning," Stone replied. "Make a fast run and hope that we aren't being watched."

The Ysabel Kid and Johnny Raybold drew their horses to one side and allowed the others to ride on by them. For three days since leaving Tombstone they'd been on the scout and what they'd found confirmed that the Apaches were about, just waiting for a chance to hit the herd.

Hooking his leg up over his saddlehorn, Johnny looked around with some considerable care. "We're being watched, Lon," he stated.

"Sure," was the laconic reply.

"Scouts for the Apache?"

"Likely."

Johnny extracted a sack of tobacco, took out papers and rolled two smokes, his fingers working as if they had eyes of their own. He passed one cigarette to the Kid, who rasped a match on his thumb and held it towards the tip of Johnny's weed. The smokes were going and the two men sat their horses drawing in the tobacco fumes and exhaling them once more.

"Never rode scout against Apaches," Johnny remarked, not for the first time. "Hoss-Indians, like your kinfolk, are more my line."

"Man'd say they're the worst of all the tribes," answered the Kid. "Grandpappy Long Walker always used to tell me he claimed one Apache coup counted for two against any other tribe."

Johnny thought over the words and they gave him little comfort. It was not bad praise, coming from a war leader of the Dog Soldier Lodge, a branch of the Comanche Nation noted for being great fighting men in their own right.

"Where'd the scouts be?" Johnny asked, as he finished his smoke and carefully put out the stub before throwing it away.

"Out there somewhere," drawled the Kid, waving a hand to the open land before them.

The smoking had not been the sole reason for Johnny and the Kid staying out here after the others had all gone in. All the time they'd been smoking their eyes had been flickering around, checking every inch of the ground ahead of them for some sight of the Apache scouts their instinct warned were watching.

Johnny had been born and raised in Indian country and had learned the tricks of the Indian scout early and from necessity. He knew the ways of Indians—but as he said, they'd been Comanches, Southern Cheyenne, Kiowa, horse-Indians all. The tribes Johnny knew did their moving, scouting and fighting from the back of the "god-dog", that wonderful four-legged creature which came to them from the early Spanish Conquistadores. Johnny knew the ways of such Indians and knew little or nothing about Apaches. The horse-Indian scorned excessive stealth as a way of war and any fighting he did was from the back of a racing war pony, plainly, openly and with spectacular results. The Apaches were different. They used the horse, but not to the extent of the plains tribes. True, given a war relay, an Apache would run a grain fed cavalry troop into the ground, but the Apache would do that same thing on his own two feet given a start across his type of country. The Apache was just as at home on his two feet as he was on a horse and he would fight from cover, in ambush if he could, preferring to take life in war, rather than lose his own through lack of caution.

"I don't see them any place," Johnny remarked after another moment's hard searching of the ground ahead.

"You wasn't expecting them to stand on top of the rocks and wave signal blankets, now was you?"

"Was they Comanches, I might. Comanches don't have no better sense," scoffed Johnny, then became more serious. "You got any of them spotted, Lon?"

"Think maybe I spotted one, about half a mile away out there. By them two rocks that are side by side. I could be calling it wrong though."

Johnny reached down to his saddlepouch, where he carried a pair of powerful field glasses for just such an emergency. Before he could take out the glasses he was stopped by the Kid shooting out a hand to grip his wrist.

"No go, *amigo*," warned the Kid. "They can see us and likely know what those glasses are for. Happen they reckon we've got one of them spotted they pull out and hide up again, only this time we won't get to see them. Let's ride on in and tell Stone what we've seen."

"We haven't seen anything," Johnny pointed out.

"Sure, that'll please him. Show him we're doing our work."

The other men were already in the grounds and dismounting when the Kid and Johnny rode towards the gates. Already Vance's foreman was showing the men where to leave their horses. Stone looked around, saw that his men were being attended to and got down to serious business.

"Let's ride out and see the herd, shall we?" he asked.

Vance nodded. "Sure. I'll take you while Birdie and the cooks throw a meal together for the hands. Are you coming, Dusty?"

"Sure, you've got me puzzled, where you're holding the cattle."

The Kid and Johnny rode up at that moment, dismounted and walked up to the trail boss. In something that might have been called a military brace and with his hand raised in a mocking salute the Kid asked, "You ready to hear a report of the activities of your scouts, Colonel, sir?"

"Sure, make it fast, we want to ride out to the herd," Stone answered.

"They're watching us."

Stone waited for a moment, but the Kid remained silent, so he grunted. "That's a tolerable fair report."

"Tells us about what we already know," Dusty went on. "They're not going to try and hit the herd where they'll be up against men with rifles, men who know the ground. That's not the Apache way. They know the herd's been gathered for shipping and they're just waiting and watching until they know which way you're headed before they hit."

"They'll pick their time and place, when they know which direction we're headed," agreed Stone. "How many scouts are there, and where?"

"Now you've hit a point, Stone," replied the Kid with a grin. "Two at least, three at most. I reckon I'd got one spotted for sure and could make a fair guess where the other two are."

"There might only be the one, if that was all you saw," Vance objected.

"Sure, there might, but I didn't see him for sure. Just finding one's as likely as drawing a queen into the middle of a four card straight flush," the Kid replied. "Apaches aren't fools, Vance. Don't you sell them short on either brains or military knowledge; that's where the blue bellies make their mistake and it costs them lives."

"You'd better explain to us then, professor," Vance replied, but he was listening attentively for all the light-hearted way in which he spoke.

"Sure, one lone man gets bored. Gets to thinking about his squaw, or some pretty lil gal who threw a stick at him, which same means to get herself all set up to be courted kind and loving. Two or three of them on scout, they watch each other as well as what they're scouting for and make sure there's no sneaking away done. Likely they meet up somewhere each night and stay together, no Apache likes being alone in the dark. That's why I conclude there's at least two and at most three of them watching you out there."

"But this is fairly open country. Where would they hide?"

"Not too close in, Vance. They could see you moving the herd from a fair piece back. But don't go betting they're not in close. An Apache can hide where you might reckon a jack-rabbit'd show up real plain."

"Could you find them, Lon?" asked Dusty. "And get rid of them?"

"Likely, given two or three days, Johnny and Peaceful to help me and a whole lot of good luck. If we went out and started looking now, they'd just pull back and we couldn't chase them far enough away to let you get the herd moving without their knowing it."

"The Apaches would be suspicious if you tried it," Stone remarked. "We'll pull out at dawn and play them as they fall."

"Which same's the only chance we have right now," Dusty agreed. "Let's leave this hard-worked scout to get a meal and head out to the herd."

The three men took their horses once more and rode out through the gates. Vance took the lead and looked around him with some curiosity. He'd covered most of the ground ahead of him hunting or bird shooting at various times and thought he knew it well. Now he was beginning to wonder if he did know it so well after all, if three Apaches could be hiding so close, watching every move made at the ranch.

Then Dusty saw a narrow gorge in one of the hills, an opening with a pole fence across it. Two men sat by the fence, smoking, each with a rifle across his knees and a belt full of bullets slung over his shoulders. They raised their hand in greeting, dropped from the rail and advanced to meet the three riders.

"The herd's in there," Vance remarked, indicating the opening.

On drawing closer, Dusty could see that the opening might be narrow but beyond it a wide valley was exposed to view, a valley where a fair-sized herd of cattle were grazing. A nearer approach showed that the slopes of the valley were very steep and in places had been made steeper by human hands. The area was a large blind canyon and being used as a natural and very useful corral. The cattle in the canyon were all well fed and looked healthy enough.

"There's a spring and a small stream in there. It goes under-ground at the blind end," Vance explained a point which puzzled Dusty before the small Texan could ask about it. "I can hold up to five hundred head in here for a fortnight or so. More if I hay them down to help out the feed."

"That's not a bad idea," Dusty answered.

"'I found this canyon while hunting for wild turkeys," Vance replied. "Saw how it could be put to use, steepened the sides where cattle might be able to get out and tried it. It works all right. How about the herd, Stone?"

"They look fit and well enough," Stone replied. "I'll not go in and disturb them. You've got a fair head of white faces among them."

"It's part of a herd I brought in with me. I hope to change the cattle all to whitefaces soon, they make better beef and cause less trouble than longhorns."

"Sure, but will they live off the country like longhorns do?" Dusty asked.

The technical discussion lasted until they had stabled their horses and were entering the house. Vance insisted they were his guests and would stay in the front where he and his wife lived instead of bunking with the hands in the now overcrowded bunkhouse section. The invitation was also extended to Mark and the Kid, for Stone wanted to hear their view on the conditions the drive would be made under.

With the meal over, their gunbelts and hats hanging on the pegs by the front door, the men went out to sit on the porch. Birdie, dressed now in a gingham frock, came out with a tray containing coffee pot and cups. She poured out coffee and handed the cups around, then sat on the arm of her husband's chair and looked towards the men who were risking their lives to bring the herd in.

"How do you figure to get the herd to Tombstone?" she asked. "And don't tell me walking, that I know."

"The way we came out here. Swing up to that ford and miss the wooded country. That way we'll be in clear land all the way. We could lose half the herd if we got into the woods, even if there was a ford and we don't know of one."

"Reckon Lon could scout the woods, just in case?" Dusty asked. "We know the Apache are thinking they'll grab the herd and the river's their best spot."

"That's for you to handle," Stone replied. "You're chief of scouts on this drive. I don't like the idea of going through those woods unless we're hide-bound forced to do it."

"I don't like that gap we have to run the herd down about a day's drive from Tombstone," Mark put in. "I thought as we came through it'd be a good place for an ambush."

"Not from Apaches that close in," objected the Kid. "I reckon if we can get the herd across the Carne River we're clear of the Apaches. They'll not come too close to Tombstone."

"I wasn't thinking about Apaches," Mark answered. "Rambeau's not going to give up that easy. No Syndicate man ever does."

"That's what's puzzling me," Dusty remarked. "I've heard some about the Syndicate and this sort of thing isn't in their line at all. They run saloons, gambling houses, places like that. They don't bother with cattle rustling, for that is what Rambeau's play comes down to. Why'd they risk getting involved in something that could blow up in their faces and cause real trouble?"

"The money on the herd will be a tidy sum," Vance replied.

"About half of their take for the day across the country," Dusty answered. "I reckon the Syndicate doesn't know what Rambeau's doing. That he and Parsons were planning a private deal. We'll have to hope that Rambeau keeps quiet about it. The Syndicate wouldn't want it known one of their top guns was planning to pull a deal on the side with a saloon operator."

"Then it might be as well if they found out," Vance remarked.

"That depends on how much word has got around. The Syndicate run because of their reputation for being tough. How's it going to look to the folks who they keep down by fear if word gets out that somebody has bucked a Syndicate man's play and shoved his face into the mud?"

The others did not speak for a moment. Then Stone said, "They'll make Rambeau back his play on his own and either come through or go under."

"He could have hired some more guns by now," Mark pointed out. "The Syndicate won't send him any more of their top-grade stock and he'll be on his own, sink or drown. That's why I reckon he'll hit at us in that draw. It's his first and last chance. He won't want to risk it too far away from town and then likely wind up with Apaches riding over him. Nearer, folks might hear, then come to see what all the shooting's about."

Vance Brownlow looked at the other men. They were all so calm and cool, not one of them showing the slightest apprehension at the thought of fighting their way by a horde of Apaches only to find more fighting against the guns of a power-greedy man. He felt confident that his herd would get through now. He also saw that had he been left to make the drive alone, he might have been wiped out without even knowing where he'd gone wrong.

"Do you think we could pull out now, make a fast run for it and be gone before the scouts know what it's all about?" he asked.

"We could try, but I wouldn't want to. The scouts aren't alone, there's a decent sized bunch somewhere, maybe two, maybe five miles away, maybe even more," grunted the Kid. "The scouts would hear the herd being moved and they'd light out. They don't like fighting in the dark, but they'll move by it. They'd get to the bunch who're near at hand, then we'd have them hit us at dawn, when the hands are all getting tired and slowed down. They'd do enough damage, run off the remuda, wreck the chuckwagon and be gone. And they'd go right to the main crowd to let them know we're on our way."

The other Texans nodded their agreement. They'd all a fair knowledge of tactics and knew the Kid called his shots right true to the centre of the target. The surprise moving of the herd would not remain a surprise for long and the pursuit would come faster than any herd of cattle, much less a herd of whitefaces, could be pushed.

Mark opened his mouth to make some suggestion, then closed it again as he came to his feet along with the others. They all heard the distant crash of shots and Vance Brownlow's face lost much of its colour as he looked at the others.

"The herd!" he gasped.

"Too far off for that," replied the Kid. "There's a fair bunch of riders coming this way."

It was some moments before any of the others could even hear the sound of rapidly approaching riders. By that time the Kid could make out certain sounds which gave a clue as to who it was approached.

"I'll get the hands," Vance said.

"Don't get all into a mucksweat," replied the Kid. "Shod hosses, leather creaking and metal clinking. Them's white men coming. An Apache couldn't make so much noise even if he wanted."

"We'll just get our guns afore we open the gate though," Dusty answered.

Guns in hand, Vance carrying a magnificent double-barrelled shotgun, the men sprinted towards the gate but, despite the Kid's warning, Dusty opened the barred slot, keeping well to one side and called, "Shout up, who are you?"

"Open the gate!" came the answering shout, "Cavalry here!"

Dusty threw open the gate just wide enough for one man to enter at a time, "Come ahead slow and easy," he ordered.

"And come with your hands empty."

The first man to enter was a grizzled and tough looking cavalry sergeant, riding with one hand on the reins, the other held waist high and well clear of his gun. He did not look alarmed or surprised at the caution shown by the occupants of the house.

"Take it kind if you'd hurry, gents," he said. "We just had a run in with a small bunch of Apaches and one of our men's carrying lead."

Mark caught Dusty's nod and opened the gates to allow a double file of blue clad, campaign hatted cavalry men to ride by him, followed by a young officer who holstered his long barrelled Colt as he came through the gate.

Sliding down from his horse, the young man looked towards the group of armed cowhands, then towards Birdie, who was coming with a lamp, then to the armed men who came pouring from the house, carrying lights with them. His face was pale and it showed signs of having been involved in the first fight. For all that he was in full control of himself as he saluted Birdie politely.

"Good evening, ma'am, gentlemen," he said. "We've just had a brush with the Apaches. One of my men caught a bullet, so when we saw your lights I came down here."

Birdie turned to where a young trooper was leaning forward in his saddle, a wound in his shoulder running blood down the blue tunic.

"Get the boy off his horse," she snapped. "Doc! Doc Leroy! Come and look at this soldier."

Doc came fast and the trooper was helped down from his saddle, to be taken up to the house. The young officer told his men to take care of their horses, then stood looking back through the look-out slot of the gate.

"How many of them did you get, mister?"

The lieutenant turned quickly, for he knew that sort of voice. It was something a green young shavetail fresh out of West Point could tell well enough, the tone of a tough officer addressing a junior. His eyes went to the small Texan who stood ahead of the others. There was something in the way Dusty stood that warned the officer his guess was not wrong. Here was a man used to asking questions and getting quick and accurate answers.

"I believe we dropped three."

Dusty swung around and snapped, "Mark, get Lon's old Nigger hoss, Lon, happen the lieutenant here'll let you. I want you to go out with the sergeant and take a look around where they hit the Apaches."

"I'll do just that," answered the Kid and headed to the house for his gunbelt, going at a dead run.

The young officer stood beside Dusty and looked with open admiration at the huge white stallion Mark led up. "I wish it was time of war," he said. "The Army's allowed to make compulsory commandeerings of remounts then, you know."

"I'd heard something about it," Dusty answered dryly. "Mister, there aren't enough men in your whole regiment to commandeer that horse from the Kid."

Once more the tone was there. The voice of a senior officer addressing a West Point plebe who gave unasked for information. There was more to this small man in cowhand dress than first appeared. It was with a considerable effort the officer managed to avoid stiffening to brace and making a formal apology.

The sergeant touched his hat and requested permission to ride with the Kid and the young officer gave it. The gate was opened and the two men rode out into the night.

"Could I night here, please?" asked the officer when Vance introduced himself. "I'm on a long sweep out of Fort Grant, checking on Apache movement. There's been a lot and I have to swing back up to Black Falls, then make my way back to the Fort."

"Stay here if you like," Vance replied. "I'm afraid we're a bit crowded at the bunkhouse, but they'll make out."

Dusty remained by the gate when the others went back to the house. He'd been standing there for a few moments when dark, then Stone asked:

"You thinking the same way I am, Dusty?"

"Why, sure. The time's only eight o'clock now. We could work up a tolerable head start if things fall right."

They heard the sound of hooves and, although neither spoke, both knew the other was tense and eager to hear what the Kid had to say when he returned. The horses drew nearer and Stone opened one side of the heavy gate, then closed it behind the Kid and the sergeant.

"Three of them," growled the Kid, sliding from his saddleless white.

"We rode into them by accident," the sergeant went on. "Young Darcy's all right. It's his first time out on independent command, but he never lost his head. Got the men through, was the last to leave himself."

"Did you hear any Apaches getting away?" asked Dusty.

The sergeant was a thirty year man, he knew a born leader when he saw one and knew that small, or tall as a redwood tree, here was a leader born, bred, raised and fully ready to lead.

"Were just the three of them as far as I know," he answered.

"Call it that way myself, Dusty," agreed the Kid. "Was I asked, that is."

"Take it you're asked."

"Three of them, small camp, likely no more," drawled the Kid. "Man'd near be safe betting it's the scouts."

Stone and Dusty's eyes met and there was the same thought in both their heads. However, the ultimate decision rested on Stone as the trail boss. He made it fast, without asking Dusty to share in the final responsibility if things went wrong. That was the way of a man like Stone Hart, or of a man like Dusty Fog. It was the way of a leader of men, of a trail boss.

"Roust out the crew, Dusty," he said. "I'll tell Vance and his lady to be ready. We ride in one hour."

Dusty turned and went without another word. Time was valuable now. The three scouts were dead and the herd could be got started without word reaching the waiting Apaches until late the following day. The actual time would depend on when the scouts were due to be changed or to report to their leader.

In the big dining-room of the bunkhouse section Dusty found a crowd of men, Vance's regular crew, the Wedge cowhands and the soldiers. There was much good natured chaff among the men and Dusty stood at the door for a moment. The talk died down and he raised his voice.

"You Wedge hands all comfortable after your long ride?"

"We sure are, Dusty," whooped young Rin.

"I aims to go to bed and sleep until the drive starts," one of the new hands went on.

"Which same's in lessn' one hour from now."

"Good, then I'll—WHAT!" The answer began cheerfully enough but ended in a wild yell as the full import of the words hit the man.

"One hour at the most," Dusty answered. "Get them moving, Waggles. Stone wants the herd headed up and moving before nine o'clock."

The segundo did not need twice telling. He'd made this sort of fast move before and was on his feet giving orders without even having to think twice about what he was saying or doing.

"Rusty, Silent, go with young Rin and help the night hawk with the remuda. Peaceful, you'll take point with me. The rest of you know where I want you. Grab your gear and hit the front of the house—*pronto*!"

It was lucky that the men had not unloaded their bedrolls from the wagon, Vance had offered the loan of blankets for the night to save them unpacking and time would be saved. So there was little to do in the orderly rush as the men prepared to pull out.

Birdie, dressed in her jeans and shirtwaist, still tucking the flap in the back of her waistband, came into the room, paying no attention to the choice and highly coloured language which was flying around. She found Chow Willicka, who was throwing his borrowed apron off, leaving Vance's cook to deal with the feeding of the newly arrived soldiers.

"I bet your wagon's nowhere's nearly ready to roll," she jeered.

Chow sniffed loftily and chose to ignore the words. He and Birdie got on very well, although they were in a state of feud all the time, which kept them amused and which the hands found highly stimulating. The old man turned to a young soldier who sat near at hand.

"Huh!" he grunted. "Women. Don't you never go and trust one, son."

The sergeant was standing close at hand and gave his agreement. "Had me a gal back at home. One night I told her that if she didn't marry me I'd up and join the Army."

"And what happened?" asked Birdie.

"She said yes, I married her—and joined the Army a month later."

"Which same only goes to prove what I allus said——" began Chow.

"Go boil your fool old head!" Birdie snapped, then she and the cook were headed for the door to harness the team of the chuckwagon.

Out in the grounds before the house, the scene lit by lamps brought from the house, men were mounting their horses. The two wagons were ready with teams harnessed and ready to roll. Chow gave his louse a gentle warning that he'd best stick up real close when they pulled out, then swung on to the box of his wagon. Birdie, carrying a wolfskin coat, climbed up beside him. She meant to ride the herd later, but knew she would be more use here out of the way during the tricky night drive ahead.

"Best put that coat on, ma'am," Chow said. "The night air get's a mite cold late on."

"Chow, honey," she replied with a grin as she struggled into the heavy and warm coat, "I didn't know you cared."

He grinned at her. "I don't, but if you come down with a

chill you'll likely blame it on my cooking. I knows you women."

The young woman's blistering reply almost seared the paint off the wagon seat, if there'd been any paint on it. Chow chuckled, then took up the reins and started the chuckwagon forward. The gates were open and the men riding through, into the night, making for the herd.

CHAPTER EIGHT

Dust Has Its Uses

THE MEN came towards the blind canyon, riding at an easy trot and saving their horses for the work which would come later. The two guards had heard the noise and rightly guessed what was happening. They'd worked fast and the fence was down by the time the trail crew arrived.

Stone Hart moved back and let the men through into the canyon. This was going to be a ticklish business and one that the slightest slip could ruin. The cattle had to be eased off their bed ground and got moving without being scared and sent off in a wild stampede. Stone wanted the herd moving fast, but not at stampede speed. With lesser men he might have been worried about starting the herd, but each man here was an expert, even the new hands had worked on the big inter-state drives from Texas and knew what to do.

The riders entered the valley without fuss or undue noise, keeping to the edges until they reached the blind end. Then they started forward, riding slowly and stirring up the sleeping cattle as they went. Steer after steer came to its feet and began to move before the riders, not panicking, not running, just moving ahead. On the two flanks of the line of men Waggles Harrison and Peaceful Gunn gauged their time right and started to move along the flanks of the herd, the other riders following, tightening the herd of cattle, cutting the bunch down into a thin line. There was a big steer forcing his way through the herd, and as he came out of the canyon opening he found a rider on either side of him. Peaceful and Waggles had the lead steer now, they were at the point with him and would stay there with him until they reached the shipping pens. The rest of the herd followed out of the opening, the swing riders coming in about a third of the way along, then the flank men joining two-thirds of the way from the point. The last steers came out and the drag riders followed them. Back in the canyon Mark Counter and Vance Brownlow were making a careful sweep to make sure that none of the herd had been left behind. Mark was riding with the herd this night, then he would be free of all duties so as to be able to ride with Dusty and the Kid as part of the free-ranging fighting force.

The herd came out, Waggles and Peaceful steering the big leader towards the east and Tombstone City. Then as the cattle moved away Rin and the night hawk came in with the remuda, holding the horses behind the herd at a distance. Chow sat on the wagon box with Birdie beside him. He started his team forward and the wagon lurched into line behind the remuda, the bed-wagon, with the hands' bedrolls, spare gear and some equipment brought up the rear.

To Vance, riding from the canyon towards Dusty and Stone, it was nothing short of a miracle the way his herd had been got moving in so little time. Stone's hour was hardly over yet and the cattle were on the move, under control and headed for the market.

Dusty was lounging in his saddle and thinking fast. He was not bothered about the cattle, although he could admire the skilled way in which the Wedge hands got the herd up and moving. He was thinking about the three dead Apache scouts and trying to decide how their death could be turned to further advantage.

"Vance," he said as the rancher rode up. "Call back at the house. Tell your foreman to keep his guards on the canyon as if the herd was still there. Have the fence erected." Before he could say more Dusty was interrupted by the arrival of the Ysabel Kid and Johnny Raybold, reporting for their orders as scouts. This was Dusty's department, although usually it would have fallen on the trail boss to tell them what he wanted doing. "Johnny, get ahead and make a scout. Don't go too far in front, though. Lon, I want you to take a couple of Vance's hands out to those dead Apaches. Hide them and try to cover up all their sign. I know you won't be able to do it perfect, but make sure they can't be found too easy."

"I get the idea," Vance said. "You want to try and fool the Apaches into thinking the herd's still in the canyon. Then they won't follow us."

"It won't fool them long," Dusty answered. "But I always allow that any time saved is worth while."

Stone nodded in agreement to this. He was not interested in the way Dusty handled the defence or planned the strategy of the herd. Stone had been a Confederate cavalry officer too, but he knew Dusty was his master when it came to out and out planning of a campaign. Dusty was in charge of tactics, that had been the agreement they made in Tombstone and

Stone was willing to let it ride that way. It was a pleasant change to have no other duties than those of handling the cattle.

Dusty and Vance headed back to the house with the Kid, and there Vance gave the necessary orders to his foreman. Turning, Vance and Dusty rode through the gates and headed after the herd. Vance was far happier now than he'd been for weeks. This was his chance, the money the herd brought in would enable him to start on the improvements he planned for his ranch.

Vance Brownlow was a man with vision and forethought. He knew that it was a matter of time, months maybe, two years at most, before the pressure of the U.S. Army brought the Apache nation to peace. Then a man could start and build up his herds, put whiteface cattle which gave good beef on to the range to grow fat on the prime grazing. The half-wild longhorns were a hardy race of cattle, but they left much to be desired in the way of beef and Vance was sure he could improve the stock. The money this herd brought in would go far to doing that for Vance. That was the prize Vance struck for. The herd would make his dream or see it ground into the dirt for nothing. It all depended on the skill of Stone Hart as a trail boss, the loyalty of those hard riding and reckless cowhands and their chances of slipping through the Apache net.

Stone Hart was sitting his big grulla horse to one side of the herd and waiting for them to catch up. His teeth flashed white against the dark blob of his face in the night.

"Nice so far," he said.

"Easy," agreed Dusty, stopping his seventeen-hand paint and looking ahead to where a cursing cowhand was chasing a steer back into the moving line. "We'll make us good time tonight."

That was only to be expected. The herd were range bred stock and not used to being penned down in one place for long, even in a place as well watered and offering such good and safe grazing as the blind canyon. Once they were out of the canyon mouth they were willing to head off at a good clip. They would stay bunched for safety, with the exception of the odd attempt to break off and hunt pastures new. Right now the steers were wanting to put as many miles as they could between themselves and the canyon, which had been their prison for so long, and the trail crew were in full agreement with this desire. Every mile they could put between themselves and the ranch before dawn gave them just that much time and distance ahead of the Apaches.

The wagons rolled by and Birdie raised her hand in a cheerful wave to which the three men replied. Stone smiled:

"Your lady'll be real tired come morning."

"Right now she's like me," Vance replied. "Too happy and excited to feel tired at all."

The three men started their horses again and Stone asked: "Where's Mark?"

"Riding the swing," Dusty answered. "He thought he'd give a hand until dawn."

Soon after the Ysabel Kid came up, his big white stallion moving like a ghost through the night.

"Got it settled," he said. "Vance's foreman'll attend to things. He's been around in Apache country."

"Cut off ahead then, Lon," Dusty answered. "Make a big circle and see what you can find. If you see Johnny, watch him—he might shoot you in the leg."

"He couldn't hit me unless he got the gun resting on my levis," scoffed the Kid, turning his horse. "Don't let 'em sneak the herd away from you."

The Kid's horse faded once more into the night and Stone turned his horse to head for the point. Vance rode alongside Dusty, having decided to cut himself in on the fighting side instead of riding herd.

"How does a boy as young as the Kid come to know so much about Apaches?"

Dusty grinned towards Vance. "Reckon his grandpappy might have taught him."

"Was his grandfather an Indian scout?"

"Well no, I don't reckon Indian scout quite covers it. See, the Kid's grandpappy is Chief Long Walker of the Comanches."

The herd was kept moving on through the darkness. The hands took turns to make for the remuda and change their mounts, selecting an animal from their own string even in the blackness of the night. Dusty, Mark and the Kid had spare horses borrowed from Stone's remuda and they would be able to rest their own mounts, although the three stallions would follow the herd and not be mixed with the other horses.

The time was four o'clock when Stone joined Dusty and Vance again.

"No sign of the Kid yet," he said.

"He'll likely be along when he's good and ready," Dustv replied. "You know him of old, Stone."

It was at that moment the Kid and Johnny rode up. Stone grinned. "Talked of the devil and up pops the Ysabel Kid."

"You'll be hurting my feelings soon," warned the Kid.

"Not your better feelings, you never had any," growled Stone. "Did you find anything, or have you just come back because you felt lonely?"

"I don't feel lonely," replied the Kid. "Didn't out there anyways, not with a camp of about thirty or more Apaches laying out in the brush."

Vance tried to keep up the same laconic posture and expressionless mien of the other two, but could not restrain an ejaculated "Apache camp?"

"Which same's just what I said, Colonel," drawled the Kid. "Comes dawn they'll all be awake and on the lookout. They'll see the dust kicked up by the herd and know something's gone wrong. Then they'll trail us and hit us when we least expect it."

"We've got to stop that," Dusty said quietly, showing neither excitement nor worry. "We don't want them hanging on our flanks."

"Could you take some of the men and pin them down while the rest of us push the herd on?" asked Vance.

"Not a whoop and whistle in hell's chance, *amigo,*" Dusty replied. "They'd soon know just how few men were against them, leave ten or so braves to hold us down and the rest come after the herd. You couldn't run the cattle in flat stampede far enough and fast enough to get clear."

"If it wasn't for all the dust we might run around them out of sight and hearing of the camp," Stone put in. "A camp that size will make things real awkward for us, Dusty."

Dusty did not reply, he was looking to where ahead of them the herd was moving and at the dark pall of dust which hung in the air. Then he turned his attention back to the Kid and asked:

"I don't reckon they knew you were about, Lon?"

"I'm back, aren't I?"

That figured to a man who knew Apaches and Dusty Fog knew them. The Kid would not have blundered blindly into the Apache camp, and walked out again. He must have found it with the aid of his big white stallion, then reconnoitred on foot and in complete silence.

"About thirty you say?" Dusty went on.

"And all braves, not a single, solitary squaw to keep them company."

Again that figured. The Apache brave did not take his woman along when he put on the paint, took up the war hatchet and went forth to do battle with the hated white-eye brother. With women there the camp might have been just a bunch headed to a fresh camp ground. Without them it only meant one thing. War, fight for the herd of spotted buffalo the white-eye ride-plenties were taking to market.

"What we really need is either a troop or so of cavalry for protection, or more men," Vance remarked, cutting in on Dusty's racing thoughts. "And quite frankly, I can't see us getting either."

"You've got a fair idea," Dusty agreed. "A troop of cavalry is just what we need. Or at least a whole big bunch of men."

Stone was silent and watching Dusty's face, trying to pierce the darkness and read what was on his mind. He'd seen Dusty in action before and knew that already the small Texan had a plan worked out.

"Stone," Dusty said and, although Vance could not tell any difference in the tone, Stone knew things were going to move fast, "I want Mark, Silent, Peaceful, Rusty if you can spare him, and Johnny. You too, Vance if you'll get your rifle out of the saddleboot."

"It'll leave us short-handed, but we'll make out," Stone replied. "Reckon Birdie'll lend a hand with the herd, Vance?"

"Try and stop her, old boy," Vance chuckled. "I'll ride on and tell her."

"Hold hard there, Vance," Dusty cut in. "Don't go off until you know what I want doing. Tell Chow I want some empty sacks, then stop the bedwagon and cut eight lengths of rope from that coil in the back. Make them long enough so they'll hang down from the saddlehorn and reach the ground with some trailing. Tell Chow I'm real sorry, but that Stone'll pay him double time, seeing as it's after midnight."

The men scattered and in a short time Birdie was afork a cowpony riding the flank of the herd, while on the other side Rin, fetched up from the remuda, proudly rode as a cowhand. The men Dusty called for lined up before him, peering through the darkness towards the man they knew as the finest light cavalry commander the Civil War had produced. There was a tense and expectant air about them all, for they knew that something was afoot. Half the crew were here, almost all of Stone's loyal and hard riding hands. Taken with Mark Counter, Dusty Fog and the Ysabel Kid, and not forgetting Vance Brownlow, it was a fighting force to be reckoned with.

"What's on your tricky lil ole mind now, Dusty,' asked the Kid.

"Real army strategy, *amigo*," Dusty replied. "And when Vance gets back I'll explain it to you."

From ahead they could hear the blistering, hide-searing curses which came from Chow Willicka as he lent Vance a hand in the back of the bed wagon. There were many highly original curses heaped on the head of Dusty Fog, for Chow did not wish to fall behind the herd, not when he might have to tire his horses catching up. For all the curses, Chow would no more have thought about arguing or disobeying Dusty's command than he would of not following Stone's word.

"Now, gentlemen," Dusty drawled as Vance rode up carrying the sacks and lengths of rope.

"Something tells me I ain't going to like this," Silent Churchman whispered to the Kid.

"Out ahead of us there's a camp of about thirty head, all bucks and all armed unless Mr. Loncey Dalton Ysabel's called the play wrong," Dusty went on, ignoring the interruption. "So we're going to outnumber them."

"Never figured you'd forget how to count, Dusty," Rusty Willis put in and waved a hand along the line. "There ain't nowhere's near thirty of us."

"That could bring a ticklish point," admitted Dusty. "Especially if the Apache get to know how few of us there really are. We've got to make sure they don't—until it's too late. That bunch has to be stopped following us and maybe picking us off one at a time from behind rocks. We've got to try and slow them down some so that they can't get to the mainbunch in time to warn them we're out. Or at least slow them so they'll not give the main bunch a chance to pick their place and hit us."

"That's fair enough, Dusty," Mark drawled. "How're we going to do it?"

"We're coming in at them just before dawn, with the wind behind us, and we're coming in whooping and yelling like a drunk Comanche coming to make talk. I want all the noise you've got, shooting, hollering, that's why I've got Silent along. Pass out the ropes and sacks, Vance."

"Chow would only part with five sacks," Vance replied.

"The rest will have to haul mesquite scrub or anything heavy behind them to stir up the dust. Pass the sacks around and then get them weighted down with rocks!"

The men all got Dusty's idea. It was a good one and, given any amount of good Texas luck, it would work. If it didn't—well, there wouldn't be too much time to worry over it. If it failed, the only thing they could do would be try and take as many of the Apache with them before they went under.

The Apache camp was silent, the first streaks of dawn's light coming in the east. Not a brave stirred as they lay around the small fires, blanket wrapped and still, their weapons sharing the blankets with them. Every brave lay there, some dreaming of the fighting and the coups they would take, others were dreaming of the loot from the ride-plenties who were with the herd of white man's buffalo. It would be hard-won loot, for no ride-plenty ever was taken without a fight. The cattle meant little to the Apache except as a means of trade. Below the border, where the soldier-coats could not follow, were men who would trade repeating rifles, blankets, whisky or tequila for the spotted buffalo the cowboys drove.

There were no guards around the camp; the Apache was too light a sleeper to need any. Each brave slept in peace, for there was no word from the scouts that the herd of cattle had been driven from the blind canyon where it had lain safe under the rifles of the ranch crew. It was not a luxurious camp, with no wickiups set up, for there were no women along to perform this menial but essential task. The braves wore paint, they were ready for war and in war women had no place.

Of all the Apache band, only the two young boys brought along to tend to the herd watching were not in their blankets. They sat their wiry ponies, asleep on the job of watching the war relays of the warriors. The two bangtail scrub ponies of the herd-boys were also sleeping, standing, and the rest of the bunch of horses was settled down, giving no trouble and making no noise.

The wiry paint pony ridden by one of the herd boys suddenly came awake, its head jerked up and it snorted loudly. The boy astride it woke, jerking erect and staring around him, his mouth opening to let out a wolf-howl of warning. He was a full twenty seconds too late. The horses of the warriors were coming to their feet in a wild and snorting panic, eyes rolling and ready to bolt.

Deadened by the soft sandy soil, the hooves of horses sounded. A large cloud of dust welled up and from it came a hideous cacophony of wild cowhand yells, whoops, screams and the blood-chilling scalp howl of a Comanche Dog Soldier.

The young horse herder went backwards from his pony's blanket, a hole between his eyes, his startled yell ending unborn by a fast taken shot from one of the riders of the dust.

The second horse herder was lucky. His pony gave a wild leap which sent him flying from its back. He lit down with a catlike agility but was an instant too late, for the entire bunch of horses were up and running. The boy turned, hurdled a small bush, landed rolling into the shelter of a rock, where he lay out of sight until the raiders went by.

"Get the horses through the camp!" Dusty Fog's voice peeled out even above the rest of the noise.

The chief of the small band was fast asleep and dreaming of the great killing of white-eyes he would make when he traded his part of the herd for a repeating rifle. Yet from fast asleep and pleasant dreams to full awake, blankets thrown off and on his feet holding a single-shot Springfield carbine looted from a dead cavalryman in some long-forgotten frontier fight, was work of a second. The rest of the band were also waking, coming up to their feet with wild yells, grabbing their weapons. But like the herd boy they woke full twenty seconds too late.

Into the camp area came the charging, stampeding horses, the dust they kicked up more than doubling that stirred by the hooves of the attacking party's horses and the weighted sacks or mesquite scrub each man dragged.

Yelling, shooting, almost half-blind by the dust, the men charged their stampede in among the Apaches. It was one of the few times the Apaches were taken by surprise. They did not know for sure how many men were attacking them, and before their startled, sleep-slowed minds worked the horses were gone, the cloud of dust settling on the camp and billowing high over the cowhands who kept the stampede going, making sure the horses were not easily found again.

It was over and done with now. Two miles from the camp Dusty allowed his men to remove the sacks, empty them and cast off the mesquite scrubs. He wanted to be sure they were out of sight of the Apaches before allowing the dust to settle. The camp had been disrupted, the braves scattered and running in all directions, disappearing behind rocks and under bushes in the Apache way. It would never do to let them see how small a force was involved in the raid. The Apaches might run before a sudden and unexpected attack, but they'd be ready and willing to take on the cowhands if they found out how few the party numbered. They would hit all the harder and with more savage rage to recover their lost face.

The Apache horses scattered, sped on their way by shots and wild cowhand yells. Not one of those half-wild broomtails would stop running until it was exhausted and that would not be for miles. The Apaches would have a long time ahead of them before they caught their scattered mounts. It would take them time to get to the main bunch on foot, too, Dusty was sure of that.

Bringing his big paint to a halt, Dusty waited until the dust settled, then turned to the others, a grin splitting his face, which was covered in dust.

"Coil up those ropes and empty the sacks," he ordered.

"And take the sacks with you. We might need to pull that game again."

Through the mask of dust and grime the Kid grinned, his white teeth a strange contrast. "It's not likely to work twice. Fact being I didn't even reckon it would work once."

"We were lucky," Dusty answered.

"Lucky nothing, Dusty," snorted Vance. "You planned to hit them while they were asleep, take them when they least expected it. Now they don't know for sure if the herd's moving or how big an escort we have."

"Could be your guess's a meat-in-the-pot hit," chuckled Mark. "Only don't let ole Dusty know it. He'll take on airs and then half a dozen or so of us'll have to settle on him and talk him back to normal. Last time he took on airs that way was when he read what some Yankee colonel said about how he handled Troop C of the Texas Light in the war. It took eight of us and a couple of hours to tucker him out and throw him in the hoss trough."

Vance laughed, then he turned to look at Dusty with fresh interest. "Of course," he said. "You're *the* Captain Fog. I never connected you with him. You couldn't have been very old then."

"I was seventeen," Dusty replied. "Almost eighteen when the war ended."

"Gad! I heard about you. Colonel Houghton-Rand, my old commanding officer, was out here as a military observer with the Union Army. He met you when you killed that General in a duel."

Dusty smiled, lounging back in his saddle. That was long ago, but he still remembered the day when he faced General Buller on the field of honour and killed the Union Army officer. The British colonel had been his second and Dusty remembered him well. That Vance had heard of Dusty was not surprising, for in the War Dusty's use of his troop had changed military thinking on light cavalry tactics.

There was no time now to think back about the old days, to dream of what might have been had the South won the War. No doubt Dusty would now have been at least a colonel handling a regiment. However, he was not worried, he was content with his lot and the men he led. The OD Connected ranch's crew were as good as any regiment.

"Let's get back to the herd," he ordered as his raiding party finished emptying the sacks, casting off the mesquite bushes and coiling the ropes.

Vance rode by Dusty Fog, silent for a time, then he laughed.

"Something amusing you, *amigo*?" Dusty asked.

"I've been cursing this dust ever since I came out here," Vance replied. "But now I'm going to change my mind. Yes sir, Dusty. Now I know that dust has its uses."

CHAPTER NINE

The Kid Brings Word

"COME AND GET IT afore I throw it to the hawgs!"

Chow Willicka rubbed his hands on his apron and let out the time honoured bellow which served the cowhand as did mess call the soldier. The old cook stood by the big stewpot, ladle ready to fill the plates of the hungry trail crew as they filed past him.

It was the fifth day out from the ranch, the herd was making good time and there'd been no sign of Apaches since busting up that bunch on the first morning. For all that, Dusty did not relax his vigilance. He, Mark and Johnny rode a circle around the moving cattle, the Kid ranging far ahead. Then two days back the Kid had come to the chuckwagon as Chow and Birdie served out the morning meal. He asked for and was given dry rations for three days, then rode out. That was the last they'd seen of him, where he'd gone and what he was doing was known only to Dusty Fog and Stone Hart.

Dusty collected his food and joined Stone by the fire. Not even the trail boss was allowed to take his meal off the lowered boards at the rear of the chuck-wagon, that was the cook's private domain. So Dusty and Stone settled down on their haunches, as they'd both done so many times before.

"No sign of the Kid yet?" Stone asked.

"Not likely to be tonight," Dusty replied. "The river's still two days away. He's not riding a relay."

Stone nodded thoughtfully. The Kid was scouting the ford of the Carne River for possible Apache ambush. It would take him time and he would have to rest his big white stallion after so much hard and gruelling work. On the Kid's news depended an important decision. The Carne River was for most of its length fast and with high sheer walls dropping down to it. There was only one way to get the herd across that Stone knew of. To the north lay a place where the banks shelved down in a gentle slope and the river widened to make a deep, slow moving pool through which the cattle would swim with little or no difficulty. It was a two-day drive, about twenty-four miles to this ford, although the river itself was only about one day's drive from them in a straight line. There was a small snag to that. Stone did not know in what manner the river stood straight ahead, for this side's banks were thickly overgrown with trees and bushes. To try and push a herd blindly into thick wooded country like that would be asking for trouble and could result in the loss of a good half of the cattle.

The woods had been a source of much discussion between Dusty and Stone. It didn't take a master-mind to figure the Apaches would have the main ford under heavy guard, if not actually covering it in full strength. But there was no sense in pushing blindly into the woods if they were to find the river impassable through the same high banks which marked most of its length. It would be foolish and worse than foolish to drive the cattle into the woods, then find they had to turn upstream and use the main ford anyway. That was one of the reasons the Kid was riding scout now. To see what the ford in the open country looked like and then try and find a second way they might cross the river.

Dusty finished his meal. It was dark now and other men were starting their usual horseplay, engaged in what had become a favourite pastime, stirring up a feud between Birdie and Chow.

"Say, Miz Birdie," Rusty Willis called. "I sure bet you made this stew."

Birdie grinned. "I did, how did you know?"

"Easy. Old Chow's tastes like he's washed his shirt in it," Rusty answered. "Now yours, why ma'am, it tastes the same, 'cepting you use that fancy smelling ladies' soap."

"How long have this bunch been like this?" Birdie demanded, eyeing Chow belligerently.

"They was all right until they started eating women's fixings," Chow answered. "Which same goes to prove——"

"It doesn't prove nothing, 'cept that they've had their tastes spoiled by a wored out old chow wrecker," Birdie yelled back.

The argument grew more heated by the minute, yet for all that there was nothing in it. Chow found having Birdie working with him a most novel and stimulating experience. On the ride out to the ranch she'd left him to handle things and he'd been polite, well spoken, on his dignity around her. Their relationship was strained for the first day, with Chow bottling up his feelings and admonishing his regular louse in so gentle a manner that the gangling youngster thought he was ill. Then on the second morning he'd heard Birdie cursing one of the team horses in a manner which left nothing to be desired to breadth of knowledge or depth of fluency. From that moment on Chow carried on as normal and his louse breathed a sigh of relief.

Dusty and Stone listened to the argument growing, laughing at the retorts which flashed back and forwards. Then, with their meal finished, they went to the bin of hot water and dropped the plates in. Coffee mugs in hand, the two men headed for the bed wagon. The back was let down and a lantern hung inside it. Birdie used the wagon for sleeping and her bed roll was spread ready. Stone climbed into the wagon, went to where a small box was firmly fitted to the side. He lifted the lid and took out a large Army map of the area which he'd brought from Vance's ranch. Moving back to the end of the wagon, he sat on the board and spread the map out. Dusty leaned by the wagon and in the light of the lamp they started to study the map once more, checking over the details of the range with their memory of the trip out.

"Still worrying over that map?" Vance asked as he walked towards them.

"Sure," Dusty agreed. "Have you ever run a herd into Tombstone before?"

"No, this's the first shipping herd I've been able to move since I took over. The man I bought the ranch from ran two in."

"Which way did he go?" Stone inquired.

"Up to the ford where we crossed, but the Apaches were at peace then. He told me he'd seen a small hunting party as he was crossing the river."

Stone ran a finger along the map, following the course of the Carne River. He tapped a cross marked on the river's coarse.

"There's another crossing here."

"I know," Dusty agreed. "Six days' drive over rough country. We'd never make Tombstone in time for the Fair and a herd this size wouldn't bring much of a price there at any other time."

"We'll have to decide by noon tomorrow at the latest," Stone warned. "That's when we'll have to start swinging north to the open country ford, or south where we might be safe, even if we don't get the herd in on time."

"I'm in your hands, Stone," Vance replied, then showed the sort of spirit which made the English gentleman what he was. "If it'll save lives, I say hang the Fair and the money, take the southern route."

Stone and Dusty looked at Vance with open admiration.

The Englishman's hopes were based on this herd, on the money selling it at the Fair would bring in. Yet to prevent them losing men he was willing to sacrifice it all, take the long route to Tombstone and miss the big money which the herd would undoubtedly command in the meat-starved town.

Stone grinned. "Thanks for saying that, Vance. There's few enough who would have. You took me and my boys on to get your herd to Tombstone in time for the Fair and that's what we aim to do. The Wedge has never failed to push a herd on to market and this isn't going to be the first time. How do you feel, Dusty?"

"I'm in this root, hog or die," Dusty drawled. "And I'm sure not fixing in to let any Apaches push me any place."

"Then I——"

Vance began to say something to show his gratitude, but the words ended before they'd really begun. Dusty and Stone came off the wagon, their hands bringing the guns from leather as they peered into the darkness.

"Douse that light, Vance!" Dusty snapped. "We've got visitors."

It was then Vance heard the sound of horses approaching. He vaulted into the wagon and put out the lantern, plunging the area around the wagon into darkness. From out in the light a voice he recognised called:

"You're about two minutes too late with that, Vance. I could have dropped all three of you had I wanted."

The Kid, unshaven, dirty, his black clothes smothered in mud, the shirt sleeve torn open, rode up. He was not riding his big white stallion but sat a wiry Apache pony with two more following on a lead rope. The huge white horse came after them, without a saddle and looking as if it had done some travelling. The Kid himself had the appearance of a man who'd ridden far and done plenty.

"Rusty, Doc!" Stone snapped as the talk around the fire died down, the trail crew staring at the apparition by Stone's side. "Get over here and take care of the Kid's horses."

The two men in question rose, but Mark also came to his feet. Rusty and Doc were good hands with horses and could handle the three Apache broomtails, but the Kid's huge white stallion was another proposition. The old Nigger horse would allow only the Kid to handle it with any impunity. Even to the other members of the floating outfit Nigger showed no friendship and merely tolerated them. For any man, other than the select few, to try and handle the big white was dangerous in the extreme.

Birdie grabbed a mug from the table, filled it with hot

coffee and darted forward to hand it to the Kid. He took the mug and drank, conscious that every eye was on him and that every one of the crowd was seething with questions.

"You made good time, Lon," Dusty remarked as the Kid finished the coffee.

"Man'd say you're right," answered the Kid. "I met up with an Apache headed for war and discussed him out of his relay. Made me a fast ride up towards the ford."

"How is it?" Vance asked.

"Bad, there's a good two hundred braves waiting on the ford and likely more of them about if needed."

"Two hundred?" Stone put in.

"Waal, I didn't stop to make no herd count, Stone. Just took me a quick peek, then headed out again. I've seen me two hundred Injuns afore now and know about how many it is. There's that many there, at least."

Stone did not doubt the accuracy of the Kid's words. There probably was not an exact two hundred braves there, but Stone was willing to take bets that the Kid called it to within twenty one way or the other. That many Apache would be a rough and hard handful for a full battalion of cavalry. They hopelessly outnumbered the trail crew. He asked no questions as to how the Kid came to be riding an Apache warrior's war relay. Somewhere out there the Kid must have come on a lone scout or a brave headed for the fight. What happened after that was anybody's guess. The Kid probably had not risked using his firearms for fear the noise would attract other Apaches. That meant there came a sudden, silent rush, the flash of sun off the blade of a James Black bowie knife and an Apache went to the happy hunting grounds.

"We'll have to pull down to the south ford and forget the Fair," Vance put it. "I don't want to risk losing lives."

It was not just a speech made to raise his prestige in the eyes of man. All the trail crew knew the store Vance set on getting the herd to Tombstone and they also knew he was sincere in what he said.

"There's another way."

All eyes went to the Kid as he spoke. Dusty knew that Indian dark and grim-looking young man as well, if not better, than any of the others and asked:

"What're you getting at, Lon?"

"There's a crossing on the Carne River—downstream—in the woods."

"Can we use it?" Vance asked.

"Sure we can. The banks are easy, the water's not even as fast as up at the other ford. It's fairly open country on the other side. We can use it all right—if we can get rid of five young Apache bucks who're watching it night and day."

"Like that, huh?" Dusty drawled.

"Just like that," agreed the Kid.

The others all fell silent, Birdie and Chow were no longer bickering and the rest of the hands sat waiting to hear what their fate was to be.

"Five of them couldn't hold the ford against us," Vance remarked, putting his thoughts into words.

"Nor even mean to try," replied the Kid. "See, Vance, they're not aiming to hold us up, or even fight us, not on their own. That'd be a foolish play and whatever else they might be, Apaches aren't fools. They'll be waiting on the river there, watching all day, for the first sight of the herd. They know the country, know how a herd'd have to travel to have grazing and water. They know that come noon tomorrow if you're in sight of the woods that's where you'll be going, not up to the open ford to the north."

"They might have more men in the woods then," Vance remarked.

"Not unless they moved in since I left."

Something in the way the Kid spoke warned Vance, told him a story. He looked at the unshaven, gaunt and tired face and knew that the Kid must have personally searched the woods, moving in complete silence to find the Apache scouts.

"Tell it, Lon," Dusty said gently.

Sinking to his haunches the Kid went on, "I came downstream after scouting the other ford. Found the tracks of five hosses and followed them. The hosses were staked out with a couple of young 'uns guarding them. I was afoot and went quiet. The other three were resting just inside the woods, but watching all the same. I let things lie, didn't figure I could take five of them and any noise'd send the others heading off fast. I didn't figure you'd want them either killing or scaring just yet awhile, Dusty."

"That's good figuring," Dusty answered. "It's no good warning the Apaches up at the other ford that we know about this one. I reckon their chief's just covering all the bets by having this ford watched. He doesn't expect us to use it."

"You called it right. The scouts are boys, look like they've just been took in on the lodge and are being given this chore as a test. They likely have been told to run as soon as they see the herd, if it comes their way."

"What would happen then?" Vance inquired. "You said the main bunch was at the other ford, right up to the north."

"They are, but they could get down here and on to us

before we could get over the river and far enough towards Tombstone, so it wouldn't be safe for them to follow us further."

Birdie came forward, halting to stand before the men, hands on hips and glaring at them.

"That's enough for now," she snapped. "Lon, I've got a plate of stew for you, it's over on the wagon boards. Go and eat it."

The Kid looked up at Birdie. He knew she was born and raised in the cattle country, she knew that only by the cook's permission could the right to eat at the wagon board be given. Then he saw Chow giving a nod of agreement and realised he was being granted the supreme honour of the trail drive, he was being allowed to dine on the cook's sacred territory.

"Dusty may not have finished with the Kid, dear," Vance put in.

"He has," she snorted, eyeing Dusty and daring him to object. "That poor boy looks as if he's not eaten since he rode out two days ago and I'm not seeing all you well fed yahoos standing around asking him questions until he's good and fed."

Vance smiled, then said, "One thing I learned early during my marriage was never to argue with Birdie. You always wind up in second place."

The Kid rose and followed Birdie to the chuck wagon and was soon eating a good meal. The men around the fire all sat back now. They'd done their day's work and most of them would be taking a turn at the night herd soon.

"How about it, Dusty?" Stone asked, for this matter came under the province of the fighting leader rather than the trail boss.

"It's the woods, down to the south or an early grave," Dusty answered. "And given the choice, I'd take the woods to the river. The crew would only have to try and hold them in something like a bunch. We might lose a few head but we'll get the rest over, what's more we'll make Tombstone alive, instead of some Apache's wickiup as a war trophy."

Stone chuckled. He might have felt annoyed at Dusty suggesting a way to get the cattle through the woods, but he did not. Dusty had put into words the thoughts Stone himself had on the problem of the woods and the solution. Now it all depended on whether Dusty's fighting scout force could get rid of the Apache scouts and make sure any more who came were also dealt with.

"When that poor, tired lil boy's had his food, took a bath and rested a mite, we'll ride," Dusty said. "He can use one of the remuda horses. I'll take Mark, Johnny and Lon with me. You'll have to let Peaceful ride close in scout."

"Could I come along?" Vance asked.

Dusty looked at the rancher and grinned. "You're getting to be a regular ole glory hunter, Vance."

"Was his hair shoulder long I'd call him Custer," agreed Stone, also grinning.

"Dash it all, there's nothing in that," Vance answered. "I merely want to go along and see how you handle things. I've done a considerable amount of hunting and hope I won't get in the way."

"You come along then," Dusty answered. "What sort of things have you hunted?"

"Bear, mountain lion, bighorn sheep out here, stag in Scotland, boar in the Westphalia of Germany," Vance replied.

"Man who's done that much hunting shouldn't need us to help him then," drawled Dusty. "Say I met a rancher up on the edge of the Indian Nations. He come from England. He told me about hunting wild pigs with a spear and from a horse, did you ever try that?"

"You mean pig-sticking," Vance replied, grinning. "Only once, while I was on leave at Canton, in China. At least the chappie swore they were wild pigs. It turned out later we'd skewered some rich chappie's prize breeding hog. He was annoyed."

It was gone midnight when Dusty led Mark, the Kid, Vance and Johnny Raybold from the camp. The Kid had eaten well, been to the waterhole near the camp site and scrubbed himself free of the dirt and dust, changed into a fresh black outfit from his warbag and caught up with a brief sleep. For all the fact that he'd been sleeping lightly and uncertainly for the past couple of nights the Kid looked fresh and alert as if he'd been safely in his bed at the OD Connected each night.

Vance and the Kid drew ahead of the others. It was a rare tribute to the rancher that the Kid allowed him to ride up front on what amounted to a scout, as much a tribute and honour as was the Kid's allowed to feed off the chuck wagon boards.

The two men rode along in silence, but after a time they brought their horses to a halt. A sudden noise and crashing through the night ahead of them again brought movement. Vance's hand shot down as he leaned forward to jerk the Winchester rifle from his saddleboot. The Kid swung across and caught the rancher's shoulder.

"Don't bother, it's only an old scrub bull taking off," he drawled.

The sound of the animal's rapid departure faded into the distance as Vance straightened once more. He peered through the darkness towards the Kid.

"How could you be sure it wasn't a man?"

"Ole Nigger here told me."

"But he didn't do anything," Vance objected.

"That's how I know. If it'd been a man ole Nigger'd have pointed him like a deep south bird dog aiming at a bobwhite quail."

"The Apache might have men out there though," Vance went on.

"Might, but it's not likely. All their men are gathered up there at the open ford, except for the scouts. The braves have gathered. I reckon I must have got one of the last on his way. Just stop your hoss a minute and listen."

The horses halted and Vance strained his ears, listening, trying to catch some light sound which might tell him what the Kid could hear. There was nothing but the ever present yipping of coyotes, the more distant bellow as an old scrub bull let out a challenge to the world in general and other bulls in particular. In the distance another bull answered. Off in the other direction, faint yet still with the menace it always held, came the scream of a cougar. These were the only sounds Vance could hear, these and the ever chirping noises of the night insects.

"I can't hear anything but the usual night noises," he finally said.

"Or me," admitted the Kid, "and as long as they're there I'm happy. Man comes along and those same noises stop. I bet that Johnny knows just where we are, from back there a piece by the way the coyotes have stopped yipping our way. Listen, see if you can tell where Johnny's bringing Dusty and Mark along from."

For a moment Vance did as he was told. The coyotes appeared to be calling all around, then he realised that the sounds were not coming from behind. A few seconds after he made out the faint noises of horses' hooves.

"Listen real good and you'll hear the leather creaking," the Kid went on.

Vance strained his ears but the riders were in view, dark blobs against the blackness of the range, before he could catch the faint sound of leather creaking. The Kid's Indian keen ears had picked up the same faint sound at a far greater distance. Vance could see now why back at his ranch Dusty showed such complete faith when the Kid said it was soldiers who approached through the night.

The three horses loomed up out of the night and Johnny asked somewhat tactlessly, "All quiet, Lon?"

"Nope," sarcasm dripped heavily from the Kid's soft spoken reply. "We're fighting Apaches off on both sides."

"Let's go," Dusty answered before Johnny could think up a suitable answer. "I want to be on those Apaches before they know we're about. That means getting to the woods before dawn."

The men rode on and once more Vance was amazed at the way the Kid acted. This was a new range for him and yet without the slightest hesitation he was taking them where they wanted to go. Vance knew that with compass and map he might be able to aim for a given point and reach it, but the Kid used neither. He relied on the inborn instinct granted to him by the blood of his Comanche forefathers. It was the ability of a travelling Indian to find his way from one point to another without any aids other than his sense of direction. This time the Kid had traversed most of the journey in daylight, coming from his scout of the river to the herd. For all of that it was no mean feat for him to find his way back to the river through the night.

Soon after the others catching up, Dusty and the Kid held a quiet conversation, then the Kid faded away, his big white stallion moving in the silence of a wild thing. The Kid had refused the loan of a remuda horse to use on the scout. He had used the captured Apache relay for his work and the white was still fresh enough to handle this raid. The Kid had complete faith in the huge white stallion he called Nigger, the horse had been specially trained for such things and was able to locate hidden men, then give the Kid a warning of their presence. Also the white would stand, not fastened, like a statue for as long as the Kid wanted and would never make a sound to betray it or its master.

Time passed, the other men rode in a straight line, not talking now, for they were approaching the river and Apache ears were very keen. It was surprising how far the sound of a voice carried at night. Vance had seen some action against Chinese bandits while in the British Army and knew that as well as did the Texans.

Vance's ears were working at full power but he still received a shock when the Kid's white horse stepped from behind a bush. He heard the Kid's gentle chuckle and knew the others were almost as surprised as he was.

"They're in there someplace, Dusty," whispered the Kid. "Ain't camping the same place as last night. Never thought they would be. They won't sleep the same place two nights running if they can help it."

"What do you reckon?"

"There's a hollow ahead, got water, good graze. We could leave the hosses down there, then move in on foot and find the camp."

"Lead on to it, *amigo*."

The men left their horses standing in the hollow and gathered. Dusty told them what the Kid found out. He looked them all over and then made his decision.

"Johnny, stay here, keep the hosses out of sight and quiet. Vance, you'll come with us. Take rifles along."

Johnny did not argue at this moment. He knew Dusty well and knew that this was not the time for argument. He was better able to handle Dusty and Mark's big stallions than was a comparative stranger like Vance. Those two horses did not take kindly to strangers being around them, or trying to nandle them and it would take a horseman of the first water to control them.

Vance drew the rifle from his saddleboot, slowly worked the lever to put a bullet into the chamber, doing it so as to make as little noise as possible. He was just a little worried, for the slightest slip might mean the Apaches would be scared off, running to warn the others. If that happened, the main bunch would come down to attack the herd.

CHAPTER TEN

In the Woods

"THIS'S FAR ENOUGH!"

The words, no louder than a whisper, came from Dusty Fog as he sank to one knee under a tree. Behind him Mark Counter, the Ysabel Kid and Vance Brownlow also sank down. They'd made their way to the edge of the woods and moved in only a few yards when Dusty came to a halt.

"What is it, Dusty?" Vance whispered.

"No sense in busting around here and making noise in the dark. We'll just settle down and wait until it's light enough to see."

The four men settled down as Dusty said, resting their backs against three trunks. Vance was more tired than he could remember, for he'd been on night herd the previous night and spent the day in the saddle. His head was nodding and the Kid whispered in his ear:

"They're not too far off. I can hear their hosses moving."

"Are we moving in on them, then?"

"You find them and I'll move in," breathed the Kid in reply. "They're not by the hosses, that's one thing you can bet on. Try and get some sleep. One thing though—happen you're going to snore—don't."

Vance rested his head on the hard, upstanding root of the tree against which he leaned. He shook his head slightly, trying to clear it. To the best of his knowledge he did not snore and doubted if he would even go to sleep with such a hard pillow.

A hand clamped down on Vance's mouth, while another shook him. He tried to struggle but the grip was too strong. His eyes opened and he found that it was now almost fully daylight. Mark held on to Vance until sure that the rancher was fully awake and would not make any sound, then released him. Vance sat up, carefully working his stiff and sore limbs, he looked around. Dusty was leaning against a tree, keeping out of sight behind the trunk. Of the Kid was no sign at all for a moment, then he was back. Coming through the bushes with the silence of a ghost, his rifle in his hands.

"You full awake yet?" Mark asked gently.

"Awake and ready," Vance replied, working his fingers to get the stiffness out of them.

"Found them, Lon?" Dusty asked, although he knew the answer.

The Kid's answer was grimly eloquent. He jerked his head towards the bushes and gave a gentle warning. "Go quieter than quiet, all of you."

The others rose and exchanged looks. This was the moment. Right now could be the beginning of safety or the end of the herd and most probably the lives of every man and the woman who rode with the cattle.

The men fanned out, they used every bit of cover they could find, flitting from bush to bush like shadows, avoiding treading on any branch which might snap underfoot and give warning. Vance showed the others their faith in him was fully justified and he thanked his stars that he'd always loved the outdoors and hunting. As a boy he'd poached rabbits and pheasant on neighbouring estates, done it in a day when a keeper would not think twice before firing on a poacher with a shotgun. Right now the training was standing him in good stead. It was a dangerous game he was playing and there was much at stake.

The breeze, light, shifting constantly in direction as it surged through the trees, came to Vance and his nostrils caught an aroma. It was there for a moment, then gone again, but he could have sworn he smelled the rich and appetising fumes of cooking turkey.

The Kid was ahead of the others, moving with the silence of a black dressed ghost. Then he halted, seeming to freeze in midstride. He looked back to the others, held up his hand, then moved his arms, spreading them out in a signal. The other three men advanced, fanning out. Vance was on the outside of the group, with Dusty next to him. The rancher reached a bush, peered over it and stiffened.

They were just ahead, four dark, squat, half naked young braves around a small fire. Even as Vance watched he saw one of the braves carve a slab of meat from the breast of a cooked turkey which was impaled on a stick placed in the ground. There was a small hole dug in the ground in the very embers of the fire. Vance noticed this, even more than he noticed that all the young braves had knives at their belts and their weapons were stacked nearby.

Slowly the Kid raised his rifle and the others also started to lift their weapons ready to shoot. There was no time to think of the rights or wrongs of shooting down the braves without a chance. These were Apaches, tough young braves who were on the warpath. At such a time no Apache would think twice of shooting down a white man from ambush and without warning.

There was a slight movement which caught the corner of Vance's eye, a splash of colour where no such colour should be. His senses were alert and he started to turn, dropping into a crouch as he did so. That movement saved his life. There was a hiss and he felt a burning knife-like agony well through him as the feathered shaft of an Apache war arrow drove into his shoulder. He saw the young Apache standing in the bushes, his own rifle fell from his hands. With pain welling through him Vance stood dazed, unable to force himself to make a move as the Apache fetched a second arrow from his quiver, set it and started to draw the bow string. Time seemed to be standing still for Vance and later he would never remember the incident in terms of seconds, which was how it happened.

Dusty heard the slight sound and turned, his short Winchester carbine coming up and spitting even as the brave was pulling back his bowstring. Dusty moved and shot fast, Vance later was to swear he felt the wind of the bullet on his face. The Apache spun around, his arrow jerked from the string and clattered to the ground, then he followed it.

There was no time to waste on the shot Apache, or even on caring for Vance's wound. Not right now, for the four braves by the fire were on their feet, startled and not sure where the attack was coming from. The confusion was only momentary, the turkey went into the fire, knocked over by a brave who leapt for his rifle. Three of the Apaches were moving, hurling for their weapons, the fourth turned to run.

Mark Counter's rifle crashed and one of the braves reeled, went to his knees then crashed down. The Kid's old yellow boy spat out, hunching over and dropping a second warrior even as his reflexes started to propel him towards his weapons. The third young brave was fast, he dived forward with hands reaching down and missed a fast thrown bullet from Dusty's carbine by inches. Lighting down rolling, the brave brought off a fast taken shot which ripped a hole through the brim of Mark's costly white Stetson hat. The penalty for missing came fast, thrown through the .44 barrel of the Kid's old rifle, slammed home on the end of a flatnosed Tyler Henry bullet.

The last brave was older, more battle wise. He also knew his orders in case of a surprise attack by the scouts of the ride-plenties, the cowhands. Not for him to stand and fight. Leave that to the young braves, the name-making braves with no coups to show for victory or tales to sing around the camp fire. The old warrior had done both things and needed no boosting to his name and fame so he could leave the young men to fight and die while he headed upstream as fast as his war relay could run, make his best time to warn the main band that the herd of white man's spotted buffalo would come through the woods and cross the Carne River here.

On his knees, wincing with pain, Vance tried to withdraw the arrow. He'd seen the sudden, wild and explosive burst of action and saw the brave running for the trees even as the others went down before Texas rifles.

"Quit that fooling, Vance," Dusty warned as he saw what was happening. "Set back and watch the Kid."

Vance released the arrow and Dusty helped him to his feet, allowing him to see what was going on and take his mind from the agony he was in. Vance, even though his shoulder throbbed and hurt, could not help but admire the cool way the Kid handled his rifle.

The Apache was gone, diving into the bushes like a greased weasel. He appeared for a brief instant and Mark's rifle kicked bark from the tree behind, while he went from sight once more. The Kid did not fire. He held his old rifle to his shoulder, left eye closed, right sighting carefully along the scuffed old barrel. The Kid knew that rifle, knew every vagary of it and he knew that he would have just one good chance to down the Apache.

There was a red flicker between two trees, the flicker made by the trade shirt of the Apache as he darted between two bushes on his racing way to where the horses were staked out. Vance saw it, then saw the Kid alter his aim slightly. Once more that red flash showed and the Kid's rifle barked. The red shirt jerked, staggered, crashed down. There was a thrashing in the bushes and then all was still once more.

Bounding forward with the speed and grace of a buck Apache, the Kid went into the clearing. He hurled the bodies of the three young braves, seeing in passing there was no danger from them. He also found time to cast a disappointed glance at the charred remains of the turkey on the fire. There was nothing the Kid liked more than Indian-baked turkey. Right now he had other things to worry about. He knew he'd sunk lead into the fleeing Apache but must make sure the brave was dead. He'd seen a badly wounded Apache cover ten miles once, to get where he wanted to go. If the brave was not dead he might even now get away and succeed in his duty of warning the main bunch.

Moving fast the Kid came to where the Apache lay. There was a hole in the side of his shirt, it was small, at the other side the exit hole of the bullet was large and ragged. There was no danger, the twenty-eight grain load used in the old Winchester 66 rifle might not have long range hitting power, but up to fifty yards would stop a man, especially when it smashed through the chest and burst the heart in passing.

The Kid did not stop by the Apache, he went on, ears straining to catch any sound which might warn him that there had been one or more braves with the horses and that they were now running. No such sound greeted him and he came on the Apache ponies hobbled and grazing in a small valley. The Kid made a quick circle of the valley, then after making sure no Apache had left, he turned to head back to the camp. There were five war relays and three horses each down in the valley, they would make a useful addition to Vance Brownlow's remuda.

"We'd best look to that arrow, Vance," Dusty remarked as soon as the Kid went from sight.

Vance was still gripping the arrow shaft, trying to pull at it, although he felt as if the strength was drained from him. He was on his knees and the sweat rolled freely down his face. Mark came forward, rested his rifle against the trunk of a tree and grunted:

"You stop that, Vance," he said, then to Dusty. "The danged fool's trying to pull himself inside out."

"You always did reckon a man who settled in Arizona didn't have good sense," Dusty answered. "Best tend to him or we'll have Birdie after us for not taking good care of him."

Taking a knife from his pocket Mark stepped forward and cut the rancher's shirt away from the wound. He worked fast and Vance stayed on his knees, making no sound of protest. The arrow's tip just showed from under his collar-bone and Mark only needed the one look to tell him all he needed to know.

"That's a barbed war arrow, Vance," he warned. "It won't come out the way it went in so——" Mark spoke gently, put his left hand against Vance's shoulder to hold it firm, gripped the arrow shaft with his right and forced it forward so the barbed head was clear.

Vance's body gave a convulsive heave but that was the only sign of pain he gave, except that the sweat was pouring down his face. Through his clenched lips he managed to grit out:

"Don't worry none about it. It's only me."

"Which same's why I'm not worrying," Mark answered cheerfully, cutting the barbed head off. "It's all over and done with now, isn't it Dusty?"

Then before Vance realised what was going to happen it was all over and done with. Mark gripped the wounded shoulder again, took hold of the headless arrow by the flighted end, gave a quick pull and it slid back through the hole and out. This time Vance did give a yell, the world appeared to be roaring around him. He clutched weakly at Mark's leg as blood began to flow.

"Whisky—flask in my pants pocket——" he gasped.

Mark nodded, he felt for and extracted the small hipflask from Vance's pocket then removed the cork and poured the raw liquor into the hole. Vance's entire body writhed and jerked in agony as the whisky bit into the wound. He groaned but did not cry out, although his eyes were suddenly filled with water. By the time he'd recovered and cleared his eyes Vance found Mark was ripping his shirt to make a bandage. The Kid was back from his scout, grinning broadly as he examined the arrow-head.

"Wonder if this here arrow's all poisoned?" he asked, knowing full well the Apache never poisoned his arrow-heads. "Had me an uncle one time, back home to Texas. He took him a poisoned arrow in his shoulder, swelled up like a fattening shoat. My drinking uncle, Si, mistook him for a shoat and butchered him for dinner. There wasn't half a to-do when they found out the mistake. See, Uncle Ezra, him that got butchered, he'd stashed away a whole jug of corn likker and none of the others knew where it was."

"You damned black heller," growled Vance, with a blanket curse which took in the whole Ysabel family. "Can't you think of anything more cheerful to talk about than that?"

The Kid grinned and went to the fire, examining the large patch of embers. He scuffed some of the back with his boot, drew his knife and started to dig until he brought forth a large ball of what appeared to be mud. Carefully juggling the hot ball the Kid got it clear of the fire and broke it with the back of the bowie knife blade. The mud cracked and came away to expose the plump shape of a wild turkey as big as the one which was still spluttering and burning on the fire. The dried mud stripped off all the feathers as it came away and the bird lay ready for carving and eating.

"I sure could talk about something more cheerful," he told the watching Vance. "But you being all shot to death like that, you just wouldn't be interested."

"I'm not that badly hurt," Vance replied. "Besides, turkey's good for a sick man. I had an Uncle Thadeus, he always insisted on eating turkey when he was ill."

The Kid grinned, his razor-edged knife went around and carved a generous slab of breast meat from the bird, then he pulled a twig from the fire, impaled the meat on it and passed it to Vance.

"This's what I call a well cooked bird," the Kid remarked. "And more than enough for us——"

"Yowee! Food!" whooped a voice from the trees and Johnny Raybold appeared, leading the horses.

"You spoke a whole heap too soon, *amigo,*" growled Mark disgustedly. "Reckon we could insult him so he'd go away?"

"With *food* here?" Dusty replied. "That's about as likely as finding an honest Ysabel, now isn't it?"

Johnny saw the bandaging attempts and opened his saddle pouch to take out some strips of white cloth. He cast a critical eye around him and remarked: "That was a tolerable amount of shooting for just three dead Apaches."

"There's two more in the bushes," Dusty replied. "We got them all. Settle on down and have some turkey."

"I wouldn't say no," Johnny drawled.

"You've never even tried," growled the Kid.

Dusty waited until Vance's wound was attended to then gave his orders. "Eat up, then I'm riding back to the herd. You come with me, Vance, I want Doc to take a look at that shoulder."

"I just helped with it," Johnny pointed out.

"Sure," agreed Dusty. "That's what I mean."

Stone saw the two men riding towards him, saw Dusty's hat make a wild wave to him and knew everything was all right, except that Vance had his arm in a sling. Sending his horse forward, Stone rode to meet the other two, he glanced at Vance and asked, "Everything all right?"

"Got them all and Vance's our only casualty."

"Head back along the line, Vance," Stone ordered. "Tell Doc to look you over. How about it, Dusty?"

Dusty cast a glance back at the herd and nodded. "They look thirsty enough."

"They're ready for it."

Dusty and Stone had experienced the way of a herd of cattle when it was thirsty and got a scent of water. With luck the cattle would run right through the trees and could be picked up at the edge of the water. There would be some time lost but it would be worth the extra trouble.

"I left Mark, Lon and Johnny to watch out. They've got

orders to down any Apache who shows any sign of coming their way, looking for the other scouts."

Time passed and the herd moved on. It had been allowed to graze but now the riders closed in on the flanks, pushing the animals closer together and the pace increased. The previous days had been at a steady drive and without trouble, now the extra pace did not unduly worry them.

Birdie had seen Vance with his arm in the sling but neither fainted nor went into hysterics. She realised that the wound was not over serious or he would hardly have come riding back in such a manner. She left her place on the herd for a few moments just to make sure, then went back to handle her part and follow the lead of Doc Leroy who was called back to check the wound. From then until Doc's return Birdie covered his and her own section of the line. Doc came back after a time, he rode alongside Birdie as she cursed at a steer.

"He'll live," he said cheerfully and raced his horse up the line.

The woods were in sight and the wind was blowing towards the cattle from it. The big lead steer threw back his head, snuffled the air, then lumbered on again for a time. Once more he sniffed as the wind bore the scent of water to him.

"Watch 'em now!" Stone roared. "They've scented the water."

The change in the cattle was instant, heads flung back, snorts rang out and they started to move faster. Stone watched them, not wanting a stampede and not wanting them to run off too much fat in a wild race.

It was now the skill of the cowhands showed itself. They rode like centaurs, keeping the pace of the herd under control. Dusty appeared to be everywhere and wherever Dusty was not Stone Hart was. Riding with the wildest, sending her cow-trained horse into the herd, around it, chasing on the cattle, rode Birdie. This was the chance for her husband's dream to come true and she meant to see that it did.

Now the herd was headed for the woods and Mark Counter boiled up out of the dust to help the others. Johnny and the Kid did not appear, they were well to the north, ready, willing and both very able to handle any chance Apache who came within range of their rifles.

In the woods it was a wild tangle, the riders all took time out to get fresh mounts from the remuda and then charged back. There was no time for refinement or gentle handling, the steers were on the scent of water and headed for it. Not one of the herd had any other thought but to sink his nose into the cool water he could smell ahead. There was no thought of scattering and escape to freedom in the trees, not while thirst ruled.

Full into the water went the leading cattle, pushed on by the steers behind. A big roan longhorn went down, thrashing in the water and risking life and limb. Dusty was after it, his rope flashed out and the huge paint churned wildly as it hauled the steer clear by brute strength alone.

"Just like a herd of women," Stone growled disgustedly, speaking to, without looking back at, the rider behind him.

Something hard thudded into his ribs and he turned to find himself looking into Birdie's laughing eyes. For a moment he flushed red, then he grinned also. The present conditions gave a man no chance at all of feeling embarrassed and he had come to know Birdie quite well on this cattle drive.

"Move them across!" he roared and Birdie was the first to send her horse into the water.

The cattle, those which had drunk their fill already, were eased across the river with little or no trouble. On the other bank the woods were neither so thick nor tempting to the cattle and the herd moved on through them, encouraged by cursing riders. Stone held half the men back to make a search of the woods and the odd strays were picked up, sent over to join the long and winding column of cattle on their way to Tombstone.

The remuda was watered and moved over by Rin and the night hawk, then the two wagons brought across. By this time the day was well advanced and Chow decided to set up his night camp on the river bank. The herd was pushed on for a couple of miles and then salted and allowed to bed down for the night. There was no trouble in getting the cattle to settle down for they were leg weary and the grazing on the bed ground was good. Stone kept his usual double night herd out, for they were not out of danger yet.

There was a light-hearted and happy-go-lucky air about the camp. They were past the most serious danger now, or would be by nightfall tomorrow. Birdie went to the bedwagon and collected a towel, some soap and a change of clothing. She also dug out her husband's razor and clean clothes, strolled over to him and remarked:

"You look like you've spent a week in a hawg-pen. There's all that clean water down there, let's go try some of it."

Birdie and Vance were away a long time. They walked back towards the camp, passing several of the trail crew who were headed upstream to wash the dirt and dust from them. Vance had his good arm around his wife. She smiled up at him.

"Vance honey," she said gently. "Wouldn't it be funny if our first baby got his start on the banks of the Carne River?"

Vance chuckled and squeezed Birdie. "I think it would, anyway, I hope it's a girl."

She looked the cowhands over on their return, remarking they all looked like strangers. This brought Chow in with a growl about them being all right until they had to eat woman's fixings and the feud was started afresh.

Laughing in delight because she'd put one over that Chow couldn't top, Birdie walked away before he could find an answer. She found Doc Leroy sitting on the edge of the bed-wagon and joined him. Doc's long, slim and almost boneless looking hands were busy, rolling some cloth to form a bandage.

"Is Vance's shoulder going to be all right?" she asked.

"Sure," Doc replied.

"Where'd you meet up with Dusty first?" she went on, talking because she was too happy and excited to think of sleep.

"Up to Quiet Town, in Montana just after the war. We ran the law there under him. He taught me there's a whole lot more to wearing a badge than hauling a drunk to jail and settling back to take a cut of the fine."

"Is he fast?"

"He's faster than fast and twice as accurate," Doc replied. "Mark's real fast too. They've got a boy rides with them now, he bust his arm and couldn't come with them on this. His name's Waco and he's near on as fast as either of them." Doc chuckled. "I bet young Waco near turned the air blue when he heard he couldn't come. That boy'd walk into a gun, knowing he was going to get killed, if Dusty told him to."

"Dusty's only a small man, I suppose," Birdie remarked thoughtfully. "It's a funny thing though. I can never think of him as being small."

"Neither can I. He stands a full seventeen hands high from where I ride. Put me a choice between him and Stone—well I surely wouldn't want to make a choice."

Birdie sat back. "You handle doctoring real well."

"Sure," Doc answered. "I read medicine for a time. Then my folks were killed in an Indian raid and I lost a brother on one of the early drives with Stone. I was just on eighteen when I left it. I've learned all I could, read books, talked to doctors. One day I'll maybe get a chance and go back to medical school and really be able to put M.D. after my name."

That day came, but it was not for four years and by that time much had changed in the hectic life of Doc Leroy.

Birdie climbed down from the wagon and headed back to

her husband. She thought of the men who rode their herd. In the few days she'd come to know them all probably better than she knew her own ranch crew. They were a varied bunch, each man a rugged individualist in his own right, yet they formed a good team, even the new hands taken on in Tombstone just for the drive. The regular Wedge crew were loyal to each other and to their boss. Yet she also felt that a good part of their admiration and loyalty was also given to that small, soft talking, fast moving man from the Rio Hondo, the man called Dusty Fog.

"We're through the worst of it now, aren't we?" she asked squatting cowhand style on her haunches by her husband, Dusty and Stone.

"Just about," Stone replied.

"I still think we'll have to watch ourselves at that draw near Tombstone," Dusty warned. "That'll be Rambeau's first, last and best chance to hit at us."

CHAPTER ELEVEN

Orders From The Syndicate

KING RAMBEAU stamped into the King Saloon in no mood to make conversation or even think of returning the greetings of the bartender who handed him a small and unopened package. It was four days after the death of Iowa Parsons and he was returning from a very unpleasant interview with a leading member of the Syndicate who had come by fast coach from Tucson.

The inquest on Iowa Parsons was long over and the verdict had been brought in 'Died of a case of slow', a verdict which had been used more than once on the victims of the killer.

"A kid brought this in while you was out, boss," remarked the bartender.

Rambeau did not need to ask or even think what was in the parcel. It contained the most expensive bracelet he could buy in Tombstone and had been delivered with a note suggesting a meeting, to Cindy Alban. The girl had not even opened the package and the note, torn into pieces, was found inside the envelope, which was stuck to the back.

At any other time this might have driven Rambeau into a rage but not with the worries he had on his mind. The Syndicate man had been brief, brutally brief. Iowa Parsons had been sent to Tombstone to handle trouble at the saloon and the Syndicate wanted to know how he came to be killed. There was no lying or arguing either, the man knew about Rambeau's manipulations, knew that Parsons was breaking one of their strictest rules when he sat in a game which did not concern him.

Stamping up the stairs and opening his room door, Rambeau still could hear the man's cold, impersonal voice:

"You started this game, Rambeau. Now you've got to finish it. The word's all through the Territory that a Syndicate man started in to take over a herd and folks are waiting to see how it goes. You've got to handle that herd, get it one way or another."

To Rambeau's request for more guns the man merely pointed out that there were any amount of men around Tombstone who would be pleased to hire out their skill with a Colt. Not another man would the Syndicate send. They'd lost one of their best and nothing was worse for their kind of business than to have it known their guns were capable of being beaten.

So it all fell on Rambeau. He must succeed or—well, the Syndicate had no use for living failures at whom men who lived under Syndicate inspired terror might point a finger and gain courage by.

"Forget that actress and concentrate on the herd," the Syndicate man had said before dismissing Rambeau with a casual wave of his hand. "You've too much on now to become involved with the likes of her. You can't afford to buy her fancy bracelets. The men you hire to take that herd are going to come out of your end."

That was the first time, although he'd suspected it all along, that Rambeau was sure he was being watched by spies for the Syndicate. He found himself wondering who they might be; the bartender? possibly; any of the dealers. It could be any of the people he employed. Or it might be anyone, for the Syndicate was a large organisation with members in all walks of life.

On the table in Rambeau's room was a carpet-bag. He galnced at the bag, not knowing what it was, then realising it would be Iowa Parsons' belongings, released to his ownership. He did not know if there was anyone who might want the killer's belongings and was about to sweep the bag to the floor when he realised that Parsons was a frugal man who never spent money if he could help it. The man was one of the best paid guns of the Syndicate and his fees for killing ran to four figures. He might have banked his money, if so there could be a clue to where the money was. Rambeau needed money, for his share of the profits would hardly cover what he would need to pay out to get the herd.

Tipping the bag upside down over his bed Rambeau allowed the contents to fall out. There was little enough, a change of underclothing, a new shirt, two boxes of bullets, one for the .45 Colt revolver, the other .41 Remington rimfire loads, and a wooden box.

Rambeau was about to sweep the articles back into the bag and toss it out of the room when a thought struck him. He lifted up the box and opened the lid, hoping to find some hint as to where Parsons stashed his money. Inside was nothing of the kind. The box contained only two things. One was a

Remington double derringer, the weapon the second box of bullets would be used for. The other object appeared to be a type of card hold-out machine. Rambeau knew something of card hold-outs, they were made to be strapped to the wrist and by an arrangement of springs would catapult the held-out cards into the palm. Rambeau ignored the hold-out for a moment, then a thought struck him. Parsons would never risk any of his money on gambling, in fact, never played any gambling games and so would have no need for the hold-out.

It was then that Rambeau saw the clip, instead of the usual shape, being wide enough to hold the desired playing cards, was made in the shape of a U, just large enough to grip the barrels of that derringer.

Quickly Rambeau removed his coat and dropped it on to the bed, then turned up the cuff on his right shirt sleeve and fixed on the straps of the hold-out. He took up the derringer and clipped it into the restraining U. Then he opened his wardrobe door and faced the full length mirror. Pressing his arm against his side he saw the derringer jerk forward. It did not quite reach his palm so he adjusted the hold-out lower. This time the squat little weapon came correctly into his palm. It arrived in a split second and he brought it up and lined. That was fast, almost as fast as the way that small Texan drew his guns.

Turning down the shirt sleeve after setting the gun again Rambeau donned his jacket and then tried the hold-out. There was no pause as the derringer flashed into his hand and lined again. That was just what he needed, a secret, hidden weapon which could be produced with the speed that these fast men drew their Colts.

Going down the stairs once more Rambeau halted and looked around. Two of his men lounged at the bar, the two who had been with him earlier that week when he tried in the barber's shop to force Vance Brownlow to his will. They caught their boss's nod and came forward, falling in behind him like courtiers following their liege lord. Where he was going they did not know, what he was going to do was not yet explained to them, but they followed him.

Cindy Alban and Miles Hamish followed their usual route from the boarding house in the respectable part of Tombstone to the theatre, where they were due to rehearse their new play. They had to pass through one of the rougher sections of town to reach the theatre but so far had met with nothing but friendly nods and politeness.

In the few days since her arrival Cindy had become well known in Tombstone and well liked. Her songs, her pathetic actions as the poor, down-trodden heroine of some tear-jerking drama, met with almost universal approval. She brought with her a nostalgic note of home, the comfort of a good woman, to men who saw little of female company and less of good women. Of all the men of the town only King Rambeau showed any sign of having designs on her virtue. He was the type of villain which nightly met his well-deserved fate at the hands of the handsome hero, Cindy mused, although he was by far more dangerous, for his threat was real.

"I was always taught never to escort the same lady twice running," Miles Hamish remarked with a smile at the girl. "This makes the fourth day, doesn't it?"

"It does," she answered. "You'll be having me think it is something serious soon, Miles?"

"Don't you think it is?"

Cindy was about to make a reply when she saw the three men who came from a sidestreet and stood blocking the sidewalk. Her fingers bit into Hamish's arm. "Miles, look! It's Rambeau."

Hamish looked forward, saw the way the men stood and knew there was likely to be trouble. The young actor was neither a coward nor a rash fool. He could handle himself in a rough-house brawl but he knew he would have no chance against three men. He also knew Rambeau meant to force his attentions on the girl and could not stand by watching it.

"Hello, songbird," Rambeau said, nodding as the man and girl approached. "I sent you a letter and present."

"Which I returned to you," Cindy answered. "I'm not interested in you or your presents, now I'd like to come past, please."

"Is that so?" Rambeau sneered, then his eyes went to Hamish. "You're not saying much, play-actor. Maybe you're not so much of a hero off the stage."

"Send your two men away and we'll see about it."

Rambeau grinned. "Hear that, boys. The play-actor's getting all uppish. He needs taking down some, doesn't he?"

"We could handle him I reckon, boss," said the taller man, a tough, who was known by the name of Dutchy Schwarz in Tombstone.

"You know, I reckon we could," Rambeau agreed. "Let's see."

Hamish pushed Cindy aside and the girl moved clear, having more sense than get in his way when he would need every chance to move freely. Her eyes went to the three men as they moved towards Hamish. She thought of running for help, but knew that before she could get to the theatre and bring back

Joe Raymond and a couple of stagehands it would be too late. Miles Hamish would be battered into a bloody wreck and never able to play a hero again.

"Three to one. Now that's what I call good odds."

The words were spoken from an alley nearby and brought the attention of the entire group to it. Standing with one shoulder resting against the wall was a thin, sallow man in gambler's dress but with the butt of a ten gauge shot pistol showing from under the left side of his coat, where it was held in a shoulder clip.

The three men halted their advance. They froze like rabbits when faced by a weasel and the description was very apt for that thin man was Doc Holliday and his reputation built him to be every bit as wild and dangerous as any weasel.

"Are you cutting in, Holliday?" Rambeau asked.

"Now that's a good question," came the mocking reply. "Make your play and find out, one way or the other."

Rambeau felt scared and could almost feel the fear in his men. They might chance stacking against Doc Holliday in a pinch, or when primed for it by bottled brave-maker. They were neither primed, nor fighting drunk right now and they were not willing to match shots with Holliday. He was a dying man, they knew that, his life meant nothing to him, or so rumour had it. A man did not stack against someone who was not worried if he lived or died, without great provocation, or great risk. There was another thing stopping those hired guns. The shot pistol Holliday carried had only two barrels but each barrel carried a deadly nine-buckshot charge which would tear a man in half at close range. He would certainly get one of them, possibly both. If a survivor killed Holliday he would be no better case for he would have the Earp brothers hunting him to avenge the killing of their friend.

"Reckon you boys have business some other place, haven't you?" Holliday asked coldly, his eyes flickering to the two gunmen.

The two men licked their lips and glanced nervously at their boss. For a moment Rambeau thought of using his wrist holstered derringer, then a nagging doubt hit him. He was far from the East and in New York the gangster's weapons were his hands, feet, a club, a knife, or a set of Tammany mittens, as knuckledusters were called. The gun had little or no use in the work of the New York crook and Rambeau was such a man. He had made the incredible blunder of not checking to see if the derringer was loaded. If he started to draw and the weapon was empty he would be dead before he even knew it, for there would be no hesitation in the way Holliday acted.

"Clear the sidewalk, all of you."

There was no mild request in Holliday's words. It was an order and one which only a roaring Colt could refuse to obey.

"Do you want to hold his men off my back, Doc?" Hamish inquired, for he knew Holliday, having been introduced at a party given in the show's honour by a prominent Law and Order Party member.

"I'm doing it for the young lady, not for you, Hamish," Holliday answered. "I reckon a fist fight might be amusing, but she doesn't want her hero with his face all marked up."

"Please, Miles," gasped Cindy urgently, gripping the actor's arm once more.

Hamish wanted to stay behind and try conclusions with Rambeau, to prove to the girl that he could handle things off-stage as well as on. Yet he knew that Rambeau would go all out to damage his face and he did have the show to consider. Without Hamish to play the hero roles Madame Paula would be in trouble. Regretfully, dealing with Rambeau must be postponed until some later date.

Rambeau and his men cleared the sidewalk and Cindy took Hamish's arm, forcing him by the other men. Holliday stood as he had all the time, his sallow face showing nothing of what he thought.

"The actor might find himself a shy girl one of these days," Rambeau snarled, watching the man and girl walk away.

Holliday's lips drew back in a cold smile like the death's head grin as his tallon-like right hand lifted towards the butt of his shot pistol and for a moment Rambeau thought he'd gone too far.

"You've got a yeller streak, King!" purred Holliday, his eyes catching the fear which flickered across the saloon-keeper's face. "Now listen to me, and listen real good. If anything happens to that girl, or the actor, I'll kill you on sight. Just remember, anything at all. You can take my word on it."

Rambeau looked at the thin face and read death on it. Any attempt at revenge on either the girl or the actor would have to wait now. Holliday was a strange man and might easily forget the stand he'd taken in a few days' time.

For all that, in the days which followed, Rambeau found a cooling air in the way the Earps acted towards him. No longer was his saloon on their list of places to stop for drinks. There was a different air around the town too, the men who had backed away from Rambeau as a Syndicate man now grew bold again.

There was another problem facing Rambeau. He could not get men to handle the stealing of the herd. The hired guns who hung around Tombstone grew evasive or even disdainful when he asked them. Those hired fighting men knew the reputation of the Wedge trail crew and more, they knew the reputation of the three men from the Rio Hondo country who rode with the cattle.

It was a worrying time for Rambeau. He had the contract for the sale of the herd arranged; they would be driven to a small place near Tombstone and butchered by skilled men, then the meat sold in town. The end was prepared, there only remained the most vital detail, getting hold of the herd.

It was two days before the herd was due to arrive and Rambeau still had not managed to hire the men he so urgently needed. He was worried as there had been a cold warning from the Syndicate. They were having trouble, people were sitting back and waiting for the first failure of a Syndicate man's project. It could break them if he failed to get the herd. Yet for all that they still could not supply him with gunmen, they needed every man they could lay hands on to hold down the restless spirits on whom they preyed.

At noon Rambeau entered his saloon after a fruitless morning looking for men. He was crossing towards the stairs when he saw a tallish, round-shouldered and prematurely bald man sitting with back to the wall. The man looked up, a cold grin on his Indian dark face as the saloon-keeper approached.

"Howdy, Burt," Rambeau greeted. "Are you working?"

"Depends on what," replied Burt Alvord.

"Something that will pay well."

"Sorry, King, that's not my line," growled the dark man. "I don't know if the herd got through the Apaches, but knowing the men who're driving it I'd bet they did. In that case I'm not stacking up against them."

Rambeau felt cold disappointment. Burt Alvord was a man well fancied by some for the two shooting matches. He'd been a fast-gun deputy with a reputation for bringing in dead prisoners. He was known to have contacts on both sides of the border and of either steering a wanted man across, or killing him for the reward on his dead body.

Taking out his wallet, Rambeau said, "No hard feelings, Burt."

"Could put you in the way of somebody who might take on."

"Who?"

"How much?—Then who."

Rambeau looked at the Indian dark face and felt anger. There was only one of two ways to deal with a man like

Burt Alvord. Pay him or kill him. Rambeau had the sleeve-hidden derringer loaded now but he did not intend using it.

"That depends on what you have to offer."

Alvord grinned. "Say a dozen bad-hat Mormons who need money to skip the border. I stood to gain on them one way or the other. Figured to win a hundred at your poker table tonight. I'll lose that if I go for them."

"Fifty down and fifty when the men show."

"Don't be a piker, King," Alvord purred. "Make it an even hundred now and the same when I bring Pilbourne in. There, I've given you that much."

Rambeau frowned. He'd heard of Pilbourne. The man was wanted, badly wanted, by the Elders of the Mormon Church. He was a bad Mormon who'd robbed and killed Gentile men and stolen their livestock. This was not regarded as too serious a crime in the Mormon book, but he'd killed an Elder of their church and looted the church funds.

"You couldn't find him, King," Alvord warned, seeing the expression which crossed the other man's face. "And I'd surely take it unkind on any man who tried."

"I want them tonight at the latest."

"That could cost you more money, but I'll be generous," Alvord answered. "I'll have him here by ten o'clock."

Rambeau watched the other man slouch away, then went up to his room. He took a map from the desk and spread it out. It was an Army survey map of the area around Tombstone and he ran his finger along a pencilled line from the Carne River to the town. He tapped the X Parsons made on the map when they first planned this business. The original plan had been to allow Brownlow to run his herd alone, then hit it and wipe out the trail crew at the draw near Tombstone, well beyond the area where a large band of Apaches might be expected. They planned that first, then to force the rancher to take them in as partners. This was their second plan, allow the herd to reach the draw and ambush it, wiping out Brownlow and his crew.

The rest of the day dragged by and Rambeau had little interest in anything which happened in his place. A miner hit a lucky streak on the roulette wheel, a streak so lucky that it licked even the crooked wheel which ran a large percentage for the house. Normally Rambeau would have either steered the man out, or arranged for him to wake up in some dark alley with his pockets emptied. Tonight Rambeau did not even give the man a second glance.

Sharp at ten o'clock Alvord arrived. He was alone and Rambeau felt a momentary annoyance, then realised that a man like Pilbourne would never show himself in a saloon, especially a well-known one in Tombstone.

"Go in the back room, King," Alvord said. "Hand me the hundred now, open the back door and he's waiting out there."

Rambeau handed over the hundred dollars, turned and went into the back room. He opened the door and for an instant thought Alvord had robbed him. Then a man stepped into the light, a big, gaunt, whiskered man in a dirty black suit and with a low tied Colt at his side. He came into the room with a wolf-cautious step, but shook his head when Rambeau went to close the door.

"I've two men out there," warned the gaunt man. "They are stood so they can cover all the room."

"I'm not armed," Rambeau answered, showing his gunless sides. "Take a seat and I'll pour you a drink. You're Pilbourne, are you?"

"I am."

"Can your men all handle guns—and cattle?"

"We have often handled both."

"Then I want you to dress as Apaches. I've got clothing stashed away that'll fit your men, and I want you to hit a trail herd of about five hundred head. You'll have to kill all the men and a woman who are riding with it. Make it look like real Apache work."

"Just that?" asked Pilbourne. "Why can't you get men from town to handle it?"

"Because the herd's being handled by the Wedge. You've maybe heard of them. And riding with it are Dusty Fog, Mark Counter and the Ysabel Kid."

"They are men I've heard of. All can handle their weapons well and it will not be easy to take them."

"The way I plan it they *will* be easy," Rambeau answered. "It's near enough to Tombstone for you to hit them when they're relaxed and thinking they're safe and far enough out for the shooting not to be heard and attract attention."

"In that case what's to stop me and my men just hitting this herd for ourselves?" asked Pilbourne.

"You don' know where to hit, for one thing. For another, not even the Clantons could pay you as well as I can. You don't know anyone in town who would take it off your hands and it is here in Tombstone the money's to be made. I'll give you a thousand dollars and the same to be split among your men if you pull it off."

"Do you know when the herd is coming?"

"Neither when nor if," Rambeau admitted. "The Apaches may have got it, although I'd bet that crew could get through.

But at latest it should be coming through the draw I'll point out on the map in two days' time. I'll make an agreement with you. If the herd comes through and you get it before the Fair I'll pay you what I said. If it hasn't got through I'll pay Alvord to get you and your men out of the country. If it comes through after the County Fair is over, which isn't likely, then you can have it and sell it for what you can get."

"I want that in writing," Pilbourne replied.

It was some moments before Rambeau would agree to put his name to anything so incriminating, but he gave in at last. This was his only chance, his last hope of getting the herd. He took out a sheet of paper, a pen and ink, from a desk in the table. The back room was used for big stake poker games and writing materials were often needed when some player ran out of ready cash and wished to give a note on a bet. The letter Rambeau wrote would be enough to hang him and might leave him open to blackmail later, but he doubted it. Pilbourne and his men were fleeing from something more deadly than United States law, they were fleeing from the Danites, the dreaded Avenging Angels, the police, regulators and avengers of the Mormon people. Once this business was over Pilbourne and his men would make the most of their time heading for the comparative safety of the Mexican border.

"Where are the clothes?" Pilbourne asked, folding the sheet of paper and sliding it into a special slot between the leather and lining of his riding boot.

"I've got them in a trunk up in my room. We can get them without going through the saloon. I'll tell you where to deliver the cattle. I'll leave the money waiting for you there and I'll want that letter back then."

It was midnight before Pilbourne left, but he had a clear plan laid out for him, one he could follow. Rambeau was contented as he went to bed that night.

The following day there was excitement for a soldier, riding despatch between two of the Forts, came into Tombstone with word that he'd seen a trailherd. From what the soldier said Rambeau guessed the herd would be arriving at the draw the following day. His main plans were all made, a fast horse ready to take him with all the money he could get down below the border before the Syndicate could know he was planning a doublecross. There was only one thing left to do. He called in all the hired men of the saloon and told them he expected trouble that night and they would, on pain of offending the Syndicate, back him in it. Lastly he called aside Dutchy

Schwartz and the other man and offered them a sizeable chunk of money to do something for him.

There was a hard and evil grin on Rambeau's face as he sat waiting for the night which should bring him word that the herd was in Pilbourne's hands and his money was on its way. It would bring something more. He took a sheet of paper from the desk in his room and wrote a letter which would bring Miles Hamish forth to a murderous beating and leave him disfigured for life and would also bring the girl Cindy Alban into his clutches. He would leave Tombstone with something to remember the name King Rambeau.

CHAPTER TWELVE

At the Draw

"DAMN THE HEAT, the flies, this stinking stain, everything!"

Pilbourne looked at the speaker with a cold, grim expression on his face. He and all his men wore the trade shirts, buckskin trousers and headbands of Apaches, with long lank black wigs and dark stain adding to the picture they made. They were lying in whatever shade they could find, all eyes on the rolling dust cloud which was coming closer all the time. It didn't look a whole lot of dust for five hundred head, Pilbourne thought, but he did not know for sure what the country was like out there.

The draw through which the herd must pass lay below Pilbourne and his men. There was a flat and open trail running down the centre of the draw, but on either side of it rocks and scrubby bushes offered good cover. The slopes rose up on either side, in some places gently, in others sheer and steep. Pilbourne's men were halfway down one of the more gentle parts, an area which offered good cover to them and places where they could lay concealed, their rifles lining on the trail. He'd split his gang into two parts, one at either side of the trail, the men taking up fighting positions ready, each picking his own in a way which showed they knew what they were doing. The herd would be well within the killing area, the cowhands holding the cattle bunched and so would be under the guns. Pilbourne's men were fair shots and could be expected to cut down the cowhands in one roaring volley. The herd would break, stampede, but Pilbourne had told half of his men to run for horses as soon as the cattle broke. The horses, up over the rims, tethered and waiting, would be grabbed by three men from either side and sent after the herd. The remaining men would deal with any of the trail crew who might have been missed by the first volley.

There was a cold, cruel and efficient way about Pilbourne's plan, he took no chances and was callous as to the fact that he might cause the death of a dozen men and a woman. They meant nothing to him, nothing more than a thousand dollars with which to get well clear of the vengeance of the Danites.

"Stop whining," he snarled at the man. "I feel those things as you do. This is far better than facing the wrath of the Danites, isn't it?"

"It is," the man agreed. "With the money for those cattle I will go south and make sure they do not find me."

"Then stop whining," snarled Pilbourne.

"What of the horse I thought I heard in the night?" asked the man worriedly.

Pilbourne looked across at the other man with cold eyes. They made camp in a bosque near the draw and the previous night this man, while on sentry, had wakened the others, saying he thought he'd heard a horse moving in the darkness. There had been no sound to greet the ears of the others and they tended to scoff at the idea.

"You were either hearing things, or it was a stray," Pilbourne replied. He looked to where the dust was getting very close, although there was still no sign of the men who handled the herd. "Get to your place and I will find mine."

Over the bank the other men were moving into their places ready. Pilbourne darted to a place where the cliff rose steep for a way and underneath the shelter offered by the slope were two rocks behind which he might hide and fire his rifle in some safety.

Nearer the dust rolled, vague shapes showing in it where men rode the herd and kept them coming. Pilbourne was not a man who had done much work with cattle, no matter what his boast to Rambeau had been. He'd worked on a Mormon farm and his knowledge of legitimate cattle herding had been gained with slow and docile milk-cows. His other knowledge of cattle herding had been on the wrong side of the law, when speed was of an urgent necessity if a man did not want to feel the hairy touch of a hangman's noose around his neck. So Pilbourne saw nothing unusual in the speed the dust cloud was approaching and did not think it strange a herd of cattle being taken to a legitimate market was getting pushed too fast.

Now the cattle were near the opening of the draw, or those dust wrapped shapes were. The ground was hard and stony here and as Pilbourne opened his mouth to let out a wild Indian yell to alert his men the "cattle" came into view from the dust.

Pilbourne's hands gripped his rifle, sighting it down ready to tumble the point rider nearest to him. His finger rested lightly on the Winchester's trigger and was about to squeeze when he saw—and so did every one of his men—that no cattle were running from the dust cloud. Only horses, riderless horses, streaming along. Of the men who drove the herd there was no sight at the moment.

"It's a trick!" screamed one of the men, rearing up into view and waving his rifle. "They're——"

That was his last word alive. Johnny Raybold came out of the dust cloud, towing a heavy weighted sack from his saddle. Once more they'd proved that dust had its use and Pilbourne's men fell for it as had the Apache braves. Johnny gave no time to gloating over the success of the trick. His Winchester rifle was in his shoulder even while his big horse ran at full speed. The rifle cracked and the exposed man went over backwards, a bullet in his head.

Even before the draw threw back echoes of the rifle shot Johnny had unshipped from the saddle of his racing horse and lit down running. He hit the ground behind a rock, his rifle coming out to make another man duck back before he could send a bullet at the other riders.

The horses, the herd's remuda, went on, coming out of the dust cloud where it ended on the hard ground. Rusty Willis, Doc Leroy and two of the new hands were with the horses, each man dismounting as fast as he could. One of the new hands was not quite fast enough. Pilbourne and his men were over their surprise and the rifles bellowed out. The cowhand was leaping from his horse when lead caught him and he seemed to collapse in mid air, his body hitting the dirt of the trail rolling and then laying limp against a rock. Doc and the others made it to the rocks by the side of the trail, flattening down and waiting for their chance. They'd heard the wild war yell, seen the Indian-like shapes and thought Apaches were attacking them. This gave them little worry, for they could see this was only a small band and their escape through the encircling Apache net made them a little contemptuous of the much-vaunted Apaches.

It was at that moment they saw that there was an urgent need for them to shoot and shoot accurately.

In the rear of the herd, wild with excitement, rode young Rin, the wrangler. In the heat of the moment, carried away by the wild ride through the dust and out into danger, the boy forgot, or ignored, every order Dusty Fog had given him the previous day. Rin should have turned his horse, racing it up the slope and around, clear of the shooting beyond the top of the rim, then come down and picked up the racing remuda when they tired from their run.

Now was long past the moment when he should have turned for, whooping like an Indian, flattened along the neck of his horse, fanning its ears with his hat and working his Kelly petmaker spurs like wild, he sent his horse after the remuda. Rin was young, not yet having reached his sixteenth birthday. On the last drive north with Stone a bunch of Osaga renegades tried to run off the remuda. Rin turned, drew his old Navy Colt and charged the men even before Johnny, Rusty and Doc came sweeping back to aid him. He'd fired three wild shots and before his three friends opened fire, saw one dirty, vermin crawling Indian go backwards from his horse. Rin knew in that moment he'd had his man for breakfast. He'd ridden away from the herd and been violently sick after that, but his courage was untouched by the incident. Courage or pure blind wildness it might have been, putting himself out like that. He did not know which it was, only that he did not intend to allow the remuda to scatter if he could help it.

Lead slapped the air and whistled around Rin as he rode. Johnny was on his feet, racing forward, his rifle crashing as he darted from cover to cover, trying to save the wild and reckless boy. The others all fired fast too. The men on the slopes were all shooting, throwing lead and it seemed that some of it must catch.

It did.

Johnny jerked under the impact of a bullet, staggered and crashed down into the hard ground. He fell in plain view but was still alive, as showed in the way he tried to crawl to some kind of safety and avoid the lead which kicked up dust and dirt spurts around him. Pilbourne and his men saw the cowhand was wounded, saw they had no chance of getting the fast riding boy who was now through their ambush and streaking after the remuda like the devil hunting down a yearling. So the rifles were turned to make an end of the wounded man and cut down any man who tried to help him.

Everything was in favour of Pilbourne and his men now. They had the others under the guns and were preparing to make the most of it. Already one of the cowhand bunch, Rusty Willis, was darting forward to try and rescue his friend. He should make the next victim. The herd would be coming along, shorthanded and could still be taken. Everything was in favour of the Mormons? or so Pilbourne thought, and it was a good thought.

Yet it was not correct.

Dusty Fog, Mark Counter and the Ysabel Kid came into view on the rim above Pilbourne. They came riding their big stallions and each held a saddlegun in his hands as he came into sight.

Dusty had known men were waiting at the draw, known it

because the Ysabel Kid had seen their camp and only the alert ears of the sentry prevented his getting in close enough to know more of the waiters. He'd not taken any chances, but had slipped away in Indian silence and warned Dusty, who laid on this surprise move. That it had cost one man his life was not Dusty's fault.

The Kid's old yellow boy rifle flowed to his shoulder and spat out, lancing flame down towards the valley. The bullet caught one of the watching men between the shoulder blades and tossed his lifeless body forward on to the rocks.

Dusty and Mark sent their horses down the slope in a wild sliding run that would have unseated a lesser rider. They were cavalrymen in training and their belief was that the best way to take an enemy was charge him while he was unprepared.

Down the slope they came, the Kid following them on foot, sending the big white stallion back over the rim to safety. Yet even as he ran the Kid kept up a rapid and accurate fire which did much to save Johnny's life, for no man before the Kid dare stay up long enough to take a careful aim. Then the Kid found a spot and came to a halt. His pants pockets bulged with fodder for his old rifle as he forced the flat-nosed .44 bullets through the loading slot and fired again with barely a pause.

The surprise attack from above shook Pilbourne and his men, but they rallied quickly to it. So far only one of the six on Pilbourne's side was dead, having been caught by the Kid's bullet. The rest turned their attention to the attackers from above them.

Dusty saw a man come up from behind a rock, saw the Sharps carbine as the man brought it up. Dusty left his saddle, hit the ground running, went over a rock in a diving roll. He heard the crash of the Sharps and the impact as the lead hit the rock over which he'd just dived. Dusty ended his roll on his feet and the Winchester carbine spat, held hip high. The man with the Sharps spun around even as he opened the breech to insert a fresh load.

Swinging from the hips, Dusty levered another bullet into the carbine's breech and threw a fast shot which dusted stone chips into the face of a Mormon who showed himself in an attempt to throw down on Mark.

Mark left his saddle and the big blood bay went on down the slope as its rider hit the ground. Following Dusty's paint, the stallion turned back up the slope and over the top and slowed down, joining the Kid's white and waiting for its master. Mark, however, was laying behind a rock and shooting at the men across the valley as he saw they were trying to get Rusty in his attempt to save Johnny.

The Kid's rifle suddenly beat out a tattoo, blazing as fast as he could work the lever and take a fresh sight. One of his shots, thrown at a man on the opposite slope, caused the same man to rear up. Below, Mark's sighting eye lined on the man, trigger finger squeezed and the Model 78 Winchester kicked back hard. The man's upwards jerk changed direction as the .44.40 bullet struck him and he went down once more.

In rushes from rock to rock Rusty made for Johnny. He hurdled one rock and went rolling over another, flattened for an instant behind yet a third, then darted forward to pull Johnny back behind the largest rock, into a place where he was out of danger from the rifles above him. Rusty knew, even though only a matter of a couple of minutes had elapsed, that he owed his life to the Kid's riflework. There had been times when lead sang close to him and he knew that but for the Kid spoiling any chance of a careful aim the lead would have been much closer.

Even as Rusty brought Johnny to safety there was another man moving in. It was Doc Leroy, his jacket pockets carrying his simple surgical tools and some bandages. At times like this, when going into a fight, Doc always went prepared for any wounds which might come his way. He knew Johnny was in need of his help and was going to do what he could.

Looking around, Rusty saw Doc coming and knew there would not be room for all three of them behind the rock. So without a word he hurdled from cover and went racing along through the gauntlet of fire again. Just ahead the side of the draw rose sheer and there was something of an overhang which would shield him from the men on that side, while a rocky ridge would give him shelter from the others. Rusty made it, diving the last few feet and landing in comparative safety, then rolled over to fire up the slope. He could see Mark, Dusty and the Kid, lifted his hand in a cheery wave and jerked it down as a bullet slapped the rock near to it.

Behind the rocks Doc Leroy was working fast. He cut the cloth away from around the wound, cleaned the blood as best he could and grunted. Johnny was still alive, which meant the bullet had not pierced anything vital. Doc knew much about the care and attention of gunshot wounds and he used every bit of skill he possessed now.

"How is he, Doc?" yelled the second of the new hands as he fired up the slope. "We'll rip the heart out of those red devils if he dies."

Doc, never too amiable while working, growled out a curse

and ignored the question. Right now he was too busy, his thin, seemingly boneless hands working fast as he probed for the bullet. He found the hardness with the tip of the probe and with care opened the gripping end. The probe had been made on his special design for just such work and he felt the ends close on the bullet. Carefully he drew back. A moan from the now unconscious Johnny brought an end to the movement. Doc was sweating but cool enough. He waited until Johnny was still again, then withdrew the bullet. Not until then did Doc breathe a sigh of relief. Johnny was far from being safe yet, but he was better off now the lead was out of him.

Rusty Willis, in his place under the slope, was worried as to how Johnny was, but he knew better than bother Doc with questions at such a time. His eyes scanned the slope, picking out where Dusty, Mark and the Kid were and spotting the remaining "Apaches". They were now exercising some caution and he could not get a clear shot at any of them.

One of the men above Rusty started to make a careful advance down the slope, sliding from cover to cover like a buck Apache. So good was he and so close the cover, that he had made a considerable distance before any of the men on the other slope saw him. The Kid was first. He saw a splash of colour where no such colour should be. It was only there for an instant, then gone, but that was long enough and more to alert a man as keen sighted as the Ysabel Kid. Now the Kid's rifle was silent. He ignored the slap of a bullet into the rock close to him as he concentrated on that splash of colour and what caused it.

The crawling man was almost on the overhang before he gave the Kid a chance to do anything. Even then there was little to aim at. There was enough for the Kid to send a bullet whistling at and the lead struck close. The man gave a yell, rolled himself over the rock and down the slope.

Rusty saw dirt, then small rocks trickling over the edge of the overhang, he saw a shape falling and dust got into his eyes, partially blinding him. The man fell, turned in the air, and lit down on his feet. His rifle crashed and the bullet sent chips splattering Rusty's face. Rusty flung himself to one side, his Winchester held in his right hand. The rifle crashed and the butt lashed back to hit hard into Rusty's side. The bullet caught the man under the chin, angled up and burst out of the top of his head, sending the long black wig and headband flying.

Up until that moment Rusty and the other cowhands had believed they were fighting Apaches. Even the Kid did not know for sure they were not, although something had been nagging at his thoughts as he shot. Rusty saw the man reeling back, saw the wig go flying and the band of white skin where the dye had not covered.

"A stinking renegade!"

So excited and annoyed was Rusty that he exposed himself and then flopped back as a bullet grazed his neck. He felt something hot running down under his collar even as he hit the ground.

"Renegades!" Dusty barked to Mark.

"I thought they handled the ambush bad for Apaches," Mark called back. "We'd best show them!"

Not even a bad Apache was hated as was a renegade, a man who raided dressed as an Indian. The renegade could never feel safe in his disguise, for the hand of white and red men was against them. Only the most cold-blooded and murderous outlaw would adopt such tactics and to such a man no mercy was shown.

"I got it," whooped the Kid, as he also watched the man reel back and lose his wig. "I knew there was something wrong. That bunch're all wearing boots."

The Kid had been worried by some nagging doubt from the start of the fight. The men looked like Apaches, from what he could see of them, yet some instinct, some stirring of his wild Comanche blood, insisted that these men were not Indians. Now he could see clearly what it was. The Apache would take many things from a white-eye as war trophy and for use. He would take a hat, a shirt, perhaps a set of pants, even underwear. He would take any kind of rifle and sing praises to his Gods all night if the rifle was a Winchester. He would take a revolver and a gunbelt to wear it on. He would not take a pair of boots. They were something he had no use for and would never wear. A white man's boots were useless to the Apache, too noisy for his silent way of moving.

Pilbourne looked around him, saw the last man on his side of the draw crumple over and go down. Then he looked up and saw a larger cloud of dust was approaching. There was no doubt what the dust was caused by. It was the herd and with it rode reinforcements for these cowhands.

The Mormons, on the opposite slope, saw it, those who were able to see anything. That was all they needed to see and started to back away up the slope. Only two made it, passing over the slope fast, the others were still shapes on the ground or moving in their last throes, for from their cover only their heads showed and a hit was likely to prove fatal.

Dusty saw the men go and saw a danger in their going.

They'd lost out here and were running, but they might come on young Rin with the remuda. The boy alone would be a good target for the hate and the horses make up in loot for the herd which was safe from them.

"Lon!" Dusty barked. "Take out after Rin and the remuda!"

The Kid gave a wave and started to move back. It was lucky he was always cautious and did not expose himself any more than he needed. Even so, the damage was serious when it came.

Pilbourne found he'd made a basic and deadly dangerous mistake. The place he picked for the fight gave him real good cover, but there was only one way out of it. And covering that escape route were two men who had already showed they could call down their shots with accuracy. He was trapped, the only ways left out were surrender and a certain hanging or fight to the death and try to take as many of them as possible with him. With the wolf-savage hate and lust for killing which drove him on to the outlaw trails, Pilbourne picked the latter way. He saw that black-dressed boy who handled the rifle so well, saw him for an instant, brought up his rifle and took a fast shot.

Fast taken or not, the shot came as close to taking the Kid's life as a man needed and caused more concern to the Kid than a wound would have. The Kid felt a sudden jarring shock and the rifle, the old yellow boy, was torn from his hands. He saw the gun hit the ground and dived forward, scooping it up in passing. Landing in the open, he rolled fast, felt lead strike just behind him and was in cover again.

One look was all the Kid needed to tell him the rifle was finished. The old yellow boy, one of the first of the model which came to be known as the 1866, had come to him just after the war when he first joined Dusty Fog in his quest to bring back Bushrod Sheldon from Mexico. Since then the rifle had never left the Kid, had been in his saddleboot or his hands ready for use. He knew that rifle, knew how it threw at ranges beyond anything the light load of the bullet was meant to be reliable at. Now it was gone, smashed by a bullet which had wrecked the breech mechanism.

The Kid might have been thankful the bullet wrecked his rifle instead of his body, but he was not. All too well the Kid knew the calibre of the men he would be matched against in the Tombstone Rifle Shoot. They were men who knew their rifles as he knew his, men capable of calling down their shots with an accuracy that the Kid would find hard to equal with a new weapon in his hands.

Cold rage gripped the Kid and it took all his self-control to prevent a wild rage-filled rush towards where Pilbourne was hidden. Then sanity came back and he knew that he must get after the remuda. Without his rifle he was of no use against the men in his defensive position and Dusty could far better deal with the man. So the Kid turned and went up the slope, went fast and keeping in cover, for he'd seen how well this renegade could shoot.

Passing over the ridge, the Kid gave a whistle and his white stallion loped back to him. He caught the saddlehorn and swung astride in a lithe Indian-like bound. Turning the white stallion, he headed along the rim over the draw to where he could get down to the bottom in safety and head after the horses. There was anger in his heart, anger and disappointment, for his chances of winning that magnificent "One of a Thousand" Winchester were well below the odds of three to one the bartender at the Bucket of Blood first started him.

The Kid found Rin three miles down the trail. The youngster had caught up with the fleeing horses and now had them under control. He was allowing them to graze and settle down and rode eagerly to where the Kid approached.

"Did we get 'em, Kid?" he whooped excitedly.

"Some of them, boy," answered the Kid. "Why in hell didn't you go around them like Dusty told you?"

"Shucks, it was quicker the way I come and they didn't hit me."

For a moment the Kid felt anger and almost knocked the boy from his saddle. Then the anger went. Rin was young, wild, reckless, but young. He'd sand to burn and that should never be held against any youngster. Johnny was hit bad but could just have easily have taken the lead in the normal course of the attack. It would do no good to blame Rin for it.

"That's right," he growled. "*They* didn't hit you. But Dusty's going to whale the tar out of you when he lays hands on you."

Rin grinned. The prospect of a hiding did not worry him any. He'd been chapped, held across the wagon tail and had a pair of bull-hide chaps applied to his pants seat without yelling; that had been when he grew slack and nearly lost the remuda in a drive. He reckoned he could take another chapping for the risk he'd run by not following orders.

The Kid sat his big white for a moment, then came to his feet, standing on the saddle to scan the surrounding country. He could see no sign of the two fleeing renegades and guessed they would be headed for the border as fast as their horses carried them. They had seen their gang cut down by the guns of the Texas trail crew. They wanted only to get out of this country and would not bother the remuda.

"We going back to the herd, Kid?" Rin asked.

"Start the remuda back slow, boy," answered the Kid. "I'm headed on to Tombstone. Tell Dusty I've gone to see if I can get another yellow boy."

Without knowing what the Kid was doing, Dusty got down to the business of dislodging Pilbourne from behind the rocks. In this Dusty was acting in the manner of a trained lawman, not as a cowhand. There was a cold determination about the way Dusty flattened down behind a large rock and glanced at Mark. They had been in the same position before and not just the once.

Rusty and the other cowhand made their way up the slope in darting rushes and flattened down near to where Dusty and Mark crouched with their rifles. The cowhand lifted his head and called:

"Dusty, Doc says Johnny'll live."

"Keep down!" Dusty's words cracked like a whip and were echoed by the flat crack of Pilbourne's rifle.

The cowhand flattened down again, his Stetson spinning from his head, so close had the bullet come. A grin came to the man's face and he turned to look across at Dusty, expecting to see an answering grin. There was none, only a cold hard and grim stare and a harsh:

"Keep your fool head down, this's no kid's game!"

Rusty moved fast, darting across the open space and flattening down by the other cowhand's side.

"You do what Dusty says," he warned.

"You in there!" Dusty barked out. "You behind the rocks. Throw out your guns and come on out with your hands raised."

"Go to hell!"

Pilbourne screamed the words back and fired a fast shot in the direction of where Dusty and Mark knelt. He jerked the rifle back and forced bullets into the breech, waiting and wondering what the cowhands meant to do.

"This's your last chance!" called Dusty.

The cowhand looked towards Rusty, surprised, and said:

"I once saw a company of Texas Rangers taking a bad wanted man. The ranger captain sounded just like Dusty."

There was a grim smile on Rusty's face. "I was a deputy under him in Quiet Town just after the war. I tell you, Frank, no ranger captain could see the day when he can teach Dusty anything about handling something like this."

Behind their rock Dusty and Mark studied the situation.

They thought as lawmen still, hard, tough and efficient lawmen. In the make-up of such men there was no taking foolish risks. They would face a man, even one in a position like this, alone, and chance being killed if they had to. Yet they would also take no chances and use the resources of all four men to take the killer now if the affair could be played that way.

"Reckon I could bounce a couple in on him, Dusty?" Mark asked.

"Make a try if you like," Dusty replied.

Mark aimed carefully, while Dusty and Rusty raised their own rifles ready to fire and hold Pilbourne down if he tried to retaliate. Mark fired, trying to send his bullet bouncing from the rock face and down on to the hidden man. The bullet flattened and left a leaden blotch on the wall. It did no damage. Nor did the next Mark threw and the big blond knew there was no chance of sending a ricochet in and dislodging the man.

"No go," said Dusty.

Behind the rock Pilbourne eased himself into a position where he hoped he would be able to shoot at the four men. His eyes went to the sky, it was gone noon and he could hold out until dark. Then there might be a chance to escape. He was alone and would take his chances in the dark against men who would hesitate to shoot for fear of hitting their friends.

The herd was moving along the draw now, the bedwagon already there and with Johnny loaded into it. Short handed as they were, the trail crew could not leave the cattle to see if they could help Dusty and the others. Pilbourne twisted around and got himself into a position where he could see and shoot down at the hands.

"Pull back or I'll cut down the riders!" he yelled.

Now there was a real urgent need to dislodge, either capture or kill the man or have their friends run the gauntlet of bullets from the rifle of a man who had proved he could call down his shots with some skill.

"Dusty!" Mark said suddenly. "Mind that time we were hunting cougar with your Cousin Betty? Just before we made that drive to Mulrooney?"

Dusty looked at his big friend and was about to growl out an angry demand as to the reason for the question. Then he recalled which hunt Mark meant, although it was far from the only hunt they'd had with Betty Hardin.

"Sure, I remember," he answered. "The dogs treed that ole cat and we couldn't see it. Then Betty saw the tip of its tail hanging down from the branches and she lined at——"

The words came to a halt as Dusty saw what Mark was getting at. From the edge of the rocks something black showed. It took Dusty just a bare split second to realise what that something was. The man behind the rock had moved, settled down to a safe shooting position where he could fire down on the trail below and in doing so was exposing the toe of one boot.

"You or me?" Dusty asked, without looking at Mark.

"My rifle likely hold closer," Mark replied. "But you're the better shot."

Dusty settled down and lined his carbine. It was a real tribute coming from Mark, who was a better than fair shot with the rifle. Mark knew that there was only one man living who might possibly equal the Kid in the skilled aiming of a long gun, and that man was Dusty Fog. The toe of the boot offered small enough target in all account and Mark knew there would be only the one shot at it.

"This's your last chance!" Dusty barked, even then not willing to kill the man if there was a chance of forcing him to surrender. "Come out or die."

Pilbourne had heard that kind of tone. It was a tough lawman speaking to a dangerous killer and meant every word said. He could come out and risk a trial, or he could force his play to the bitter end.

"I'll drop the point man!" he roared. "You make——"

The carbine lined, there was no time to ask again. Dusty knew without needing to look that Mark's rifle was lifted and ready to take up the second card of the deal. It was only left to Dusty to haul the ace from the hole and bring off the showdown, Dusty and that twenty inch barrelled Winchester carbine which the Kid always scoffed at as being grossly inaccurate at over ten feet.

The carbine spat and suddenly Pilbourne felt something strike his toes, sending agony through him, bringing a scream of pain from his lips as he reared up. The scream was cut off abruptly by the bark of Mark's rifle and the bullet it spewed out right straight into the up-jerking head. Pilbourne never knew what hit him; he spun, crashed into the wall behind him and went down.

Dusty, Mark and Rusty ran forward, but they came with their rifles held ready for instant use. They came from both sides, moving in fast towards where the killer was sprawled, arms thrown out and rifle laying well clear of him. If he had been holding the rifle they would have shot again, for that was how they were trained, never to trust a man who held a gun.

The cowhand watched the three men and wondered how

he could have ridden with them for the past days without knowing all their traits. Rusty was acting like Dusty and Mark, acting like a well-trained lawman in this moment. The cowhand did not know of the hard lessons Dusty forced home on Rusty while they wore law badges in Quiet Town. Rusty had never forgotten those hard, firm rules Dusty laid down for dealing with a dangerous killer.

"He's cashed," Dusty said. "Cut down to the trail and ask Stone to hold the herd clear of the draw and get a couple of the boys back here."

Rusty went fast and Mark turned up the slope to collect the horses. Dusty looked down at the dead man's boot; the bullet had torn the sole badly and the toes were a bloody mess. The stitching of the upper was split and Dusty saw something white. He bent forward and extracted a sheet of paper the man had kept concealed in a hideout of a kind Dusty knew. Unfolding the paper, Dusty looked down the writing and read King Rambeau's death warrant signed by the saloonkeeper himself.

Stone Hart came up the slope as the herd came clear of the draw. He saw Dusty and Mark standing side by side, their faces grim and cold.

"Rambeau's men?" he asked.

"Sure, read this," Dusty replied.

Stone read the message and nodded grimly at the end. "How'll you handle it?"

"Ride on to Tombstone now," Dusty answered. "You're in the clear and likely be in tomorrow around noon. Mark and I'll deliver this, us and Lon."

"Lon's already gone," Stone drawled. "He doesn't know anything about this. Sent word with Rin he's gone to buy him a new Model '66."

"We'll likely find him," Dusty said gently, but there was no gentleness in his eyes. "Haul the bodies someplace and leave them for John Behan to look over—happens he wants to. They're renegades and there might be posters on them."

Stone watched Dusty and Mark mount their big horses. "I could spare Rusty and Doc," he said. "Rambeau's friendly with the Earp boys."

"I wouldn't spit in Wyatt's face if it was on fire," Dusty drawled as he turned the big paint stallion. "But I wouldn't see him backing a play like Rambeau just made."

"Nor me," agreed Mark, reining his bloodbay around. "Not with certain proof like we've got against Rambeau. No sir, Stone, it wouldn't be Earp's play at all."

CHAPTER THIRTEEN

King Rambeau's Mistakes

CINDY ALBAN sat in the buggy, her arm around Miles Hamish's waist as he handled the reins. They'd been on a picnic and had completely forgotten how the time was flying So now they headed slowly towards the distant lights of Tombstone not talking, each thinking. There was no show for them that night, for they were taking their last chance to relax before the opening of the Fair in two days' time.

The girl had a black Stetson hat on her head and wore a light dress under her coat. The night was not too cold and yet there was a bite in the air which made Hamish pleased that he'd brought his cloak with him. He swung it around his and the girl's shoulders, the white silk lining showing briefly in the night.

"Paula will be worrying," Cindy finally remarked. "I hope she doesn't send that young Earp boy out to look for us. This is the first time we've managed to throw him off and have a few moments alone."

"It's more than a few moments we've had," Hamish replied. "We went out at noon and it's dark now. Young Earp has got it bad where you're concerned."

"I manage to hold him off," laughed Cindy.

Warren Earp, youngest of the brothers, had been one of Cindy's most constant attendants over the last few days. The girl liked him, found his boastings of travels to far-off cities like Sacramento or Saint Louis amusing. However, she did not care to have him around all the time as he tried to be. So it had been with something like relief that she slipped out of town and away from him for the picnic. He would undoubtedly be waiting at the boarding house, but she was sure he would now see he had no chance at all.

"I don't like having you out here after dark, Cindy."

"There's no danger this close to town," she answered.

"Howdy, Miss Cindy."

Hamish gave a startled exclamation and twisted around

with his hand fanning towards his coat, where he had a shoulder holstered Merwin & Hulbert pocket revolver. The big white stallion had made no sound as it came up behind them and the first warning they'd been given was when the Ysabel Kid spoke. He'd seen them from a distance just before dark and only just caught up with them.

"Lon!" Cindy gasped.

Hamish brought his hand from under his coat and a smile came to his face, for he now knew that the Ysabel Kid was no rival. "I nearly shot you," he said.

"Folks're always doing that," came the Kid's drawling reply. "Must be something about me that makes 'em."

"My grandfather was a United States Customs Officer," Hamish answered, remembering stories he'd heard about the Kid's past. "That must be why——"

"Shucks, fancy admitting that afore a lady," chided the Kid. "Don't you hold it against him, Miss Cindy, he couldn't help it."

"I suppose not," Cindy replied. "And I could hardly hold it against Miles. You see, *my* father was head of the Border Patrol in Texas for a time after the War."

The Kid started to rein back his horse. "I knowed there was something about you pair that I didn't like."

The girl laughed and the Kid rode alongside the buggy again. The days when he rode as a border smuggler were long past, but his friends often teased him about them and he was never ashamed of the wild nights when he and his father ran contraband over the border.

For her part, Cindy was delighted that Miles Hamish was acting as he did. He was less stuffy and superior now and acting friendly with the Kid. It was at that moment the girl remembered what had happened to take the Kid from town.

"Where's the herd, Loncey?"

"Back there a piece. I came on ahead so I could hear you sigh."

The girl laughed and looked towards him, seeing that the big white stallion had covered a considerable amount of miles.

"Did you have any trouble bringing the herd this far?"

"Nope, not what I'd call real trouble."

For the rest of the ride Cindy tried to get the Kid to tell her some of the exciting things she was sure had happened. For all that, the Kid's version would have her believe the herd left Vance Brownlow's place and came through without anything worth talking about happening.

They reached the outskirts of Tombstone and made their way through the quiet backstreets to the boarding house. At

Cindy's suggestion, the Kid left his leg-weary white stallion in an empty stall of the boarding house stables. Then with the white and the buggy team cared for the three walked towards the house.

The owner of the boarding house came to answer Hamish's knock. She looked out and her smile broadened as she looked at the girl, then faded a trifle at the sight of the unshaven, trail dusty young Texas cowhand who was with her.

"That's my friend, Loncey Dalton Ysabel," the girl remarked. "Can he wash up and tidy up in Miles' room, please?"

Cindy was the woman's favourite and could do no wrong. So the permission was willingly given and the Kid went with Hamish up the stairs. The woman stood looking at Cindy with a smile playing on her lips. The girl looked radiantly happy, her cheeks showing a touch of colour which was not entirely due to the Arizona sun.

"This Arizona climate seems to agree with you," she replied. "Miles is from New England, Warren Earp's from Iowa and the Kid's from Texas."

The Kid managed to get most of the dust from his clothes before he came down and found Cindy in the living room entertaining young Warren Earp. The youngest of the Earp brothers was a good-looking young man who wore cowhand dress and had a low-tied Colt holstered at his side. He was just removing the gunbelt when the Kid entered the room and frowned.

"Warren," Cindy said, leading him forward. "This is my friend, the Ysabel Kid."

Young Earp nodded a greeting and gave the Kid a broad grin. Doc Holliday was something of a hero to Warren Earp and from the deadly ex-dentist Warren had heard much about the Kid.

"Howdy, Kid," he greeted, then remembered the news which all Tombstone was awaiting. "Say, they were offering five to one that you didn't get that herd through Apache country."

"They were wrong," drawled the Kid. "She's got through and'll be here in a couple of days."

"Yowee, the men and old Doc's won us some money to bet on Brother Wyatt in the shooting matches."

Cindy felt relieved. She knew there was little love lost between the Earps and the cowhands and did not want trouble in the boarding house. Now it appeared the two young men were going to be friendly.

There was a knock on the outside door and the girl excused herself. She left the room, went along the passage and opened the door. A ragged Mexican boy stood outside, a piece of paper in his hand.

"For Señora Alban," he said.

The girl took the note, told the boy to come in while she found a coin to pay him. Then after seeing the boy depart she closed the door and opened out the paper. Her eyes went to the writing, read the first line and a hot flush came to her cheeks. The contents of the letter were vile, insulting in the worst degree that could be spawned and poured out by King Rambeau's mind.

That was the moment when the saloon-keeper's plan started to go wrong. His first mistake was in his judgement of Cindy Alban's character. The girl might allow herself to be saved from the villain when on the stage, but off it she was completely self-reliant. She was burning with a mixture of shame and anger at the message and determined to go along to Rambeau's saloon and shame him before the customers. She knew the ingrown chivalry of the Western men and knew that Rambeau's letter would be enough to see him run from Tombstone.

That was Rambeau's first mistake. He'd expected the girl to run to Miles Hamish with the letter. The two men outside the house were waiting for the young actor to come out, their orders to beat and mark him for life.

Cindy pulled her Stetson on, then she took Hamish's cloak from the hall stand and flipped it across her shoulders. Once the sun went down there often came a bit of cold in the air and she wanted the cloak, although her anger was warming her. She opened the door, the light in the hall behind her as she went out, the white silk lining of the cloak swinging out into view of the two men who stood by the gate. Miles Hamish was coming down the stairs from his room as the girl went out. He saw her closing the door and opened his mouth to call out.

In the darkness the two gunmen waited by the garden gate and there Rambeau's second mistake began. Neither of the men intended to risk a fist fight with the young actor, for they'd seen him bounce a drunken cowhand clear through the doors of the Bon Ton Theatre and were not meaning to tangle with him. The end product would be the same. The rest of the show were attending some function in town and the two gunmen expected the girl to come running out when she heard the sounds of Hamish being worked over. Their orders were to grab Cindy and take her to a cabin on the edge of Tombstone, where Rambeau would collect her.

One of the gunmen lifted his gun as he saw the shape come

through the door. He knew that cloak and the Stetson hid any sign of Cindy's hair from his view. He brought up the Colt and fired, saw the shape at the door stagger and went through the gate.

Then hell broke loose.

Hamish heard the shot, saw the door panel split as a bullet came through and heard a shrill scream of pain. Then he was hurling down the stairs and towards the door, and even as he tore it open he heard a crash of glass from the next room.

The Ysabel Kid was pacing the room. He was never really at home in such a place as this boarding house. He passed the window and through a slit in the curtains saw two shapes by the garden gate. He gave it no thought and crossed to the door of the room, glanced at Cindy as she was putting the cloak on. Warren Earp was seated, relaxed and at home, watching the cat-like way the Kid prowled the room. He opened his mouth to say something as the Kid went to the window again. Then he saw the Kid tense, heard the shot and started to come to his feet.

The Kid brought both hands in front of his face and went straight through the window, carrying sash and glass with him in passing. He hit the ground outside, making havoc among the owner's flower bed. His old Dragoon Colt was gripped in his hand as he saw one of the two men running forward and heard the startled curse as the man saw it was Cindy and not Hamish he'd shot.

Even as the Kid started to bring up his Dragoon he saw the house door burst open and Miles Hamish hurl out. Full on to the gunman, clearing the girl's weakly moving body, hurled the young actor. The revolver crashed once wildly, sending the bullet into the ground, then the gunman was smashed down with a savage fighting fury on him, battering him with hard fists.

The second gunman had seen the Kid come through the window and his Colt was listed, but against the darkness of the house the black clothing worked as a cloak of invisibility and nothing of the Kid showed as he tensed, ready to move in and take the gunman.

The gunman could see nothing but a whirling tangle as Miles Hamish and his companion fought. He could not risk a shot at them. Then he saw a second shape at the window and his Colt crashed. Young Warren Earp had leapt to the window, making a basic mistake; his gun was in his hand ready, but the bullet which came from the night taught him a lesson. He spun around, his shirt torn wide open and a bloody gash appearing on the flesh of his shoulder. With a yell of pain the young man spun around, back against the wall and out of sight.

The Kid was halfway across the garden before the gunman saw him. The man began his turn, but flame blossomed from the barrel of the old Dragoon even before any action could be taken. The gunman let out a scream of pain as the bullet caught him high in the shoulder, smashing flesh and bone as only a round, soft lead ball powered by a full forty grain charge of prime Du Pont powder could. The gunman was thrown backwards, hit the ground and lay screaming in agony, his arm almost torn from his body.

By now the owner of the house and other people from along the street were coming, carrying lamps and lighting up a scene they would never forget. Cindy was holding her shoulder, crouched against the door, with her face white as she stared at Miles Hamish, who knelt beside the man who shot her and smashed his head brutally on to the hard soil of the path.

The Kid came forward, his Dragoon in his hands, the hammer drawn back under his thumb. "Get off him, friend," said his voice, the growling snarl of a Comanche Dog Soldier taking his lodge oath.

Miles Hamish looked up with unseeing eyes. His left hand knotted into the man's hair, his right came across to smash knuckled into the bloody face. The head crashed on to the path with a satisfactory thud and Hamish gripped the head once more.

The Kid had no intention of stopping Hamish killing the man, that was for sure. To him it was nothing that did not require doing and the young actor had the right to do it. The other people were gathering around fast, some looking down at the badly wounded gunman in the street, others crowding into the garden, where the boarding house owner was already bending over Cindy.

Weakly the girl forced herself up and gasped, "Miles! Miles, stop it!"

Possibly there was not another thing in the world which could have stopped the young actor's blind and savage rage. He heard the voice and released the man's head, allowing it to drop back to the path. Then, rising, he turned and went to Cindy, dropping on his knees beside her.

The girl was hit high in the shoulder; it was a painful and nasty wound, but she would live. Her eyes were open, full of pain and not a touch of pride in the way Miles went to save her. The kneeling woman, by Cindy's side, looked at the neighbours who were running up the path and took command of the situation.

"Miles, carry Cindy inside and watch her shoulder," she snapped. "Mrs. O'Neil, would you be so kind as to go for the doctor?"

The Ysabel Kid stood in the garden for a moment, then something white caught his eye. He stepped forward and picked up the note which brought Cindy through the door. The people who were close at hand saw him open it and glance at the writing in the light of the lamp. Then they saw the change which came over his face. No longer was it the innocent, handsome, yet somewhat babyish face of the Ysabel Kid. Now it was the war-mask of a Comanche looking for an enemy.

Warren Earp was by the door, holding his bloody flesh wound. He saw the Kid crumple the paper and asked, "Who were they, Kid?"

"Rambeau's men," the Kid answered and went to where men were gathered around his victim in the street. There was no chance of questioning the other man, he was unconscious and would stay that way for some time. The man the Kid shot was conscious, though only just, and he was in agony. The Kid shoved by the watching men and bent down. He knotted his fist into the man's shirt and hauled him into a sitting position, bringing a scream from him. "Who sent you?"

The gunman screamed again and gasped out, "Rambeau!"

For a moment the Kid stood holding the wounded, screaming gunman with his left hand, right curled around the butt of the old Dragoon Colt. There were big men in the crowd, tough men, but not one of them would have dared to interfere. Go up against a she-bear with new-born cubs, go into a cave where a scared cougar was in hiding; but go against the Ysabel Kid at this moment and the other two would seem like nothing.

Dropping the man's shirt and allowing him to fall back to the ground, the Kid turned. The man was a cheap gunman, just a trigger to be pulled. His arm would never be of use to him again. He had been punished enough. It was the man behind the trigger who must pay.

Turning on his heel, the Kid glanced towards the house and to where Warren Earp was pushing through the onlookers.

"They were doing it for Rambeau," said the Kid gently, yet there was no gentleness in his tone.

"Can I help you?" asked the youngest Earp.

"Get your shoulder seen to, Warren. I'll tend to Rambeau."

Before Warren Earp could open his mouth to either object or warn the Kid that Rambeau had several men at his place, it was too late. The Kid was walking along the once quiet, now disturbed street, making for the King Saloon, where he was going to kill a man or die in the trying.

The shooting brought Virgil Earp, but he came from the other direction and so missed the Kid. From his younger brother he learned of what happened and looked along the street to where the Kid was already out of sight. A man came from the house with word that Cindy had fainted but was in no serious danger. Virgil Earp stood looking at his brother's wound and a hard, grim look came to his face.

"I thought we'd taught you better," he said. "Coming in front of a window with a light behind you. Say—Wyatt, Morgan, Bat Masterson and Doc Holliday are at Rambeau's place."

"We'd best get down there, they might side Rambeau," Warren answered.

"I'll go," Virgil snapped. "You stay here, get that shoulder tended to, then move those two gunmen down to the jail."

Even as he turned, Virgil Earp knew he would be too late. One thing was sure, no matter which way this thing went, King Rambeau was done in Tombstone. It would do the Law and Order Party no good to be friendly with the man who caused the shooting of Cindy Alban, a favourite of the Bon Ton Theatre and darling of every man in the wild and sprawling town.

The King Saloon was booming open. Rambeau moved through the crowd, greeted his friends, or those who were in such a position as to make it worth while to appear friendly.

The batwing doors of the saloon opened and Rambeau felt a sudden cold and raw ache of fear biting into him. This was yet another mistake he'd made. He had not known the Ysabel Kid was in town. In that moment Rambeau knew that his plan had gone wrong, although the noise of the four-piece band, laughter, sounds of his place, had drowned down the shots.

"Rambeau!" the Kid's voice cut across the room. "It didn't work, you lousy, no-good yellow rat."

The first word came in a slight lull of the noise and with each succeeding word the silence grew. The roulette wheel clicked unheeded to a halt, the laughter and curses at the vingt-un table ended, the band trailed off to a discordant chord and died away.

Rambeau knew what had happened, knew that his plan was wrong, knew it from the slip of paper in the hand of the Ysabel Kid. He was near to the Earp brothers' table and threw them a look, but so far Wyatt was not taking cards, was sitting fast until he knew what was wrong and where public opinion lay before cutting in.

"What's eating you?" Rambeau asked, knowing his men were moving in ready to help him.

"Your boys shot Miss Alban, reckon it might have been a mistake, but they shot her."

The words carried to every man in the crowd and the silence was more deeply ominous than ever before. Rambeau could feel the soft, cold hand of death on him and knew he must kill the Kid before too much could be said. There was enough on that sheet of paper to hang him and he knew it. His eyes went across the room to where his last two gunmen were moving through the crowd, making to where they could flank and side him.

The gunmen moved forward, then a foot came up, across the gap between the two tables they were passing. They halted, eyes going to the leg which was so clearly blocking their passage. Then they looked along it, up by the gambler's coat from under which showed the butt of a shot-pistol, up to the sallow face of Doc Holliday. The thin killer's lips drew back in a grin and he shook his head gently.

"That's private, boys. Let's keep it that way."

Rambeau saw what had happened to his gunmen, saw it and knew they were out of the game unless they fixed to tie in with Doc Holliday. He knew, however, the rest of the saloon workers would back him, thinking they were tying in on a matter for the Syndicate. The odds were good, the crowd moving back and allowing his own men to come forward and make a half-circle behind him. They were not professional gunmen, all worked in some capacity in the saloon, but they could all use their guns and no one man could stand against them.

Wyatt Earp shoved back his chair and came to his feet; with two brothers, the tall, derby hatted, Eastern dressed Bat Masterson and Rambeau's men backing him he ought to be able to stop the Ysabel Kid from causing trouble. It would be something of a feather in his cap if he could.

"You'd best go out to Mrs. Satterlee's boarding house, Earp," the Kid spoke evenly. "Warren took a bullet in the shoulder in the shooting."

One of the few good points any Texan was willing to concede about the Earp brothers was their loyalty to the family. Cut one Earp and all the brothers bled. Morgan Earp was now on his feet by his brother's side.

"What're you meaning, Kid?" he asked.

"Rambeau here sent two men to wait outside where Cindy

Alban is living. He sent her this note, thought either Miles Hamish or me would get shown it and come out to be killed. Only Cindy didn't show it us. She put Miles' cloak on and started to come down here, reckon she aimed to face this stinking rat down and show him for what he is—only she didn't make it. One of them shot her as she came through the door."

There was a rumble of anger at the Kid's words. His left hand lifted and he threw the paper towards the Earps. Morgan caught it but did not open it, he was more concerned about his brother.

"What about Warren?"

"Like I said, he caught a bullet from one of Rambeau's men."

"Is that true, Rambeau?" Morgan growled.

"I don't know what the hell he's talking about."

Rambeau could feel the touch of the hold-out and the stubby Remington Double Derringer. It was his chance to finish the Kid before he could say any more. His hand twitched and he was about to press the spring to send the grip of the little gun into his waiting palm. The saloon workers would back him even now if he moved fast.

The batwing doors of the saloon opened and two men stepped in. Two Texan men, one tall, one short, but both wearing two guns and both alike in their cold and deadly menace as they flanked the Ysabel Kid.

"We got your hired men, Rambeau," said Dusty Fog. "You played the wrong card when you wrote out that agreement."

"He's mine, Dusty," warned the Kid.

It was at that moment Rambeau found he stood alone. The saloon workers were not gunmen, but they knew who these two men were. This was the small Texan who had beaten Iowa Parsons to the shot and the big Texan who, by all accounts, had brought his gun clear of leather before Rambeau's best gun, top hired killer of the Syndicate, cleared leather.

Rambeau felt the sweat run down his face. The Earp brothers were walking out of the saloon, going to see how badly Warren was hurt. Bat Masterson and Doc Holliday were still here, but both showed they'd no intention of siding with him. It now all stood or fell on him. He was done and there was nothing but a rope before him unless he could kill the Ysabel Kid.

"Three to one?" he asked, fighting wildly for a chance.

Dusty Fog turned and walked to one side, halting with his

hands resting on the top of the nearby vingt-un table. Mark Counter swung away, also presenting his back as he went and sat with Bat Masterson, not looking around and in no position to bring rapid aid to his friend. At the same moment the saloon workers faded back. Now they knew this was no Syndicate matter and Rambeau stood alone in it.

"One to one, start when you like," drawled the Ysabel Kid.

Rambeau pressed the spring catch of the holdout, felt the Derringer flick down and into his hand. He started to bring the weapon up in a fast move even as the Kid twisted his hand palm out to lift clear the old Dragoon. Then Rambeau hesitated, the short barrelled hide-out gun lining. Was he aiming at the Kid, could he be sure of a hit? The thoughts raced through his mind in that flickering second between the Kid gripping the old Dragoon and bringing it out to line. Only a brief time did the man hesitate—but it was long enough.

Never, by the wildest stretch of imagination could the Ysabel Kid claim he was fast with a gun. It took him all of a second, starting from empty hand and ending with lead flying, for him to make his draw and a second was a whole lot too long at a time like this.

The old Dragoon came up even as Rambeau hesitated, trying to decide if the Deringer was lined. Flame lashed from the old Colt in the Kid's hand, there was no hesitation about the heavy .44 ball and went backwards, arms flailing, into the table behind it, fell on to it, rolled off and to the floor.

There was not a sound through the saloon as all eyes went to King Rambeau, who had just made his final mistake.

The batwing doors opened and Virgil Earp stepped in. He came quietly and without hurry, but he came with his hands held well clear of his belt. A man did not take chances when dealing with a situation such as had been enacted in the King Saloon. The Ysabel Kid was too fast to take any chances with when he'd just dropped a man and might suspect anyone who came behind him.

The Kid turned, holstering his Colt as a sign of his good faith and Virgil Earp felt relieved. The Texas memory of Kansas towns did not tend to give any son of the Lone Star State trust in any man who bore the name of Earp. Virgil stepped forward with a nod towards Rambeau's body and the crowd saw there would be nothing more happen.

"You got him, Kid," he said. "Miss Alban's all right. She'll live, be off the stage for a time, but she'll live."

"You'd best take a look at this," replied the Kid and handed over the note Rambeau sent to Cindy.

Dusty and Mark were by their friend now and from the

pocket of his shirt Dusty took a second sheet of paper.

"You'd best take this while you're at it."

Earp read the two notes and the crowd moved forward, trying to hear everything that was said. Slowly Virgil Earp looked up after he read the two notes. One he could understand, the one which brought the end to Rambeau's life at the hands of the Ysabel Kid. The other puzzled him and he asked about it.

"I took it from one of the gang of renegades who hit at the herd some ways back, at that draw," Dusty explained. "Reckon you'll find it's in Rambeau's hand if you take a look in his office."

The story of the drive came out, bringing whispered remarks of admiration from the crowd. The fight at the draw was glossed over, but there was an angry rumble at the Kid's old yellow rifle. Every man in the saloon knew that the Kid was one of the top favourites in the shooting, or had been. His chances of coming anywhere with his old, tried and trusted rifle bust were small.

The problem was worrying the Kid and Mark Counter moved forward from the crowd. They stood looking at each other for a moment, not noticing Doc Holliday stood close behind them, listening to every word.

"You've used my Model '73," Mark said quietly.

The Kid nodded in agreement. He'd used Mark's rifle on more than one occasion, but that did not give him the knowledge he would need of its ways to enable him to win the Rifle Match.

"Happen I could take it out of town for a couple of days, with plenty of bullets, I might learn how it fires in time."

"That'd be easy arranged."

"It'd cost more money than I've got to spare."

Mark dipped his hand into his pocket and grinned wryly. "I near on spent out myself."

Holliday turned back to look around the room. His eyes fell on the roulette table, where the dealer was idly spinning the wheel ready to start business once more when the crowd returned. Crossing the room, Holliday removed his wallet and tossed a pile of notes on the table, landing them casually on the seven. The dealer looked up and the cold eyes of the killer brought an uncomfortable and uneasy chill to him.

"Your boss caused the Kid's rifle to be bust," said Holliday. "Reckon it's only right he helps make up for it. I'm betting one hundred and fifty dollars to help him."

The dealer grinned. He'd got ten dollars riding on the Ysabel Kid's rifle skill and hoped Doc Holliday called his guess right.

With a practised flick of the wrist he started the wheel spinning with one hand, the other going to the small marble ball. Then Holliday spoke, his voice mild, gentle and yet cold and freezing as the bite of a Texas blue norther storm.

"We don't need to bother with that—now do we?"

Slowly the dealer's eyes went to Holliday's face, then to the thin hand as it hovered the butt of the shot pistol. He let the ball rest on top of the wheel spindle and his tongue tip flickered across his lips.

"No sur, Doc, I don't reckon we do. Seven's the winner."

The Ysabel Kid and Mark Counter were still wondering how they could get around the money problem and if Frank Leslie or Texas John Slaughter could help them lay in a supply of bullets.

"Kid," the word brought them both around to face Doc Holliday. "Here, take this. See that fat jasper playing vingt-un? Go tell him I said for him to sell you anything you want."

The Kid accepted the money, asking no questions. He knew Doc Holliday slightly and wondered what made the killer give him a pile of notes. Then he glanced to the vingt-un table and the fat, prosperous looking townsman who was playing. The crowd were rapidly getting back to the interrupted pleasures now.

"Reckon he'll do it, Doc?" asked the Kid.

Doc Holliday grinned. "I reckon he will. Just tell him I saw him in Bignose Kate's last week, while his wife was on vacation."

So it was that at dawn the following morning the Ysabel Kid rode out of Tombstone with Mark Counter's Model 1873 Winchester, the packhorse, his white stallion and over a hundred and fifty dollars' worth of cartridges. He had the first five days of the fair and all the Sunday to learn enough about the centrefire rifle to let him enter the Rifle Match and win that magnificent "One in a Thousand" Winchester.

CHAPTER FOURTEEN

The Cochise County Fair

THE COCHISE COUNTY FAIR had been a roaring success so far. It came up to all its organisers had hoped for. From the East, brought from the railheads in the best and most comfortable coaches Wells Fargo could supply, came the rich dudes, eager to see the wild, wide open town of Tombstone at play. They flocked in and with them came much money to be spent over bars, in the hotels, at the gambling tables.

The dudes came, stared with amazement and delight as steel thewed miners sank steel drill bits into the rock and hard soil. They cheered to delight as Chow Willicka of the Wedge drove his lathered chuck wagon team to victory in a thrilling race. They watched, trying to imitate the wild cowhand yells as bucking horses were rode and riders piled into the dirt. They stared at the men who would provide the main attraction, the Pistol Shoot. Tall Tom Horn, in buckskins and looking like a bold Apache war chief. Bat Masterson, in derby hat and eastern clothes, but with a brace of Colts in a fast man's rig. Wyatt Earp, looking for all the world like a prosperous trail-end town undertaker. Burt Alvord, who the dudes whispered behind their hands, had been a lawman who never brought in a living prisoner. The dude ladies sighed and fanned their faces vigorously when that blond giant, that rangeland dandy from Texas, Mark Counter, strolled by or attended some function to which the ladies were invited. There was a man, what a man. The milk faced dudes paled into nothing in comparison with such a man.

Walking the crowded streets with Mark Counter was a small man, a nobody in the eyes of the dudes, and few, if any, asked his name. Those who did were surprised when told he was *the* Captain Dusty Fog of Civil War and later fame. The dudes who were told this laughed, suspected that they were being jobbed, as was known to be the Western custom. Few, if any, of the dudes bet their money on that small, soft talking and insignificant Texan. For this Buckskin Frank

Leslie and other odds giving gentlemen were grateful.

The day of the rifle shoot dawned clear and fine, there was little wind and conditions were ideal for shooting. The Ysabel Kid had returned that morning early, paid a visit to Cindy Alban who, with arm in a sling, was able to walk around. Then he went to the line in a shooting match which would long be talked about in the West.

It is possible that no man ever was at such great disadvantage as was the Kid when he went out to the line with Mark Counter's rifle under his arm and the remains of the ammunition he took from town with him. Where he'd been and what he'd done with the rest he never told anyone and there were few who would have dared to ask.

The match was arranged so that there was an emphasis on the fast handling and repeating quality of the Winchester and such rifles, and one rule was that the same rifle must be used all through. This rather put a block on Wyatt Earp's plan to use his Winchester for the ordinary shooting but to bring in a Sharps Old Reliable when accuracy over a long distance was called for.

Details of the match were reported on by the *Tombstone Epitaph* and repeated in papers throughout the length and breadth of the United States. The editor of the paper began in grand terms to describe the scene, meaning to carry on with how his friend Wyatt Earp cleared all before him. By the time the first three parts of the shoot were over it was clear that, good though Earp was, that black dressed boy from Texas was much better.

For all of that, the Ysabel Kid did not get everything his own way. The rifle in his hands was still strange to him and he had to concentrate all the time to remember the traits he'd learned on his lonely ride for the past days. Let him but relax for one moment and he slipped back to handling the rifle in the manner of his broken old yellow boy. It cost him points and kept the crowd in a state of tension. So much so that on the last shoot it was still possible for any of the others to take the Kid's precariously held lead from him.

The last test would be the one which would decide who owned that wonderful rifle and an engraver specially sent out by the Winchester company was seated poised and ready to carve the name of the winner on the silver plate. It was a test which would bring out the finest qualities of the men who now stood on the line. There were only eight men left and the crowd was tense as they waited.

At a distance of some twenty feet before each man lay a spread out handkerchief; beyond this were three foot high hurdles spaced some five feet apart. The idea was to fire bullets so close as to bounce the handkerchiefs into the air, over the hurdles, in the fewest shots and faster than the other contestants.

The Kid relaxed on the line, the tensions of competition not bothering him as he gave Cindy Alban a wave. The starter for the event raised his hand, his Colt pointing into the air.

"Are you ready, gentlemen?" he asked and received the nods in agreement. "Get set, then go!"

The word was echoed by the deep bark of his Colt and re-echoed by the flat barks of eight rifles. The eight handkerchiefs were bounced into the air, sailing up by the force of the close landing bullets. On his third shot Burt Alvord pulled off slightly and his bullet ripped through the handkerchief, at which he aimed. He was out, the handkerchief, torn by the shattering impact of the bullet, resisted all his efforts to bounce it again.

The Kid's eyes focused along the barrel of the rifle. The bouncing handkerchief was a gaudy hue which reminded him of his friend Red Blaze's bandanna. The various colours caught the eye and were easy to pick out, but they had the disadvantage of blurring and becoming indistinct, making the exact place to aim at hard to locate. For all of that, the Kid's third shot bounced the handkerchief over the first hurdle before any of the others made it. The Kid's sighting eye never made any mistake and slowly the mumble of the crowd grew. He was over the second hurdle and there were only three men left in it now. Wyatt Earp was throwing his shots fast, trying to catch up on the Kid's lead. His very haste caused him to miss a chance, his handkerchief hung over the second hurdle, caught on it, resisting three fast thrown bullets to tear it free.

The Kid's eleventh shot sent the handkerchief into the air; it spread out and came down. There was a gasp of dismay from the onlookers, for the handkerchief had caught by its very tip on the face side of the hurdle. Tom Horn, last man in the contest, saw this and fired again; the handkerchief before him sailed into the air and fell short of the hurdle, just too close for him to hope to bounce it over, but he lined his rifle. The Kid was also sighting and the crowd held his concerted breath. The two shots sounded almost as one and the crowd let out a yell which rang out and threw back echoes.

Tom Horn's handkerchief hung over the top of the hurdle. From the Kid's hurdle had burst a shower of splinters and the handkerchief tore free to float down on the other side. With a wry grin Tom Horn lowered his smoking Winchester and spread his hand in the Indian sign talk way of saying finished.

A band started to blare out a stirring tune. The civic dignitaries of Tombstone crowded forward eagerly. In a tent the Winchester engraver was poised ready to work. The judge of the match emptied the Kid's rifle magazine and counted the remaining bullets, then did the same for Tom Horn. The big buckskin man was grinning, knowing he had fired more shots than had the Kid.

Slowly the referee raised his right hand, the band gave a final roaring fanfare and silence that could almost be felt spread over the crowd.

"Ladies and gentlemen," announced the judge in a booming shout which carried over the vast crowd. "The winner of the Cochise County Fair's Rifle Shoot and winner of the One of a Thousand Winchester Model 1873 rifle I give you, Number Ten on your programme, Loncey Dalton Ysabel."

The crowd gave out their approval in traditional style, from the dudes came polite and well-bred applause, from the miners cheers of louder and more raucous style. It was from the cowhands that the most noise came. Those hardy sons of the saddle bellowed out their wild yells, fired their Colts into the air in their delight. The "yeeah!" battle yell of the Confederate Army rang out loud and clear, and for once the Ysabel Kid's face showed its true feelings.

It was only with a considerable effort that the Kid restrained his impatience to get hold of the magnificent Winchester which was brought from the tent where the Winchester engraver had done his work fast and with skill.

Holding the rifle, the Mayor of Tombstone began a speech, praising the Kid's shooting skill and tossing in a few words of praise for his town, the Fair and for Cochise County in general. Then he held out the rifle and the Kid, trying to look normal and nonchalant, as if winning such a wonderful rifle was an every-day thing, took it. From the first moment of gripping it the rifle felt good in the Kid's hands. He slipped bullets into the breech and at a word from the Mayor stepped forward on to the firing line. A man ran down the line of hurdles and placed three beer bottles on the farthest, just where the handkerchief had hung. He moved to one side and the Mayor nodded.

Up came the "One of a Thousand" Winchester, the Kid's eyes lining along the barrel, his finger caressing the set trigger. The flat crack of the Winchester was followed by two more in quick succession, but with each shot one of the bottles was burst by the bullet.

"Yes, sir, Mr. Mayor," drawled the Kid. "That's a tolerable close shooting rifle."

The crowd were wild in their cheers of delight, yelling their approval, and the Kid walked to where his two friends waited for him. He handed Mark back the rifle he'd used for the match and grinned. Dusty was also grinning.

"Lon," he said. "I never saw you look like this since that day when Tom Alden gave you that yellow boy just after the War."

"I never thought to own a rifle like this," replied the Kid. "Let's get out on the range and see how close she shoots."

Dusty shook his head. "We're all invited to a dinner by Vance Brownlow and his good lady. And I promised on my word as a Texan that you'd be there."

"Which same means you'll be there all right," Mark went on. "Likewise, I gave Miz Birdie my solemn oath you'd be along."

The Kid grinned and cursed the unguarded moment when he let Birdie Brownlow know his aversion to attending formal dinners. He also recollected that he had annoyed her and Chow both with his comments on their cooking, and this appeared to be a way of getting their revenge on him. The thought was confirmed soon after when the old cook came ambling up.

"Hear tell you coming to this fancy dinner tonight, Kid," he said, then leered at the Indian dark face. "I always telled you evil got paid back in the end."

Cackling hoarsely, Chow Willicka ambled on and the Kid made a mental note never to rile Chow again—unless he was sure there was a good avenue of escape left for him.

The dinner was far from being as formal as the Kid imagined, although there was a fair crowd along for it, the trail crew, Vance, his wife, all Madam Paula's troupe, several town dignitaries and a few dudes who had managed to get themselves invited.

After the meal the men stood around talking while preparing for the show Madam Paula promised them. Dusty leaned by the bar at the corner of the room. He was looked over by the Dudes and passed off as some minor member of the trail drive drew, although the same dudes were puzzled at the deference the others showed to this small and insignificant Texan.

Sheriff John Behan, one of the guests, joined Dusty, a broad grin on his face. Jerking his thumb towards the editor of the *Tombstone Epitaph*, he said, "Clem looks real down in the mouth. The Kid spoiled a good story for him."

"Likely, John, likely," answered Dusty. "Wyatt Earp's not here."

"Nor likely to be," Behan replied. "He got to boasting about winning just after you pulled out, so I made a bet with him. Things stand this way, if he loses both the shoots he doesn't stand for sheriff against me."

Dusty looked at the other man for a long moment, then grinned. "That was a mite tricky, John."

"Like my pappy always told me, Cap'n Dusty, if you can't lick 'em, trick 'em."

At that moment the show started and for the first time the Ysabel Kid managed to hear Cindy Alban sing. Later that same evening the Kid's pleasant untrained tenor voice was matched in duets with the girl, but she had eyes only for Miles Hamish and on the third finger of her left hand was a diamond ring.

The following morning found an air of expectation over the crowd as they moved out of Tombstone to the place where the shooting would be performed. There were only nine men left in now, the others had realised they stood no chance and so bowed out.

There was some talk among the crowd when the contestants lined up for the first shots. Wyatt Earp had his long barrelled Peacemaker holstered at his left side and all there knew a fast draw was impossible with such a weapon but it would give him a good chance of scoring well in the long range work.

The first tests rolled by, shooting with sights and by rough alignment at targets, then at a can thrown into the air. Earp scored well, so did all the other men, but when the scores were added it was found that the small man who was marked down at number nine was the highest scorer of them all and next to him that blond giant called Mark Counter.

"That long range work will show a difference," Vance Brownlow remarked to Stone Hart as they stood in the forefront of the crowd, watching a man who was setting up an empty whisky bottle in the centre of a patch of cleared earth some hundred yards from the firing point.

"Likely," drawled Stone. "Likely. I'd still bet on Dusty for it."

By the time Earp took his stand no man had managed to hit the bottle in less than five shots. There was a grin on Earp's face as he lined the long barrelled Colt and fired, watching the dust puff up where the bullet slapped into the earth near the bottle. There was a rumble of approval from the watching crowd, for no other man had come so close to the bottle with his first shot. Earp stood sideways, holding the Colt shoulder high as he sighted. His second shot dusted the bottle but did not break it. On the third shot there was a crash and a flying hail of splintered glass, and cheers rang out from Earp's supporters. Here was one part of the ranch they were sure he would win.

Mark Counter took his place with the seven and a half inch barrelled Cavalry Peacemaker in his right hand. His first shot was just as close in as Earp's, but it took Mark four shots to hit the bottle. The third shot had been close, it should have been a hit by all fair means, but the four and a half inch difference in the gun barrels gave Earp a big advantage. Mark grinned and walked back to where Dusty stood. The big Texan was satisfied, although now Earp stood slightly over him in the scoring. There was the test for fast gun handling next and Earp's long barrelled gun would put him at a disadvantage.

There was a mutter from the crowd as they saw the type of Colt Dusty was using. It had taken Bat Masterson six shots to range in the four and three-quarter inch barrel of a Civilian Model Peacemaker and none of the crowd thought to see the small Texan do any better.

Dusty sighted carefully, watching how the breeze stirred the grass, then made his calculations and cocked back the hammer. Another pause to make sure of the aim, then Dusty fired. There was a roar from the crowd as dust erupted within a scant inch of the bottle. For a moment every one of the crowd thought a hit was scored and a yell rolled high then died away.

Unruffled by the noise, Dusty set his sights again, waiting for a moment when the breeze was at its steadiest. There was not a sound from the whole crowd as the people waited for the crack of the Peacemaker. Then Dusty fired! The bottle burst, shattering under the impact of the .45 bullet.

It took the crowd a long five seconds to realise what had happened. Then, as Wyatt Earp threw down his cigar in disgust, the cheers rolled out.

Earp's temper did not improve on the test for fast gun-handling. For this the contestant walked down a valley and targets, mansized and shaped, were pulled up from behind cover with the aid of ropes. He shot well, but knew that he might have scored even better. This was the event for which the long barrelled Peacemaker was the prize, and he hoped to take it. However, Mark Counter scored higher, getting the highest points so far. Dusty followed and went the line of the valley, shooting fast and equalling Mark's score.

"Toss you for it," Mark drawled as they walked towards the judges.

"Spin a coin and make a call," Dusty answered.

Mark laughed, flipped a coin into the air and made a correct call, so he took the cased presentation Peacemaker.

It was now, as the men went to the line for the last event, that the interest of the crowd really worked up. The other shooting had been good, very good, but it was something they could have seen any time. Right now was the big moment, the star attraction which the organisers of the Fair planned. This was the test to see who was the fastest man with a gun.

The Colt company had been hard put to think of a way to test the speed of the draw and after much thought came up with an idea. To one side of where the shooting had taken place the special targets were set up. They were mansized and cut in the shape of a man drawing a gun. The posts on which these targets were fixed rested on, but were not fastened to, a bar. Beyond this and placed so that the target support would hit it when moved by the force of a bullet, was a second bar with spring-loaded grips attached so as to catch and hold the target supports. The target line was made so that the first shot to hit a target moved it and the support back to hit the second bar. This in turn loosened the spring-loaded grips on to the other targets and prevented them from falling over backwards.

In tests conducted both at Hartford and on the ground at Tombstone the system showed it worked even when there were only split seconds between the impacts. It was possible to tell which bullet hit first, for that was the only target which could fall over.

The nine men took their places on the line. Each one was set, making sure his holstered Colts lay just right. They were probably the fastest men alive, those who toed that line, each one having proved his right to be there, with a smoking Colt in the heat of a gunbattle. This would settle one argument, who was the fastest of them all.

"Gentlemen!" boomed the judge of the match, holding a Colt in his right hand, "I'll count to three, then fire a shot. On that shot you make your move."

The line of men stood ready, hands poised to grip the butts of their guns. The count was given, then the Colt crashed. As if springs were released, hands snapped down. Dusty's hands crossed, the curve of the Peacemaker butts fitting into his palms as they so often had before. There was no conscious effort about the move, no straining to gain extra speed. The thumbs curved over the hammers, drawing them back to firing position even as the Colts cleared leather. Dusty's eyes were on the target before him, twenty feet away, the guns came up and lined to fire while still waist high. The thunder of his Colts sounded and was lost in the crash of the other eight men's weapons, which came as a ragged crash. Dusty saw his target rock back, saw the others jerk, then his target tipped over and crashed to the ground.

The crowd were silent for a moment, then wild were the whoops and yells from those watching Texans, the other cowhands joining in. Every cowhand here was wild with delight, for one of their kind, one of the leading names of their trade, had just proved he was the fastest gun of them all.

Dusty holstered his Colts as the yells and cheers of the crowd died away to allow the judge to announce the winner. He was smiling, this small Texan, knowing that the test proved little or nothing. It was one thing to send a bullet into a target but another again to throw lead at a man who might be faster and was capable of throwing bullets back. Dusty Fog knew that the crowd would not think of that, they had seen Wyatt Earp, Bat Masterson and the other fast men beaten by the Rio Hondo gun wizard. Arizona was safe from the Kansas lawmen.

THE END

J. T. EDSON OMNIBUS VOLUME 1

Of all the characters created by J. T. Edson, Dusty Fog – that small, softly spoken hero who strikes when least expected – is surely the most famous, the most popular.

Here, for the first time, are three Dusty Fog stories in one volume. *You're in Command Now, Mr Fog: Kill Dusty Fog!: The Devil Gun* all deal with Dusty Fog's exploits during the Civil War.

0 552 13602 6

J.T. EDSON OMNIBUS VOLUME 2

The Ysabel Kid is one of J.T. Edson's most vibrant and colourful characters. Half Comanche, half Irish, the Kid was raised as a Comanche brave. From his Irish father he learned superb rifle skill, and from Dusty Fog he learned how to be a fighting man on the OD Connected Ranch. Dressed in black, riding his white stallion, the Ysabel Kid is a character no one can ever forget.

Here are three stories, all featuring the Ysabel Kid –
COMMANCHE;
SIDEWINDER;
OLD MOCCASINS ON THE TRAIL

0 552 13603 4

J. T. EDSON OMNIBUS VOLUME 3

Waco is one of J.T. Edson's youngest characters. Wild, brave, and sometimes inexperienced, Waco has the best teachers in the West. For characters like Dusty Fog, Mark Counter, and the Ysabel Kid have all taken a hand in training Waco to be as fearless and skilled as they are themselves. The three stories in this volume feature Waco, holding his own with the most dangerous characters in the West.

Three Waco Stories
TRIGGER FAST
THE MAKING OF A LAWMAN
WACO'S DEBT

0 552 13604 2

J. T. EDSON OMNIBUS VOLUME 4

Mark Counter, six-foot-three, big, blond and dangerous, is certainly the most handsome character ever created by J. T. Edson. From the top of his low-brimmed Stetson to the soles of his cowhide boots, he is one-hundred-per-cent a fighting man.

Here are three stories of the Floating Outfit, all featuring Mark Counter –

TROUBLED RANGE
THE WILDCATS
RANGELAND HERCULES

0 552 13605 0

J. T. EDSON OMNIBUS VOLUME 5

Life was wild and dangerous in the West – particularly in the Trail End towns where violence and corruption ruled and the only law was that of a gun. Dusty Fog and his friends, quiet, tough, and as quick on the draw as any gun slinger, were the only people able to cope with taming the West. When they moved in the citizens of the Trail End towns knew that the law had arrived, and the best Lawman in the West – Dusty Fog.

Three Lawman stories featuring Dusty Fog –

QUIET TOWN   THE TOWN TAMERS
THE SMALL TEXAN

0 552 13606 9